MW01222213

Shadows In The Sun

By
Jack A. Sariego

authorHOUSE™

1663 LIBERTY DRIVE, SUITE 200
BLOOMINGTON, INDIANA 47403
(800) 839-8640
WWW.AUTHORHOUSE.COM

First published by AuthorHouse 11/30/05

ISBN: 1-4208-8687-8 (e)
ISBN: 1-4208-8685-1 (sc)
ISBN: 1-4208-8686-X (dj)

Printed in the United States of America
Bloomington, Indiana

This book is printed on acid-free paper.

AUTHORS COMMENTS

This is a work of historical fiction! Few stories have been written about the pre-Civil War days of Spain that include the uncertaintities, the wide immense poverty that resulted in a time of prolonged misery throughout the country! The government was corrupt! There was very little employment and mass poverty was everywhere, especially in the northern provinces that were mostly farmlands who had been struck by one of the most severe droughts in history!

I remember only too well stories that were told by our mother to her children consisting of five sons and one daughter! During my youth I can still recall the tales of her own prolonged suffering in Spain that finally resulted in migrating to the United States hoping to live a new and better life in a land that she knew very little about! We spent many dull afternoon hours listening to those stories, and it wasn't until I was much older that I felt a need for sharing some of those moments with the public!

The historical elements outlined in this story are factual and have been well documented by official files of the Spanish historical archives! The names of many of the characters are based on persons that were instrumental in shaping the future of Spain but have long since passed away! The names of some of the characters, although based on stories that were told by my parents, have been changed for a number of obvious reasons!

*A special tribute has been paid to His Majesty **KING JUAN CARLOS**! After having been grossly underestimated by many of his subjects and despite having been personally trained and schooled by **Generalissimo Franco** himself he rose above his critics and became a true leader! From an early age he was expected to rule Spain with the many imposed Fascist doctrines that were in existance following the Spanish Civil War! The young King quickly showed his maturity at an early age! He quite masterfully headed off a coup that sought to endanger his throne and threatening to return the country to its pre-Civil War days of turmoil and unrest. His intelligence, his perseverence, and his love of both his country and all of its people soon resulted in* *an overwhelming success for the monarchy once again! He was also a forceful factor in establishing for the first time a practical constitution which is still in existance!*

*Thanks to **King Juan Carlos**, Spain today is one of the best ruled countries in Europe! It is a model for democratic reform! The King is as famous today among his people as he was when first appointed to rule a troubled nation! It would be a gross injustice to assign his true role to any fictitious character!*

It is with admiration and a sincere appreciation that this book is respectfully dedicated to my late parents, my four brothers and one sister, all of whom always had one thing in common, the love for Spain and the undiminished pride of being second generation Spaniards! It is this legacy that those of us who are still alive will always cherish and those members of my family who are no longer with us have taken with them to their grave!

It has been a great pleasure for me to once again relive those days of the past and to perhaps even feel a bit nostalgic over days and events that disappeared so long ago! My hope is that whoever reads this story will appreciate and enjoy its contents as much as I have enjoyed creating a special moment in time to share with the world!

Jack A. Sariego

SYNOPSIS OF CHARACTERS

The years leading to the Spanish Civil War had the once prosperous country in complete turmoil. Poverty and unemployment were widespread as families were torn apart and people moved from place to place in their struggle to survive! They will soon learn that strange things happen during a war!

SOLEDAD ALONSO — A young, determined woman born into poverty in the northern province of Spain! She has loved her childhood sweetheart all her life until fate drifts them apart!

MIGUEL (Flaco) ROMERO — Soledad's childhood sweetheart who becomes a rising young military officer in Franco's post-war Spain and will need to make a choice between love, honor and duty!

GUILLERMO TORRES — A life long friend of Miguel's and a fellow Guardia Civil who will be tried for desertion when he falls in love with a nurse.

MARIPAZ ROMERO — Soledad's young daughter who will become an ETA Basque activist accused of murder!

ANDRES TORRES — Guillermo's son, an attorney, will play a key role in transforming Spain from a military to a civilian government and will assist the King in creating a constitutional monarchy!

Each person in his own way will need to make harsh decisions that will forever change his life! Each one will make a contribution in restoring Spain to the level that it is today! One thing is certain! Their lives will never again be the same!

Shadows in the Sun
Book 1

CHAPTER 1

Salinas, Spain

1920

It was a beautiful, crisp Autumn morning in Asturias! The summer harvest of the small farm located behind the large masonry house in the northernmost province of Asturias had yielded enough potatoes, onions and kale to last them through the cold winter months. All of the vegetables that had been provided by the small track of land had been carefully stored away for the winter months when the cold harsh winds blowing from the Mediterranean Ocean prohibited the people from any outside work. The small square, "Horrio", that had been constructed behind the house was filled to capacity. The wooden structure, mounted on four vertical columns several feet above the ground, had been locked only to spring into action once again after the first winter frost when the pummeling temperatures caused by the freezing winds were upon them.

For some unknown reason, it seemed that everything had suddenly changed! It seemed that nothing in the small seashore town of Salinas would ever be the same again! For young Soledad Alonso, it should have been a day much the same as all the others when her mother would call her early in the morning and ask her to go to the well for a pail of fresh water. Things were different today!

The first thing that the young girl noticed was that her mother who always had a smile on her face was not smiling! Her eyes seemed swollen and puffy as if she had been crying! It was something she had never seen before! She arose from her bed in the small room that was located at the rear of the two-story masonry house. The front of the house had a large bedroom complete with a wood burning stove that served to provide the house with warmth as well as to cook their meals and to provide the warmth and comfort of her small bedroom on the first floor. Soledad put on her wooden "Madrenas", wooden shoes that were always used for walking through the mud and the dirt to the well. As she walked the narrow pathway, she had a feeling that something was different. Her father, who had always walked into her room, had not come in this morning to kiss her and to remind her that she was his little "Muneca" (doll), as he had always called her!

She filled the pail with water as she did each morning and struggled to hold the heavy pail, afraid that it would fall and spill the fresh water on to the ground. Struggling back to the house, she pushed away several of the chickens that were in her way and one of the small pigs that had found its way into the house to get away from the morning chill! Soledad called out to her mother and told her she had returned! Upon hearing her voice, the young girl's mother opened the large wooden door and asked her to sit down because there was something she needed to tell her. Seeing the sad look on her mother's face was enough to alert her that whatever her mother had to say was not going to be good! She took her place and sat down in a wooden chair waiting for her mother.

For a long time after her mother had left the room, the young Soledad remained seated as she tried to make some sense of what had happened! It was difficult for her to understand the reason why her father would no longer be there to kiss her and hold her as he had always done. Fathers were not supposed to do such things, she thought! Could it have been that she had done something wrong and had offended him? As hard as she tried, she couldn't think of anything she could have possibly done to make him angry.Her mother had tried to explain in her own words what death was and how it always affected all of them, one way or another! Unfortunately, for a young pre-teenage girl, there were no explanations that were convincing! After all, death was something that always happened to other people, but not to her! Her home was secure and she had always felt safe there despite the poverty that had engulfed the country for many years.Poverty was something they all had felt at one time or another; and, as far as she was concerned, it was something she had always known from the time when she had first been able to think and reason for herself! Even though they were poor, she knew that her mother would routinely test the chickens each day, and separate those that were still capable of laying fresh eggs away from those that were no longer capable of producing them! These were the chickens that were then put aside, and would be systematically slaughtered in time for their Sunday dinner!

Soledad carefully opened the door to her parent's room and tried to understand what she was seeing for the first time of her young life! At the far end, her eyes went to her father who was dressed in a white shirt and was fast asleep in a wooden box! She also saw that her mother was all dressed in black, sitting by the wooden box and reciting the rosary! She thought of interrupting her, but, she also knew that her mother had insisted that she not be interrupted whenever she recited the rosary! After a few moments, her mother raised her eyes and asked her to go to the small patch of land on the far side of the house. She was to pick some of the wild flowers and place them inside the box where her father was sleeping. It seemed like a strange request, but then, everything about this day had been strange! Why was her farther lying in a wooden box that was barely large enough to accomodate his frail body? Why was he there instead of in his bed where he always slept? She did as she was told and selected a handful of the fresh yellow flowers that were still in bloom. After all, these flowers were for her father and she wanted him to have nothing but the best! She walked slowly into the room and gently placed the armful of fresh flowers inside the box on each side of her father's arms!

Soledad had waited until her mother had gone out to milk the cow before she went up to her father and shook him gently as she had often done in the mornings! She waited patiently for him

3

to open his eyes, but they remained firmly closed! She shook him again, this time a bit harder, but again, there was no response! It just was not like him not to answer her! After all, any time she went into their bedroom and had shaken him, he would open his eyes, sit on the side of the bed and take her into his arms! It served as a reassurance to her that everything was well with the world and that no harm would come to her! Today, things had been different! Her father had not awakened nor had he taken her into his arms! Instead, he had decided to remain asleep and ignore her silent pleas!

Late that afternoon the priest from the local church, Padre Joaquin came to her house for a visit! He gently cradled her in his arms and tried to explain that her father was now in heaven and that he wouldn't return because now he was in a much better place! Out of respect, she remained silent and didn't answer the priest, but what he was saying didn't make any sense to her! After all, how could he possibly be in a better place than where he lived and where he belonged with his wife and young daughter who adored him? If this place called heaven was so good, then why had he gone there by himself and had not taken his family? None of what she was hearing for the first time was making any sense to her, especially when she saw that four men from the village had come to her house, closed the wooden box, and carried the box with her father on their shoulders into Padre Joaquin's church and then to the small cemetery behind the church where a large hole had been dug in the dirt! She stood surprised as she saw the box being gently lowered into the hole. Many people were crying as was her mother, and the happiness she had enjoyed every day in her young life had suddenly been taken away from her! There was only sadness and grief everywhere! A short while after the wooden box had been lowered into the hole, the few people who had been at the cemetery gathered in her home, sitting and talking to her mother and drinking coffee! Whatever they were talking about remained a mystery because they had deliberately excluded her from the conversations, and every time she came to say something to her mother, she soon noticed that the conversation would stop until she again had left the area. Only Padre Joaquin had come up to her after everyone else had left and had spoken to her!

"Soledad, you must remember that now only you are left to help your mother! You need to be a brave little girl and do whatever she asks of you! I want you to know that if at any time you find the need to speak to someone, I am always available to you!" the Padre told her.

"I don't think that will be necessary, Padre! You see, I find it hard to believe that my daddy will never return! He loves us too much and I know that he would never leave us! After all, I know he was only sleeping!" she answered.

"No, my child!!" he replied. "Your father is now in heaven with the angels! You must go to church and pray for him! I'm sure he is looking down on you, but he won't be back!" She glared at him and he could instantly see that this young girl was angry and didn't really accept what he was telling her.

"No! No! No!" she cried. "Ustedes son unos mentirosos! No es verdad! Mi pappi ha de volver, ya lo veran!" (You are all liars! It isn't true! My father will return, you will see!)

"No, Soledad! We are not lying to you! I'm afraid he won't be back! Please child, try to understand!"

By the time he had finished speaking she could no longer hold back the tears! They were all wrong, she mumbled to herself. Tomorrow when she awakened, she would go into her mother and father's bedroom and she would nudge him if he was sleeping! She was determined that he would awaken, sit up on the side of the bed and lift her up into his lap. She knew it would happen! She just knew it! After all, what did she know about death? Once or twice she remembered her mother mentioning the word, but it always applied to someone else, never to them! As far as she knew, these things didn't happen to her family. The fact that she was angry and confused by what she had been told meant absolutely nothing. If only she knew what to do! She couldn't approach her mother! After all, she had spent the entire day crying and she didn't want to pester her nor worry her more than she was. She did notice that her mother had been speaking seriously to the village doctor, Don Jose Perez who had arrived at her house in the afternoon. He was

5

dressed all in black, with a black hat and his medical bag and had arrived in his horse and carriage. He had tapped her on the head as he always did when he came, kissed her gently on the cheek and had gone upstairs to speak with her mother. There was nothing she could do except to wait for answers she needed to the many questions now on her young mind!!

Flaco, as he was called, was a young neighborhood friend, a few years older than Soledad. He lived in a small farm house with his parents just a short distance away from where Soledad lived. His real name was Miguel Romero, a name that he simply disliked and would prefer to forget! The story went that when he was an infant, his mother would always call him "Miguelin"! The young man thought that the name was much too infantile, and hated the way it sounded whenever his mother would call him into the house. It was his father who had given him the name of "Flaco" mostly because he was tall and skinny and knew that his son disliked being called by the name of Miguel. From that time on, everyone knew him by the name of Flaco! Even his best friend Soledad had begun calling him by his nickname. One day she had forgotten and had mistakenly called him "Miguelin"! He became furious and had kept his distance from her for several days. She finally apologized and promised never again to call him by that name again! She had kept her promise; and, as a result, they had become inseparable friends! Theirs had almost become a perfect union! Although Soledad was small in stature and dainty, she had the physical strength of some of the boys she knew who were much older. Unfortunately, Flaco lacked the strength of most boys his age, but everyone knew that he was the smartest young man in the group. He was the person she would always go to when something came up that she didn't understand. Today she felt it was going to be one of those days because she needed him to explain to her what was suddenly happening to her life. There was no point in asking Padre Joaquin or Don Jose because she probably wouldn't be able to understand what they were telling her. No! Thank goodness for "Flaco"! He would certainly know! She made up her mind that tomorrow after all of the ceremonies of the funeral were over, she would approach Flaco and ask him for advice! He would make more sense and he would certainly understand! For now, it was getting a bit late and the sun was no longer shining! She kissed her mother goodnight and had gone to bed; but she could hear her mother still crying inside her bedroom! She admittedly found it strange that for the first time she couldn't hear her father's voice! Could it have been that they were right after all? Could it be that he had no intention of returning to them; but, if so, why would God decide to punish them this way? Wasn't it enough that they were poor and the small parcel of land they owned was barely enough to provide them with enough vegetables to sustain them during the harsh winter? Whatever His reasons may have been, she needed to go to sleep! It had been a tiring and confusing day! Besides, she had decided to awaken early so she could talk to her friend and ask him to explain what was happening in simple words that she would understand.

As the days and nights went by, there were two thoughts that continued to come up in her mind! One was what Padre Joaquin had told her about her father not returning! She was beginning to realize that what the good Padre had told her was probably the truth! Several weeks had now gone by and there were no encouraging signs that her father would ever return. She had hoped and prayed eagerly that she would wake up one morning and he would be there to pick her up and cradle her in his arms the way he had always done, but it hadn't happened! Unfortunately, the days had passed and every morning when she awakened she would run into her mothers bedroom, but the side of the bed her father had slept in was always empty. Her mother would pass the days and nights praying the Rosary and crying! It was almost becoming a daily ritual! The other troubling thought was that nothing in her young life would ever again be the same! The happiness and the tranquility she had felt in her young life had begun to vanish and every semblance of happiness was slowly withering away! Even the times she had enjoyed speaking to Flaco soon began to vanish as she became more involved with her house chores and was unable to devote as much time to their friendship as before!

On one occasion, she remembered overhearing a conversation between the village doctor, Don Jose speaking to her mother. Their voice was purposely low enough for her not to hear, but, she could tell something was wrong when her mother began to cry! It seemed quite obvious that whatever they were speaking about could not be very good! At one point, she remembered the doctor telling her mother that he had gone and had told them what she wanted him to say, but they steadfastly refused to offer her any help! It was then Soledad remembered the stories told to her by her mother how she had come from a wealthy family, but they were adament against her marriage to her father. It seemed that her father was somewhat older than her mother, and had the unfortunate reputation for drinking more than his share of wine! She remembered her mother telling her how much her grandparents had been opposed to her marriage. When her mother decided to disregard the feelings of her family and had married her father without their blessing, her family had disowned her and had refused to have anything else to do with them. They had provided them with the large, stone two story house they lived in and a few farm animals. In exchange, they insisted on having nothing else to do with their own daughter or their grandaughter! The only connection her mother had been able to maintain with her family had been by way of Don Jose Perez, a trusted family friend who had tried many times to reunite them, but, all of his efforts had been unsuccessful! She could only imagine that her mother was in a state of desperation and was facing a critical time of her life when hard decisions would need to be made!

The only solution was for her mother to be trained as a nurse by the old doctor. It was decided that she would then use the second floor of the large house as a hospital for patients that were in need of minimal care but couldn't afford to take the trip to the larger medical clinics in Aviles, a larger city located thirty miles away from Salinas. There was another much larger hospital in the city of Oviedo, but that was much farther away and was hardly accessible to the people from the northern villages. Travel by horse and carriage to any of those areas was time consuming and expensive! The old doctor had explained to Soledad's mother that such an arrangement would provide her with a source of income with which to live. The arrangement was finally accepted out of necessity and the results were that her mother would now need to spend most of her time upstairs in the hospital while she, a youngster would now be compelled to do all of the major chores around the house! It was an alternative that she had no choice but to accept. Being so young she soon realized that the work would be difficult for a child. By the end of the day, she was so exhausted by her work that there was little time for her daily conversations with her friend Flaco!

Flaco, on the other hand, had his own problems! His father was also out of work, and the small parcel of land that provided most of the vegetables had been left to be worked by him during the day. The small farm required his daily attention, and during the spring and summer months, he would begin working the land at sunrise and wouldn't be finished until sunset. By that time, he felt so tired that there was little time for interest in anything else. He would go directly to bed and get his much needed rest for yet another day! His father had been unable to work the small parcel of land due to a persistant cough that had him suffering frequent spasms as soon as he did any physical labor. On one occasion, Don Jose had made a house call and had suggested moving him to a hospital fearing that the man was suffering from Tuberculosis, a common illness among the elderly. Unfortunately, the family was much too poor, the badly needed medicines were much too expensive; and the care he required could only be provided by someone who had been trained and had the proper medical knowledge! There was also a time when Don Jose had spoken to Soledad's mother, and she heard him suggest that Flaco's father be moved to their house. He said something about the man being terminally ill and he was afraid that moving him there might contaminate any of the other patients that were in the house for medical treatment. When they realized that Soledad had been listening to what they were saying, they made her promise not to say anything to Flaco fearing that the illness would only contribute to their own desparate situation. Shortly afterward, Soledad was down by the creek doing her daily wash. Now that the second story of her house was used as a hospital the amount of clothes to be washed had increased and there were times when she would need to spend most of the morning washing clothes. The blood stained sheets and pillowcases had to be washed daily down by the edge of a small river flowing behind the house.She heard the sounds of footsteps and was startled when she turned her head and saw Flaco standing behind her!

"Que haces aqui?" (What are you doing here?) he asked when he saw the large straw basket filled with the soiled clothes that needed to be washed. "How long is it going to take you to wash all those clothes?"

"I don't know!" she replied. "My mother said she needs them right away! Flaco, why haven't I seen you lately? I thought that perhaps you were angry at something I might have said!"

"No, of course not! I've been kept busy working on the farm; but, unfortunately, the crops have not been good! We have a small supply of potatoes and onions in this year's crop! It seems as though the long, hot and dry summer has parched the land and it didn't give us enough vegetables to hold us over for the winter!"

She noticed immediately that her friend was worried and concerned. If only she had more time available she could help him with the farm, she thought! After all, she could see that he was a skinny kid and didn't have very much physical strength! If only she didn't have so many chores to do around the house, she would be free to help him!

"Don't worry, Flaco! As soon as I am finished here, I will go over and help you on the farm! You'll see, everything will be okay!" she lied, knowing well that it was foolish to hope for better times. As young as she was, she was well aware that times were tough and every indication seemed to point to the fact that things were getting worse and certainly not better!

"It's no use, Soledad! Besides, my father is very ill and it certainly doesn't look good! It seems that he is now coughing all the time! This morning, as I was watching him, I saw him spitting up blood!"

"Did you send for the doctor?" she asked.

"No, what for? Don Jose already told us that he was very ill and probably wouldn't last very long! He mentioned something about moving him into your house where your mother can attend to him!"

"I'm sorry to hear that; but, if they move him to our house, I'll be able to spend more time with you!"

"Yes, perhaps! Who can say what will happen? My mother has been talking about moving to Aviles or down to Oviedo! She wants to find work as a house maid and perhaps make enough money to support us both!"

"Oh, no, Flaco!!" she replied, worried and concerned by the news. This was something she had not thought about. How could his mother even think about moving away from Salinas? What would happen to her if they should move? She would have no one to speak to who could teach her things about life that she didn't understand! "You can't move, Flaco! What would happen to me? Who else will I have to speak to who will teach me things I know nothing about? Perhaps you could talk her into remaining at my house! I'm sure that my mother wouldn't mind!"

"No, Soledad, it is much more than that! The land has yielded very few vegetables and the "Horrio" is almost empty! We have little food to store up for the winter months! We need to do something and we haven't any money!"

"But what will I do without you?" she asked, sounding worried and desperate.

"If we move to Aviles, I could still come back to see you! Unfortunately, if we should move to Oviedo, it is much farther away. I doubt I'll be able to return! We don't have the horse and carriage any longer, my father needed to sell it to pay for the fertilizer!"

Soledad's world suddenly fell apart! For some unknown reason, the thought of being without Flaco had never once entered her mind. With the passing of time she had reconciled with herself that her father was not coming back, but how could Flaco even think about leaving her? Her day was suddenly ruined and she started feeling lonely in this large, oversized world that had no time nor pity for small girls! Why did life need to be so unfair? Why couldn't people just live forever? It didn't seem fair that her father had simply died and had left them so much grief. Now Flaco's father was also dying and she knew that it would also add to her own grief! This time the grief would be passed on to her best friend, and she didn't want him to be sad! After all, he was smart and knew many things! She needed his knowledge as much as he needed her help in working the fields, anything just as long as he didn't move away!

"Flaco, suppose I come over each day after my own chores are finished and help you with the farm? This would give you an extra hand and together we can grow more vegetables!":she said almost pleadingly.

"It still wouldn't be enough! Besides, someone would still need to milk the cow and feed the few animals that remain!"

"I could do that! I could milk the cows, and, I could also feed the animals. Remember, I feed our chickens and our pig! I could just as easily go over to your house and feed your livestock!" she said, trying to convince him that her help would cure all of their problems.

"I'll need to speak to my mother and see what she says! It seems that every time we hire one of the local men who is not working, he charges us "tres perronas" a day! We just cannot afford to pay them the nine cents a day that they charge for doing a day's work!"

When Soledad returned home, she saw that Flaco's father had already been moved into her house and had been put to bed in the upstairs hospital. Don Jose was busy getting him settled while her mother had gathered two large wooden frames made up from scrap lumber that were being set up on each side of the bed and out of sight by the other two patients. Soledad, seeing what was happening, tried to prevent Flaco from going upstairs. The scene was all too familiar to her! She had seen those frames set up before and installed on each side of the bed while waiting for the patient to die! Don Jose had obviously given the sick man some barbiturates, hoping to reduce the coughing spells. Now, he was administering some analgesics hoping to reduce the pain in the patient's chest. This was a familiar pattern she had seen many times before when she knew that the end was near! Now she needed to brace herself across the wooden set of steps hoping to stop Flaco from going any further.

"No te vayas!" (Don't go!) she pleaded! "Your father is very ill and isn't expected to survive much longer!"

"But, I must go! I must see him before he dies!" he said as tears began to roll down his face. "He mustn't die! He has to know how much we need him!"

"No Flaco! There is nothing you can do! It is best that he remains with those who can help him!" she lied. She had seen her mother and Don Jose spread some clean white sheets over the wooden frame to prevent the other patients from seeing him when the time came for him to leave this world. It didn't seem right that other patients would have to witness another patient who was dying.

"But Soledad, I don't know what to do! There has to be something that can be done!" he answered. She remained adamant! She had seen her father's death, and she found it necessary to spare him the same grief she had felt when she had to remain outside while her father was in his eternal sleep.It was something that had happened a long time ago and it had taken her a long time to overcome the sick feeling. She also knew that Flaco was weak and needed her protection!

"No, Flaco! There is nothing you can do!" she insisted. "It will only make him feel worse if he sees you standing there! Your mother is with him now; and I think it's best if you remain here with me! You mustn't worry!" she said. "I will always be with you and I will never allow you to be sad!"

Flaco remained downstairs while she kept him busy feeding the chickens until she received a sign from her mother, asking her to take Flaco outside until the body was removed from the house!

"Suppose he wants to see me or has some instructions for me, I must go to him!" he insisted.

"Flaco, he is much too ill to see you! I doubt very much that he even knows who you are! I think it is best that you remain out here with me!"

Flaco already knew from experience that there was no point in arguing with her once her mind had been made up! She

was a youngster but already life had made her wise beyond her
years. Perhaps she was right, he thought as he tried desparately
to hold back the tears that were streaming down his face. Soledad
walked over to him and carefully wiped away the moisture! It was
important that the strain of the loss be lightened! Already she had
taken it upon herself to be his protector, and a part of her job was to
be with him in the time of need. She led him outside and skillfully
began asking him questions about life and why it was that some
people were much too poor to survive through bad conditions?
He tried his best to give her the answers to her questions but his
mind was on other more important things at the time. His thoughts
were fixed on a father who was dying knowing that he would never
speak to him again; and it was going to be necessary for him to
assume the role of being the man of the house after he was gone!

His father had lingered a few more days than Don Jose had
expected! When the end came, Flaco was busy working out in the
field preparing the ground for the spring planting. It was now up
to him to provide a crop sufficient to feed his mother and him. The
funeral was simple with only a few mourners to accompany the
wooden box to the church. After the mass, several of the young
men had carried the plain wooden box to an area behind the church
where it would be buried in the small cemetery that contained most
of the departed souls from the area. Her own father was buried
just a few feet away! When she saw for the first time the simple
grave marker with his name, all of the sadness, the sorrow, the
disappointments of her young life came back to remind her of what
she had lost. She knew how long she had suffered and how long it
had taken her to realize that her father was not going to return. It
seemed important that she spare Flaco from this pain. She stood
next to him when Padre Joaquin recited the final funeral prayers,
and held his hand tightly when they lowered the casket into the
empty hole. It was only when he began to cry that his mother came
over to him and comforted him. Soledad quickly intervened telling
his mother that she would take care of him just as she had taken
care of everything he needed to do to complete his work out in the
field.

In the days that followed, Soledad was always at Flaco's side! After completing her own work of washing clothes, attending to the animals, she would rush over to his house and help him turn over the soil at night time when she was tired and ached all over from the strenuous work. She soon developed hard calluses on her hands from using the hoe and the pick and fullfilling the tasks that needed to be done. By the time she returned home she was so tired that all she wanted to do was to go to bed, knowing that the sun would soon rise again; and the daily ritual of doing her own chores would begin all over again. She didn't mind it at all! It was a necessary evil that needed to be done because it was the only way to make sure that Flaco and his mother remained in Salinas and wouldn't move away from the town where he was born!

Several years had passed and nothing had happened to improve the economic conditions of the country. Soledad was no longer a child! Instead she had turned into a beautiful young teenager, full of enthusiasm and hope for tomorrow! Despite her changes, the strength and determination she had from childhood always remained a part of her. Both she and Flaco had weathered many storms, but she had always remained at his side ready to come to his aid if anything happened where he would need her! She had been convinced that among her duties was the one she cherished the most, being always at his side to help him in every way! After all, as long as she was there to help him he would continue to be happy and contended! It was a form of security that she both wanted and needed, not knowing what she would do if he ever decided to leave her. Then one day, from out of nowhere things suddenly changed! She would never know whether or not the changes had been for better or for worse, not that it mattered! Everything was intended to be a part of growing up! It was a dangerous time for both of them; and she quickly knew she would need to take control of things regardless of the dangers that came with foolishness!

It was a hot, summer day and Soledad had gone down to the river to wash her clothes as she always did each morning! Flaco had been there with her and because it was so hot, he removed his shirt and decided he would jump into the shallow river and cool off his body. The sky above was cloudy and it seemed as though one of the frequent violent summer storms, that were always drenching the area in the summer months, was about to drench the area once again! He had ignored her pleas when he told her of his plans! She knew how vicious the summer storms could be and Soledad was fearful of the lightning, especially if he was in the water. Several meters away from the shore there was a small island. Occasionally, Flaco would jump into the water, swim out to the island, and then swim back! He had done this many times before without any problem! Today, Soledad was fearful! She had urged him not to go into the water, but he continued to ignore her warnings and jumped into the cold water waving his arm at her as he allowed the cold water to chill his body! All of a sudden, from out of nowhere, the storm suddenly appeared, complete with the ominous clouds and treacherous streaks of lightning everywhere. Soledad immediately stopped washing the clothes as the river water began to rise with a dangerous flow of the storm. As he reached the island, she knew immediately that the currents were much too strong to risk returning to shore. Flaco became frightened and called out to her, telling her that he was unable to swim back! The storm had interrupted their afternoon and it was getting late! She knew that if he tried to return and swim against the tide, the downward currents were also too strong and it was doubtful that he would be able to overcome them and arrive safely back to shore.

"Soledad," he yelled frantically. "Que voy hacer?" (What can I do?) She could see that he was frantic and was afraid that he wouldn't be able to return to the shoreline!

"Don't worry!" she yelled back. "Stay where you are until the storm passes and then you will be able to swim back!"

"But I can't!" he yelled back. "The water is rising and it will soon cover the island! I can't remain here! What can I do?" he asked. She could see that he was in trouble and needed her help desperately.

"Don't move, Flaco!" she ordered. "Don't try to swim back, the currents are much too strong! Stay there until the storm passes, then, you'll be able to return!"

"But I can't do that!" he pleaded. "Look, the water is almost covering the island! I can't stay here! I'll need to take my chances and swim back!" The tone of his voice alerted her that he was getting desparate and frightened! If she let him try to swim back, he might do something foolish that would put his life in danger!

"No! Don't you dare!!!" she yelled back. "The water is too deep and the currents are very strong! You'll never be able to make it! Just stay there and don't worry, I won't leave here without you!" Even though she had done her best to remain calm, in silence, she was also frightened at what was happening! With the water rising and Flaco not being able to swim back, she needed to do something and it had to be done quickly! Her mind was full of ideas and none of them were good! There was no point in her swimming out to the island for fear they would both be stranded! On the other hand, Flaco, her Flaco was in trouble! She needed to save him, but how? How could she possibly get him back to shore while the storm was in full force? There had to be a way, but how? What could she do? She needed to come to his aid! He was her everything! There was no way she could let him remain in danger on that small island! All of a sudden, an idea came to her! If she could get a long branch from one of the trees and extend it across the water, he could hold on to it and she could pull him back against the tide!

"Listen to me!!" she yelled back. "I want you to stay where you are! I'm going to try to find a large broken tree branch and try to reach the island. Whatever you do, don't dare leave that island! Give me a little time to find something I can push across to you!"

"But you can't! It's raining too hard and it's thundering and lightning! I'm afraid of what will happen to you if you get struck by lightning!" he told her. "You must go back home and I'll try to remain here until the storm passes over!" His calm voice didn't fool her one bit! She could see that he was trying to act calmly but all the time he was frightened. She also worried that he might do something foolish that might harm him!

"Just stay there and I'll be right back! Don't move; do you hear me?" she ordered.

She stood idly watching some of her fresh washed clothes drift down stream while she ran off to search for a tree limb that was long enough to reach the island. Soaked from the downpour, nothing else mattered! Flaco was in trouble and she needed to be there for him! His voice had sounded much too weak to expect him to ride out the storm without her help! She ran off into the woods, stumbling, tripping and falling several times. Her clothes were filled with mud as she stumbled through the brush until her eyes saw a fallen tree limb that seemed long enough to extend from the shore line to the small island. She grabbed hold of the limb and dragged it across the mud until she reached the water's edge! By that time the island was barely visible as the rising currents were quickly covering the island. Knowing that she had little time, she quickly dragged the tree limb to the water's edge. She could feel the strength of the currents fighting her; but she knew that it was going to take all of her strength to push the tree limb against the tide until it reached the island. It took all of her strength as she pushed and tugged the branch floated across the water until it finally reached the island.

"Hurry! There isn't much time! The water is almost over my head!" he yelled back at her in frantic desperation.

"No te preocupes! No voy dejar que algo te pase!" (Don't worry! I'm not going to let anything happen to you!) Then, with a sudden renewed burst of strength, she gave the tree limb one final shove as it landed on the island. "Now, when it gets a bit closer, grab hold of the limb and I'll pull you back!" she said with determination.

"No, I can't! The currents are too strong! You won't be able to hang on to the tree limb!" he told her, terrified at what she was asking him to do.After all, she was only a young woman, and he felt that there was no way she had enough strength to pull him across to safety!

"Don't worry!" she yelled back."You need to have faith in me! I have never failed you and I won't fail you now! Do you or don't you trust me?" she asked exhibiting a defiant determination! He knew better than to doubt her strength whenever she was determined to do something that she needed to do!

"Of course, I trust you! I just don't think you are strong enough to battle the currents!" he answered.

"Then, stop hollering! Save your strength and do as I tell you!" it was no longer a request. It came as a firm order knowing that she needed to take complete control of the situation. After several attempts, she finally maneuvered the tree limb into position. She took one quick look at herself and realized that her clothes were soaked from the rain water. Her long dark brown hair was drenched and the water was dripping down her face. "Okay!" she hollered. "Now hold on to the tree limb and I'll bring you back on shore!"

Flaco did as he was told! He took hold of the tree limb and held on to it tightly as she started to move backward holding tightly on to the other end and pulling him back and back and back until he was finally on shore! When she saw that he was back, she dropped off the limb and fell exhaustedly to the ground. Flaco went over to her and tried to keep her from falling, but he was too late. He took hold of her arms and pulled her back on her feet holding her against him! It suddenly occured to him that she was only inches away as he remained still staring into her eyes. He realized that she was no longer a child and neither was he. Both were teenagers and both were feeling strange sensations throughout their bodies that they had never felt before. It was difficult to describe what they were feeling! Whatever it was, it made them feel both good and bad all over! Suddenly, he felt that the young girl had turned into a woman; and, for the first time he noticed that she had long, brown hair and a fair, smooth pale complexion! Her lips were full and smooth, and her eyes were like deep dark caverns, tantalizing and yet mischievous, but with a secret beauty that seemed to go right through him! It was a strange feeling as he felt he was seeing her face for the first time! She was also having the same frightening feelings! It almost seemed that he was no longer her friend, her mentor her dependable aid! No, he was something else! Yes, he was thin and tall, but there was also a rugged beauty about him she had never noticed before! At first, the thought of what she was experiencing was frightening because she still remembered that in church they had always said that these feelings were sinful and needed to be controlled! Although it was something she needed to do, it was something she didn't want to fight if only because she liked the way she was feeling. They remained standing, soaked from the rain and looking at each other as if for the first time. All of a sudden, she knew it was necessary to break the spell when she noticed that he had cut his hand from holding on to the limb! The blood was rolling down his arm; strange, she thought, that she had failed to notice it!

"You are bleeding!" she told him. "Let me wrap it up for you with one of the bandages!"

"That's okay!" he answered. " It will be fine! I think we had better go back!" He knew that it would be dangerous to remain where they were, especially with the new found feelings!

"Not yet!" she answered. "There is something else I want to do! I'm going to cut myself because I want to have my blood mix with yours!"

"But Soledad, that is crazy! Why should you cut yourself?"

"Because I want my blood to mix with yours! That way, we will both know that no matter what happens to us and no matter where we are, there will be always a part of you that will be with me, and a part of me that will always be with you! No matter where I am, there is always a part of you that will be with me! That way, we'll always be together and no one will ever be able to separate us!"

"Okay, if that's what you want! I still think it's crazy! I'm not going anywhere and neither are you, so we'll always be together! Perhaps, that is our destiny!" he told her, not knowing that there destiny was about to change! Shortly, the only thing they would have in common was the blood oath they had taken this day!

Soledad did not answer! She looked at him with sadness and despair! It was almost as if she had a strange feeling telling her that they would soon be separated and that each would soon be going his separate way. The poverty in Spain had worsened and she was wise enough to realize that eventually the security she had felt as a youngster would soon end! The day would come when she would need to face the bitter world all alone! Nothing would ever remain the same! Already, an exodus of Spanish citizens had begun and those that could afford a passage by boat had begun to leave the country at an alarming rate. They were going to other places, such as the United States and Cuba, where it had been theorized that the leaves on the trees were filled with dollars. The utopia they mentioned had offered them a decent living abroad, away from the squallor and the decadence that was being felt thoughout the country. The blood exchange she had insisted on with Flaco was necessary, if only to give her a false sense of security that nothing between them would change. It was something to give her reassurance knowing that wherever Flaco went, she would always be with him!

In her search for a better life, she had spoken several times with the local parish priest, but Don Joaquin had not been able to give her any assurance that things in Spain would eventually get better. Praying for miracles did not put food on the table, and the small parcel of land was not providing enough vegetables for their survival. Just a short distance away in Flaco's house, things were even worse! Flaco's mother would pass away the time sitting outside in a small wooden chair. Eventually she would roll a cigarette, making sure she used the tobacco sparingly, just enough to satisfy her craving while her son worked the land doing his best to produce just enough vegetables to last them for the winter. Soon, he noticed that his mother had started having coughing spasms! As time went by, the spasms became more severe and more frequent! They were nearly the same as the ones his father had suffered before he died. Soledad was seeing a repetition of his father's illness just before being transported to her house for his final days.

Reality soon told her that the work in the land was much too difficult for Flaco! The land was becoming more and more parched and unyielding! All of his best efforts in making it produce was going to waste. There had been times when she would go to his house and would help him farm the land and work the soil! Soon, she developed calluses in her hands until they ached so much that she was unable to help him. By the time she would return home, she felt tired and her body ached all over feeling as though it were on fire from the hard work. Never once did she ever complain about the work knowing that it would sadden Flaco to know that, he, as a young man, had not been able to supply the work that was needed. She remembered once hearing her father telling her that it required a special person to work the fields; and, whatever that meant, one thing was becoming abundantly clear! The work was much too difficult for a thin young man; and even while she considered herself to be the strongest, she had to admit that the work was much too difficult for her young body! Soledad fought hard to hide her feelings for fear that he might eventually leave her and seek work elsewhere, perhaps even as far away as Oviedo, where it was doubtful she would ever see him again.

By the end of the decade, "La Tierra del Sol", or the land of sunshine had turned into "La Tierra del Infierno"! The warm, comforting Spanish sun had turned into a scorcher and when combined with a severe drought all summer long, it had truly become the land of Satan! All of the small farms in the area had been scorched due to a lack of rain that made a bad situation much worse. None of the lands produced nearly enough vegetables and all of the Horreos in the area were empty, except for a few heads of "kale" or "Verzas" that managed to defy the elements and continued to grow, but with a stunted growth. Several heads of the cabbage-like vegetable were required for making the traditional, "verzas" soup, the mainstay of the people from Asturias!

Soledad woke up one morning, washed her face and accidentally looked into a broken mirror that was hanging on the wall of her small bedroom. It was the first time that she had noticed that her youthful appearance had disappeared and she was now growing up into a woman! Her body was developing into maturity and her chestnut brown hair was hanging loose and long! She had mixed feelings about the way she looked! She hesitated for a few moments, long enough to admire herself and no longer did she see the young child she had been. Her dark, piercing eyes had grown even darker and larger; and her warm smile was starting to fill her body with all sorts of mixed thoughts and desires. In silence, she wondered if Flaco had taken notice of the way she looked! Slowly, she turned to her right and then to her left, and was pleased with what she saw, perhaps for the first time in her life. She almost dreaded the thought of having to wear the frumpy, blue, unglamorous garment, white stockings and the wooden shoes she always wore whenever she did the house chores. Today was threatening to be another scorcher and the only comforting thought was that she would need to go down to the creek and wash the clothes and bandages! She was thrilled when she found out that her mother was earning a few coins working with the sick patients that occupied the second floor. Of course, with poverty all around her, there were many times when the patients did not have the money to pay; and they would settle their debts with a chicken, or a loaf or two of freshly baked brown bread, called "borona" that she gladly accepted knowing that at least it was nourishment for her and her daughter.

Soledad went down to the waters edge carrying the large, circular straw basket carefully balanced on her head. It was better to complete the laundry before the hot, afternoon sun would be much too strong and would prevent her from washing the clothes. Soon afterward, she heard the sound of footsteps and smiled at herself without bothering to look and see who was coming! There was no need to look, she could tell by his footsteps as she did every day when she went to wash her clothes! Little did he know that this was the only moment in her life that she cherished and looked forward to each day. After he greeted her, she paused long enough to look at him! It occured to her that she was now seeing him as she had seen herself in the mirror! He had grown up and was now a handsome young man! Yes, he was still thin; but, then, he had always had a thin frame probably the result of being undernourished for most of his life!

"Ya estas trabajando?" he asked. (You already working?) It was his regular morning greeting, not knowing what else to say. She had the feeling that he also had looked forward to those few stolen moments together by the edge of the river. Since the day she had saved him from drowning, their relationship had grown even fonder; and it almost seemed as if they depended upon each other for a few stolen moments of well deserved happiness! Today was no exception! That is, until he started to speak and she quickly felt her heart sink to her feet!

"Soledad, I won't be able to come here anymore to see you!" he said. It seemed strange that for the first time she heard him say that his reason for coming there each morning was to see her! It was something she already knew, but hearing it from him made it sound even better! It had been something she had known since they were youngster but had never dared to admit it to anyone, not even to themselves!

"Porque?" she asked. Her eyes were following his every move as she watched him getting nervous as he searched for the right words to say, trying to avoid the look of disappointment!

"Tomorrow, I will be reporting to the "cuartel of the Guardia Civil" There was a small garrison of the prestigious Guardia Civil or Civil Guard that had been assigned to Salinas in place of a police department. It was not at all unusual for some of the young men to join the Guardia Civil! Because of the poverty throughout the area, it was a way through which they would be amply fed even though the pay was very minimal. Of course, it would be necessary for them to spend their nights at the cuartel or the garrison while they received the required training. The length of training varied from trainee to trainee, depending on their intelligence and the dedication to their work! It was a vigorous program and one that would require him to be away from his home! Soledad was stunned when he told her the news!

"Why do you have to join the Guardia Civil? It isn't necessary!" she said, trying not to show her surprised disappointment. If the living conditions at her house were poor, the situation where Flaco lived had to be even worse! Still, there had to be a way! It didn't seem right that she should be doing her chores and knowing that she would no longer be looking forward to hearing his footsteps as he came down by the water to visit her each day!

"It's no use, Soledad! My mother and I talked about it and we both decided this was the only way! The "finca" is no longer yielding a harvest and we have no money for food! Your mother has asked us to come to your house for our meals, but I need to do something more to help our situation! It is bad enough that your mother will be feeding one extra person without also having to feed me!"

"But why? Why must you become a Guardia Civil? Why can't you come to my house with your mother and have your meals with us? Surely, a pot of 'verzas" will feed two people instead of one!You can eat at my house every night!" she told him.

"I can't do that! Besides, I am a grown man and I need to do something worthwhile with my life! It just wouldn't be fair to your mother nor to me! You are the one who is doing all of the work and I am doing nothing! Even the farm refuses to produce! What is there for me to do? " he told her. He was trying hard to defend his position knowing very well that she wouldn't understand the way he felt. His pride would not allow him to accept handouts, especially realizing that he was in good health and that he needed to do something besides work of a piece of land that produced very little.

"If you don't want to work on the land, perhaps you could help my mother working with the patients! I'm sure that if I spoke to Don Jose, he would welcome your help!" she told him.

"Be honest, Soledad! There is hardly enough work for one person much less two people! Besides, what is there for me to learn? At least if I went to the cuartel, the Guardia Civil would teach me how to read and write. With any luck, who can say where that would lead? My decision is made up; please, don't try to change it!" he pleaded.

"But what will become of me? What happens to the oath we took with our blood saying that we would always be together?" she said. For the first time, she felt her eyes fill with tears as she spoke and struggled hard to conceal them so that he would not see how disappointed she was. There had always been a side of her reminding her that this day might come; and this had probably been the reason why she had unknowingly insisted on the blood oath they had taken several years ago.

"It isn't that I won't be seeing you! I'll be returning home on weekends! At least, I will be well fed and there will be enough money for my mother to buy food! Please try to understand! I don't want to hurt you nor would I ever hurt you, but, this is something that I need to do! You'll see! A day will come when you will be proud of me and this will make me a better man, and perhaps a lot smarter also!"

"You are already a smart person! Think of all the things you have already taught me! Who am I supposed to turn to? There is no one who will listen to me, I may just as well be dead, because without you, that is what will happen to me!" She hated herself for sounding so desperate, yet she knew how much it would hurt her if he left!

"No, Soledad! You won't die! You are now a very attractive woman and I am certain that someday a man will come along who will marry you and will make you happy!"

It was this last remark that surprised and saddened her more deeply! She had always lived with the anticipation that they had been meant for each other. This had been why she had insisted on their blood oath! To her it was a silent omen, not only that they would always be together, but also that they belonged to one another.When the time came and they had grown up, she assumed they would be married and have their own family! It would be their children and no one else's! The thought of her having someone else's children had never crossed her mind! She had accepted the fact that poverty was a way of life! Still, she was optimistic that the times would eventually change for the better! It didn't matter that they were poor. Everyone was poor! It was a way of life that had to be dealt with! After all, had not Don Joaquin preached all along that poverty was a way of life, and that if their hearts were pure and without sin, how could anyone consider themselves to be poor? One thing was certain! Her own sins had been minimal! She had never harbored an evil thought in her life! All of her life had been spent thinking about others who had less than she, and she had prayed often at home and at church that things would change! She had learned to live for that day and waiting for her wishes to come true! What little of her world was left, had suddenly been taken away from her by Flaco! He had been her security ever since her father had died! Now, what little security she had left was being taken away by someone with whom she had taken an oath in blood! There was no point in insisting, his mind was obviously made up! She realized, finally, that it was a cruel world after all, realizing that she would need to provide for herself if she had any hopes of surviving! Perhaps he would return one day! There was always the chance that he would be unhappy or that he would miss her and would want to come back home! All that was left for her to do was to pray and hope! If Flaco no longer wanted to listen to her wishes, perhaps there was still a God in Heaven who was willing to listen to her pleas!

"In other words, what you are saying is that the blood oath we once took means nothing, is that it?" she asked coldly, as she rolled up the sleeve of her dress and showed him the long scar made the day she had saved his life. Flaco looked at her and realized how much he had hurt her! It had been something he swore he would never do!

"No, Soledad, you are wrong! The oath we once took and the blood we exchanged is something that I will never forget. I'm sorry if I hurt you! I never wanted to do that! Besides, I will still be home on weekends, and I'll come here every day I am home and be with you! That won't change nor will I ever forget you! There comes a time when everyone needs to do what must be done in order to exist! It has nothing to do with being happy! Unfortunately, we are living at a time when it is hard for us to create any life for ourselves. You may not realize this now, but there will come a day when you'll know that I was right. Perhaps, in your own way, you'll even be grateful for what I am about to do!"

There was no point in getting him to change his mind! It seemed inconcievable that he would make such a rash decision without having first discussed it with her! During their lives, they had always confided in each other. It had almost been as if they were both one person. They thought alike, acted alike, and their needs and wants were the same! How could he have done such a thing? Did he not realize how much she needed him? Didn't he stop to think that if he left, there was a part of her that would leave with him? How could he have been so insensitive to her feelings? Many thoughts were still struggling for reason within her mind. If this was the way it needed to be, then, so be it! She was much too proud to beg him not to leave her! Her father had always reminded her that she was an Asturiano; and, despite their poverty, Asturianos were proud people who never begged for anything!

"Bien! Pues ve te ya, que no te necesito!" (Go now! I no longer need you!) she told him finally as she got down on her knees and started to wash the clothes. Flaco remained watching her hoping that she would at least say something encouraging but she remained silent. It was necessary for her to do whatever she could so that he wouldn't see her eyes filling with tears. Her heart was broken and she had the need to conceal this from him! It was a time for her to be strong and resolute in her determination. Flaco had wanted to be out of her life! Well, then, so be it! She wouldn't stand in his way! Instead, she would get out of his new life; but deep inside, she also knew that he would never be very far away. Wherever he went and whatever he did, there was a part of her that would always be with him! There was also a part of him that would never be very far away from her heart! The pent up anger she was feeling made her work more feverishly as if her work was a way of getting rid of her frustrations and her broken heart. She heard the same footsteps again; but this time they were moving away from her, something he had never done before. For a few seconds, she fought off the urge to call him back, tell him how much she needed him; but, then, the voice of her father came back reminding her that she was a proud Asturiano! She was much too proud to urge him to return!

It seemed amazing how quickly everything in her life had changed! She knew that dire needs required extreme remedies, and there was no denying that things were going from bad to worse. There had been one occasion when she had gone to the "Horrio" for some fresh vegetables only to notice that it was nearly empty. It was only November and the coldest months of winter were yet to appear. If the temperatures of the previous years were any indication of what the winter was going to be, she knew it would be terribly cold and that there would be a persistant shortage of food. Other steps were imperative if they were going to survive the cruelty of the season.

The seashore of the town where it faced the Mediterranean Ocean was equipped with a small wooden pier where the fishing boats would return from the sea with daily catches of fish which were to be sold on the open market. Soledad decided that from

that time on, she would go down by the pier each day after the
fishing boats came in just before sundown. Once the fishermen
came ashore, they would carefully review the catches of the day
and retain only the fish and sardines that were large and meaty
enough to sell. The fish that were too small for market were
discarded and tossed back into the sea. Soledad had watched the
fishermen discard the small fish for several days and realized that
most of the fish that was being discarded back into the ocean were
small sardines. She put on her jacket before the sun had set for
the day and went down to the pier where many of the boats had
already come in and were busy selling their catches of the day. She
waited until one of boats arrived and just before a young toothless
fisherman was about to discard the small sardines into the ocean,
she called out to him!

"Senor, por favor! Quiero que me den el pescado que no
sirve!" (Sir, please! Give me the fish that you cannot sell!) she
asked.

"Si nena! Como no!" the large burly man answered as he
reached into a large round basket made out of straw and pulled out
several of the smaller fish and gave them to her! She placed the
fish into the lull of her white apron and quickly took them home.
When her mother saw her coming and holding on to her apron,
she wondered what her daughter had been up to. Ever since Flaco
had gone away, she had noticed that her daughter had started to do
certain things on her own without saying anything to anyone. Her
mother knew how badly she had been hurt by his absence; and she
wondered if some of thye things she was now doing were merely
a way of getting even with Flaco for abandoning her! Hoping that
she would eventually overcome her grief, her mother had decided
to leave her alone without interfering hoping that time would allow
her to heal her wounds!

"Que tienes ahi?" (What do you have there?) her mother
asked.

"The "horrio" is nearly empty! We haven't any food, so I
decided to go down to the pier and ask the fishermen to give me the
small sardines that were too small to sell at the market! The man

looked through his basket and gave me enough for dinner!" she answered.

"Buena idea, hija!" (Good idea!) her mother answered.

Soledad knew that it had been a good idea! It was so good in fact, that she wondered why she had never thought of it before! Suddenly, Flaco came to mind! Perhaps had she thought of it sooner, Flaco would still be with her and there would be no need for him to leave! Not that it mattered! This was now survival and she was determined to survive if only to show him that she didn't really need him! Her daily walks down to the pier had become a daily occurence. She would rush through her chores and try her best to finish early so that she could meet the boats when they came in from the sea with their catch! As time went on, she noticed that after a while she was not alone! Several of the other girls from the area had seen her and had also gone down to the pier to gather up the fish that was going to be discarded. Soledad noticed that some of the dirty fishermen, many with heavy unshaven beards would routinely pay more attention to those young women who would smile and wave to them as they were docking the boat to the pier. She soon learned that in order to continue getting the fish, she was going to need to give the young man a flirtatious smile, hoping that the added attention would provide her with more fish!

On one occasion she had stood by the pier waiting for one of the arriving boats to dock when she saw an old man standing on the deck with a younger man, both waving and smiling at her! She quickly flashed them a smile and waved back hoping that this added attention would be rewarding. She heard the older man telling his partner, "Oye! Mira que guapa es esa guaja! Dale todo el pescado que quiera!" (Look at the pretty young girl! Give her all the fish she wants!) As soon as the lines of the boat had been secured, the young man jumped on shore and went directly over to her. She slowly elevated her apron making the cradle for the fish. As he placed the fish into her apron, she felt him pressing with his hands against the lower part of her body! Soledad quickly moved away from him taking the young man by surprise!

"Que pasa, guaja? No quieres el pescado?" (What's the matter? Don't you want the fish?) he asked. She returned his stare and noticed that he was smiling through several missing front teeth. He almost looked like one of those bad-men she had once heard about called "piratas", and quickly realized that she was going to need all of her strength in order to thwart him away quickly!

"Claro que quiero el pescado! Perso si me vuelves a tocar, to meto un punal!" (Of course I want the fish! But, if you touch me again, I'll kill you!) She had no way of knowing whether or not she could ever be capable of such a thing. The only thing she did know was that the feel of his dirty hand on her was repulsive! If this is what she needed to do in order to get some fish that was going to be discarded, she would rather starve! The man gave her a hearty laugh as some of the other boats were starting to come in to the pier and soon joined in the laughter. The frown that was on her face made him know that she wasn't kidding! She meant every word! The young man went back on board, came out with an armful of sardines and handed them to her!

"Toma, nena, que bien las mereces! (Here, young lady, you deserve them!) he said, still grinning. From that day on things had changed! No longer did the young fisherman make any more advances toward her. Instead, he would look for her at the pier when the boat docked! The first bundle of fish he took off the boat was for Soledad, who had been anxiously waiting for them to arrive from the sea. The fish was able to sustain them through the winter months! She knew that she had learned her first cruel lesson in survival and had passed the test with flying colors!

CHAPTER 2

The cuartel of the Guardia Civil was intended to respond to any civil unrest, violence, or other disorders. They were expected to lend a hand during disasters or any other emergencies that required the aid and assistance of the local garrison. It was a prestigious honor not only to serve but also if selected for training. Because of who and what they represented, the men were admired and respected by the people of the communities where they served.

The garrison of Aviles was smaller than most! It was staffed by a limited number of guards with only fifteen or twenty men. Most of them were youngsters from the local areas who had been selected for training. After the training had been finished, they could be expected to be transferred to other garrisons around the country. El Flaco was one of those young men who showed promise and was immediately selected for advanced training. Because of his calm demeanor, his superiors felt that he had a natural good sense of objective reasoning and should be trained in the field of civil disobediance where his judgement could more adequately be utilized. After a few weeks of physical training, it was soon felt that this tall, young recruit was showing all of the requirements for leadership. After completing his initial training consisting of strengthening his body muscles, one of the main requisites, several of his superiors targeted him quickly for advanced training. It was a necessary field that needed more and more recruits because there was a growing sense of instability throughout the country and several sqirmishes with the local authorities had been reported throughout the country. It was no secret that the political situation in Spain was worsening as more and more people were losing their jobs; and unemployment was beginning to spread in the industrial areas of the country. Many of the unemployed citizens, especially in the small towns were openly expressing their displeasures with the government and were asking for reforms that would enhance the economy of the nation and would restore the jobs that had been lost. This problem was being felt not only in the larger cities; but it was also spreading to the smaller towns, particularly in the north, that depended largely on farming. The area was also being hit by a dry, hot summer and the small farms had failed to produce sufficient amounts of vegetables to sustain the local farmers throughout the winter.

Flaco had been away from home several weeks before being allowed to mount a horse and return home for the weekend! He was happy with the way he looked as he took one last look in the mirror! His brand new olive green uniform, complete with a black shoulder strap that started at his shoulder and ended up on his hip where his holster for his revolver was heavily polished, gave him a feeling of pride knowing that he had qualified out on the pistol range and was now qualified to carry his own weapon. The "tricornio" or odd shaped three corner black leather hat was smartly tilted forward over his forehead. It was a display of authority yet carefully designed not to obscure his field of vision. He was proud of what he had accomplished in so little time! Now that he had become the envy of many other young men his age, he was quite sure that Soledad would be proud to be seen walking with him. Flaco had made many plans, hoping to spend a few days with her.There was that certain spot down by the river where she had once saved him from drowning that had become a favorite meeting place. He also knew where to find her in the early morning hours when she was washing her clothes and the white bandages from the previous day.Now that he had been paid the handsome amount of "four pesetas" (eighty cents) as payment for one month of service, he felt both a feeling of wealth and elation knowing that, for the first time in his young life, he had some money in his pocket that he could spend on her. Hopefully, there was enough for him to go into town and buy her a present; something she would be able to hold on to and cherish during his absence. It would have a special meaning knowing that it had come from his first pay check as a "Guardia Civil"! Perhaps it could be a kind of symbol between the two of them that a part of him had remained with her! Then, everytime she thought about him, she had something that she could return to! Something special that he had brought only for her with his own money and realize that a part of him was still with her!

The angry look on her face was still very much on his mind the day he told her that he was leaving Salinas to join the Guardia Civil. He had never seen her look so hurt and angry, especially realizing that it had been the first time that he had made a decision on his own without asking for her help. Ever since they had been youngsters they had always been together. They had even both agreed the day when she wanted to unite their blood as a secret omen that they would always be together. Even now when they had grown up to be young people, that special bond of attraction had remained a secret bond between them. He was certain that his absence had given her enough time to forgive him for having left her. Of course, he wanted her to see him all dressed up in his new uniform knowing that once she saw him, all of the hurt and anger would be forgiven and forgotten. He had the chance of being with her once more and assuring her that never once had he forgotten their blood oath! Perhaps he would even conjure up enough nerve to tell her how he had never forgotten her during the time when his formal training had occupied most of his time.

Flaco mounted the chestnut brown stallion, placed his feet into the stirrups and started his trip to Salinas. He stopped frequently, just enough to allow the horse to rest briefly and drink water for the trip.Also, he deliberately avoided the city streets and instead guided the horse through the small trails in the woods heading northward. Seven hours later, his legs stiff and tired, he finally reached the old farmhouse. Slowly, he dismounted, tied the horse to an old tree and ran inside to see his mother. His first stop was at the rear of the empty house! It was the portion of the house that remained open for a few animals and provide them shelter from the weather. He paused momentarily and looked down at his black boots. After all, he didn't want to be seen with boots that had stepped into the mud and had lost their shine. When he was satisfied with the way he looked, he walked forward several more steps and opened the large wooden door. Normally, he knew that his mother could always be seen sitting on the old wooden rocker, rolling a few cigarettes that she would smoke when outside the house. Everything seemed exactly as it had been the day he left, except that his mother was not sitting where he had expected her to be! The old wood burning stove located at the far side of the large room was cold, a sure sign that it had not been turned on even though the air was chilly! The stove hadn't been turned on even though the house was cold and damp. He called his mother's name several times, but there was no answer. He was worried! Then, he ran up the wooden stairs at the other side of the room hoping to find her. Unfortunately, she wasn't there! By now he was becoming concerned and worried! It just was not like her to leave the house unattended! He stole a look over the dry and arid farmland, hoping to see her but there were no signs of her. For a while he remained still trying to collect his thoughts and wondering what he should do! The only solution was that she had perhaps become ill and had been transferred to Soledad's house and was now being cared for in the upstair hospital.

Flaco went out of the house and ignored that the horse was still tied to the tree. Instead, he removed the "tricornio" as well as his belt and holster and ran over to Soledad's house. This had certainly not been what he expected when he made plans to go home for a visit; but his only solution was to ask Mrs. Alonso about his mother and then about Soledad! Certainly she would know! The narrow dirt road conneted both houses through the farm as he rushed down the pathway until he reached Soledad's house. As he walked in, his eyes focused on Mrs. Alonso as she was coming down the steps!

"Mrs. Alonso," he said excitedly. "Do you know where my mother is? I've just returned and saw that the house was empty and she was nowhere!" The older woman eyed him curiously from head to foot, silently admiring the way he looked. One look at her

35

face, and he knew immediately that the news was not going to be good!

"Sientate!" (Sit down!) she told him. "There is something that I have to tell you!" She motioned with her hand to an old wooden chair that was away from the door and the cold wind that was coming in from the farm. "I had hoped I wouldn't be the one to tell you the bad news! Unfortunately, your mother passed away several weeks ago! You should also know that she was not alone during her final days! Don Jose and I were at her side when the end came! You remember, she had been ill for a long time! Eventually, her condition became worse and she developed fluid in her lungs! Don Jose did everything he could for her, but it wasn't enough to save her life! She is buried behind the church beside your father; should you want to go there!" she said.

Flaco was both saddened and stunned by the news! Of course he knew that she had been ill, but he didn't think she was sick enough to die! Why did she need to die? Couldn't she have waited long enough to see him dressed in his new uniform? Soledad had been right all along when she told him that life was unfair! Slowly, he lowered his head between his hands and began to cry! Sra. Alonso reached out to him and gently stroked his head and did her best to console him while at the same time reassuring him that they had done everything they could for her. After several minutes, he got up from the chair, thanked the elderly woman, and began walking in the direction of the church! There were pains of guilt that came over him! Perhaps his mother would have still been alive had he not gone away and joined the Guardia Civil! He could only wonder if his mother had realized that what he had done was for her? It seemed that he too had been tossed into the wind, and now he was all alone! The only person who would be capable of understanding him was Soledad and she was nowhere to be found! It was more improtant than ever now that he find her! All through his training he had never given it any thought! Now that he was alone, he could only think how much she meant to him! Since his mother had now passed away, the only person he had left back in Salinas was Soledad! More than ever before, he needed to find her!

On the way to the church and a visit to the cemetery, Flaco decided to walk down by the river where he felt Soledad would be washing her clothes! There was no point in delaying his visit any longer! By this time he was anxious to see her, if only to tell her how much he had missed her! He went down to the one spot that they had both known so well! It was the spot where he knew she would always go to wash the clothes. It was also the spot where she had saved his life what now seemed so many years ago! Yes, he knew the spot well and could still remember how she dragged the old fallen tree limb and carefully edged it over the side until it reached the island where he had been marooned! Smiling, he remembered the look on her face as she tugged and pulled the limb until it finally reached the island. Also, he recalled how that day she had decided to cut herself so that her blood would mix with his as an omen or perhaps a promise that from that day forward the two of them would always be together. The more he thought about her the more anxious he was to see her! Whatever wrong he had done in leaving her, he knew that he could make it up to her if given half the chance! As the thoughts were on his mind, he was determined that this time he would not leave Salinas again until he was convinced that Soledad and he had once again recaptured the closeness they had once depended on and needed more than ever!

The road down to the edge of the river was longer than he remembered! Since that was the meeting place where they had always discussed everything that was on their minds, it seemed only natural that it would be where he would find her. Perhaps she would understand how sad he felt that he had not been home when his mother had passed away. Surely she would understand! If there was someone in the whole world that would understand the way he felt, it would be Soledad! After all, she had always been his strength and she was someone he could always depend on to be there to comfort him if he needed it! Flaco walked briskly, a product of his training, as he anxiously looked forward to seeing her! With a stroke of the hand, he pushed away several small bushes growing between the trees. Off in the distance he saw several young girls from the village also washing their clothes. His eyes scanned the area from side to side, but he failed to see

her! There didn't seem to be any reason to be concerned! She
was probably somewhere with the other youngsters and probably
had turned her back away and hadn't seen him. It was better that
way, he reasoned! This way she would see him all dressed up in
his uniform and would run to him when she noticed how well
he looked. As he approached the water's edge, he could feel the
approving looks of some of the young girls as they smiled at him
and he smiled back! Still, Soledad was not among them! Suddenly,
he felt concerned and disappointed that she wasn't there. He went
up to one of the young women and asked her if she had seen
Soledad Alonso!

"No, senor!" the young girl answered. "Soledad no longer
comes here!"

"No puede ser!" he answered. (It can't be!) "She used to
come here at the same time each day to wash clothes! Do you know
where I can find her?"

"No, Senor Guardia!" the young girl told him. "We haven't
seen her nor do we know where she is! Perhaps her mother might
know! The only thing I can tell you is that we come here each day,
but we haven't seen her! Either she comes at another time, or else,
she goes somewhere else!"

The disappointment that showed on his face was noticeable
as the young girl looked at him, secretly hoping that this young,
good looking Guardia Civil might have been looking for her! Flaco
remained silent! Instead, he rushed back to Soledad's house and
was anxious to talk to her mother. Could it be that something had
happened to her? After all, her routine had always been to be there
washing her clothes early just as she had done for many months. He
was worried and could only wish that nothing had happened to her!
He felt reasonably certain that her mother would have an answer
for her absence! Today more than ever before, he felt the need to
see her and be with her! Could she ever know how much he needed
her comforting words and her assurance that everything would
again be the same as it had always been? Perhaps if he was lucky
she might even decide to hold his hand as she had so long ago, a
simple symbol that would give him the strength and courage that
he desperately needed. For sure, she would have forgiven him for

going away just as she had always forgiven anything he did! Her anger would be replaced with pride and admiration when she saw him in his uniform! He turned around, thanked the young women and went back to the house in time to see Soledad's mother tossing feed to the chickens just as he walked up to the house.

"Senora, donde esta Soledad?" he asked. The uniform had done something to him! He was no longer the shy youngster he had been! There was the unmistakable sound of authority in his voice that he had been taught in school. It was a tone that he had never used before and he noticed that the old woman was looking at him more sternly than before but with a sign of respect! She was obviously seeing him, not as the shy young man she had known from his youth, but rather as an officer of the law who was now speaking to her in a more commanding tone of voice! True he was still calm and inquiring, but he now had an air of authority that caused her to stop and listen.

"No esta aqui!" she answered coldly. (She isn't here!)

"Do you know where she is and when I can see her?" he asked, once again showing signs of authority, while inside him he was more eager than ever with anticipation, not knowing where she was.

"Senor Guardia!" she answered in the same tone of voice. He found it a bit curious that it was the first time she was not referring to him as Flaco as she had always done! Now he was Senor Guardia! It was a name that signified respect and authority. "Perhaps you should come inside! There is more that I need to tell you!"

Her words were troubling and caused him to remain silent! She had used the same words before when she told him about the passing of his mother. All he could do was hope that the same news would not apply to Soledad. Something had happened! Whatever it was, there was a need for him to know! If someone had harmed her, he wanted to go out in search of whoever it was! For some reason the blood bond they had shared many years ago came back to haunt him! He walked slowly inside the house using his hand to disperse the chickens that were in his way. Now, he had already made up his mind that whatever the reason for her absence had been, his air of authority would not change. This was now an official visit! His training had been to investigate these matters; and for this, he needed to be at his best. At this point, he was no longer a friend; that relationship had obviously withered away! Now he was a servant of the law!

"Mrs. Alonso," he began. "Please, I need to know! Has anything happened to Soledad?"

"No Flaco, she is fine! There is, however, something that you should know. When you first arrived, I told her you had come to visit and had asked about her! I thought she would have been interested in seeing you especially knowing that your mother had recently passed away! Instead, she looked at me sternly and told me emphatically that she didn't want to see you! When I asked her why and I told her how well you looked in your uniform, she merely shrugged her shoulders and told me firmly that there was nothing between the two of you! She had no interest in seeing you again! As soon as she had finished, she walked out of the house not wanting to run into you!"

Suddenly, it was now Flaco's turn to look surprised, angry and show a stern side of him that she hadn't seen before! He had been certain, knowing her that she would have certainly forgiven him for going away! Yet, there was a tone of finality in what her mother had said that bothered him! His mind became full of doubts as to whether or not he had made the right decision! In addition, he needed to know whether or not his decision had been worth the price he had to pay? He lowered his head and was staring at the floor for several moments before being able to speak again!

"Do you know where I can find her? I will need to leave here shortly and would like to see her again before I go away!" It was almost as if he were pleading for a chance to see her again!

"I don't know where she went! All that I can tell you is that she sounded very final! She simply doesn't want to see you again! Perhaps it might be best if you were to return to the cuartel!" the elderly woman told him.

He arose from the chair, planted a peck on the cheek of the elderly woman and returned to his house. It seemed strange to realize that all his life the town of Salinas had meant everything to him. Suddenly, the two women who had meant the most to him were now out of his life! The stubborness of Soledad was well known to him, especially on those occasions when she didn't get her way. It now seemed obvious that all of the hopes and wishes he had been eagerly looking forward to had suddenly disappeared. His own world had taken on an entirely different direction and there was little of the old one! Even the pride he had with his accomplishments had all been without meaning. There was nobody to care about them and certainly no one to ask him! The words of Soledad rang out in his mind when she told him that her world had fallen apart when her father had passed away! Although she had been merely a child, she still had felt a certain loneliness, the likes of which she had never experienced before! She had turned to him and he had responded by soothing her wounds and had even assured her that he would always be there for her! Flaco placed the "tricornio" back on his head and put on his shoulder stray and gun holster. Taking a final look around the house, he went outside and untied the horse! There was nothing more for him in Salinas! All that he wanted to do was to return back to the cuartel as quickly as possible! The cuartel had become his home as well as his security! He made himself a promise that he would rise within the ranks as high as possible so that he would never again need to return to Salinas. Whatever success he expected to have, he would owe it all to Soledad! It seemed like such a pity that she would probably never know how much a part of him she would always be!

Only a short distance away on the clear, sandy white beach, Soledad remained all alone on a late and chilly afternoon staring aimlessly at the far off horizon! During the winter months, it was difficult to gather up enough scrap lumber for the stove. Besides, if the wooden scraps were dry, she had seen how quickly they would burn when used for the fire. She remembered how many times she had stood at the same spot and had looked at the freighters as they emptied the cauldrons out at sea. Then, she would watch them dump the particles of coal into the ocean and would see them drifting into shore with the tide. On one occasion, she had asked Don Jose what would happen if they decided to mix the burned coal with the wooden scraps. His answer had been vague but it was certainly worth a try! So, she walked down to the shore carrying her large straw basket. Carefully, she filled the large basket with as much of the coal as she could carry. When she arrived home, she spread out the coal in the sun, long enough so that it would be perfectly dry. When all of the signs of moisture had been removed, she would open the stove and mix some of the coal with the wood that was already burning. It didn't take long for her to realize that the stove remained lit for longer periods of time and that the coal could be burned again! The results soon became rewarding; because, instead of the house being cold and damp during the night, the burning coal now provided more heat for their own comfort as well as for the comfort of their patients upstairs in the hospital!

What had begun as an experiment became a regular chore! She now had another reason for going down to the beach. As soon as she collected the sardines from the fishing boats, she would deposit the sardines at home and would return to the water's edge for the lumps of coal that had washed on the beach! Today, she was alone; and, for the first time, she felt lonely! The evening clouds had begun to gather and the sun was going down! Nobody would ever know how badly she wanted to see Flaco! Why did her father's words have to ruin her life when he told her that 'An Asturiano never begs for anything?' Her father could be happy now, she thought! By obeying him she had missed out on seeing the one person who had shared her childhood! He was gone now and it had all been of her choosing! The chances were that she would probably never see him again! After all, there was no longer anyone for him to come home to, and she had been the one that had sent him away! Could it be that her father may have been wrong when he told her that Asturianos never begged? It didn't really matter now, because she would never know! The only thing that was certain was that her heart was aching like it had never ached before! One thing was certain! There would never again be anyone that would take Flaco's place in her heart! His place had always been special; after all, had they not once been joined with their own blood? At least the silly symbol she had insisted on many years ago now took on a new importance. It was the only thing that remained of her childhood, but it was something that no one could ever take away! Soledad continued to stare at the horizon and reviewed her thoughts! The world around her no longer mattered! There was no one to see the tears that had been falling down her cheeks since she had arrived at the shore. Flaco had always considered her a strong woman; and now she was happy that she was all alone and that he didn't see her crying. Although he had gone away, it was necessary to spare him the pain of seeing her weaknesses for the first time. The sun was slowly setting and it was getting dark. She knew that she should be going home; but, unfortunately, she had the need to speak to someone who could understand what she was feeling, and the reasons why the sanctity of life she had always revered, had suddenly lost its meaning. Would there ever be a time when she would again be happy, the way she had been during her youth? The only person she felt would understand her feelings and would be able to help her was the priest of the local church, Padre Joaquin! It wasn't that she had ever gone to him for advice before, she hadn't! Unfortunately, this was a special occasion, and she needed to speak to him!

Don Joaquin, the priest from the local parish, was a pious man that had spent most of his adult life caring for his people and saying mass for them! The tall, thin, middle aged man no longer had the physical ability of days gone by when he would spend countless hours each day working the fields for an ill member of his parish who were too sick to care for their land! There had even been times when she had seen him all alone down by the river washing his own clothes, as well as the clothes of another sick parishoner who was in need of his services. Never once had he uttered a complaint! Being the pious man that he was, the good priest had always considered these added chores to come with the territory; and, if that was what God wanted him to do, then, why should he complain? His calm demeanor and pleasant sounding voice made him easy to talk to. Soledad remembered her mother once telling her that Don Joaquin was a distant relative. It was something she had never known for certain, because everyone who happened to be a close friend of a family was somehow granted the honorary title of being a relative. This was a catch-all title that was given, when no other titles were available! These people were always considered to be cousins! Don Joaquin had fallen into this catagory! Her mother had once said that the good priest was a distant cousin which probably meant he was nothing more than a good family friend!

Her father had never been a God-fearing man! She had once mentioned to Flaco that the only time her father had seen the inside of a church had been when he passed away and had been taken to the church for Mass before burial! Don Joaquin had visited them on several occasions, especially after her father had become ill. Soledad had always had the feeling that the good Father, despite his family affiliation, had never been welcomed in her house! She noticed that his visits were short and would soon leave her house when her mother or father would tell him that his services were not required! Today, things had changed! She needed his assistance and needed his kind words badly! She had to know why it was that she felt so sad and dismayed, not merely because Flaco had come home for a visit and returned to the "cuartel", but she needed to know why she considered life to be so worthless! It didn't even matter whether she were to live or die! She was wise enough to realize that this was not normal behavior for a young girl barely in her teens! Her own image of a young woman her age was one of happiness and optimism! Unfortunately, she did not know happiness, nor could she afford another disappointment in her young life by being optimiistic! After all, her life was a cloud of monotony and had not changed since her childhood! Why could there be any reason for her to think that things would eventually get better?

She walked back from the seashore slowly; her "Alparagatas" or cloth shoes with a cordoned sole were still wet from her disregard of the ocean spray while gathering coal. She felt a bit of apprehension not knowing exactly how she should approach the priest, nor even knowing what she would say to him, assuming that he was interested in the things she wanted to say and his willingness to listen! When she reached the small, white stucco house, she knocked on the large wooden door! Her knock was weak and for a moment, she had thought about running away! Before her knock was answered, she took off her wet "alparagatas" and entered the house barefooted! It wasn't that she felt uncomfortable; she didn't! It was only that she wondered whether or not this was the thing to do when a person approached the house of a priest!

Don Joaquin opened the door and she immediately noticed that he was dressed in a long, black cassock, probably the same one he had worn the day he had said the mass for her father's funeral. "Soledad, hola! Que haces aqui?" (Hello Soledad! What are you doing here?)

She paused for a moment trying to collect her thoughts, but not before noticing that the expresion on his face was one of kindness and concern, a far cry from what she had expected to see. It occurred to her that the walk to his house was made even longer as she thought about the things she would say to him! During the few times she had seen him at church, she had always seen him reading a large, book with a black cover and a gold cross, that he always referred to as "El Libro Doctrina!" What Doctrina meant was foreign to her! She had no idea what it meantand nobody had explained it to her! For a brief moment, she wondered if she had perhaps made a mistake by coming here! Had it not been that he had quickly asked her to enter, she would have gladly run away in fear of speaking one on one with this stranger dressed all in black! She had somehow conjured up an image of him bringing out that big black book and would start by reading it to her as he always did in church! How would she be able to tell him that she didn't really understand what he was reading?

"Pasa p'ca nena!" he said gently. She walked past him still carrying her shoes in her hand! "Put your shoes next to the stove, so they'll dry!" he told her.A feeling of calm came over her as she felt how easy it was to speak to this man, all dressed up in black and standing before her. "Dime, que te pasa?" (Tell me, what is wrong?) he asked, when he saw ther her eyes were still red and puffy from crying. "Tell me, is your mother ill or is something wrong?" She was again having mixed feelings about pouring out her heart to this stranger. Instead, as she carefully thought of what she would tell him, she started to fumble nervously with her fingers, acknowledging that her mother was not ill!

The priest saw immediately that this was a troubled young woman! All of the training he had received while at the seminary was going to be needed! He was going to need to be patient, supportive and understanding. It had obviously taken a great deal of her young courage for her to come to him and he was grateful that she had taken him into her confidence. "Soledad, I can see that you are troubled and you have come to the right place! I want to assure you that anything you say to me will be held in the strictest confidence! It troubles me to see you looking so sad, and I can also see by your eyes that you have been crying! Tell me, my child! Tell me what is bothering you?"

She walked over toward the warm stove, placed her cloth shoes by the fire and quickly buried her head into her hands and began to cry! The priest went over to her, stroked her head gently and waited a few more moments before asking her again what was making her cry!

"Don Joaquin," she began. "I have been at the sea shore and I have never felt so sad! You know that Flaco and I have always been together. Today, he came to see us. I told my mother that I didn't want to ever see him again, nor did I want him to return!" she admitted.

Soledad watched him curiously as he began to rub his chin as though he was deep in thought! He knew from experience that this was going to be a problem that young people her age would sometimes need to face and it was important that he show her sensitivity and concern for what she was feeling. It might have been much easier to dismiss the problem by telling her that she had simply done what she wanted to do! Unfortunately, he also knew that this was not the answer she wanted to hear!

"Tell me, child, why were you so angry that you never wanted to see him again? Certainly, you must have had a reason!" he told her calmly. Without being aware of what was happening, she suddenly felt that it was very easy to speak to him, especially since he seemed to be showing sympathy for the things she was feeling!

"We were always together ever since childhood, Father! You already know that! He just came and told me that he was going away to become a Guardia Civil! I never thought I was going to be so lonely without him!"

"Perhaps, you shouldn't have asked him to leave!" The priest was happy with himself with his answer. It seemed like a logical and simple solution to a complex problem! Certainly it wasn't the type of answer that would appease her for the things she felt, but, it was an answer never-the-less!

"Father! I wanted him to stay and I was angry with him! He didn't need to go away and just leave me alone! He had no right to do that!" she said as she tried to defend her feelings.

"Did you tell him the way you felt?" he asked while paying attention to every word.

"I told him that I needed him and I didn't want him to leave!" she replied.

"It seems to me that you may be thinking only of yourself and you didn't stop to think about what he was feeling or why he was leaving" he explained. It seemed like such a simple explanation, but he knew that for him to succeed, it served as a way of getting her to open up to the things that were really bothering her.

"For one thing, he told me that it didn't seem fair for me to be working his land that was so unproductive! The horrio was almost empty, and he had no money! I explained that it didn't matter, and that I would help him to work the land! Also, I told him that I needed him to explain things to me that were beyond my comprehension! Now, I have lost him forever and I have nothing left! I don't care whether I live or die!" she said, as she began to speak more freely and he had the feeling that she had taken him into her confidence.

"Soledad, there comes a time in everybody's life when they feel the same way as you! There are times when we feel that we are facing the end of the world whenever something happens that displeases us. It isn't really that way at all! The world doesn't end just because an important part of our lives goes away! The world continues to go on and so must we!" he said, but he was also noticing that he wasn't being very convincing.

"What good is life for me without him?" she asked.

The priest was taken aback! It was not the kind of question he had been prepared to answer! This was a delicate subject, especially knowing the intense poverty that was being experienced throughout the country. He could only wonder how many other young people were feeling much the same?

"The gospel of Saint Thomas tells us something that I have always found very interesting! It tells us that 'within a person of light, there is light'! It is up to us to radiate that light to others. For example, each one of us is a bright light and with every light, there are also shadows! It is up to us to make that light shine through all the shadows! When you get the chance, stop for a moment and look up at the sun! Notice how bright it is! Unfortunately, there are, at times, shadows that tend to block out the brightness! It is during those times that the sun needs to shine even brighter so that the light does not become obscured! Unless we can do that, then, the light will not be seen by the people that we care for, and all we'll have left are the shadows!! No matter what we think at that moment, those that we care about need to see that light! You are a young and beautiful young lady and you are good and kind! You are a light to many people and you must never allow it to be hidden behind the shadows that often get in our way. There will come a time when those shadows that seem so important will disappear, and the light will then shine through! But, only if you let it! I think that is what Saint Thomas wanted us to do!"

"But what kind of life do I have, father? I have no life and I have less hope that it will ever change! The only thing that gave me happiness was Flaco and I chased him away.What kind of light can I possibly give to others when my own life is so full of shadows?" she asked.

"I somehow have a feeling that your young man knows that you didn't really mean what you said. If it is your destiny that he return, then, he will! If not, then, he won't! It's all very simple! But I am also sure that if he doesn't return, someone else will one day come along and take his place! Things will get better but you need to have faith, my child! As for being the light, I think you are a light to your mother, to your friends, and, yes, even to me!" he answered.

"How can I be a light to you, father? I hardly know you! Also, how can I have faith when there is nothing but ugliness all around me? There is no happiness nor is there anything to look forward to!"

"These are the times when you need to have faith! Nothing ever remains the same! There will come a time when you will be happy, my child! Don't ever lose faith, because, in the end, faith is the power that sustains us all! Whenever you are happy, that's when the light shines the brightest! Your job is to make the shadows vanish so that the light can shine through again!"

It occured to her how easy it was to speak to this stranger and how much better he made her feel! Flaco had to know that she had probably not meant what she said and that he was feeling as lonely as she was! No, he would return!! She knew that he would! It had been this stranger, dressed in black, who had spoken to her softly and calmly and had given her a new hope for believing in the future. The only thing he hadn't told her was how long it would take? Perhaps he was right and she really needed to be that light that he had spoken to her about. The fact that Flaco was not with her was probably only one of those shadows that had come into her life. After all, the stranger had reminded her how there are times when a dark cloud casts its shadow on earth; but, eventually, the cloud passes and the sun begins to shine brightly once again! Life was indeed worth living, she thought as she smiled warmly and thanked the priest for listening to her.Slowly, she walked over to the stove, gathered up her "alparagatas" and said goodbye!

"Soledad," he said moments before she opened the door, "before you leave, I want you to promise me one thing! I want you to promise that whenever you feel sad or that life no longer matters, you'll come back here and talk to me! Will you promise me?"

"Why father? Why should you care? I don't even go to church on Sundays!" she said.

"Because I want to help you become the bright light I think you can be! If I can erase some of those shadows, then, I have done my job as a priest!" he answered.

Soledad returned home feeling better than she had felt all day. It had been a good decision to stop and visit with Don Joaquin! He was easy to talk to and she had a feeling that he had felt her needs and had offered a ray of hope that she would now be able to live with. In the back of her mind, she remembered his homily when her father had died. It was then that he quoted Jesus saying that "He was the way, the truth and the light!" It seemed to her that he was now saying that even though she could never be the way, or the truth, she still had the prospects for being a bright light to others. If that was to be her destiny, then, so be it! She decided that she would become that light and wait patiently until the day when destiny would decide that Flaco should return to Salinas! It would give her a new approach that the next time she would be more understanding and would realize that he would do whatever he needed. It was her duty to wait patiently for him to return. She knew that he would indeed return; and, when he did, she would be more understanding and would welcome him home where he belonged!

Flaco arrived back at the garrison just before nightfall! He quickly took his horse to be watered, hung a pail of oats around the neck of the animal, making certain that the chestnut colored stallion would be well fed for tomorrow's exercises! The disappointment he felt as he left Salinas was still very much on his mind! It occured to him that there was nobody left in his home city who cared whether he lived or died. His mother had now passed away and the only person capable of understanding how he felt had made it clear that she no longer wanted to see him. After making certain that the horse was sufficiently in the stall, he went inside the orderly room and saw a message in his box! The message was brief and to the point! It told him that the Post Commander, Colonel Garcia wanted to speak to him as soon as he returned. Flaco went down to the small office at the end of the orderly room, knocked on the door and waited until he was told to enter. He waited anxiously for the few moments until he heard the familiar deep, manly voice asking him to enter and to close the door! He did as he was told, standing before an old man wearing an officer's uniform and also wearing a set of eyeglasses peering at him from behind a large stack of papers piled up on his desk. Flaco stood before him, saluted the Colonel and waited until he was asked to be seated.

"I have been reviewing your record! I noticed that you have received outstanding grades in areas that are of great interest to us. Your instructors have remarked that you have become very knowledgeable in the field of civil disobediance. It seems that your grades are among the highest of your class! As you know there have been a number of social problems throughout the area, especially in the city of Oviedo! I want you to pack your things and prepare to move out with a cadre of twelve men into that city. Your job will be to restore peace and quiet against the uprisings against the government! Do you think you are capable of handling this assignment?" the colonel asked.

Flaco thought about it for a few moments before replying! The prospects of going so far away was troublesome, especially since he knew nothing about the city except that it was the capitol city of Asturias and was much farther away than Salinas or Aviles. Of course, with this assignment it was going to be necessary for him to familiarize himself with the city especially since he had never been there. The first thing he would need to do was to learn the causes for the uprisings and then to step in and try to stop them! There was no way for him to know in advance whether the assignment was going to be either large or small! What he did know was that there was no longer anything in Salinas for him to return to, and this assignment was offering him a chance to go forward and advance in his new career!

"I don't know whether or not I'll be capable of handling this assignment!" he answered. "I suppose that if I can have proper guidance and someone who is familiar with the city, we'll be able to do the job!"

The colonel eyed him sternly and gave him an accomodating smile! "I am placing you in charge of the cadre and you will do whatever you think is best to quiet the situation before it becomes worse! Of course, you will report directly to me and you'll keep me posted on everything that is happening! Is that clear? We don't want the problems to get out of control; and I am depending on you to see to it that they are contained and resolved! Are there any questions?"

Flaco was stunned! This had been the first time he had been entrusted with a command and didn't know whether or not he would be capable of handling that responsibility! Of course, he knew that he had everything to gain and nothing to lose! If he was successful, it would increase his value in the eyes of the commander. On the other hand if he didn't, he could always say that he knew nothing about the city and that the problems might be better served by someone that had already been trained in this area of expertise and who would know what to do!

"No, mi coronel, I have no questions! Please give me a list of the other guardias who will be going there with me! I will gather the men early in the morning and I'll instruct them on what will be expected of them!" he said.

The colonel seemed genuinely pleased! The young man was already showing definite signs of confidence and determination! It would be his first command; and, if he was successful, it was very doubtful that it would be his last!

"Muy bien!" The elderly man said, as Flaco stood at attention and gave him a snappy salute. The colonel returned the salute, after which he then extended his hand in friendship and told him, "I have every reason to believe that you will be successful! Remember, I will be here to help you if you need me! That will be all!" he said as he watched Flaco leave his office. During the time they had been speaking, the colonel was secretly thinking about the awful mess this young man would be going in to, and the terrible time he would have with what was happening in Oviedo! All of the virtues he had learned were going to be needed, including patience, firmness and determination! If this was a test to determine his abilities as a leader, he was going to need all the help he could get! All of the reports were saying that the civil disobediance problems in Oviedo were going to get worse before they turned around for the better!

The thirteen men piled into a slow moving truck as it started to trudge its way into the capital city! All of the men were busy laughing and talking while Flaco remained sitting in the rear of the truck and was silently thinking about his new assignment. It occured to him that this had been the very first time in his life that he had been so far away from home! As he turned his head upwards, he noticed that the cloudless sky was bright with sunlight, a sure sign that Soledad was probably down by the river washing clothes as she did each day about the same time. The brief visit to Asturias had been a disappointment and had hurt him deeply. The death of his mother had been unexpected only to be followed by the news that Soledad, his faithful confidante, had not wanted to ever see him again! He was wondering if his mother had the sufficient medicines and food to survive or had his mother left this world believing that he had abandoned her also. Surely, everyone had to know that there was just no employment and money was necessary commodity for survival. The few pesetas he still had in his pockets had been intended to pay for the medicines his mother needed and also to buy a small gift for Soledad, something she could have as a reminder of what they had been to each other! In Aviles, there had been many occasions to go with many young women, but none had measured up with Soledad! He had remained alone while some of the other guardias had begun dating some of the local young women as soon as they had finished their studies for the day. He had preferred to remain in the garrison, read his textbooks and prepare for the many tests and quizzes that were routinely given to them more often than he would have liked! This was a whole new life for him and he began to like the career he had chosen! The new uniform made him look more handsome than he was, and the flirtacious glances of the young ladies whenever he went into town with the other guards, had not gone unnoticed! None of his new friends were remotely aware of his problems, only that something about him seemed strange because he made to attempts to date the young ladies that were always available to all of them!

For the first time in his life he had been given an authority that was greater than any he would have expected! It seemed to be a trust that had been thrust upon him and made even more difficult by the fact that he had no knowledge of the unrests that the colonel had mentioned. During his training he had been taught how to read and shortly thereafter he read published reports talking about riots and insurrections in some of the smaller towns and cities.The problems mentioned by the colonel had been in Oviedo, and his instructions had been vague and inconclusive. It seemed unusual that he would consider sending out a new recruit on such a mission without any specific instructions to follow. One thing he did know was that after he had learned to read he became aware of the problems throughout the country; and the problems that had been reported were no different from the problems of unemployment and poverty that was being felt not only in Salinas but also in the towns of Norena, Piedras Blancas, and Burgos! Since these towns were mostly farming areas, they didn't get the attention that the unrests in the larger cities such as Oviedo had received. The only areas in Asturias that had not been plagued by unemployment were in the southern areas of the province where there was an abundant amount of work, mainly in the coal mines, where the devastating coal dust would eventually decay the lungs of the workers, creating the employment turnovers! It was already considered that working in the coal mines was akin to preparing for an early death! While he had once thought of going there in search of work, he decided on becoming a Guardia Civil instead. It wasn't that the pay was going to be great, but he liked the authority and the responsibility that came with the job. In addition, he had been taught to read and do mathematical problems, something he had never learned as a youngster! He still felt certain that Soledad would have been proud of him, seeing how he looked in his new uniform, and seeing how intelligent the schools had made him! Unfortunately, his plans had now been upset; and she would never know how much he had thought about her and how much he had been hoping that she would be waiting for him when he returned home!

Oviedo

The large wide open, slow moving truck finally entered the city of Oviedo after travelling the bumpy roads southward! It was the first time in his life that Flaco had ever seen the "trambias" or streetcars in the city's downtown areas! His first observation was that most of the streetcars were travelling nearly empty without any passengers. The slow moving, electric powered streetcars seemed like a novelty to him; and he wondered for how long could the city afford to have them running if the people couldn't afford the "one perrona" that it took to pay for the transportation? He immediately made a mental note while the other twelve guardias of his cadre were passing the time eyeing the few pedestrians that were walking the streets. Some of them were in search of work, while some of them were merely passing the time away attempting to avoid the monotony that always came with unemployment. Flaco immediately told himself that this challenge was going to be much greater than it would have been if it was in Salinas where the men were kept busy cultivating their lands and the women kept busy at work inside their houses or else feeding the animals or washing clothes! When the truck approached the center of the city, Flaco quickly saw a crowd of several, hundred people gathered outside a large, white stone building that appeared to be the "City Hall" or "La Casa del Ayuntamiento"! Most of the people were dressed in traditional peasant clothes, many with small children holding on to their hands.. Some of the older women were dressed in black just the way his mother dressed after his father died. The only difference was that she also wore a black veil over her head showing that they were widows of men who had passed away, probably from working in the coal mines or from long hard hours in the hot sunlight trying to bring some signs of life into infertile lands. In many ways he became aware that they looked no different than they did in Salinas! All of a sudden, memories of his mother, dressed all in black with a veil covering her head came to mind! Now that the scene was being repeated again, he felt a shiver across his back as he remembered the suffering his family had also endured during the difficult times of his young life!

Inside the garrison and after they had been settled, Flaco summoned a large, burly guardia that had been assigned to the cadre. The large man was asked to go inside into the small make-shift office that Flaco had prepared for himself. This man who towered over him was named Guillermo and had gone into

the guardia civil from the hometown in Norena! He had met
Guillermo when both men were in training. After talking about
their backgrounds, they soon learned that they had a great deal
in common. Their backgrounds were similar and Guillermo had
joined the guard because he was tired of spending endless days
working a land that refused to yield enough vegetables to sustain
them through the cold winter months. Flaco had noticed that
Guillermo had walked with a slight limp, but he had never gotten
up enough nerve to ask him about his walk.Not that it really
mattered, because what Guillermo may have lacked in intelligence,
he more than made up for it with his brawn! In addition, he also
felt that this man could indeed be trusted, and when he learned that
the colonel had assigned Guillermo to his group, he was pleased to
have him as a member!

"Sientate Guillermo! Quiero Hablarte!" (Sit down
Guillermo! I want to speak to you!) Flaco ordered. The tall man
sat down in a small chair opposite the old desk and waited for
Flaco to tell him the reason why he had been signalled out! "When
everyone had been settled in their new quarters, I want you and
another Guardia of your choice to go into town and go to where we
saw that large crowd today! I want to know who are the leaders of
the group! Take their names and tell them that I would like to meet
with them this evening here in the garrison! Tell them that they
don't need to worry! No harm will come to them!"

"But, comandante, what do I tell them the meeting is
about? They will be upset if they come to the garrison and see all
the Guardia Civiles! You already know how the politicians have
ignored the pleas of the people.They'll probably think that you
called them here to arrest them or to do them harm!"

Flaco hesitated momentarily! It was the first time anyone
had called him comandante and he wasn't yet accustomed to
hearing him being addressed in this manner.

"It will be your job to convince them not to be afraid!
Between you and me, I want to listen to their complaints and see if
there is something we can do to help them!"

"Are you kidding?" Guillermo said laughing. "If word gets
out that we want to help them, the politicos will be all over us!"

"When I was given this assignment, the colonel made sure that he was vague with his instructions! True, he didn't tell me to see what we could do to help these people, but he also didn't say that we shouldn't try to help them!" Flaco told him.

"I saw some of the ladies that were very old! They were all dressed in black and were walking with the demonstrators! I kept thinking about my mother!"

"I did too! I saw visions of my own mother and the poverty we all felt! I have to do something! I haven't yet decided what I can do, but perhaps, if we can get the leaders here, I may be able to get some suggestions!"

By the time some of the leaders came into the garrison, Guillermo was standing at Flaco's side! Flaco noticed immediately that the men appeared to be frightened, especially as soon as they saw the cadre of other guardias mulling around the garrison. He had thought of sitting at his desk when meeting with them, but since the men were all standing, he decided he would make a better impression on them if he too was standing!

"Gentlemen," Flaco began. "I asked you here because I saw the demonstrations this morning near city hall! Fortunately, the demonstrations were peaceful! I get the feeling that there are some people would like for them to become troublesome so they could send the Guardia Civiles to maintain order! I don't want to see that happening, so I hope you will do everything in your power to keep the demonstrations under control!"

"Senor guardia!" one of the men said. "The people are starving! The children are hungry! Some of the children are ill, but there is no money with which to buy medicines! There is no work for us, and there is no one who is willing to listen to us! The people have good reason to be restless and we don't know how much longer they can continue to be tolerant!"

"How long have these demonstrations been going on!" Flaco asked.

"We have been out there for more than a month! The winter is now upon us and things can only get worse! We have asked to speak to the politicians, but they have repeatedly refused to listen to our pleas! How many "obreros" need to die before they listen to us?" another man asked.

"I have only arrived here today and my men are just getting settled! I can tell you that I am not here to cause harm to any of you! If you will give me your word, I will give you mine! As long as you maintain order and there is no threat to anyone, you will be left alone! In the meantime, I will do my best to do whatever I can to help you! I don't know how or what I can do; but, with your help I'll do my best! On that you have my word!"

The group of six men paused to look at one another bewildered by the things that this guardia civil was telling them! He was the only person that had cared enough about what he saw to do something. Although they all had their doubts, at least they felt comfortable that finally someone of authority had been willing to listen to their pleas. Suddenly, the men broke out in a smile as one of them extended his hand! Flaco took hold of the extended hand and held it in his own for a few moments before letting it go. "I don't know what I can do, but, I'll do whatever I can!" Flaco repeated.

"Senor guardia!" another man said. "I have two young children who are sick and I have no money for medicines! They also have nothing to eat! I don't know what to do or who to go to for help!"

Flaco watched the man and was feeling sorry for him! Before he had finished speaking, the man broke down and began to cry! Flaco reached into his pocket and pulled out "three perronas" and handed them to him. "Here, take them! I want you to use them to buy medicines and make sure that the children have enough food!" he said. The man took hold of Flaco's hand and brought it up to his own lips kissing it and thanking him with tears of gratitude still streaming down his face!

"Gracias, senor guardia! Que Dios se lo pague!" he said over again! (Thank you! May God repay you!) as the small group left his office bowing and nodding until they reached the door. When they were outside, he heard the voice of one of the men say to him, "Que Dios lo bendiga, senor guardia!" (May God bless you!)

He felt good and relieved that he had been able to help the poor man! He knew from past experience what it was like to be both young and hungry! How many times during his youth had he also gone to bed hungry because there was no food in the house? He continued to think about the poor man with his sick children, and suddenly a thought came to mind! He knew it was going to be a long-shot, but he had finally come up with an idea that would help the people! Of course, he already surmised that the politicians would be opposed; and he also wondered how the colonel would feel when he found out what he was doing. Perhaps he would be reprimanded for what he was about to do, but it was a chance that he needed to take, and it was well worth the risk!

"Guillermo, entra y cierra la puerta!" (Guillermo, come in and shut the door!) Hell, Flaco thought! If he was going to get into trouble for helping these poor people, he might as well also enlist the services of one of his men who was just as fearless as he was!

"Si comandante! Aqui estoy!"Guillermo said as he entered the office and closed the door behind him so that none of the other men in his cadre could hear what they were saying!

"I want you to send a dispatch to Colonel Garcia and tell him that I will need to have two pesetas for each of the guardias in my cadre! Tell him that I need to have these pesetas quickly!" Flaco ordered.

"What? Estas loco?" (Are you nuts?) "Si le pido esto, me cuelga por los huevos!" (If I ask him for that, he'll hang me by my testicles!) At first, he thought that Flaco might be kidding him, but it wasn't until he saw the stern look on his face that he realized that he was serious! "What shall I tell him the pesetas are for?"

Flaco thought about it for a moment! He needed to come up with a good answer and he also knew that asking for more money was not going to be taken very lightly. "Tell him that since we are in a large city, everything is much more expensive and that the men need more pesetas with which to live!"

"But comandante! Don't you think you are asking for too much? Perhaps if you asked for one peseta, he wsould be more agreeable! But two pesetas, I think he will refuse you!" Guillermo told him.

"I know, Guillermo! Actually, I only want one more peseta for each man! If I ask for two,he'll argue with me, but in the end, he'll agree to give us one more peseta for each man! If I only ask him for one peseta, he'll liable to give us only twenty or thirty perronas and that isn't enough for what I want to do!" Guillermo looked at him and started to smile! His young Commander was much wiser than he had expected! All that was left to do was to find out what he intended to do with the extra money, that is, assuming he would succeed in getting what he wanted!

"How are you going to distribute the money among the peasants? One peseta is not going to go very far!" he asked.

"What is the legal exchange rate at the bank? In other words, how many "perronas" will they give me for a peseta?" Flaco asked.

"I believe the banks will give you ten perronas for one peseta! I'm afraid it won't go very far!" he replied.

"I think you may be right! There has to be something more that we can do! Think of something, Guillermo!"

Guillermo thought for a moment before breaking out into a hearty laugh! "Senor Comandante, I think I may have the answer for you! You are talking about the banks, but if we were to go to the private exchange houses on the street, they would probably give you as much as thirteen or fourteen "perronas" for each peseta! That would make the pesetas stretch farther! Unfortunately, I believe that those exchange houses are illegal! I think it may be against the law to go to them and exchange currency!"

"Good idea! But, since we are the law, who will go against us? Think of it, Guillermo! If we can get thirteen extra pesetas and exchange them with a private money changer at the rate of thirteen perronas for each peseta, we could end up helping almost one hundred and seventy people! Although one perrona per person may not seem like much, it will pay for food! Will you go with me and listen to the needs of the people? I won't order you to go, but you are the only person that I can trust! We may get into trouble for what we are about to do, but I think it is the right thing to do!" Flaco said.

There was another hearty laugh from Guillermo! He always liked doing the things that were unconventional and now he had a commanding officer who thought and acted the same way. "Of course, I will go with you! I also don't think you should say anything to any of the other guardias! They may not agree with what we intend to do with their extra money!"

"They won't know anything about the extra peseta! I have no intention os saying anything to them just yet! If we are successful, then, they will eventually be told! For now, I think it would be best if we kept it a secret between ourselves!"

Two weeks later he received a communication from the colonel reprimanding him for asking for more money after such a short time. The refusal appeared absolute as he was told that he didn't need the extra twenty six pesetas he had asked for. His request was considered exhorbitant and was totally unnecessary! The colonel did agree however, to give him one extra peseta for every man in his cadre, and that was as far as he was willing to go! Flaco put the letter in his pocket! The small cloth bag containing the extra thirteen pesetas had already been tucked safely away. It was now time to call Guillermo into his office again and tell him that tomorrow they would need to visit the local bank and the exchange houses! His friend flashed him a mischievous smile knowing that the reply had been well received!

The two men decided that if they were going to go to visit the money changers, they would be much better received if they were dressed in regular civilian clothes! They started out early in the morning going from one money changer to another until they finally found one who was willing to give them the exchange of fourteen "perronas" for each peseta! They quickly decided that it had been the best offer they had received! Most of the others had offered them exchanges of twelve or thirteen, but they also believed that by bartering with the money changers they would receive a better rate of exchange and they had been correct! After a few moments of bartering, Flaco finally left the small office with a bag full containing one hundred eighty two coins that would be distributed among the most needy. They interspersed the crowd, giving their attention to the older women dressed in black they had seen the previous day. To those women, Flaco would hand them two coins, while the rest of the people received one coin each! Those people he had not been able to help would need to wait until the following month; but, for the time being, he was pleased that he had been able to help more than one hundred fifty of the demonstrators. Nobody in the large crowd of over five hundred people knew who these men were! They were recognized only by one of the leaders who had attended the meeting in the office of the guardia civil! The leader smiled when he saw Flaco but said nothing to the others. As Flaco walked past him, the man simply nodded his head in acknowledgment and moved on to one side allowing him to pass!

By the end of the second month, every demonstrator had received a coin from the stranger although nobody knew that he was the person in charge of the Guardia Civil! Everyone was grateful for the mysterious handout, knowing they would now be able to buy a few basic foods for the table. Flaco and Guillermo continued on with their handouts for several months until they realized that the unhappy crowds they had seen gathered each day had begun to disperse without any encouragement from the local guardias. Flaco had been given the responsibility of patrolling the southeast section of the city where the crowds had been more vocal! The news reports were saying that the other areas of the city were becoming more intolerant while the politicians began to notice that the southeast section of the city had become uncharacteristically quiet and contained, a tribute to the recent arrival of the Guardia Civil! Several months later, Colonel Garcia arrived for a visit and raised the question about the additional money Flaco had requested. Before arriving at the garrison, neither of the men realized that the colonel had spoken to some of the townspeople who had told him that a certain stranger had been handing out bronze coins to them. They only knew that the benefactor was a stranger they had not seen before. When the colonel discovered what Flaco had done, he became angered and considered a reprimand; but after thinking it over, he soon realized that the young man had done the right thing for all the right reasons. By his actions, he had also shown success, had contained the rowdy crowds; and, most importantly, he had shown sensitivity toward the people. All of these qualities were in the best traditions of the Guardia Civil and he was pleased that he had assigned the proper man to do the job!

Flaco was smartly dressed in his uniform when the colonel arrived at the garrison! He quickly stood up, saluted the elderly man and remained at attention! "I suppose you know that what you did was wrong!" the colonel said without looking at him. He had decided to give Flaco a mild reprimand after all, if only to teach him a lesson. The decision had been made with some reluctance, not wanting to hamper the young man's sensitivity toward other people!

"I don't know what you're saying!" Flaco replied.

"Oh, I think you do! You deceived your Commanding Officer, that's what!" he told him. "I should give you a reprimand for what you did, but instead, I decided against it! I am taking the opportunity of promoting you to the rank of sergeant!" He removed a small pin from his pocket containing three small stripes that were to be affixed to the front of Flaco's "tricornio"!

"Thank you, sir!" Flaco answered. For a few moments his thoughts went back to Soledad and wondered how proud she would have been! Unfortunately, whatever he had with her had ended; and, he feared that, as time went on, he would probably never see her again!

"One more thing, sergeant!" the colonel said, "The next time you decide to go into the crowds and hand out bronze coins, I suggest you do it while in uniform! The Guardia Civil has to seize every opportunity to maintain its good reputation! I want you to wear your uniform at all times! Now that you have been promoted to the rank of sergeant, there is a good chance that you may be transferred away from here! Do you have any objections?" he asked.

Flaco thought about it for a few moments! It didn't really matter where he would be transferred! He had no family back in Salinas and only a few casual friends in Aviles. There was no longer any point in returning to his old home town! If he was needed elsewhere, it was his responsibility to go to wherever he was ordered! "No sir!" he finally answered. "I have no objections!"

CHAPTER 3

The economic and political situation in Spain failed to change as time passed by! Unemployment became widespread throughout the country and even the coal mines that had provided livelihoods for many peasants began to discharge miners in rapid succession. There was unrest! Public demonstrations mainly around the political offices of every major city quickly became more numerous and more vocal as the people began clammoring for work. Unfortunately, they soon learned that no one was willing to listen to their pleas nor did they do anything to alleviate a bad situation that only seemed to be getting worse. All of the doubts Flaco had felt when he first joined the Guardia Civil were vividly on his mind! After all, if things were so bad in the capitol city of Oviedo, what could they be like in the small town of Salinas that had no industry and was comprised mainly of farmland? Guillermo and he had formed a sort of partnership! Each month when they received their payment of five pesetas, eight for Flaco because he was elevated to the rank of sergeant, they would go to the money changers, trade their coins for "perronas" and would return to distribute the coins among the needy people. To many of the demonstrators, Flaco and Guillermo were considered saints, especially as they mingled among the people, listening to their complaints. They would then give them one or two perronas, just enough to buy food or medicines for the hungry families. It was a situation that was becoming increasingly deplorable and there were no signs of improvement in the horizon!

So bad had the political situation become that in April 1931, news began to circulate that the reigning king, Alfonso XIII, had been convinced by many of his followers that he should consider going into exile! Because of his autocratic rule, he had never been a favorite of the politicians around the country. He had ruled Spain with an iron hand since 1902, and his problems began seven years later when he personally ordered the execution of a popular radical leader by the name of Ferrer Guardia who was denouncing the king in Barcelona! The ruling king, with the help of Miguel Primo de Rivera had methodically suspended the Spanish consitution, had established martial law, and created a strict system of censorship! It was their way of restricting the news that would find its way down to the towns and villages where the dislike of politicians was the greatest. Miguel :Primo de Rivera had, at the kings insistance, agreed to rule the country only for a period of ninety days. If things were difficult, they quickly became absurd, especially when he started spending money on the establishment of public works as a way of reducing the unemployment throughout the country. This quickly caused the added problem of an immediate inflation; and, after losing the support of the army, he had been forced to resign his post. After the democratic elections authorized by King Alfonso XIII when the people overwhelmingly voted for a Spanish Republic, the king was advised that the only way to avoid large scale violence throughout the country was for him to go into exile. A year later, he took the advice of his consultants and left for another country.

The unrest worsened after the king went into exile! The small demonstrations that had been seen in many of the cities started to expand and grow until every city and town was now being subjected to the demonstrations of the people seeking employment, better living conditions, and a chance to make a decent living! Unfortunately, the patterns of unrest were no different in Spain than they were throughout the world. It soon became a problem that would need to be solved by Spain and Spain alone!

Now that Flaco had been relieved of his command and had been recommended for officer's training, he was told that he would be transferred to another garrison near the capitol of Madrid. This decision had been made by Colonel Garcia as a reward for his handling of the demonstrations in Oviedo! The colonel had noticed that in some of the other garrisons, the Guardia Civil would at times become physical with the demonstrators; but, Flaco had found a way of soothing their displeasures by handing them a small pittance from his own salary if only to curb the needs of the people for a short time. Even though the colonel had shown some displeasure, he had to admit that what the young man had done was a novel idea. For a short period of time, he had gained the support and the confidence of the people. It was then that the colonel decided that this young man had the intelligence and the integrity to do whatever needed to be done, while at the same time, projecting the image of the Guardia Civil in the eyes of the people! Flaco had voiced a few objections at first, but the colonel quickly convinced him that his leadership qualities and his sensitivity toward the people were qualities that the Guardia Civil always looked for when recruiting new members. After voicing a few objections, Flaco told the colonel how his friend Guillermo had also helped him in handing out the "perronas"! The colonel, with many years of experience behind him, saw something in the two men that he hadn't seen for a long time. Both were friendly and were well suited to work together! As long as they were happy working together, he would be a fool not to allow them to continue!

Everyone had thought that once the king had gone into exile, things would get better! Instead, they became worse! Primo de Rivera, who had agreed to remain as a ruler for ninety days, appeared to like the post he held and continued to rule until July 1931 when another election was held and a provisional government of the Second Republic had called for a new general election. By that time the Socialist Party or PSOE won an overwhelming victory. Another member by the name of Niceto Alcala Zamora became the prime minister and included in his cabinet several radical figures such as Manuel Azana, Largo Caballero, and Indalecio Prieto! By the end of 1931, Azana replaced Zamora as prime minister. With the support of the Socialist Party, he did his best to introduce a program of agrarian reform and regional autonomy; but, these measures of improving the country were consistently blocked by the courts.

Azana, a confirmed Socialist, believed that the Catholic Church was the culprit and was responsible for Spain's backwardness! He strongly defended the elimination of special privileges that the church had enjoyed, on the grounds that Spain had ceased to be Catholic! In retaliation, the church started to criticize Azana for not doing more to stop the burning of its buildings throughout the country. In response, Azana further infuriated the Catholic Church by saying publicly that 'the burning of all the convents in Spain was not worth the life of a single Republican'! This created a further revolt among the people; and, by mid 1932, there was a failed military coup in the country that was led by Jose Sanjurjo! This allowed the Azana government to finally pass the Agrarian Reform Bill as well as the Catalan Statutes that were finally passed by the courts. Unfortunately, the modernization of the Azana administration was undermined by a lack of financial resources. In 1933, new elections saw the right-wing CEDA party win an overwhelming 115 seats whereas the Socialist Party could only manage to win a mere 58. CEDA then formed a parliamentary alliance with the Radical Party, and over the next two years the new administration had demolished the reforms that had been introduced by Azana and his government!

Salamanca

The small classroom in a one story concrete building in Salamanca was hardly large enough to accomodate the group of thirteen Guardia Civiles who had been selected to receive advanced training. For the first time, Flaco was exposed to the new training, concentrating on crowd control and the treatment of crowds who were now demonstrating more frequently and in larger numbers than before. He had seen the crowds that had gathered in Oviedo, and fortunately, he had been able to contain them with the help of his cadre. His instructions were to contain the uprisings and not to inflict any harm to any of the demonstrators which

could further infuriate the people that had gathered outside the
Ayuntamiento. It was hoped that some of the politicians would have
the decency of coming outside, face the crowds and try to explain
if not to justify why it was that no one seemed to be listening to
their desparate pleas! It had only been because of the donation of
the "perronas" that Flaco and Guillermo had distributed among the
most needy that had kept the crowd contained. Despite his stern
manner, he knew that the colonel had been pleased with the results,
and had been the one who personally had selected Flaco to travel
to Salamanca, a mid-sized town located a few miles northwest of
Madrid for advanced training. He had made the request to have his
friend Guillermo go with him, telling the colonel how he, too, had
given up his own "pesetas", trading them into the smaller coins
for distribution among the needy! The colonel had refused his
request without reason, only to say that he had other plans for the
large, burly man who had also joined the Guardia Civil, a victim
of unproductive farm land that had repeatedly failed to provide
sufficient vegetables for the winter months. There was no way
for Flaco to know where his friend was being assigned since the
colonel had refused to give him any information of his plans. The
only instructions he had received had been to pack his things and
prepare to travel by truck to his new assignment!

Travel to Salamanca seemed a world away from the small
towns that he had visited. Much to his surprise Flaco noticed that
in Salamanca the uprisings were not as many nor as boisterous as
they were in other places. The angry citizens would gather into
small groups and would go to the gates of politicians, very orderly
and well contained. His first impression as the large truck made
its way into the city was that it was loaded with an abundance of
catholic churches on every street corner.He had been told about
the political conflicts that had been taking place in Madrid! Now
that Manuel Azana and his hand-picked cabinet had again gained
control of the government, he could only wonder how long it would
be before the churches here would be subjected to the mysterious
fires causing them to burn to the ground? After all, it was common
knowledge that Azana, who in 1936 had helped to form a coalition
of Socialist parties, such as the Socialist Party (PSOE), the

Communist Party (PCE), the Esquerra Party and the Republican
Union Party, all of which were asked to help him rule the country.
Unfortunately, none of the parties were particularly fond of the
church, blaming them for many of the uprisings, and were secretly
hiring needy people to start the fires and do their best to abolish
the stronghold of the catholic church in Spain. The small groups
that had been united had given themselves the name of the Popular
Front (El Frente Popular). They strongly advocated autonomy
for the Catalanes that were located in the eastern section of the
country, in the area of Barcelona. This area always considered
themselves to be Catalanes with their distinct dialectic Spanish
language that made it difficult to be understood whenever they
travelled into other sections of the country!

The Frente Popular also aspired to do other reforms that
they thought would greatly help the crisis in the country. Among
other aims on their agenda were to provide amnesty for any
political prisoners, agrarian reforms, an end to political blacklists
that had been created to single out those people, who because of
need or ambition, had formed their own small groups protesting
against the politicians. One of the other ambitions of the Frente
Popular was to provide immediate indemnificatioin to those land
owners who had sustained damages to their properties during the
revolt of 1934. The remaining peasant workers saw this as a way to
indemnify the rich while again forgetting the poor. Because of this,
the Anarchists refused to support the coalition and established a
widespread campaign urging the people not to vote in the General
Elections of 1936. The result of the election ended up with the
Frente Popular being rewarded with a total of 263 seats in the
parliament, or more than half of the available number of 473 seats.
The courts had no other alternative than to form a new government
that would eventually lead to an upset of the conservatives who
were comprised of many of the land owners. This upset was greatly
enhanced by the immediate release of all of the left-wing political
prisoners. The government also quickly introduced agrarian
reforms that penalized the recognized aristocracy with more taxes
and more erosion of income in order to support the public projects
that had been started as a way of putting people to work and allow

them to receive a pay check, however small, in order to feed their families!

One other serious project was also taking place! The new authority also included the transfer of right-wing military leaders such as Francisco Franco to be stationed to posts outside of Spain, therefore practically outlawing the Falange Espanola and granting Catalonia political and adminstrative authority to the eastern area of the country. Flaco quickly realized that all of these changes were quickly taking place, but he had no idea as to how they would pertain to him! After all, he was nothing more than a Guardia Civil, and that was all he had ever wanted to be! The fact that all of these political changes were taking place only seemed to portray many more problems in days to come! His job as Guardia Civil was only to maintain law and order and to help the citizens in any way possible if the need should arise! Suddenly, he was now studying such things as riot control! When the subject of C & C was first given to him to study, he had no idea of what it meant nor what to do! These terms were unknown to him! As he studied the subject matter with more interest, he found the elements of Containment and Control puzzling, and became skeptical of the explanations and uses that the instructors were offering. True, there had been some problems when he was in Oviedo, but the unrest or the discomfort of the people were neither unlawful nor unreasonable. The only thing the people wanted was to air their grievances to the civilian authorities hoping that someone would listen to them. They seemed happy when Flaco appeared and was willing to listen to them and give them a coin to buy food or medicines. During his early years, he had always been taught that the government was supposed to attend to the needs of the people; and, while he had seen a continuing erosion of confidence between the people and their government, he felt certain that at some point, the government would listen to the pleas of the poor and that eventually necessary corrective action would be taken! His studies did not seem to imply that any corrective actions were being contemplated! What he was studying was simply an expansive overview of what to expect in the way of demonstrations in major cities such as Madrid, something that had been unheard of in previous times! His grades were among the highest in his class; and, he was happy when he learned that his studies would soon be ending, and he would be re-assigned to yet another location. So, he was surprised to see the large figure of Colonel Garcia walk into the school, peek into the classroom and make a motion to the instructor to wait outside. The instructor excused himself and was seen in a discussion with the Colonel until, finally, he returned and asked Flaco to go outside! He gathered his things and approached the colonel outside in the hallway!

"I've come to take you away from the classroom!" the colonel told him. "I need you to go on a new assignment! I must tell you that this time, I don't really know whether or not the assignment will be right for you!" Flaco watched as the elderly gentleman toyed nervously with his large, handle bar mustache as he studied the look on Flaco's face.

"I'm here to obey your orders!" Flaco replied. "I'm sure you know that I haven't yet finished my studies here! However, if you feel that my services are needed elsewhere, I'm willing to do what you direct, sir!"

Flaco was pleased with his response, but not nearly as pleased as the colonel! He liked this young man from the beginning; and, now, without questioning a new assignment, he was telling him that the needs of the Guardia Civil were first and foremost in his mind. This young man was certainly destined to go places within the service and he was happy that he had been the one who had recommended Flaco for advanced training. The matter at hand was one of urgency, and would require that he leave the classroom before completing his classwork!

"What would you say if I told you that I needed you to return to Asturias?" the colonel asked. Once he again his eyes were on Flaco's face as he studied it carefully for any reaction! As before, there was none!

"I'm willing to go wherever I am sent!" Flaco replied. "If I may say so, sir, I am a bit surprised to be returning back to Asturias! What will be my assignment?"

"Flaco, what I am going to tell you must be kept in the strictest of confidence! It is not to be repeated to any one under any conditions; is that clear?"

Flaco looked at his commanding officer quizzically. It was not like the colonel to reveal any secrets about an assignment! Flaco was ware that in going to Oviedo, he knew nothing about the assignment nor did he ask any questions! In the Guardia Civil he had learned to accept assignments without question; nor was he to give any thoughts, either for or against, whatever he was asked to do! Things were now different! He was obviously being taken into the colonel's confidence; and he had a feeling that the assignment was not going to be a good one! In silence, he was rather looking forward to return to Asturias if only to see his old homestead and see how things had changed since his departure. He also wondered if Soledad might still be living there with her mother? The time had passed by quickly and it had been several years since he had last seen her! He couldn't help but wonder if he would even recognize her if he saw her again! He doubted very much that she would recognize him! Just like her, he was now considerably older, his hair was turning prematuredly grey, especially around the temples. The name of Flaco was still with him! Not that he had changed very much! He was still tall and thin! Only his arms and muscles had strengthened, and he had even taken notice of stares from young women whenever he walked down the street in his uniform. Also, he had grown a thin mustache that was also turning grey. No, he was certain that she would no longer recognize him although he was equally certain that he would recognize her anywhere! The more he thought about it, the more excited he became thinking of the prospects of seeing her again! However, he had to be careful not to appear overly enthusiastic; but the hidden desires and expectations were certainly on his mind!

"Whatever you tell me will be held in the strictest confidence!" he answered. "My job is to go wherever I am sent and to perform my duties! That is what I have been trained to do, sir!"

"Good!" the colonel answered. "That was the answer I was hoping for! We have received reports that there is going to be a general strike and an armed uprising in Asturias! It is our belief that there will be a serious problem and we need you to keep the uprising under control!"Do you think you can handle that?"

"No se!" he answered."I suppose we can do it provided we have sufficient manpower distributed in the major cities! I don't think the problem will be unmanageable in the small towns such as Aviles, Campiello, Piedras Blancas; but the problem may be more severe in some of the larger cities like Oviedo! The unrest there has been bad and it can only get worse! How many men will you be sending into the area?" he asked.

"I can only spare one brigade or about one hundred guardias!" the colonel answered.

"Hay carajo!" Flaco answered with a whistle. "Sir, are you aware that in the southern part of Asturias we have the Cordillera Cantabrica? Those mountains are filled with unhappy citizens who are living in those mountains. These will be hard to contain! We also have the cities of Burgos and Valladolid that will need to be patrolled! When I was in Oviedo I was told of the unhappiness of the mine workers in Burgos and in the areas of Valladolid! Sir, Asturias is a large province! We are going to need more than one hundred guardias to do the job effectively!"

"That's why I decided to send you into the area! You did an excellent job in Oviedo, and I am confident you'll also do a good job on this assignment!"

"But how am I supposed to keep the people from demonstrating? In many ways, I agree with their demands! Remember, I have seen first-hand the poverty and the starving children! Those people have absolutely nothing and no one is willing to listen to them!" Flaco said.

"Perhaps! Flaco, you know the Asturianos and I feel that you will be able to control them! Besides, we also have reports that Manuel Azana is encouraging the disturbances and may even be supplying arms and weapons to the insurrectionists! That is what frightens me the most! If the Asturianos should decide to drink large quantities of cidra or wine and become enraged, anything is liable to happen! That's why I need you to be there!"

"Then sir, I request that you transfer Guardia Guillermo Torres, from wherever you have sent him! Don't forget that it was he who worked with me in Oviedo! He also understands the people and he is strong enough to use force if he has to! I need to have Guillermo there with me!"

The colonel rubbed his chin in thought! This had been one request he hadn't anticipated and he didn't know whether or not he would be able to grant that request! "I can't promise you anything! I'll do my best to have him transferred to you, but I don't know how successful I'll be!"

"Sir, if you are going to toss me into the "gallinero" (henhouse) the very least you can do is to give me the necessary tools to work with! I need to have Guillermo Torres with me if I have any hopes of being successful!"

"Muy bien! Veremos que se puede hacer!" (Very well! We'll see what we can do!)" the colonel answered. "I'd like you to leave for Asturias tonight! Is that alright? I also suppose you will want to be stationed in Oviedo!"

"No sir! It it's permissable, I would prefer to have the garrison in Aviles! I will ask Guardia Torres to go into Oviedo and establish himself there!"

The colonel gave him a suspicious look! Why would he prefer to be located in a small town like Aviles instead of being in a major city like Oviedo? The young man obviously had a reason. For whatever reason, it didn't matter! If he preferred to be in Aviles, then, so be it! Perhaps he had a girlfriend in Aviles and wanted to be closer to her! As long as he had known him, he had never seen nor heard of him being with any young woman in any of the cities where he had gone! No doubt, he had his reasons; and whatever they were, the colonel realized that he was much too handsome a young man to escape the roving eyes of young women! There was an air of mystery about him that was strange! Despite his efficiency, there was always the unmistakable look of depression and unhappiness that seemed so strange in a young man his age! Who knows, the colonel thought, perhaps a change in assignment was just what he needed to make him happy!

Many thoughts ran through Flaco's mind as he started to pack his things in preparation for the transfer! It occured to him that he was no longer the young man he used to be; but, now he was a man who demanded authority and respect! Not that he had given these matters any consideration, nor did he ever think he would achieve what he had achieved from the Guardia Civil! All that he had wanted was to have something to eat and a place to sleep each night! The idea that he would one day become an officer in the guardia had never entered his mind when he decided to enlist! The admiration and respect he had received when he was in Oviedo had been well received; but there was a side of him that felt sympathy for the people. It was the first time in his life when he had been exposed to such misery and poverty on such a large scale. It had made an impression on him that he would never forget. He had seen youngsters starving for food and old women who needed to work the fields because their husbands had died. He had been exposed to these calamities in Salinas, but had never thought that those facts could be multiplied in such large numbers as he had seen in the larger cities. All of the childhood thoughts had returned to him many times as he repeatedly thought about the days when Soledad would be by the river washing the clothes! Suddenly, he had been transformed into an important somebody in society and wondered if she too had made such a transformation! No one certainly deserved it more than she did! Even as a young woman she had all of the likely characteristics to rise above the young women of her age. She was brave, strong and persistant! Maybe now that he had been deployed to that area, he would again visit Salinas and try to see her again! Perhaps now that they had both grown up, all of their youthful foolishness could be left behind and they would be able to be together as they had promised each other the day they had exchanged their blood oath! All of a sudden, his eyes drifted down to his hand and to the large scar that reminded him of the promise they had made. She had told him that wherever he went a part of her would always be with him! He couldn't help wondering if she still remembered the promises they had made? She had been beautiful as a child and might be married to someone else. Nah! He thought! She would never do that! Soledad would never marry anyone else but him, nor would he ever consider marrying another woman. The woman that he wanted had remained a part of him through the passing years.

He locked his small cotton travel bag and went to the kitchen for something to eat! The fact that he hadn't finished his studies in C & C (Containment and Control) was no longer important! He was quite satisfied that he was well familiar with the subject and would be able to handle any problems that might come up! Flaco was also well aware that a successful completion of a course in C & C meant that he had come a long way and that it was a final step before going into Officers Training! A certain fear came over him as he thought of himself as being an officer! Could he really be able to handle the job? It was something he needed to think about! And what about Guillermo? He had thought about him and wondered where he might have been sent! The two men had become very close when they were dispatched to Oviedo. If he was lucky, the colonel would see fit to transfer Guillermo to him in his new assignment. If so, then leaving the school was not as bad as it had seemed; because it now gave him something to look forward to. With Guillermo with him and Soledad near him, he would be happy once again! What he didn't realize was that in his new assignment, he was going to need all of his capabilities without either person!!!

Salinas

It was early in the morning when Dona Balbina opened her tired eyes with the first rays of the morning sun as it shined into her bedroom window. With every passing day, she noticed that she needed to force herself out of bed, something she had never done before.There had been a reduction in her energy and it had become so obvious that she had discussed the problem with Don Jose. After examining her he ordered her to drink a strange concoction that consisted of a tall glass of red wine, mixed with one or two raw eggs and a spoonful of fresh honey. The mere thought of mixing the foul-tasting drink each morning was enough to make her ill! She decided against drinking it especially on those days when she knew that he would not be coming to the clinic. Now that Soledad was no longer with her, she felt all alone in the large house. It had been several weeks since an old man in his eighty's had been taken to the clinic with a severe case of pleural effusion, an accumulation of fluid between the membrane lining the lungs and the chest cavity. The situation had become so painful that Don Jose had taken him to the clinic where he could receive the medical care that he needed. The elderly man, a wealthy landowner, could well afford to pay the required two pesetas per day, but it was also necessary to insert a tube into the chest cavity and aspirate the fluid in order to alleviate the breathing. It was a simple procedure that she had seen many times while working with the doctor; but, in this case, the health of this patient had worsened because of other illnesses as well as his advanced age. The elderly man had enjoyed a series of successes in agriculture during years that were profitable and had a considerable amount of wealth. When he was released from the clinic, the doctor realized that he was going to need special care on a daily basis, making certain that the aspiration tube was inserted and cleaned every day. Since the elderly man had no living relatives, he had offered to take young Soledad with him to his home in Mieres where he would pay her for watching over him! They had agreed on a total of three pesetas per month and that also included the general housework that the young woman would be expected to supply. Soledad, with some reluctance, had accepted the work and had gone with him to Mieres. The salary she had been offered was enough to pay for the daily costs of food and care at her mother's house. No one had bothered to ask her whether or not she liked the work, but none of that mattered. The living conditions in Spain had deteriorated to the point where there was no work to be had! Now that she had been given the chance to work and earn a living, she decided to go if only to see a new town that she had never seen before in her life!

Soledad seemed satisfied with her new employment. She was now able to send her mother the tidy sum of two pesetas every month, enough to help her purchase some scraps of lumber for the stove and a few vegetables to feed the patients and the animals. The fact that Dona Balbina was also earning a few pesetas had not come without a cost! Dona Balbina missed her daughter! It was the first time they had ever been separated and now all of the house chores were left to her since her daughter had gone away. The woman was not young and often found herself working until late evening, at times without supper, washing clothes and bandages or feeding the animals while also taking care of the patients.

The elderly man with whom Soledad was staying had been spared from the excessive taxation that had been imposed by the newly established government. He had not made any arrangements that precluded him from payment of taxes. It had been well established that all of the wealthy land owners were being heavily taxed in order to pay for the public works that had been started throughout the country as a means to create badly needed employment for its citizens. He had already been taxed to capacity! The only reason for being relieved of a heavier tax burden was because the government was aware that he had no living relatives. They had decided that with his advanced age and poor health, he would soon be dead! Since he had no relatives to receive any inheritance, the government felt that once he was gone, his wealth, whether big or small, would eventually be turned over to them. They could afford to allow him to live his remaining days in comfort knowing that they would soon inherit all of his estate!

Don Jose, however, was another matter! There had been the emergence of motor driven cars that had made their way into Aviles! Most of the cars were owned by wealthy merchants and politicians! Don Jose had faced many of the patients wanting to know when he planned to purchase one of the motor cars to provide faster transportation when going from house to house instead of using the old horse driven buggy! The aging doctor had consistantly denounced the use of the motor driven vehicles, saying they were invention of the devil. He was convinced that buying one of these new vehicles would eventually cause his death! It had been a premonition that many of his friends had accepted with a smile. Nobody had given the matter any importance knowing that the good doctor would often refer to his premonitions of death! However, he also silently felt that perhaps the purchase of one of these vehicles would allow him to see more patients in much less time! There was little doubt that the new vehicles would allow him more efficiancy in seeing his patients.In these days of tumoil, his workload had increased and he was now seeing himself being kept busier than ever. When he finally decided to buy one of the motorized vehicles, one of his first visits was to Dona Balbina's to show her his new purchase! Everyone who saw the car was curiou; after all, it was a novelty the likes of which was rarely seen in Aviles and hardly ever seen in the town of Salinas. He had avoided the purchase as long as possible; and now that he had finally gone against his better judgement and finally purchased the car! He was still reluctant to use it fearing that his new purchase would somehow contribute to his death!

The doctor had offered to transport Dona Balbina in his new vehicle to the hospital in Oviedo, hoping that she would be examined more thoroughly! It was obvious to him as a doctor and to her as the patient that she was not improving and that her health was, in fact, deteriorating further! She had taken the wine mixture that the doctor had prescribed, but she was well aware that he needed her at home and working in the clinic and could not afford to take the time! The small amounts of money she received from him and those she received from Soledad were needed for other more important purchases. It frightened herto think of what the doctor would do if they decided to keep her in the hospital for a longer period of time? Who would be available to care for the other patients now that Soledad was no longer living at home? It was because of this that she remained adament against going! The wine mixture while it had helped her in the beginning, had now lost its power; and, even though she drank it every morning upon arising, she felt herself getting weaker and weaker each day. Today had been no exception! She had started the day by praying for herself and for Soledad, hoping that she would find a man that would love her and provide a good home for her, knowing that whoever the young man would be, would certainly need to fight an uphill battle with her! Deep within her heart, she also knew that Soledad had never forgiven nor forgotten Flaco! Many years had passed since hearing from him; and although she constantly told her mother that she no longer cared about him, it was the pain she had lived with since that memorable day when he first told her that he was leaving to join the Guardia Civil! Although he had gone out of her life, he had never gone out of her heart! Of course, she was much too proud to admit it to anyone even her mother, but Dona Balbina knew very well that there was nothing she could do to relieve her daughter's pain! The only thing she could now do was to hope and pray that someone else would come along and capture her daughter's heart! Unfortunately, her prayers had gone unanswered, and there was nothing more that she could do but to keep on praying hoping that God would eventually hear her pleas, before she left this earth!

The elderly woman got out of bed, washed her face and went down to feed the animals! It was the ritual that she followed each morning! It was the first time that she became annoyed with the blend of fragrances between the wood burning stove that was needed for warmth, the antisceptic odor of the clinic and the blend of odors from the animals in the back of the house that were making her ill! True, she had gone through the same ritual every morning, but today, things were different! She found the repugnant odors offensive and wished that things could be different! Unfortunately, they weren't, and there was little she could do about them! She walked slowly up the long flight of stairs, as she did every morning, making certain that her patients felt comfortable and that they had spent a peaceful if not comfortable night! She knew that Don Jose would arrive a bit later, and she wanted to be sure that the patients had been well attended, that the bandages, where necessary, had been cleaned and changed! The patients were anxiously waiting for the arrival of the doctor.It was during this respite that she would then go downstairs and feed the animals. The chickens would be fed and any discarded morsels of food that remained would be unceremoniously deposited inside the pig-stye to feed the hogs that always seemed to be hungry! By the time she had finished, she felt tired and needed to rest for a few moments! As she sat down, she would have given anything for an hour's rest; but the cow needed to be milked so the patients would be able to receive their daily ration of fresh milk! It had been one of the chores that had been routinely done by Soledad! Now that she was gone, there was no alternative but for her to go to the barn with her pail and work the utters until the slow of milk had stopped. Dona Balbina had just finished and had taken the pail into the house when she heard a commotion near the house. She deposited the pail and went outside to see what it was, thinking that it was another patient that was being brought to the clinic for medical care. If so, then she was going to need to put fresh sheets on a bed until the patient, whoever it was could be taken upstairs to await the arrival of the doctor.

Outside, she saw a small gathering of men carrying a patient and walking in the direction of the rear of the house. "Espera!" she said. "Primero tengo que arreglar la cama!" (Wait! First, I have to prepare the bed!) There was no point in taking the patient upstairs until the bed had been made up! She took a step closer to see who the patient was and was startled and taken aback by what she saw! Shocked and dismayed, she brought her hands up to her lips when she saw that the patient the men were carrying was Don Jose, the doctor.She ran up the steps and placed a fresh sheet on a bed. From what she saw, the old doctor was covered with blood from his head to his feet! Whatever the cause had been, it was obvious that he had been dangerously injured!

"Dios mio! Que paso?" (My God, what happened?) she called out, demanding an answer from the men.

"We found the doctor at the bottom of a ravine just off the road! He must have lost control of the motor-machine, and it went off the edge of the road and into the ravine! It seems that the force of the accident must had thrown him out of the car and he was unconscious when we got there!" one of the men told her.

"Take him upstairs immediately!" she ordered. Quickly, she ran out to the well for some fresh water in order to wash away his wounds.As soon as she started sponging down his injuries she knew immediately that the doctor was much too badly injured to survive! There was an ugly opening at the top of his head, and she could see by his difficulty in moving that he had sustained several broken bones.

"No te preocupes, Don Jose!" she said calmly as she tried to comfort him and assure him that everything was going to be alright!

Peering through moments of consciousness, the old doctor had seen too many accidents and knew that he was too badly injured and would not survive! He made a lame effort to speak but the words would not come out! Instead, he grabbed hold of Dona Balbina's hand and tried to smile! His lips were moving as if trying to tell her something, but she watched as he took a deep breath, turn his head to one side and close his eyes. The end had come quickly! This had been another person in her life who had been taken away! All the comments he had made before he bought the motor car came back to her as she remembered how many times he had told her that the motor car would eventually result in his death! She could only wonder if he had merely a premonition or had he known for sure! No one would ever know; and now, there was no one she could turn to! All that was left for her to do was to send word to Soledad and ask her to return to Salinas for the funeral. More than before, she knew that her daughter would not be able to remain with her! She had committed herself into taking care of an elderly man and needed the work in order to put food on the table. Don Jose was gone and there was no one else she could go to and ask for help! All that she knew was that she was becoming weaker and weaker with every passing day; and, although she had thought of no longer taking the wine mixture, she now felt she owed it to the doctor to continue even if it meant that it was losing its ability to provide her with strength!

Several weeks had passed while Flaco tried to arrange things with his battalion in preparation for the demonstration that was being expected in Asturias! Several of the guardias had already been dispatched into the small towns and the remaining brigade troops had been assigned to protect the capitol! Oviedo, as the key city, was loaded with politicians who were well maintained in their plush offices.The rumors continued to flow saying that Manuel Azana had been behind the insurrections; and, it had also been reported that Azana and his men had transported weapons into the northern areas of the province. For the most part, the demonstrations of the people were nothing to fear; but Flaco knew from experience that if the insurrectionists were equipped with weapons and a jug or two of fresh made cider, the results could be disastrous! The area that needed to be protected was large, and he had no idea how he was going to spread his men making certain that most of them would be dispersed into the areas that were the most vulnerable.

One problem that bothered him was that of communications! It was difficult to transmit messages from one place to another since all of them needed to be transported by a person! The areas of the towns would take longer, but so far the messages would eventually be delivered. Those that gave him the most trouble were the messages intended for other guardias that were stationed in the cities of Burgos, on the south side of the Cordillera Cantabrica! A messenger would need to cross the narrow mountain paths before arriving in Oviedo or Aviles. Also, the length of the trip by foot would take several days, assuming that the weather was pleasant and the messenger didn't decide to take many rests while on the way to one of the locations. Flaco was well aware that he was sitting on an explosive situation that was liable to erupt at any moment! If he were needed in places such as Burgos, it would require several days for him to arrive there! Of course, he would need to have a truck for transportation and he didn't yet have enough faith in the motorized vehicles to take him there safely. One alternative that he considered was to have a guard dispatched at regular intervals between Burgos and Oviedo; but then, doing so would mean that he would need quite a few men, enough to cover the relay over the rough terrain knowing that there were times when it was impossible to pass safely.

Flaco was sitting at his desk attempting to seek a solution to his problem when the door suddenly opened! "Guillermo!" he shouted out surprised at seeing his old friend. "Que haces aqui? Why didn't you send me word that you were coming?"

"There wasn't time! You see, I was in school when the colonel came for me, took me out of the classroom, and asked me to report to you! I asked him if I could take a day or two to visit my family but he couldn;t afford to give me any time off! The only thing he said was that you would explain everything to me once I got here! Now, if you want to go to the taverna with me, I'll buy you a glass of wine and we can talk there!"

Flaco considered the invitation for several moments! Ever since joining the Guardia Civil, he had learned to enjoy a glass of wine during his meals, something he had never done before! It might be a good idea if the two of them would speak away from the garrison! After all, he still wasn't sure how much of what was happening could be told to his men!

"Tienes razon!" he answered. "Let's go, but this time you pay for the wine!"

They walked to the local tavern, sat at a table far away from the door, making sure that whatever was spoken between them would be out of reach by the other patrons. They ordered a healthy serving of tapas, including several generous portions of tortilla de patata, pimientos morrones with cheese, and ordered two glasses of wine for each of them.

"So tell me!" Guillermo asked. "What is so important that the old man saw fit to take me away from school and asked me to come here?"

"I can't give you very many details! I do know that there is supposed to be a major demonstration all over the province against the government! I've been told to maintain the peace! That's all I know!"

"So what? We've had demonstrations before! Those 'hijos de puta' sitting comfortable inside the government buildings have nothing better to do with their time! It seems that every decision they make is wrong! We've never had any problems before, why all the preparations now?"

"The demonstrations are not the only problem! We've been told that the government of Manuel Azana is passing arms to the local peasants. The fear is that all-hell will break if the peasants have both weapons and a jug of fresh cider! This is what they fear!"

"So? Where do I fit in? What the hell am I supposed to do?" Guillermo asked.

"I asked for you! I wanted you here with me! There is a serious problem with communications if something should happen in Burgos! Have you any idea how long it will take to get a message from there to here? Once you realize the problem, and, assuming you wanted to begin a demonstration, what area would you concentrate on?" Flaco asked.

"If I wanted to do damage, then, of course I would start with Burgos! If not there, I would start in Oviedo, the capitol! It doesn't take a genius to figure that one out!"

"Exactly, that was what I also was thinking! That's the reason why I want you to go to Burgos and command a company of men I will be sending there!"

"Yes, but then what do we do in the region of Puerto Pajares in the South? That is also a large area! We won't have enough men if things go bad! How will we get word to you for reinforcements if we need them?"

"I think I have an idea that may work! I want you and another man that you feel you can trust to dress out of uniform as "campesinos" and mingle in the crowd! You and the other man will mingle in as many groups as possible and try to keep up with what they plan to do! As soon as you hear of any plans that you consider critical, I want you to immediately send word to me! Hopefully, if something should happen, we'll be able to tackle the problem quickly!"

"So, you want me to remove my uniform and dress like a 'campesino'! Does this mean that I can also act like one, especially if I see a group of "muyeres guapas"? he asked smiling.

"I don't care what you do as long as you get the news to me! What you do with "las guajas" (the young ladies) is your business! I need you to keep me posted on what you hear, especially if you hear of any plans to deliver weapons into the area! What you do down there is exactly what I plan to be doing here in Aviles!" Flaco said.

"Yes, and what are you going to do with 'las guajas', Guillermo asked.

"I'll call for you, how's that?"

"Haces bien! Sabes que soy mas guapo que tu!" (That's because you know I am better looking than you!) he answered as the two men returned to Flaco's office.

Several days later, Guillermo went to Burgos while Flaco remained in Aviles! Each day he could see the crowds getting larger and even the moods of those gathering was beginning to change. The people were in an ugly mood! Poverty was rampant throughout the country, and many of the smaller business had started to close their doors. It was felt that there was no point in remaining open if the townspeople had no money to pay for their purchases.The ruling party was now taxing the landowners to the extent that most of the money was needed to finance the public projects that were on the increase throughout the country!

Flaco did in Aviles exactly what he had urged Guillermo to do in Burgos! They started to mingle with the crowds of people, dressed in farm clothes while trying to listen to any comments that would tell them that Azanas party was actively planning to deliver weapons to the demonstrators. It seemed odd that the news persisted about the weaponry; and, yet, no information was heard that would give any credence to the rumors. Several weeks later, it was reported that Manuel Azana had been arrested on October 7th and had been interned on a ship that was anchored in the Barcelona harbor. Guillermo was ordered back to Aviles, pleased that the demonstrations had not gotten out of hand, and no one had been injured! Both men remained in Aviles while the government began to take the necessary steps to ease the situation and return the country to some degree of normalcy. Six months later, Azana defended himself in court in which he gave a three hour speech declaring his innocence! As a result, the Tribunal of Constitutional Guarantees acquitted Azana; and he was subsequently restored to his post! By that time, the Socialist Party, the Communist Party and the Republican Union Party were firmly in control of the country.As the demands began to grow from both the Popular Front on the left and the National Front on the right, the situation was getting worse!

In the days that followed, the parties in power released all of the political prisoners while the government introduced some new agrarian reforms that only continued to penalize the aristocracy. Flaco and Guillermo remained at their duties in the area without any direction, nor any knowledge as to where their next assignment was going to be. In yet another surprise move, the Popular Front transferred right-wing military leaders such as Francisco Franco to posts outside of Spain. Although he had not been specifically told, the two men believed that Colonel Garcia had also been re-assigned to the army and had been transferred to posts outside of Spain. They believed he may have been sent to join Francisco Franco in some unknown post where they would not be a destructive force to the ruling government!

A few months later, Flaco and Guillermo were ordered from Aviles to report to the regular army barracks in Madrid for training and re-assignment! This was the one move that they neither expected nor were looking forward to! It was a move to show that the Guardia Civil was now being conscripted into the regular army; and although they would retain their regular uniforms, the Guardia Civil would now be under to military control. Before leaving for Madrid, Flaco made one last effort to find Soledad! He knew that time was scarce, but he needed to see her again if only to be certain that she had survived the unrests. Guillermo agreed to drive Flaco to Salinas. Together, they drove northward to the seashore town where Flaco had been born and raised. His first stop was again by the river where he saw a few women washing clothes and ignoring the presence of the two men still in uniform.

"Oye guapa!" he said to one of the women, "Sabes donde esta Soledad Alonso?" (Young lady, do you know where Soledad Alonso happens to be?)

"No senor guardia! Have mucho tiempo que no la veo! Creo que ya no esta por aqui!" (No sir! I haven't seen her in a long time! I don't think she lives here anymore!)

"Do you know where I may be able to find her?" he asked.

"No sir! I know that she used to go to the docks almost daily and I do remember seeing her speaking to one of the fishermen! He would always give her some of the sardines he would otherwise toss back into the ocean! I think he liked her and would give them to her instead of tossing them back into the sea!"

"Has she been to the docks lately?"

"It's been a long time since I've seen her! But I also don't see the boat arriving with the fisherman that used to speak to her! Perhaps she went with him, I don't know!"

There was no point in asking any more questions! This young woman seemed frightened to death facing two large men in uniform! The answers he got were certainly not what he expected! Could it be that she had fallen in love with a fisherman and had gone away with him? He began feeling the unmistakable pangs of jealousy! How could she do such a thing? Damn it, didn't she know that she belonged to him? If that were true, then, she had one hell of a nerve! The only way to find out for sure would be to return to her house and wait for her to arrive! Could it be that the fisherman was living in that big house with her? He paused for a moment trying to think of what he would say if he saw her there with someone else!

Flaco went forward when they arrived in Salinas while Guillermo walked a step behind him! He realized this was going to be a very personal matter for his friend, and it was best for him to be left alone. Flaco looked over the small farm and saw that it was covered with ugly weeds and even the big white stucco house where he had been born was deserted and badly in need of repair. There was no point in going inside! Since his mother had died, he knew there would be no one else to care for the property. He did his best to fight a lump that appeared in his throat as he remembered the happy times he had spent at home with his family! Soledad had been his friend from the time they were youngsters; but the necessities of life had turned them both into opposite directions, something that was not supposed to happen. The path leading to Soledad's house was also unkept and overrun by large weeds and strange pieces of wood he didn't remember seeing! Of course, now that Soledad was probably with a fisherman her interest would no longer be on the land, it would have turned to the sea! He had a strange feeling that she would still be at home, and if not, then Dona Balbina would be there and would certainly tell him where she could be found!

The rear of the house was still opened when he and Guillermo arrived! It was that area where he still remembered the animals entering the house to avoid an impending storm or as an escape from the hot, summer sun! Flaco stopped for a moment not quite knowing what to think! He saw that there were no animals! Even the two cows, "la Pinta y la Fosca" that Soledad would milk each day were no longer in the barn.The pig pen was left opened and the three pigs they had raised from birth had also been taken away. The house was empty and deserted! He walked slowly into the living quarters and went upstairs to the second floor that had once served as the medical clinic! The small, narrow beds were still in place, but there were no patients to attend! The house was empty! He stood alone looking at the clinic and gently lowered his head into his hands realizing that his eyes were filling with tears. There was basically nothing left of his childhood that had been the happiest days of his life. What happened? Was this the way that life was supposed to be? Life had provided him with a few short years of happiness and security, and just as quickly, they had left him alone and lonely. Both families had assumed that one day Soledad and he would be together; yet now, she was nowhere to be found! From what he was able to see, no one had been inside the house for a long time. It was almost as if a cloud had covered his mind and removed from memory all of the happy moments he had known. He opened his hands and again saw the scar in his left hand, a product of their youth. There was no one he could turn to! The only thing he had been able to save as a souvenir had been the scar on the palm of his hand.He had tried to find Soledad but had failed! As far as he was concerned his life had ended the day he joined the Guardia Civil! It almost seemed as if he was now being compelled by the forces of nature to begin his life all over again. He tried to brush away the tears that were rolling down his cheek, but it was no use! Finally, it happened! He broke down and started to sob with his head buried into his hands.After he again felt composed and had wiped away the tears, he walked slowly down the steps and paused momentarily to take one final look at the hollow emptiness that remained.Then, he turned quickly away and walked out to meet his friend, knowing that he had visited the place of his birth perhaps for the last time!

"Anda, vamos Guillermo! Ya vi lo que vine a ver!" (Let's go, Guillermo! I've seen what I came to see!)

"Pero todavia no sabes donde esta la guaja! Quieres ir al ayuntamiento?" (You still don't know where the girl is! Do you want to go to City Hall?)

"Pa que? Ojala que donde este, sea mas feliz que yo!"
(What for? Wherever she is, I hope she is happier than I am!)
"Let's go, Guillermo! I want to get the hell out of here!"

The following winter Francisco Franco had joined a group of Spanish Army Officers, namely Emilio Mola, Juan Yague, Gonzalo Queipo de Llano and Jose Sanjurjo discussing what they should do about the Popular Front Government. Mola had been appointed the leader of the group, but, at this point, Franco was not yet willing to commit himself to joining any uprising. Unfortunately, there were other problems that were taking place! As a result of the government's policies, the wealthy people starting taking large sums of money out of the country. This sudden decline in capital created a worsening economic crises and the value of the "peseta" began to fall creating a steep decline in trade and tourism! As the consumer prices began to rise, the workers, many of whom were employed in the government projects started to demand higher wages. This situation led to a series of labor strikes thoughout the country. Flaco and Guillermo who had been receiving combat training at an Army base near Madrid were once again re-assigned! Flaco remained in the capitol city but his friend was ordered to report to Sevilla and to await further orders. It was several months later when the conservative Niceto Zamora was ousted as president and was promptly replaced by the left-wing Manuel Azana!

Flaco was commissioned as a Lieutenant in the Army and was invited to participate in secret meetings with other Army officers who were discussing how to overthrow the Popular Front government. Several months later the new president Azana appointed Diego Martinez Barrio as Prime Minister and asked him to negotiate with the rebels. Emilio Mola was offered the role of Minister or War! Only when he refused the appointment did the president realize that the Nationalists were unwilling to compromise. He immediately fired Martinez Barrio and replaced him with Jose Giral. In order to protect the government, the Popular Front, Giral issued orders for guns and weapons to be distributed among the left-wing organizations that opposed the military uprising. Flaco was worried! He had spent most of his time trying to avoid bloodshed! Now the government had decided to issue arms and weapons to people that hardly knew how to use them. How was he ever going to stop the killing of innocent people? It seemed almost inevitable that there would be a civil war; and, from the initial unrest among the people, there was little to stop the bloodshed that was sure to follow, and all upon the orders of the government! He was shocked when word was handed down that General Emilio Mola had issued a proclamation of revolt in Navarro on July 19th 1936. It had gone bad for the coup, especially when Jose Sanjurjo was killed in an air crash the following day. The uprisings were unsuccessful in most parts of Spain, but Mola's forces had been successful in the Canary Islands, Morocco, Seville and Aragon. There were even reports circulating that Francisco Franco, who had been appointed as commander of the Army of Africa, had joined the revolt and began to conquer the southern areas of Spain. Flaco was stunned when he read in one of the reports that Franco's aid was a Lieutenant Guillermo Torres! If the reports were true, it meant that his friend and he were fighting on opposite sides! Unless the revolt could be stopped, who could say what might happen?

CHAPTER 4

Manuel Azana expressed his desire to retire from government, opposing to head a government that was militarily trying its best to defeat another group of Spaniards. Following a period of persuasive discussions, he was finally convinced to remain in power by the Socialist Party and the Communist Party who felt that he was the best person to persuade foreign governments not to support the military uprising.

Socialists and Communists from all over Europe began to form International Brigades and travelled to Spain to protect the Popular Front government. They arrived from a variety of left-wing groups but the majority of the International Brigades were almost always led by Communists! This began to cause frictions among the other parties; and, of course, also among the Anarchists! Spain, during late 1936, had two separate armies. The Peninsular Army, the largest, consisted of more than 110,000 men. Unfortunately this Army was poorly trained! By the start of the war, there were more than 40,000 men who were on leave. It was the Army of Africa consisting of 35,000 men that was considered to be militarily superior to the Peninsular Army that was comprised mostly of Spanish Army units that were based in Morocco. The force was small in numbers, but it was composed of regular Spanish Army units and the Spanish Foreign Legion.

Guillermo Torres was one of the officers that was present when Francisco Franco held a high level meeting of all of his Field

Grade officers and announced his plans to airlift almost 11,000 men across the Strait of Gibralter in airplanes that were owned by the German Luftwaffe! Lieutenant Torres was unhappy with the decision! Some of the strategies that were discussed simply didn't make any sense at all. The government in power had insisted on retaining the leadership of Manuel Azana because he was the best person they could think of to persuade other foreign governments from supporting the military uprising. Now, Franco was making plans to allow the Germans to fly his troops into the heart of the battle. As an elite paramilitary force, other members of the Guardia Civil as well as the Assault Guard had joined the Nationalists; but strangely, the regular Guards gave their loyalty to the Republican government.Only a handful of officers joined the Republican Army; and some of them were left wing members of the Union Militar Republicana Antifacista (UMRA).

Franco looked at Guillermo standing by his right; and, from the frown on his face, he could see that the young lieutenant was not at all happy with what was being planned.

"Sir," he said, "how can we expect the government to persuade foreign governments not to interfere while we take the advantage and do the same thing? Don't you think that once we allow Germany to transport our troops, they will then assume complete control? What will happen if one of the aircraft should be downed by ground fire? If they retaliate, every country in the world will want to interfere into Spanish affairs in order to fight the Germans! Personally, I think we may be asking for more trouble than we want to handle! It will force Germany to fight the Russians on two fronts! I see this as being very dangerous!"

Franco eyed the young lieutenant for several minutes as if he were thinking over the logic of what he had just been told.Then, in an abrupt move with his hands, he told him, "You lieutenant, will be in command of the ground forces! It will be up to you to make certain that none of the German aircraft are shot down!"

Guillermo did not like the assignment! He had served as a proud member of the Guardia Civil! Most of his training had been in domestic disturbances and crowd control.His military background had been limited to the training he had received while serving in the Army camp near Madrid. Military strategy and planning were new to him, but there was another thought that troubled him. Franco's African Army was comprised mainly of Black People from the Northern part of the African continent. The people of Spain knew very little about them and a sudden influx of Black Soldiers in a predominantly white environment was going to be trouble! The Spaniards were a proud people and they didn't like to have any outsiders becoming involved in their affairs. He realized that Franco had taken him as an aid because of his intelligence; but, he also knew that the General was a vicious person who was likely to kill you as to speak to you! Suddenly, he found himself wishing that his friend Flaco could have been there! After all, Flaco was much smarter than he was, and he had a certain persuasive quality that would have probably been well received by General Franco. He hadn't received any word from Flaco, but he had to believe that he had become a member of the Republican Army, because most of the Guardia Civiles had joined the army. If he was still in Madrid, he was certain that Flaco would have had some hand in the military plans! After all, he was much too intelligent not to be used in planning military strategy! Could it be that after their friendship, destiny had brought them to opposite sides of the war? If he were to meet Flaco on the battlefield, would he possibly get up enough nerve to kill him? For that matter, if the situation were reversed, would Flaco be able to kill him? Guillermo had watched him working the crowds as they pleaded for alms for the needy, and had also been with him when they cashed in their pesetas for "perronas" so that they could distribute them among the needy. Flaco was not a killer; but then, neither was he!

Franco was successful! The Republican Army was about one third larger than the Nationalist Army. However, by the time the rest of the Army of Africa arrived on mainland Spain, the number of men in each of the armies was almost equal. It was during the early stages of the Civil War that members of the Falange Espanola, Carlistas and other right-wing political parties joined forces with the Nationalist Army. The fighting became fast and furious as both armies did their best to control certain areas of the country. After the first few weeks of the war, the Nationalist

Army controlled most of the northern provinces of Spain. The northernmost areas such as Galicia, Asturias, Leon, Navarre and large sections of Old Castile and Aragon were in the hands of the Nationalist Army. They also held the areas in the south such as Cadiz, Seville, Cordoba and Granada! In all, the Nationalists controlled about one third of the country. By August 1936, the National authorities introduced conscription, and this enabled them to recruit an additional 270,000 men during the next six months.

Since the capital of Madrid was under the control of the Popular Front, Emilio Mola and Francisco Franco were extremely anxious to capture the capital city as quickly as possible.They began their first introduction of air raids on the capital city at the end of August 1936. Lieutenant Guillermo Torres became disillusioned quickly when he saw first hand the devastation of the air raids on the capital city! The once beautiful city had been destroyed; and, for the first time, he saw people without arms or limbs seeking medical assistance. There were bodies of dead civilians everywhere and the persistant swarms of summer flies were feasting on the decaying flesh that was everywhere! More than once he wished that he could have spoken to General Franco and tried to stop the bloodshed; but, by that time,.it was too late and he feared that by doing so he would have been branded as a traitor! In a short period of time they had come a long way from the days of peaceful demonstrations that could be easily quieted with a simple "perrona", just barely enough to buy a few vegetables for the table! He had wondered many times what had happened to Flaco? It was ages since he had received any word from him, and could only wonder what would happen if he too became exposed to the same atrocities that he was now seeing!

Oviedo

Flaco was eating dinner when word was received that Madrid had been bombed from the air! There had been previously circulated reports saying that a major air raid was being planned; but he had hoped that the nationalistic spirit of the people would finally prevail and that such destruction might be avoided. His biggest fears had now come true as the reports were all saying that the casualty rate had been enormous. The war that had started as an insurrection had grown into a full-blown civil war and nobody could predict how it was going to end! If the Soviet Union was going to come to the aid of the Socialist and the Communist Parties, it seemed only fair that Germany would come to the aid of the Nationalist party. He had wondered how it was that they had come into a war so quickly, never realizing that secret meetings had been held between the German authorities and Emilio Mola who had travelled to Germany in search of aid!

He had just finished his dinner when Colonel Garcia came to see him! As he had been taught, he quickly put down his fork and stood at attention before him!

"Sientate!" the Colonel told him. "Sit down, Lieutenant, I want to speak to you!" Flaco nodded politely and sat down. He already assumed that for the colonel to come looking for him, the news was not going to be good!

"I suppose you have already heard that the war has taken a turn for the worse! Madrid has been bombed from the air and there are many reported casualties! I'd like you to go there and give me you assessment of the situation! We need to know how to react to what is happening and we don't have a sufficient Air Force to stop the bombing! Also we'll need to know how many more troops we will need in the South to fight off the Nationalist Army!"

Flaco thought about it for a few minuted before answering! The entire strategy made no sense at all to him! How could they possibly expect to fight an air war without using airplanes? Also, he wondered what would be the good of sending more troops to the capital? It would mean that the Northern cities would then be left unprotected! "What is it you want to know, sir? We can't fight an air war without any airplanes! Furthermore, it seems to me that every effort should be made to contain the war to the South! Colonel, the people who live in the northern provinces are simple people; most of them are just farmers! To them, war is something they know nothing about!"

"That is the reason we drafted them! We will need to train them on how to use weapons, and also they will need to learn the basic army tactics! Unfortunately, we won't have much time!" the elderly man explained.

"But do they know what you want them to do? Sir, I have seen these people during the demonstrations! They are peaceful people who want nothing other than to be at home with their families and taking care of their small particles of land! I doubt we will be successful!"

"That's why I want you to go there and see for yourself! Return to me with the information! They need to protect the "Frente Popular"!"

Flaco looked at him and smiled! He was a subordinate in the army and knew there were some things that couldn't be said to a superior officer! He wondered to himself what had been so wonderful about the Frente Popular that needed protection? Everyone knew that it hadn't produced any vegetables for several years! He also knew that the people were poor and underfed! Really, he thought, what did they have that was worth defending?

"I will leave for Madrid in the morning!" Flaco said.

"Muy bien! Vete y regresa pronto!" (Good, go and return promptly.)

By the time Flaco arrived in Madrid, he saw that many things had already taken place! A Lieutenant Colonel Walther Warlimont of the German General Staff had already arrived from Germany and was immediately appointed as the German commander and military advisor to General Franco! The following month Colenel Warlimont suggested that a German Condor Legion be formed to fight the Spanish Civil War. Shortly thereafter the conduct of the war began to change when the Condor Legion was quickly equipped with more than 100 aircraft and more than 15,000 troops. As soon as Flaco saw the vast destruction of the air raids, he already knew it was going to be extremely difficult to defeat this enemy! There had been a reluctance among Spaniards to kill other Spaniards; but that attitude began to change as more foreigners were brought into the fight. He wondered how he had allowed himself to get into this mess? The only thing he had wanted to be was a Guardia Civil; now he had turned into a military officer, something he believed was far beyond his abilities! Once again his thoughts drifted back to Soledad! The thought of her trying to talk him out of becoming a Guardia Civil was vividly on his mind even though it had been many years since he had last seen her! Perhaps she had been right all along, he thought!

The area of Badajoz is a Spanish province that lies on the border with Portugal. Just like many of the other neighboring provinces the vast area, mostly agricultural, was rigidly controlled by the Republican Army during the early days of the Civil War. General de Yague and a full brigade consisting of more than 3000 Nationalist troops began a vicious attack on the capital city of Badajoz. The area was surrounded by a series of small mountains to the north and flanked by Portugal on the west! By the time the attack took place, General Hugo Sperrle had arrived from Germany and had been appointed commander of the Condor Legion. His chief of staff was none other than Wolfram von Richthofin, the cousin of the First World War flying ace, Manfred von Richthofen and had already been placed in complete control of all the ground troops in the area. The three thousand troops stormed the area after several days of non-stop bombing raids that had completely destroyed most of the infrastructure of the city! Houses had been completely destroyed and most of the public buildings had been flattened.The casualties were high and became even higher when bitter street fighting and hand to hand combat began to take place as soon as the Condor Legion entered the city.

Captain Guillermo Torres had been sent as an observer to the area, and later to report to his Commanding Officer what he had seen. The sights on the streets were unbelievable as he saw dead bodies being tossed about like discarded rags throughout the city.The few hospitals that had been set up to receive the wounded were filled to capacity with many wounded civilians and soldiers outside of the makeshift tents waiting to be attended! Guillermo entered one of the hospitals and saw scores of wounded people. The odors emanating from decaying flesh were repugnant, and for a few moments, he had to fight the urge to run outside feeling that he was getting ill! As he entered the tent, he saw that the wounded men had been separated into two sections. One section of about five Nationalist soldiers were receiving medical attention, but the other remaining group were patiently waiting to be attended. The captain soon noticed that the men of the second group were more seriously wounded than those from the first group. Some of them were still bleeding from the open wounds on their bodies. He noticed that one of the men had his head wrapped up in a dirty white cloth while yet another man had his hand over his eye with fresh blood rolling down his arm. Guillermo looked at both of them but remained silent! Just then a young nurse dressed in a blood stained white uniform, passed in front of him. He decided to stop her and find out why the men were not being treated since they seemed to be the ones who needed immediate attention!

"Muyer, porque no estan atendiendo a estos hombres?" (Lady, why aren't these men being attended to?) he asked.

He could see by the annoyed look on her face that she didn't particularly like to have her judgement being questioned by a stranger! He did notice, however, that the nurse was young and very attractive! She had long dark hair that had been pulled up into a circular bun behind her white cap. Her dark, expressive eyes seemed to go right through him as though she was looking beyond him when she spoke.

"Solo tengo dos manos, y las dos estan ocupadas!" (Because I only have two hands and they are both occupied!) she answered.

"I can see that! But don't you think that these men who are more seriously wounded should be attended to first?"

"Who are you? Are you a doctor?" she asked.

"No! I am a representative of the Nationalist Army, and I've been sent here to see what was happening!"

"Then you should know that those men are prisoners from the Republican Army! I've been told to treat them last!"

Before he was able to answer, a young man entered the tent with a rifle slung over his shoulder. Without making any announcements, he lowered his rifle and opened fire on the five wounded Republican Army soldiers. Two of the men made an ugly sound as they fell to the floor.He saw that the young man, probably not older than seventeen years of age was delirious! The rapid, uncontrolled spray of bullets was going everywhere! Guillermo reached for the nurse, knocked her down to the ground and quickly threw himself on top of her protecting her from the assault. When he saw that the young man's rifle was empty, he got up and jumped on the youngster, ripping away the rifle from his hands. Several other men dressed in white went over to them, restrained the young man and led him away!

"Ahora puedes ver lo que esta pasando!" (Now you can see what is happening!) she told him as she dusted off her uniform. He could see that her eyes were filling with tears as she spoke. "Those poor men will not be needing any medical attention now!" she said through the tears.

"Does this happen very often?"

"No! This is the first time! I want to thank you for saving my life!" she said. "I would have been killed had it not been for you!" Suddenly, she buried her head in her hands and began to sob! It almost seemed that she was ashamed that this stranger was seeing her at a weak moment. He gently placed his arms around her and held her against him! He had no idea why he had been so brazen, but it seemed to be the only thing he could do.

"No llores, nena! Esta guerra pronto va terminar!" (Don't cry, woman! This war will soon end!)

She looked at him almost as if she was seeing him for the first time! "You called me, nena! Where are you from? You obviously aren't from around here!" she asked.

"No! I am from Asturias! In fact, I was born there!"

"Then why are you wearing the uniform of the Nationalist Army?"

"It's a long story! I enlisted in the Guardia Civil! Before the war broke out, I received Army training near Madrid! From there I was sent Southward, where I became assigned as a member of General Franco's staff! That's the reason why I'm here!" He paused for a moment, noticing that she was intently listening to his every word. "By the way, my name is Guillermo Torres! What's yours?"

"Dolores Pineiro," she replied. "Yo soy de Galicia!" (I come from Galicia!)

He noticed that she had lowered her voice when telling him that she came from the next province to the west of Asturias!

It was best that he not ask more questions! It seemed obvious that the hospital had been set up to care for the Nationalists soldiers since they had now conquered the city! All of the available medical facilities had now been re-assigned to care for the winning army! If they found out she was from Galicia, there was no way of telling what they might do to her! The Moors that Franco had transported into Spain from North Africa, were vicious people; and it was difficult to judge how they would act or feel in the presence of a young, attractive woman that they knew would be vulnerable because she would not receive any protection from their own army.

"How can you attend to these people knowing what they have done?" he asked quietly. In some ways he was questioning her loyalty; and, he could see by the look on her face that she had been offended.

"Que quieres que haga?" (What do you want me to do?) I was working here in the hospital and as soon as your Army took control of the city, they took control of the hospital as well! If we had any hopes of caring for the Republican soldiers, we needed to do exactly as we were ordered to do! By the way, mi Capitan, I somehow get the feeling that you are less than overjoyed with what is happening! What will happen when you move up to Asturias? Whose side will you be on?" she asked.

It was a question that he always felt would one day be asked, but, he never thought it would have been asked so quickly! At least it seemed as if this young nurse was harboring equal feelings; and, although he needed to speak to her with extreme caution, he felt comfortable while in her company! After everything he had seen, she had been a welcome surprise!

"I wish I could be truthful with you! The truth is that I really don't know! Whether I like it or not, I am now a Nacionalista! I began as a Guardia Civil and we were taught never to take sides! I hope I won't be transferred up to the north because it will be very painful for me!"

"For me it was equally as bad! We would have all been killed had it not been for the many reports of Cholera that is breaking out in many areas! The "facistas" decided to spare our lives as long as we pledged our service to them! You see, they realize that they didn't have enough medical people to handle the outbreak of illnesses! This enabled them to have their staff just in case they are needed in some of the towns!"

She flashed him a smile and remained silent as she soon realized that he was finding it difficult to take his eyes off her. Whenever she smiled, it seemed that her entire face became lit with a fresh sunrise! She had a smile that was contagious and one that would be hard to forget!

"Porque me miras tanto?" (Why are you looking at me?) she asked.

"Because you are the first ray of sunshine I have seen since the war began! I didn't want to come here, because I wanted to avoid seeing the casualties that the war is causing! Now, I need to admit, you made me happy that I came!"

She smiled again and gently lowered her head as if she were shy that this officer had given her a compliment! She had never received a compliment before and certainly not from any Army officer who was as kind and as sensitive as she was!

"What time do you get off work? Could we go somewhere and perhaps get something to eat?" he surprised himself that he had been so bold as to ask her to eat with him. He had admired many of the young women when he was in Aviles with Flaco; but, he had kept away from the women, especially those that were openly flirting with him while in uniform! Now he had met a stranger and without any regrets he had asked her to spend a few more moments with him. Not that it really mattered, he thought! She would probably turn him down anyway!

He received the surprise of his life when she looked at him again, and softly answered. "Con mucho gusto!" (Of course, gladly!) "I will be free in about an hour! If you like, I'll hurry and change clothes so we can look for a place that sells something to eat! You certainly wouldn't like the food here in the hospital!"

"I'll be back in an hour!" he said excitedly. "No!......Instead, I'll be here in half an hour! I don't want to take the chance that you'll change your mind!" he said smiling.

She returned the smile as he watched her start to walk away! Strange that she no longer seemed to be shy! His only hope was that she was looking forward to being with him as much as he was looking forward to be with her!

Later when they met at the hospital, he saw that she was even more beautiful than she was before dressed in a nurse's white uniform! Her hair was still pulled back into a "mono", but now she had applied just enough makeup in order to accentuate the smooth lines of her face. He gave her a big smile when he saw her again, and she knew immediately that he was pleased with the way she looked. They walked down the dark, deserted street and noticed an eerie silence that loomed everywhere. Some of the dead casualties were still laying on the streets and had not yet been removed! Guillermo wished that things could be different and that the two of them could enjoy a liesurely stroll down the street in better times. They could have been talking about themselves and getting acquainted with each other instead of being reminded of the hardships of war. But, this was not to be! He had heard somewhere that the Nationalist army had massacred almost eighteen hundred people while taking control of the city. The ugly scenes he was seeing were a grim reminder that the totals he had heard were probably true! A few blocks away they arrived at a small taverna that for some unknown reason had decided to remain opened during the siege. Guillermo and Dolores went inside and selected a small, cozy table that was away from the glass window! Although the city was now under control of the Nationalists, there were still many individuals that were dazed and incoherent walking the streets with rifles on their shoulders. The safest place he could think of was to keep away from the windows and away from any of the dazed citizens who were still walking the streets. Guillermo held the chair for her as she sat down, but he noticed that the charming smile had not hidden the tired look of her face!

"I can see by your face that you are very tired!" he said as he watched her flash him a forced smile and stared at her hands, ashamed of the how she felt.It occured to her that back in Galicia she had never felt tired! She had enjoyed her young life to the fullest, and now, suddenly all of her youth had seemed to vanish!

"I'm sorry, mi Capitan! I wish I could look better for you!" she said meekly.

"Oh, no, no, no!" he answered. "I didn't mean that! In fact,. I think you are one of the most beautiful people I have ever seen!" he corrected himself."Tell me about yourself! I want to know everything about you!! By the way, please call me Guillermo!"

"Okay, Guillermo!" she answered. "What would you like to know? My life has not been very interesting! I was born in a small town called Guisamo, a few miles east of La Coruna! I am the youngest of four and my parents still live there! I studied nursing at La Coruna, after which I was sent to Badajoz because they were having an acute shortage of nurses! Your army took us by total surprise; and, before long, we were in the hands of the Nationalist army. Because we were medical people, they decided to leave us alone as long as we promised to care for the wounded Nationalist soldiers first!"

"Are you satisfied with what happened?" he asked.

"What does it matter whether or not I am satisfied? The only thing left to do is for us to find the means for survival! We have been lied to, and abandoned by our own army! We had every hope that the Republican Army would be able to defend the city, but you know better than me what happened!"

"Can you be loyal to the Nationalists?" he asked.

It seemed like a strange question coming from an Army officer; and she knew immediately that her answer was going to be vague and incomplete, barely enough for him to draw his own conclusions! "What is loyalty, Guillermo? How can you be loyal to a government that has deceived its people? Tell me the truth! Can you be loyal to the Nationalists?" she asked.

"I suppose you're right! I, too, had many dreams and desires when I first joined the Guardia Civil! They faded away! I was happy and without a care back in Asturias! I had it all, honor, prestige and respect! Then, all of a sudden, I awoke one morning and I was an army officer! Loyalty is no longer an option, I guess! I do my job and hope that one day the war will end and we can all go back home!"

"Do you ever hope to return to Asturias?"

"Of course! I don't know whether or not I will ever go back, but I can always hope and dream! Those are the things that a war can never take away!"

"I feel much the same as you! I would have liked to have met you back in Asturias or in Galicia as two happy young people. I think I could have become very attracted to you!" she told him. He immediately noticed that her cheeks had turned a crimson red and felt embarassed that she had revealed more of her feelings than she wanted to!

"Don't be embarassed!" he said as he reached across the table and took her hand! "I feel the same way!" Slowly, his eyes looked down at the table as if his mind was many miles away!

"You are a very strange person for a Nationalist officer! It almost seems as if you are being compelled to do a job that you don't really like! I was watching you back at the hospital when the young man fired his rifle at the wounded officers. Any other Nationalist officer would have killed him on the spot! I got the feeling that you lacked the nerve to kill the young man in cold blood, no matter who he was! I think that was when I began to admire you! I still don't know very much about you, but I do admire you!"

"Thank you!": he replied. "It's been a long time since I heard someone be so frank and truthful with me!"

"Are you married? You needn't answer me if you don't want to!"

"No! I am not married nor do I have a girlfriend! Any more questions? he asked smiling.

"None that really matter! Will I be seeing you again or will you be going away?" Once again she saw him deep in thought and gazing down at the table! "Do you want to tell me what you're thinking? I can see by that serious look that there is something on your mind!" Slowly, he raised his head, held her hand tightly, and stared into her eyes!

"Dolores, I want you to leave this place! Is there any chance that you can return home to Galicia? I realize that it may not be easy for you, but, if you want me to, I can arrange for you to get immediate transportation out of here!" he told her.

She seemed surprised! She had hopes of seeing him again, perhaps on a regular basis, and now, here he was, asking her to leave this place without him! "I suppose that is your way of telling me that you don't want to see me again, is that it?"

"Heavens no! That isn't it at all! It is because I do want to see you again, and I worry about your safety! That's why I want you to return to Galicia where you'll be safe!"

Guillermo had returned to headquarters when a company consisting of black Moors from Franco's African Army arrived in the city! He had heard some of the officers repeating the orders of General de Yague, encouraging the dark troops to rape all of the supporters of the Popular Front government without fear of being admonished or reprimanded by their acts. He knew that despite her work as a nurse, down in her heart, she was still very much a sympathizer of the Popular Front. With her beauty she would be a prime target for any of the animals, especially those who had not had a woman's company in a long time! He dreaded the thought of what might happen to her! If he could convince her into leaving and returning home, he would be satisfied knowing that she would be safe! Who could say that at some point he might not be transferred to the northern provinces where they could again meet under better circumstances!

"I would still like you to go home! I'm sure I can arrange that! Also, I think you will be much happier there!" he told her.

"No!" she answered. "What difference does it make? How long do you think it will be before the army travels into the north? The entire country is at war and there is no place in which to hide! Besides," she said smiling, "As long as I'm here, I still feel I have you whom I can trust! I have a feeling that you will see to it that nothing happens! Am I correct?"

"Yes!" he answered quietly. "Of course! I'll be watching over you and I'll do my best to keep you safe!"

"See that? Already I feel better! I have nothing to worry about!"

They ordered a strong cup of black coffee and a piece of 'pan dulce', a piece of regular, fresh baked bread coated with sugar! Most of the conversation centered around their lives back home. They discussed their families and friends and compared the hardships they had endured as children. They parted with their hands held together and with him promising to see her again the following day! She reached up and gave him a friendly peck on the cheek and quickly turned her head so that he wouldn't see that she was embarassed!

"What was that for?" he asked feeling pleased that she had kissed him.

"Just for being who you are, and also, for having come into my life!" she answered. She then quickly withdrew her hand and started her walk back to the hospital while he began to walk in the opposite direction toward the cuartel!

It had been an enjoyable evening and perhaps one of the happiest moments he had in a long time! Suddenly, he heard the loud screams of a woman who seemed to be in distress! He turned around and saw that Dolores was only a block away from him. There were two black Moors, still dressed in their African Army uniform, who were attacking her! One of the men was trying to hold her arms while the other man was doing his best to rip away her clothes! He started to run toward her!

Guillermo rushed over grabbing one of the assailants by the neck and shoving him away! Quickly, he grabbed hold of the other man's arm who was the one trying to rip away her clothes! Then, he took hold of the assailant's arm and bent it behind his back as far as he could until he heard a loud snap making the black intruder let out a horrowful yell! The first person that had been holding her, reached for his firearm and was pointing it directly at Guillermo's head! In an instant, Guillermo quickly reached for his revolver and fired away three quick shots! Two of them entered the assailant's body in the chest and head! Standing over him, he watched the wounded man gasping for air and trying to let out a yell before falling down to the ground! His eyes remained opened and a steady flow of blood was gushing out of the large hole in his chest. The other man made another move toward Dolores! He quickly pointed his gun at the assailant's head ordering him to let her go! The large black soldier then released Dolores and started to run away still holding his arm!

The young woman, having been taken by surprise was in tears! The cotton top of her dress had been ripped away and her flesh was exposed! Her tears were partly because she felt embarrassed that Guillermo should see her naked and partly because she had never expected an attack so close to the hospital. "Are you alright?" Guillermo asked.

"Yes, I'm alright, but what about you? Will you get into trouble for killing this man?" She knew that killing a member of the African Army would not be taken lightly by the authorities. There was a good chance that he would be reprimanded, especially since the other man had escaped and would certainly tell the convening authorities his version about what had happened. The only thing left for Guillermo to do was to alert her as to what she should say if she was asked.

"It is important that you insist that you are not a sympathizer of the Republican Army! Tell anyone who asks you that you are a worker for the Nationalists and that he attacked you! You can say that I came to your rescue, asked him to leave you alone; and, when he disregarded my orders, I then took the liberty of killing him in order to protect you!" he told her.

"If I tell them that, for certain they will come after you and then you'll be in trouble!" she answered, afraid of what the consequences would be.

"Now you know the reason why I wanted you to go back to Galicia as soon as possible! Maybe you may want to think it over again?" he asked.

"No!" she answered. "My mind is made up and I want to remain as long as you are here! I feel safe, and besides, I don't want to leave here without you!"

The investigation into the death of the African Army soldier had been swift! The person that had run away after attacking the nurse had filed a grievance; and Guillermo had filed his version of the complaint and outlining the events that had taken place! His excuse for doing what he did was well explained. Franco had established certain rules of military behavior and he insisted that all matters be resolved quickly! In his remarks, Guillermo had explained that any attack on a provider of medical care would undoubtedly give the Nationalist army a poor reputation that could not be disregarded since reports were already circulating about the atrocities that were being committed. If the control of the country was going to be determined by a war, it was going to be necessary to retain all of the medical help that was available that was needed to care for the injured troops! The reports were already cautioning about shortages of medical staff and there were many who had worked for the Republican army that had been adamant in refusing to provide medical assistance to the enemy! Such a ferocious attack on a woman who had worked many hours attending to the casualties of war would only serve to further the reluctance of attracting badly needed medical help! The report about Guillermo had been sent to the office of the "Mariscal" somewhere in Madrid. The punishment could be anything from being a 'justifiable homicide' to a death sentence for killing a member of the African army that was considered to be an elite group of soldiers. The opinion came down quickly that the killing of the Moor had been justified and strongly recommended that no further action be taken against the defendent! It was a hollow victory for both Guillermo and Dolores since it showed that the dismissal of the charges had been ordered by a "Mariscal" who seemed to be just man! Since the decision was final both he and Dolores felt relieved by the prompt resolution! Almost as soon as the decision was reached, word began to be circulated that the two people involved in the crime were romantically linked and deserved the respect of all Army personnel! This was the "Mariscal's" way of assuring them that there were to be no reprisals or further attacks against the two people by other disgruntled army personnel!

It was difficult not to admit to the rumors, since after the incident, they had been seen regularly every evening and had begun to spend most of their free time together! Guillermo had proclaimed himself to be her protector, and, for the first time, she felt completely safe and secure while in his company! For the sake of security, both of them made certain that the rumor was not denied, adding to her security in troubling times. The Moors who had been a part of the African Army were well trained soldiers and had no scrupples against raping women who had been suspected of being Republican sympathizers before having been taken by the Nationalists! It soon became known that this nurse as well as all other medical people were not to be raped nor attacked in any way under punishment of death! It seemed strange that the edict had been given after the incident! Guillermo could only wonder if it had not been an added condition that had been imposed by the Mariscal when informed of what had happened!

Upon the outbreak of the Civil War, the President of Portugal, Antonio Salazar, immediately offered his support to the Nationalists in their struggle against the Popular Front government. Salazar feared that if the Nationalists were to win the war, his own authoritarian government would certainly be threatened! Concerned over the effects that the events in Spain would have on his country, he quickly established his own militia that was intended to serve as auxiliary police throughout the country! The newly established police force quickly began to arrest a growing number of dissidents and removed politically unreliable people from many of the educational and governmental institutions throughout the country. It also began to arrest supporters of the Popular Front who were living in Portugal. In addition, he closed off the Portuguese frontier to all Republican sympathizers and issued orders that any violators of his new edicts would be severely dealt with! Although this new series of mandates soon came under considerable pressure from Britain and France, Salazar refused to allow any international observers to be stationed on the Portugal-Spain borders. Officially, it was his claim that by allowing the observers to be stationed in those strategic areas would violate Portuguese sovereignty! In reality, his true reasons behind the new mandates were intended to keep the world from knowing of the large amounts of aid that were crossing the borders into Spain in support of the Nationalist forces!

Burgos

Ths situation in Burgos had changed for Soledad! The elderly man she had been caring for had been strickened by a fatal heart attack; and now that her mother had passed away, she had no one to turn to. After a simple funeral, she had often wondered

about what was left of her life and for her to do now that she no
one to turn to. Don Martin had been kind and generous to her. He
had left her some money to care for herself once he had passed
away! The thought had entered her mind about returning to Salinas
and caring for the large house that her mother had left her; but the
work that needed to be done was much too strenuous and time
consuming for a young woman. The animals had already been
sold at a public auction for a few pesetas; and, even if she felt like
re-starting the farm, she also realized that the conditions in Spain
were getting worse. There was no assurance that once Franco's
army marched through Asturias, she would be able to continue to
farm the small parcel of land that surrounded the large stone house.
As soon as it became known that the house had been used as a
medical clinic, she was certain that it would be confiscated by the
conquering army; and all the work she would have invested in the
land would have been forgotten!

For the first time in her life, she felt all alone and lonely!
Her youth was quickly passing her by as she began to realize
that the best time of her life were now behind her. She had been
raised with poverty; but, with her mother to protect her, she had
developed a certain strength that she thought would always be
with her. Strange that at these moments her thoughts would return
to her youth when she had saved the life of a skinny friend who
had almost drowned in the river as she was washing clothes. He
had also walked out of her life in search of something that he was
unable to identify! So many years had gone by since those days!
She even remembered the foolish prank when she had deliberately
cut her arm allowing the flow of blood to mix with his! Smiling to
herself she remembered the stupid things that young people would
often do! The lifelong dreams, fantasies, and expectations had
always shielded her from the dismal realities of poverty throughout
her youth! Her thoughts centered on the skinny boy who had
always gone down to the river and kept her company while she was
busy with her chores. He was probably married by now, stationed
in some remote place in southern Spain, working as a Guardia
Civil and earning just enough "pesetas" to raise a family of four
or five children! In fact, she now had forgotten his real name

because he had always been known as Flaco! He was probably
fat or perhaps overweight with a receding hairline, the result of
worrying about how to feed his family. Not that it really mattered
now! Those were childhood fantasies and dreams; all of which had
ended with childhood! No, this was the real world, she thought,
as she looked at herself in a mirror and became unhappy with the
woman who was looking back at her! Her face had become drawn
and hard-looking with ugly wrinkles around her eyes! Her hair was
disheveled and untidy, a product of the many hours of work and of
taking care of Don Martin!

When she first arrived, Don Martin had been ill but easily
manageable! Her job consisted of taking care of him and doing
the regular housework, things that had been very familiar to her
during her youth. The elderly man soon became too old and too
ill to pay attention to her youth! There had been rumors that a
man living alone would sometimes take in a young girl to care
for the house, and would also use his house guest to feed his
male appetite for sex! This had never been the case with her! Not
that she actually knew what sex was all about! There had been a
strange attraction with that Skinny kid, but certainly nothing that
could be considered sex! The only thought she had about sex was
the time when the young fisherman that gave her the sardines had
made a pass at her! She remembered how disgusting and repugnant
it was! It infuriated her that he had taken liberties with her that
were dispicable! She still remembered how ugly it felt the day that
he had tired to fondle her with his ugly and dirty hands. In a sign
of determination, she had walked away but not before threatening
to kill him if he ever touched her again! From that day on, they
had remained friends and still gave her the sardines that would
be tossed back into the ocean; but he never again tried to fondle
her!Perhaps, one of the things he had never known was that the day
it happened, she had gone home and looked at herself in the mirror.
Her hair was neatly combed and she had put on a new dress! She
recalled liking the way she looked, and there was a certain feeling,
a certain satisfaction she felt knowing that someone of the opposite
sex had been attracted to her. It was a feeling that she never forgot
even though it was never repeated! She was much older and wiser

now! During the cold evenings, Don Martin and she would sit by the wood burning stove and would discuss things that troubled her about life! What little she knew, she had learned from him who regarded her almost as if she were his daughter. Luckily, he had warned her about men such as that fisherman, and had stressed that she needed to remain strong at all times! She was a lovely young lady and needed to protect herself from the evil thoughts of men who were hungry for flesh! After their little talks he would insist that she remain by his side while they repeated the evening prayers. In the absence of her own father, it had been Don Martin who had taken on the role of advisor and protector!

Soledad had come to love him as a father, especially after her mother died and there was no one else to turn to. Don Joaquin, the village priest, had been transferred away from Salinas, after a fire of suspicious origin had demolished the church and only the charred wooden supports remained. There had been a cursory investigation, but the outcome had never been established! It had been Don Martin who had explained to her about the ruthless aims of the Socialist government; and how they wanted to rid themselves of many of the Catholic churches, because they felt that the churches had done little to stop the demonstrations of the needy who protested against the government for their failure to provide employment for those who were the most needy! In the beginning, none of these things made any sense; but now that she was much older, she started to notice a pattern of churches being set on fire as a way of removing the church from the functions of the government! With the death of Don Martin, she soon realized that all she had left was her pride! The comments her father had made that ' an Asturiano was a proud person who never begged for anything' rang out in her mind! She had never begged and had always been proud of her heritage! It was something that no one could ever take away! Despite all of life's adversities,she had always remained strong and proud! As conditions changed and her life was becoming more unsettled,who could predict how long her pride and strength would continue to support her?

Everybody knew that the government was in an upheaval! There were personnel changes being made every day and things seemed to be getting worse instead of better! There was a new army commander by the name of Francisco Franco, who had made his move with a brigade of Moor soldiers he had brought with him from Africa; and, reportedly, they were marching their way northward in their quest to take over the government. Not that it meant much to her! After all, any new move would almost have to be better than the government they had! It had already abandoned the people who were hungry and in need and had no one to turn to! She felt luckier than most because Don Martin had seen to it that she was never hungry! He had little time nor interest in politics because he had confessed to her that he really didn't trust any politician, and she was starting to believe what the elderly man had told her!

The latest reports coming out of Madrid was that President Azana had appointed a man by the name of Francisco Largo Caballero as Prime Minister of the country! All that was known about him was that he was a felt-wing Socialist! His political affiliations were quickly confirmed when he brought into the government two left-wing radicals by the names of Angel Galarza as Minister of the Interior and Alvarez del Vallo as the Minister of Foreign Affairs. To a young woman with nothing to share, this meant nothing! It only meant the shifting of yet more names and people but with the same results. Every one of the Ministeries was firmly in control by a group of Anarchists and Socialists. The two Ministries that remained were those of education and agriculture, and those were staffed by well known Communists, Jesus Fernandez and Vicente Uribe! Once the cabinet had been formed, Largo Caballero announced that he was now concentrating on winning the war and was not pursuing his policies for a Social revolution! In an effort to gain the support of foreign governments, he announced that his administration was, "not fighting for Socialism but, rather, for a Democracy and a Consitutional rule!" It was this declaration that infuriated the leftist people in the new Spanish government! The new changes included conscription, the introduction of ranks and insignias into the militia and the abolition of workers and soldiers councils! He also established a new police force, the National Republican Guard and agreed that

Juan Negrin would take control of the Carabineros! None of these names mattered very much to Soledad who was now spending much of her own time pondering her future. Many of the other villagers had grown a strong distrust for the government, and Don Martin had insisted that she make a small hole in the farm behind the house and bury in the hole all of the "pesetas" he had given her. The banks could no longer be trusted to protect their investments! Some of the villagers who had deposited money into the banks would routinely try to make withdrawals only to be told that, under a new rule, the funds on deposit would need to be taxed in order to finance the war effort! After several denials, many of the local villagers decided to bury their money in the ground where it would not be taxed by the government. It was a move that further depleted the reserves of the banks and created the failure of many banks under the new government! Soledad had decided that her own funds were secure as long as the "pesetas" were safely buried in the ground! Now all that she needed to do was to protect the property from being confiscated by the government. She had purchased a rifle and had sworn to Don Martin that she would defend the property as well as the "pesetas" with her life if necessary!

Madrid

It was near the end of 1936 when the generals involved in the military uprising came to the conclusion that Francisco Franco should become the commander of the Nationalist Army! At the same time, he was appointed to the post of Chief of State. General Emilio Mola agreed to serve under him and was quickly placed in charge of the Army in the North! Franco immediately started his quest for total control! He started removing all of his main rivals for the leadership of the Nationalist forces. Some of the leaders were forced into exile and nothing was done to help the rescue of Jose Antonio Primo de Rivera from captivity. However, when Jose Antonio was shot by the Republicans at the end of the year, Franco wisely exploited his death by making him a mythological saint of the fascist movement!

Mariscal Romero was sitting in his office when he received word that Francisco Franco had been named as Commander of the Nationalist Army! The youthful looking Mariscal had mixed feelings about the nomination! He had seen reports of the atrocities that had been committed by his forces, especially by the brigade of Moros he had brought with him from his African Army. All in all, he had been more fortunate than most young men! Need and logic had prevailed in his acceptance of a responsible assignment in the Nationalist Army! He had been assigned to a battalion in Granada as a senior officer in the Guardia Civil! His reputation for success with demonstrations had preceded him, and the people soon realized that he was a capable and considerate leader and one of the few leaders they could trust! After it was brought to Franco's attention that such a man was within his grasp, he travelled to Granada to interview him and determine what political affiliations he would need to work with! Several things impressed Franco from the first interview! For one thing, many of the reports that had been circulated showed that the man was well respected by the people and that they trusted and had faith in him when he listened to their demands. Franco was aware that if he was going to be successful in his conquest of Spain, he would need people of this caliber to serve in his cabinet. The young Mariscal was tall and thin with handsome light features, probably a resident from one of the northern provinces. The interview began by making Franco wait for more than one half hour, because the young man was listening to the petitions of the local villagers on complaints they wanted to make about their local government. To have Franco wait for an interview was totally unheard of! Wherever the general went people would go out of their way to accomodate and welcome him, some of them out of fear and some out of fear for his position, but never would he be kept waiting! Yet, this young Mariscal appeared to have little regard for protocol, considering the needs of the people far more important than a simple interview that he knew was only intended to gain his support! At first the general was angry that this young man had not given him the proper respect, allowing the people's needs to take precedence over the interview. But, on second thought, he rather admired the nerve of this young man, barely into his middle years, that was willing to take such a bold step. If the general hoped to gain the support of the people, he was going to need as much support as possible from the leaders serving him. Wherever he was trained, it was soon obvious to the general that he would be a powerful leader to have under his command. Any of the thoughts he had entertained about walking out of the interview were quickly set aside as he decided he would sit and wait his turn! More than one half hour later, the young Mariscal Romero made his appearance, apologized for allowing the general to wait, and quickly asked the General to sit down!

"En que le puedo servir, mi General?" (How may I serve you, my General?)

There were no signs of ambition, excitement nor concern as he spoke to the general! Franco noticed that he was nicely dressed in a fresh starched officer's uniform! His hair was neatly groomed and there was an unassuming seriousness about him that drew the admiration of the general.

"I want to know where your allegiance lies?" the general asked. It was neither a threat nor a coercive approach! Instead it was said as a point of interest!

"My allegiance is to the people of this nation!" the Mariscal replied. "I feel that the Spanish people have been misled and abused enough! No one has listened to their needs! Most of the peasants are hungry and unemployed! The present government of Spain has ignored them for many years. If this country is ever again going to reach a point of greatness, they need a leader who is willing to listen to their pleas!"

The general nodded his head! It was a response that he hadn't expected to hear! Unlike many of the other young officers under his command, this man obviously held allegiance to no one! It seemed obvious that he was a born leader and knew enough about the people to realize that in order for him to succeed, he was going to need young men such as this to gain the respect of the people!

"Where do you come from?" the general asked.

"I was born and raised in Asturias! I joined the Guardia Civil; and , because the current government has done nothing to curb the needs of the people, I decided to join the Nationalist army as soon as the opportunity arose! Personally, I am opposed to a Socialist government that is in control! The will of the people has been abused and exploited! Their needs must be attended, and, if it can only be obtained through a change of government, then I am in favor of what needs to be done, my general!"

"As you know, the war is moving rapidly in our direction! We will need men such as you to protect the people! What we are offering is a government that will be democratic! A government that believes in free enterprise; but it will need to be one that takes the people's needs into consideration! As you know, there have been many Republicans who have already come over to our side. Would you be willing to accept a Commission in our Army to help us achieve these goals?"Franco asked.

"If you will provide the guarantees that we need, then, I would be honored! I must also tell you general, that I am aware of the atrocities that have been committed in the western parts of the country. Many of these atrocities have been committed by your legion of troops from North Africa! The perpetrators have gone unpunished and I have been told that some of your own officers have allowed these atrocities to take place! Atrocities are evils against the people! To me all the people are the same and they all require equal treatment! If this trend should continue, then tell me, my general, how is your Army any different from the Republican army?"

Franco looked at him with silent admiration! The young man was extremely handsome, tall and lean! Still there was a rugged maturity and a muscular body, all of the required characteristics for a good fighter! He felt a wave of jealousy that nature had made him rather short and stocky! He could only imagine how much more successful he might have been if some of these qualities had been given to him instead of to this young man standing before him! His answers had been deliberately vague and uncommitting! There would be no point in trying to inflict fear on him as he had done with many other young men who had changed sides in the war!

"Should you decide not to join us, you could be executed by a military court if it becomes known that you have helped the Republican army!" Franco told him, not that he had any intentions whatsoever of following through on his threat! This man was not easily frightened! The Mariscal stared at him seriously for several moments before continuing! Franco found it hard to determine whether or not his fearful approach had been successful!

"I have already seen that your vision of a military court is whatever you want it to be! I have seen reports of many members who have joined your army and others that have been executed! Atrocities are atrocities, any way you look at it! They are wrong! The fear of execution does not frighten me, General! I have lived my entire life in a world of uncertainty! I had no life in my past years, and I doubt that it will improve in the future no matter who may ultimately win the war! If the Republican army should win, I will probably be executed for helping the enemy! If the National army is victorious, then, I will be executed for helping the Republican army! Either way, I can consider myself a doomed man and your comments have just confirmed mine!"

This young man was making a great deal of sense! He didn't appear to be one bit shaken by the threat of execution! All of his determiantions seemed to be directed toward the outcome of the conflict. It had been the first officer he had interviewed that had not tried to sway him with his own contributions to the war! Life was meaningless to him! Whatever his young life may have been was a total mystery; but, whatever it had been, it had obviously hardened him to the penalties for the living! The more Franco spoke to him, the more he was convinced that this young officer would go very high in his army! He was a natural born leader and would be a great governor at some city after the conquest. Also, he had the ability to capture the respect of the people and could also be instrumental in establishing a form of government that he needed to maintain control of a nation in turmoil!

"I want you to join us! I want you to become a part in a new Spain! There are many of us who agree with you! We also want to create a better life for our people; and we need young men like you who understand the Spanish people and want to help us reunite the

nation!" Franco said. Almost as soon as he finished, he realized
that he had been impressed by this young man and, in his own way,
he was hoping that he wouldn't be turned down!

"I am willing to join you, my general! But I am a Mariscal;
and, as such, I need to have the rules of war meticulously
followed!" he said. "I want the atrocities to end immediately! If I
may continue to serve as a Mariscal, I want to seek punishment
for any offender! I want the Spanish people to be able to attend the
church of their choice! The burning of churches and the criminal
acts that are done on the convents and of the rectories need to be
eliminated! The church is an important way of life to our people!
In times of turmoil there is little more than faith that the people
can believe in! The Socialist and the Communist movements have
been burning down the churches and killing the priests and the
nuns! This must end! It can only stop if you issue a stern warning
that any offenders will be severely punished and then give the
Mariscals the power to impose punishment! If you can make me
this promise, my general, I will be honored to join your army!"

"You have my promise!" Franco told him. After all, he had
no control as to what happened whenever his troops entered a city!
No one could actually blame him if some of the troops decided
to defy his orders and destroy whatever the Republican army had
accomplished! He would issue the edict and would allow each of
his commanders and the Mariscal's to decide on the appropriate
punishment! He felt pleased that he had been able to convince this
young man to fight on his side! If only there were more Spanish
loyalists such as him, conquering Spain would be such an easy
task!

Both men shook hands, and, for the first time, the Mariscal
saluted the general in parting! Franco looked at him as though
he hadn't expected the salute! Instead, he extended his hand and
announced, "No hay necesidad en saludarme! Ahora eres uno de
los nuestros!" (There is no need for you to salute me! You are now
one of us!)

Both men agreed that the Mariscal would remain stationed
where he was but agreed to become available if needed in any
of the areas that had been conquered. Franco felt that since this

young man seemed to have things under control, there was no
need to make any immediate changes although he would still
be available if needed for consultations on other areas. Romero
remained seated and in deep thought at his desk long after the
General had left! He wondered if he said the right things and if
he had made the right decisions! Despite his rapid advances, the
truth was that he had become disenchanted with the Republican
army and of some of the things that had been reported. From
the atrocities that had been charged to both sides, it seemed that
one side was as bad as the other! There had persisted troubling
reports that some of the troops had been ordered to go into the
cities and to burn down the churches. The Socialist government
had been against the establishment of the churches, blaming them
for the uprising of the people! They had consistently argued that
it had been the church and not the government that had drawn
the wrath of the people! They had asked for entirely too much in
the means of support and of improvment of their lifestyles! Until
recently, they had allowed the church to remain untouched by the
government; but, in recent times, he had already noticed that as
more and more Socialist and Communist people were admitted into
the government, they could no longer enjoy the freedoms they once
had! Many of the catholic churches had already been burned and
destroyed; the priests had been either killed or badly beaten and
had been accused of disobeying government orders. Many of the
nuns, especially the older ones, had also been killed, and those that
were young, had been systematically removed and had been taken
to secret locations where they had been raped repeatedly by army
officers and were later executed! It was the communist way of
getting rid of the churches and eliminate any interference in their
ultimate goals for complete domination! The most expeditious way
of accomplishing this was to burn them and then blame it on the
Nationalist army sympathizers and the Moor troops that had been
brought into the country by Franco! Romero knew that this was not
entirely true and that it was nothing more than a fabrication of the
true facts. However, he also knew that if he became too vocal, he
might be regarded as a Nationalist sympathizer and would face a
punishment tribunal! It appeared that there were two evils glaring

at him from either side and it was difficult for him to decide which one of the two was worse!

Badajoz

It was another warm day when Dolores and Guillermo decided to take a casual stroll through the downtown streets of Badajoz now that the fighting had eased and the city was in full control by the Nacionalistas. All week long they had been looking forward to a day of rest when they might take a casual stroll, stop in one of the small tavernas, drink some wine and eat a few tapas! These had been bare luxuries that had become non-existant during the fighting! They began their walk down the street to the small taverna they had gone to in the evenings after work! A few of the Nationalist soldiers were seated at one of the tables drinking wine! When Guillermo walked in, Dolores and he took their usual table at the rear of the small tavern. Amost immediately some of the drunken soldiers began to criticize him for being in the company of a Republican sympathizer! At first, Guillermo decided to ignore the remarks until they became louder and more defiant! After he had heard enough, he got up from the table and walked slowly to where they were sitting. One of the men who seemed to be older than the others was the most vocal. Guillermo walked up to him and grabbed him by the throat! The soldier, having been taken by surprise, was unable to speak!

"Since you seem to have the most to say, I want you to repeat those things to my face!" he demanded. The soldier seemed to be frightened to death as Guillermo tightened his fingers around his neck! The other two soldiers got up from their places and walked out! They knew that the penalties for fighting with an officer were severe and once he had approached them, they wanted no part of a fight!

"I'll ask you again! Whatever you have to say, I want you to say it to my face!" he insisted. The soldier had a plate full of a fresh made tortilla sitting in front of him. Guillermo grabbed the back of his head and slammed it down hard on top of the egg omelette! His face was quickly covered with egg and there were food droppings on his uniform and the floor. The man tried to say something, but quickly decided against it. Instead, he got up from the table and followed his friends out of the building still wiping his face as he left! When Guillermo returned to the table, he saw that Dolores was upset with what had happened! He tried to convince her that it had been the effects of the wine, but she knew that the comments were deeply rooted and mired in hatred! Also, she began to fear what would happen to her if Guillermo was transferred away from Badajoz!

"Guillermo, we mustn't see each other again!" she told him.

"Why not? I thought you were happy with me!" he answered.

"That's just it! You make me much too happy! If I stay here there will be nothing but trouble for both of us! I want you to do me a favor!"

"Of course, I'll do anything for you! What is it?"

"I want you to arrange for me to return to Galicia! I need to return home, back to my family!"

"But why? You probably will be no safer there than you are here! It's only a matter of time before the troops go into Galicia! I want you here with me where I can protect you!" he told her.

"That's just it! Things here are not good and they don't seem to be getting any better! I have two younger sisters at home! How do you think I would feel if something ugly were to happen to them, and I was here with you safe and sound because I was under your protection?"

"But what about us? What happens to us? I had hoped that we would stay together! I'm not happy with the way things are here either, but what do we have to look forward to? At least here, we have protection of the Army, something we won't have if we return to Galicia! Besides, I would be considered a traitor, and you know what they would do to me!"

"I have heard that there are groups of people that are organizing under ground movements! I've also learned that a guerilla movement has already started to fight the war in the under ground! I've heard that this is the only way to fight the Republican army! Once the Moors go into Galicia, they will commit all sorts of atrocities to the women just as they have done here! I need to go back there and be with them! They are in dire need of medical assistance to care for the wounded. I feel that I can be of more help to them than I can be here where my safety depends entirely on your being here with me!"

"I'm not happy here either! But there isn't very much we can do!"

"That's not true! There is much you can do if you are unhappy! We can join the under ground brigades and fight them on their terms! I can't expect you to go with me nor to understand what I feel! I need to be with my family!"

"And what about me? I thought you were starting to care about me?"

"It's much more than that! I have fallen in love with you; and I can't stand the thought that some of these men, like the one's who were sitting here, may harm you because of me!"

"Have you stopped to consider that I, too, have fallen in love with you?"

"It will break my heart to leave you without knowing if I'll ever see you again! I wish there was some way I could get you to go with me, but I know it wouldn't be fair of me to ask you to come with me!"

"No, Dolores, if you go, then, I go with you! We'll face the future together! If God wills it, He will protect us and keep us safe until this war is settled! When would you want to leave?" he asked her.

"I'll go whenever you think it is convenient! Do you think you can arrange for safe passage?"

"Of course! I'll ask for a furlough and tell my commander that I have sick relatives that I want to see! I'm sure he will allow me to go! As for you, you can simply walk away! We'll meet at the train station and leave together!"

"Are you sure that this is what you want?" she asked. "I want you to be happy! I want us to be married and be together, but I can't ask you to give up your life for me!"

"Dolores, without you I have no life! What kind of life could I expect if all I did was to worry about you? Why can't you understand that I want to be with you? The life we now have is terrible! Atrocities are being committed everywhere we go and each side is blaming the other! The truth is that both sides are to blame! I have no family in Asturias, and I would have no life without you! We can get out of here now! I'll arrange to go on leave and take you with me! As long as we're together, there won't be anyone who will question us. The only thing for me is to go with you; and, then, don't come back!"

"But do you think you could be happy living the life of a guerrillero? All of our work will be under ground! There are units in Galicia who will help us, but it won't be an easy life! We will all need to depend upon you for guidance and protection! It may not be very rewarding! I would marry you here and now if you were to ask me; or we can wait until we reach Galicia and can then be married in a church, providing there is still one standing when we arrive!"

"Then, it's settled! Maybe that is where I really belong! I would like nothing better than to do my part in eliminating the bloodshed! I realize that our life won't be easy; but, I do love you! I'm willing to wait and hope for a brighter tomorrow when the war is over and we can again live in peace!"

"But do you love me enough to give up everything for me?" she asked.

"Yes, I do! I only know that life without you has no meaning! Whatever I can do to protect you and your family will serve as my reward! If it will make you happy, then, I'll be happy too!"

"I love you, Guillermo!" she said softly.

"Yes, I know and I love you too, Dolores! Tomorrow we will begin to finalize our plans and return to the North where we both belong!" he told her. He held her hand tightly, almost like a symbol that they belonged to each other! They had seen the bloodshed and the atrocities on both sides; and they had become tired of the bloodshed and the fighting, knowing that nothing would be accomplished! Their love had grown with every passing day and she wondered if she was doing the right thing? The only solution seemed to be for them to join the underground and do whatever they could to stop the fighting and to protect the lives of those that were unable to protect themselves! It would be a new beginning for both of them, and she could only hope and pray that the life they were seeking would never end!

Even as the preparations for the trip were underway, Guillermo noticed a change in the way he was being treated by the other junior officers. The change had begun shortly after he had submitted the request for military leave. There was no point in withholding any information! They would certainly soon know that Dolores was going with him! The fact that they already knew that she had been a Republican sympathizer before turning her allegiance to the Nationalist government did little to help the situation. No sooner had he made his request for leave when the seeds of suspicion were quickly sown! Being truthful was imperative because if anyone should stop her along the way, she would need to show her permission to travel! If she didn't have any travel documents with her, she would be arrested and might even be charged with treason the way many other professional people had been unfairly charged. It didn't seem to matter who it was that they were assisting! The law was the law and could not be changed!

Every morning the cadre of junior grade officers would assemble in a large room and would discuss military plans as well as the projected plans for occupation in the areas that had fallen and were now under Nationalist control. Guillermo had been an active member to these gatherings; but, suddenly, the invitations had stopped coming and no plans were discussed in his presence! Everyone seemed to know that he was under suspicion and many of his friends who had always been friendly toward him, began to change their appearance and would avoid being seen with him. His formal request for a leave had gone unanswered; and he knew from experience that this silence almost always signified a bad omen! Approvals were generally returned quickly, but it was the refusals that were long in being answered! If the request was denied by his immediate superiors, there was always the chance that he would be able to able the decision to a higher authority in Madrid. The appeal would go to an officer called a "Mariscal" who would render the final decision! Of course, his approval or denial would have to be carried out by Guillermo's immediate superiors.

The fact that he had heard nothing probably meant that an appeal would have to be filed. Since he was being isolated from the other junior officers, he had already been planning an appeal in silence for when the news was finally received that the request was being denied. He had noticed that the meetings consisting of the other officers were now coming more frequently; and there were even times when the other officers would be summoned at a moment's notice! It was fairly obvious that there was something big being planned and he was deliberately kept in the dark! If there was going to be another push on another city, it was almost a certainty that the decision of the "Mariscal" would not be in his favor! On the other hand, it could be advantageous! After all, he would still need to go through the capital city of Madrid and having him visit the area could provide the Nationalists with valuable intelligence! It could also provide his superiors with information as to what defenses were going to be needed. However the decision went, there was nothing he could do but to wait and see what would happen! Dolores had spent several days pressuring him for a response, but experience had told him not to seem to anxious for a response, lest it be taken the wrong way! The only issue that troubled him was not knowing how long Dolores would be willing to wait, and what would she decide to do if his request was denied? The other troubling thought was what he, himself, would decide if the final answer was a denial? It would be extremely dangerous for him to leave the garrison without permission! He would be considered a deserter, and he knew from experience that the penalty for desertion was almost always an immediate execution by a firing squad!!

CHAPTER 5

The daily military strategy meetings that were held at the garrison began early in the morning and would often continue until late in the afternoon! Word had been circulated that all military leaves had been cancelled; and there would be no time off from the military rank of field officers down through the regular soldiers. Guillermo had disregarded the rules and had decided to submit his request for a leave anyway! It came as no surprise when an orderly approached him the next day and told him that his request had been denied! Dolores became angry when he first told her the news! They both knew that the chance of acceptance had been slim, but the blunt denial seemed offensive and unnecessary, especially since she had been looking forward to going home and be with her family! The forward advances of the Nationalist Army were becoming well known! Everyone knew that the army had moved Northward and had successfully conquered the cities of Badajoz, Merida! There had also been reports that some of the troops had advanced near the city of Caceres. The advanced garrison had already been established along the banks of the Tagus river that flowed from the interior of Portugal eastward to the city of Toledo and beyond! The only thing that kept them from advancing more quickly into the area was the long stretch of mountains called 'The Extremadura' that were located east to west just before arriving at the river. The Nationalist army had practically been able to move at will, and the siege of Badajoz became a resting place where the troops would be rewarded with well deserved R and R's before again moving forward! From past experience Franco had learned while fighting in Morocco, that the Moroccon troops would require frequent rests along the way. He also soon learned that his troops had lived many years in periods of unrest, and could easily begin their own government if they were to become disenchanted with the way things were going! In order to satisfy his troops, Franco ordered frequent rests and would reward his troops by allowing them to commit rapes and robberies of the townspeople without fear of punishment!

Since that night when there had been attempted rape in the streets of Badajoz, Dolores had feared the Moors and quickly realized that her own safety was entirely dependent on the protection of Guillermo! If he were to move forward with the rest of his troops, there was no way to predict what would happen to her during his absence! Guillermo told her that he had filed an appeal immediately when he was told that his request for a leave had been turned down! He also knew that normally the approvals generally were quickly returned, but it was the denials that always seemed to take more time! Now that he had filed his appeal, it would need to be passed on to the office of the Mariscal and almost always a period of at least one week would go by before an answer was returned. He had no way of knowing the reasons behind all of the strategy meetings; but, since many of Franco's senior officers had been arriving from other parts of Southern Spain, Guillermo theorized that whatever the reasons were, it would be a very large movement and would be very soon! If there was to be an all-out offensive of Madrid before receiving a reply to his request, there would be virtually no chance for either of them to leave Badajoz! He had the feeling that their every move was being carefully observed and checked thoroughly! Franco demanded nothing less than absolute loyalty from his people! Anyone who chose to depart from this loyalty would either be jailed or executed by a military tribunal that would routinely hand down a sentence within hours after the tribunal had been assembled!

The dilemma he had discussed with Dolores was whether or not they should risk the chance of escaping before any word was received from the office of the Mariscal! If they decided to escape, the exit would need to be made quickly and they would be leaving without any travel documents! If captured, they would become deserters and would be treated accordingly! If, on the other hand, they should wait for a decision, it might arrive too late! Any projected military movements may already be taking place before the arrival of the courier telling them of the decision! At that point, he would be unable to leave and Dolores would be needed at the hospital to care for the wounded. It was no secret that she had once been a member of the Republican army! So, if she were to decide to leave, they would certainly execute her on the spot! The only real chance of escaping was to leave at night and try to use the benefit of darkness to shield their travel. If their luck held out, it would be morning before they were reported missing! However, if they could be on the ten o'clock train, there was a good chance that they could be in friendlier territory before being reported missing! It was a dangerous plan that might just work; unless, of course, the train was subjected to a surprise search by the authorities as sometimes happened! The evening train would travel northward along the banks of the Duero River which was very near the Portuguese border! Guillermo felt confidant that he would be able to bluff his way through if the search was made by Portuguese authorities! Unfortunately, he also realized that the Spanish authorities were much more thorough and this was what he feared the most!

"Entonces que vamos hacer, Guillermo?" (Then, what are we going to do?) a very worried Dolores asked! "Do you think the train will be searched?"

"There is always that chance!" he replied.

"What do you think we should do? We could steal one of the cars and drive there!"

"No! That would be worse! The car would almost certainly be stopped! Remember, it would be displaying the insignias of the Nationalist army! Our best chance is to leave by train!" Suddenly, he paused for a moment as an idea came to him. "Dolores, why not bandage my arm and put it into a sling? If I leave here dressed in my Army uniform and the searchers see my arm in a sling, they may take pity on me and let me go unchecked!"

"But you still won't have any travel documents and neither will I" she told him.

"I know! But I also think it will look much less conspicuous if they think I have been wounded and that you are my wife taking me home on leave! If they ask us for travel documents, we'll tell them they were lost and hope they believe us!"

"When do you think we should leave?"

"I think we should be separated for a while so as not to arouse any suspicion! I'll stay at the garrison where everybody will be able to see me. In the meantime, I want you to go into town and purchase two round trip tickets to Zamora! Hold on to them until we leave tonight!"

"But why buy two round trip tickets if we have no plans to return?"

"Because it will go to 'intent' if we happen to get caught! If they interrogate us and they see that we have round trip tickets to Badajoz, it will show that we aren't deserters and that we had intended to return to our base!"

"Do you really think it would matter to them if we were caught?"

"It will matter if we need to go before the Mariscal! That would need to be our defense! We'll both say that I was wounded in battle and that we were going home to be married! After the ceremony, we had every intention of returning to Badajoz! That's the reason why we deliberately purchased round trip railroad tickets!" He reached into his pocket and handed her several 'pesetas' to pay for the train tickets! He then kissed her gently and wished her luck as he returned to the garrison!

It was a cold, rainy evening several nights later when Guillermo and Dolores arrived at the train station! Dolores had wrapped his left arm with a clean, white bandage and had carefully placed the arm in a sling. The long concrete length of the station was deserted as the two walked slowly to the far end where they would be less conspicuous. Together, they had rehearsed every word they would say if they should be stopped and questioned by the authorities. It seemed that everything had been carefully covered. They had agreed that if asked for travel documents, he would fake a struggle to get them out of his pocket hoping that whoever was asking for them would take pity on him and would allow him to continue freely on his word without any more inconvenience. Guillermo was still wearing his freshly ironed Nationalist uniform that had just been cleaned. At the far end of the platform, he looked both ways just to be sure there was no one in sight watching them. Through the misty haze, the visibility had been reduced to almost zero! Good, he thought! It seemed likely that on a miserable night such as this, there would be few people at the train station at that hour of the night! Travel had been critically reduced during the days of the civil war, and, what little travel existed was done by people that needed to go somewhere on business or travelling for the government! Indeed, travel for recreational purposes was greatly reduced to a very limited infuential few and these people rarely travelled at night! Guillermo once again looked both ways to see if anyone was within sight! There was a moment of alarm when he saw the faint shadows of two figures, presumably of soldiers, who had been sent to guard the station. At first, he decided to simply ignore the shadows hoping they would go away before the train arrived. He was hoping for time allowing them to board the train that would start them on their journey.At least it would allow them the luxury of passing the first hurdle of their several day journey to the north of the country. As he was about to say something to Dolores, he was stopped momentarily whewn he heard the voice of one of the soldiers who had arrived out of nowhere and was now standing behind him. His heart sank to his feet! The obstacle he had hoped to evade was upon him. The young recruit had spotted them and had come over to speak to them. Guillermo took a few deep breaths before turning around to address the soldier. When the young recruit first saw the silver bars on Guillermo's shoulder, he immediately snapped his ankles together, came to attention and flashed him a smart salute which Guillermo quickly returned. Instead of returning the salute, he wanted to shake his head in disgust when he saw that the young soldier was barely fifteen or sixteen years old!

"Buenas noches, mi Capitan! Puedo preguntar donde van?" (Good evening, Captain! May I ask where you are going?) the young man asked.

"Si, como no! Estamos en luna de miel y vamos a visitar nuestros padres que estan enfermos!" (Of course! We are on our honeymoon and are going to visit our sick parents!) Guillermo answered.

Guillermo felt a bit uneasy as he followed the young man's eyes drift down to his arm that was all warpped up and in a sling! He was wondering if the young man had noticed something strange that he and Dolores had accidentally overlooked? It was important that he retain his composure and not bring on any doubts to his plans!

Finally, after staring at him for several minutes, the young man asked. "Fue herida de la guerra?" (Were you injured in the war?)

"Claro, que te parece? Por eso me dieron permiso para ir en luna de miel!" (Of course! What do you think? That's why they gave us permission to go on our honeymoon!)

Suddenly, they heard the loud metallic noise of the large engine as the locomotive roared into the station making a deafening sound! Guillermo and Dolores were anxious to board the train as soon as it came to a stop! No sooner had the forward movement been halted, when Guillermo nudged Dolores onto the steps while he remained close behind. As he looked back, he thought he had heard the young man say something; but the hissing noise of the large engine drowned him out! Guillermo decided it would be best to ignore him and board the train as quickly as possible. He could only assume that the young man must have remembered to ask for his travel documents, but, by that time, it was too late! Both he and Dolores were already on board as he heard the loud voice of the conductor yell out something as he too climbed on board as the train left the station!

Once they were both seated, he glanced over at Dolores and wiped his brow! "Whew!" he said. "That was a close one, but at least we have just passed our first hurdle! Who can predict how many more hurdles we will need to cross before we arrive at

Galicia!" She held on to his arm tightly as if she were afraid that he
would suddenly leave her all alone. They were both aware that their
future together would be unpredictable now that they had broken
the law by deserting from the Nationalist army. They also knew
very well what the penalty would be if they were caught before
arriving to Galicia! It was fortunate that they had decided to leave
when they did! Shortly after the departure they learned that a total
of 25,000 troops under the leadership of General Jose Varela had
reached the western and southern suburbs of Madrid. Several days
later, General Varela was joined by General Hugo Sperrle and the
Condor Legion! It was the beginning of the siege for Madrid which
was to turn into a blood bath for both sides and would continue for
a long time!

Francisco Largo Caballero and most of his cabinet decided
to leave Madrid on November 6, 1936. It was this decision that
was severely criticized by the four anarchists in his cabinet
who regarded his leaving the Spanish capitol as being an act of
cowardice! At first, the cabinet members had been reluctant to
leave their posts, but they were eventually persuaded to move to
Valencia with the remainder of the government.

The defense of Madrid was critical! It was the capital city
of Spain and most of the central areas of the government were
still located in that area. If Madrid were to fall to the Nationalist
army, it was more than possible that the remainder of the country
would soon follow. Largo Caballero appointed General Jose Miaja
as commander of the Republican Army. His chief aid was Colonel
Edmundo Garcia who had been recently promoted to the rank
of General de Brigada (Brigadier General). General Miaja was
given specific instructions to set up a Junta de Defensa (Defense
Council), consisting of all of the parties of the Frente Popular
(Popular Front) and to defend the capital of Madrid 'at all costs'!
He was given the aid of Vicente Rojo who was later to become
his Chief of Staff. Miaja's task was later helped with the arrival
of the International Brigades. The first units reached Madrid on
November 8. Led by the Soviet General, Emilo Kleber, the 11th
International Brigade played an important role in the defense of
the city! The Thaelmann Battalion, a volunteer unit that consisted

mostly of members from the German Communist Party as well as the British Communist Party were also deployed and ordered to defend the city!

One week later, Buenaventura Durruti arrived in Madrid from Aragon with his Anarchist Brigade. Durruti was killed in action while fighting in the outskirts of the city just one week later. Durruti's supporters in the CNT were soon to spread the news that he had been killed by members of the Communist Party. Shortly afterward, the Nationalists attempted to cut the Madrid-La Coruna road to the northeast of Madrid. After suffering heavy losses, the offensive was finally brought to an end before the end of the year! The Nationalist had been able to use this brief respite to restock their units with ordinance and resumed the attack just two weeks later. In the short span of four days they had regained ten kilometers of roadway. The gain had come at a large toll in human lives as they reluctantly reported the loss of about 15,000 men. The International Brigades, who had assisted in defending the roadway, had also reported heavy losses during this battle. Benito Mussolini had also started supplying the Nationalists with both men and equipment. He had supplied a total of 30,000 men from the Blue Shirts Militia and an additional 20,000 men who had been actively serving in the Italian Army. These men were eventually incorporated into the Italian Corps (CTV) and fought side by side with both the Nationalists and the Moors.

The long train ride heading North toward the city of Zamora had been uneventful. Guillermo felt relieved that nothing had happened during the ride to upset their plans. The only unsettling characteristic came when he stared out of the window in the daylight hours and saw a vast movement of Nationalist troops moving forward in the same direction. They had gotten out of Badajoz in the nick of time! He could now theorize that the lengthy meetings that had been held in the strategy room had been the planning of a major offensive toward Madrid! Had he remained at the garrison for a few days longer, leaving the city would have been virtually impossible! There were troops everywhere he looked! Some were travelling on foot, others on horseback, and still others were riding in large military trucks! The men were all dressed in full military combat gear and were all moving in a northward direction! He remained silent as he looked at what was happening! The last thing he wanted to do was to frighten Dolores! In his own mind he considered it quite obvious that the Republican Army was no match for the vast army of men that was now heading northward! If Madrid should fall into the hands of the Nationalists, how long could it be before they reached the outskirts of both Galicia or Asturias? Once that point was reached, the only resistance that could be given against a military onslaught would be limited to Guerilla activities, which, at best, could be troublesome but certainly no match against a moving, well equipped army!

Guillermo's plans had been well made! The train was to take them northward into the city of Caceres, a small town located several hundred miles west southwest of the capital city of Madrid. Once at the city, they would need to change trains, and get a train that would take them to the town of Santa Catalina that sat at the edge of a small set of mountains that began at the north side of the Rio Tajo! There, they expected to be met by someone who would take them to where they wanted to go! Of course, the further north they went, the friendlier was the territory! The Nationalist army had not yet travelled that far north although there were already signs that certain advance units had arrived to scout the territory before making a major assault on the city! The instructions he had received were to get off the train at Santa Catalina and wait! Someone from the guerilla movement would be sent there shortly and would transport them all the way northward to Galicia during the night hours. They did as they were told even though the train had been late arriving by about one hour! For the first time, Guillermo was finally able to breath a bit easier knowing that he was arriving into areas that had not yet been taken over by the Nationalists. It was dusk and it occured to him that it had been raining all day! From where he was on the platform, the visibility was once again limited; and it was doubtful that he would be seeing any of Franco's advanced troops so late at night and with the weather being so dismal! Dolores held on to his arm as the two of them left the train and walked to the far end of the platform, away from the curious stares of other passengers who had also gotten off the train at the same station. He looked carefully around him making certain that there were no soldiers or other military men standing on guard around the station! It was the first time that he had felt comfortable enough to hold on to Dolores arm and huddled with her at the far end of the station just as he had done while in Badajoz. The station was soon deserted except for the arrival of several vehicles that had arrived to pick up passengers, but none that had been meant for them!

Several minutes had passed and then several more when he heard the voice of a soldier call out to him! "Alto! Donde van?" (Stop! Where are you going?) The young soldier and his partner were smartly dressed in a traditional Nationalist uniform in full military dress! The approach of these soldiers were a surprise and far different from what he had previously been told! He had been assured that there were no Nationalist guards within the area! He was now facing the two young soldiers with no where to go and no place to hide! His only hope was that whoever was supposed to come to meet them would hurry and would be there in time to rescue them from the guards!

"Vamos al norte! Estamos en luna de miel!" (We're going North! We are on our honeymoon!) It was the same excuse he had used while in Badajoz and it had worked there. There was certainly every reason to hope that it might work again!

"May I see your travel authorization?" the young soldier asked. Guillermo made a motion to reach inside his coat pocket with the arm that was not bandaged. Perhaps, if the young soldier could see he was struggling to reach the pocket of his jacket, he would let them go! Unfortunately, this was not to be! The young man remained waiting silently, all the time with his rifle aimed at Guillermo!

"I must have lost my travel papers on the train!" he answered. It was a weak and very lame excuse, but it was the only one he could think of at that moment!

"I'm sorry, sir! Unless you can show me your authorization, I will need to place you under arrest!" the soldier answered. This young man was certainly nothing like the other young man he had confronted at the station in Badajoz! This one seemed much more serious and determined!

"Look," Guillermo tried to plead. "We are on our honeymoon and I've been injured! Can't you give us a break and let us go on?"

"I'm sorry, Captain! Orders are orders! There are many people who have become deserters and are travelling without authorization! I am sorry for your misfortune; but, as an officer, you should have been more careful! I must ask you to please come with me!" he ordered. The guard lowered his rifle and held it closer to him with the stock of the weapon resting against his abdomen!

"What about my wife?" Guillermo asked. "Must she also come? Also, where are you taking me?"

"Yes sir! Your wife will also come with us! Both of you will go to the cuartel! My superiors will then decide what to do with you!"

"But why? All of this is absurd! Can't you see that I an Army officer?"

"Yes sir! That is the problem! There have been other officers who have deserted and have travelled northward dressed in military uniforms! We have been instructed to watch carefully for these people and to take any suspicious people back to headquarters!"

"What will they do to me once I get there? Am I to be charged with anything, just because I don't have my travel authorization with me?" he asked.

"That isn't up to me to decide! I suppose that if your status cannot be proven, you will be charged with desertion and will need to go before the 'Mariscal' and explain your reasons to him! Now sir, can we please get started?"

He looked cautiously at Dolores realizing that his well planned escape attempt had one fault and it was that fault that had turned against him! Had he decided to travel in either a Republican army uniform or in plain civilian clothes, no one would have detained him! He was now facing discovery simply because of the uniform he was wearing and there was nothing he could do about it. There was no point in trying to contact his previous station! It

certainly would come as no surprise that he had been a northern
sympathizer and that he had chosen to defect! Either way, he
knew he was in serious trouble! If he claimed to be a Republican
officer dressed as an officer in the Nationalist army, he would
obviously be tried as a Republican deserter. On the other hand,
if it was proven that he was travelling without any authorization,
he would be considered a deserter! He knew that the penalty for
desertion was execution by a firing squad! Therefore, he decided
to be obedient and follow the young soldier to the garrison! The
rain was now coming down hard and he realized that there was
virtually no chance of escaping his capture. Once inside the
garrison, he was escorted into one small room while Dolores was
escorted into another! He was immediately surprised when he
saw that the small room was filled to capacity with many other
Nationalist soldiers, all of which were dressed in civilian clothes.
It was a clever disguise that was intended to avoid detection by the
Republican soldiers. Seeing these men dressed in regular civilian
clothes made them cleverly disguised from being soldiers from the
northern armies. This had been another tactic he had overlooked!
Everything had been carefully thought out and controlled; but his
one mistake had been in walking out with his Nationalist uniform,
a dead give-away as to who he really was! He wondered where they
had taken Dolores and hoped that they hadn't treated her harshly!

Early in his training, Guillermo had been taught to remain
calm and to listen to what was being said! Obviously, they were
waiting for someone to come to question him; and it seemed
important to remain calm and to answer all of the questions as
best as he could without revealing his true reasons for being
there. Of course, he also knew that the outcome was not going
to be favorable! If he was believed to be a Nationalist officer,
the punishment for desertion was death! If he argued that he
was actually a Republican officer in disguise, they would almost
certainly transfer him over to the Republicans who would also
consider him a deserter and would also execute him. There was
no point in asking for clemency! From experience, he already
knew that clemency was not a word worthy of any consideration!
The only two alternatives that remained opened was the fact that

he had escaped before receiving a reply from the office of the Mariscal! If by any chance he had been granted permission to be on a honeymoon, there was still an outside chance that his escape had been legal and would be obeyed. This was a long shot that he considered much too far-fetched to be practical! Unfortunately, these were critical times and critical times required critical decisions! The other alternative was that once the death penalty had been imposed, he could ask for an appeal to the office of the Mariscal. As an officer in Franco's army, this appeal would have to be granted! He could then go before the Mariscal and argue his case with the hope that the office of the superior would have pity on him and would spare him from the obvious fate! Either chance was highly doubtful! At this point there was little that he could do except to play out the game and see where it would lead! It really didn't make any difference who would be the one to execute him, the end result would be the same! The only thing he could do was to buy time and hope that he would be successful! As he now sat alone in the small cell awaiting the outcome of his fate, his thoughts went back to Dolores! He hoped that some of the large, black African Army Corps troops hadn't decided to abuse her as they often did in these circumstances and with permission of their superiors. It was several hours later before one of the civilian guards went in and unlocked the cell. The young man was armed with a rifle that had been loaded and pointed directly at him! The soldier asked him to get on his feet and to follow him! Guillermo did as he was told! The guard then gave him a stern warning not to try to escape since had had been ordered to shoot him if he tried to run away! He knew better! Many of these young men had served in the field and most of them were trigger happy, and anxious to use their weapons at the slightest provocation!

"Where are we going?" he asked.

The young guard did not reply! Instead, he made a motion with the the barrel of the rifle implying that Guillermo was to follow him! It was nearly midnight when another slightly older man walked into a larger room, sat at a desk, and started thumbing through a stack of papers that were neatly piled on the desk! Guillermo stood before him, his arm still bandaged! The small caliber pistol he had taken with him had been taken away, and he remained standing for what seemed like hours before the man sitting at the desk began to speak to him!

"Cual es tu nombre?" (What is your name?) he asked.

"I am Captain Guillermo Torres!" he answered. He quickly realized that it would be foolish to go into a long diatribe trying to explain the reason for being there. Those questions would be asked quickly enough! The only thing that was important at the moment was to reply only to the questions he as asked and nothing more. This was also a part of the advanced training he had received when he was a simple Guardia Civil, before all-hell had broken loose!

"Are you aware of the charges that have been brought against you?" the stranger asked.

"No sir! I have not been advised of any charges! I was asked to come here and I did so voluntarily!"

"You are being charged with desertion! You have no apparent proof that you are an officer in the Nationalist army! I was informed that when the guards asked you for your travel documents, you were unable to produce them!" the stranger said behind a pair of granny eyeglasses that had been positioned just above the bridge of the nose, probably hoping it would make him look a bit older than he was!

"The fact that the papers are not on my person, does not, in itself, classify me as being a deserter!" Guillermo answered. He knew in advance that his answer was nothing more than a lame excuse, but, now, he was locked into a struggle against time and needed to play every card that he had been dealt!

"Where are your travel documents? I understand you said that you were on your honeymoon and that you had permission to do so!" Now, the inquiry was getting a bit personal. There was really no reason to lie at all! He felt that it wouldn't have done him any good anyway!

"I was stopped by the guards before I boarded the train and was asked to produce my travel documents! The guard allowed me to board the train, so obviously, the documents were on my person at that time! You can see that I have been wounded; and it was a little hard to get the travel papers out of my pocket!" he lied.

The officer looked at him suspiciously from behind his granny glasses, nodded his head and continued. Guillermo had no way of knowing whether or not the young officer asking the questions really believed him. He knew that he had remained calm and had been straight forward with his answers! Perhaps it was now time to ask the inquisitor what had happened to his wife? After all, if it was true that he was on his honey moon, it was only logical that he would be worried about his wife and would want to know where they had taken her.

"Before answering any more questions, I want to know what happened to my wife? She was taken from my side when I was brought here and I refuse to answer any more questions until I know she is safe and has not been abused!"

"Your wife is fine; I can assure you of that! She has been taken to another room where she is being de-briefed by a woman! She will be with you shortly!" the man answered. "Now, I need to know what happened to your travel documents?"

"I can only tell you that they were on me when I was questioned before boarding the train! I can only assume that they must have been lost at that time!" he again lied.

"As an officer of the Nationalist army, were you not told to have those documents on you at all times?"

"Yes, of course! However, as you can see, I was wounded in battle; and, unfortunately, it isn't so easy to keep track of travel documents when you are unable to move your arm!" Once again, the man sitting at the desk gave him a suspicious look, peered at him from behind his glasses and moved on!

"Captain, I get the feeling that you are a deserter in uniform! If that is the truth, you certainly know what the punishment will be for deserters!" he said.

Good! Guillermo thought! He already seemed to be drawing his own conclusions without giving him the benefit of a doubt! It now seemed to be the right time to act defiant and pull rank on him if necessary! He needed to continue to play the hand that he had been wounded in a Nationalist battle! "Sir, if I were a deserter,why would I risk coming here still dressed in my army uniform? Would I not have come dressed in civilian clothes where I might not look quite so obvious?"

The man asking the questions looked at him sternly but did not reply! He had obviously made his point! If he was a deserter, he wouldn't have been so careless as to be dressed in an army uniform knowing that it would stand out wherever he went. Also, he was heading in a Northward direction, an area not very friendly with soldiers who were fighting on opposite sides! The man asking the questions knew that this was not going to be an easy decision! Soldiers changing sides was frequent and could be easily dealt with; but, this man was different! He was a Nationalist officer; and, if by chance the story he was telling was true, a bad decision on his part could make a large difference to his otherwise unblemished military career. The only thing left for him to do was to keep him and his wife detained until such time as he could find out more information about him, even if getting information from his headquarters would take some time!

The worry lines appearing on the inquisitor's forehead was telling Guillermo that the stranger was uncertain about what he should do. It was this delay that he needed to exploit! In order to do so, he would need to remain firm and persistant and not allow this inquisitor to get the upper hand. "I need to know what you plan to do with us? Being in this hell-hole has deprived me of a day of honeymoon! You know as well as I that a major movement will soon be underway and I will need to be back at my garrison before that happens! (This too had been a lie! Officially, he had received no word about what was going to happen! All that he knew was what he had seen from the large train window! It seemed like a reasonable approach for him to take!) If the young inquisitor knew anything about the prospects of a new offensive, Guillermo's comments would have confirmed what he had already thought might happen! If not, he would need to treat this as new information, and, in his present capacity, it was information that he needed to have!

"Frankly Captain, you have me a bit undecided as to what I should do! I can't release you because you have no travel authorization! It's going to be necessary for me to get that

authorization from your garrison before I can release you! I'm
sorry, sir! There isn't very much more I can do!" he answered
almost as if he was apologizing for his indecision!

"But I can't wait that long! I don't have much time! Isn't
there anything you can do to allow me to be with my wife?" he
asked. "By the time you receive a reply from the garrison, my leave
time will have expired! There has to be something else you can
do!" the young man looked at him once again! The worried lines
on his face had disappeared, and it seemed as if Guillermo was
about to have his way!

"This is what we'll do!" the inquisitor said with a tone of
finality. "We'll allow your wife to be with you! In the meantime,
we'll by-pass your garrison and refer this matter directly to the
office of the Mariscal which is much closer! It will be his decision
to make and I will be free of any misconceptions or errors!"

"And where is the Mariscal's office located? Is it near
here?"

"The office of the Mariscal is in down town Toledo! With
any luck we can have a messenger deliver this case to his office and
we should have a reply probably by tomorrow!"

The handling of his case by the Mariscal had been the one
condition he had not planned for! True, the one incident involving
the Mariscal had been when the African soldier had been killed
when he tried to rape Dolores in Badajoz. It had been an unusual
move for the Mariscal to rule in his favor! It was generally known
that most Mariscal's would nearly always rule on the side of the
government! The fact that he had gone against the African army
had come as a surprise. It would be too much to expect him to rule
in his favor again! There was no reason for optimism! His luck had
run out and he had been apprehended in his efforts to escape to the
North. It was obvious that this case was different from the last! He
had nothing to go on! There was little known about the Mariscal
in Toledo, only that he could be severe or forgiving! Guillermo had
the feeling that if the case went to Toledo, the punishment would be
swift! He felt himself with doubts about leaving for the first time!
The fact that he didn't like what was happening politically in Spain
meant absolutely nothing! The entire country was undergoing

a rapid change and none of the changes seemed to improve the conditions in Spain! The Republican army was being run by Communists and Socialists! There had been change after change in people at the top and nothing good had come of it! People that were good were disappearing for no apparent reason! Many of the Catholic churches were being deliberately destroyed; and priests and nuns were disappearing and were not to be seen again!

On the other side of the change was the Nationalist army that was nothing less than an absolute dictatorship! The same atrocities were being committed with the permission of the military officers that had now assumed control of the people! Guillermo dreaded the thought of what would happen when Franco's army marched into the northern provinces of Asturias and Galicia. Most of the citizens were uneducated and simple farmers, but they were good people who deserved better! All of their lives had been spent in working small parcels of land and now time had passed them by and they had nothing to show for their efforts. The abuses in the system were unbearable! Those people that owned a large parcel of land had been heavily taxed in order to pay for the public works and could no longer afford to work the land! Despite all of the hardships, the people loved their country! Most were idealists who believed in whatever they had, and all that they wanted was to live in peace without any interference from either side of the political spectrum. Unfortunately, he, too, had been caught up in the impasse and had been transferred from the ranks of the simple Guardia Civil to that of an officer in the Nationalist army! The change had not been of his choosing, but, considering the circumstances, it had been the right decision at the right time! Things may have been different had he not fallen in love with another idealist like himself! She also had become disenchanted with the new movement and had decided to return home to help her family!

Everyone knew that a victory over the Nationalist army was virtually impossible! The peasants that lived in the northern provinces knew very little about war! Conscriptions into any organized militia had been unheard of during their lifetime and was now beyond their dreams. Many of them had decided to

take matters into their own hands and had formed small bands
of underground fighters who were hiding along the foothills of
the Cordillera Cantabrica in the southern part of the provinces.
If a major movement by the Nationalists was inevitable, they
were committed to fight and create as much damage as possible
to Franco's army as their way of defying submission to a new
leader. It was this movement that was of interest to Guillermo
when he decided to desert his unit in Badajoz! At least, he and
Dolores would be able to live their lives in peace, even if it meant
being holed up in some small cave in one of the mountains. They
would be together, even if now things were looking a bit bleak! If
he refused to appeal the decision to the office of the Mariscal, he
would be giving himself away and would immediately be branded
as a deserter by this young man. On the other hand, he had no way
of knowing who this Mariscal was! It was fairly obvious that he
had to be someone held in high esteem since he had been elevated
to a very prestigious and responsible position. If he had been alone
he might have considered trying to escape! He also knew that to
do such a foolish thing, they would probably take it out on Dolores,
God knows what they might do to her! The chance he had, and a
slim one at that, was to hope that the Mariscal would take pity on
him and would rule in his favor!

"Very well!" he answered, although not very convincingly.
"I agree to have my case forwarded to Toledo and hope the
Mariscal will clear me of these ridiculous charges! I would
however, like to have my wife with me!"

"I will see to it that your wife is brought to your cell! I see
nothing wrong with that!" the young man answered. "Besides, we
expect to have a reply from the Mariscal in a day or two!"

Dolores was escorted into his cell and Guillermo looked
her over carefully making certain that she hadn't been abused. She
started to cry when she saw him and he explained that the situation
was being referred to the Mariscal in Toledo! She was aware that
if he should refuse them, it would result in an execution! This
had all been her fault! Had she not insisted on returning home,
none of this would have happened! The civil war had suddenly
taken on a new dimension! Already they could listen to the troops

Jack A. Sariego

gathering outside their cell, probably preparing to make a new rush
on the capital city of Madrid! Had they remained in Badajoz, he
would almost certainly been assigned to the front lines while she
remained at one of the rear hospitals working on the steady stream
of casualties that were arriving each day! For a few moments he
was stricken by a lethargic feeling of not caring what happens!
He already knew that the situation of going before a Mariscal was
merely a routine function and that the final decision would be
obvious! Whatever was to happen, he was happy that during his
life he had known the happiness of having a woman by his side.
If it meant his giving up his life for her, then, so be it! He was
prepared to pay the price! All that was needed was to settle the
uncertainty of finalizing their fate and that was beyond his control.
Guillermo had insisted that Dolores do whatever she could to join
one of the underground units and return to her family! That is,
assuming her life was spared! He had received some reports that
many of these smaller guerilla units were well armed and were
staffed by brave men who had no fear of dying! If this was true,
it was also possible that these men would somehow get her out of
prison and return her to her home where she belonged!

More than one week had passed before one of the guards
approached the cell and asked him to gather his things! Despite
his request, very little information was given for the move! The
only thing he was told was that they were about to be moved to
Toledo where the petition would be heard quickly. Apparently,
a major drive was about to begin by the army for the capital city
of Madrid, and the Mariscal was anxious to clear his desk of all
unfinished business before his office was moved to a new and safer
location! Both he and Dolores took the time to wash their faces
and comb their hair! After all, if they were going to be executed,
it was important that they meet their creator with a clean face and
with their hair combed! Strangely, one thought came to his mind!
Why was it that a woman would want to wash her face before
being executed? Might it be that God would not want you in heaven
with a dirty face? The idea was almost humorous if it wasn't so
serious! One of the other guards came into the cell with a loaded
rifle and they escorted the two prisoners into a large opened army

truck ready for the long, bumpy trip to Toledo! All along the way
they saw brigade after brigade of Nationalist soldiers dressed
in complete army gear moving in the same direction. Once in a
while they would see a smaller brigade of troops from the African
army who were riding on horseback! There were small mortars
mounted on each side of each horse near the stirrups, almost as
though it were a play toy from someone's imagination! He had
already seen the African army troops in action when at Badajuz,
and knew from experience that although they were undisciplined,
they were excellent fighters who were not afraid to die! At a later
time, Guillermo learned that there had been one large assault on
the capital city that had ended in failure! He had learned from
listening to some of the guards that there was going to be another
frontal assault on the city, and that General Franco had issued
orders for his troops to cut off the road that linked the city to the
rest of Republican Spain! There were some comments that the
assault was to consist of 40,000 men and would also include troops
from the African army as they were preparing to strike by crossing
the Jarama River into the outskirts of the city! None of that was of
interest to him now! His mind was on many other things that were
more important! What the hell, he thought! He would probably
be executed in a few hours anyway, so it didn't really matter who
would be in control of the capital city! His only concern was in
trying to get Dolores released from jail so that she could contact
some of the underground people! If the assault was going to be as
great as the guards were saying, they would be needing a great deal
of medical help on both sides since the casualty rate was probably
going to be very high! She would at least be in demand as a nurse;
and the best way to remain alive was to be in demand!

It was nearly midnight when the large, opened truck finally
arrived at the rear of a small stucco, one story building in the
outskirts of Toledo. The building consisted of several small rooms
where the prisoners who were to face reviews by the Mariscal
were taken until it was time for their review. The rooms located
immediately behind the main office on the first floor consisted
mostly of jail cells; each one about six by eight feet. They were
sparsely equipped with a thin used mattress laying on the cold,

damp concrete floor, a small commode and a tiny wash basin! From the cell the prisoners would be taken in handcuffs to a much larger room where the Mariscal was seated on an elevated platform. It was a physchological weapon that had been introduced by Mussolini in Italy. Because he was so small in stature, he believed that by sitting on an elevated platform, it gave him a psychological advantage whenever an offender ws brought before him! It not only provided Mussolini with an egotistical feeling of superiority; but it also gave the defendent a feeling of inferiority as the spot where he was standing was well below that of the one who would be deciding the defendent's fate! The Mariscal, it was said, had adopted this procedure not because he was a small person. Standing well over six feet and blessed with a muscular body of a young man, there was hardly any need to express his superiority! Guillermo would never know whether he had taken this position because he actually believed in what it represented or whether it had been one of many edicts imposed by General Franco because he too was rather short in stature and believed that the appearance was consistent with the way he was supposed to look as a conquering hero!

Guillermo and Dolores were taken into one of the small cells! They both laid down on the thin mattress holding on to each other realizing that this was probably the last and final time that they would be together. From the small cell window, they were able to hear the happy voices of a group of men, probably the death squad, who had nothing better to do than to sit around, smoke their hand-rolled cigarettes with a rare blend of strong tobacco that had been brought in from Morocco! It had been intended primarily for the African troops but had been used by the Spaniards who soon learned to enjoy the strong smoke as well as the feeling of power and relaxation that it gave them. From what they could see, it seemed that the executions were performed in the rear of the building and away from the sights of the few residents that still lived in the area. It seemed like an ideal way of ridding themselves of undesireables who could be quickly, easily carted away and disposed of as soon as the bodies stopped moving!

The early morning sunshine crept in through the small
cell window much sooner that they had expected! Since it was
probably the last night they would spend together they had passed
the night away speaking about their childhood, the happy times
as well as the more disappointing times of their youth. They had
lived with a pessimistic feeling of doom created in large by the
mass poverty they had known. They both believed that the way in
which Spain was going, everyone would soon be dead anyway! If it
became known that someone spoke in favor of Franco and against
the Socialist government, they were executed on the spot. If, on
the other hand one were to speak favorably about the Socialist
government, it would then be the conquering Franco who would
perform the executions. Either way, it was a no-win situation!
Eventually, everyone would be dead, long before God had wanted
it to happen! At least, lying on the mattress they felt an inner peace
within themselves and had made peace with their God! Nothing
else was really important! They were ready to be executed! In
order for a person to have a desire to go on living, there had
to be something that was worth living for! As far as they were
concerned, there was nothing left of value! Furthermore, there was
no indication that things would eventually become any better; and
even if they did, who would it benefit? Would it be the Socialist
government who had destroyed the churches, killed the priests and
raped the nuns, or would it favor instead the conquering heroes
who savagely killed anyone standing in their way? What difference
did it make anyway?

Two young men arrived! One of them was a Spanish
speaking guard who spoke with an accent from the south, perhaps
from Andalucia, who was not more than eighteen years old! The
other guard was somewhat older and very obviously a member of
Franco's beloved African army. The man's skin was very dark;
and when he smiled, Guillermo noticed that several of his teeth
were missing, probably the result of another battle, another place,
another time!

"Ya estan listos?" (Are you ready?) the Spanish guard
asked, smiling as if he was about to be entertained by a beautiful
young virgin instead of a no-nonsense officer of the law!

"Cuando quieran!" (When you're ready!) he answered. The guard asked him if he wanted to wash his face or go to the bathroom! Guillermo nodded his head that it wasn't necessary! During the night, he and Dolores had agreed that she would remain in the cell while he went before the Mariscal! Suddenly, she had changed her mind! If he was going to be executed, then, she insisted on being there with him! If possible, she would spring her body at one of the members of the firing squad so that he would execute her as well! It was her way of thinking that if they were to be deprived of life together, they would be together in death!

"No, Dolores!" he pleaded. "Ya sabes lo que acordamos!" (You know what we agreed!)

"No importa!! Quiero estar contigo hasta el final!" (It doesn't matter! I want to be with you until the end!) she said, disregarding the plans they had made during the night! Both of them remained standing side by side as the African army soldier opened the door of their cell. After giving them a hand motion, they were led out of the cell, one guard in front and the other in the rear as they walked down a long, dark, poorly lit hallway! Guillermo paused to take one final look at Dolores just before being led into a large room, probably the court room, that was empty except for a desk, several wooden chairs and desk lamp! Both prisoners were nudged and asked to go inside, remain standing and wait for the Mariscal who would be coming out of a side door. They did exactly as they were told and waited for what seemed like hours waiting for the "pompous ass" to arrive! It seemed odd to him that here he was, expecting to die; and yet he had no regrets nor second thoughts about what he had done! There were no reflections about his life, what it had been, what it might have been, or what he wished it had been! All of those precious thoughts had vanished from his mind during their last evening together.

The large wooden door creaked noisily as it opened up and the tall, lean figure of a man entered! His facial features were pleasant, his hair was showing signs of grey at the temples; and despite his age, he had a strong muscular body of a man many years younger! Guillermo immediately found it a bit strange

that the tall man was not wearing a uniform! He had expected
the Mariscal to be dressed in a well starched Nationalist army
uniform! Instead, he was wearing a simple white shirt that was
opened at the collar, and a pair of regular civilian trousers! The
'granny' eyeglasses were perched over the bridge of the nose as he
sat down behind the desk and began reading some of the papers
that had been neatly piled on the large oak desk. Never once did
he look up nor did he glance at the accused who were standing
before him waiting for him to speak! Instead, he ignored them and
continued to look at the papers on his desk! Finally, when he was
finished reading, he removed his reading glasses and lifted his head
to face the accused! If he was shocked by who he saw standing
before him, he didn't show any signs of surprise as he looked at
them and remained silent. There was only a few feet separating
the two men! Both of them stared at each other with a firm look
of determination! Between them there was an uneasy feeling
of silence as they glared at one another, almost as if they were
already assembled at a gravesite! For several moments the two men
continued to outstare each other, patiently waiting for the other
to flinch! Neither man flinched their eyes as they both stood their
ground, almost as if they were both mesmerized by each other's
presence! The two guards who had accompanied them inside were
beginning to get impatient and were moving around nervously
waiting for the final decision to be given!

Outside of the courtroom they could hear the faint voices
of one of the members of the execution squad saying to the other
men. "Oye muchachos! Recarguen las escopetas, que todavia nos
quedan dos para liquidar!" (Hey fellas! Reload your rifles, we still
have two more to liquidate!)

Madrid

In response to the battle for Madrid, General Miaja sent
in three International Brigades including the Dimitrov Battalion,
to the Jarame River valley in order to block the advances of the
Nationalist army. It was then that the fierce fighting that occured
on one of the hills named 'Suicide Hill' that the Republicans
suffered a large amount of casualties. Tom Winteringham, the

British Commander, was forced to order another retreat to the next ridge! The Nationalist army then took advantage of this retreat to move forward to Suicide Hill, but were then routed by Republican machine gun fire! On the right flank, the Nationalists had been successful in forcing the Dimitrov Battalion to retreat! It was this move that eventually enabled the Nationalists to virtually surround the British battalion. The British came under heavy fire and the casualties continued to increase! They had been reduced to a mere 160 men out of an original battalion of 600 troops, and were forced to establish defensive positions along a sunken dirt road. Unwilling to follow up the retreat with another forward attack, the Nationalist army decided to retreat!

General Franco was coming under heavy pressure from Adolf Hitler and Benito Mussolini to obtain a fast victory by taking over the capital city of Madrid. He eventually decided to use a force of 30,000 Italians and 20,000 legionnaires to attack the city of Guadalajara, forty miles northeast of the capital. The Italian force eventually took over the city and began their forward move toward Madrid. A few days later, the Republican army with their Soviet tanks began a counter-attack of the city. The Italians suffered many heavy losses; and, as a result, those that were left alive were then forced to retreat! The Republicans had also captured secret documents that proved that the Italians were actually regular soldiers and not the volunteers that had been reported. It was unfortunate that the Non-Intervention Committee refused to accept the evidence and the Italian government boldly announced that no Italian soldiers would be withdrawn until the Nationalist army was victorious. At the same time that Franco was forcing the unification of the Falange Espanola and the Carlistas with other small right-wing parties, the Republicans were secretly forming a band of guerillas, who were fighting underground with the fragments of the army that were still available. This band was known as "Los Milicianos"! Franco had appointed himself as the new leader! He began by circulating pictures of himself, imitating the tactics of Adolf Hitler in Nazi Germany! In Spain, the huge posters of Franco were shown with the dead Jose Antonio and a display that read, 'One State! One country! One chief! Franco!

Franco! Franco!' These large posters were distributed throughout
Spain and soon gave "Los Milicianos" a new reason to continue on
with the fight!

Francisco Caballero came under increasing pressure from
the Communist Party to promote its members to senior posts
within the government! He also refused the demands to suppress
the Workers Party, and this caused the Communists to withdraw
from the new government that was being established. In an
attempt to maintain a coalition government, President Azana fired
Largo Caballero and asked Juan Negrin to form a new cabinet.
Negrin began by appointing members of the Communist party
to important military and civilian posts. It was the Communists
who regained control of the prestigious posts such as propaganda,
finance and foreign affairs. This led the Socialist Luis Araquistain
to describe the newly formed Negrin's government as being the
'most cynical and despotic in Spanish history'! Shortly afterwards,
Franco's death squads were kept busy assassinating a large number
of anarchists while living in their homes. The next day more
that 6,000 Assault Guards arrived from Valencia and gradually
took control of the large port city of Barcelona. Someone had
remarked that more than 400 people had been killed during what
later was to become known as "the May Riots". President Manuel
Azana agreed and asked Juan Negrin to form a new government.
Negrin had been a communist sympathizer and from that date
Joseph Stalin finally obtained more control over the policies of the
Republican Government. All of the upheavals of the Republican
government allowed Franco to maintain better and more complete
control of his conquest! This was to lead to a new experiment
suggested by Adolf Galland of the Condor Legion! The plan was
to experiment with a new bombing tactic that had not been used in
previous raids. It was given the name of 'carpet bombing', because
all of the bombs would be dropped on the enemy from every
aircraft at one time in order to obtain maximum damage. The
Nationalist army finally broke through the Republican defenses
and managed to reach the sea. General Franco then moved his
troops toward the city of Valencia with the objective of encircling
Madrid and the central front! This move allowed "Los Milicianos"

to finally get better organized with other guerrilla fighters in the neighboring provinces and moved collectively to re-conquer Spain from the Nationalists!

CHAPTER 6

Aviles

These had been trying times for Soledad! For the first time in her life she felt all alone and lonely as never before. After her mother and father had died, she lived in the house of Don Martin and had nursed him during his illness until his death. Their relationship had been strained at the beginning; but, as time went on, he came to regard her as a daughter and had taught her many things about the world that she had never known, nor had she considered in the years of her youth! As a young child she had been physically strong and had always had an unlimited supply of natural energy which enabled her to perform her daily chores without any problem.

Don Martin would always go out back and feed the chickens each morning and would feed the two hogs a bit later in the day! It had been a ritual that she had grown accustomed to each morning! It also meant that the only chore left for her to do was to milk the large oversized cow who would always give them an ample supply of milk each day. The elderly man had gone into town and had purchased the cow for her on one of her birthdays! He had selected this particular one because he remembered her speaking about a cow at home that was white and black and was called 'La Pinta'! She still remembered the smile on his face when he came home that afternoon with the cow and told her, "here is

La Pinta for your birthday!" She was surprised when she saw the large animal especially since it had been the first time she had ever received a present on her day of days! There had been no way of knowing what had become of the first cow after her mother had died, but, by naming her, it was almost as if the animal was a connection with her past! Every morning, her first stop was at the barn just to make sure that the cow, her cow, was still in the barn! There was also a feeling of pride she felt because now she finally had something she could call her own and didn't need to share with anyone else!

Today, for the first time, following the death of Don Martin, she felt tired! All of her chores had been completed and the animals had been fed! Afterwards, she had gone down to the river to wash the clothes as she did each morning. The day seemed overcast and it seemed that a summer storm was forming over the horizon! She had arisen early wanting to complete all of her chores before the storm which would further retard the plans she had made for the day! These were troubled times for the Spaniards! It wasn't that she understood all of the things that were happening within the government! Whatever was happening was beyond her comprehension!There had been some talk about the politics of the country, but these were conversations that were shared mostly by men at the local taverns! Her world did not exist beyond Aviles and Salinas, and all the land beyond those two towns was a world apart as far as she was concerned! At some point, she had heard men speaking about some unknown general by the name of Franco! It was said that he had been the commander of the Army in Morocco and had invaded the country from the South and was moving Northward in his attempts to take over the country. If what they were saying was true, she had nothing to worry about! Her life was pretty much established and it didn't seem probable that it would ever change, whether for the good or for bad! After all, how bad could it get? Everything she had loved in her life had been taken away! Her parents had died; the cow she had loved had been removed from the barn! Now, the kind old man who had given her love and attention had also passed away! As she recalled her life in retrospect, she was unable to remember the times that her life had really changed at all! Her family had always been poor and had struggled to make a living since she was born! If she had any other living relatives, she would never know; because, according to her mother, they had disavowed her family when her mother married her father, Don Francisco! Those things had never bothered her before! Now as she grew older and felt more alone, they seemed to be gaining importance!

The little money that Don Martin had saved had been left to her before he died! It seemed as if he had a premonition that he would soon be leaving this world because he had taken it upon himself to teach her many things about life! One of the first things he had taught her was how to save and how not to spend her money foolishly! Among his teachings he had also told her that the banks were not to be trusted, and that the only real savings she would ever have was in the small hole she had made in the dirt behind her house. It was there she had hidden the few pesetas he had left for her! Don Martin had also noticed that as the time passed by, she was growing into a beautiful young woman and would undoubtedly become the target of hungry young men who would constantly try to outdo each other in order to capture everything she had to offer as well as those things she didn't want to offer! Don Martin had insisted that she not give herself to anyone other than a person she could trust and would promise to care for her for the rest of her life! It wasn't that he felt that all men were bad, but, rather, that women were more vulnerable and had a sympathetic way about they that could be easily swayed if she wasn't careful! She remembered what he had told her as she recalled the incident at the dock when she arrived to get the sardines and a dirty fisherman had tried to place his filthy hands on her! Just thinking about his dirty hands on her was disgusting! She was nearly ashamed to admit that it had been the first time that she had felt wanted as a woman, and the thought had given her a passing satisfaction that she had never forgotten! Of course, that had been several years ago and the feeling had never been felt again, especially now that there were few men who were available. All of the young men in the area had been conscripted into the Republican army, and those that hadn't been, had found ways of leaving the area. Some had even travelled to foreign countries such as the United States and Cuba, or else had crossed the mountains into the Southern part of France! Maybe if she had some money, she would have considered also going elsewhere if only to see for herself if life was better elsewhere than it was here in Spain!

One thing was puzzling on her trips into town! There was an abnormal movement of troops wherever she went! Some of them were being transported in large, ugly army trucks, and others could be seen walking around in regular civilian clothes. The only way she was able to tell that they didn't come from Asturias was because some of them spoke in a different accent othet than Asturiano! There were also many others whose skin was black in color and didn't speak any Spanish at all! These army men, whoever they were, had not been seen in Asturias, and she wondered why it was that many of the local peasants would run and hide inside of their homes whenever they saw a group of these black men together! She had listened to stories about some things they would do, especially to the women who were walking along the street. For that reason, many of the young women had decided not to walk the streets alone, especially during the night hours when it became more dangerous. Soledad had no fear! She felt confident enough with her own strength to know she could fend off anyone who treated her unkindly. She also knew that there was always the chance that someone with more strength would take advantage of her youth and beauty!

Soledad had gone into town to buy a few groceries and was surprised at the number of strangers she saw eyeing all of the local peasants as they went about their daily chores. She hadn't remembered seeing so many at any one time and felt uncomfortable with what she was feeling! It wasn't any wonder that things had seemed to be different! After everything that was happening, it soon became difficult to tell the strangers from the villagers. As she was about to leave the town bakery where she had gone to buy a small loaf of 'borona' (Brown bread that could be held for several days before it became moldy!), she came upon a group of young men; two of the men were olive skinned, and the other two had a deep, brown color she wasn't familiar with! There seemed to be little doubt that these men were members of Franco's African Army! At first she had no idea what they were doing in Asturias, but, this was an entirely new world, where everything could happen! The thought of Don Martin came back to her! He had cautioned her about strangers and had tried to convince her into buying an 'escopeta' (rifle) to keep in the house for her protection! After all, he knew that she would soon be alone in the big stone house and would need to have something to protect herself! His only hope was that she would find some young man who was kind to her and would give her protection from any intruder. Unfortunately, he also knew that she was a free and self-supporting person, and finding someone she could love for the rest of her life was not going to be an easy chore! It would be best if she had a rifle in her bedroom where she could defend herself against anyone who tried to invade her privacy; but, she had refused to buy a rifle, telling him that she was strong and capable and could fight off anyone who was to come to her house uninvited!

In the beginning she did her best to ignore the four men as she walked briskly down the street, but then she realized that they were following her! It made her feel a bit uneasy as she began to think that perhaps Don Martin had been right after all! When the comments became more abusive and more salacious, she decided to turn around and face them directly!

"Que demonios quieren?" (What the Hell do you want?) she asked. One of the men began to laugh and passed off another dirty and offensive remark that offended her!

"Vete con tu madre!" she told him angrily. (Go with your mother!)

The black man made an ugly motion as he held on to his crotch, saying something that she couldn't quite understand, but could easily imagine what it was! Again she walked away and tried to ignore them; but she knew that these men were persistant and would not walk away. Her eyes searched up and down the street hoping to find a Guardia Civil who might come to her rescue, but there was none within view. Ordinarily, there would have been any number of Guardia Civilies walking the streets who would have come to her aid, but these were different times and many of the

Guardia Civilies had been conscripted into the army! One of the
olive-skinned man made another gesture at her and asked her to
go with them! She scowled at them and didn't reply! She had the
feeling that her temper was about to overtake her emotions; and she
realized that this could be real trouble! None of that mattered now
because she was much too angry to care!

"Dicelo a la madre que te pario!" she said angrily. (Tell that
to the mother who gave you birth!)

It was a nasty expression that she had not used before; but
in view of the comment he had passed, it seemed appropriate at the
time. The group became interested in another woman who was also
walking down the street and began to say unpleasant things to her!
Soledad seized the opportunity to quicken her pace and get out of
their sight!

The sun was starting to fade as Soledad completed her
daily chores, making sure that the cow and the chickens were fed!
It was a daily ritual that she had followed before going to bed!
The large stone house was equipped with a large wooden door
that separated the rear of the house from the living quarters. It
was an area where, in the cold evenings of winter, the animals
were permitted to come inside and take advantage of the warmth
from the wood burning stove in the living portion of the house. It
provided just enough warmth to make them comfortable and to
provide them with protection against the cold night winds. Soledad
was certain that she had closed the large doors before going to bed!
The night was cold and damp and she longed for the warmth of her
small bed and the heavy woolen quilt that would keep her warm
during the night. She had barely rested her head on the pillow
when she was startled by a strange sound coming from the rear of
the house. At first, she tried to ignore what she heard knowing that
there had been times when either the chickens or the cow would
make strange sounds, but this time, the sounds were strangely
different! It sounded as though someone was walking around
the area where the animals were allowed to roam. She became
frightened when the sounds persisted and wondered who it could
be! It was possible that someone had entered the house to steal one
of the chickens! Occasionally, there were times when someone

was ill and needed to make chicken soup and had no chickens! The person would come into one of the houses and would steal one of the feathery creatures as they were preparing to rest for the night! This, however, was not one of those sounds! Even though she was frightened, she felt it necessary that she remain perfectly still! Sleeping alone in her bed had never frightened her before, but this was different! Everything was different! Damn it, she said to herself! Why did Don Martin need to die? He would have known what to do! It was a struggle to keep from getting panicky, although her feelings were hard to control! The noises seemed to be getting louder and louder, and now she could hear men talking among themselves! She remained in bed, not wanting to confront whoever it was and hoping they would go away and leave her alone!

All of a sudden, the large wooden door opened and she saw the four men she had seen in town! They had probably followed her home and had seen that she was living alone! With her closest neighbors a long distance away, they could do anything they wanted to do! Franco had issued orders to his army that the members of his African army were allowed to rape any of the Republican women they met! Since they were in Asturias, they knew that she was fair game because she was a Republican! She could almost see them salivating at the thought of all of them raping her if only to give her a lesson that she would never forget! Although she did her best to conceal her true feelings, she felt panic-stricken and didn't know what she should do! The one thing that was certain was that she was about to be abused in an ugly manner and there was nothing she could do about it! The only thought she had was in wondering what Don Martin would tell her do under the circumstances! Giving in to their desires would be shameful and would not prevent the attack! Despite her fears, she was becoming angry! Don Martin had once told her that one does crazy things when they are angry! Well, this was one of those times! She was angry and knew that she needed to control that anger and make sure she diden't do crazy things that would make her feel sorry that she had been unable to control her temper!

"Que quieren?" she asked. There was a firm determination in her voice as she spoke, whether real or make believe! Still, it was defiant and without any signs of surrendering to those animals!

"Pues guapa! Queremos pasar la noche contigo!" (Well beautiful! We want to spend the night with you!) one of the olive skinned men told her!

"Quiero que se vayan de aqui! No necesito compania en mi cama!" (I want you out of here! I don't need company in my bed!) she replied. She sat up in her bed and made certain that the long cotton frock that she slept in was covering her ankles.

"Mira guapa! Primero te van a joder los Moros, y luego los Andaluces! Asi puedes escoger quien te gusta mas de los dos!" (Look beautiful! First, the Moors are going to screw you and then the Andaluces. This way you can chose which you like the best!)

One of the olive skinned men who had been doing the talking walked over to her and in one swift move grabbed her by the arms. She struggled and fought them off while they laughed as she tried desperately to break their hold. One of the Moors had taken hold of her white cotton gown and had started to rip it apart exposing her nude body! While the two olive-skinned men held her down, the black man was removing his pants getting ready to mount her! She shuddered at the thought of being raped by any man, much less these animals who were considered her enemy!

"Cochino, marrano, puerco!" she cried out. "Vete a joder a tu madre, degraciado!" (Pig, swine, hog! Go and screw your mother!) she cried out as they laughed while the black man started to fondle the inner portions of her thigh, in preparation for the invasion! She was furious and fearful of what was about to happen! Suddenly, she remembered something that Don Martin had once told her. Keep your anger under control and you'll be able to think more logically when in a desparate situation! Quickly, she became calm and stopped fighting the invader! There was no point in fighting him because it only seemed to make him more eager to penetrate her! Instead, she would try to relax, hoping they would finally leave the house when they were finished and would not return!

"Mira! Dile a ese, que no me aguante mas! Ya que me van a joder, que me dejen en paz!" (Tell your friend not to hold me! If you are going to screw me anyway, leave me alone!)

"Ahora si muneca! Creo que desde ahora vas a ser muneca mia y de nadie mas! (That's it, doll! I think that from now on, you are going to be my doll and no one else's!)

He slowly let go of his grip on her hands as the black Moor was on top of her, fully aroused! She grudgingly wrapped her arms around his back as if she were lending him a helping hand as the other men cheered him on! She made a few noises with her mouth, as if she was enjoying what he was doing to her for the first time in her life! The other three men were excited and could hardly wait their turn! From the bulging of their pants, she was able to see that they too were being aroused by what they were seeing! This had been the scenario she had expected! When the black man was at the point of climax, she carefully slipped her hand beneath the mattress unseen by the others who were too busy enjoying the attack! When she felt no one was looking at her, she took out a long kitchen knife that she had hidden under the mattress! It had been another clever suggestion from Don Martin when she refused to purchase the rifle! As they all stood awaiting their turn, she withdrew the sharp knife and, in one quick movement, stabbed it into the back of the Moor! Once, twice, and then again! She continued to stab the large black man until she saw his eyes roll back into his head and he slumped over her body, blood rushing out of the stab wounds all over his naked body. The other men were shocked by what they were seeing! One of the olive-skinned Andalusian men took one step toward her as she quickly pushed aside the dead man's body and stood naked in front of him still holding the blood soaked knife in her hand!

"Quien quiere joder me ahora?" she asked. (Who wants to screw me now?) "Ven! Hijo de puta! Apunale a tu amigo, y ahora te toca a ti!" (Come you, son-of-a-bitch! I stabbed your friend and now it is your turn!)

The men rushed out of the house as she followed them, using the renewed surge of energy she had received from somewhere or from somebody! She was no longer frightened; but, instead, she was damn angry and promised herself that no man would ever abuse her again! She had chosen the right moment to stab the bastard! He had not yet penetrated her and her virginity was still in tact! It had been a close-call, but it had taught her a new lesson! This bastard would never again force himself on another woman! She had seen to that! All she needed to do was to wait until they came to her farm and started to investigate the black man's disappearance! At least she had her work cut out for her knowing that in the morning she was going to need to make a large hole behind the house and bury her attacker who had tried to rape her!

Aviles

Soledad felt alone and depressed, wondering if she would ever erase the image of the assault! Over and over in her sleep she had seen the dead face of the black Moor as he hungered over her like a hungry animal in seach of prey! The thought of his weight touching her naked torso was vividly portrayed in every thought! As hard as she tried, it was next to impossible to get the thoughts out of her mind. Her life had been uneventful until that day, but, in that short time, she had learned much about life and had prayed often for the soul of Don Martin who having taken her under his wing, had filled her with knowledge of the world that she would have been otherwise unaware! It was a cruel and desperate world made even worse by the greed and harmful effects of man! She had seen both! She had seen the good in Don Martin and had seen the bad with the attack on her body by a black stranger! One thing had happened for sure! The name of General Franco, who had barely received any recognition before, had now become a hated and despised individual in her opinion!

She was resting in the house the next day following a day or work that had left her tired! As she was about to sit down, she heard an unexpected knock on the door! Instinctively, after everything that had happened, she was now more careful! Before opening the door, she went to the knife hidden beneath the mattress and held it tightly before turning the doorknob! If it was another one of those ugly men, this time she would be ready for them!

They would need to kill her before she would allow anyone to climb on top of her and invade the sanctity of her body!

"Quien es?" she asked, before opening the door.

"Mi nombre es Gomez! Soy de Salinas y quisiera hablar contigo, si me permites!" (My name is Gomez! I am from Salinas and would like to talk to you, if you let me!) the person said. She noticed that the voice seemed kind and gentle, not intimidating or frightening at all! This man, whoever he was, seemed to be well spoken and courteous! Many thoughts ran through her mind! The most frightening was that it was the authorities who were investigating the disappearance of the black Moor and that the trail had led to her! In any event, there was no point in rejecting him because doing so would only make things worse!

"Un momento, por favor!" she said, as she struggled to open the large door. A large, well dressed elderly man waited courteously outside until she asked him to come in!

"What I have to say is private! I hope you will respect our wishes and will continue to retain our privacy!" he told her. She was surprised that he was speaking more about privacy than about the murder! She found it difficult to consider him an investigator, or else, why would he be so well spoken and courteous?

"You have my word! Now, what is it you want?" she asked. She was also polite, but remained curt and to the point! If she was not interested in what the visitor had to say, she would turn him away, shut the door, and return to rest!

"As you know, the situation in Spain is getting worse! The Republicans are changing the government every day; and, in the meantime, they refused to see that the dictator Franco is gradually conquering more and more of the country!" What he had told her had been interesting, but it had nothing at all to do with her!

"So, what can I do about it? she asked. "I live alone and I have no money!" She started to tell him about the assault, feeling a need to tell someone about the incident, but quickly decided against it! After all, she knew absolutely nothing about this stranger other than he was courteous and obviously harbored a strong dislike for both the government and the fascist movement!

The man spoke to her in a gentle voice almost the way Don Martin would often speak to her! It wasn't long before she felt she could trust this strnager and the things he was telling her were making sense. There was a side of her that wanted to ask him to leave and not return, but the look from the face of hell on the black soldier was too vividly implanted on her mind! It was a look of evil, of hatred, of lust and destruction all into one! That look would remain with her for the rest of her life! He had been a member of Franco's African Army, and the bastard had no reason to bring such men into the country to wreak havoc on innocent people! No, she thought! Let this stranger talk! She was suddenly interested in what he was telling her!

"It isn't money we are looking for! We need spirited people such as you who will help us! There are groups of civilians from the provinces of Leon, Galicia, Asturias and eastward to Vizcaya! We are uniting and working together against the fascist movement! Spain has been lost! The fascists are already in Madrid and God alone knows what they'll do to us once they get further north! In the meantime, the government has allowed themselves to fall into the graces of the Communists! They are already burning down the churches and destroying the religion of our people! Also, their answers to the fighting is to change the people in the government and send them out to fight a war that nobody wants! We believe that as an underground movement we can do more than the enemy! We are having a meeting tomorrow night at our secret meeting place in Pola, at the base of the Cordillera! I would like you to come and join us and decide for yourself whether or not you would like to join our unit!"

Soledad looked at him strangely, without knowing what to think! She kinew that the one thing they both seemed to have in common was their dislike of the Nationalist army. There was no way of telling what his reasons were, but she knew what her own reasons were! Perhaps it might be best if she were to tell him what had happened!

"I don't know your reasons for hating the Nationalists, but I have my own reasons! Several days ago, a group of four men came to my house at night! Two of them sounded like Andaluces, but the other two were members of the African army. One of the Andaluces held me down while one of the black Moors took off his clothes and assaulted me! That 'hijo-de-puta', tried to invade my body! Fortunately, I was able to stop him from raping me!" she told him.

He looked at her without showing any expression waiting for her to continue. Finally, when she had finished, he asked her. "How did you stop them?"

"How did I stop him???? I killed the bastard, that's how!!" she answered excitedly.

He was able to see the fierce look of anger in her eyes as she told him the story! This woman had more guts than many of his fighters, he thought! Now more than before he was hoping that she would agree to join their group!

"What did you do with the body?" he asked, in a calm voice without showing any signs of being surprised.

"I dragged the body out of my house and into the back yard! I then dug a large hole and buried him there where he belonged!" There was no remorse for what she had done! Unfortunately, she had paid little attention to such things as an investigation once the man was reported missing! If the others managed to escape, the trail would obviously lead to her!

"Don't you know that they will probably investigate the murder? They may return here looking for you!" he said, trying to get her to be a bit more cautious.

"For what? Because I killed an animal that should have been killed by a firing squad?? I don't care what they do to me! If they want to, I'll gladly go before the Mariscal and tell him what I did! I will never forget the look of lust, fire, and hunger in his eyes as he tried to penetrate me! No man has ever done those things to me, and now neither will he!"

"Yes, but remember that the Mariscal has been appointed to his position by none other than the General himself! The murder of any of his troops will not be taken lightly!" he told her.

"Then, let the general go to bed with him if he thinks so highly of him! I'm not ashamed of what I did, and I would do it all over again if I had the chance!"

"I think it would be wise for you not to mention what you did to anyone else! It may not be safe! I believe that now more than ever, you may be needing our help! If they send you to jail, we'll do whatever we can to free you, no matter what the risk may be!" he assured her.

Perhaps this stranger had spoken the truth! There would probably come a time when she would need their help! She had been so angry that she hadn't had time to think about the possible consequences, but, this stranger had alerted her to some of the risks that she hadn't considered!

"So, if I were to join your group, what is it called?" she asked.

"We're called, 'Los Milicianos' ! We have a great deal of support that has been promised! There is the Brigada Lincoln, from the United States. Also, there is a member club called the UHP, and several others. In addition, there is a long list of entertainment stars that have been giving concerts and shows with all of the proceeds coming to our cause!"

"What stars? Who gives a damn what becomes of us? Nobody has cared about us for many years, why would they change now?"

"That's where you're wrong! There are people in the United States such as Consuelo Moreno, Xavier Cugat, Andres Segovia and many others who do care and who do want us to succeed!"

She thought about it for a moment! None of the mentioned names were familiar to her, but, if it was good enough for them, then, why not? Perhaps she should join the group! "Are there any women in the group?" she asked.

"Yes, there are some! There is also one of our leaders who you will be meeting who is also a woman! Perhaps you will meet her tomorrow night if you come to our meeting!" He paused for a moment before continuing! "If you join our group, we don't want any of our true names to be revealed! You will be given a nickname; and that is the name you will always use! We have a list of names you can select from!"

"No!!! I have my own name! If you want me to join the group, then you'll need to agree to my own selection of a name!"

she said adamently. "I want to be known as 'La Muneca'! That is the name I want to use; and, unless I can use that name, I want no part of your group!"

"Why, 'La Muneca'" he asked. "The name is okay as far as I'm concerned! But why are you so insistent on that name?"

"Because those men who came to my house to harm me, one of the Andaluces called me a Muneca and said that I was going to become his own private Muneca! By using that name, I will be reminded of his ugliness, and how much they looked and acted like the wild animals of the field! Since he wanted me to be his private Muneca, I want him to have his wishes; but this time, he will have her but only on my terms!!" she answered.

"Very well!!" the man said, "It is settled! Shall I come for you tomorrow evening? I will come for you and take you back home! You need not fear any person in our group! Most of them are married and have their own families! I will see to it that nothing happens to you!" he said with reassurance.

Soledad remained silent while nodding her head! At that moment she had no idea of whether or not she had made the right choice! The only thing she felt was that of a new involvment in a group that was unknown to her. The feeling was that this group was about to embark her into yet another direction that would again change her life! Maybe a new change in her life was what she needed after all! The stranger had seemed kind and caring! If she was going to remain in that big house, she would need someone to depend on now that Don Martin was no longer around to protect her. She only knew that these were people who seemed to share her wishes and her dislikes! Until the untimely event in her bedroom, she had never given much thought of what might happen to her. Indeed, she had been much too pre-occupied with her own problems for survival! Also, she remembered hearing that the Mariscal in Toledo had been personally appointed to his post by General Franco. Although he had acquired a reputation of being a fair and just person, if he was a member of the Fascist movement, one thing was certain; he was not a person to be trusted! Life had compelled her to do something she had never thought she would have been able to do in killing another human being! It was true that she had done so out of necessity; but it was the taking of another life that continued to give her mixed thoughts about what she had done! If the investigation into the disappearance of the black man led the investigators back to her, she knew they would probably find the burial spot in the back of the house! The small mountain of fresh dirt would certainly tell the story, but, it would be their story and not hers! For the first time she felt that she needed someone to protect her! If it became necessary to kill other people in order to retain her own freedom, then, that would be the price she would need to pay!

The stranger had offered her the help of 'Los Milicianos' if something should happen to her! She took one look into the mirror, and for the first time, didn't particularly like what she was seeing! The attractive facial features that had always stared back at her had disappeared! There were no dark circles under her eyes from not sleeping! Despite her outward strength, the episode she had faced alone had taken its toll on her! She was now frightened! Since that horrible night, every slight creak in the house became grossly magnified. Every movement of the wind made it seem as though someone was hiding inside the house. The nights were restless with the thought that the person who had tried to invade her body was lying behind the house with his eyes wide opened! There was a side of her that was trying to convince her that he would never again return! Unfortunately, there was the other side that told her that the other three men who had escaped could possibly return, and this was what she feared the most! All of those things were running through her mind when she noticed that the tears were rolling down her cheeks! It was one of the few times when she felt the need to cry, realizing that perhaps, just perhaps, she may not be as strong as she once thought she was! Although she had agreed to attend the meeting, she still had mixed feelings! There was no way for her to know what it was that these people wanted from her! She certainly did not have any of the abilities that other people had. Hers had been a simple life in a simple environment and any activities that would take her away from the things she was familiar with was a bit frightening!

It was already dark when they arrived at the small
secret cave in the village of Pola! The village itself was sparsely
populated consisting mostly of small farms and houses! Gomez
had parked his car behind one of the houses; and they walked for
a long time until they reached the end of the Cordillera Cantabrica
along the southern end of the province of Asturias! Soledad
followed the elderly man as they walked along several narrow
mountain passages that were spiraling in an upward direction
until they reached a darkened cave that had been carved deep into
the mountains! The only lights that were available were the few
candles that had been lit awaiting their arrival. Inside the cave
there was a group of five men, each of them elderly and all of
them untidy with long beards and mustaches, each man wearing
the customary boina on their head, and each one sipping from a
leather pouch that had been filled with red wine! There was an
old woman, dressed in black, who was giving out the orders to the
other men! She wondered if this old lady was the person in charge
of the group? Gomez greeted the others and introduced Soledad to
the group! They all smiled courteously and some of them shook
her hand! It was nothing more than a friendly gesture, but they all
seemed happy that she had come to the meeting! Gomez then took
Soledad by the hand as he took her to meet the woman dressed in
black!

"Soledad, ven aqui! Quiero que conozcas una de nuestros
lideres!" (Soledad, come here! I want you to meet one of our
leaders!) Gomez told her.She walked over to the old woman
dressed in black who was now wiping her hands on a black apron
before extending her hand in friendship. "This is Dolores Ibarruri!
She comes from a small town in Vizcaya called Gallarta! She
served as a seamstress before joining us and now she has become
one of our leaders!"

"Mucho gusto, Senora!" Soledad said. She extended her
hand but the elderly woman placed her hands on her hips as if
she disapproved that this young woman had been brought to the
meeting!

"Es demasiado joven! Porque la traiste aqui?" the old woman told Gomez! (She is much too young! Why did you bring her here?)

"I brought her here because she is all alone and needs someone to look over her! Besides, it is likely that she will be investigated for murder and she shouldn't be left alone!" Gomez replied. Suddenly, the eyes of the elderly woman opened wide and she let out a toothy grin, nodded her head up and down!

"Who did she kill?"

"A group of four Nationalist soldiers went to her house! Two of them were from Andalucia and two were from the African army! One of the Andaluces held her down while one of the African soldiers jumped on top of her and tried to rape her! She withdrew a knife from under the mattress and stabbed him several times until he was dead!" Again, the elderly woman smiled as if she was listening with interest to everything that Gomez was telling her and enjoying the conversation!

"And what did she do with the body?" she finally asked.

"I dragged it outside and buried it behind the house!" Soledad answered.

"Ay! Que bueno! (That's good!) "Perhaps you will do just fine!" She then went over and placed her arm around Soledad's shoulders! "Hiciste bien!" (You did good!)

"By the way," Gomez told her. "Nobody is to call her Dolores around here! This woman has a reputation throughout Spain as "La Pasionaria"! You will be hearing much more of her if you remain with us!"

"What name do you want us to call you?" the elderly woman asked.

"I want to be known as 'La Muneca'!" Soledad answered. The woman looked at her a bit strangely. She didn't know whether or not La Pasionaria had been surprised by her selection of the name or the anxiety she was showing in making certain that everyone had heard her.

"That is a strange name! Is there a story behind that name?" La Pasionaria asked.

"Yes!" Soledad answered with determination. "When the men came into my house, one of the Andaluces had the nerve to call me his muneca! He told me that I would become his own private muneca and it made me angry! I hated those men and I wanted nothing more than to harm them! Unfortunately, I was a woman and wasn't strong enough to take them on! To me, "La Muneca" is a name that I want to remember every time I see one of the fascist troops! It will remind me of what they did and how much I hate all of them!"

"Oye Gomez! Mira, que esta chica si que tiene cojones!! Creo que nos va servir muy bien!" (Gomez, this young girl certainly has testicles! I think she is going to be just fine!) "Oye Muneca! How would you like a hot cup of coffee with a little brandy?"

Soledad accepted the hot drink but only poured a few drops of the brandy into the black liquid! It felt good as she sipped it and bought warmth to her body! She had been feeling cold inside the cave, and the coffee was what she needed to warm her body! The elderly woman then led her to a far corner of the cave where a small fire had been lit! She motioned with her hand for Soledad to sit down beside her and asked her to tell her all about her youth in Salinas!

The battle for Madrid was costly to both sides! In an attempt to relive the pressure on the capital city, Juan Negrin ordered an attack across the fast flowing Ebro River. General Modesto, a member of the Communist Party, was placed in charge of the offensive! More than 80,000 Republican troops, including the 15th International Brigade and the British Battalion began to cross the river on boats in mid July! The men then moved forward toward the cities of Corbera and Gandesa. Shortly afterward, the Republican army attempted to capture Hill 481 which was a key position in Gandesa. The hill was well protected with barbed wire, trenches, and bunkers. After the bitter fighting and the many casualties, the Republicans were forced to retreat after only six days to Hill 666 on the Sierra Pandols. From there, the Republicans were finally able to defend the hill from a Nationalist offensive, but once again suffered the loss of many soldiers. The very next day, following the reports of large numbers of troop losses, Juan Negrin, the head of the Republican government, announced that the International Brigades would be unilaterally withdrawn from Spain. That same evening many of the volunteers moved back across the Erbo River, began their journey out of the country and made their way back to their own countries! The remainder of the Republican army had to stay behind and tried to withstand the steady flow of attacks by the Condor Legions! General Gonzalo de Llano also moved forward a total of about 500 cannons which fired an average of 13,000 rounds a day at the Republicans. Before the end of the year, the Republicans were forced to retreat. In the battle of Ebro, the Nationalist army had killed more than 6,000 troops and had wounded more than 30,000 men. These were the worst casualties of the war and it effectively ended up by destroying the Republican army as an effective fighting force!

Juan Negrin made a mild attempt to gain support of the western governments by announcing a plan to de-collectivize many industries.It was May 1938 when Negrin published a thirteen point program that included the promise of full civil and political rights as well as the freedom of religion! Later that year, President Azana attempted to oust Negrin from office, but unfortunately, he no longer had the power he had before with the aid of the Communists in the government and in the Armed Forces. Negrin was however able to survive the ouster attempt! Several months later Barcelona fell to the Nationalist army. Azana and his government were forced to more to Perelada, a city near the French border. With the Nationalist forces still advancing, Azana and many of his colleagues crossed into France! After this final escape, the underground began most of their destructive activities and the only reasonable resistance to the Nationalist army. Because the band of guerrilas known as "Los Milicianos" had the advantage of concealment within the caves of the Cordillera, they were able to perform most of the destruction during the night hours and would hide in the caves during the day in order to avoid capture!

Soledad became one of the group's fiercest fighters, having been taken under the wing of "La Pasionaria"! It wasn't long before she became one of the planners and a much respected member of the group. No one dared to call her by her real name! Everyone knew her as "La Muneca," and, after a short while, she became one of the most feared guerilla fighters in the region! "La Pasionaria" was pleased with her progress, but often wondered if perhaps she hadn't become a bit too daring! One careless mistake could end up by costing her life, but none of the mattered now! She became a woman on a mission! Her life meant nothing at all! There was virtually nothing to live for; but, at least, she knew that she was taking her revenge on an enemy that had tried unsuccessfully to invade her body! The words of her father came back to haunt her once again when he had stressed over and over again! The Asturianos were proud people, and would never allow themselves to be abused by anyone! Well, she had been abused and she was still proud! Now it was up to her to do everything within her power to defeat her enemy!

There was an urgent meeting that was scheduled the following evening! Gomez, the leader of the group, had come to her house with another member called "Chato"! She had recognized him from the previous meeting because he had spent his time playing with his rifle while the other members were talking and planning their next moves! At first she thought he might be mentally impaired, but she soon learned that he was an expert marksman with the rifle and would always accompany Gomez whenever he went to someone's house!

"Que pasa Gomez?" she asked. It seemed strange that nothing had been said about having another meeting so soon! Chato walked past the leader and remained at the door!

"Muneca, a serious problem has come up! It seems that the Nationalists are preparing to move northward into Asturias! We have learned that the entrance into Asturias will be by crossing the River Nalon! There is a large bridge that the fascists will need to cross near the city of Langreo! If we can destroy that bridge, they will need to march much further to the east where the fascists will have to encounter the Basques! They are better prepared to fight them than we are!"

"Are they also members of "Los Milicianos?""

"No! Not directly! They have their own guerilla movements! You see, they have wanted to gain independence from Spain for many years! They have their own criteria and they are very strong, both in armament and in manpower! We are working together with them! In fact, it was they who gave us the information about the forward movement!"

"What do you want me to do? I know nothing about blowing up bridges! I'd be willing to help wherever I'm needed, but I doubt I would be very useful working with dynamite!"

"Muneca, the only way for you to learn is to go with us! Do you think you can handle an 'escopeta'?"

"I can if someone teaches me! I have never handled a rifle in my life, but I'm willing to give it a try!" she answered.

"If you like, when we get back to the cave, Chato will take you outside and he'll teach you how to handle a rifle! He has taught most of us and has even taught 'La Pasionaria' how to aim and shoot!"

She thought it would be thrilling to learn how to use a rifle! There had been talk about buying a gun when she was living with Don Martin, but she was always afraid that something bad might happen! Still, if she had a rifle when the four men came barging into her house, there would have been four graves behind her house instead of just one!

"Of course I want to learn! I can probably be more useful to the group if I learn how to defend myself and to defend others!"

"Hecho ya!" (It's done then!) Gomez told her. "Now get your coat and let's go make our plans!"

She did as she was told and returned with them to the cave where they had met before! She looked and smiled when she saw "la Pasionaria' standing and offering her a cup of strong, black coffee. She took a sip from the steaming cup and sat down next to the others. There was Chato, a middle aged thin man without any front teeth; El Ingles, an older man with a large belly, probably the result of drinking too much wine and smoking too many strong cigarettes, and an older man named Ramon! He was a bit older than the others, with a heavy grey beard but a bit on the quiet side! The only time he would say something was when he was asked a question! At other times, he would remain silent and listened to everything that was being said! La Pasionaria had mentioned something about his wife and two daughters that had been raped by the Nationalists. Since he had no place else to go, he had joined their guerilla movement! His contribution to 'Los Milicianos' was that he could listen carefully to a plan, and, after a few moments, he could tell them of any flaws or any potential risks that might have been overlooked!

"What do the people of Langreo think about the plan?" she asked.

"They're in agreement! The don't want to have fascists in their town! They have agreed to give us their support!" Just then, she noticed that Chato was playing with several large round sticks by tossing them into ther air and catching them with his bare hands! Gomez looked at him and remained silent while he took out a large piece of paper and spread it out on the ground! "Chato!" he finally said. "Deja eso ya!" (Leave them alone!) he ordered.

"Que son esos palos?" she asked. (What are those sticks?)

"They are dynamite sticks!" Gomez replied. "If they go off, they are powerful enough to blow up the entire cordillera!" He had no need to say anything more! She went over to him, grabbed the sticks out of Chato's hands and handed them to Gomez! Chato looked surprised, but the angry look on her face warned him against saying anything!

"Estas loco? Si te quieres matar, son cosas tuyas, pero yo no tengo ganas de morir!" (Are you nuts? If you want to kill yourself, that's your business, but I have no desire to die!) she told him as he walked away and lit another cigarette!

They went over the plans in detail! Gomez made the decision that only he, Chato and El Ingles would go with him and would be leaving tonight! Muneca looked at him! She was disappointed that she had not been asked to go after having gone there to prepare their plans! "Porque no quieres que vaya?" (Why don't you want me to go?) she finally asked.

"Because what we need to do has to be done quickly and efficiently! We need to plant the dynamite sticks and run the detonation line a long distance in order to get a maximum result!

We have been told that there is a unit that will be marching over the bridge tomorrow night! That's the reason why we have called a meeting tonight, so that we can destroy the bridge before they arrive!"

"What do you plan to do if there are already some of the advanced troops that will be guarding the bridge? We already know that some of the troops were in Aviles! You don't have enough rifles for protection! I want you to give me a rifle and allow me to go along!" she insisted.

"Muneca, you don't even know how to use the weapon! We can't expose you to any danger, just yet! Wait until you get the proper training!"

"No!" she insisted. "I didn't ask you to join 'Los Milicianos', you were the one that came to me! Now, I am either a part of the group or not! If you want me to learn, then, it's important that I go along or else I may as well go home!" she demanded.

"Muy bien!" Gomez said. "Perhaps you are right! It may be best if you are exposed to what we have to do! I want you to take a rifle and stay with Chato! He will teach you how to load it and use it!" Good, she thought! She had won her point! If she was going to become a guerilla fighter, there were things that she would need to learn and would need to learn them fast!

The older man, Ramon looked at her and was smiling, shaking his head from side to side! "Que atrevida eres, mujer!" (You are quite daring, lady!)

The group entered Gomez' car and drove off to the town of Langreo, a few miles east southeast of Oviedo! The town was little more than another farm village much the same as those in the north, except that the streets were empty and there was no one around to see what they were doing! Gomez drove his car into a small cutaway in one of the foothills where it would be out of sight! He decided that he would let the engine continue to run! It had been calculated that the entire plan would not take any longer than fifteen minutes if they worked quickly.

Muneca remained in the car with Chato while Gomez and El Ingles walked over to the edge of the bridge and went out about one hundred yards over the span. Ingles took with him four or five sticks of dynamite, all neatly wrapped with adhesive and gently lowered the cache over the edge of the bridge until it settled on one of the main vertical supports. Then, he climbed over the low steel rail and gently lowered himself to the area where the dynamite sticks had landed. He saw them resting on a large steel hinge that supported one of the long horizontal spans across the river. Carefully, he lowered himself to a lower distance until they were within reach! He then attached a long thin wire to the package and gently climbed back onto the span! The roll was neatly coiled as he unravelled the thin wire and carefully stretched it out as far back as it would go until he was back across the approach where he then attached the other end to a small square box that Gomes had planted a short distance away from the car. Once again, he made certain that the wire was securely attached and walked back to where Gomez had been waiting for him. Before igniting the fuse, he asked Muneca to look around and make sure that no one was watching! She took the rifle away from her shoulder and pointed the barrel of the gun toward the ground as she looked carefully all around until she was satisfied that no one was looking!

"Esta bien!" she told Gomez, as he nodded his head and continued to attach the loose end of the wire to the detonation box!

"Vete pa'tras, nena! Que va hacer mucho ruido!" (Get back, girl! It's going to make a lot of noise!) he said.

She did as she was told and shielded herself behind the metal at the rear of the car. All of a sudden, he pressed down on a lever, and in a second or two, there was a loud explosion as pieces of steel began to plummet down to the river! After a few more seconds, there was another loud rumbling and the fierce shaking of the ground beneath them as a large portion of the bridge span broke away and also fell down to the river! The force of the rumble had created a large opened section of the bridge several meters wide making the bridge impassable! There was nothing below except the smooth flow of the river as Gomez quickly detached the wire, grabbed the detonation box and got into the car! As they were about to drive away, they saw the arrival of three fascist soldiers, each wearing their Nationalist army uniform, who had come out of one of the nearby buildings! They quickly aimed their rifles and began firing their weapons in a steady stream of gunfire that soon disturbed the tranquility of the night. As they started to drive away, Muneca decided that someone needed to return the fire! This had been Chato's job, but he had been caught with an empty rifle and was busy trying to re-load quickly in order to return the fire! Muneca felt a cold sweat on the palms of her hands as she realized that unless the fire was returned the group would be in danger! After all, the soldiers had been well trained in military tactics; and, for the most part, her group was comprised only of simple peasants who had never felt the need to fire a rifle! Muneca quickly lifted her own rifle and pointed it in the direction of the soldiers. Never before had she felt the need for a rifle, but this was not an ordinary situation! The cold metal of the housing felt uncomfortable against her bare arm and, she had no idea as to whether or not she was doing the right thing! All that she knew was that she was facing the enemy and it was her job to keep them away! The anger she had felt when the four men came into her house to harm her came vividly into view! All the hatred and scorn she had felt had returned once again! Slowly, while the car was moving, she aimed the gun through the opened window and took steady aim! The rifle refused to keep still as the movement of the car spoiled her aim! Finally, she pulled the trigger, her arm snapped upward from the small explosion as the gun re-coiled, but not before she saw that one of the soldiers had fallen to the ground. The other two stopped the firing and turned their attention to their fallen comrade! It appeared as if they were attending to the wounds of a large man that was lying on the cold concrete, his uniform stained with fresh blood as he remained lifeless at their feet. When they were finally back at the cave, she saw one of the soldiers say something to the other man and shake his head from side to side! There was no need to wonder what was being said, the somber look on their faces had said it all! There was little doubt that their partner was dead!

The men congratulated her on her first mission as she remained confused as to whether or not she had done the right thing! The use of the rifle had been easy enough, much easier than when she had to use the kitchen knife under the mattress to

kill a man. It soon dawned on her that she had felt nothing! She
didn't even feel nervous or apprehensive for having killed another
man! It was not like before, when she had fallen asleep every night
seeing the large black man laying dead on her bed with his eyes
wide open! Could it be that she had become hardened to such
things? Perhaps she would never know! She would also never know
that she had embarked on a new career that was going to make
'La Muneca' a feared legend in Asturias that would not soon be
forgotten! Despite the many set backs, the band of guerillas known
as 'Los Milicianos' would create a nightmare for General Franco
long after he had conquered Spain!

      With every mission Muneca became more efficient even
though some of the men considered her too young to be an
effective guerilla fighter! They soon learned she had acquired
nerves of steel and wouldn't hesitate to use her rifle anytime she
felt that a member of her group was being threatened! Chato,
who had at first refused to teach her how to use a rifle because of
her youth, had now taken on a new interest and had often taken
her into the hills of the Cordillera where he had taught her the
art of aiming the rifle and shooting straight! She had become
so efficient that it wasn't long before she became more accurate
than her mentor and could outshoot any male member of the
group. In addition, she had learned everything she could from 'La
Pasionaria'. She had mastered the different types of explosives that
they used depending on the circumstances and had memorized the
capabilities of every stick of dynamite and every explosive that
was in their arsenal! It wasn't long before she became more than
just another "Miliciano'; she had become one of the leaders and
was always considered a leader whenever the group decided to go
on a mission to retard the advances of the Nationalists. Perhaps
the Republican army had not been able to stop Franco's advances,
but she and the small group of guerilla fighters were known to do
the impossible! There was no way for her to know whether or not
the soldier she had recently killed would end up in an investigation
and she would become the accused! The only thing she knew for
certain was, that from that moment on, she would never again
be able to return to her home! This was obviously the first place

they would go to look for her! If she were found, she would have to go before the Mariscal, and her only defense would be that she had been assaulted by a group of fascists. This defense would do little to spare her execution immediately after the mock-trial was conducted! Her only salvation was to remain concealed inside the cave where she would receive the protection from her new friends!

Several days had passed when Muneca heard a strange noise outside the cave! She went outside and saw Chato about to enter the cave with a strange person who had been blindfolded and had his hands tied behind his back! All of the other group members had gone about with their menial chores and had left her alone! She looked at Chato with a surprised look and saw that the prisoner was not speaking, but instead, was being led with a rifle pointed at his back!

"Chato, que haces aqui"? she asked. (Chato, what are you doing here?)

"Este hombre estaba en una taverna y estaba hablando de los planes de los Nacionalistas!" (This man was in a tavern and was talking about plans being made by the Nacionalists!) I brought him here to interrogate him and to find out what he knew about the Nationalist movement!" he told her.

She watched him carefully as he led the prisoner inside the cave and slowly removed his blindfold as well as the restraints of his arms. He ordered the prisoner to sit down on an old wooden bench at the far side of the cave! Muneca saw immediately that the man was tall and handsome! His body was lean and thin, and he had a smile that seemed to go right through you! Whoever he was, he had attracted her eye, and he could see that she was also attracted to him! "Why don't you wait outside and leave me alone with the prisoner! Let me talk to him and see what he has to say!" she told Chato. He nodded his head with some reluctance and went back outside as he had been ordered to do!

"Sit down!" she told the prisoner. The man did as he was told, but not without flashing her an endearing smile! He could see by her reaction that she posed no threat to him! The truth was that he was tired of fighting and had welcomed his new role as a prisoner! "I want to know everything you spoke about in the tavern!"

"What is it you want to know?" he replied, still flashing that enticing smile that seemed both threatening while at the same time attractive!

"Where are you from and what are you doing here?" she asked, trying her best to sound very professional and yet not letting him know that his smile was making her feel uncomfortable!

"I'm from Sevilla! I fought with the Nationalist army and was sent here as a forward scout to find out about your defenses! I was to report back to my garrison tomorrow with the information they wanted me to obtain!"

Muneca noticed that he seemed to be a pleasant man, kind and gentle and rather easy to talk to! This seemed so different from other prisoners who had been far more defiant! This man appeared to be happy that he had been captured and that his fighting days may well be over!

"What information can you give me about your army and when do they intend to make a major drive into Asturias?" she asked.

"I can tell you that it will be soon! But, why is an attractive woman like you fighting a losing battle with these guerillas? Don't you realize that the Generalisimo will soon overrun this area and your activities will be stopped?" he answered.

Muneca resented any talk about stopping their activities! She looked at him sternly and tried to find the proper answers of assurance that their work would not be stopped!

"We are well equipped to handle and to stop any forward movement! Now, I want you to tell me everything you know about troop strengths and when you plan to invade this area!"

He took a seat on the long wooden bench and noticed that she swat down next to him! It was annoying that all the time she had been talking to him he was smiling at her as if he didn't care; or, at least, as though he realized that she was being attracted to him!

"Look!" he said. "I am a poor farmer from Sevilla! I really don't have very much knowledge about the war!" Although she was sitting next to him, she felt that by being at his side he might be willing to speak to her about what she wanted to know.

"Our man said you were talking about troop movements! That was why he brought you here!"

He got the impression by her tone of voice that she was almost apologizing for having been brought here. If so, this would certainly help his cause! He already had the feeling that he had an upper hand with her, and all he needed to do was to build up his advantage to this poor, young, attractive woman that was trying her best to act even stronger than she really was!

"I admit that I may have said things that I shouldn't have said! You know how it is! You drink a little wine and you start to talk without realzing what you are saying!" he told her. After a few minutes of an uncomfortable silence, he asked her, "Tell me, why is an attractive woman like you living here like this? You deserve so much better!" he said.

Suddenly he noticed that her face became flushed and she seemed embarassed by his comments! There was really no point in telling him the way she felt about Franco's army! She again sat down beside him and he could see that she seemed uncomfortable sitting so close to him!

His smile was penetrating and infective as it went right through her! He was handsome enough with his tall lean body and she felt embarassed as she silently envisioned what it would be like to be in bed with him! It was a feeling she had never felt before and it seemed so different from the repulsive feeling she felt when the other members of the Nationalist army had broken into her house! They were repulsive but this man seemed kind and gentle; and he knew that he had attracted her attention! As they spoke, he started to run his hand over her thigh, stroking it gently as if it were made of silk! Ordinarily, she would have shoved him away, but there was something about this man that was pleasing to her! His hand touching her was stimulating; and it gave her a strange, numbing feeling as he stroked gently at first, then applying a bit more pressure as he watched her squirm uncomfortably while sitting next to him! He saw that she hadn't turned him away; in fact, she seemed to enjoy every stroke of his hand! She took several deep breaths knowing that she was feeling things she had never felt before! He was watching her as her breasts were rising and falling with every breath of air! When he felt confident that she was finally within his grasp, he whispered to her, "I'll tell you anything you want to know if you'll spend the night with me! I want to be with you, even though I don't even know your name!"

"My name is La Muneca!" she answered, unable to sound convincing as she felt once again his strokes on her thigh and wishing she had met this stranger at another time and another place!

"Que nombre mas linda tiene la hija de tu madre!" he whispered. (What a beautiful name your mother's daughter has!) "Que bendita debe de ser, con una hija tan hermosa!" (She has been blessed with such a beautiful daughter!) She didn't reply! Instead she remained seated where she was listening to his warm, kind words that no one had ever said to her! She closed her eyes and was enjoying every minute of his comments!

"Mi nombre es Javier!" he told her. (My name is Xavier) "I come from a small town outside of Sevilla! My parents owned a citrus farm that produced Oranges! Everything was fine until the Republicans began to tax our income and began taking away portions of our land to distribute among some of the other unemployed peasants! Eventually, there was nothing left of the land; and, the few pesetas we had in the bank were also confiscated by the socialist government to finance the government projects, most of which were unnecessary, just to put people to work! I grew up disliking both sides, but I knew that the government could not continue the way it was going and when it came time for conscription, I decided to join the Nationalist movement!"

Muneca quickly recognized the truth in what he was saying because the same things had happened in Asturias! It had been because of this that Don Martin had insisted that she make a hole in the ground behind the house and bury the few pesetas that were left where nobody would find them. At least these would be available to help her pay for her needs! If they had remained in the bank, the government would have taxed the small income and there would be nothing left to pay for her needs! She also knew that this man produced an unwanted danger! There was little known about him and for all she knew, he might have been one of Franco's top officers! None of that seemed to matter now as she sat down with him, her head resting against the wall, while his hand kept pressing deeper and deeper into her upper thigh! She realized that he presented trouble for the unit, but yet nothing seemed to matter! She rather liked what she was feeling! Her mind was filled with many thoughts, some good others bad, but none that really mattered! The war was going to have to wait! She was enjoying this stranger's manipulations even if she knew that it meant immediate expulsion from "Los Milicianos", if it became known that she had intimate contact with the enemy! Muneca noticed that the stranger edged his way even closer until their thighs were touching! The stroke of his hand was sending her into another world that was far away from the troubles she felt while on earth! As he came even closer, none of that seemed to matter, as he placed his strong arm around her shoulders and drew her closer to him!

CHAPTER 7

Toledo

It had not been a particularly good day as the Mariscal sat down behind his desk and was thinking about the three people he had condemned to death! All three men had been charged with desertion; and, as Mariscal for the area, he was aware that the mandatory sentence he had given them could not be appealed to a higher authority. Condemning people to death had always been an regrettable occasion, especially if they were peasants whose only crime was going against the policies of General Franco! There were so many policies that he had disliked and wished that they could be changed! Unfortunately, this was war; and in war there are many unpopular policies that need to be enforced! Today's accused had been simple peasants, poorly educated, and had been so confused by the current state of Spanish politics that they found it difficult to decide for whom they should be fighting, or who was really the true enemy! They had survived decades of starvation, hoping for the day when they would be able to settle down in their homes, harvest a small tract of land, and raise their children without the need of answering the dreadful drums of war. These men had known nothing about wars! All they knew was that wars meant death and destruction, and, in their young lives, they had already experienced enough death and destruction to last a lifetime! The faint smile on their faces as they were led out of the large room was still very much on the mind of the Mariscal! He had listened to the sounds of gunfire many times before from his office behind the courtroom, but there was something troubling when he heard the shots this time, knowing that three young men had met their death and had not been traitors! These men had been peasants just like him not many years ago! Making matters worse was the fact that they had come from the same province where he had been born and raised! Two of the them, one eighteen years of age, the other one twenty years of age had come from Asturias! The remaining prisoner was a bit older! He had a wife and two small children and had come from Galicia! Damn, how he hated this job!! There had been a new law that these men had to be considered as common criminals because they had deserted their army units! No one would ever know how many times he had wished in silence that he had the nerve to desert his unit and perhaps escape to another country where all of these senseless killings could be forgotten!

Desertion had been a serious problem for both sides! There were members of the Republican army who had deserted their units and had joined the Nationalist army! It wasn't that they were idealists and believed in the causes! The causes were much too complex for them to analyze! There were also just as many Nationalists who had abhorred the civil war, many with relatives that lived in the Southern provinces and who had escaped to the North in order to avoid the battles that were raging every day!

The Mariscal had been more fortunate than other men! He had escaped poverty by enlisting in the Guardia Civil and soon was selected to study advanced civil disobedience and riot controls! Out of need, the fascists had conscripted many of the Guardia Civiles; and he had been highly recommended by a previous officer Colonel Garcia who had also changed sides and was now fighting with the Fascists! The turning point came when the colonel became a personal aid to Generalissimo Franco; and when he thought that the time was right, it was the colonel who recommended the young lieutenant for advanced studies in law and in social studies that would eventually benefit Spain. So pleased was General Franco with the young man that he had made a personal trip to interview him! Franco was quickly swayed when he saw that, unlike many others his age, he was not easily intimidated nor was he frightened by authority! He had spoken to Franco clearly and truthfully and had expressed his own ideas for the law and for fairness in the social systems.Franco saw that this young man's desire for fairness, respect and honor would be qualities that would eventually be well received especially in the northern provinces where these qualities were demanded of the men of authority that would be left in charge.Shortly after his graduation from advanced studies, he was awarded the post of "Mariscal" for the region! His duties as the Field Marshal were many! Because he was a rising star in the new movement, his appointment was over the military as well as the civilian matters that came before him! He had also been appointed as a liaison between the military and civilian authorities for the entire area! The young Mariscal Romero knew that he had come a long way from the days of his youth when he was painfully thin and barely surviving in a dying environment. His own allegiance was torn between both distinctive sides! There was a sense of gratitude that had taken him to the Nationalist government who had recognized his capabilities and had given him social status! Yet, there was also the other side of him that had never forgotten his home town in Asturias! His entire family had been poor, and he had been raised in the poverty that gripped the nation! There were times when he would go to bed hungry and praying that the following day would be more fortuitous than today! Silently, he knew they would not be, but his life had a meaning and with meaning there was also a sense of happiness that came with the expectations that something might happen the next day that might change his life forever! He wondered how many other young men his age had gone to bed each night with similar wishes? Despite his assignment he hated the finality of death and despised meaningless killings! This had been the way he had interpreted the Civil War! In many ways, he knew that he was being hypocritical in his beliefs! Every time he would condemn a peasant to death, he had felt the penalty and hated himself for discharging the dark duties of his responsibilities. No one knew nor realized the many times he had been awake all night when he knew he would have to render another life or death sentence on someone that had been taken before him! The allegiance he had for the Nationalists was genuine, but it had been for all the wrong reasons! Neither of the governments, whether old or new, offered very much hope for the future of the country! It was merely an attempt for survival, and he had chosen his fate!

The Republicans had also burned many of the Catholic churches, thus depriving the citizens of the only ray of hope that had been available to them! The people within the government, firmly in command, had determined that the churches had not done nearly enough to quiet the demands of the people! They had systematically removed many of the priests from their churches, many of whom had turned up dead along some uninhabited country road! The nuns had been raped and ravished, many of them buried in small parcels of land along with the skeletal remains of unborn babies that had been unmercifully killed before having a chance to enjoy the good concepts of life! Even the few animals that were alive had shown more decency than the government, and it had been all in the name of justice! These had not been merely crimes against mankind, but they were also crimes against the dictates of God! How could God have allowed these ravishings to go on in a land that had always been devoted to Him? Shortly after the elimination of religion began, the Nationalists had decided to continue their own destruction of the church, each one blaming the crimes on the other! He had wondered at times what had happened to the young priest Don Joaquin! The Priest had devoted his entire life to God and the church by helping those in need! Also, he had served admirably the small town of Salinas in Asturias, often lending a helping hand to farmers that were too ill to tend to their lands! Was this Christianity, he thought? Was this what God had intended when He blessed Spain with world-wide supremacy?

The young Mariscal paused momentarily to stare at the young couple standing before him! What crime could they have committed? It was a struggle for him to hide his surprise when he saw his best friend Guillermo staring at him from the other side of the desk! Both men stared at each other quietly, neither person showing any signs of recognizing each other! Instead, theirs had been an uneasy silence that made the entire court seem uncomfortable! The penalty was final and they both knew it! The person standing before him had been accused of desertion! Even though the woman had not been named, he could only assume that the one standing beside him was either a girlfriend or his wife! Not that it mattered! All that mattered was his official charge of desertion; and yet the only crime he had probably committed had been to fall in love, just as any young man might be expected to do! There was an immediate attraction that he felt with the young woman even if he didn't even know her name! Here she was, willing to sacrifice her life for the simple pleasure of being by his side when they both took their last breaths! Even as they stared at one another, he wondered if Guillermo's thoughts were the same as his! Was he also thinking about the times that they had been Guardia Civiles and had exchanged their few pesetas into perronas to be distributed among the poor and needy. Something needed to be done, but what could he possibly do? The bailiff, a die-hard fascist, was applying pressure for him to pass down the obvious sentence! He had already heard the loud voices of the firing squad asking the men to load their rifles for another execution! The eager voices of those men in the firing squad had resonated over and over in his ears and were distoring his thoughts! Guillermo had always had a strong will; and he knew that he would never risk the other person's identity by putting before them their past friendship! Those few moments had seemed like hours as he tried to think of reasons why these two people standing before him should not be put to death! He needed more time to think! It was necessary for him to review in his own mind the crimes, if any, that these two people had committed and that had brought them to this end!

"What are these people charged with?" the Mariscal finally asked his bailiff.

"They were apprehended without any documents, Don Mariscal!" the bailiff told him. "The Captain was taken into custody while still wearing his army uniform! It is our understanding that the woman is a nurse who has also deserted! Both of them arrived here from the city of Badajoz and neither wants to answer any questions!"

Damn, the Mariscal said to himself! How could Guillermo have been so stupid? He should have at least removed his uniform and worn civilian clothes! If he had been caught wearing a pair of coveralls and a shirt, no one would have suspected him of being an army officer! The woman could have avoided execution simply by saying that she was his girlfriend!

"Was she also without any documents when she was apprehended?"

"Si senor!" was the reply.

"Is that true?" he asked the prisoner! "Is it true that you are a deserter?"

"I am what you say I am! I can neither deny nor affirm what you say!" Guillermo answered.

"Are you married to this woman?" the Mariscal asked.

"No! We were going to be married, but we were caught and they brought us here!"

"Well then, if you aren't married, I hardly consider her to be a deserter!" the Mariscal answered. At that moment the woman raised her hand indicating that she had something to say! The bailiff tried to silence her, but the Mariscal raised his hand and silenced him, allowing her to speak!

"Senor Mariscal, we were in Badajoz and arrived here by train! We have both served in the Nationalist army! It is our desire to live together; but, if that is impossible, it is our wish to die together! Spain is lost and there is nothing to live for!" she said.

"No es verdad!" (That's not true!) the bailiff interrupted. "She has been accused of killing a member of the African army! It is our understanding that it was the Captain who did the actual killing!"

"Is that true?"

"Yes sir, I'm afraid it is! What the bailiff is not saying is that she was attacked while she was on duty as a nurse! The assailant was trying to rape her! In defense of her honor, I admit to killing him! If that is wrong, then, I'm prepared to take my punishment! It is up to you to decide!"

So that was it! Guillermo had lost nothing of his skills! What he had just told him had been said knowing how the Mariscal felt about honor! If it was up to him, there would be no way that the Mariscal would consider executing him for killing someone who tried to rape his woman! If one of those animals tried to rape this woman, it would have been just like Guillermo to intercede! He was quite sure Guillermo had asked in silence, what would you have done if you were in my shoes?

"Senor Mariscal, the firing squad is ready for the sentence! It is almost two o'clock and they had expected to execute this pair before siesta time!" the bailiff said with an air of annoyance!

Good! The Mariscal said to himself!! Without realizing what he had done, the bailiff had just given him several valuable hours in which he would think of a way to help his friend! Of course, he knew that the two or three hour siesta was almost sacred! No one dared to work during this time! The Mariscal knew that the streets would be deserted and there would be nobody working during the hours of siesta! In general, the time allowed for the afternoon rest was two hours; but there were also times when circumstances would demand an extra hour! With any luck, he knew he would have at least three hours to think of what he could do to help Guillermo! Perhaps it would be best if he sat quietly at home during this time in his own study and think over calmly the alternatives that were available to him!

Without addressing the bailiff, he stood up from his desk and glanced at the two prisoners standing before him. "It's almost siesta time! There are still some questions that I want to ask this prisoner! I am, therefore, directing you to return these people to their cell and we can continue with the trial after 'la siesta'!"

"Pero, Senor Mariscal, no es necesario! La ley es la ley, y para los que han desertado, la pena is final!" (But sir, it won't be necessary! The law is the law and for deserters, the punishment is final!) the bailiff said. "If you will say the word, the sentence can be carried out before siesta time!"

"Quien es el Mariscal? Eres tu o soy yo?" (Who is the Mariscal? Is it you or me?) "I will decide what the penalty will be and when it will be carried out!" he answered.

The bailiff knew better than to interrupt or contradict his boss! His job was secure as long as there were no altercations, and he liked what he was doing! It did however, seem a bit strange that the Mariscal had never before shown any reluctance in handing down a sentence, but there was something about this prisoner that was making him act strangely! It was almost as if he had no fear of the firing squad! Whatever it was, it was none of his business! As far as he was concerned, he was happy to use the extra time to visit his young lady friend who would be waiting for him! It would be his time to relax with a couple glasses of red wine and, perhaps if the Mariscal was will to extend the siests time for an additional hour, he might have time for a little sex with his young friend! Since his boss had appeared anxious to hold off the execution, maybe he would see if the siesta time could be extended by another hour!

"Don Mariscal, que le parece si la hora de la siesta es extendida una hora mas?" (How about extending the siesta time by another hour?)

He knew that ordinarily the Mariscal had always been a stickler for time and would probably turn him down! But today, he didn't refuse at all! "Esta bien! Nos veremos dentro de tres horas!" (Very well, we'll return in three hours!) was all he said. As soon as he had made his decision, the bailiff went over to the prisoners and guided them back to their cell! As they were about to leave the courtroom, Guillermo hesitated for a brief moment and turned his head for one last look at the Mariscal! The Mariscal, still standing by his desk, returned the stare! For one split second, he thought he had seen a slight smile appear on Guillermo's face as he was led out of the room and back to his cell!

Everyone seemed happy with the decision! The bailiff immediately locked the cell and went home! Before leaving, he dismissed the members of the firing squad who had been waiting for the prisoners. One of the men asked him what happened and why the decision had been delayed; but the bailiff was in too much of a hurry to offer an explanation! Instead, he merely told him, what difference did it make? At least now you have an extra hour to go to the taverna and drink your wine! As for me, I'm going home and I'll see you when I get back!

The Mariscal ordered his driver to take him home! The young man asked if he should wait. He was told not to wait and that he should come for him within three hours and return him to the courtroom! His mind was on many things as the slow moving car travelled down the Avenida de la Luz through the downtown area. His mind was on the two prisoners that had been taken before him! At first, he almost wished that they had been taken to another Mariscal in some other area, but the more he thought about it, he became satisfied that they had been taken to Toledo instead of to someone else who would have passed the mandatory sentence and would have executed them immediately! At least he now had the advantage of some extra time! Not that it was great; because after all, he only had three hours in which to do something to help his friend! He removed his shoes and lay on his cot trying to think of what he could do! Nobody except him had known that he had never been able to accept many of the new laws imposed by the Fascists! Even if he wanted to go against the Fascists, he couldn't do it while dressed in a military uniform! No, if he did something illegal, he would need a disguise where no one would be able to identify him or else all his efforts would have gone for nothing! Whatever he decided to do, now was the time! He would need to be quick and he would have to be thorough! Also, there could be no turning back because he would only have one chance! Hell, he thought! If he was going to be thorough and have only one chance, he would find a way to free the prisoners! Guillermo would know what to do once he was freed! If he succeeded in what he was about to do, his friend would be a free man; if not, he would be compelled to pronounce sentence! Then, both Guillermo and Dolores would have to be executed! That was the law, and damn, how he hated the law!

There was nothing he could think of that would help his friend while still protecting his own job! He had noticed an air of suspicion with the bailiff when he decided to put off sentencing the two prisoners! Whatever he might decide to do, he was going to need to be careful and not arouse any suspicions! One of the edicts that the Nationalist government had put into effect was to pay a handsome reward to any informer that reported anything that

would be treasonous to the new government! Although he and the
bailiff had a reasonably good working relationship, he also knew
that in these days of uncertainty there was no one that could be
trusted! Nobody was above suspicion! These had been but a few
of the many new laws that the new government had already put
into existance! The more he thought about Guillermo and what he
could do to help him, the more his mind became a blank! He found
himself trying to put aside the images of the past when he and his
friend had gone to the money changers to distribute the 'perronas'
among the poor! It was difficult to imagine how he had been able
to rise so quickly in the new government, and his friend had come
down to a point where he was about to be executed? How was he
to live with himself if he passed on a death sentence to his friend?
There were so many things about this new government that he
had found deplorable; and there were scores of many innocent
people who were going to suffer for no reason! One other annoying
fact was that it was now early spring; and the British Prime
Minister, Neville Chamberlain had issued a report recognizing the
government headed by Generalissimo Francisco Franco. One day
earlier, he had learned that Manuel Azana had resigned from office,
had unceremoniously declared that the war had been lost, and no
longer wanted any more Spaniards to make useless sacrifices!

Juan Negrin had promoted Communist leaders such as
Antonio Cordon, Juan Modesto and Enrique Lister to senior
posts within the army. The commander of the Republican army
of the center, Segismundo Casado was thoroughly convinced that
Negrin was planning a Communist coup and with the support of
the Socialist leader Julian Besteiro and several other disillusioned
anarchist leaders, established an anti-Negrin National Defense
Junta. Several days later the news reports said that General Jose
Miaja and Colonel Garcia had joined the rebellion and had ordered
the arrests of the Communist leaders in the city. It was reported
that Negrin had made an attempt to escape into France, had
ordered Luis Barcelo, Commander of the First Corp of the Army
of the Center to try to regain control of the capital! His troops had
entered the city and there were many fierce battles within the city
of Madrid! Anarchist troops led by Cipriano Mera were able to

defeat the First Corp.capturing Barcelo who was quickly executed! There were also some reports that Segismundo Casado had tried to negotiate a peace settlement with General Franco, but Franco refused and instead demanded an unconditional surrender. The members of the Republican army that were still alive were no longer willing to fight and allowed the Nationalist army to enter Madrid virtually unopposed! The reports were circulating, saying that General Franco was planning to announce the end of the Civil War the following day!

The Mariscal realized that while the formal end of the Civil War was at hand, there was no way of stopping the guerilla movement that he knew would soon be accelerating in the Northern provinces! Up until now, the activities of the Milicianos had been rather subdued, but these could be expected to increase now that the war was officially ended! The peasants living in the northern provinces were simple people but very idealistic in their own beliefs! Adding to their hatred was the fact that Franco, who had been born and raised in the province of Galicia, had brought the African Army into Spain! To these people the introduction of foreign Moors into the country was an unpardonable sin that could never be forgiven!

Now as he lay in bed thinking about the problems that remained, an idea suddenly came to mind! He had previously wrestled with his need to help some of the poor people who had suffered so much in the war! As much as he wanted to, his job as Mariscal prohibited him from getting involved! As an alternative, he had thought about disguising himself somehow while he was helping the people! If he were caught giving aid to the enemy in his uniform, he would be executed on the spot; but if he wore a disguise, then no one would know who he was! The idea had been planted in his mind! Now that he needed to help his best friend, the time had come to put his plan into action! He smiled to himself, pleased by what he decided to do, jumped off the bed and quickly left the building by himself to an unknown location! There was no way of knowing where this new idea was going to take him; but, the first time, he felt it was something that he needed to do immediately! Once he thought about it, it almost became an obsession! There was a firm determination that there was no one who would stop him! At least he now had an idea as to how he was going to help his friend!!

At some point in time during the siesta, a tall, sinister looking figure dressed in a pair of coveralls and a simple white shirt entered the jail through the rear entrance! He looked carefully in every direction making sure that no one was seeing what he was about to do! The tall figure was wearing a full face mask with small cut outs for the eyes and mouth! He wore a pair of 'alparagatas' as he quietly opened the door and walked directly to the wall where all of the keys to the cells were hanging. Good, he thought! They were all there! Positive that the cotton slippers with the cord soles would be quiet and wouldn't attract any attention, he walked briskly down the long hallway passing empty cell after empty cell that had housed prisoners before their execution! Far down the hall, he thought he heard voices! At first he was startled, but soon realized that the voices were those of the two prisoners that were awaiting their punishment in their cells. Quickly, he went up to the cell making certain that no one was watching him and raised his forefinger to his mouth as a signal to Guillermo and Dolores to remain silent! Then he took one of the keys from his pocket and quickly slipped it into the lock on the cell door! What he needed to do had to be done quickly and quietly making certain that he was not arousing any suspicion from anyone! When he was satisfied that he was alone, he unlocked the door of the cell, slipped a note under the cell door and quickly ran away!

Guillermo was the first person to raise the piece of paper and wonder who this strange visitor had been! Could it be that someone had set up a trap and would kill them as soon as they were seen walking away? For the first time, he felt shivers going up and down his spine as he thought of Dolores possibly facing the end of her life in such a manner! These were certainly strange days in Spain when anything could happen, and it usually did! He noticed that the visitor had still been holding his index finger to his mouth when he signalled with his hand to Guillermo and pointed to the note! Before he had retrieved the note he noticed that the strange visitor was out of sight!

"The door is open! Leave immediately through the rear door!

Someone will be waiting to take you and Dolores to Galicia! You

will be happy there! Say nothing to anyone!"

There was still some apprehension as to whether or not he whould do what the note instructed him to do! The fact that whoever the stranger had been knew the name of his future wife was puzzling! If it was a way of getting him to try and escape, why would he have apparently made arrangements for them to be taken to Galicia! No! Whoever it was, it was not intended as a trick! Someone had come to their rescue and there was little time for him to make what might well be the most important decision of his life! As mysteriously as he had entered, the masked stranger had disappeared and was no where in sight! It was a mystery how the stranger could have disappeared so quickly without anyone seeing him!

"I'm wondering if we should take the chance, Dolores? I have no idea who the stranger is! For all we know there may be someone waiting to shoot us if they see us trying to escape!" Guillermo said.

"Don't be a fool!" she answered. "There is no need to do that! You know as well as I that they plan to execute us as soon as the siesta is over! Whoever it was obviously knows us! But who could it be?" she asked.

Guillermo did not answer! Instead, he let out s slight smile and nodded his head! The thought came over him that somehow the Mariscal had been involved! It would be too risky for him to give them their freedom, but he must have had someone who had done the work for him! Could it be??......he thought! Nah!....he reasoned! The Mariscal was much too important a person in the new government to do such a thing......still.....who knows? The more he thought about it, the more he reasoned that whoever it was had been sent by his friend! As soon as he saw the Mariscal, he knew immediately that he wouldn't have the nerve to order his execution! They knew each other very well and had gone through too many different matters together! The only thing he knew was that he had one chance to escape and a stranger had entered the jail and given him that chance! If the masked man arrived unnoticed, then, he was almost certain that he and Dolores would also be unnoticed if they tried to escape!

"Tienes razon!" (You're right!) he told her. "C'mon. let's get out of here and see where it takes us! At this point we have nothing to lose!"

As soon as they got outside, Guillermo tried to shield Dolores with his body against anyone that might be waiting for them. Fortunately, there was no one around except for an old car that was slowly making its way up the street. Guillermo's heart sank to his feet when he saw the car approaching them! He waited momentarily, frightened yet eager to escape until he saw the door of the car open! A stranger came out of the car and called out to him, "Anda, ven con nosotros! Ya vamos esperando muito tempo! Ya va sendo tempo!" the man said. Whoever he was sounded like a Gallego, and Dolores began to smile! "Tio Eduardo, estamos aca! Gracias a Deos!" (Uncle Eduardo! Here we are, thank God!)

At least they were both on the way to Galicia! This had been where they had wanted to go before all the trouble began! They had faced many problems along the way and the journey had turned into a nightmare! Now, finally, a stranger had come to set them free and start them back on their journey! They had no way of knowing who he was; but now it was obvious that the Mariscal had tipped them off and they had arrived at his request! One thing was certain, he owed the Mariscal his life and he would never forget it! His only hope was that whoever his contacts were or whoever he had contacted to give them their freedom would not create a problem for him! Guillermo was hoping that someday, somehow, they would meet again but under different circumstances, perhaps to ask him who the masked man was! Somehow, he felt that there would come a time when they would meet! The hands of fate that had brought them together would make sure that they would meet again! There was no government, no war that would ever be able to destroy the spirit of the people! The road back to Galicia was long and there was still a great amount of work that needed to be done, the sooner they got started, the better!

There was a whirlwind of confusion back at the Mariscal's office in Toledo when word got out that the two prisoners were not in their cell! The Mariscal appearing angry and disturbed over what happened summoned the bailiff into his office and asked him why the prisoners were not in the cell! The elderly bailiff, unable to explain what had happened, was at a loss for words as he did his best to explain that the two people had been escorted to their cell and had been secured before going to their siesta! The explanation was unsatisfactory as the Mariscal paced the floor in search of answers that were not forthcoming! He reminded the bailiff that he had given specific instructions as to what to do with the prisoners and the instructions had not be carried out!

"Pero, Don Mariscal! Los prisioneros estaban dentro la celula cuando fuimos a morzar!" (But Mariscal, The prisoners were in their cell when we went to our siesta!) he said. The Mariscal made believe that he knew nothing about what had happened, but he also knew that the bailiff could not be trusted! This is what the Mariscal needed to give him an edge over the court employee!

"Que quiere que haga!" the man cried, seeing the angry Mariscal pacing the floor, and unable to find a proper excuse for what had happened! Secretly, the Mariscal was elated! He had never trusted the bailiff and he now realized that he had just gotten the upper edge on him! Regardless of his efficiency, the elderly worker knew very well that the penalty for an error such as this was execution! The only thing he could now do was to plead for clemency knowing that the prisoners had been released into his care and were no longer where they were supposed to be!

"If they were in the cell when you went on your siesta, then, how could they have escaped?" the Mariscal asked. He could see the beads of perspiration accumulating on the forehead of the poor man, fearing the worse!

"I don't know, sir! The keys were hanging on the wall where they belonged! I have no idea what could have happened! I can only tell you that the prisoners were in their cell before I went to siesta!" he said.

"Do you know the penalty for such negligence?" the Mariscal asked calmly.

"Yes sir! I know that the punishment is death! Please sir, I am pleading for my life! I don't know what could have happened; but I do promise that it will never happen again if you will spare my life!" he pleaded.

It had been an interesting plea but it was also one that he could easily have used on other prisoners that had been brought before him for disposition! It was the first time in their working relationship that the Mariscal felt he was holding the upper hand, and it was now within his power to manipulate his new power however he chose!

"I will spare your life!" the Mariscal finally said. "But it will have to be after you agree to the following conditions! From now on you will do whatever I ask of you without any questions! Whether or not you agree with my findings is irrelevant! You are to do exactly what I ask of you! If you should depart from any of these directives I will remind you how you allowed the escape of two prisoners that had been entrusted to you! I will then deal with you in my own way; is that clear? Do you have any questions?"

"No sir!" he muttered as he felt his bottom lip starting to quiver. "I promise to do exactly as you say! There will be no more questions asked to any of your rulings, sir!" he said.

Good! The Mariscal thought! This would now allow him some leeway in dealing with prisoners he felt were not really deserving of the death penalty! He realized that he had been fortunate in allowing one prisoner to escape, but who could say how many more prisoners he would need to help escape from the arms of the Fascists! One thing became perfectly clear! For the first time, he had been able to finally get the bailiff under his complete control! The rest should be easy!

In the small town of Lugo in the province of Galicia another meeting was taking place! A group from 'Los Milicianos' had called a meeting with their counter parts in Galicia attempting to form a combined effort to fight Franco in the northern provinces! Gomez, Ramon and Chato had travelled to Lugo hoping they would be able to combine their efforts and form their guerilla unit as a combined force to fight off the Fascists advances. The preliminaries had already been arranged! The only important question that remained was in trying to decide who would be given the responsibility of passing on the orders for the destructions that were being planned! The group from Galicia had one advantage! There had been an unknown stranger who had appeared with them from time to time and had come to their aid on several occasions. This person always wore a hooded mask with cut-outs for the eyes and mouth! He dressed just like one of the peasants with coveralls and usually a white shirt and always wore a pair of work gloves when he was working with them. Nobody knew who he was; but they did know that he seemed to have a thorough knowledge of their movements as well as the movements of Franco's armies. The person was a stranger; and the only person who had seen him had been the new fighter that had been released from jail just moments before his execution. All of the communications with the masked person had been by written notes and nobody had ever heard him speak! It had been he who had contacted the underground and had asked them to go to the jail and to pick up a man and a woman who were being tried for desertion! He had freed both people and just as mysteriously as he appeared, he quickly disappeared out of sight! Whoever he was, it seemed quite obvious that he was bitterly opposed to the Nationalist movement! Guillermo listened to what was being discussed, but offered no opinions! The person had been as much of a surprise to him as he had been to the others! All that he knew was that he and Dolores had been spared from execution and both of them were among friends and in a safe place!

Now that Franco's army had assumed complete military control of the country, the only resistance he had was from the underground efforts of a few true patriots that remained. By combing their forces, each had a distinctive advantage over the others! The group from Asturias seemed to have both the know-how and the manpower; but it had been the Gallegos who had been able to steal the necessary weapons that were going to be needed! Before Franco had entered Galicia, the small band of underground fighters had raided many of the ammunition storages and had stolen a large quantity of grenades, many sticks of dynamite and the rifles that were needed to arm their operatives. The reports of their activities had flooded Franco's headquarters; and having himself been born and raised in Galicia, he knew very well of their tenacity in fighting and their determination to give the invading armies as much destruction as they could! Franco had issued a firm order that anyone accused of being an underground fighter would be subjected to an immediate death sentence by firing squad. This information had been passed on to all of the Mariscals in every district of Spain! The reports of the executions varied throughout the country, but it was believed that as many as 50,000 people had already been executed! The only pockets of resistance that remained were those in the northern provinces! With the surrender of the government, firing squads seemed to be popping up everywhere! The killings had turned into massacres of entire families and villages around the country! Anyone who seemed the slightest suspicious of helping the enemy was quickly executed! The Republican army, in retaliation for the atrocities committed by the Nationalists, also began their own systematic executions! It was believed that the total executions carried out by what was left of the Republican army had also exceeded 50,000 people! Most of the executions were carried out in hidden kangaroo courts among the southern provinces. Simple peasants feared walking outside their homes for fear of what they might be accused of doing! The only place that the people could go for safety was the few existing Catholic churches; but many of them had already been destroyed, first by the Republicans upon orders from the Communists, and later, by the Nationalists who were eager to blame the destruction of churches on the opposing party! The truth was that both had been deeply involved and only a few churches had been left standing! Spain had always been a deeply religious country and had been left without any semblance of organized religion! Priests, in order to escape execution and torture, were compelled to abandon their clerical robes and Roman collars and wear regular civilian clothes in order to avoid detection. Nuns had also disappeared from view! Many of them had been raped! When sections of convents had been unearthed, they were faced with the skeletal remains of young infants that had been killed; and the remains of many younger nuns who had committed suicide rather than to face the cruel and torturous advances of the attackers, primarily from those that were members of the African Army!

An organized resistance seemed imperative if only to bring some order to Spain! The underground guerilla units remained hidden when they grew in numbers and strength. Fortunately, they had found protection in many of the caves that had been excavated along the base of the Cordillera Cantabrica! The peasants who had lived along the northern provinces had been well trained and had learned every one of the caves that was available for their concealment. So great was the movement that Franco soon encountered problems within his own armies from soldiers that wanted no part of tracking down the members of the underground! The large growth that the underground was experiencing was because it was becoming the only source that provided safety for its members. Women and children became part of the movement and would remain hidden inside the caves when the men would go out on missions and create as much destruction and havoc as possible while trying to stop the advances of the conquering armies!

Cuevas en Asturias

Soledad had been left alone with Javier, and was now feeling uncomfortable with the stroking of her thighs, which she felt was indecent! For several moments she had to admit to herself that this handsome person seemed likeable, and not at all like some of the men she had known! In the back of her mind she remembered the words of her father telling her that Sevillanos and people from along the southern provinces were decendents of gypsies who had invaded the southern areas of Spain years ago in search for social acceptance! Her father had also told her that many of these people had migrated from countries such as Hungary and Roumania and were people who lived on whatever they could steal from the people! She remembered him saying something about how they had been chased out of their own countries and had settled along the southern coast of Spain because they liked the warm and temperate climate! Since they lived mostly in the outdoors, the cruel winters of the North would no longer hinder them since they could live in their carriages and tents without any fear of the weather!

There were many other thoughts that were slowly coming to mind! The vision of the intruders that had entered her home had also said that they came from Andalucia and from the southern areas! Each time she blinked her eyes she could still see the hungry look on their faces when one of them announced that he was going to rape her and that she would become 'his muneca'! These words and the vision had never left her! As far as she was concerned every person who came from the South was evil! Now that this handsome man had come into her life, yes, she had found him pleasing but not quite acceptable! After all, he was a prisoner and an enemy of their group! Here he was trying to manipulate her by stroking her thighs that would lead to a violation of her body! Was he really so much different than the other intruders? Without any warning, she arose quickly from where she had been sitting! In a fleeting second she grabbed hold of her rifle; and, before he was able to get out of her way, she swung the stock of the rifle and slammed it with all her might against the side of the prisoner's head! Javier was forced to take a backward step to get away from another blow! There was a steady flow of fresh blood coming out of an open wound and soaking his clothes with the red liquid! He began to feel dizzy and felt as though he were about to pass out! Soledad raised the rifle again and slammed the stock of the weapon into his crotch, causing him to yell out in a fresh burst of unbearable pain!

"If you touch me again," she told him angrily, "I'll put a bullet in your heart!"

Javier was undecided as to whether he should attempt to hold his hand over the opened wound on the side of his head or to hold on to his aching crotch!

"Hija de la gran puta!" he cried out. "No tienes compasion de nadie!" (You son-of-a-bitch! You have no compassion for anyone!)

"Sin verguenza! Vete a tocar a tu madre!" she said.
(Shameless one! Go touch your mother!) "Now, you are going to
tell me everything you know if you want to continue to live! When
my partner returns, he will deal with you; and if he has lost his
nerve, then, I will!" There was fire and venom in her eyes and in
her voice as she spoke. He knew she was quite sincere in what she
was saying! This woman was obviously a real bitch and wouldn't
hesitate to do what she said!

"Give me a cloth to place over the open cut and stop the
bleeding!" he asked.

She handed him a dirty cloth that had been laying on
the ground and tossed it at him while he quickly placed it on the
wound trying to stop the flow of blood! Just then Chato came back
inside and was surprised to see the prisoner's clothes covered with
blood! He wondered if perhaps the prisoner had tried to molest her!

"Quieres que lo lleve pa'tras y que lo liquide?" he asked
her. (Do you want me to take him into the rear and liquidate him?)

"No!" she answered. "Todavia no! Vamos ver que libre
tiene la lengua!" (No! Not yet! Let's see how loose his tongue is!)
she answered.

Chato noticed a certain coldness in her voice as she spoke!
She was young and attractive, but he would never want to be her
husband! The poor man would have been dead after their first
argument! He did mention that Javier had told him something
about a large ammunition depot that was located on the outskirts of
Madrid. He had tried to get his prisoner to tell him what he knew,
because one of their main problems had been a lack of ammunition
that was available. If he could find out where the ammunition was
being stored, perhaps Gomez would want to plan a raid, salvage
what they could get, and then blow up anything that remained!

Javier was still in pain as his hand was still holding the
dirty cloth he had been given to stop the blood. When he refused to
answer their questions, La Muneca raised the stock end of the rifle
over her head and was about to strike him again! "No hagas eso,
Muneca!" Chato ordered. (Don't do that!)

"Y porque no? Este cabron no quiere hablar!" (Why not!
This bastard doesn't want to talk!) she told him.

Chato asked him once again the same questions but this time his tone had been less threatening! The man squirmed in his chair while eyeing Muneca who was still standing over him with her rifle in her hands. After a few moments, he gave them the information they had been seeking! He outlined exactly the spot where the depot was located and even told them the number of guards they could expect to be guarding the area! Chato wrote everything down on paper then, handed Javier a cup of coffee and allowed him to drink it with no further questioning. He had been promised his freedom if he answered the questions, and, while it had been an option, he had his own doubts that this bitch would ever allow him to leave the cave alive! Just by sitting inside the cave he had learned too much about their movment and knew exactly where they were located!

"Cuando me van dejar salir?" (When are you going to let me go?) he asked.

Chato remained silent! It was these decisions that he hated to take on his own! His idea was to wait for either Gomez or 'La Pasionaria' to return! They were the ones who would know what to do! Muneca got up from her chair and walked slowly over to the prisoner!

"Ven conmigo! Ahora te voy a dejar salir!" (Come with me! I'm going to set you free!) she told him.

Chato gave her a surprised look! This young woman had turned into a blood-thirsty fighter! Experience had already told him that these types of fighters were the worse kind!

"Wait until Gomez returns!" he said.

"No! That won't be necessary! I know what to do!" she said as she poked the barrel of the rifle into Javier's rib cage and ordered him outside and into a wooded area just behind the cave! After a few seconds, Chato heard the sound of gunfire! It had been just a single shot, but he instantly knew what she had done! Ordinarily, he would have reprimanded her or said something, but he could see that this was not the kind of woman that would have accepted being reprimanded by anyone! All that he could do was to leave her up to Gomez or to La Pasionaria and let them reprimand her! They would know how to handle her! As for him, seeing her in action only added to his own fears! With her, the secrecy of the group would be compromised and he started to wonder if perhaps they might not be better off without her?

Toledo

It was almost midnight when the Mariscal decided he had had enough for one day! Today had been one of the days when he had not been expected to have anyone executed! It was a welcomed relief! Nobody knew how much he dreaded pronouncing a death sentence on some poor peasant who probably didn't know what he had done in the first place!

Unfortunately, the death penalties under Franco's orders had become a daily ritual! Executions were carried out nearly every day; and while some of them may have been deserving, there were many others who didn't know what crimes they were being accused of! As time went by, the more he had gotten to hate his job! Many times while in the loneliness of his room he had wondered how he, coming from a poor environment, had ended up with such a responsible job? The jurisdiction of a Mariscal exceeded civil responsibilities but also included military matters that required rapid dispositions! The thought ran through his mind of the day that General Franco himself had come to interview him! All of his life he had spent being truthful and straight forward, and now he felt he had been successful in convincing the General that he had been well suited for the job! He now wondered if he had been truthful? Had the job turned out to be much too painful for him?

At first, he had dealt mainly with civil matters! There was always the problem of excessive taxation that was being applied to some of the peasants! These were easy cases to resolve! All that was needed was to order a tax reduction, and everyone was happy! Everyone knew that any tax reductions would be temporary; but, at least, a short term relief was better than none at all! As time passed by, the work became steadily more rigid because it now involved more serious penalties and the infractions dealt with desertions on both sides! The penalties were a quick execution! If a person had deserted the Republican army and had joined the Nationalists, he would be given the death penalty by the new government! If, on the other hand, the person had been a member of the Nationalist army and had been charged with desertion, he would also be given a death sentence by the Mariscal! Military desertions without any meaning were one thing, but there had also been cases where the desertions had been justified! He had seen times when a man would choose to desert because his family was starving and had nothing to eat! Other times, a member of the family had been taken ill and needed medical treatment! Even though he had always tried to remain objective and fair, there had been times when his own objectivity had began to fade; and he wondered if there would ever come a day when the entire country would be at peace!!

Things had gotten worse now that Franco was in complete control of the country! There were many guerrilla underground units, some more proficient than others that seemed to be popping up in every province! The area that presented the most problems to the new government continued to be the northern provinces of Galicia and Asturias! Most of the units were made up of peasants who had managed to escape capture and had somehow made their way to their small farms and houses! Galicia was particularly embittered by Franco's advances and blamed him for bringing the African army into the country! He still remembered how as a Mariscal he had received notices that any African army member who appeared for prosecution was to be granted leniency! It was a way of showing discrimination that he simply did not approve! Since many of the guerilla units began as vigilanties who had banded together and had taken the law into their own hands, this resulted in having the army also taking matters into their own hands and fiercely attacking the small groups whenever or wherever they were spotted! The results were that the army intensified their pursuits, and the groups became larger in numbers and better organized to deal with Nationalist army troops that were better equipped and had the strength in numbers to put down the pockets of resistance that were coming out all over! There had been some unofficial reports that an alliance had been established between the guerilla troops in Galicia joining forces with their counter parts in Asturias.At first, he didn't pay very much attention to the reports, because one of them had mentioned that one of the leaders in Asturias was a frail looking elderly woman known as 'La Pasionaria'! Any group that needed the strength of a frail looking, elderly woman could not possibly pose any threat!

It had been some time since he had to face Guillermo, a move that surprised him! He was able to feel the hurt of their stares as they stood eye to eye, looking at each other without acknowledging that they had once been close friends! He wondered what had become of him and if he had joined the guerilla forces in Galicia? The memories he had about when they had been Guardia Civiles had been happy ones that he would never forget! He still remembered how it had been his friend that had introduced him to the local tavernas and the relaxing effects of red wine when the day was done! He had been a true friend who would have gladly given up his life for him if the situation were reversed! As soon as he saw him with the young woman, he wondered if his friend realized that he would never be able to sentence him to death no matter what offenses he had committed!

It was nearly midnight and he was still wide awake! He got up from his bed, put on a pair of alparagatas and decided to treat himself to a fresh bottle of wine! He had made a vow never to drink when he was on duty; but now his duty day was over and he needed something that would help him overcome the thoughts and fears of the times! As he was about to open the bottle he heard a light knocking at the door! It was late and the Mariscal felt a little apprehensive about opening the door to strangers so late at night! Who could possibly be calling on him, he wondered? He paused for a few moments thinking that whoever it was would probably go away! The person, whoever it was, did not go away! Instead, he knocked once more, this time a bit harder than before!

"Quien es?" he asked, but there was no reply. The Mariscal felt a cold sweat creeping over him! He wondered if it wasn't one of the guerilla units who had come to cause him harm! Quietly, he walked over to his uniform and slowly withdrew his revolver and cocked the weapon as he went to the door!

Once again he asked who it was and once again there was no answer! The Mariscal hurriedly put on a pair of pants and held the revolver in his hand ready to fire as soon as whoever had come to the door decided to enter the room! He unlocked the door and allowed it to open just a bit while he remained inside shielded by the wall with one hand on the door knob and the other clutching to his revolver and aimed at the intruder! The door opened just enough for him to see the tall figure of a man! It was a man that he would have recognized immediately no matter where he was!

"Guillermo!" he said, still surprised to see his friend. "Que haces aqui?" (What are you doing here?)

"I wanted to thank you for what you did! I needed to come back to see you after such a long time has passed! Como estas, hermano?"

The Mariscal took his hand and gently pushed him inside the room. He glanced both ways to make sure that no one had seen him! When he was satisfied that they were alone, the two men embraced and held on to each other, in love and in friendship, as they had done many times so long ago!

"So, you are the Mariscal!" Guillermo said smiling. "I should have known! You've come a long way, Flaco! Tell me, what happened to that skinny guy that used to go to the money changers to trade our pesetas for perronas to feed the hungry?" Before Flaco was able to answer, he reached into his own pocket and pulled out a perrona that had been cut in half! Guillermo looked at the half coin and slowly handed it over to the Mariscal! "Here, I made this for you!" he said. "I am keeping the other half as a reminder of things we did when we were both much happier and were united in a common cause!" Flaco took the half coin, looked at it carefully and placed it in his pocket!

"Not much has changed, my friend! I am still Flaco and my own personal ideas have not changed very much! I was awarded this job after being interviewed by the General! I was then appointed to this office!"

"Ah yes!!But now you are a rising star in the new regime! You can no longer afford the luxury of going against your mentors!" Guillermo kidded.

"It's good for you that I am here! Don't forget, I was the person that needed to pass on the ruling when you decided to kill an African army soldier who tried to attack your girlfriend! Think of what would have happened if you had gone before someone else?"

"I guess I should have known it was you! Only you would have had the sensitivity of knowing what it was like to see the love of your life being attacked in your presence!"

"So tell me! What happens now?" Flaco asked him.

"We have organized our efforts with those units in Asturias! At first, we wanted to create as much trouble as possible for the Nationalists, but, now the situation is much too serious! Flaco, people are starving and dying everywhere! Remember the days when we used to trade our few pesetas for perronas just so that the peasants could buy some food? The situation now has gotten much worse! The Nationalist army has cut off many of the food supplies and they have created an economic blockade in Republican controlled areas! The peasants are dying and there is malnutrition everywhere! There have been reports of about 20,000 deaths that have been the results of these blockades! Flaco, why don't you leave the military and come join us? We need all the men we can get!" Guillermo urged.

"I can't do that, Guillermo! Remember, everybody knows me! If I were to go to the other side, word would get out and I would get executed on the spot!" His friend noticed that he was frowning! It was the same frown that he always showed when he became overly concerned over a problem! "How many people do you have in Asturias?" he asked.

"In Asturias we have a small group that is being led by 'La Pasionaria'! She is getting along in years and is no longer as active as she used to be! There are also several men and another young woman that is known as 'La Muneca'! We don't know very much about her other than the fact that she comes from the town of Salinas and has been on her own for a while! We hear that she was keeping house for an elderly man who died! She had no other place to go, so she decided to join the group! From what I hear, she can be a real bitch! She has no fear of anything and she won't allow anyone to stand in her way! If you ask me, she is much too daring to be any good! It's those daring fools that eventually get you into trouble!" Guillermo told him.

Flaco nodded his head and his friend could see that he was hoping he could join the group! He listened to his friend rave on and on about the group's efficiency, until he was suddenly interrupted! "Guillermo, I think I have an idea that may please you! Now that you know where I live, why don't you come here in the evenings when no one is here? Tell me what your plans are and maybe I'll be able to help you! I can at least tell you whatever I happen to know about the areas or the things you may want to destroy! I usually get my information from the guards, where they are stationed, what they have stored inside the depots, and the problems you may expect! The more I think of it, the better I like the idea that may help you and your group!"

"I like what you say! But what happens if you should get caught?"

"Then, I'm going to need the help of you and your friends to get me out!" he answered.

"Flaco," he said with hesitation, "There is something else I need to know! When Dolores and I were in jail, a man appeared out of nowhere! He was wearing a face mask with cut-outs for the eyes and mouth! He slipped a note under the cell after unlocking the door and told us to leave by the back door! Who in the Hell was this guy? He had to be someone you knew!"

Flaco thought about it before answering! "Actually, I don't know him! I have heard stories of how he has helped some people, but he seems to be a bit strange!"

"How well we know! He slipped into the rear where the cells are located and slipped out just as quickly without once saying a word!"

"I know! There have been stories about him! Some of the peasants he has helped in town call him, "El Raposo" (The fox!) Apparently, they call him by that name because he never says anything but is always there when they need him!"

"Have you ever met him? Maybe you could get him to work with us! We could certainly use his help!" Guillermo said.

"I don't think so! I never met the guy! I didn't even realize that he had helped you escape! My plans had been made up to keep you in jail until I came up with a plan to help you escape!" Flaco told him.

"I'm going to have to leave, my friend! One of our operatives will soon be here to take me back! Also, Dolores will be wondering where I went!"

"She seems to be a nice lady! Probably too nice for you!" he said jokingly.

"I refuse to get married until I am sure I can have you for the best man!"

"That could take some time! Take my advice and don't wait too long! Who can tell where all of this will finally lead!" he told him.

"Are you sure I can't convince you into coming with us? Flaco, it would be just like old times, you and me!" he said.

"No! I think I can help you better where I am! As a Mariscal, I have a great amount of authority and I can help you when you go out on missions! Just come here at night, make certain that no one sees you! Knock three times on the door and I'll know it is you! From there, I can give you advice or whatever information you may need to know!"

"Very well, my friend! I guess I'd better leave!" Guillermo told him. "Hasta pronto!"

"Vete con Dios, amigo! (Go with God, my friend!) "Don't wait too long before coming back to see me!" Flaco told him as his friend opened the door, looked both ways and disappeared into the night!

Franco's blockade of Asturias was having serious effects on the people that lived there! They were no longer dying because of the war, they were now being starved and were dying of malnutrition. The rate of death became so great that it soon became impossible for the few standing churches to accomodate the surviving people that wanted to remember the loss of their loved ones with a mass! Don Joaquin had been compelled to remove his Roman collar and his black cassock, attempting to disguise who he actually was! He had found himself tossed between two separate worlds and no one seemed to be giving the respect he had been accustomed to and had rightfully deserved after so many years of faithful service. People everywhere were afraid of being seen in his company fearful that they would be branded as a friend of the church which was just as fearful as being a member of the clergy! The small church in the town of Salinas had been burned down! He had been forced to find refuge in the house of an elderly couple he had helped by working their small farm in better days! They had taken pity on him after seeing that he was homeless and agreed to take him into their home! His work in performing his profession was limited, but his own desire to return to the position he once had was always on his mind! The Republican government had been steadfast against the church from the beginning, and now that General Franco had assumed control over the government, the situation had become worsened!

One day as he was returning to his house following his evening prayers and meditations, two young men, each armed with a rifle, came up to him and asked him where he was going? When he refused to disclose his house, they took him into the cuartel at gun-point as if he was a common criminal! They continued to poke him and jab him as they walked along, with the barrels of their rifles firmly placed on his back as he accompanied them without speaking! It was well known that many of the clergy disappeared mysteriously and many of the nuns had also become victims of the new conquerors! At least they were able to find some consolation as they prayed for a better day as well as for the country that everybody had once loved! He walked flanked by the two guards, careful not to say anything nor to upset them in any way for fear of what they would do! As they reached a dark turn in the road, he heard the sound of more footsteps and saw three men coming up to them and approaching them from behind! One of the guards saw the dark shadow and made a move to turn around; but it was too late! Before being able to aim his rifle, one of the strangers came up behind him, slipped a strong arm around the guard's neck and held it tightly until the guard fell unconscious to the ground! The other guard was about to point and aim his own rifle; but, just as quickly, a woman walked up behind him and stabbed the guard several times, burying her dagger repeatedly until the life of the guard had ended and he was laying in the street soaked in a pool of his own blood!

Instead of running away, Don Joaquin remained standing over the fallen soldier and murmured several prayers after which he made the sign of the cross over the fallen soldier's forehead and his lips. Before he was able to conclude his services for the dead, he heard the voice of a young woman holler out to him, "Don Joaquin, apurate, y ven con nosotros!" (Hurry and come with us!)

"Quien me llama?" he asked as he looked around to see who it was that had apparently recognized him! (Who is calling me?)

"Te llama la Muneca!" the young voice answered. He turned quickly around and was speechless when he saw Soledad standing behind him!

"Soledad, que haces aqui?" (Soledad, what are you doing here?)

"We came to get you!" she answered. "And Padre, for your information, Soledad Alonso is no more! I am now 'La Muneca' ! Now, please, come with us where you will be safe!"

There were many unpleasant things happening here! For a moment, he wanted to remain over the body of the young soldier! It didn't matter that he was the enemy! As far as he was concerned he was a human being; and as a human being, he deserved to have the proper care and respect, whether he was alive or dead! Unfortunately, he also realized that if he were caught standing by the body of a dead soldier, he would probably be blamed for the young man's death; and he dreaded thinking about the penalty! He paused momentarily for several moments trying to decide what he should do; but, the young woman walking behind him didn't allow him the luxury of a decision! Instead, she pushed him gently into a waiting automobile as they drove off for the cave in the Cordillera! They had acquired a new member in the group even though the new member knew absolutely nothing about what he would be expected to do!

CHAPTER 8

Asturias

It was during the cold days of winter 1939 when the Spanish Civil War finally came to an end! Generalissimo Franco had become the victor and the conquest of the country was now complete. The British Prime Minister announced its recognition of the Nationalist government! Manuel Azana, after some hesitation, finally announced to the people that the war had been lost. He ordered everyone to lay down their weapons and give recognition to the newly formed government! There were some sporadic pockets of resistance in some of the southern provinces that were quickly dealt with by the newly formed government! It was the northern provinces of Galicia, Asturias and Bizcaya that continued giving the new government resistance, mainly in the towns and cities, using the benefit of the mountains along the southern coasts for camouflage and concealment from the occupying troops that were stationed in every region. For the most part, the Gallegos and Asturianos were now on their own with little, if any, support from the peasants, each one voicing their own ideas as to what was wrong with the new government!

The victory for Franco did not come without any cost! Many of his troops had been either killed or wounded and the disbursement of troops throughout the country were scarce! Hitler was well on his way to conquering Europe and he needed every man that was able to carry a rifle! Those that were too old were used to drive the vehicles that would support the troops! It became known that as soon as it was universally known that the Civil War in Spain had come to an end, Hitler immediately recalled all of the German officers and troops that had been aiding Franco during the war. It was this movement that angered Franco! He quickly sent his emissaries to negotiate with both Hitler and Mussolini asking them to allow their troops to remain in Spain and help with establishing order within the country! Hitler immediately refused the request saying, 'the Civil War had been much too costly and there was no need to continue rendering any assistance!' Mussolini, who had also dispatched several brigades of well trained troops, had followed Hitler's orders and also ordered the Italian troops to return to Italy!

Franco was left with a small army and a few units that had remained from the African army that had been under his command! In the meantime, the Soviet Union who had also sent army officers to aid the Republican army, also recalled its men back to Russia. Hitler was on a western swing through the Soviet Union; and, in many ways, he was making the same mistakes that Napolean had made in trying to conquer the Soviet Union during the coldest months of winter! Strategists have firmly believed that this was a serious tactical error that prevented the Nationalist army from staging any reprisals against Franco! Had the Soviet army officers been allowed to remain in Spain, they would be facing a badly beaten Fascist army that would have been vulnerable to any counter attacks! The problem was that both armies, the Nationalist and the Republican, had taken a serious beating; and both sides had grown tired of fighting! The enthusiasm of the people had also waned! The people as well as the troops were now starving and there was barely enough food to feed the remaining people!

The only provinces that were capable of giving Franco any resistance at all were along the northern coast! Galicia and Asturias had joined forces with the underground movement and were a constant barrier to a total conquest! Both organizations were active in cutting off supply lines and destroying ammunition depots that the General desperately needed in order to retain his superiority over the people! 'Los Milicianos' became well known as a fighting group; and it wasn't long before they were feared, not only by the peasants living in those areas but by the Nationalist army as well! So strong were their capabilities that Franco issued a directive to exterminate any member of the group who was caught and brought to trial!

The secret meetings between Flaco and Guillermo became more frequent and much more detailed! Flaco made it a point to advise Guillermo on any missions that had been planned by 'Los Milicianos' and would give him his own ideas and strategies that they should use! The missions that he considered to be much too dangerous would be discouraged as Flaco tried to recommend only the missions that had a good chance of success! It was a convenient arrangement that allowed Flaco to help his friend and at the same time allowed him to continue serving as the Mariscal for the area! Guillermo went into detail explaining the newly formed alliance between Galicia and Asturias, and even though he was initially afraid of the consequences that might result, it did seem like a unique way of combing forces and obtain maximum results!

"Guillermo!" Flaco said, "I've been advised of a convoy consisting of three trucks that will be carrying food to feed the troops in Asturias! It would be a good idea if 'Los Milicianos' could overtake the trucks before they discharge their loads! It is my understanding that they will be carrying large amounts of food and vegetables! Instead of feeding the troops, they could be used to feed the people! From what I hear, the security is not very strong on these movements!"

"Do you know when the convoy will be arriving? Also, will they be going into Oviedo or Aviles?" Guillermo asked.

"I believe they are destined for Oviedo! Do you think that your people can handle the mission? It may not be easy!"

"I'm sure they can handle it! Besides, we have a young woman working for us that can be a "real bitch on wheels"! Her only problem is that she is much too trigger happy, but we have people that can keep her under control!"

"It needs to be handled with the greatest of care! You cannot afford to have someone eager to pull the trigger of a rifle!

There are too many people and one of them could alert the guards! It needs to be handled with utmost care!"

"I'll pass on the information! Are you sure that you still don't want to join us?"

"No, Guillermo, I can be of greater use to you where I am! My only fear is for the group in Asturias! If they are anxious to use their guns, it could turn out to be a disaster! The General has already issued new orders that any member of the underground that is brought to trial must be turned over to a firing squad! I wouldn't want to need to pass sentence on any member of the group if they should get careless!"

"Don't worry!" he replied. "I'll tell them what you said!" Guillermo left the back room of the Mariscal's office and quickly disappeared into the night! After he had gone, he started to think about what they had discussed; and, if the group from Asturias had people that were too eager to use their weapons, it could only lead to a disaster! He would need to help them and make certain that there were no disasters!!

The day finally arrived when the food trucks were expected! Some of the superiors had told him that there would be military people assigned to protect the vehicles against theft and pilferage! The more Flaco remembered what Guillermo had told him about the guerilla units in Asturias, the more worried he became thinking about the young women that seemed more anxious to use her rifle than she was to use her common sense! It was a problem that would need to be dealt with because it could become disastrous if people became careless!

The rumble of the army trucks could be heard for miles while inside one of the caves, a small group of men had completed their plans and were waiting for their arrival! Guillermo had informed the group what the Mariscal had told him and everyone was in agreement! They would wait until the trucks were upon them before making any moves! After all, if they were travelling North from the city of Leon, it would be a major distribution for supplies needed by the troops that were stationed in the northern provinces! Both groups had gone over the plan many times until they knew by heart what they would do! Not one minor point had been omitted! After all, this was considered a major attack! If they could succeed in overtaking the trucks, there would be enough food in the cargo compartments to feed scores of peasants already starving from malnutrition! They had decided to wait for the truck arrivals until they were about to cross the Cordillera Andina and until they had entered the boundaries of Asturias where they knew there would be only a limited amount of resistance. Once the trucks were in their possession, the contents would be taken off the vehicles and taken to one of the more obscured caves where the food could then be evenly distributed between Asturias and Galicia!

Chato had been ordered to watch for the arrival from a high perch on top of the Cordillera where he would have a clear view of the road below! The plan was then to have Gerardo and Guillermo from the Galicia group, working with Ramon and La Muneca from Asturias, to be on the lookout below! As soon as the trucks were spotted, Ramon would go out and block the narrow roadway with a small wooden donkey driven cart, making it impossible for the trucks to pass! When the trucks came to a halt, the other guerillas would come out of their caves, overtake the drivers as well as the guards who would be seated next to them!

From the time they had planned the operation, Guillermo had been a bit apprehensive about the young woman that had been introduced to him only as La Muneca! Her previous exploits had not been overlooked! He had come to the conclusion as a military man that she was much too immature and impatient to be effective! True, she had already inherited the reputation of being a fearless fighter, one who seemed to enjoy killing! It appeared to him that she had been put in charge of the group from Asturias! If she should become careless and begin to fire her weapon, the results could give away their position and might be disastrous for all of them! It wasn't that he had voiced his opposition to anyone about having her in charge of the group, still he felt uncomfortable about what she might do! There was something he had noticed about this young woman that he didn't trust!

It was important that the group remain inside the cave and out of sight until the trucks arrived near to the area of the cave!

After all, if the trucks were spaced too far apart from one another, there was the fear that the drivers would have enough time to seek cover and would be a safe distance away! If, on the other hand, the trucks were closer together, it would be much harder for the drivers and the guards to seek cover around the bushes! The group remained perfectly silent as they heard the labored motors coming closer to them! After leaving the main road, they would need to turn into a narrow dirt road that was narrow enough to prevent them from turning around! The group was waiting while Chato was watching the convoy make their turn onto the dirt road which would take them to the northern parts of Asturias! The loud rumble of the slow moving vehicles drowned out their voices as they continued to wait anxiously for them to get closer! The group had already cocked their rifles and were ready! All that was needed was to hear the voice of their leader, Guillermo, ordering them to make their move! When the lead vehicle made its turn, the truck slowed down just enough to wait until the other two vehicles to get closer! Guillermo gave the group a hand signal to wait! La Muneca, either disregarded the hand signal or didn't see Guillermo's hand, pointed the rifle directly at the leading truck! Gerardo saw the signal and moved the wooden cart and the donkey into the middle of the dirt road. He found himself struggling with the animal as it sat down on the road and resisted Gerardo's attempts to get him to rise, but he had sat down appropriately enough to prevent the truck from passing! The driver of the truck stopped the vehicle and went to see what had happened!

"Mueve ese carro y el burro!" he ordered. (Move that cart and donkey!)

"Pero Senor! Es que el burro no quiere moverse!" he answered. (Sir, the donkey doesn't want to move!) The driver took hold of the thin strap around the donkey's head and tried to nudge him but the animal refused to move! Watching them quietly from the inside of the cave the others could see that the driver was getting angry and frustrated and insisted that the road be cleared! The frustrations were beginning to show as he hollered out to Gerardo to help him! La Muneca was watching what was happening and saw that the driver was now turning his anger toward Gerardo! Without waiting for Guillermo's order, she came running out of the cave firing her rifle until she saw the driver fall to the ground! The other drivers upon seeing the lead driver on the ground immediately brought their trucks to a sudden stop! They quickly jumped out of the trucks, leaving the doors open just enough to shield them and began to aim their rifles in the direction of the cave! La Muneca continued to fire repeatedly without aiming in the direction of the five men who had trained their own weapons on her! There was a loud burst of gunfire as the others inside the cave came out and began firing relentlessly into the direction of the vehicles!

"Que conho haces?" Guillermo yelled out! (What the Hell are you doing?) He came out of the cave in a burst of gunfire that could be heard for miles! He realized immediately that his initial distrust of this woman had been justified! This damned woman had just ruined their chances for success! They were suddenly outnumbered, as the drivers and their guards had beeen well protected behind the opened doors of the trucks! He also knew that the loud gunbursts would probably bring in troops stationed in the nearby garrisons! There was little more they could do other than to retreat to the safety of their cave! The driver that had been shot by La Muneca was struggling, trying to grab his rifle! If he was successful, he would be in an excellent position to return the fire and would probably hit La Muneca who continued to fire at them from behind a large tree! The wounded man finally grabbed his rifle and was about to fire his weapon when a masked stranger appeared from out of nowhere! He was dressed in a pair of coveralls and a white cotton shirt! There was a mask covering his face with cutouts for the eyes and mouth and nothing more! The man leaped on top of the wounded driver and swiftly kicked the weapon away and out of reach! La Muneca looked stunned by what she saw and didn't know what to do!

The masked stranger made a motion toward her to go inside with the others! He grabbed hold of the guard riding in the lead truck, and wrapped his arms around his neck gradually tightening his grasp until the guard offered no more resistance and fell lifelessly to the ground! From the corner of his eye he saw that the soldiers from the other trucks came to the aid of their fallen comrade! Good, he said to himself! At least now they are all together! The stranger made a quick turn and swiftly kicked one of them brutally in the groin! His fists were swinging wildly at the other two men until they also fell down on the ground! Just as one of the guards was pointing his rifle at him, he grabbed hold of it by the barrel and swung with all his strength striking the soldier on the side of the head! One of the two men that was on the ground had recovered enough to begin fighting! He grabbed hold of a rifle and fired it in the direction of the attacker as he watched him fall and remain motionless! Then, he took a hand grenade from his pocket, pulled the pin, and tossed into the direction of the remaining guard! The explosion missed the guard! However, the concussion and the sudden blast tossed him several feet into the air, and he fell to the floor! The men who had been hiding inside the caves came running out with large ropes, tied up the crews and immobilized all of the soldiers, disarming them and making them helpless! Once all of the crews had been tightly secured, they quickly began to empty the trucks loading the goods onto the cart and into the nearby caves!

La Muneca was aiming her rifle at the tied up men and was getting ready to fire off another blast! The masked stranger went up to her in a flash, quickly grabbed hold of her rifle and pointed the gun into the air! She stood still for a few moments wondering who this masked stranger could be! She was confused and unclear, not knowing whether she should thank him for what he did or hit him with the stock of her gun for spoiling her aim! She tried to move the rifle slowly downward and aimed it at him; but, he was much too strong! His grip was overpowering and firm as he nodded his head from side to side!

"Dejame matar a estos cabrones!" she yelled out. (Let me kill these bastards!) but the masked stranger continued to nod his head! Both of them were standing face to face while she was still holding the rifle! All of a sudden, she felt a shiver and a creeping feeling come over her as she continued to stare at him! She could only see the pupils of his eyes but they had a strange look, almost as if she were being hypnotized by this strange man!

Guillermo was standing at the entrance to the cave but decided not
to interrupt! The more she looked at him, the more uncomfortable
she felt! It almost seemed as if the stranger's eyes were looking
right through her! Once again, she tried to aim the rifle at him,
and once again she felt completely helpless! His eyes were much
too dark and expressive! She again felt the strange sensation creep
over her body and felt goose-bumps all over her body! Slowly and
without effort, she gently lowered the rifle; and instead of pointing
it at him, she slowly turned the gun over to him! There was a brief
hesitation as he gently laid the gun at her side!

It felt so wierd that this stranger had appeared at a critical
time from out of nowhere only to help them! She had no idea who
he was! Maybe it was one of the unhappy peasants who had arrived
in the nick of time! The way she felt had nothing to do with who
or what he was! It had been those penetrating eyes that had left
her mesmerized! They were so unlike any that she had ever seen
before! Still, the more she thought about them, the more she felt
something strange that troubled her! Quite obviously, they were
not the eyes of any man she had known to do her harm! But yet,
there was something very familiar about them! They were hard and
deep, but yet sympathetic! Could it be that these were the eyes of
an angel, she thought? Perhaps she would never know! The only
thing she did know was that the eyes would torment her and cause
her many sleepless nights wondering who the masked man was and
how he knew that they needed his help? All of the fury she had
felt while running out of the cave had mysteriously disappeared!
She remained calm but she was still frightened! The only thing
she could hope for was that somehow their paths would cross and
she would see him again! Those eyes seemed so venomous and
yet they also held a great deal of kindness to her! It had taken
her a long time to reach the level of daring that she had attained!
The stranger had looked at her with kindness, and, after her short
relationship with Javier, she no longer felt the way she was feeling!
This was just not like her! Soledad Alonso had died and was no
longer alive! She was now La Muneca and had promised herself
to make that name feared by everyone she would eventually meet!
Instead of helping the others, she went back inside the cave but she

had fogotten the rifle that the masked stranger had placed at her side! It was several moments before reality set in and she realized what she had forgotten. For one brief moment, she was hoping that she might get another look at the stranger; but, by the time she went outside, the stranger had disappeared and was not seen again!

"Quien era ese estrangero?" (Who was that stranger?) she asked Guillermo. He looked at her but didn't answer! He was still angry at her for what she had foolishly done that had increased the danger to the group!

"No se quien era!" (I don't know who he was!) he answered angrily. The strange look appearing on her face when the two had been looking at each other had not gone unnoticed. The only thing he remembered was what the Mariscal had told him, that he was a friend who had helped him before! Whoever he was, he had certanly arrived at the right time! He could still remember the time he had come in to the jail and had slipped the note beneath the door of the cell! He too had wondered who it might be; but, he also knew that the Mariscal, for some strange reason had not mentioned his name! Perhaps they would meet again! One thing was certain, they could certainly use his help! Guillermo promised himself that the next time he spoke to Flaco he would ask him again who he was! For now, there was another business point that needed his attention! He would talk to La Muneca and remind her of the rules of the game! She had been much too impetuous and impatient; and he wondered if she would be a danger for the group? One thing was certain! He would need to calm her down before the next mission! Although this mission had started out carelessly, everything had ended up well! All of the fruits and vegetables and the other provisions were now safely in their possession, and it was time for them to move on! The drivers of the trucks had been released as they turned the trucks around and headed back to Leon. None of their men had been injured, and they now had enough food to distribute among the hungry! It was a moment for feeling elated! He felt that the group might still be able to defeat General Franco after all! The only thing that remained was to conceal the cave and to find another cave where they could again find protection. This mission had been much too risky! They would obviously need to move away from the current location to one that would not be nearly as accessible to the enemy!

Caves in Asturias

In one of the larger caves in the Southern section of Asturias another meeting was taking place! The truckloads of food from the trucks had already been distributed among the many peasants of the area who had little to eat! Guillermo was watching happily while the food was being distributed, thinking that things were finally going their way! It was the first time that La Muneca had come face to face with the newest member of the group, Don Joaquin! He stood awed by the sight of vegetables being distributed by the small group of fighters whose only interest seemed to be in helping the people of the province! A very subdued Muneca was watching the distribution! Guillermo had already promised himself that he needed to speak to her and to calm her ambitious motives, if only for the sake of safety of the entire goup! She seemed pleased that the priest had agreed to join their group and wondered if he would remember her visit from the early days when she had come to him for his help?

"Father!" she said meekly. "Can I have a talk with you?"

"Of course," he answered. "That's why I'm here!"

"I guess you already know what happened yesterday! I know that I was wrong and should have listened more carefully to the plans, but, I guess I went on my own and placed the entire mission in jeopardy!" she told him.

"From what I hear, it seems that everything worked out fine! The mission was accomplished and now, as a result, many people have food on their tables!" he told her.

"Father," she said with some hesitation, "what I need to speak to you about has nothing at all to do with the mission! I already know it was successful; but something happened that has been bothering me since last night! There was a masked stranger who appeared from out of no where! I wanted to kill all of the Nationalists guards when he appeared mysteriously! All that I could see was his eyes and mouth! Yet, when he looked at me I felt something I have never felt before! In the beginning I wanted to kill him for getting in my way! Then, suddenly, he took hold of my rifle, pointed it to the sky and gently nodded his head as if telling me not to kill my enemies! I did my best to look away and pretend he wasn't there! It was then that I found myself unable to get his pair of riveting eyes away from me! I felt threatened and scared as they seemed to go right through me! I considered running away but I couldn't do it! Why, Father? Is it so strange to believe that a perfect stranger can have such a strong hold over you? I tried to forget him staring at me, but I found it impossible! What's worse, I think he knew how I was feeling!"

"No, that isn't strange!" he said calmly. "Soledad, whenever a person takes away a living creature whether it is a person or an animal, something very strange happens to them! The taking away of a living creature has a profound bearing on the person! Once the concept of life has been removed, there is a certain euphoria that comes over that person! It is nothing more than a temporary victory and the person feels that he has triumphed over the life of another being! Whether that life is a person or an animal, doesn't matter because the feeling remains the same! God has placed all of the creatures on earth for a definite reason, and what you felt was precisely what most people feel, triumph over death! Maybe you think you wanted to kill them all, but there was something inside of you telling you that it was wrong! What is important was that you realized that what you were doing was wrong, and that is always a good, healthy sign, my child!"

"No, Father, it was more than that! The stranger that appeared seemed to have power over all of us! I wanted to kill him, until he stared into my eyes! It was almost as though he held a grip on me telling me that it was wrong to kill! I hoped he would leave me alone and get out of my way, but he didn't move! It was as if his staring was going right through me from behind a piercing set of eyes that I can't get out of my mind! It was the first time that I felt frightened! The stranger made me feel helpless and weak in his presence! It was almost as if he was controlling my life! I became scared, not knowing what to do! Now, I have gone to sleep every night thinking about those piercing eyes! What can I do, Father?

I need to be strong and to be an asset to Los Milicianos; yet, I am afraid of what will happen if I should see him again!"

"From what I've heard, you have nothing to fear! Whoever he was, was on your side! You may not have prevailed if he hadn't come along when he did! From what I've heard, he fought gallantly at your side! He seemed to know that what you were doing was for the benefit of the people, and that was really what mattered! If that stranger had a hand in prohibiting you from killing someone, then, it was all worthwhile!" he explained.

"You still don't seem to understand, do you Father?"

"What is there to understand? I do understand that because of what happened, many starving people are able to have food on their plates tonight! People that have been mal-nourished will be able to eat! Isn't that all that really matters?"

"No, Father! It goes far beyond that! I need to know who that stranger was and why he came to us at a time of need? I need to know why his stares were so controlling that they prevented me from doing what I had promised to do! I need help, Father! I need help in getting those eyes out of my mind! I also need for him to know the effect he had on me, and why, because of him, I haven't been able to sleep at night!"

"I know that to these people you seem to be fearless! They have come to know you as La Muneca! I remember once a young girl came to me, upset because she was about to lose a young man that had enlisted in the Guardia Civil! She seemed frightened and worried; but eventually, she learned to overcome her feelings! Well, once again you need to get those feelings out of your mind and forget about him! Chances are you may never see him again!" She nodded her head, but in her mind, what he had told her had no real meaning! She had felt no better than before with the feeling that she would never forget!

"Oye Muneca!" Guillermo called out interrupting her throughts. "Come in here, we need to talk!" She walked slowly over to him and gently took her place beside him!

"What we are doing is dangerous work! If we are to be successful, we need the cooperation of everyone in the group! Today, you almost got us all killed! It cannot happen again!" he told her. "If you decide to take matters into your own hands, it has to be without our cooperation! When we give out an order, we expect that it will be followed! If you decide to change your plans, think first of what it may do to the others! From now on, I don't want you to take these things in your own hands! If you do, I will personally see to it that you are excluded from this group, do you understand? We are doing dangerous assignments and they can only work as long as everyone does their job! It was your impatience that almost got us all killed! We can't afford that! From now on, you will do exactly as you are told! If we see another incident where we feel you are not capable of doing as we say, then, we will have no choice but to give the job to someone else! We just can't afford to let those things happen again!" He was speaking calmly, but she could see that he was very angry as he spoke!

"Guillermo, please!" she asked calmly trying to change the conversation! "I need to know who that stranger was who came to help us!"

"I don't know!" he answered. "I'm sure happy that he came when he did! If it hadn't been for him, we might have all been dead, thanks to you!"

"I'm sorry for what I did and promise it will never happen again! But please, Guillermo, I need to know who that stranger was! Is there any way for you to find out?"

"I doubt it! The only thing I know is that he is known as "El Raposo"! He always seems to be on our side and appears when things seem to be going against us! I can't tell you who he is, but, I'm sure happy he was there when we needed him!"

"Do you think we will ever see him again?" she asked.

"Who knows? I only hope that he continues to know when we have a problem and comes to our aid! From all appearances, he seems to be on our side, but I have no idea who he is or how he finds out when we need him! I do know that he is getting a personality all his own of 'El Raposo' and that his actions have been a thorn to the Nationalist movement! I have asked the Mariscal, but he has said nothing!" he told her.

La Muneca walked away from him not quite convinced that he didn't know who the stranger could be! Neither he nor

Don Joaquin had answered any of her questions and she felt just as confused now as she was when she went to them. She was still troubled and unsure of what the future held for any of them! The only thing she knew with any certainty was that she would not be able to sleep tonight with those mysterious eyes still imbedded inside her mind! Without needing to elaborate on what had happened she felt reasonably certain that the hooded stranger's entrance into her life was an omen of things to come! If his mission was to help Los Milicianos, then hers would be to get this piercing magnetism out of her mind and try to forget what he was doing to her without even knowing!

Secret meeting place near Leon

It was a dark rainy night when Guillermo met once again with the Mariscal in a secret meeting place just a short distance from Leon! Flaco had felt that meeting in Toledo was much too risky, and it would be better if they met away from the courthouse! This time Guillermo had taken with him his fiancee, Dolores who wanted to meet the Mariscal under more friendly circumstances than when he was about to sentence them for desertion! There had been some reluctance to meet him, but she finally gave in to Guillermo's insistance and went with him to meet the man who had spared their life. The memory of how close they had come to being executed was still troubling; and she wondered if it was safe for her to have as much faith in this man as Guillermo? They entered through a secret doorway and into a deep cave! She was completely surprised when she saw that Flaco was not wearing a Nationalist army uniform like he did when they were taken before him! Instead, he was dressed in civilian clothes, and the warm greeting he gave her soon eased all of her fears!

Flaco quickly opened a bottle of wine when he saw them and placed three glasses on top of a makeshift table. They lifted their glasses in the air while toasting their success for the food they had been able to take from the trucks! "I understand you ran into some trouble!" Flaco asked.

"It was because of an unfortunate move by one of our members who started to fire her rifle before she had been given the order! Luck was on our side when El Raposo appeared and quickly took care of the problem! In this line of work if you succeed in a mission without any any casualties, then it is considered successful!" he explained.

"Who was the woman that became impatient?" he asked.

"We really don't know very much about her, other than the fact that she has no family and comes from Asturias! Gomez brought her into the group and she quickly turned into a hell-fire! It bothers me that she is always anxious to kill! Frankly, I don't like it! I've heard that she had some problems with Nationalist soldiers who tried to rape her, so I guess her hatred for them is understandable! There are times when she becomes impatient and that could become a problem!"

The Mariscal looked at him and remained silent as if he were deep in thought! After a few moments, he looked at Guillermo and told him,."I'm going to ask something of you! In the future I want to know everytime you are going on a mission that includes this young woman! There have been reports saying that the underground activities in the Southern provinces have been stopped! If they are true, then it means that the Nationalists will be re-directing their troops and concentrating on the Northern provinces who seem to be giving them the most trouble! If she is so anxious to kill, it can only mean trouble for those who remain! My personal opinion is that it may be wiser to control her now before she gets out of hand! There is a time to kill and a time to be patient! This woman has evidentally not yet learned which is which! I want you to tell me when she is slated to go on a mission with the other members and I'll tell you whether or not I think it's adviseable! You need to be extra careful now in what you do and the way you do it!"

"You're asking a hell-of-a-lot from me! From what I hear, she wants to go on every raid! In many ways she takes a firm stand on everything that is happening! La Pasionaria has taken her under her wing and has encouraged her! If I tell her that she can't go she'll be angry with me! Who can say," he said smiling. "She may want to eliminate me!"

Suddenly, Dolores who had been listening to the exchange interrupted the conversation! She had no idea that this Mariscal was so interested in the activities of the underground! She would have never guessed that he had been one of them all along judging by his stern approach when they had been brought before him!

"You surprise me! she said. "If you are one of us, then, why are you wearing the uniform of a Mariscal? We have been told that you have been selected by General Franco! Why are you so much against the Nationalists?" She didn't know where she had gotten the nerve, but she needed to know!

"Like Guillermo, we both began as Guardia Civiles! I too came up through the ranks! At first, I looked at the Civil War as an opportunity to strengthen our country and to have a government that was more receptive to the needs of our people. Unfortunately, this has not happened! The last Spanish government was full of corruption and with the changes in government, came more and more Socialists and Communists that were in control of the people! They started out by burning down churches, the only ray of hope that the starving people had! Little by little they wanted to control everything and the poor remained hungry while the affluent were taken care of by those in the government! In the beginning, I welcomed the change, thinking that the Fascists were capable of restoring the country to the greatness it once had! But the opposite happened! The Government of Franco was filled with even more corruption and with more disregard of the people! It was then that I became disenchanted with them! Tell me, do you know the difference between Fascism and Anarchy?" he asked.

"No!" she told him. "To me they are only two names that apparently have a meaning, but I don't know what the meaning happens to be!"

"For your information, Fascism is the principles or methods of a party that is in favor of governmental control of both industry and labor! It is usually strongly opposed to either Communism or Socialism! The term Fascism began in Italy back in the year 1919! By contrst, Anarchism is the absence of a system of both government and laws which can only lead to disorder and confusion! Think of it, if you will! Does it really matter to the people who is in control of the government? Is there really any difference? Either you have Fascism which is nothing less than a form of dictatorship that controls the very bloodline of the nation; or else, you have Anarchism, where everyone rules! In effect, you have no government! When I was first studying Political Science, we were taught that for a short period of time, Fascism could actually be good for a developing country, but unfortunately, things started to change! What we now have is no government at all, and where everybody rules you....end ...up...with absolutely nothing! That is exactly what is happening! The reason we need to do what we are doing, hoping that eventually luck will be on our side and that things will change.....for the better!"

"Do you think we have any chance of winning in the end?" she asked.

"Who can say? One thing is certain! Unless we give it our best effort, nothing will happen; and we will then have no one except ourselves to blame!"

"You never cease to amaze me!" she told him. "When I first saw you in the courtroom, I thought for sure that our life was going to end! The only person who retained his optimism was Guillermo! I didn't mind dying just as long as we were together! Even now, I doubt that I would want to go on living without him!"

Flaco let out a smile! "He is a very fortunate man to have someone like you at his side! He and I go back a long way! I could never pronounce a death sentence any more than he could pass one on me, if things were reversed! That was the reason why I needed to ask a friend for help and I was grateful that he didn't fail me!" he answered.

"Flaco, I need to know! Who is this person that wears a mask and is known as El Raposo? The young woman I told you about asked me to find out who he was!" Guillermo asked.

"Why does she want to know?"

"I don't really know! It seems she came eye to eye with him and he left an effect on her! He grabbed the gun out of her hands and laid it down beside her! That was no small fete! To her, the rifle is her lover! She is never without it being at her side!" Guillermo said, smiling.

"That's why it is important that she be contained! If she gets angry, then, so be it! It's better that she stays alive and angry than to make a foolish move that may cost the lives of others beside herself! By the way, when are the two of you getting married?" he asked. They could see that he was now anxious to change the subject!

"Very soon! We have a priest that has come over to our side and we've already asked him to marry us!"

"But, there is something that Guillermo isn't telling you!" Dolores interrupted. "He refuses to be married until he is certain that you can be his best man! He doesn't care how long it takes!" Flaco started to smile and placed his arm around the shoulders of his friend.

"Ordinarily, I would have told him to go on with the wedding! But, I want to be honest with you! I don't want you to get married until I can attend the wedding!" he replied.

"What happens if we have a child before you are able to attend the wedding?" Guillermo asked.

"Then, it will be an even happier occasion! I will have the chance of not only being the best man at the wedding; but, also, the Godfather of the baby!"

"Will you make us that promise?" she asked seriously.

"You have my word! Perhaps one of these days when the pressure lets up, I'll be able to get away and we'll have that wedding! By the way, who is the priest that has joined the group?"

"His name is Don Joaquin! I hear he comes from the town of Salinas! Wasn't that also your home town? Maybe you know him!"

Flaco nodded his head in silence! Guillermo saw that the expression of happiness had disappeared; and, its place, there was the pensive look of sadness as though he was carrying a heavy thought. "Yes, I know him well!" he suddenly replied. "He was the priest that buried my mother! Please give me my kindest regards! Tell him I continue to hope and pray that the day will soon come when he will have his own church once again so that people can return to their faith which has always been their strength!" He glanced at his watch and saw that it was getting late. "I think you had better leave now! The guards will soon be changing and will be making their rounds in the area! I don't want you to risk being caught!" he said as Guillermo finished his glass of wine and stood up!

"You know, I used to feel much better when we were exchanging pesetas for perronas!" he said as though he was getting a nostalgic feeling creeping over him!

"For whatever it's worth, my friend, so did I!" Guillermo was the first to leave the cave as he looked both ways making certain that no one had seen him leave! Dolores followed closely behind but not before she gave Flaco a brief peck on the cheek! "What was that for?" he smiled, pleased that she had seemed to have accepted him as a friend.

"Guillermo has always told me that you and he were like brothers! I guess that makes me your sister-in-law!" she said.

"Nothing could please me more! Besides, I still think you are much too good looking for him! He is much too ugly!" he said kiddingly as they both disappeared into the darkness!

Galicia

Several weeks had passed since Guillermo and Dolores met with the Mariscal! The group had been alerted to a meeting that was expected consisting of several army officers! The meeting was to be held in the city of Lugo; and judging by the preparations that were being made, it would appear that the attending officers were of field grade importance! Flaco could only guess that the purpose of the meeting was probably to discuss more effective ways of dealing with the underground movements that seemed to be getting more frequent and more destructive. Los Milicianos were getting a great deal of attention; and it was reported that they had been successful in weakening the the Fascist defenses all along the northern provinces! Eliminating this threat seemed to have reached a critical moment! General Franco had issued stern orders that these people were to be eliminated by whatever means possible and that the attacks on the convoys would need to be ended!

The Mariscal had received a list of who was expected to attend and he noticed that his old mentor Colonel Garcia was on

the list! The Colonel was now an elderly man, but his mind had
remained sharp and his physical ability had not diminished! As he
thumbed through the list it occured to him that while the Colonel
was still a senior member in the Nationalist army, his rank had
not increased! This seemed a bit odd since it had been well known
that General Franco had increased the rank of many of his senior
officers and had given out promotions to other lesser officers
serving in the army. For several moments he wondered aloud how
it could be that the Colonel had never been advanced? It had been
a long time since Flaco had seen him, and, even then, he noticed
that the elderly man who had once been so military, had reached a
point where he seemed unhappy with the way things were turning
out! Of course, he had been cautious with his comments! After all,
Flaco had been made a Mariscal, a prestigious officer of the new
army and had been specifically appointed by the General himself!
He was wondering what could have caused this oversight! If it
became known that the Colonel was a republican sympathizer,
Franco would have seen to it that he would be executed! The mere
fact that he still retained his status as a senior army officer was a
sign that he was still a member in good standing with his superiors!

Despite their guarded friendship, Flaco had the idea that the
Colonel was disappointed that he hadn't been elevated to the rank
of General, especially since many of the other officers who were
much less knowledgeable or efficient had been elevated! Although
he was the Mariscal, it was going to be necessary that he be very
cautious in speaking to him, not knowing what the consequences
might be! It seemed fairly obvious that the old Colonel felt
the same way! Whatever the reasons may have been no longer
mattered! It was going to be necessary to make certain that any
activity against the group would spare the colonel! If for no other
reason the two men had always been friendly and had been treated
well when he served under his command! There had been times
when the Colonel could have issued severe punishment for some
infraction, but he had always looked the other way! Even though
he may not have condoned some of the things he did, he had
always escaped without being punished! As he recalled, it had been
Guillermo who had always been a constant companion to him and

had also escaped the wrath of the colonel! Whatever happened to the other officers attending the meeting didn't matter! The Colonel was to be protected at all costs!

When Guillermo and he discussed the planned meeting, they both agreed that they needed to spare the Colonel! It wasn't that he thought it wise to rescue him or to take him into their confidence; after all, the meeting was intended to find ways of curtailing the underground activity and they had no idea whether or not they could really trust the elderly man! One other restriction he had told Guillermo was to make sure that La Muneca was not involved in any way! They both knew that this was going to be a critical attack, and they couldn't take the chance that she would again decide to take matters into her own hands and maybe destroy the mission! It was decided that they were going to need two caves! One cave would be used for the attack on the army officers; and the other, a good distance away from the first one would be used for their escape after the attack! They agreed that since the group from Galicia had a better knowledge of the mountains, it would be up to them to spy on the officers attending the meeting. The Asturiano group would be responsible for the actual attack with the Gallego group ready to follow in the event that something should go wrong and they would need more firepower! It seemed to be an excellent plan as they discussed in fine detail all of the terrain where the meeting was being held!

La Muneca was pleased when the group was told about the plan! She had spent all day cleaning her rifle and making certain that the weapon was in excellent firing condition and fully loaded in anxious anticipation of what was about to happen. Guillermo, who had taken charge of the group looked at his watch and decided he would need to go to the young woman and tell her the news that she was not included in the mission! He had thought about how he would break the news to her easily, knowing she would be furious! He, of course, could not tell her that the exclusion had been at the request of the Mariscal! After all, she had never met him; and if the news about him was true, he was a person that needed to be feared! Besides, there was no need for her to know the truth!

"Muneca," he said, "Come with me outside! I need to talk to you privately!"

"Espera un poco!" (Wait a minute!) she answered. "I've been cleaning my rifle and I am almost finished! I'll only be a few minutes!"

"No!" he ordered. "I need to speak to you now!" She put down her weapon, mumbling something under her breath and followed him outside!

"On this mission, you will not be going with us!" he said. Since he really had no good escuse to give her, it was just as well that he had been blunt and to the point with her!

"What do you mean, I won't be going? Estas loco? (Are you crazy?) Don't you realize you will be needing all the firepower you can get? You need me to go!" she argued.

"No, Muneca! The job is much too risky and we can't take the chance that something will go wrong! You won't be going with us and that's final!" He saw the look of disappointment and anger on her face, as she began kicking at the dirt beneath her feet! She was furious that she had been excluded!

"You must have a reason! Was it because of what I did when we went after the food trucks?" she asked. In truth, he had already forgotten the problem; but since she had been the one to bring it up, maybe he could use that as an excuse!

"That's one of the reasons!" he lied. "If something should go wrong, Dolores is going to need all the help she can get! We need you here to tend to the wounded, if necessary!"

Suddenly, all of the anger and frustration she had been harboring exploded, and he knew he was going to need to treat her with utmost care! "Suppose you now listen to me! I am one of the Guerrilleros; and my obligation is to be with them, not to be back here in the cave playing nurse maid to someone that may have been injured! I didn't do that when I was a child and my mother had a clinic at home! I'm sure as Hell not about to do it now either!" she said.

"Perhaps now you should listen to me! I am in charge of this mission, and I am the one who decides who goes and who stays! You aren't going and that's final!" he argued as he began to walk away from her!

"Was it because I made a silly mistake?" she asked. The anger was in her tone of voice! "Is that what you are holding against me? Who was the one that suggested that I not be included? Was it that masked stranger who came to help us? Have you been speaking to him? Besides, I asked you to find out who he was and you never paid any attention to me!"

"I can assure you that I don't know nor do I care who he is! I was thankful that he appeared when he did, but whoever he is is still a mystery! This mission is going to be much too risky, and it is in everyone's interest that you remain behind! The decision is final!" he told her.

She paused momentarily as though she was thinking over what he had told her! Guillermo was disliking himself for excluding her knowing how much she had enjoyed fighting their enemies! Still, he had done so after the Mariscal had spoken to him; and he must have had a good reason for doing what he did! "Well...since you don't think I can handle it, I want out of the group!" she told him.

Guillermo knew that what he had dreaded the most had now appeared! It was something he knew would happen and something that he wasn't sure how he was going to handle it! "If that is what you want, I can't stop you!" he said calmly. "Just remember before you leave, you know a great deal about our operation! We cannot afford to have one of our members leave us while angry! You know where all of our ammunition and supplies are being stored!" He realized that what he had just told her had been a veiled threat that he disliked making; even though, in many ways, he was being truthful with her!

"So, what do you plan to do, kill me?" she yelled. "Who gives a damn? My life isn't worth anything anyway! What do I have to show for my life? I was born and raised in poverty and I am still poor! What difference does it make whether I live or I die?" she answered. He could see that she was defeated and injured by what he was implying!

"You may be poor," Guillermo said calmly and without raising his voice. "but at least, you have food to eat! You didn't have food when you came to us! Maybe you aren't able to realize that it is because we value your life that we want to look out for your safety! Muneca, we know you're good!! You're damned good! But you are much more valuable to us alive than dead! No Muneca, we would never kill you! But we also don't intend to sacrifice your life foolishly!" His calm words had soothed her anger and she began to cry! It had been the first time in her young life that she had heard someone tell her that she was a valuable person! He walked over to her, placed his arms around her and said to her calmly, "There are some of us who don't want anything bad to happen to you, and I happen to be one of those people! Please don't leave us, Muneca! We all need you, especially me!" he said as he gently stroked her hair and led her inside the cave for a hot cup of strong coffee!

A small part of the group had been eyeing carefully a large concrete building located on the far side from the main garrison! They had seen a great deal of activity and had noticed an increase of troops that had been sent to guard the area! It was a clear indication that something big was about to happen! They had seen large, oversized cars, left over from the Germans, who had come to Franco's aid, arriving in a steady stream since early morning. Every member who arrived was smartly dressed in their fresh, army dress uniforms; and each had their own personal valet as they entered the building! The group noticed that as soon as they arrived, the officers were hustled out of their vehicles along with their escorts while the drivers were sent to a large parking lot located on the opposite side of the garrison! They immediately realized that if the building was going to be destroyed, there was also the need to place another explosive in the area where the cars were being parked to prevent any of the attending officers to leave the area! The group wrote down every minute detail that they felt would effect their strategy! If the building was going to be demolished, they would need to run another wire between the parking lot and the detonator. It was plainly obvious that they needed more explosives than they had estimated and there was little time for them to get the needed supplies! When they discussed their plans with Guillermo, it was decided that someone would need to go into the city and get more wire! The amount of explosives they had in their arsenal seemed sufficient for the job, but enough wire had to be obtained to run between the parking area and the cave! Since the building was made mostly of wood, they felt that upon impact it would quickly ignite and burn before the fire could be extinguished. The only thing that was important was that the parking area would have to be destroyed quickly so that the officers gathered inside would not be able to escape! Gerardo, a senior member of the group from Galicia, knew where he could steal additional supplies of wire! There was a hardware store in town and he had been friendly with the owner. He had decided to tell him a story that he needed more wire in order to repair a fence that was in need of repairs. Guillermo gave him the go-ahead and told him to be careful! They certainly could not afford an arrest of any of their members at this critical time since every member had been assigned a job and was going to be needed!

It was almost noon when they saw another car arrive! When the valet opened the car door, they saw that Colonel Garcia had been invited! Unlike the arrival of many of the others, there as no fan fare when he arrived! There were no formal greeters nor troops standing at attention and saluting him when he got out of the car. The information they had received was that the meeting would last for two days! The first day had been set aside for orientation while the second day was set aside for the meeting itself! After the meeting, all of the officers would then be free to leave! Guillermo soon realized that it was going to be extremely difficult to protect the Colonel against the planned explosion! The group decided that during the night, when the officers were sleeping, they would plant the explosives and run the wires between the building and the parking lot to the detonator! Of course, they would have to conceal the wires making certain that they remained undetected by the soldiers. Someone was going to need to be standing by the detonator, set to go off if and when they saw that the Colonel was outside the building!

When it was dark, the group from Galicia began their task! Gerardo had been successful and had returned with the large spools of wire! It was now necessary to have one of the men sneak inside the garrison and place the explosives in an inconspicuous place where they would not be seen by the guards! Manuel, the smallest member of the group, volunteered to sneak under the fence, enter the area of the garrison and plant the explosives. The building that was housing the officers was the priority! After the explosives around the building had been set, they would then go to where the cars were being parked and would plant some additional explosives in that area and run the undetected wires back to the detonator!

Manuel led the way and Guillermo decided to go with him as protection in case he should be seen by any of the guards. When they saw that the guards had disappeared inside the building probably getting ready for a change of guard, Manuel cut some of the wires that had been placed around the perimeter of the building! He had sneaked around the back and planted some sticks of dynamite underneath the building and had gone unseen by anyone! Then, he ran the wire back to the cave, making certain that it was covered with dirt as he hooked it up quickly to the detonator that had been placed on top of a small incline about one hundred feet away! When he was finished, he went over to the parking area and started to do the same thing! This was where his luck had run out! One of the guards went up to him and was about to shoot him when suddenly, Guillermo approached the guard from behind and swiftly wrapped his arm around his neck! He tightened his grip around the neck until he could see the guard's eyes bulging out of their sockets and he fell lifelessly to the ground! Both men needed to take time away from their plans to drag the dead guard away from the area and conceal the body among the trees in the Cordillera. A short time later, they returned to the parking area and completed the work! Manuel clipped away the barbed wire enclosure and crawled inside until he reached the first car. He placed several sticks of dynamite under the car and ran the wire back while he crawled on his stomach until he was a safe distance away from the lot. Once he was back, he looked both ways making certain the dead guard had not aroused the others.

"Good," Guillermo told him. "Ya esta listo!" (It is ready!) "Now, let's get the hell out of here and wait until we see the Colonel going outside to smoke one of his cigars!"

"How did you know that he smoked cigars?" Manuel asked.

"Because I once served under him! At that time, he was a chain cigar smoker, but the damned things smelled so bad that he needed to go outside to smoke them!"

"So, you are hoping that his old habits haven't changed, is that it?"

"No! He may not be smoking any tonight! It would probably make the other officers angry! Instead, he'll probably do it tomorrow! That's when we will have the best chance!"

"But suppose his plans have changed, then what?"

"Then, my friend!" he said laughing. "We'll have to wait and hope that he needs to go outside to 'pee'! He can't hold it in forever!"Guillermo said as both men had a hearty laugh!

The following morning everyone was up bright and early when the first rays of the sun were shining down on them! There was a feeling of excitement as each man went out to their assigned positions. Guillermo remained by the detonator with a set of binoculars pointed toward the garrison waiting for some movement by the officers. From the top of the small incline he saw a steady stream of officers going outside, apparently for a breath of fresh air! He had already assumed that their stay outside would not be long because there was a chill in the air! Some of the officers had come from the Southern provinces and were not accustomed to the Northern winters where the temperatures were quite different! As far as they were concerned, the damp, cool evenings were good for harvesting the lands and little else! As he stood along, he had asked La Muneca to keep her eye on the garrison but from a higher ledge that would give her a much wider and unobstructed view of the grounds in search of more guards that might be stationed elsewhere in the area! As far as he could see and prepare, everything was now in place! If they were successful, this would have been a major accomplishment and would set back Franco's efforts against

Los Milicianos for a long time! Guillermo was anxiously hoping that the delay would be until spring when he would have a new contingent of men that would be ready to replace any that might be lost! Manuel was hiding in the foothills near the parking lot, just in case something went wrong and one of the guards might have seen an exposed wire or else had seen the cut barbed wires and had aroused the rest of the guards!

At the last minute Guillermo had a change of heart and had asked La Muneca to use the pair of binoculars and look inside the compound! It was a way of making her think she was still very much a part of the team! The group waited and waited; and it seemed that every one of the officers had decided to go outside, some to smoke, some to simply standing around to kill time and speaking to each other! After what seemed like hours, they finally saw the heavy set officer appear! Muneca made a motion with her hand toward Guillermo, indicating that the Colonel had just gone outside and was lighting up a cigar! Guillermo grabbed the binoculars and trained his sight on the old man! His first observation was that the old man now appeared older than he remembered! The elderly Colonel was standing all alone at the far side of the building! Because of the morning wind, now blowing out of the south, they could see that he made several attempts to light the cigar without success! All of a sudden, he made a move away from the building trying to once again avoid the wind and tried to light the cigar! Then it happened! From out of nowhere, they saw an unexpected sight! It was the stranger again, this time dressed in a concealing mask! In a flash he jumped over the enclosure, took hold of the old man by his belt and with one strong shove, he pushed him away from the building!

"Mierda! Que have ese cabron ahi?" (Shit! What is that bastard doing there?) Manuel was the first to ask as they both saw the hooded stranger struggling to take the older man further away!

"Que se yo!" (What do I know!) Guillermo answered, as in one swift move he pushed down on the handle of the detonator! There was an immediate explosion as parts of the building flew into the air as did everything that was inside! Within a matter of a few seconds there was another explosion as the parked cars scattered into pieces! Some of the parts were set on fire and in turn ignited the other cars! A few of the guards that had been assigned to that area came running at the sounds of the explosion, not quite knowing what to do! After all of the dust had finally settled, Guillermo again looked through the binoculars and saw the hooded stranger laying on top of the old man protecting him from the blast! Once the dust had settled the old man stood up and began dusting off his clothes. In a matter of seconds the masked stranger disappeared while the Colonel stood, all alone and confused, wondering where he had gone! The attack had been a success as he and Manuel shook hands knowing that the attack had been carried out exactly as planned. The old man had been spared and the building was in shambles as fire broke out and quickly engulfed whatever remained of the structure. Whoever had been inside at the time of the blast could not have escaped! Hopefully, most of the officers had been killed and Los Milicianos could now have some breathing room until a new batch of officers was created to take the place of the ones that Franco had lost! They quickly disengaged the detonator and took it with them as they disappeared into the woods and the safety of the secondary caves!

In the meantime, and not seen by anyone else, something else was happening! The intensity of the blast had thrown La Muneca from her perch on top of the hill and threw her down a long steep incline to the bottom! She remained there, unable to move, her foot badly injured and she was unable to move! In yet another strange move, the masked stranger appeared and slowly made his way down the steep slope until he reached her! Without speaking, he looked at her foot and realized that it didn't seem to be broken! He tried to help her back on her feet, but she was in too much pain to walk!

"Dejame conho!! No necesito tu ayuda!" (Let me be, damn it! I don't need your help!) she barked angrily. She was angry with herself for allowing herself to fall and was unable to walk! To add to her anger, this masked stranger had once again appeared and she didn't want him to see her in need of help! He looked at her and without saying a word, took away the rifle she was holding and laid it down by her side. Before she could resist his actions, he picked her up in his arms and carried her down the steep slope until they reached the cave where the others were waiting. Still holding her in his arms, he carried her into the cave and gently laid her down on one of the cots! He had completely disregarded her angry comments about putting her down and ignored her pleas, making absolutely sure she was okay before leaving. Guillermo had seen him and was standing by his side! In those few moments, just as he was placing her on the cot, he saw a small metal coin fall out of the stranger's pocket! Guillermo stooped over and picked it up! Smiling he handed it to the masked stranger who quickly placed it back into his pocket! As quickly and as mysteriously as he had arrived, he quickly disappeared without waiting for anyone to acknowledge his presence or to thank him for having taken La Muneca to safety! In a split second he waved his gloved hand at Guillermo as he was leaving, but not before he noticed a smile that appeared on Guillermo's face!

After he was out of sight, Guillermo was again smiling as he remembered the object that had fallen out of the masked stranger's pocket! It was the same, 'half-perrona' that he had given Flaco when he met with him in Toledo! Now he knew that his own suspicions had been confirmed, and he knew exactly who El Raposo was! The stranger could be assured that his secret would remain a secret and nobody would ever know except him!

CHAPTER 9

Asturias

La Muneca was not the same following the episode with
the masked stranger! Something about her had changed and she
acknowledged to herself that her feelings had been changed when
the masked stranger picked her up in his arms and carried her
inside the cave! After the bad experiences she had with men, she
was determined to never again be interested in a man! It wasn't
that she didn't like them; indeed, she did! Her activities with Los
Milicianos demanded all of her time and there was little time left
for anything or anyone else. There had been those few moments
when she had been swayed by Javier's advances, but she had
also realized that her interest in him would be short lived! It was
troublesome to think of this masked stranger as simply another
man! She had no idea how he was different but he was! Whether
she was willing to admit it to herself, she had to agree that she
was attracted to him. First, it had been the tantalizing effects of
his large dark eyes that were troublesome. Now she had seen him
again, and there was little that she could do except to stare into
those eyes that seemed to go right through her! She needed to
know who this stranger was and why without any effort, he had
such an effect on her! There was something in the soft and gentle
way he had taken her into his arms and carried her inside the cave!
It had been foolish enough to wish at that moment that the cave

was much farther away, so that she could relish in her own feelings in the arms of the stranger whom she had never met. The more she thought about it, the more she felt that Guillermo knew much more about him than he was willing to tell her! The smile that appeared on Guillermo's face when something metallic had fallen out of his pocket had not gone unnoticed! There was no point in asking him again! She had done that once before and had received no answer except that he didn't know who he was! The only person she could confide in was Don Joaquin! At least he could explain to her the feelings she had! Once again she felt the need to speak to someone; but, she also needed to fight the feelings that were threatening her and the things she still had to do as a woman. There was a persistant feeling that this was a sign of weakness; and, in her line of work, there was no room for weaknesses, whether it was because of a woman or a man!

The other members of the group had also noticed the difference in La Muneca! Suddenly, she had become more subdued as time went by! Often she would sit alone inside the cave and there was a far away look in her eyes as if her mind was on other things, other than the work that was being planned. In some ways, Guillermo was pleased that he had limited her participation in the work of the group. At first he didn't pay much attention to her, thinking that perhaps it was a sign that she was growing up! There was no longer the desire to fire her rifle that she once had! The alliance between her and the elderly woman La Pasionaria continued to grow. It was almost as if the elderly woman was protecting her from the evils of communism! Muneca had listened to the elderly woman with respect, even though she had her own ideas about the new movement as well as her doubts about its success! Foremost in her mind was the poverty she had experienced as a child and the way her mother needed to convert her house into a medical clinic, just to receive a few pesetas desperately needed for survival! She also would remember how, as a child, she would go to the pier and wait for the fishing boats to arrive, so that she could gather the few sardines that were too small to be sold at the local market! All of these things had been allowed to continue while she heard of change after change of the politicians in Madrid! All of them still maintained their luxurious houses despite the widespread poverty. Expensive clothing was another luxury that was available only to the affluent few who could afford them! There was also the plight of Don Martin, and how hard she needed to work only to survive! All of these things had taken place under a Communist or Socialist government! In many ways, she blamed part of the poverty on the Civil War, thinking that had it not been that the country was in despair, the war would probably never have taken place! Now, because of, or in spite of it, here she was wearing clothes that were worn and haggard while she remained dirty and hungry! Nothing had really changed! Many of the women her age would have preferred to be at home with a husband that cared about them, raising children and training them to carry on the traditions of a proud nation! All of these things were non-existant as far as she was concerned! She hated men for what they had tried to do to her! Franco had introduced the people of Spain to the African army, and while well trained in the military and in combat, their social graces were nothing short of being barbaric! Still, the government that sought to rectify the country, stood idly by condoning their actions, allowing them to rape and attack people without the fear of being punished! No! As far as she was concerned, the war had done nothing to alleviate the hardships she had endured! It had been the result of the war that had left her bitter and pessimistic about the future! For her and other like her, there was no future! She had joined Los Milicianos out of necessity rather than of idealism! At least this group treated her with kindness and care, something she had craved for but had never had! In order for her to survive in this environment it was necessary for her to forget that she was a woman! Instead, she needed to compete in order to become an equal warrior! Certainly, she was smart enough to realize that her future was bleak and she would need a great deal of luck just to survive and reach middle age! Life was meaningless and it was only the talks she had with Don Joaquin who tried to make her feel that she was more important as a human being than she could ever imagine! Don Joaquin, was the elderly priest that she had gone to for advice many years ago when she was still a child! Now he was older and still unsettled! He had joined their group simply because, thanks to the Socialist government, he had no church nor any congregation to lead! If this was the type of world God had intended for them, might it be that almighty God Himself, had become disappointed with His own creations? This wasn't living! Instead, it was Hell on earth! Now here was this kindly old woman trying to convince her of how wonderful things would be under a Socialist government! Well, she had already seen the effects of a Socialist government; they were no different from those of a government formed by a dictator!

She was interrupted in her thoughts when the priest walked up to her and said, "Que pasa, Muneca? Te veo triste!" (What's the matter! I see that you're sad!)

"Nada padre!" she replied. "Estaba pensando! Solamente pensando!" (Nothing Father! I was thinking! Only thinking!) He walked over beside her, took her hand and sat down next to her! It seemed like the right time for them to have another talk!

"Que pasa, nena?" he asked."I somehow get the feeling that you have lost some of the fire you once had! Is there anything you want to tell me?"

"I can't really explain it, Father! I just get the feeling that everything we do is for nothing! Whoever will ultimately rule the country will rule it their own way and nothing will be improved! It almost seems as if we are fighting a losing battle!" she said. There was an unmistakable look of sadness on her face as she spoke!

"As long as we have life, there is always hope!" he replied.

"What are you hoping for, Father? Do you really think that you will one day receive whatever you hope for?"

"Why shouldn't I?" he said. "I am still hoping for the day when all of our churches will be restored and the people will have a place to vent their frustrations and pray for help!"

"Religion is dead, Father! These bastards have seen to it that it died! Nobody wants religion anymore! Look at what they did to the churches! They burned them all down and then raped and attacked the nuns! Look at you, Father! What is there left of your faith?"

"Soledad!" he said. "To me you will always be Soledad! They can destroy all of the churches and the clergy, but no one can destroy the power of the church! That will remain forever! They have burned down the small Capilla back in Salinas, but do you really believe they had destroyed my faith? Of course not! That is what keeps me alive! The church can never be destroyed, God will not allow it! But, I think there is something else that is bothering you! I saw the change written on your face when the masked man carried you inside and laid you down on the cot! Is there anything that happened that you want to tell me about?"

"No, Father! Nothing happened! I have only seen him two times, and both times he made an impression on me that I can't seem to get out of my mind! The first time I saw him I was about to kill several Nationalist soldiers. He came from out of nowhere, grabbed the barrel of my rifle and turned it toward the sky! He then nodded his head, almost as if he was telling me not to kill them!"

"That seems logical! There has certainly been enough killing in this war! Don't you think that enough people have already died?"

"But....it..wasn't that!! It was the way he stared at me! His eyes were dark and mysterious as if they were looking right through me! Father, in his eyes I saw all of the emotions of man! I saw love and hate, hope and despair, sympathy and happiness! I have never felt anything like that before! The problem is that I can't forget him; yet, I don't even know who he is or where he came from! There are times when I get the feeling I have seen him before; and, yet, he is a total stranger! Why do I feel this way, Father?" she asked.

"Perhaps it is nothing more than an infatuation! Maybe his mysterious presence is that he represents something that you are fighting for! That isn't so strange and it can sometimes happen! I find the person, whoever he is, to be daring and fearless! Yet, I don't know who he is!" the priest answered.

"But how can I find out who he is? Why are his entrances so mysterious? If he wants to help our cause, then, he should be willing to reveal himself to us!"

"Have you stopped to think! If he wanted you to know who he was, he would have revealed himself to you? Whatever the mystery of his disguise, he probably has his own reasons and we should respect them!" he answered.

"No, Father! It goes beyond that! There is something about him that has become an obsession with me, and I can't get him out of my mind! I haven't been able to sleep very much thinking about him! Father, there has got to be way for us to find out who he is!"

"Don't let it upset you, my child! Whoever he is....he is! If the time ever comes when he wants you to know, I'm sure he will tell you! If not, you should just accept him for what he is and be thankful that he was there to save you from making mistakes that could have ended your life!"

"Father, I almost hate to admit this....but.....do you know that because of him, I have almost lost the will to fight? It's almost as if he is holding his strength over me asking me not to kill and not to fight! It's a personal thing! Whenever I hold my rifle, I see him standing there beside me and pointing the barrel into the air. It's almost as if he is telling me not to fight anymore! Father, what am I to do? I need to fight! That was the reason why I joined Los Milicianos!"

"You need to do whatever your heart tells you to do! If your heart tells you not to kill another human being, then, that is what you must do! Forget 'El Raposo'! If he wants to see you again, he will return! If not, then, accept him for what he is....nothing...but ..a.fox! Be thankful that he was there when you needed him!" he said.

"Thank you, Father! I'll try, but I don't know how successful I'll be!"

"That's all you can do, my child! If he wants to reveal himself to you, he will do so! If not, then, be grateful that in a way, he was your guardian angel! We all need one of those from time to time!"

Muneca laid down on her cot! Her foot was still in pain from the fall! She went over in her mind how the mysterious stranger had known she had fallen and had been there at the right time. She agreed with everything Don Joaquin had told her, but, in her mind, there were still many unanswered questions! Could it be that at some point in time she had met this person? She doubted it! Certainly she would have known if she had! Her life had been much too sheltered, and she knew no one who would be as daring and as protective as he was! Perhaps the priest had been right after all! He was nothing more than a stranger; and, maybe, she should leave it at that! She had already tried desperately to get him out of her mind, but sleep just wouldn't come! Those bewitching eyes were still on her mind! Perhaps she would try again and ask Guillermo who he was! She was certain that he did know but had his own reasons for not telling the group! Now perhaps it was time to ask him again, but this time, she wouldn't allow herself to appear satisfied with some flimsy answer as she had done before!

Madrid

The next morning all of the newspapers were reporting stories about the way that 'El Raposo' had come to the rescue of an old army officer and had thrown himself on top of him to shield him from a devastating explosion at a local garrison! The publicity given to 'El Raposo' had suddenly changed! Before he had been identified only as the Fox and was reported to be fighting on the side of the Republicans! Now his reputation had changed! He was being regarded as a hero for having saved the life of an army officer and had sacrificed his own life in the process. Guillermo burst out in laughter as he read the news! What he was now reading seemed almost comical! A staunch enemy of the new government had now suddenly become a hero! There were also reports that Generalissimo Franco had been anxious to learn the identity of this stranger so he could reward him with a medal for bravery!

The Mariscal was still reading the heroic exploits about 'El Raposo' when Guillermo arrived at their usual meeting place! It had been a typical sunny day when he entered the cave wearing a broad smile! The two men embraced as the Mariscal opened up another bottle of wine and set two glasses! The news had been favorable and interesting! El Raposo was given celebrity status in the newspapers! It had even been suggested that perhaps more people should take notice and do their part in restoring law and order to Spain now that the Civil War had ended! Because of his heroics, all of the attention was given to the way in which the hooded stranger had jumped on the back of an elderly military officer of the Nationalist army and had risked his own life while in the process of saving his life! So much acclaim had been given that no one had stopped to ask how El Raposo knew precisely how and when the explosion of the garrison was going to take place! It had been this omission that made the incident even more humorous as the two men read the article together!

"Why didn't you tell me who you were?" Guillermo asked the question that caught the Mariscal by surprise!

The Mariscal looked at him but remained silent! It was several moments before he finally answered that it would not have served any worthwhile purpose; and now that the masked man had received hero status, there was all the more reason for keeping his identity a secret from everyone!

"The young woman I told you about, La Muneca, has asked me again who you were! It appears that she became very impressed with you, first, when you took her rifle away and then when you carried her into the tent after she fell off the ledge!"

Flaco started to smile! He too had been taken in by her beauty; but, with all the work that still needed to be done, it was important that no one else be implicated in his work other than Guillermo, now that he had discovered his identity by accident!

"It's important that no one else knows the truth! Everything will work out much better that way! As the Mariscal, I can alert you to what is happening and I can be there to help whenever I feel that extra help may be needed! If anyone else knows who I am, of course I will be removed from this office! If I'm caught, think of what will happen! Remember, I was personally selected for this job by General Franco! It would be a severe shock for him to learn that a member of his own select group had become an adversary! No, Guillermo! Whatever you do, please, conceal my identity!"

"And what about La Muneca? What do I say to her when she asks?"

"She is a young woman who is enraptured with heroics! She'll get over it! Let her continue to be the dedicated warrior that she has become! All that you need to do is to keep her away from where the action is because she is much too eager to kill! You know as well as I, that could be very dangerous! It isn't so much that I worry about her, but I also worry about the group! She is young and reckless, and we cannot afford to have that! After this is over, she'll probably get married, have a bunch of kids and settle down in Asturias! All of this will be behind her, and I'll be nothing more than a forgotten relic! Let it remain that way!"

"Are you quite sure you don't know her? She said that she comes from Asturias!"

"No! There are many people who come from Asturias! It's been so long since I have been to my old home town that I would probably wouldn't know anyone that remained! I'll be happy when all of the killing has ended, and we can go back to being Guardia Civiles again!"

"Would you really want to go back to being a Guardia Civil again after all that's happened?"

"I don't know! It might be a welcome change! As strange as it sounds, I was actually happy being a simple Guardia Civil! Guillermo, think of what we have now! Do you know that since the end of the war, the Nationalist army has executed 75,000 people? The Republican army also has not been exactly a regiment of angels either! They have killed more than 55,000 people! Think of how many of these poor people were innocent peasants whose only sin was that they didn't want to fight; or else, they were caught fighting on the opposite side! That doesn't even begin to take into account the other 25,000 deaths from malnutrition in the Republican controlled areas because of the economic blockades! In all, approximately 4% of the Spanish population has been killed and nearly 8% have been injured! It will take years to overcome these losses!" Flaco told him.

"Is that the reason why you decided to disguise yourself as El Raposo?" Guillermo asked.

"That was part of the reason! The other part is that we have learned from some very reliable sources that the Franco government is systematically arranging the execution of another 100,000 Republican prisoners. That will result in another 35,000 Republicans left in the concentration camps that will surely die within the next few years unless we can find a way of liberating them! These are the people that El Raposo is interested in! I can't stand seeing so much killing and not do anything about it! As a Mariscal, I am a part of the killing machine! As El Raposo I can be something else, even if it is only a particle of hope!"

"It seems strange that here we are on different sides, and I now learned more about you than when we were young, drinking wine and exchanging our few pesetas for perronas so that people could eat! You have changed, my friend! Do you think there will ever come a day when you and I can sit down and drink a bottle of wine together, out in the open, without having to fear getting caught?"

"I certainly hope so! Remember, I already made a promise to Dolores to be your best man, and also to be 'El Padrino' to your first child! That in itself gives me something valuable to look forward to!"

"And what about you, Flaco? Why haven't you ever married? I never once heard you say that you wanted to be married, settle down and have children!"

"Those are a lot of questions to answer in a short period of time! I don't think I would ever want to raise a family in the country we have today! What for? So they could starve to death like all of the other peasants? No, I think I would prefer being unmarried and without children! This way nobody gets hurt! It's best that I leave marriage to the other 'casanovas' such as you!", while slapping his friend on the shoulder and sipping on the wine. He waited until he had swallowed a mouthful of wine before getting serious again!

"Guillermo, with everything that has happened, we have been told that Franco is going to concentrate his efforts and stop the activities in the North! They are getting suspicious that someone is tipping off 'Los Milicianos' in advance! It all began with the two explosions when the top brass got together for their strategy meetings! From what I've been told, they will be sending two more brigades up into the provinces! One of the brigades will be made up of members from the African army!"

Guillermo nodded his head and smacked his lips in disgust! It was well known that the African troops were not well liked in the North, especially in the province of Galicia, which was where Franco had been born and raised. In silence, he had visions of a blood-bath that would only create more victims and bring more troops into the North! "Is there any way of stopping them before they arrive?" he asked.

"I've been thinking it over; and, yes, I think there is a way! It's going to require careful handling and I don't want that young woman in your camp to do anything foolish! From what I heard, they assume that the underground will expect them to take the road to the North and into Asturias! It is a much better road, more direct and without nearly as many mountain passes to cross in order to reach their destination! Instead, they plan to use the Northern road that comes from Orense! They will remain in Lugo for about two days and then head northward all the way to Tapia on the Golfo de Masma. They know that it is a much longer route, but they also think it will be safer!"

"So, which road do you think we should go after? If they are trying to trick us, won't they get suspicious that someone is telling us their plans?" he asked.

"Of course! That's why we are going to need to go after both roads but on different days! First, there is the road from Oviedo that goes to the northwest to Luarca on the Costa Verde! Send someone down there to take out the road around the city of Grado after you leave Oviedo! You will need to do this before the troops and the trucks reach Lugo! In the meantime, you should also send someone down to Lugo and remain there out of sight until the trucks arrive! As the road turns to the northeast, you have to wait until they are on the road through the Cordillera! Before reaching the end of the Cordillera, you take out that road! They will have no alternative but to turn around and head back! Don't dare try to take them on! There are too many of them for your small group to take on! That's why I want that young girl, La....La...whatever her name is, to stay away from there!"

"And where is El Raposo going to be?" Guillermo asked.

"I won't be able to get back to Galicia in time! Instead, I'll be around the city of Grado to help your group there! If I get caught back in Galicia, there may be officers in that group that know me! It's best that I keep away from there! Since the area of Grado is sparsely populated, you won't need to have more than one or two men there!"

"Do you mind if I send La Muneca with that group? I'm sure that the old lady, La Pasionaria, will also want to be there! I can keep them both there and out of trouble!"

"That may be a good idea! At least it will prove to her that she is still a viable part of the group! I'm sure that La Pasionaria will keep her subdued!" he answered.

After they had finalized their plans, both men embraced, finished their wine, and said goodbye! They both realized that this was going to be one of their most dangerous missions, and everything would need to be carried off perfectly in order to succeed!

Las Cuevas de Asturias

It was time for the group of Los Milicianos to meet in one of the caves along the Southern part of the Cordillera! The group from Asturias was busy planning the destruction of the road leading into the Northern areas. It was a move that would compel the Nationalists to turn the vehicles around and head back over the Codillera. Everyone knew that the mission would not be the most important part of the attack, because the largest portion of the shipment would be heading into Galicia. El Mariscal had carefully outlined the plans in advance with Guillermo and both men knew what needed to be done! If the Fascists decided to use the province of Asturias as a decoy, then, so be it! The Milicianos would be ready and waiting for them! Flaco had explained that there would be a minimal number of troops that would be assigned to that mission, and that only a couple of his Guerilla fighters would be required for the attack! As soon as she heard the plans, La Muneca got excited She always felt a sudden surge of excitement when told she would be going on a mission, and it was this uneasy eagerness that always worried some of the group! It almost seemed as if she would get some a certain sadistic satisfaction knowing that she was outsmarting a hated enemy! As Guillermo was carefully going over the plans, she was listening to his every word of what needed to be done! They decided that Chato and Gomez, their leader, would be the men assigned to bury the explosive land mines along a remote section of the road that was not frequently used. The plan was that since the trucks would be using this road, they would explode when they passed over the buried land mines. It was a simple enough mission, and one that promised to be successful!

"Que quieres que haga yo?" (What do you want me to do?) she asked Guillermo.

"I want you to be on your guard when Chato and Gomes are burying the land mines! It is possible that they may send along an advanced contingent of soldiers to make certain that the coast is clear! If so, they will need you to be their cover! If, for any reason, you notice their arrival before the land mines are buried, I want you to give them a hand signal so they will stop what they're doing and will be able to defend themselves! I have faith in you if there are only one or two guards, but if they send more than two soldiers you are going to need help! Whatever you do, I don't want you to become a heroine and try to take them out by yourself! Remember, they have been well trained in combat and you will be outnumbered! I don't want anything to happen to you!" he cautioned.

"I know! I know! It's that damn Raposo, isn't it? He still thinks I am unable to defend myself just because I happened to fall down an incline during the last mission!" she told him.

"That's where you're wrong!" he lied. "It has nothing to do with El Raposo! He has said nothing to me other than what needs to be done! He never mentioned you at all!"

"Is he going to be there?" she asked. She had an uneasy feeling that he wasn't tell her the truth! It occured to her that he must have known who El Raposo was because he had never denied knowing his identity! Even now, it would have been easy for him to simply tell her that he didn't know who the masked stranger was; but the only thing he had told her was that she had not been mentioned at all! It was a clear indication that Guillermo had at least spoken to him and that he had every intention of concealing his true indentity! Even as she was speculating, she had nearly forgotten how spellbound she had been when she first saw his piercing eyes! What was happening now was much more serious! This was a matter of life or death! In her mind at the moment, she only had one thought! She hoped that he would again be there if they should run into trouble!

"I don't know whether or not he'll be there!" Guillermo told her."Just don't plan on it! Rely instead on your own instincts, and don't wait for anyone to come to your aid! That's the rule we need to follow in whatever we do!"

"How long do you think it will be before the road leading into Galicia gets destroyed?" Gomez asked.

"I was told to plan the destruction two days apart! We're probably going to need more men there, especially if this is the main route! The road to Asturias is only going to be decoy! It is also possible that they will be testing us to see how much we know! If that's the case, we'll have to destroy both roads so that we don't draw too much attention to what we know! Is that clear?"

"Yes, sir! I'm ready whenever you are!" Gomez replied.

"Do you have all of the necessary equipment?" Guillermo asked.

"Yes! I've checked it myself over and over! I think we're ready!"

"Good!" Guillermo told him. "It's time to go then! I'll be waiting here until you return!" They all grabbed their coats and the bags containing the land mines and took off to their target! La Muneca wsa the first to enter the car as they drove along the bumpy dirt road through the small foothills of the Cordillera until they finally reached their destination. The trip had been uncomfortable and tiring as they travelled through the giant holes in the road that added to the discomfort of the seats of the car! After about two hours, they arrived at the almost completely deserted town of Grado! They took the road to the left, passing through the town and noticed that the once bubbling town, full of people was practically deserted. They finally reached a small cave that was hardly large enough to conceal the car! Just like a well conditioned machine, they quickly unloaded their equipment, laying it out carefully along the ground before making the holes in the road where they would bury the land mines! The idea was to let the weight of the trucks pass over the area. The result of the force would set off the explosion and destroy the truck!

La Muneca jumped out of the car, looked both ways and made sure that no one was watching them. She gave the others a hand sign indicating that the area was deserted and no one was in sight! Chato, who was the expert was in charge of the land mine, got out of the car and immediately started to make round holes on the dirt road from one side to the other! There were a total of six holes, each one about eight inches deep, just enough to conceal the mines and cover them with dirt. No sooner had he finished when he heard a noise coming from the nearby bushes. Gomez aimed his rifle and walked slowly to the far side of the area, but there was no one in sight! As they were returning to the work area he again heard a rustling noise that sounded like someone walking! La Muneca signalled to the others to continue working! She walked quietly into the bushes, her rifle aimed at anyone who should appear before her! Still, there was an uneasy silence as she saw no one! Just as she turned around to join her partners, the unexpected happened! Five men with their rifles aimed at them came out of the woods and promptly encircled them! La Muneca wanted to fire, but, she also knew that if she did it would be the death of all of them! Most of the soldiers were dark skinned, probably members of the African army who had been well trained in field operations. She stood motionless, stunned and surprised, not knowing what to do!

"Alto!" one of the soldiers said. "Que hacen ustedes aqui?" (What are you doing here?) She saw that they were slowly taking their places around them and realized it would be foolish to fire her weapon!

"Estamos trabajando!" (We're working!) Gomez replied. He knew that it was a flimsy excuse but he hoped it would perhaps allow them some time to return to the car and get their weapons.

The only person who had a rifle was La Muneca, and she was certainly no match for the five soldiers.

"Es mentira!" (You're lying!) one of the men told them. "I want all of you to come with me!"

The tone of the soldiers voice told them that it was not an invitation but an order! Obviously, someone had been alerted and the men had been hiding in the woods waiting for them! Just as they laid down their rifles, getting ready to follow the guard, they were startled by another noise coming from above! Before they were able to focus on what was happening, a masked stranger leaped down from the top of one of the many inclines and landed on top of two of the guards! He fought them off unmercifully, punching them fiercely until they dropped their weapons and ran away! The brief fight had allowed Gomes and Chato to return to the car! Fists were flying everywhere, as the masked man summoned every ounce of strength in fighting the guards. Gomez picked up his rifle and slammed it against the head of one of the guards and watched as he fell to the ground! As El Raposo was occupied with the other remaining guards, the other guard pointed his rifle at him and was about to fire! Seeing what was happening, La Muneca aimed her gun at the guard and with one single shot, the bullet hit the guard in the forehead making a small hole before he died! Raposo paused when he heard the shot and saw the smoke still coming out of the barrel! He gave her a salute as if he was mocking her but at the same time admiring what she had done! She flashed him a smile and was hoping that he had seen it as she began to reload the rifle! One of the guards construed this as a moment of weakness! He grabbed his gun and pointed it at her! Before he was able to press the trigger, El Raposo pulled out a small revolver he had taken with him and fired off several shots in the direction of the guard! Everything had happened so quickly that there was hardly time for anyone to think! El Raposo unfortunately, failed to see that when he fired his weapon, La Muneca had accidentally entered into the line of fire! It was too late! One of the bullets had struck the young woman! She let out a blood curdling yell, as she dropped the rifle and also fell to the ground! El Raposo, fighting anguish and anger, pointed his gun once again at the two

guards and killed them quickly! He quickly placed his revolver
back into the case and ran over to where she was laying! Blood
was everywhere! Her light blue cotton dress and white apron were
covered with blood, her blood! As he did his best to revive her, he
began to panic when she didn't respond! Chato went over to him to
see what had happened and Gomez was holding his arm! A bullet
had found its way to him!

"Muneca!! Muneca!!! hablame!!" El Raposo pleaded with
her but she did not answer!

Her eyes had remained wide open but the pupils had gone
to into the back of her head and the only thing that remained to be
seen was the white of her calm, lifeless eyes! Chato handed him
a large white towel that he used quickly to stop the flow of blood
and cover her wound! Raposo was in despair as he leaned over
her and listened for any signs of life, but there were none! There
was no indication that she was breathing, and as he gently placed
his fingers on the side of her neck and was feeling for a pulse in
the carotid arteries, there were no pulses to raise his hopes that
she may still be alive! Could it be that, after all this time, he had
been the one that had killed her? It seemed like such a foolish and
careless thing for him to do!! Damn it, he knew better! Sure it had
been an accident, but it had happened, and it had happened because
of his revolver! He slowly picked up her limp body, thankful that he
was still wearing the mask and no one could see the tears that were
falling from his eyes! Then, he carried her carefully into the car as
they quickly drove away! It was important that they return to the
cave immediately! At that point, he didn't even know whether or
not they had a doctor they could send for!

Damn it!! How could he have been so careless? The car
seemed to be moving much too slow as he held Muneca in his
arms! "Damn it!" he yelled at anyone that would listen. "Forget the
holes in the road and get this car moving faster!!" he ordered.

Chato was looking at him and could see that he was upset
with what had happened! There was no point in answering! One
the way back to the cave, El Raposo was speaking to her and
hoping she would answer him, but there was no response! It almost

seemed like hours before they were finally back inside the cave! Guillermo, who had remained behind was the first to greet them!

"Caminate! Llama un doctor, inmediatamente! Esta muy grave! (Hurry, call a doctor quickly! She is very grave!) he ordered as he gently took her inside and carefully laid her down on one of the beds! He was careful when he took her limp arm away from around his neck and laid it gently at her side. Once again he was surprised by what he was seeing! It was something he had suspected, but all this time he had lived with the hopes that he was mistaken! As he raised her arm, his eyes focused on an unmistakable, large, ugly scar on the inside of her forearm! He stood there alone staring at the scar! All of his childhood moments returned in a flash! That day had now seemed like an eternity ago when he had almost drowned in the river, and she had pulled him to safety! He could still hear her words as she looked at her own wound and was happy that her blood was mixing with his! It had been an oath that he had long since forgotten, but it now returned in all of its vivid reality! Soledad had been so insistent, that wherever he went, her blood would be with him; and wherever she went, his blood would always be with her! It had been a simply childish prank that had seemed so important to her that day! It now seemed that it had meant nothing at all! He had killed her, and that was something he would have never done! How could she now know that he had never loved anyone else except her? Would it even be fair for her to know that he had suspected it was Soledad when he first saw her; but so much time had passed that he had never been certain! He was still there looking at her body and stroking her head! Her arm now showing the scar was very visible, almost as if in death she wanted to be certain that he was aware of what he had done! Could she ever forgive him for what he had done accidentally? Now it was too late! He watched carefully as Don Joaquin began to whisper something over her, making a small sign of the cross on her forehead! Only then did he break down and began to sob uncontrollably! Chato had gone for the doctor, but it would probably be too late! Soledad had lost too much of her blood! Once again he looked at her and it occured to him that, for the first time in her life, she looked so defenseless and frail! It was almost as if she were once again a child, playing and talking to him by the river while she washed her clothes. Perhaps she would never know how much he had missed her all of his life! The promise he had made to her so many years ago had never been broken! It had been the day when he promised her that there would never be anyone else in his life but her, and now he had been faithful but it mattered only to him! How could he ever tell this to her? Through his tears he waited until Don Joaquin had finished! He waited for a few moments before he said quietly to her, "Forgive me, Soledad! I've never broken my promise to you! Wherever I was, you were always with me, and now I am here with you! I'll never leave your side!" he whispered as he started to cry all over again and buried his sobbing face against her breasts! Then, just as he had done so many times before, he kissed her tenderly on the lips and disappeared out of sight! This time, it wasn't because he wanted to remain unknown, but rather, it was because he didn't want anyone else to see that he was unable to stop crying!

The group was huddled inside one of the caves discussing the possibility of destroying the road to Lugo! Meanwhile, Guillermo had gone to discuss the plans with Flaco! It was obvious that El Mariscal's enthusiasm was no longer as great as it had been! The guilt of what he had done was on his mind and he was unable to rid himself of remorse! It was no longer important whether Los Milicianos was successful! As far as they were concerned, their active participation in the war was over! The fighting had stopped and all the troops that had been fortunate enough to survive the vicious battles had started their return to their homes!

Franco had established a Fascist government and had been successful in joining the Anti-Cominterm Pact! One of his first moves was in declaring neutrality as soon as the Second World War was underway. Adolf Hitler had done his best to change Franco's mind; but when he refused the demands that Franco was making, the talks went nowhere and were quickely ended! Each decided to go his own way! One of Franco's demands was that any postwar settlement would need to include control of Gibralter, French Morocco, and a portion of Algeria that included Oran and parts of Africa! Hitler steadfastly refused to yield on his demands!

Franco also demanded that Hitler compensate Spain for all of the costs of the British blockade of the country! Once again, Hitler was in no position to undertake the burden and it was those territorial disputes that produced a schism betwen Spain and Germany! The only concession that Franco was willing to make was to provide logistical and intelligence support and agreed to send a new force comprised of volunteers that was known as the Spanish Blue Division, intended to help fight against communism in Europe!

After Hitler's success in the defeat of France in mid May 1940, negotiations were resumed again with Franco! The two men met secretly in a town named Hendaye later that year!Hitler's main request was for Franco to allow the German troops to travel through Spain and join in an airborne assault of Gibralter! Franco had a strong feeling that Hitler could not possibly win a long, drawn out war! Instead, Franco demanded additional arms and weapons so that Spain could then capture the important area of Gibralter! The meeting became so acrimonious that Hitler was said to remark that he preferred to visit a dentist and have his teeth extracted than to face another meeting with the General! Franco did indeed have visions of invading Gibralter while Britain was involved in the war against Nazi Germany; but quickly decided against it when he learned that if this was to happen, the British forces were ready to invade the Canary Islands! By late 1943, Francisco Franco abruptly recalled the Spanish Blue Division from the Soviet Union, thoroughly convinced that the Axis powers would eventually be defeated. As a result, he started to openly support the Allies in the war against Germany!

Galicia

Everyone knew that the war had ended and that there would be a major attempt to abolish the underground movements in Spain that were an added nuisance to the newly formed government. If Spain was going to survive, the independent cells of resistance would have to ba abolished! The group started getting together the equipment that was going to be needed to destroy the main road leading to Galicia! Guillermo had reviewed the plans with El Mariscal, but some of the interest was no longer apparent! It almost seemed as if he had acquired a defeatist attitude toward the underground movement!

Guillermo felt uneasy! If they were to succeed he knew that the mission was difficult and they were going to need the help of El Raposo! Speaking to Flaco, he noticed a lack of enthusiasm; and, it didn't matter that he had told him the news that La Muneca was gravely ill, but still alive! She had lost a great deal of blood, but was slowly on the road to recovery! The request to Guillermo had been abrupt! There was no way of knowing what he wanted, but El Mariscal had told him to meet him in yet another secret cave and to bring La Pasionaria with him! He had never met the elderly woman, but her zeal and determination had been a thorn in Franco's side for a long time! It had taken a considerable amount of coaxing to get the old woman to accompany him! There were still some elements of distrust the older woman felt for anyone in Franco's government who had such a high position! Her greatest fear was that El Mariscal had wanted her to go just so she could be captured! After all, Franco had posted signs everywhere offering a handsome reward for any information that led to the arrest of this woman! When they finally met at the cave, Flaco was surprised to see that the old woman was older and more frail looking than he had thought! It seemed fairly obvious that she was no longer the threat she had once been, and even her activity with the underground had begun to diminish! Flaco was polite as he greeted the old woman warmly and ushered her to a seat!

"Senora!" he said. "Thank you for coming here to meet me!" he pulled up a chair and sat down next to her! The elderly woman still eyed him with suspicion! "I asked you here because I need a favor from you!" Flaco paused to study the look of confusion on the old woman's face! "Tell me, how difficult would it be to get La Muneca out of the area and safely away from here?"

The elderly woman needed time to think over her answer! Certainly Guillermo must have explained that the doctor had come in time and had saved her life!She had been seriously ill and had been unconscious for several days due to the lose of blood, and while she was able to move around, her wounds were still bandaged and she was unable to use her arm! It had been her sheer determination that had aroused her from her injury and her desire to resume her anti-Franco activities with the group!

Guillermo was taken by surprise! Why would he want to take this young woman away from them, knowing that they needed everyone they could get? She had been a viable part of the group, and, although she had made some mistakes, she was fearless and a damned good guerilla fighter! Asking her to leave the group was going to be trouble!

"Where do you want her to go?" Guillermo asked.

"I want her to leave this place and go somewhere where she can enjoy life and live it in peace!" Flaco explained.

"Can I ask you why? And why now, when we are preparing another raid on the main road to Lugo?"

"It's a personal matter, but it is important to me!"

For the first time, La Pasionaria spoke! Her voice was shaky and light, the result of living many days and nights in the cold, damp caves of the Cordillera! "Quien era el hombre con la masquera que la leevo a la cueva?" (Who was the masked person that brought her to the cave?)

"Eso no importa, senora!" (That doesn't matter!) he answered.

"She is still very weak and really should not be moved away!" the old woman explained.

"I realize that! That's the reason I would like you to accompany her and go with her!"

"Flaco, tell me, why is this woman so important to you? What makes her more special than the rest of us?" Guillermo interrupted.

"Let's just say that I am honoring an old promise I once made many years ago! Let it go at that!"

The elderly woman continued to look at him with curiosity! She could see that there was pain and feeling in his eyes as he spoke! It was a rare sensitivity that she hadn't seen in any of Franco's officers! She looked at Guillermo and asked, "Puedo hablar con franqueza?" (Can I speak freely?)

"Certainly, Pasionaria! That is why I brought you here!"

"Quieres que le diga sobre el barco velero?" (You want me to tell him about the sailboat?) she asked. Guillermo nodded his head that it was okay to speak freely.

"There is a small fishing sailboat that arrives each week from Bilbao! It is disguised as a fishing boat, but it is loaded with fruits and vegetables that are gown in the Basque country and intended to feed our people. She could go back with them to Bilbao! We have a cell there that will take good care of her! So far, Franco has not interfered with our movement there and I'm sure she will be safe!" Guillermo nodded his head and looked over at Flaco to see his reaction! There were still many questions that needed to be answered, he thought!

"Flaco, what do we tell her and what reasons do we give? Certainly, she will want to know why she is being taken away from the area! Even if we lie to her,she will be furious with us knowing that we have taken her away with asking her permission!"

"Tell her that....that....after careful consideration, the Mariscal has ordered her out of the area! Place the blame exclusively on me! Tell her I said that she has become too much of a nuisance and that I insist she leave the area, or else she will wind up facing the firing squad! That's all she needs to know! Just don't let her talk you out of it!! Tell her that I insisted on her leaving in order to save her life!" he answered.

"She is going to be angry as hell when she finds out, you know that? If you are sure that is what you want us to do, then, you must have your reasons, but we'll do it!" Guillermo replied.

"Guillermo, listen to me! We all know that our time here in Spain is coming to an end! Eventually, the work of Los Milicianos will be ended, and God only knows how many of us will end up before a firing squad! I don't want that to happen to her! I would prefer that she remain angry with me but alive, then to end up before a firing squad! Place all of the blame on me!" he told him. "If she is still as weak as you say she is, she needs to be carefully watched. I can't think of anyone that is better than La Pasionaria to watch over her! That was why I asked you to bring her here!"

"Debe de ser bastante importante!" (She must be very important!) the old woman told him.

"She is, senora! She is...." he said, as his voice trailed off and ended up almost as if in a whisper.

The elderly woman was beginning to feel sorry for him! She knew what had happened in the field, but the sensitivity he was showing toward this young woman was much greater than it should be! She was old and had been on the earth for many years, but she knew by looking into the eyes of a person when they were hurt or in pain! This Mariscal was feeling a great deal of pain, and she knew that she couldn't refuse him.

"Bueno Guillermo, entonces vamos! Tenemos mucho que hacer!" (Let's go Guillermo! We have much to do!) she ordered, as the two men embraced!

Flaco reached over and gave the old woman a peck on the cheek, causing her cheeks to turn red! "Vaya con Dios, Senora! Que Dios se lo pague!" (Go with God and may God bless you!) he told her as she waved her hand and said goodbye!

Many of the other members of the group were busy making holes in the road that were deep enough to conceal the land mines. If everything turned out as planned, the trucks would travel over the mines and they would be blown up and prohibited from entering Galicia. With any luck, any guards that had been sent with the vehicles would also be destroyed and the road would remain impassable for a long time. It wasn't that it mattered because Los Milicianos didn't need that road anyway! If, on the other hand, they were successful, the destruction of the road would prevent Franco from sending in troops intended to eliminate the activities of the underground just as he had already previously done in many of the southern provinces!

Flaco remained alone in his room thinking over what he had done! He felt certain that what he had done had been done for her safety! The sight of her lifeless body being carried inside the cave was still on his mind! She had been the victim of his weapon! As El Raposo, he saw many things about Soledad that came to mind, but it almost seemed absurd that after so many years, she had come back into his life! Strangely, as close as they had once been, they were now more far apart than ever before! Thanks to the Guardia Civil, he had been well educated, and goodness alone

knew how much this poor woman had suffered after he had left
Salinas. Suddenly she seemed so much older, but, then, so was he!
Had he remained it would have been the attempts of just staying
alive instead of actively trying to make the country that they both
loved better than it had been. Now, he was sending her away!
Knowing her as he did, she would be angry, and God alone knows
what she might say or think if she ever found out that El Raposo
had once been her childhood sweetheart! It was almost like a
story-book tale! It seemed odd that he should remember now those
impish childish talks as though they had just happened! When he
first caught her staring into his eyes, for a moment, he thought she
had recognized him! It almost seemed as if their childhood had
returned! He had no idea that it was she because she had changed
so much! She was still as attractive as he remembered, even though
he had seen in her eyes the undeniable signs of hurt and despair!
Life had obviously not been good to her; and, now here she was,
fighting a losing war as an underground agent! It didn't seem fair!
He was certain that what he had done had been the right thing
to do! Perhaps a day would come when she would remember to
thank him! In the Basque hills she would be safe and that was all
that mattered! Guillermo already knew what their fate would be!
Both he and Dolores would probably end up before a firing squad;
it was only a matter of time! He had nothing except Dolores, but
she loved him! As for him,he had no one so life didn't matter at
all! It wasn't that he hadn't any opportunities, but he had become
much too involved with his studies and his work to give very much
attention to anything or to anyone else! Here he was approaching
middle age; his temples were showing signs of grey, and the
lines on his face were a grim reminder that he was no longer the
youngster he had been! Flaco was lost with his thoughts when he
heard a knock on the door! Guillermo walked in; and, by the look
on his face, he immediately knew that the news was not going to
be good! It was the first time that Guillermo had refused the usual
glass of wine that was always offered!

    "What's the matter, Guillermo? You look worried!" Flaco
asked.

Flaco seemed upbeat and satisfied knowing that the arrangements had been made to send Soledad to the Basque country with La Pasionaria, knowing she would be safe away from the group of Los Milicianos whom he suspected were now operating on borrowed time. There were signs that the country was finally getting more stable with the formation of a new government, which although under Fascist control, was showing marked signs of improvement! There had been talks with Guillermo where he had suggested that perhaps it was time for them to begin cutting back on their underground activities. The war had ended and Franco had declared neutrality among the Allies during the Second World War! As long as he maintained his neutrality, he knew that many of the Allies would be eager to assist him in creating a democratic government while still maintaining almost complete dictatorial control.

"I think we may have a problem!" Guillermo said somberly. "It has been three days since we planted the land mines on the road to Lugo and there have been no signs of any vehicle moving to or from that area!"

"I don't think there is anything to worry about! The trucks move extremely slow and they may have encountered some delays while crossing the cordillera!" Flaco replied.

"It has never happened before, Flaco! There were occasions when some delays of one or two days were experienced, but we've never had delays of more than three days! Is there any way for you to find out if the trucks have left and are on their way?"

"I doubt it! I can't just go around asking questions without arousing suspicions! I don't think there is anything to worry about!"

"But suppose some peasant farmer decides to use that road and drives over the land mines? You know what will happen! They'll have every garrison in the area sending troops to investigate the cause of the blast! I don't like it, Flaco! It worries me!"

"Let's just wait and see what happens! If I hear anything, I'll let you know! By the way, did Muneca and La Pasionaria get off?"

"Yes, they were on the Velero yesterday! La Muneca was still very weak and was in no position to give anyone an argument! I think that La Pasionaria will have her under control! She is still improving, but, because of the loss of blood, she is still quite weak! At least she can now use both arms!"

Flaco nodded his head and aseemed satisfied with the news! The doctor had arrived in time to remove the bullet from her shoulder! The wound had been sutured and he had stopped the bleeding! Had she gone to a hospital, they would have given her a blood transfusion; but working by candlelight in a cave was difficult and there was little more that he could do! At least she was on the mend and had gone away from what he knew was going to happen sooner or later! Both the Gallegos and Asturianos were much too idealisitic to know when to stop their destruction! What no one had known was that for some time he had been giving thought to leaving his job as Mariscal and also escape to Vizcaya! Unfortunately, he too was an Asturiano and an Asturiano would never abandon his friends at a time of trouble! He had merely been awaiting his fate for the day when his own activities would be discovered and would be taken under arrest! The penalty for treason was the firing squad, but it didn't seem to matter now that the war was over! All that mattered was that perhaps the old woman would one day speak to Soledad and explain to her the reason why she had been taken away! If she was still as fiesty as she was during her childhood, she would probably be angry with everyone that had a hand in taking her away from what she was doing! Fortunately, she was no longer fighting a worthless cause, and that was what was really important!

Guillermo left Flaco's room and went back to the cave to wait for the trucks to head Northward as planned.There had been no activity, and while he didn't want to show his concern to the other members of the group, he had been worried! Even if there had been an accident along the way, surely he would have known! After all news travelled fast! Flaco was the Mariscal and any such information would surely be sent to him!

The fact that no one had said anything was beginning to worry Flaco! There had been no changes among the guards; and,

if anything had gone wrong, surely they would be among the first
to know. The atmosphere was peaceful and calm, perhaps too
peaceful and maybe too calm! There was little that he could do
except to wait and see what happened! He went back into his room
and removed his shirt! The day had been easy since there had been
no trials, so there was really no reason for him to feel tired! Flaco
went to the cupboard and opened up a bottle of wine, wishing that
Guillermo had been there to join him and keep him company.
He poured himself a tall glass of red liquid and began thumbing
through some papers he had taken from the court room! Not
that it was necessary, but he needed something to help break the
monotony! Ever since the day Soledad had been wounded, he knew
that something had happened to his spirit! There was no longer
the desire to continue with his work. The shot had devastated him,
especially when he saw her fall to the ground and he could still
see eyes roll to the back of her head as if she were dead! It was
a feeling he would never forget, nor could he ever explain even
though the image would be forever in his mind! Everytime he wore
the El Raposo mask, the thought of what had happened would
return and haunt him! His only hope was that she would eventually
find happiness, and perhaps, in time, learn to forgive him, even if
she never knew who he was!

Night time had fallen and all of the lights had been
extinguished! It was so dark that candles needed to be used, even if
he decided to go outside for a few minutes for a breath of fresh air
or to smoke a cigarette. He was suddenly startled when he heard a
knocking on the door! Whoever it was had separated him from his
thoughts, and he wasn't particularly happy to receive visitors at this
time of night!

"Quien es?" he asked angrily. There was no answer, but yet
another knock! This time it was somewhat louder and forceful!

"Si? Qiuien es?" he again asked, as he made his way
toward the large wooden door and removed the lock! As soon as
the door was opened, he received the shock of his life! "Colonel
Garcia!" he asked. He was stunned to see the old man standing
at the doorway dressed in a simple pair of trousers and wearing
an opened collared shirt. "Que have Usted aqui?" (What are you

doing here?) he asked, moving off to one side and allowing the Colonel to enter the small room.

"Flaco!" the old man began softly and with a great deal of determination. "I am here on official business! The truck movement you and your group were expecting will not be arriving!" he said in a very matter-of-fact tone of voice!

"I don't know what you're talking about!" Flaco lied. "I know nothing about any truck movment!"

"You aren't being truthful! The government is aware of what you have been doing! Let me start by telling you that you were the only officer who was told about the movement of the trucks! It was a deliberate ploy to see what you would do! We already know all about the land mines that have been planted along the road waiting for the trucks to roll over them! You have been seen receiving visitors at night, probably members of the underground in this area! I was sent here to relive you of your command and to place you under arrest!"

Although he knew that eventually his activities would be known, he was still startled that the old man had made such an accustation even if there was no point in denying it! His activities had been discovered and they now had all the information they needed to place him under arrest! His first thoughts were how happy he was that Soledad had been sent away! "So, what are you planning to do?" he asked.

"I have no choice in the matter! Of course, you know what the penalty will be!" the Colonel told him.

"I know it only too well! I have given out the same punishment to others many times!" he answered.

"You have given it to some, but not to everyone who has come before you!" The way the Colonel was speaking, it seemed more like an accusation than a bit of information. Perhaps, now that he had been caught, it was time for him to defend himself! Not that he felt it would do any good! His fate had obviously been determined!

"I did my job the way I thought it should be done! I did my best to be fair and to be just! Was that so wrong?"

"Flaco, don't be sanctimonious with me! We know each other much too well!" the Colonel replied.

"So, what do you plan to do?"

"You know the routine! A tribunal will be formed to try you for treason! If you are found guilty, you'll face a firing squad! This is one of the most difficult jobs I have ever had to do!"

"And when does the killing stop? Does it really matter if a person dies of hunger and malnutrition or if he faces a firing squad? Look at yourself! What has become of that kind and just officer who guided and taught me during the years I spent in the Guardia Civil? What ever happened to that man who gave me a few more pesetas so that they could be exchanged at the Money Traders and divided up among the poor? Does it really matter who will be seated in the capital of Madrid, as long as the end results are exactly the same? The people are still starving and where we once had a corrupted government who cared little about its people, we now have a dictatorship that is just as bad or worse! Tell me, Colonel! Did we really win the war, or did we lose the peace? Which is it, because I sure as Hell don't know?"

The Colonel looked at him but remained silent! Flaco had an uneasy feeling that in many ways, the old man was in agreement! Unfortunately, as a senior officer he had no right to agree with anything that was against the current government! After a few moments of silence, Flaco saw the old man staring at the floor as he spoke clamly, almost apologetic for doing what he had been sent to do!

"I know that it was your doing that saved me the day Los Milicianos placed the explosives under the garrison that killed many of the officers! There was a hooded man who came out of no where and shoved me away, dropping me to the ground and getting on top of me, making sure that I would not be injured by the blast! I don't really know how you managed to do it, but I have the feeling that the hooded man was you! I won't ask you who it was, but I do know it was your doing! I'm grateful that you gave me back my life!" the old man said. "You have no idea how much I hate to do what I've been ordered to do!"

"I understand, Colonel! I'm ready to face my fate! If what I did was wrong, then, I'm prepared to take my punishment! If what I did was right, then, I can only hope that somehow, I may get my reward, if not in this world, then, perhaps the next! When will the tribunal be summoned to pronounce sentence? How much time do I have?" he asked.

"The tribunal is set for the day after tomorrow! I will be seated on the panel, but I doubt that my vote will count very much! I'm sorry, Flaco! God, how I wish that there was some other way! I almost feel as if I am pronouncing a death sentence on my own son!" he answered sadly.

CHAPTER 10

Toledo

The situation in Spain had rapidly started to change! Franco soon realized that the toll of the war had produced great shortages of manpower throughout the country. If Spain was ever going to prosper, she was going to need all of the strong men she could find in order to work the fields and produce the fruits and vegetables that were needed to feed the public. In a move out of desperation, Franco issued an edict that would provide pardons for peasants if they would agree on two conditions! One, that they would never again raise an angry arm against the new government! Two, they they would agree to work the fields and produce whatever they could to feed the hungry masses! The plan had been ingenious! Since there were so many peasants that had been jailed, many of them quickly opted for the unconditional release! Some of the critics had considered it a ploy to get the peasants to work the fields, but there were others who considered the move as a way of eliminating long jail sentences and were willing to take a new chance at freedom! One thing was certain! The cases that were decided before a Mariscal began to dwindle! Only a few stray people had the nerve or the resolve to stage a revolt against the current government! Flaco was one of those that was in a precarious situation! The Colonel had come to place him under arrest for his actions against the government, and to this end, Flaco had accepted his fate! Colonel Garcia had passed along the word that he was now the new Mariscal until such time as a replacement was named! No reasons were given for the change except to say that the change was made for the benefit of the community! He feared that if the truth were made known, Flaco might well have the sympathy of the towns and villages on his side! These could also result in an uprising of sentiment that would be unfavorable for the new government! It was the middle of the night when the Colonel walked silently into the back of the building and visited his prisoner! Flaco had been sound asleep when he heard the footsteps! He had tried to fall asleep! However, the pressures of everything that happened had taken their toll, and he found it impossible to get some rest! The first thing he noticed was that the Colonel was dressed, not in his uniform, but in civilian clothes, as he walked over to the cell and called his name from the door!

"No, mi Coronel! I am not sleeping!" he replied.

"Stay back! I want to come inside and speak to you! I also want to make certain that you understand every word that I will tell you and you won't give me an argument!" the old man warned.

"How can I give you an argument? I am here inside the cell and you are the only one who has the keys! No, Colonel! Honest, I will give you no argument!" Flaco told him.

"I have contacted your people and have made some arrangements with them! Tonight they will be coming and will compromise the guards outside the building! I have in my pocket a vial of powder that I'll put into a cup of strong coffee! It is something that I use to help me sleep! Your friends will then arrive to release you! They will take you to Gijon where you will board a small fishing boat that will take you to the Basque country where you will be safe! When the authorities come here to investigate, I will tell them that one of the guards must have put some sleeping powder in my coffee! That should give you the escape that you need to get out of here! Now, don't ask me any questions and go before I change my mind! I can handle anything that happens here; and you need to get out of the area as quickly as possible because tomorrow may be too late!" the old man said.

"Pero, mi Coronel, why don't you come with me? We can both get out of here!"

"No Flaco! You are a young man and still have your life ahead of you, but I am old! What can they do to me?"

"They can certainly charge you with negligence! It doesn't matter how old you are! Come with me, please Colonel!"

"No! Don't worry, my son! I have learned how to deal with them! You go and stay alive for both of us! I will be praying to God that you make your journey in peace! Just remember, you once gave me back my life; now, it is my turn to give you yours!"

"Will I ever see you again?" Flaco asked.

"Who can say? Perhaps there will come a day when we will again be together and drink a bottle of red wine! But for the time being, it is important that you leave this place, and I will do the rest!"

"God bless you, mi Coronel! May God be with you!"

"And also with you, my son! May He always be at your side! You have done a great deal of good things for this country! Now, it is my turn to return the favor!"

It was several hours later when Guillermo entered the cell area! He and Gerardo had immobilized the guards and opened the door to the cell that the Colonel had left for them! Flaco walked out slowly, stopping for one last look to make sure that the Colonel was in his office! As they were leaving, they saw the Colonel looking at them from the window as he waved at them! It had been a sign of goodbye and letting him know that they were on their way! The Colonel nodded his head, gave him a mocked salute and then blew him one final kiss! After they were out of sight, he opened up the small vial, poured the contents into a cup of coffee, and drank the liquid that would make him fall asleep!

"Vaya con Dios, mi hijo!" The Colonel said softly as he again raised his hand in a mock salute! "Hasta la proxima!" he said. (Until we meet again!)

It was a long two day drive to Gijon as they crossed the Northern end of the Cordillera driving Northward to the ocean where the small sailboat was waiting! Flaco turned his head and kissed his friend goodbye, not knowing if he would ever see him again! There were tears in both their eyes, thinking and wondering what the future held in store for each of them. Not that it mattered now! The only thing necessary was to see that Flaco was on the boat and on his way to Bilbao! No doubt he would meet once again with La Muneca and whatever had once existed between them could be started again! He dreaded the thought of going into an unknown territory alone; but, he also knew that La Pasionaria would also be there. She would certainly do her best to get him started with a new life and a different country!

Bilbao

The sailing time between Gijon and Bilbao had taken three days in which there was little for Flaco to do other than to sit alone on the deck and stare at the blue sea and skies! Where he was going was a place he had never seen before! Everything would be new to him and he wondered how the people would treat him, knowing that he had once been a Nationalist officer? He had resigned himself to be just another peasant seeking refuge and nothing more! He had thought of La Muneca and wondered if he would ever see her again! If the old woman had explained that she had been taken there at his instructions, she would probably still be angry! At least he felt reasonably comfortable that she was safe and that was all that really mattered! Franco had never gone after the Basques, realizing that they were much too elusive and cunning for his troops to handle! Flaco toyed with the fact that he might be able to reconcile with La Muneca, but there had been far too many changes in both their lives to allow that to happen! He had managed to escape with only his clothes and a few pesetas he had earned as Mariscal! The trip had been calm and unexciting! Had it been at another time and another place, it might have been far more pleasurable! This was different! This had been an escape from reality without knowing what the future held! After three long days at sea, the small sailboat finally docked in a make-shift pier that seemed to be falling apart! He was the first to leave the boat and jumped onto the wooden pier! There was a brief glimmer of happiness when he saw La Pasionaria waiting for him at the pier!

He went directly to the old woman, placed his arms around her and kissed her warmly on both cheeks!

"Que tal Mariscal? Has tenido buen viaje?" (How are you Mariscal? Have you had a good trip?) she asked.

"Yes! The trip was good but a bit long!" he answered. She took hold of his hand and led him away onto a horse and buggy that had been waiting for his arrival! "Tell me, how is La Muneca?" he asked. "Has she full recovered from her wound?"

"Oh yes! She is fine! I told her you were coming and she was quite angry! She refused to come with me to meet you! She is still very angry because she knows you were the one that had her sent away!"

"You know I only did that to keep her safe!"

"Of course, I know that! But....she is young and impressionable! She doesn't understand! It will be up to you to convince her!" the old woman answered.

"Where will I be staying?" he asked.

"I have a small house with two bedrooms! You will remain with us until you get settled! She is also staying with me, so you have to treat her with care! Be gentle and be patient! It will take time, but I am sure that eventually she will realize that you were her friend and that you sent her away for her own safety!"

Flaco climbed onto the cart! The old woman held the reins and started their journey home! It seemed like hours until she arrived at a small, quaint, house somewhere in the outskirts of Bilbao! The area seemed isolated except for a few small white stucco houses, a small parcel of green land behind each one, much the same as he had once had in Asturias! It seemed like a nice quiet town and an excellent place to settle down and raise a family, were it not for the unsolved problems that were going to need his attention. He leaped off the cart, and carefully helped the old woman get off! Soledad came running outside, but he noticed that she refused to greet him! He felt a little sad and disappointed, hoping that she had forgiven him for what he did, but he should have known better! Also, he noticed that she was now up and walking, apparently the cool farm air and the brisk ocean breezes had been good for her! With hesitation, he walked up to her and smiled but her face remained stern and unyielding! It was going to be some time before she would forgive him, but it didn't matter! What he did had been the right thing to do! At least she looked great and was safe and well! For that he was happy!

"Buenos dias!" he said calmly. It was almost as though he were a stranger meeting her for the first time!

She looked at him sternly, but remained silent! It seemed odd to see her dressed in a light blue cotton frock with a white apron and a white bandana warpped around her hair. The more he stared at her the more he realized that she had really not changed very much at all! She was still very attractive despite her dress, and her hair was piled up into a coil in the back of her head, called a "mono"!

"No me conoces, verdad?" (You don't know me, do you?)

"No, senor! Se que eres el Mariscal de Toledo! Tambien se que por tu culpa estoy aqui en vez de estar con los amigos que me necesitan!" (No, sir! I know you are the Mariscal of Toledo! I also know that it is because of you I am here instead of being with my friends who need me!)

"Quizas tienes razon! Pero cuando la vi que estaba herida, queria que te fueras de ahi para que te amejoradas!" (You're right! But when I saw that you were injured, I wanted you out of there so you could get better!) he told her.

"Who are you to decide where I should go and who I should be with? I don't know who you are nor do I care! Why didn't you leave me where I was and where I could be useful?" she asked.

"How useful could you be if you were badly wounded?" he asked. without making it known that he knew she had been wounded by his bullet!"

"Don't you think I was capable of taking care of myself? I was able to get here, wasn't I? I didn't need you to send me away from my friends!"

"Aren't you among friends now? Have they not taken good care of you, or are you just being ungrateful?" he asked.

"That is none of your business! I am alive and well! That is all that matters! Now, I would like to return to my friends who need me!" she said angrily.

He looked at her sternly! For some reason, he felt it impossible to tell her what he really would have wanted her to know. Perhaps it would be best to wait until they had found a moment to be alone! After all, the old woman had already warned him of her anger and had cautioned him to treat her with care!

"Why have you gotten so angry with the entire world?" he asked.

"Because that is what life has taught me! I have been used and abused by people that I didn't even know! There were also times when I was attacked by strangers who wanted to harm me! How do you think I should feel?"

"Hopefully, all those things are now behind you! I am here with you, and I will protect you from your enemies! No one will ever hurt you again!" he promised her calmly.

"So that's it! What is it you want? Am I to be your mistress? Is that the reason I am here? Well, think again! I am not a whore to anyone! There is no one who will ever use me as their mistress! I may not be educated, but I am young and strong! Nobody will ever abuse me again! It doesn't matter whether I am here on in Asturias where I belong! If that is the reason why you came here, perhaps you may want to think it over again! To me, you are nothing!"

"How about you and me taking a walk down by the beach where we can talk!" he asked.

She glanced at La Pasionaria and saw that she was nodding at her and smiling! It seemed strange to see the old woman smiling! Smiling was one thing she had never seen her do! La Muneca paused for a moment to think over whether or not she should go with this stranger whom she hardly knew! She nodded her head in agreement and picked up her rifle.

"No, Muneca! This time I don't think you'll need a rifle!" he told her.

Still eyeing him with curiosity, she put down her rifle! She had no idea what he had on his mind, but if he thought of convincing her to be his personal whore or mistress, she would stop him cold! She was determined to resist any advances that he might make and it didn't matter that he was handsome!

They began their walk down to the beach, walking side by side but in complete silence! Flaco was thinking of what he would say to her! Strange that he would need to be careful what he said when there had been a time when they had been so close! He had been cautioned into treating her gently! It was a task that he feared not knowing how it would all turn out! The woman walking beside him was a far cry from that young woman he had once known. Renewing their relationship after all the time that went by was not going to be easy! For once, he was grateful that he had studied and read a great deal about psychology! If he had any chance to succeed, it would depend upon his approach and to meet her on her terms. It was a warm day when they finally reached the beach and they spread out a large cloth to protect their bodies from the discomfort of the hot sand! Flaco removed his shoes, and continued to stare at the calm, blue ocean! Soledad was showing signs of impatience as she tried to find a way to begin the conversation!

"So, what do you want to talk about?" she said bluntly.

"I was staring at the blue, clear ocean and it reminded me of when I was a child! We would go down to the river and watch all the young girls washing their clothes! Things seemed so much better then! It almost makes you wonder how things could have changed so drastically or have gone so terribly wrong so quickly!" he told her.

"Everything has to change at some time or another!" she answered. "I also remember when I too would go to the river and wash clothes! As much as I hated to do it, there was a certain simplicity that made life so wonderful! I realize now that those days were the happiest times in my life!"

"Why have you built up so much hatred for everything and everybody?" he asked.

She could see that he was being sincere and even a little sad as he spoke! Also, he had never once raised his voice and stopped staring at the ocean while he spoke! "It's all because life taught me a lesson! It taught me never to trust anyone and to always be on guard for anything that happens! It also taught me never to expect too much out of life! If you don't expect very much, then you won't be disappointed when things appear that make you unhappy!"

She was speaking to him calmly, and all the time she noticed that he was staring into her eyes! The stare of this stranger was making her feel uncomfortable! They were deep dark eyes, that appeared both happy and sad at the same time! They seemed to be looking right through her! There was love and hate,anxiety and compassion, all at once! She had seen those eyes before, she thought! Too bad that she didn't know where or when! It wasn't that it mattered, although she recalled feeling as uncomfortable and as uneasy as when she had seen them before!

"Have you ever loved anyone?" he asked, as if out of nowhere! He was once again using that soft tone of voice as if exploring her feelings without revealing his own!

"I think that is a personal question that I don't care to answer!" she told him. "Have you? Have you ever loved anyone?" She had no idea why she had asked him those questions, nor where she had found the nerve! They too were personal, but it was a way of diverting his attention away from her!

"Actually, yes! Yes, I did! I remember once long ago when I loved someone who was very close to me! I remember once making her a promise! It was a promise that I have always kept!"

"Are you married?" Here it was again! Another question out of her mouth without thinking! For a brief moment she almost having regretted asking him that question! After all, what did it matter? It was none of her business! Damn it!! Those eyes were again getting to her, as she suddenly remembered where it was that she had seen them before! It had been the eyes of the masked stranger who had rescued her when she fell from the top of the incline and had carried her into the cave!

"No, I am not married; nor have I ever been! Once I became the Mariscal de Toledo, there wasn't very much time for romance! My work kept me busy both day and night!" he answered.

"What are you, a Saint among men?" she asked smiling. "All the men I've known all seemed to think that promises were meant to be broken!" She had no idea why she found it so easy to speak to this perosn! This was not at all like her! It seemed that she was telling this stranger too much about herself, and she hadn't wanted to do that!

"No! I prefer to think of myself as a simple man among Saints! The Saints were the people that I condemned to death by a firing squad, all because they believed in something they were willing to die for!" he answered.

"Not everyone who believes in a cause is doomed to die! I remember a person wearing a hood who was both violent and yet gentle! I owed him my life! Los Milicianos went on a mission and became surrounded by Fascist troops. He appeared out of nowhere and saved my life!" she told him. She waited and watched for a reaction, but there was none! Instead he simply shrugged his shoulders!

"Was that when you were wounded? By the way, how is your wound? Are you feeling better?"

"I feel fine! La Pasionaria has taken good care of me! But, tell me, why did you order that I be taken away from my friends?" she asked. Guillermo had already told her that it had been El Mariscal who had given him the order to take her away from the area.

"It was because I wanted you to be safe so nothing would happen to you! It was a part of the prom......"he paused, realizing that he had already told her too much!

"But why? Why was I so special? I was nothing more than a stranger to you! I had no life; so, what difference did it make whether I lived or died?"

"Maybe it is because there has already been entirely too much killing! Too many people have died for no reason! I didn't want that to happen to you!" he told her. She was feeling confused and mixed-up by what this stranger was telling her! If she was nothing more than a stranger to him, why was he so concerned?

"I get the feeling there is something that you aren't telling me! I keep looking into your eyes and I get an uneasy feeling that I have seen those eyes before! I know I have! Whether you know it or not, they are very expressive! Every time you look at me, I almost feel as if you are seeing right through me and it is very troubling! I wish you wouldn't stare at me! It makes me very uncomfortable!"

"Okay!" he said smiling. "Suppose I look at the blue ocean instead!" It almost felt as if he was playing a game with her feelings and emotions! This was the one thing she never wanted to happen!

"Soledad!" he asked. "Tell me, why do you think that men don't ever keep their promises?"

"It's because they always......wait!!!! You just called me Soledad! How did you know my name? No one has called me by that name in a long time!" Here it was!! Damn it!!! He did know her, but how, and from where? She had been convinced that she had seen him before and now he had just confirmed her thoughts!

"I once knew a person by that name! It was many years ago! She too used to go down to the river and wash clothes! There was even a time when she saved my life!" She nodded her head not really listening to what he was saying! His comments about his life almost paralleled her own! All of a sudden, the thought came back to her when that young skinny kid, whose name she couldn't remember had drifted on to an island and she had to look for a tree branch that was strong enough for her to bring him to her side of the river! The talk was getting much too personal and he felt it was time to reveal who he was! He reached over and grabbed her arm, but she quickly pulled it away! He was getting too damned personal! It was time for her to go home where she would be safe! She stood up and began to walk away! It suddenly occured to her that he hadn't told her how he knew her name!

"Before I leave, you need to tell me how it is that you knew my real name!" she demanded.

She still felt angry and confused! This strange man and his eyes were slowly drawing her to him, and she hated the way she was beginning to feel! It was the same way she felt the first time she had stared into the eyes of El Raposo! All of the discomfort she felt had come back to her! She even remembered how foolish she felt staying awake at night thinking about the tantalizing eyes that were full of mystery and compassion! Now, here it was again! Damn it, she didn't want to feel this way! The only way to get away from the stare was to leave the area as quickly as possible! Her mind was made up! There was simply no way she could stay in that house with this stranger! He was far too intelligent for her! There was a certain way about him that was controlling what she was and what she had been! Who knows what would happen if they remained in the same house together! Her mind was made up! As soon as she returned, she would get her rifle and insist to La Pasionaria that she felt well enough to return to her group of underground guerillas! It was time for her to return to where she was needed, and the sooner she left Bilbao, the better!

"Don't you want me to tell you how I knew your name?" he asked. Again he seemed so calm and soft spoken as if he didn't have a care in the world!

"It doesn't matter!" she lied. "I need to get back to the house! When I return, I am going to insist to La Pasionaria that I be returned to my old group back in Asturias who needs me! They need all the help they can get and I feel as if I have had enough rest! I feel well enough to go back to Asturias!" she demanded.

"Soledad, you must forget about returning! The war is over! I'm sure you will find that Los Milicianos have all been disbanded and all of the members have returned to their families! Those that are foolish enough to remain are going to get killed! Franco now has enough forces to fight off any cells of resistance in the area! Why do you think I have come here? You and I are both renegades! If we go back, we will both be killed! I'm going to urge La Pasionaria not to return as well! Maybe it would be best if we all learned to live with one another and forget about the fighting!"

"No!!" she yelled. "You're lying to me! We can still fight them; and we'll win,,,,you'll see!" she insisted.

The moment of truth was at hand, and he now knew he would need to make his move! To prolong the inevitable would only increase her desire to return to a worthless cause! Franco had openly told the world that he preferred his neutrality! He had made some errors in judgement! There had been so many people killed in the war that there were hardly enough young men to work the fields. There were also rumors that Franco was secretly negotiating with the United States, to allow them to use several of the air bases as a stepping stone to Europe that was far away from the battlefields! Franco steadfastly insisted that this was an act of assistance to the allies, when in fact, the kindness was because he was in dire need of hard currency in order to rebuild the country. The only way to do that was to allow the United States to rent the air bases in a lease of perpetuity, for as long as they wished! With the money he would obtain from the rents and any amounts he might later negotiate for the reconstruction of Spain after the war, the country would once again be able to survive and fluorish! It was foolish for anyone to think they could fight the government! There were now too many obstacles that needed to be conquered! Those that remained in the guerillas had neither the manpower nor the required weaponry needed to prolong the fight! The only conclusion was that those that chose to remain would be killed! Those that accepted amnesty would be allowed to return to their homes and families and be allowed to work the fields and to turn over to the government a full thirty percent of everything that was produced! The amnesty was much too attractive to be overlooked! This was certainly not the time for anyone to be an idealistic fighter!

"I'm not lying!" he told her. "You can do whatever you wish, but before you go, there is something you need to know! Please sit down! I have something more to say! After I'm finished you can do whatever you want! I promise that I won't stand in your way!" It was the first time that he appeared resolute and stern! It was almost as if he was scolding her for something she wanted to do! At his insistance she returned to where she was sitting and once again took her place beside him.

"Let me see your arm!!" he said as he reached over and grabbed it! Once again she pulled quickly away, but this time his grasp was more firm and he wouldn't let go! He carefully turned her arm so that the inside of her forearm was now facing him. "How did you get that scar?" he demanded.

"It's none of your business!" she answered with anger. "How I got that scar has nothing to do with you! It's a personal matter that I don't want to talk about!" she told him as she started to pull back her arm and remove it from his grasp! Before she was successful, he turned over his palm and showed her his other hand!

"Take a good look, Soledad! Do you remember this?" he asked. He was furious as he raised his hand closer so she could see the scar on the palm of his hand more plainly! His blunt approach and angry look took her by surprise! He was now showing a side of him that she was unfamiliar with and one she didn't remember seeing before! When the shock was over, she took a long hard look at the palm of his hand! Suddenly all of the pain she had felt in her youth came back to her in one single moment!

"Ay Dios mio!!!....Dios mio!!!....Dios mio!" she called out as she covered her face with her hands. She nodded her head in disbelief and began to cry hysterically! The only words she could say through the tears were....."No puede ser!!!....No puede ser!!"! He carefully took away his hand and placed his arms around her.

"Go ahead, Soledad!! Let it all out!!!" he said soothingly. It seemed like hours before she was composed enough to ask him questions that so often she had wanted to ask him if they should ever meet again!

"Flaco....Flaco....mi Flaco!" she cried over and over as he gently pulled her over toward him! "So, you are El Mariscal! No wonder you knew so much about me! Flaco, why didn't you ever come back to me? Did you forget what we once promised each other? Everytime I would ask you who you were going to marry, you would always answer....tu, Soledad! Do you remember? When did you know that it was me?" she asked.

"The day you stared into the eyes of El Raposo, and you couldn't take your eyes away from his!" he answered, smiling.

"But you weren't there, so, how do you know? Unless...... unless.....yes...that's it!! No wonder I couldn't take my eyes away from El Raposo! Those were your eyes I was staring at, weren't they?" she asked. Flaco didn't answer, but she saw that he was smiling! "Now....darn it! It happened again! You began to stare at me, and those darn eyes of yours were tantalizing me! It was the same as you used to do when we were young! Can it be, Flaco? Please, tell me that I'm not dreaming and that I'll wake up and you will again be gone!"

"No Soledad! This time I am here to stay! That was the reason why I wanted you to be away from Asturias! Remember when we both promised to protect each other? I just couldn't take the chance of something happening to you once I had found you! That was why I had you taken here where I knew you would be safe! Once you were in Bilbao, I would always know where to find you, and there would come a day when I would be here with you! I guess it happened faster than I had anticipated!" he told her.

She was still confused, overwhelmed but very happy, all at the same time! She tried to stop crying but couldn't dry her tears! After all this time Flaco, her Flaco, had finally returned. This time she would never let him go! "Flaco, why didn't you return after you left?"

"If you remember, I did return! Your mother had told me that you didn't want to see me, so I went away! After that, I was sent for advanced training and that was where I met Guillermo! After that, I became a Mariscal and remained in Toledo! The rest you already know!" he said.

She saw that he hadn't really changed at all! His hair was starting to turn grey at the temples, and the lines of his face were a bit more pronounced; but, he was still as handsome! She had never forgotten and he had always been the one love of her life! "What happens to us now? she asked. "Flaco, I never again want to leave your side! All these years I lived with the thought that the day would come when we would meet again! I always had that feeling! Before you ask me, I've never given myself to any other man!" she told him. He smiled when he saw her embarassed by her own admission!

"What happens? I'll tell you what happens! We're getting married, that's what! I've lived alone for much too long! I have never stopped loving you, Soledad! Maybe that's why I never found anyone to take your place!" he admitted.

She went even closer as she rested her head against his shoulder! She stood there, unable to speak, for several moments looking out at the blue clear ocean!

"En que piensas, mi amor"? (What are you thinking, my love!) he said as she began to smile and slowly picked up her head so that it was touching against his face!

"I was just thinking! If we are getting married, what will we call her if she happens to be a little girl?"

"I think we should call her Balbina, after your mother! She was a wonderful woman and deserves to have a grandaughter prreserving her name!" he said.

"She stood silent for several moments before answering! Then, almost as if she had now thought it all out, she told him smiling. "No! If we have a little girl, I have another name I want to give her! I want to call her Maripaz! Mar, because of the clear, blue waters of the ocean that brought us together, and Paz, because there is now peace in the country we both love! Maripaz, that's what I want to name our daughter!" she told him.

"And what happens if we have a boy?" he asked. "I wouldn't want him to be named Flaco!"

"Why not? It has to be either Flaco or Miguel! It was good enough for his father; it should be good enough for him! But, I think I'll let you decide that one!" she told him with finality.

They both started to laugh as they began the long walk back to the house! "Wow, what a day we've both had! Do you think we should ask La Pasionaria to start making the arrangements for the wedding?" she asked.

"Are you in a hurry after all these years?" he answered.

"Well, if we're going to start working on Maripaz, maybe we'd better get started, don't you agree? Flaco, there is one more thing I would like us to have! There is a priest from Salinas, Don Joaquin who had joined the resistance! Would you mind terribly if we brought him here to perform the ceremony?"

"Wasn't that the priest from the small church near the cemetery where our parents are buried? I seem to remember that name!"

"Yes, that's him! I think he would be delighted if we asked him! He lost his church! It was burned down by the Nationalists!"

"Or the Republicans! They were also famous for burning down churches! Maybe we can concentrate on building another one!"

"Let's think about that after the ceremony! For now, I want to tell La Pasionaria that she'll be going to a wedding! After all, she has been like a mother to me! Besides, I forgot to ask you where we were going to live?"

"I've been able to save enough money as Mariscal! I have enough to buy us a small parcel of land and a few sheep to work the fields! I remember you once asking me, if I wanted you to help me, remember? Well, now you have that chance!" he told her.

"First things first!" she answered kiddingly. "At this moment I have other plans for you!" she told him as he pulled her closer and kissed her gently at first, then much longer! She again looked into his eyes; but this time, they were focused on her and nothing else! Staring at him for a few moments, she broke out into laughter!

"What are you laughing at?"

"I was just thinking! As long as you and I have loved one another, do you realize that this is the first time you ever kissed me?"

"I guess I don't have much experience since I never found anyone else that I wanted to kiss!" he said smiling.

"Flaco, how many times have I told you! You really do need me! From now on I want you to practice kissing me, and I won't allow you to stop until you learn to do it perfectly!"

"Then, you'd better be patient!" he replied. "It may take a long time!"

His eyes were no longer tantalizing and making her feel uncomfortable! Suddenly, this day had turned into the greatest day of her life; and there was nothing in the world that would ever separate them!! As far as they were concerned Flaco was right! The war was over and it was time for them to live their lives as husband and wife and forget the bitterness they had both endured!!

Book 2

CHAPTER 1

GUISAMO, GALICIA 1960

It was a warm sunny day when Guillermo and Dolores Torres, decided on a going away party for their son Andres, celebrating the announcment that he had been accepted and would be leaving the next day to attend the Universidad Nacional Autonoma de Madrid! It had been the third time he had tried to be admitted but had been turned down without any explanation! The rejection slips had been curt and to the point, only that he had not been accepted! The demand for students to go to college was high, and it was very brief and to the point when someone was turned down! Unfortunately, this was the way it was done and there was little that anyone could to that would change the system, especially since he had been accepted on the third try! Andres had always been an excellent and very intelligent student! Contrary to the other young men his age, he liked going to school and his grades were always far above average! Knowledge had always come easy to him! So easy, in fact, that his test grades were always far above average! Now as he was approaching the beginning of his adult years, his mind had been set on becoming a lawyer! It wasn't as much that he liked the study of law! He had read many books on the subject; and, more often than not, he was often at odds with himself trying to discover the type of law he would select that would show his qualifications! He had been raised in idealistic attitudes feeling that the law, in order to be effective, would need to defy common logic! Unfortunately, the more he read about the subject, the more he came to realize that most laws seemed to defy common knowledge if not common sense! Nevertheless, coming from a small town in Northern Spain called Guisamo, he soon realized that peasants needed some form of protection against exploitive landowners who did their best to boggle up every morsel of land that was available. Often, they would end up by cheating the prospective seller who had no recourse except to finalize the sale, whether or not it had been in their best interest! There had been many complaints about these coercive practices of cheating the peasants; but, in the post civil war era, there was little in the law that provided an injured seller any protection from the unscrupulous practices! This malfeasance had always been bothersome to him, and had ultimately convinced him into going to the University for the study of the law! If everything went as planned, he would return to Guisamo and serve the interests of injured sellers against exploitative buyers!

Guillermo and Dolores were proud of their son! Besides being a muscular six footer, catching the roving eye if every young women in town, his manners and his approach when speaking to older people, was kind, formidable and caring! Now that the ugly war was behind them, both of them had done their best to enroll their son in the University! It wasn't until his father had been elected mayor of Guisamo that the young son was finally selected on the first ballot and was sent the customary letter exclaiming in large letters saying "Le Filicitamos"! He had always considered this greeting to be a bit gaudy; but, as long as it heralded his acceptance, the rest of the letter was actually unimportant! He knew he would do well, and, if he became a lawyer, his parents would be proud of him and that was all that really mattered!

The young man felt a little embarassed and awkward when the people began to arrive, some that he knew from town and others were total strangers! He watched them dancing on the hard wooden floor, hopping around happily dancing something they called "La Muneira;" and another much slower dance called "La Jota"! What they had been dancing didn't really matter, because he had never learned how to dance! There had been times when he had seen his mother and father jumping around on the dance floor with many other people! Whatever they were dancing, they all seemed to be having a good time! In many ways, he enjoyed watching them giggle and laughing as they drank bottles of wine as they danced, a far cry from the ugly stories his parents had told him about the Civil War! His parents had often recounted many of the things they had been forced to do during those difficult times; but, thankfully, the war was over and things were starting to change for the better! It wasn't that things were perfect! There was still much room for improvment! But people were laughing and dancing and enjoying each other's company, and those were the things that were important! Being an elder brother to two younger sisters had been difficult! There had been another son, one year older than him who had died during childbirth, and the family had endured some pretty difficult times! His mother, a registered nurse, had taken the death of his brother badly and remained in a state of depression for a long time until he, Andres, had arrived! The birth had been a Godsend, because as soon as she discovered that the baby was in excellent health, she survived the depression and became transfixed with the idea of caring for another baby! From then on, she had given birth to two baby girls, each arriving into the world healthy and strong! She would often brag to her neighbors telling them how much her children loved her, a story that wasn't exactly untrue!

Andres was his mother's favorite! From the time he was an infant he had read any books that were available describing the politics of Spain and the implementation of the law that was intended to be uniformly applied throughout the country under the Franco government! The inconsistencies that bothered him had been discovered early in his readings! There had been many times when the statutes had not been uniformly applied, and the reasons given seemed senseless to his young mind! It was these inconsistencies that had made for some interesting discussions among the family, especially with his father who had fought in the Civil War and had personally witnessed the abuses of the new system. He had tried on many occasions to convince his son of his own idealistic principles, saying only that the law was the law; and, in the absence of something that was better, it needed to be respected and observed by the people! Most of the discussions had been friendly and informative! However, Andres was soon to learn that many of the inconsistencies that his father considered justified were actually wrong and that every case deserved to be decided on its own merits and should be treated likewise! There were many points of contradiction that prevailed throughout the country, particularly among the youth of the country, casuing some of them to be engaged in a silent rebellion, limited to small, smoke filled coffee houses that were rarely discussed publicly for fear of retaliation by the authorities. Andres had taken part in some of these disagreements as he became older! While he often expressed his own ideas, he soon came to realize that the authorities were governing the nation in a semi-authoritarian manner, mixing the inconsistencies of social reform with a military manifestation of right and wrong that bordered on dictatorship! The repressed ideas had been spreading throughout the free world, the same as they did in Spain! In some countries the movement was known as the youth uprising! In other more democratic countries that didn't have this authoritarian rule, they were simply called 'activists' !

The United States had just finished fighting the ugly war in Korea that was just as unpopular as the Spanish Civil War had been in Spain! Even though many of the ideals were similar, the exposure of freedoms mandated by the Consitution of the United States allowed for vocal dissents, especially among the youth! In Spain, unfortunately, these same movements were mandated by judicial reform imposed by a dictatorial government that forbade its exposure to the world! Unfortunately, while the growing waves of dissent were spreading throughout the region, they had been repressed by a controlled media; and often any person who opposed the rule of law could be tried for treason under the existing statutes. Andres was often reproached by his father when Guillermo found out that his son had taken part in some of the manifestations! Not that he considered them to be wrong, but he did know that the penalties could be quite severe! He did his best to prevent his son from encountering the same

fate he had encountered in earlier years when he had fought long
and hard, even after the Civil War had ended, to overthrow the
new government of Spain! He had been arrested and sent to a
concentration camp along with other members of the guerilla unit
called "Los Milicianos"! It was only when a new law was enacted
allowing the prisoners to be pardoned and released from the camps
so that they could work the farms and produce the fruits and
vegetables that were badly needed during the area of reconstruction
that he had been freed! There was fear, real fear, that his son
might be tried for treason and be punished and sent to jail for a
long time! This was when Andres decided that if he was going to
make a difference in changing some laws, he was going to do it
within the law, rather than in an outside coffee house! In order to
accomplish this, he was going to need to learn everything he could
about restrictions, decide upon their application and fairness, and
then involve himself into the humanities and try to convince the
bureaucrats that many of the laws were wrong and that they needed
to be changed. He had just returned from fullfilling his military
obligations that had sent him to Korea! Fortunately, the war had
ended before he arrived; but, having been assigned to a medical
unit, was convinced that wars were never the answer to political
problems! Just as so many other young men had done, he went to
Korea as a youngster and had returned a man! The tearful sendoff
he had received from almost everyone in Guisamo was still on his
mind! Coming from a very protective Spanish home, he had been
raised in Guisamo, a small farm town in Guisamo, where everyone
was more than a neighbor! Most of the people were like family!
It just seemed that many of the stories told by his father when he
was a young man seemed to be happening again at the other side of
the world! Perhaps it had been the influence of his father that had
convinced him into changing a troubled world for the better. There
had been a few correspondence courses in law, and that was when
he decided that upon completion of his military service, he would
apply to the University and study the law! Perhaps in some small
way, he would be able to change the country for the better without
the fear of retribution by the current government!

After the war, Guillermo had earned his release from one of the camps and had returned to Guisamo with his wife! He worked long and hard hours on a small parcel of land and had raised his children with love, attention and respect for other people! He hadn't spoken much about the Civil War, nor had he been critical of the new government in the presence of his children as they were growing up! Andres always felt that his father knew much more about the Civil War than he was willing to tell them! The only stories he would tell were about the camps and how they had obviously been constructed with a blueprint from Hell! The happiest day of his life was the day he had gotten his release and was permitted to return home to work the farm! His wife, Dolores was always at his side! Very often, the young Andres had told himself that if ever he would marry, it would need to be a woman who was as understanding and as caring as his mother had always been!

Tomorrow was going to be an important day in his young life! He would take the train from La Coruna and would travel to Madrid! The large university would become his home for the next few years! It would be a whole new world for him in a city crowded with people from every part of the country! Andres already expected to receive a great deal of friendly criticism, especially coming from a small town, but none of that mattered! His temper had always been even; and he knew he would be able to handle whatever comments were tossed into his direction! It seemed strange when his father took him to a nearby cantina, ordered several glasses of red wine, and had decided to do his fatherly chores in alerting his son to all of the pitfalls he would have! Andres smiled to himself, knowing that this was the way parents were toward their children; and there would probably come a day when he would do the same thing to his children! Guillermo had apparently overlooked the fact that his young son had served in Korea for more than a year; so being away from home was not something that was new to him!

"No te olvides de escribir!" (Don't forget to write!) his mother had repeated for the umpteenth time! Just like every other mother, they always wanted to maintain an attachment to their

children; and they hated the thought that one of their off-springs
was going off into the world in search of independence!!

"No te preocupes madre, que no te voy olvidar!" (Don't
worry mother! I won't forget you!) he told her, knowing that these
were the words she wanted to hear!

It was a long and uncomfortable train ride from La Coruna
to Madrid! He had sat next to a woman who was going to Madrid
to visit other family members that lived in the capital city! The
elderly woman had made several attempts to begin a conversation
with him; but, he continued to read his book and really didn't want
to listen to her telling him about the problems she had in finding
meaningful employment in Galicia. He knew only too well that
times in the nortehrn provinces were difficult! So many times he
had wondered to himself if perhaps, General Franco was punishing
the northern provinces because of their opposition to the Civil
War? Andres felt that if Spain was going to fluorish, it would need
to gain the support of all of its people! The bitterness that resulted
when he introduced the Moors from Africa into the Iberian
country were still strong! After all, Franco had been a native son,
who had been born and raised in the northern province of Galicia!
It wasn't until he heard the elderly woman say something about
overthrowing the government that he became interested! He had
listened to some of the agonizing stories told by others about the
war, and dreaded the thought of once again returning to the old
days and of fighting a losing battle! His father and many of his
friends had tried to fight the war and had ended up in concentration
camps as a reward for their efforts. He, too, was a Gallego and
knew very well of their determination and their stubborness,
but, fighting a cause without any future, was no way to rebuild a
country that had been torn by anger, stubborness and misguided
intentions! Everyone knew that Franco was firmly established as
the head of the government and his rule was absolute and firm!
Many of the civil liberties that people thought would come after
the war, had been left behind! The economy of the country was
in shambles; and, if any changes were going to occur, it would be
up to his generation that would return the country to its original
power! The last thing he needed to hear was a threat to organize

guerilla fighters that would prevent the country from growing either socially or economically!

"La guerra ya termino, senora! Es mejor dejar que descanse en paz!" he told her. (The war is over madame! It is best to let it rest in peace!)

"Eso es porque tu eres demasiado joven para pasar los tiempos malos!" (That's because you are too young to have endured the bad times!) she answered.

"What is there to gain by fighting another war?" was his reply.

"We need to establish the old government! Things were so much better then!"

"What makes you think that the old government was any better than the new one?" He asked the question calmly, almost in a matter-of-fact tone of voice It was almost as if he were inviting her to give him a reply.

"At least we had stability! That's more than we have now!" she told him.

"How can you say that Spain had any stability at all when the government changed faces every few weeks, and the hunger of people was never taken into consideration?" He thought of telling her about the plight of his parents, but decided that doing so would only prolong the unwanted conversation! There were too many other thoughts on his mind that needed his attention, and re-hashing the Civil War was certainly not one of them!

"At least we had our own land to cultivate! Now, the land has been cut in half and what we produce, a portion needs to be turned over to the new government!" One thing was certain, he thought! This old woman is certainly not one of Franco's admirers!

"That was one of the problems! Only a few of the people owned most of the land! The rest of the people had nothing! Also, from what I've read, the Republican party began to tax rich land owners to pay for construction work, so people could earn a few perronas to buy food for the table! The result was that the rich became poorer, and the poor were left to starve! Many of the people died of malnutrition! Was that any way to run a government?" By this time his voice had risen several octaves, and he felt himself becoming annoyed at the conversation!

"At least the old government tried to do something! What has Franco's government done for the people? Nothing! Absolutely nothing!" she said sternly.

"Franco is trying to feed the people! He knows that if the people are well fed, they will be better off and can better contribute to the rise of Spain! Had it not been for Franco, a communist government would now be in control! The people would continue to starve and there would be signs of poverty everywhere! With the new government there is hope, something that Spain has not had for a long time!" he told her.

No sooner had he finished speaking when he smiled to himself! He had just done something that he once said he would never do! But then, he was a Spaniard; and these were things that Spaniards were known to do!! He had been so troubled by the older woman and her defense of the old Republican government that he felt the urge to defend the new government of Franco! The truth was that he loathed Franco's regime as much as he loathed the old government that was riddled by corruption and malnutrition! He could sense by the sound of her voice that she was not happy with his answers! The truth was that neither was he! He finally felt relieved when she smacked her lips together and nodded her head! "That's the trouble with you young people! You have no idea how it was, because you are too young; and you always need to worship a hero!" she said.

Nothing could be farther away from the truth, but Andres felt that the conversation was becoming much too serious and it was time to bring it to an end! "Tiene usted mucha razon senora! Siempre hay que tener a alguien que sea un heroe!" (You are quite right ma'am! We always need to have someone who is a hero!) he said, as he rested his head against the back of his seat and closed his eyes. For several minutes, while pretending to be asleep, he heard her murmuring something! Whatever it was, it had been unintelligible and there was no reason to ask her to repeat what she was saying. The best thing to do was to continue pretending to be asleep and avoid any further conversation! Never would the woman know that he was not only unhappy with the old government of Spain; but, he was equally unhappy with the new one! What he hoped to do was to do something about it, but whatever needed to be done, would have to be done legally and through the system of courts. He had a compassion to help those who would need his help and try to change some of the laws that he considered discriminatory and in many cases also illegal! In order to accomplish his own aims, he would certainly need much more than an old woman sitting beside him as a professional informer!

It required several days for Andres to become enrolled and to be assigned a dormitory room! He had already noticed that the university seemed to be discriminating in favor of the affluent students who paid the high fees for their education, as against those students who came from the poorer sections of the country! His first exposure to discrimination was when he saw that the affluent students were always taught by full professors, most of which had received their education from abroad! Those students who came from the poor areas and of unwealthy parents, were taught by assistant professors or instructors who had not been able to reach the epitome of their profession! It didn't seem to matter at that time, Andres thought! He had come to study law, and had enough self confidence to know that he would be proficient no matter what professor had been assigned to his classes. His room mate was a slender young man from the city of Granada in the south of the country. Both men, while they had little in common, seemed to have hit it off well from the beginning! Carlos Perez had a dark complexion, and slick wavy hair that attracted the attention of the co-eds when he went to and from his classes. Whatever Andres lacked in personality and tact, Carlos had made up for it with the girls! He made it a point to always invite his friend to go with him to all of the social functions at school! Unfortunately, Andres felt guilty about going to these functions and he often would turn down the offer!

Despite their differences, Carlos was an interesting friend! No two men could have been more different, and it was probably the result of these differences that quickly made them the best of friends. His background had been from a modest family who had owned a large orange grove, part of which had been confiscated by the previous government and given out to some of the peasants living in the area. It wasn't until after the Civil War that the new government saw fit to provide his family with the confiscated land; and, when it was re-instated, once again provided the family with a reasonable income! The truth had been that the new government was in need of large supplies of citrus fruits for distribution in the northern provinces. This was one way of being assured that a large portion of the production would be turned over to the government, while still retaining enough to make a living on the fruits that could be sold on an open market. Andres always felt that Carlos good looks and olive complexion were probably gifts from gypsy ancestors who had migrated into the Southern part of Spain many years ago! Each man had his own ideas about the current political situation; still, his great personality was exactly what Andres needed on those days when he missed his family and wished he was back in the small town of Lugo! Whenever Carlos tried to take Andres out of his shell and develop a personality that would please the young girls, he would be repaid when Andres found it necessary to tutor his friend on those days when he had failed to study for an important exam. The fact remained that the men developed a strong bond between them and were always together. If Carlos had the same classroom as Andres, he always did his best to find a seat that was near his friend so they could be together. Carlos was a social butterfly, while Andres would frequently remain in his dormitory room studying his work and making sure that his grades continued to remain among the highest of the students in his classes!

As most of the Spanish universities, the Universidad Autonoma de Madrid was owned by the state! Admission was based upon the applicant's prior grades; and, in order to remain in good standing, it was necessary for the student to retain numerican grades of 80 for each class. If the numerical rating of the student dropped below 75, he would be expelled from the university and would be sent home! In theory, the system was fair, but he had seen cases of students that had been assigned into the elite classrooms where the grades had been consistently below the required levels and they had been allowed to continue studying in the insitution! This was just another of the discriminating characteristics that Andres had noticed; but since he was not required to pay any tuition or board, it was important that he remain quiet for fear of any reprisals!

One day, Andres had been busy studying for an examination when Carlos came in the room! He was excited as he asked his friend to put down his book because he had a favor that he wanted to ask of him!

"Que quieres ahora, hombre? No te puedo ayudar, porque necesito estudiar para manana!" (What do you want now? I can't help you because I need to study for tomorrow!) Andres said.

"It doesn't matter! Look, you have got to listen to me!" his friend said. "There is a dance at the main hall tonight! There is a girl that I have an eye on who will be going with a friend! I need you to go so you can be a partner to her friend!"

"Are you crazy? You know that I'm not a good dancer! Why do you think I never go to those things?" Andres replied.

"You are much too serious! You need to have some recreation; and, besides, you can't let me down now that I need you!"

"Nah! That's not for me! Heck, with your personality, I'm quite sure you can handle two girls!" Andres told him smiling.

"C'mon, Andres! No seas asi! (Don't be like that!) "I need you to go! Besides, I already told Dorita that I would take a friend as an escort! I knew you wouldn't let me down! You have to come!" he insisted.

Andres began to laugh! It was just like him to be involved with two women at the same time! He was obviously going to need to find a way of smoothing things out! "Sorry, not today! Tomorrow night you are on your own! Besides I have some serious studying to do and so should you! Tomorrow, you will be asking me to help you!" Andres said. Then he added, "Also, to tell the truth, I don't have very much money! I think it's best that I not go!"

He felt a bit embarassed admitting to his friend that he really didn't have very much money! The truth was that even though the tuitions and room and board were supplied by the government, there were the added costs such as meals and books that had to be paid out of the small sums of money sent by his parents each week. The few pesetas he would receive needed to hold him over until he received another letter from home! Despite his embarassment, he knew that his friend was sympathetic and understanding as he had been on previous occasions.

"Conho!! Is that all that's holding you back? Why didn't you tell me? You don't have to worry! That is why we are good friends! I have enough money for both of us! All that I need is to hear you say that you'll come along with me!" Andres was stunned and confused not knowing what to do! He had hoped that by telling him that he had no money, perhaps his friend wouldn't have insisted, but, instead, it didn't seem to matter at all! As far as his friend was concerned his problem was solved if the only thing that was needed was a few pesetas!

"What the Hell is the matter with you?" Carlos said. "How many times have I told you to see me when you're broke and need money? Damn it, what do you think friends are for? Now, put your damned books down and get dressed! There is another dance tonight that we'll both attend! If things go okay, we'll stay late! If not, we'll be in our room early! You need some distraction!"

"But I don't even know what your friend looks like! As a matter of fact, I don't know what her friend looks like either! Suppose I don't like her, or suppose they don't like me, then what do I do? Stay there and watch you dance while I feel like a damned fool?"

"If you don't like her or you don't hit it off, excuse yourself after a while, and tell them you need to study for an exam! Who can say, if her friend doesn't like you, she might tell you the same thing! That will make things easier for both of you!" he said. There was no point in looking for more excuses! Carlos had given him a convincing argument! What he said had been the truth; since coming to the University, he had no social life! All of his time had been devoted to his books and the more he thought about it, the more he realized that what his friend had told him had been the truth! The studies had taken up most of his time and some recreation would do him good! If things didn't work out, he would be free to excuse himself and leave! After all, nearly everyone knew that tomorrow there would be planned examinations in most of the classrooms! Why they had decided to schedule a dance on the night before major testing was a mystery! They should have scheduled it at a far better time!

"Okay, okay!" Andres finally told him, if only not to listen to him insisting he should go to the dance. "I get the feeling that you aren't going to let me alone until I give you my word about going! Give me an hour to shower and shave! There is still one thing that you need to know! I still need to study for a major exam tomorrow, so I can't make it a late night!" Andres admitted..

Carlos let out a hearty laugh! Then, almost as if on impulse, he reached over and planted a kiss on his cheek!

"Get out of here! Next thing I know, you'll be telling me that her friend is really a man in disguise! Now, let me get dressed!" he said jokingly!

The dimly lit hall where the dance was to be held had been decorated with multi colored streamers to create the atmosphere for the dance! A large table had been set up along the far side containing articles of food and drink! The music had begun to play and Andres was felling a bit uncomfortable as he walked near one of the speakers that was blasting over his head. Carlos immediately began to look over the young, unescorted women that were standing alone. Andres remained a step behind as he silently watched his friend spring into action! As he went from young woman to young woman hoping to start up a conversation, some would speak to him while others simply walked away! Andres's own experience with women had been very limited! The only time of his life when he had been away from home had been when he served in the army in Korea. In the province of Galicia where he had born and raised, social gatherings such as this one had been non-existant! Even on the few occasions when someone would decide to form a dance or social gathering, many of the young people were so tired from working in the fields that they either stayed away or else didn't care to engage in idle chatter! Where he came from, marriages were arranged in advance; and, if one was not interested in any of the young ladies, they would avoid any

contact and try to discourage any interest! This had been a side
of the social activities that had always bothered him! He could
never understand why the parents of a young person were the
ones to decide who and what was best for their offspring! It just
wasn't fair! His mind was filled with other thoughts, such as law,
and his desire to change the antiquated customs that he thought
were unfair. If he were to become interested in one of the young
women, the next step was to have an immediate round of secret
gatherings, each side trying to decide whether the two young
people were adequately suited for one another! The one thing he
wanted to avoid was to upset his parents, especially if they decided
to make such important decisions on his behalf. They would mean
well, of course! But these were different times and he had other,
more important plans. His parents were simple people and he had
been raised with the stories of his father how he fought against the
emergence of the new government. Because he had read about the
life in the old provinces, there was still much work to be done; and
he didn't have time for any college romances! There was an effort
to rebuilt Spain just as many other countries that were in a similar
position and rebuilding following the World War. There were
still many times of turmoil and unrest, and it was these issues he
wanted to address! The only thing he wanted to do was to receive a
formidable education that would allow him to take an active place
in the changing world! Everything else could certainly wait!

As he walked around the hall he saw groups of several
young people speaking and laughing! It was almost as though they
were oblivious to the things that were happening in the world! He
wondered how many of these young people were as serious or as
dedicated as he was? Did they really have anything in common?
He already knew that unless he was a member of a specific group,
he would be alone; and no one would approach him or begin a
meaningful conversation with him! Perhaps coming here had
been a mistake after all, he thought! He had wanted to remain in
his room and study, and had come down here only to appease the
demands of his room mate! Slowly, he worked his way over to the
large table that was filled with pastries and several large bowls that
were filled with a red liquid! He poured some of the liquid into a

paper cup, and noticed that it tasted like wine with sugar! True, he liked wine, and he did have a sweet tooth; but he certainly didn't like them together! Slowly, he placed his cup down on the table and started to walk away when a young woman came up to the table and poured herself a cup of the untasty, sweet liquid!

"Ugh!" she said as soon as she tasted it. "Este vino esta demasiado dulce!" (This wine is much too sweet!) At first, he smiled when she echoed his thoughts! He had no idea whether this young woman was repeating what he said or if she wanted to start a conversation with him.

"Tienes razon! Tampoco me gusta!" he said. (You're right! I don't like it either!)

"Are you from around here?" she wanted to know. He was starting to feel that this attractive young woman had indeed approached him with the idea of starting a conversation! He could see that she was small in stature and thin, but she had smooth lines and was very attractive!

"No! I am not from around here!" he told her."I am from Galicia!"

"Did you come alone?" she asked. At first he thought she was being a bit forward asking if he came alone! As long as she was asking, he might as well tell her the truth and let the chips fall where they may!

"Actually I was talked into coming here by my room mate Carlos Perez! He seems to be making the rounds speaking to everyone else! I was really getting bored and was just about to go to my room! I have a major test tomorrow, and should have stayed where I was!" he said.

He had no idea to reveal so much information with her; after all, what did she care? She was undoubtedly with her friends and anyone as attractive as she was would certainly have her choice of attractive suitors who would be anxious to start a conversation with her!

"You almost sound as out of place as I feel! You see, I came with my friend under similar circumstances! She came to meet a young man here and insisted that I come with her! It was my understanding that her young man was going to bring along a friend for me! I wasn't interested in meeting anyone! The man is probably an ogre with three eyes and two heads! I don't like blind dates, do you!" she said and noticed that he had begun to smile/

His mind was on the things that Carlos had told him! Could it be that this was the young woman he had told him about? For a minute he thought of excusing himself and going over to where Carlos was speaking to his young lady. He should tell him he was leaving; but, this young woman had started speaking to him and he had found her attractive enough to wait a while longer!

"I'm just wondering if I am the guy that you were supposed to meet!" he said. Just then, another young woman came over to where they were speaking! She said something as her eyes scanned the floor! Once she spotted Carlos, she quickly excused herself and said, "I have to go now! My date is on the other side of the dance floor!"

"I guess that leaves the two of us all alone!" she told him. He looked over at his friend and saw that he was enjoying his conversation as both he and his lady friend were walking toward them! Andres was undecided whether to stay or leave! If he was going to exit the dance, he would need to do so before Carlos talked him into remaining!

"I don't think so!! I'll just return to my room and study!" he told her as Carlos was approaching him.

"Ola guapa!" Carlos told her as he eyed her from top to bottom. "Cual es tu nombre!" (Hi good looking! What's your name?) The young woman looked at him; and he could see that she seemed angry that he was taking liberties she hadn't wanted him to take! She had just met this young man and they had been talking! What right did he have to interrupt? For whatever it was worth, they did have something in common! They were both bored and lonely! Maybe if he allowed her a little more time, she might have convinced him to stay!

"Mi nombre es Maripaz Romero!" she said with annoyance, making it obvious that she didn't appreciate his interruption!

"I'm sorry!" he said. "I didn't mean to make you angry!"

"I don't like strangers to call me "guapa"! I prefer being called by my real name!" It was her way of telling him that she wanted to be treated with respect as the young man she had speaking to had shown her! Only then did the young lady with Carlos interrupt them to say that Maripaz had been the young woman she had arranged for his friend. They had met quite accidentally, but, at least they were no longer strangers! The music started to play and Carlos and his young companion walked out and started to dance to the music!

"I'm sorry!" Andres said. "I am not a very good dancer! Perhaps it would be best if I went to my room! I'm afraid I would only be dull company for you!" he said as he flashed her a smile and started to walk away.

"Please don't leave!" she said, as he turned around surprised that she had asked him to remain!

"Maybe if they play a slow number, I'll be able to talk you into dancing with me! I don't really care if you aren't a good dancer! You see, I'm not very good either! At least we have something in common!" she said smiling. "Where are you from? And, as long as we're going to be together,don't you think you should tell me your name?"

"My name is Andres Torres and I come from Galicia!"

"Now, I know why it is you don't want to dance! In Galicia you need a bag-pipe and drum while they are playing the Muriego or La Jota, right?"

"Something like that!" he answered. "Although I don't dance those dances either, but I do like to listen to the bag-pipe and the drum!" he answered. It occured to him that this young woman was not only easy to speak to, but she also had a sense of humor and wasn't afraid to laugh!

She smiled at him and nodded her head! It occured to him that she had a warm smile! It seemed as if her entire face was lighting up when she smiled and it seemed to be infectuous! "It just occured to me that we seem to have something in common!" she told him. "I come from Bilbao, deep into the Basque country! We also enjoy listening to bag-pipe and drum!! I knew we had something we could speak about!"

For a brief moment, Andres felt a little embarassed that she had seemed so forward while knowing nothing about him! Where he came from, young women were not forward and he wondered if his cheeks were turning red!

"I'm sorry!" she said. "I didn't mean to embarass you! It just seems that you and I are the only outcasts here! Perhaps we should be partners!"

"Why should we feel like outcasts? I thought that everyone at school was supposed to be treated equally!" he lied.

He knew all too well that not everyone was treated equally! Those students whose parents made major contributions to the University or came from affluent families had a much better selection of classes taught by professional instructors than those that came from more modest families! The young woman was right! As far as they were concerned, they were considered outcasts from the other students; with the exception of his friend Carlos.

"C'mon. Andres! I can't believe you haven't noticed the difference! We don't have the same classrooms as do the elite! We already have two strikes against us just by coming here!"

"Then why did you come here? Why didn't you go to another University? Don't they have Universities in Bilbao?"

"Yes, of course they do! But not like this one! If you ever hope to find a good job after you finish, you need to get a degree from this University!"

"What are you majoring in?" he asked.

"I'm studying the humanities! I'd like to learn everything I can about my people! Hopefully, when I'm finished I'll be able to go back and put my knowledge to good use! What about you? What is your major?"

"I'm studying law! Hopefully, one day I'll become an attorney and try to do something about the things that I see as being wrong!"

"From where, Galicia? You won't make very much money working there! Or do you intend to remain in Madrid and practice law from here? The city is full of starving attorneys!"

"I can always go back home to eat! My parents own a small tract of farm land, so at least we do have food on the table!"

"You may need to! Either that or you can always return with me to Bilbao! We do have a lot of sheep, but not very much practice of law! Who can say? Maybe one day things will change and we'll be recognized for who we are!"

"You seem a bit angry!" he said as the music started to play a slow number!

Maripaz didn't wait to be asked to dance! She grabbed him by the hand as if he was a little boy and slowly edged him toward the center of the dance floor! "Okay," she told him. "Now, show me how you dance!"

Again, he felt a little embarassed that she had taken the initiative of guiding him into the middle of the dance floor without first asking! It seemed a bit strange that a woman could be so forward; and, yet, he wasn't offended at all! As he started to move in time to the music, he discovered that the steps were coming to him much easier than he had expected. She seemed satisfied with him as he felt her body come a bit closer until he could almost feel her breathing against his cheek! It was a feeling that he had never felt before; and for some unknown reason, he rather liked the feeling!

From that moment, Andres and Maripaz spent the rest of the evening dancing and comparing the areas they came from! The night had passed by quickly, too quickly! It seemed as if he had just arrived and it was already time for him to return to his room! There was something about this young woman that attracted him and he wished he could gather up enough nerve to ask to see her again! He told himself over and over that it had been the magic of the music and that everything would be forgotten when he was back in the classroom the following day! Besides, he didn't have very much money, so going on a date with her was beyond his expectations! The fact that she was good looking had not gone unnoticed; and she could probably have a date with any other young man in school that she wanted! After all, how could he expect to compete against someone, perhaps from an affluent family who could afford dinner, a bottle of good wine and an enjoyable evening? Whatever her own reasons had been for being with him didn't seem to matter anymore! The euphoria of the evening had ended almost as quickly as it started! It was now time to say good night; dance the final dance, and return to the room! Tmorrow would be another day and things would be back to normal!

As they were dancing another slow number, he noticed that she stepped a bit closer; but then, he reasoned that it was probably the mood of the slow music!They danced cheek to cheek without speaking! It had been the only time during the entire evening when they had found nothing to say! The silence probably had some meaning, he thought, but he surely didn't know what it was! After the music stopped, he realized that she was still holding on to his hand on the dance floor! It seemed as if they were standing there like two spellbound kids, staring silently at each other without speaking!

Finally, after what seemed like hours, it was Maripaz who broke the silence! "I guess I was wrong!" she said.

"Wrong? About what?" he answered.

"I was waiting for you to ask when you could see me again! Frankly, I thought we had hit it off rather well! I guess I was wrong! You didn't ask, so I guess this is good-bye! I have to admit that I do feel a little disappointed!" she admitted, almost as if she really was regretting that the evening had come to an end!

"Boy! Were you ever wrong? But not about what you were probably thinking! I would love to see you again! I really enjoyed speaking and dancing with you! To be honest, since I come from Galicia, we don't have very much money, that's why I don't go out very much! I suppose I was too embarassed to tell you!"

"Don't you think it should be up to me to decide whether or not I wanted to see you again? What makes you think you need to have money to see me? We could go to the park and study together, or else we could take bus ride into town and walk through the Plaza de Espana; feed the pigeons and criticize the tourists! That wouldn't cost very much!"

Andres started to laugh! He had never before met anyone quite like her! She was forward, and yet simple! Elegant but with a casual flair loaded with simple pleasures! How could he not want to see her again?

"Perhaps if we put our money together, we might even go into one of the cantinas or slse sit in the park and listening to 'La

Tuna' serenade us all afternoon! If we play our cards carefully, we might even have few perronas for a bottle of wine; that is, unless you become extravagent and decide you want an empanada to go with the wine!" she said laughing.

"You make it hard for me to say no! I really would like very much to see you again! That is, if you're sure you won't mind!"

"What's the matter with you? Haven't they taught you anything at all about women in Galicia? You think that Galicia is poor; what makes you think it is any different in Bilbao? At least allow me to preserve my honor by allowing me to wait until you ask me!" she told him jokingly.

"Okay Maripaz! When can I see you again?" he asked, completely oblivious that he and she were the only couple that were still standing in the center of the dance floor!

"Not too soon!" she answered. "I don't want to seem anxious! How about tomorrow?"

"I have a major test in the morning, but, I'll be free all afternoon! Will you be available?"

"Just tell me where and when to meet you!"

"One o'clock, by the front entrance! It will probably interfere with my siesta, but, I'll have to make the sacrifice!" she said smiling. She simply nodded her head and was happy that he had finally asked to see her again!

"Buenas noches, Andres! Hasta manana!" she said.

"Buenas noches, Maripaz! Que descanses bien!" he answered.

Andres was much too excited to fall asleep! He had tried to study his school work, but his mind was on other things! It was the first time he felt excited about someone and he couldn't get her out of his mind! She was forward, but there was a way about her that was not offensive! He tried to guess what her family was like! There had been some rumblings in the newspapers about the Basque provinces; and to many, the Basques were nothing more than a group of troublemakers! She was very direct, and there was an air of sincerity that made you believe anything she said! Obviously, extravagance did not impress her! That was another thing that puzzled him! Most of the girls he had met at school were extravagent! They all wanted to be wined and dined; and because of this, he would always refuse to go into town with other members of the group. He wondered how many of the other young women would have been so open minded and truthful as she was? Damn it! It bothered him that she had made her way into his mind and he couldn't get her out! All that he could hope for was that he had absorbed enough of the work before the dance, so that he would do well in his work!

It had been late when Andres finally went to his room only to see that his friend was wide awake waiting for him! He hadn't said anything, but had undressed and laid down on his bed staring at the ceiling!

"What's the matter, Andres? Are you having a hard time sleeping?" Carlos asked kiddingly.

"I guess so! Maybe it was too much activity for one night!" he replied.

"It was strange that your young woman was the one who came with my girl friend! It seems that she hadn't wanted to go to the dance! She also hates blind dates and had to be talked into coming! From what I could see, the two of you seemed to get along well together!" he said.

"Yes!" I had to admit that it was a pleasant surprise! Thanks for talking me into going!" Andres said.

"Well....c'mon! Tell me more! Are you going to see her again? Don't you think I should be told all of the details?"

"What is there to tell? Yes, I plan to see her again tomorrow afternoon! That's all the details!"

"What did you talk about? I saw the two of you engaged in a pretty serious conversation!"

"Not very much! Only that she comes from the Basque country; and she isn't at all the way people say the Basque women are, stubborn and selfish!"

"Andres, look! I watched the two of you after the last dance! You were the only two standing in the middle of the dance floor! Don't tell me that you were comparing notes about Vizcaya!"

"No! You're right! At that point we weren't even thinking about Vizcaya! Now, does that answer your question?" Andres said.

"All I want to know is whether or not you had a good time? If you did, I'm happy as Hell for you! If not, then, you'll have to try again!"

"Actually, I had a great time! I found her interesting and attractive! I almost hate to say it, but I need to thank you into talking me into going! Now, you'd better get some sleep! We both have exams tomorrow and we need our rest!"

"Okay, okay! I get the message! That's your way of telling me to keep my damned mouth shut! Is that it?"

"Yep, you got it! Now turn out the light! We have a busy day tomorrow!" Andres said.

The following morning, Andres was already showered and dressed by the time Carlos woke up! "Donde vas con tanta prisa?" he asked. (Where are you going in such a hurry?)

"I need to go out and I don't know when I'll be back! Don't wait for me for dinner!" he answered.

Having dinner at the cafeteria together had been part of their regular routine! Whoever returned first to the room would wait for the other to arrive! This had been their own private time when the two would discuss the events of the day and other trivia that was important. Whenever things went wrong, they had learned to lean on each other until their friendship became stronger with each day. Carlos noticed that something was different about today! He already knew that Andres was having a major exam today; but for some reason, it didn't seem to be nearly as important as the others! Andres had been unusually quiet and he knew the reasons why!

"Are you seeing that woman from last night?" he asked, already assuming what the answer was going to be.

"Yes!" his friend answered. "I don't know where we're going! One thing for sure, with my income, it won't be very far!" he answered.

"Do you need money?" Carlos asked. This had been another of many things that had strengthened the bond between them. Whenever one or the other was going out and found themselves short of funds, they would borrow from each other! It was their way of making certain that neither risked having a good time because of a lack of funds!

"No!" Andres replied. Carlos could see that he had said it with some hesitation and that he probably did not have enough pesetas for the evening!

"Here!" Carlos said abruptly.He reached in his pocket and took out several pesetas and handed them to him! "Take these! I know you are short of money! This will help you!"

"Thanks!" he answered. "I feel pretty damn lucky to have you for my room mate! If I don't spend them, I'll return them as soon as I return!"

"No me jodas!" (Don't screw with me!) he replied. "If you return them, I'll know you didn't have a good time! Now, get out of here and have a good time! This is the first time I saw you excited about going out, and it's about time! Just remember to call me, if you need any help with her!" he said laughing.

By the time Andres reached the front door of the university, he saw that she had already arrived and was waiting for him! "Ya va siendo tiempo que llegaras!" (It's about time you arrived!) she said laughing.

"I think you were a bit early! I came as soon as I got out of class!" He noticed that she was wearing a white pair of slacks and a simple blouse! She also had on a pair of alparagatas, the same as they used to wear in Galicia! He paused momentarily, just enough to notice her natural beauty! Her long black hair was pulled back just enough to accentuate the smooth clear lines of her face! He paused just long enough to tell her how nice she looked! It was a compliment he had never before said to any other woman!

"I'm glad that you like the way I look! I was hoping you would! Last night, I needed to get all dressed up just like one of those other senoritas at the dance! Today, I felt I could dress more comfortably!" She immediately took his hand the same as she had done the previous night! After a brief discussion, they agreed to go to the park, buy a small bag of peanuts and feed the pigeons!

"How did you know that pigeons like peanuts?" he asked jokingly. "Remember, they are Spanish pigeons and maybe they would rather pick on castanas!"

"They'd better take what they can get! The castanas won't be available for a few months!" she said, as they walked down the street to a small park that was located a short distance from the Plaza de Espana! After they had been there a while, he asked her if she would like to go to the Plaza Central, drink some wine and listen to La Tuna!" She accepted the invitation immediately; and they selected a smal intimate cafe with a small iron table and a large umbrella, large enough to shield their faces from the strong afternoon sun!

"I hope you like this place!" he remarked. 'This is where I sometimes come to study! I find it very relaxing and away from the noise back at the univeristy!"

He looked over the simple menu and made a mental note of how many pesetas he could afford. It was barely enough for a flask of red wine, some tortilla Espanola, and an order of Queso Manchego and chorizos! It was just enough to satisfy their appetites! They spoke about their childhood and of the things they had missed because they were no longer available! It was a surprise when they realized how similar their childhood had been! She was an only child! Her parents had been born in poverty in Asturias and had migrated to the Basque country after the Civil War! It seemed like a coincidence that Andres parents had also come from Asturias and had decided to settle in Galicia for some unknown reason! They had obviously been active with underground activity in the post-war period, but that was all he knew! He felt relieved when the Tuna finally arrived, sang a few songs and then left the table! Andres and Maripaz were oblivious to anyone else! The afternoon had passed them by and they could see the night clouds begin to gather! Never before had Andres seen the time go by so quickly, and it was difficult to believe that the time had come to return to school!

"I wonder where the time went?" she said sadly.

"I guess that is what happens when you enjoy what you're doing! I don't remember when a day has gone by so quickly!" he told her.

"I enjoyed every minute! I wish we could stay here all night!" she told him. He could see that the exhileration in her voice he had seen all afternoon had vanished and she seemed saddened at the thought of leaving! "When will we see each other again?" she asked sadly, hoping he would say that he was as anxious to see her as she was to be with him!

"I don't know!" he answered. "I have a great deal of studying to do! I can't be with you and study at the same time!"

"Does that mean you don't want to see me again?" she asked sadly. "Have I been a disappointment to you?"

"Gosh no!! That's just it! I liked being with you too much!! I could see you every day and wouldn't be disappointed!" he answered. He was being truthful! It had been a wonderful day and indeed he wanted to see much more of her! He also knew that being with her would interfere with his school work and that needed to come first in his life above everything else!

"Forgive me for not understanding! You liked being with me so much that you don't want to see me again! Is that it?"

"Of course not! That wasn't what I meant at all! It's only that my parents saved a great deal of money to send me here and I can't disappoint them!" he explained.

"Does that mean that you'll cut off all of your social life? Somehow, I find that hard to believe!" she told him.

He could see by the look on her face that she was both hurt and angry by his comments! She had every right to be! After all, why should he turn away from his social life? All of his friends had other friends they saw frequently and it didn't hurt their grades! Look at his friend Carlos! He was with a new girl almost every night and still he found time to study!

"I want very much to see you again!" he told her. "It doesn't matter if I see you for just a few minutes or a full day! I enjoyed your company and I liked being with you! I know how I feel, and I'm afraid of what may happen if we see each other too often! It has nothing to do with you, it has to do with me! Please, don't be angry! The last thing I want is for you to be angry with me!"

"And where does that leave me? Am I supposed to wait until you decide that it is time for us to see each other? Is that what you want me to do?"

"No, Maripaz! That wouldn't be fair to you! Perhaps one day when we both have finished our studies, we can then pick yo where we left off! Things will be much different then, you'll see!" he stammered trying to find the right words to say, knowing that the excuses he was giving her didn't make any sense at all! The truth was that he did want to see more of her, much more! But he was also afraid of what could happen! He could not afford to allow his studies to fail; it wouldn't be fair to his parents!

"Suppose we see each other again next week! Is that okay with you?" he asked. He had though of his suggestion as being a compromise, but he could see by the look on her face that she was much too angry to accept it as such! The fiery Asturiano temperament had taken hold of her senses and she was no longer aware of what she was saying!

"Don't bother, Andres! Stay with your books! If the day comes when you need someone to talk to, pick up a book and speak to it! Maybe it can console you and will listen to your nonsense!" she answered angrily.

"Can't we at least talk it over? We've had a wonderful day! It wuld be a shame to have it end this way!"

"I wasn't the one who wanted it to end, remember? It was you who laid down all the road blocks! I almost feel sorry for you for not recognizing sincerity when you see it! I suppose that living with your friend has made a difference in what you want out of life!" There was no point in answering! The discussion had suddenly turned ugly and he knew that what he had told her had made no sense at all! The fact was, that he did want to see her!

"Let me take you back to the university!" he said.

"Don't bother! I don't need you to take me back! I know the way!" she said as she stood up and left him alone in the plaza!

There was little more he could do as he watched her walk away, thinking what a damn fool he had been! At least they had exchanged room numbers! After things had quieted down, he would call her again hoping that by that time she had forgotten her anger and would be willing to see him again! Andres remained in the plaza sipping on his wine, thinking about how ugly the evening had turned out! It had started off so great and had gone steadily downhill because of what he said! When he saw that no one was left at the plaza, he paid his bill and returned alone to the university! He needed desperately to speak to someone, and the only person he could talk to that would understand him was his friend and room mate! He went to his room and laid down on the thin narrow bed! Carlos had obviously gone out for the evening and had not returned! The only thing Andres wanted to do was to be alone with his thoughts and his pleasant memories. A long time later, he was disturbed by loud voices and a commotion in the hallway just outside his room! The voices sounded as if they were of women and he wondered how they could have gotten into the men's area at that time of evening without first receiving permission! Not that it had mattered! Whatever it was certainly had nothing to do with him!

He opened up a book and started to read, anything that would take his attention away from his thoughts and the commotion outside in the hallway! The more he tried to concentrate on what he was reading, the louder the commotion seemed to get! It continued to get louder until it was now interfering with his concentration! Suddenly, it happened! From out of nowhere, there was a sudden knock on the door! The knock was soft at first; but it soon got progressively louder until there was banging on the door before he was able to open it and see who it was and what they wanted! He jumped out of bed and opened the door! He stood there in awe and shocked by what he saw! Laying in front of him, was Maripaz, outside in the hallway with several of her friends! One look at her and he saw that she was bruised and battered from head to toe! The white slacks she was wearing were covered with fresh blood as she struggled to stand straight up while being supported on the arms of two of her friends. He immediately picked up her limp and battered body in his arms and gently carried her to his bed! All he could do was to be astonished by what had obviously happened and wonder what could have gone so terribly wrong!!

CHAPTER 2

San Sebastian

In the small seaport of San Sebastian, Flaco and Soledad
kept busy collecting the vegetables from the farm and storing them
into the Horreo to be used during the cold winter months! This
was the usual routine during the fall months, and while the harvest
had been good and plentiful, they both realized that something
was missing from their lives. Their only daughter, Maripaz, had
gone away to the university in Madrid! Soledad had done her best
to convince their daughter to attend the univeristy at Bilbao, but
when it was time to enroll, she had decided on the Universidad de
Madrid, which she argued, had much better courses in the fields
of humanities that were of interest to her! As a child growing up
in the Basque regions of the country, Maripaz had been a loveable
child; but, at times, she could become a bit testy and a bit difficult!
Her mother, however, understood that she was young and would
overlook her youthful impatience! These were certainly not the
best of times in Vizcaya! Flaco had been fortunate enough in
purchasing a small parcel of land and a few head of sheep to grow
and breed in the rich green pastures of the land! After the Civil
War he had seen some success in his new work; and after a few
years his herd of sheep was among the largest in the country! The
land had also been productive, and he had managed, with Soledad's
help, to harvest enough fruits and vegetables for themselves and

to feed some of the local peasants who had also migrated into the area, but who had not been quite as lucky!

Success, however, had not been easy! When he first arrived at San Sebastian, he had used the small amount of money he had earned while serving as the Mariscal of Toledo! The first thing Soledad had insisted on was their marriage! Miguel had not been opposed to the marriage, although he would have preferred to wait until they had been settled in and on their way! At her insistance, they were married in a simple ceremony at a small church located on the outskirts of the city! They had enjoyed a storybook marriage that had come after many years of hardship and more unhappiness than either of them wanted to admit! In their own way, each had harbored a feeling of guilt knowing that they had contributed to each other's unhappiness! Fortunately, their love had endured the hardships; and, when Soledad again saw him, she had promsied herself never to lose him again! There had been a change in her personality from her youth! She had been known as La Muneca, but she had used that name as a reminder of the evils about life! Thankfully, those days were now gone forever! Her only interest was to be with Miguel, to care for and love him, and to help him in everything he wanted to do! Times had been tough as they had struggled during the early years of marriage! It had been difficult at first to provide enough food for the table! Fortunately, and with Soledad's great help, they had weathered the storm and were now the envy of the area!

The happiest time in their marriage had been when their young daughter was born! All of the pains and agonies were quickly forgotten when the healthy and beautiful daughter was born! The realization that her infant daughter had been the product of their love had made it all worthwhile! The only disagreement she remembered had been in the selection of a name for their tiny daughter! Miguel had insisted she be named after Soledad's mother, Balbina; but it was Soledad who steadfastly insisted she be named Maripaz as a symbol of their past and, hopefully, to their future! After all, it had been the clear blue sea that had guided them into a safer harbor, and the fact that Spain was now finally at peace! All that was left was an unfortunate memory of the suffering they had all endured! It also seemed like a sign that told them that the worse was now behind them; and they and all the others could now be focused on the future!

The small tract of farm land that Miguel had purchased was near the ocean; and he immediately felt it would be ideal for farming! From the profits out of the crops, he continued to invest in more land which in turn would also increase the harvest for market! After a few months, he invested his profits in buying more head of sheep as well as a few other barn animals for the farm. In time, the sheep began to multiply; and, after a few short years, he and Soledad owned a sizeable spread of green land and a large herd of sheep, enough to sell on the open market at a healthy price thus increasing his income! The spread of their land was among the most fertile and scenic of the entire region! They always enjoyed the clear ocean view from one side of the land. On the other side, they had the spectacular view of the giant Pyrenees mountains. that majestically separated Vizcaya from the French borders! It was an ideal location to raise a family; and, at the same time, it provided them with enough money that soon made them one of the wealthiest families in the Basque area!

It was the priest from Asturias, Don Joaquin who had performed the ceremony! He too had joined Los Milicianos, more for survival than because of fantasies and ideologies that he felt were useless! Soledad had turned to him on several occasions when she needed someone to speak to, and, after she and Miguel had gone to Vizcaya, she had asked the good priest to join them! It had been something he did with reluctance, but, it was a way of getting away from the possibility of being imprisoned for being a member of the underground! It had turned into a real blessing, as he began to celebrate mass in his own church and soon became an accepted member of the community as well as a close friend of the family! He had also helped Soledad and Miguel in working the soil whenever they would need an extra hand! Once wealth came into their lives, the good priest could always depend on Miguel and Soledad for support! Strangely, after so many years of hardships, it seemed that all of Soledad's childhood dreams and wishes had now been fullfilled! They could now face the future together in their new home!

In his spare time, Miguel had begun to read everything he could find concerning his adopted land! He was interested in seeing for himself any differences from the land he had left behind! The Basque nation, as they wanted the rest of the world to know, had been spared from the tribulations of the Civil War! For whatever reason, the new government of Franco had little interest in this part of the country! There had been some who had theorized that Franco had deliberately avoided having any contact with the Basques because of the fear of not knowing what to expect! It was believed that their determination to obliterate anyone who tried to disrupt their autonomy would be handed a devastating blow! Franco, having been born and raised in Galicia knew all about the existance of the Basques,but many believed that he feared any additional confrontations with them! Even though they were an organized force, their ability to seek refuge in the Pyrenees would have ended in an additional loss of troops that he simply could not afford to lose! The losses sustained because of the war had been many; and with the entire world in turmoil because of the Second World War, he could no longer depend upon his friends or his allies to help him defeat an area that for all intents and purposes was practically worthless and not worth the trouble! It was common knowledge that many of the underground operatives had escaped execution and capture by leaving Spain and seeking refuge among the Basques! In addition, he didn't want to interfere with their strange beliefs, customs and ways of living that he knew little about! As a group, the Basques had never considered themselves to be Spaniards! While most of them spoke fluent Spanish, they had their own language that was taught in the schools. It was a language that was not easily understood by any of the of the other people.For the Basques, the Civil War meant nothing!There was a genuine sympathy for the people but had decided to remain neutral same as Switzerland had done during the World War! Their exposure was mainly to the French and many of their fruits and vegetables were routinely carried over the Pyrenees and sold in the outdoor markets! Miguel thought that if he and his family remained in the area that had provided them with refuge, the least he could do in appreciation was to study everything he could about his new land and to convey the results of his knowledge to his family! From the beginning, he realized that there were many more complexities to this land than there were in Spain!

There had been some evidence to suggest from the archeological and ethnographic findings that the Basque people had evolved from the Cro-Magnon era for some 40,000 years before there was the existance of Spain! The distinctive features of the people were identified by scholars as far back as 7,000 years. Two thousand years later came the introduction of sheep that were not native to the area, and were followed by horses and cattle that came into being! The circumstances of these introductions made it necessary for the people to travel periodically into other areas which later contributed to cultural and sociological advances. There was also some evidence to lend support to the theories that the cultures of the surrounding areas were mostly those acquired from the basin of the Rio Ebra as well as the region of Acquitaine! Some scholars had pointed out that those areas were of particular importance in Basque archeological and linguistic history since it coincides with the seasonal migration of flocks of people in search of rich pastures in the Pyrenees and where there are still many Basques place names that can be found!

The strange sounding language of the Basques was estimated as going as far back as 6,000 B.C. The language was spoken in the entire Aquitaine area, and extending eastward as far as Catalonia. During the sixth century B.C. it seems that the Indo-European cultures systematically wiped away all of the pre-Indo-European languages that had been spoken throughout Europe until that time with the exception of the Basque language! This move created any number of serious cultural and political problems that became the after-effect of the movement. The languages being spoken during those times were Germanic, Slavonic, Celtic, Romance, Mongol as well as others spoken by the Albanians, Arabs, Greeks, Lithuanians, Berbers, Armenians, Caucasians, Irananians, as well as Basques!

Another interesting observation that was discovered was in their religious practices. Excavations showed that the direction of the corpses at the time of death were always interred facing the sun! This led scholars to believe that there was some kind of sun-worshipping in existance during those times! Their well-defined, pre-historic Basque people began to feature in the history of the area. It is unfortunate that the worse thing that can happen to a people is not to write its own history! This means that any knowledge about the people must be left up to the mercy of historians to reconstruct their past! The first evidence of Basque history was written be geographers Pliny and Ptolemy. In their writings about the "Journey of Antoninus" they mention names that show that the Basques extended not only to the Aquitaine regions of the North, but also as far down as the Rio Ebro in the South!

There had been several times when Miguel had considered the readings interesting enough to try to explain them to Soledad. Unfortunately, his wife was much too involved with the farm and their growing daughter to pay much attention to what he was telling her. As far as she was concerned, all of this ancient history meant nothing! It only meant that they were living among decent people who had accepted them, had treated them fairly, and had given them refuge! While she cared little about the past history of these people, she wanted her daughter to be well educated! In San Sebastian, there were schools that were operated jointly by the local government and the church! She wanted to be sure that her daughter learned this strange but new language! She also wanted her to provide something of value to this land! Soledad had never gone to school as a youngster! She was needed at home to do the chores of the house! As a result, she had never learned to read or write! What little she had managed to learn had been learned from her husband after she became an adult! Soledad felt grateful that their daughter had been born with enough intelligence to see through many of the obstacles of her life! She had been blessed with her father's handsome facial features, but her stubborness and her fiery temper had been inherited from her mother. Her mother had seen many of the same signs she had when growing up! Fortunately, Maripaz liked school and was willing to learn! There was no time in her young life for any nonsense, and anyone who made fun of her or decided to criticize her eagerness would soon discover her fiery temper after the school day was over! There were even times when Soledad had worried in silence that her only daughter would grow up in a life of turmoil and would fail to retain the feminine qualities that a young lady with her good looks was expected to have! Whatever characteristics she did have, when she was in school she was a far different person than she was when she arrived home. Maripaz adored her father and loved her mother as well! There were times when she would announce her disgust at having to work in the field or feed the animals. Also, sometimes her mother would punish her and prohibit her from doing the things she wanted to do! It was during these times when she also discovered that her father was a soft touch! Whenever she was punished she would go to him and cry on his shoulder until she finally got her way! When the punishment was too severe, she would expect him to intercede on her behalf until her mother finally gave in and took away the punishment! Despite her draw-backs she was an otherwise good and obediant child! When she graduated from grade school, Soledad was happy that she would now have a daughter to help farm the land and feed the animals. It almost seemed like a repetition of her own childhood, one she had learned to cherish as she grew older! So it was that she was soon shocked and disappointed the day that Maripaz went up to them and explained that she wanted to attend the Universidad Nacional Autonoma de Madrid! The first wave of displeasure came knowing that she would need to leave home and live in a dormitory room perhaps with another young woman that was a stranger! How could she know whether or not she would like her room mate, or that her room mate would like her? It was a decision she had made on her own! She was determined to study the humanities and hope that at some point in her young life, she would be able to give back to the community a portion of the good life the community had given her!

Soledad's greatest worry was in what they would do if something happened to her while she was away! Overland transportation between Madrid and Vizcaya was difficult at best! If something happened and they were needed, they would have to depend on transportation by vessel, a trip that would require several days! Another anticipated problem was that the end of the war was much too recent to expect forgiveness! It was quite possible that Soledad would be allowed to travel to Madrid; but it was also doubtful that the Franco government would be forgiving and would allow Miguel to enter into the Spanish capital! He had been well known among many of the Army officers, and his escape into Vizcaya had received a great deal of negative publicity, calling him everything from a traitor to a turncoat who had turned against his government! It had been publicized that his return to Spain would be considered treasonous against the government. If caught, he would be arrested and tried in the military courts for desertion! The end result was that if he was arrested in Spain, he would probably face execution! Maripaz had lived with risks all her life, and with her youthful ambivalence, she felt sure that nothing would ever happen to her! After arriving in his new country, Miguel had lost all previous contacts with his friends in Asturias! Even his best friend Guillermo had not been heard from! His last notice simply said that he and his wife had returned to Galicia after spending a considerable amount of time in a concentration camp! Only the dire necessity for food and vegetables saved them from a lifetime of confinement! It was this isolation that worried both Soledad and Miguel! While Soledad had been vocal in refusing her daughter, she had often argued with Miguel for not being forceful enough! There had been no reason why she couldn't stay in Vizcaya and receive her education at the local university! Unfortunately, all of the protests landed on deaf ears! Maripaz's mind was made up! The only university she would consider was in Madrid! After all, she argued, she had nothing to do with the Civil War! She wasn't even born when the war was on, so why should she be punished for what happened?

Despite the allusions of being a trouble-free country, one thing was going on that seemed troublesome! There were a growing number of town meetings that were being held in the town hall of San Sebastian! There had always been a few scattered meetings discussing some of the local problems, but these had been few and far apart! Now the meetings were much more regular and the number of people that were in attendance was also growing.. A new movement was underway that had all of the marks of autonomy! Everyone knew that the Basques had always considered themselves as being their own nation! No one had taken these views seriously, but now that the town meetings were being held, the movement was getting more recognition and was getting strong! Until that time, feelings would rise and fall after a period of time; however, now, there was a small group of young people being led by a few boisterous leaders that were actively seeking autonomy from Spain! Soledad had argued repeatedly with Miguel telling him that he should attend these meetings if only to know what these people were telling the local villagers! Every time she would mention the meetings, Miguel would simply walk away and tell her that he would not attend! He had already listened to enough pleas from people out of his past! As far as he was concerned, these meetings were nothing more than a way of allowing certain people to outline their own ideas after which nothing more would come of them! What neither of them knew was that their daughter had been taken in by these zealots who firmly believed that the solution of their problems was in ceceding from Spain and then form their own country! There had been times when she had discussed some of the subjects heard at the meetings with her father. After listening to her, he felt a bit surprised that she seemed to be more interested than he had expected! At first, she had spoken to her mother and tried to convince her, but her mother quickly dismissed her by saying that the idea was nothing more than a 'tonteria de locos' (Foolishness of crazy people). Soledad had never stopped to analyze her own daughter's interest in these movements until the day when she overheard the conversation with her father!

"The idea of autonomy or of becoming a separate country from Spain is very ambitious!" he told her. "But where will the money come from that is needed to finance the support of independence?"

"We would need to raise the people's taxes!" was her reply. Strange that his own daughter was becoming a member of a group that sought many of the things he had heard over and over during his youth in Asturias! How could he explain to her that it was these ideals that had finally resulted in one of the most costly Civil Wars in modern history!

"Maripaz, stop and look at this country that is seeking independence! There is no industry, no commerce, certainly no leaders that make any sense! The only thing we have here is farming and grazing and little else! You cannot run a country without the necessary funds or with a reasonable income in order to fullfill the required obligations!" he explained.

"But that's just it, Father! We should ask Spain to grant us autonomy but still give us the needed capital we would need to run the government!" she told him.

"What?? Are you listening to what you're saying? You expect the government of Spain to finance the independence while you want to divorce the land away from Spain? Who is filling your mind with such crazy ideas?"

"These are the things that were being discussed at the town meeting the other day!" she answered.

"But think about it! Does it really make any sense? Maripaz, we are living in an area where thirty five percent of the people live in poverty! Another thirty percent barely make enough money to support themselves! Their families and the rest of us certainly want no problems with Spain! What happens if we antagonize Franco enough that he decides to attack this area that was spared from the war! Where would an army come from that would fight them? Do you really believe than an effective army can be formed over night and be ready for battle? Where will the badly needed armament and equipment come from? Who will sell the Basques what they will need, and how will the Basques pay for it? Has anybody thought this out? It sounds like a wild dream to me!" he told her."It sounds like an old familiar story of a poor country that wants to invade another that is more advanced and superior in every way! When asked, are you crazy? That country will take us over immediately! The president said that he knew that the superior country would take them over quickly! However, he said, we have nothing to lose! If we should win the war, we'll be able to have full control of all of its wealth which we desperately need! If we lose, then, they will need to support our needs! How can we possibly fail?"

Soledad had been listening to the conversation! She hadn't injected her own ideas nor did she want to interrupt what was happening!! Of course, she felt disappointed that her only daughter had been naive enough to believe what was being said at those meetings! The argument was not very plausible, but the worse part was that her own daughter had been taken in by the troublemakers! Her daughter was much too interested and hadn't bothered to think things out! It was then that she decided not to stop her from going to Madrid! If nothing else, it would at least keep her away from the meetings and might strengthen her own common sense into thinking through the things her father was telling her. Perhaps, she had needed a change after all! From that day, Soledad had suffered in silence not knowing what would become of her daughter; but, at least, she would be away from the town meetings and from the crazy ideas of a few rebels who were voicing their opinions!

The meetings were also producing other negative effects that were adding to the uncertainties! Spain had always been mired in petty jealousies and accusations, some fabricated, others real, but none were important enough to produce the anguish that was being felt! Because of the territorial problems Spain had always known with Vizcaya, the Basques were not considered to be very good people, worthy of Spanish protection! The ideas that had been allowed to foment not because they were true, but, rather, because of the constant pressures of autonomy and because the Basques were known to speak a language completely foreign to the Spaniards, they were considered to be outcasts to many of the 'Madrilenos' from Madrid! Not that they were alone, they were not! The 'Madrilenos' considered themselves, and only themselves, to be the only Castillan Spaniards! The Gallegos and the Asturianos from the North were thought of as being stubborn and hard-headed, a characteristic that followed them wherever they would go. The people from Andalucia in the South were thought of as being Gypsies; and the people in the Northeast, from Valencia to Barcelona were known as Catalanes with the same characteristics as the Gallegos and Asturianos! What made them more distinct was that each of the provinces spoke their own distinctive dialect that made them easily identified wherever they went! Some called this a form of Spanish pride, while others believed that only the Madrilenos were the true Spaniards! All the rest were considered as being part-Spaniard or, worse yet, an imposter! These feelings added greatly to the schisms that prevailed throughout the country, and while they had been somewhat alleviated during the Civil War, the same feelings had now returned and history was beginning to repeat itself! Since only the Basques spoke a language that was their own and had no identification to the Spanish language, they received the most criticism from the others! Only the Basques and the Andaluces had the reputation for being trouble makers and were subsequently discriminated against by all of the people throughout the country. The government did little, if anything, to quiet this unethical estrangement from the whole of Spain! As time went on and nothing happened, the Basques and the Andaluces were considered to be outcasts and had little acceptance in any of the other provinces. The common idealogy was how could a person be living in the Spanish territory and not speak the Spanish language? It was an unpardonable sin for a citizen to speak a language that was not Spanish! The attitude soon became equal! If the Spaniards wanted nothing to do with the Basques; then, why should the Basques have anything to do with the Spaniards? As travel improved over time, there was more interaction with each other! Therefore, the negative feelings continued to grow until they reached the elevation, and Franco finally decreed that such actions were illegal and would not be tolerated! This move only served to create more antagonism among the Spaniards! It became little wonder why the Basques had yearned to have their own country and become permanently separated from Spain! The idea had been thought out carefully, but not the implementation of how they would support their own country with the limited means of support that were available One of the results from this schism was that each of the other dialects such as the Andaluces, the Gallegos,

Asturianos, Madrilenos and Catalanes were smart enough to seek language recognition while still being a vital part of Spain! It was in compliance with a new law trying to unify the nation! It was only the Basques that didn't want that recognition, but instead, wanted their own separate country in defiance of the new Spanish laws!

Madrid

Andres was shocked when he saw an incoherent Maripaz, badly beaten and laying in his arms! Thanks in part to the training he had received while serving with the military in Korea, he saw immediately that she was seriously injured! Whatever had happened, had taken place after she had left him alone in the plaza. Perhaps he should have asked more questions from the young woman that had brought her to his room, but he was much too dismayed to ask what had happened! Her white slacks were covered with blood and her blouse had been partially torn away and was also stained with her blood! All that was left for him to do was to make sure that she didn't have any other wounds on her body that might be causing her to lose so much blood! She was unconscious and incoherent as she lay still in his bed while he did his best to resuscitate her and get her to tell him what happened! From the appearance of a scalp wound, he could only assume that she had been hit by a blunt instrument that had rendered her unconscious! He knew what needed to be done, and also, what was prudent to do in these cases without arousing too much speculation! Prudence would need to take a back seat to imprudence, he reminded himself! It was imperative that he examine her body for any other wounds that were related to the blood loss!

Carefully, and making sure that he didn't hurt her, he stripped away her white slacks and her blouse! There were some ugly bruises on her upper torso, but her lower body didn't seem to have been injured. The major part of the trauma had been to her head, and he was thinking that she might have a fractured skull! He tore up one of the sheets from his bed, ripped them into narrow strips and started to bandage the opened wounds in order to stop the bleeding. He, then, ran out into the hallway to the ice machine;

and, while making a basket out of the sheets, he took enough ice to soothe the head wounds and wait for her to regain consciousness! After applying the ice compacts to her head and to the ugly bruises on her body, he realized that she was going to need her clothes in order to get back to her own room! The only thing left to do was for him to wash her clothes in the bathtub and try to remove the blood stains! At least they would look more presentable when she put them back on to return to her room! The proper thing to do would be to call the emergency squad or take her to the hospital himself, but he didn't have a car and Carlos had not yet returned to the room!

Experience had told him that there was little time to waste! Her breathing was normal as was her pulse! All that was needed was for her to get out of her state on unconsciousness! He could only imagine how angry she would be when she saw that her clothes had been removed, but there was no point in worrying about that now! She needed her rest and he was hoping she would soon awaken and tell him what happened! Once he had applied the ice-packs to her forehead. he covered her almost nude body with a white cotton sheet. In the meantime, he went into the bath and finished trying to remove the blood stains from her clothes! In the midst of scrubbing the blouse, there was a loud knock on the door! At first, he thought that his room mate had returned! But Carlos had already told him that he would probably not be returning that evening because he had made other plans! Before he was able to think logically, he heard the knock again! This time it was much louder than before! With his shirt sleeves rolled up and his hands full with soap suds, he went to open the door! Standing in the hallway was a very serious looking elderly man flanked by two uniformed Guardia Civiles standing on either side!

"Si senores!" Andres said as politely as possible. "En que les puedo servir?" (How can I help you?)

The elderly man, dressed in a regular suit and white shirt identified himself as the head of Security for the university! Apparently, the incident had been reported and the investigating officers had come to see what had happened! It was well known that the head of Security had a great deal of input whenever there was a disorder reported on the campus! After being notified about the incident, he had summoned the Guardia Civiles who had now come to investigate what had happened!

"I don't know what happened!" Andres said when questioned. "I was in my room when I heard noises in the hallway! When I opened the door, I found the woman laying on the ground! She was unconscious and injured, so I brought her inside! I've had medical training in the army! I cleansed her wounds and applied ice compacts to her head, hoping that she would become conscious, but she hasn't moved!"

Without an answer, the three men walked inside the door and saw the young woman, unconscious, and laying on the bed! "How did she get into the room?" one of the Guardia Civiles asked.

"I carried her inside! Why? Should I have left her outside in the hallway, laying on the floor?" he answered.

"Just answer the questions!" the head of Security said while writing everything down on a small pad!

"What else do you want to know?" Andres asked, this time trying to be more helpful.

"Were you with this girl today or tonight?" the Guardia Civil asked.

"Yes! In fact, I was with her for most of the afternoon! We had a slight argument and she walked away and was heading back to her room! That was the last I saw of her until someone brought her here!"

The other Guardia Civil walked into the bathroom when he heard the water running! He saw the clothes full of blood soaking in the bathtub! "Miren," he said. "Vengan aqui!" When they other men saw the blood stained garments, the head of Security nodded his head from side to side! Andres saw this turn of events and he already knew enough about the law to realize that the eyes of suspicion were directed at him!

"Look, if you think that I did it, forget it! It wasn't me! I was trying to get the blood out of her clothes so she would have something clean to wear when she regained consciousness!" he explained, but it didn't appear as if they were listening to his explanations! They walked back into the bathroom while the head of Security carefully pulled down the sheets that were covering the partially nude body! No sooner did he see that she was nude he quickly put down his pencil and tablet and made a motion to the Guardias! One of the Guardia Civiles grabbed hold of Andres' arm and told him quietly. "Sir, I'm afraid you will have to come with us!" it was spoken in a soft voice, but he realized that it was a demand that he couldn't refuse!

For the first time since his arrival, Andres was happy that he decided to study law! At least now he knew exactly what to say, and what he shouldn't say that might be used against him! All that he knew was that he had committed no crime! She was angry but she was quite well when she walked away from him and left him all alone in the plaza! Whatever happened had occured when she was on the way back to her room! In just a few moments, he started to review everything that took place between them, and there was nothing he could think of to justify what had happened! He remembered that when she was taken to Andres' room, one of the girls had said that the medical clinic at the university had been closed and that no one was available! It would appear that the young women had taken her to the clinic first. When no one was available, they had taken her to his room! Unfortunately, there was nothing else they could do, so they left the area as soon as they saw him carry her postrate body into his room and laid her down on his bed! What he had done when removing her clothes had been done, not merely as a necessity to determine the extent of her injuries, but as a matter of decency and respect! It had nothing at all to do with any lascivious behavior that they might be imagining! Little did they know that he was much too fond of her to force himself upon her! What he did know was that the head of Security would make up his own mind and would forward his recommendations to the univeristy! Expulsion from the university was an absolute certainty; unless, of course, he was a member of the elite! These individuals would be allowed to face a board of inquiry and explain their views before being expelled! He had no idea what was going to happen to him! Maripaz was still unconscious! Any evidence they had obtained from the room was purely circumstantial; but, he also knew that what they had was certainly more than enough to

gain a conviction! A crime of passion, as they had imagined, was
also punishable by a long prison term of thirty years! He needed
to do something and had to do it fast! With the young woman still
unconscious, they had seen him washing her blood stained clothes
in his bathtub! He had also been the last person who had seen her
and had been in her company that day! The evidence seemed very
compelling! There was little he could do, and no one to turn to! It
seemed that everything had been left to the unpredictable hands of
fate and he had no idea where it would lead!

As the two Guardia Civiles went up to him, each one
holding one of his arms, one of them said. "Sir, you will have to
come with us!" All of Andres' thoughts were on the possibility of
expulsion from the school, and how disappointed his parents in
Galicia would be when they found out that their son was in jail!

"What about the young woman? She needs some medical
help quickly!" he told them.

"She will be transferred to a hospital! I will remain here
until the ambulance comes for her! In the meantime,you will
remain in custody until the authorities decide what they want to
do!" the head of Security said as the other two Guardia Civiles led
Andres to the county jail!

Guisamo

It was a day like any other when Guillermo returned
from the local market and was told by Dolores that word had
been received that their son Andres had been arrested in Madrid!
The communication was short and the information vague and
incomplete! All that they were told was that their son, a student at
the Universidad de Madrid, had been arrested for having attacked
a young woman! The list of charges against him had already
been published! They were attempted murder, assault, public
disturbance, each one a serious violation of the criminal code! The
authorities failed to mention the name of the young woman he was
being accused of assaulting! Also the circumstances that led to the
assault, or any other information that would have given them more
details had been conveniently excluded! They did say, however,
that that the accused had been expelled by the school pending

the outcome of the trial that was to begin in about two weeks! It seemed strange, even though they knew nothing about the law, that a trial with such serious charges could begin so quickly! Guillermo had read about other cases tried in the courts; and for the most part, most of them would not come to trial for several months! The court docket was full and once the accused was being confined, there was no reason to bring the matter to such a quick conclusion! This case had just happened and already the trial had been set. There was barely enough time to engage a competent lawyer to be present and give his son adequate legal representation! Both his parents were stunned by the news! There had to be some mistake! After all, they knew their son only too well; and they also knew he was not the type of man that was capable of doing things that were illegal! In fact, if there were any doubts at all, he could be expected to turn the other way and avoid confrontations, especially in dealing with matters of the law that he had always considered unfair and also conveniently tilted against the accused!

Guillermo quickly made up his mind to travel to Madrid, visit his son and find out for himself what had happened! Dolores had wanted to go, but the cost of two people travelling a long distance was prohibitive and unaffordable! They simply did not have enough money for both of them to travel! There was a time after the Civil War when it was forbidden to have people from the northern provinces travelling freely around the country; but, in recent years, those restrictions had been lifted! Since many of the people had relatives living in other parts of the country, the government, at the insistance of the people, had lifted those restrictions! The people were now permitted to visit with relatives and friends living in other provinces! He packed a few things in a small bag, opened up a small jar in which they stored some of their small change from the store, and removed enough coins to cover the cost of the trip! As soon as she realized that Guillermo had lost none of his stubborness and determination, she could only caution him against losing his temper for fear that he too might be arrested and charged with interfering with the law!

The trip from Guisamo to Madrid took two days and it could well have been two months! Guillermo was anxious to meet with his son and get all of the details; whether, true or false, it would obviously have serious impact on the rest of his life! Guillermo hated himself for not having the foresight to have saved enough of his hard earned money that would allow him to remain in Madrid until the trial, but he needed to do whatever was within his means! The money he had taken was barely enough to pay for the cost of the trip and supply him with enough cash to pay for his room and board!

When he finally arrived in the capital city, Guillermo was sleepy and tired! He hadn't been able to sleep in the old noisy 'colectivo' that had taken him there! He went directly to one of the many 'pensiones' (a small building with rooms to rent for visitors which would include a continental breakfast and dinner) That would certainly be much more than he needed! The rooms were shabby and not very well kept at all; but, thinking about his army days, he knew he had slept in much worse accomodations than what was being offered. As soon as he deposited his small pouch that contained a change of clothes, he went directly to the jail! The officer in charge was an elderly man who had probably been given the job because of his poltical connections!

"Si? Que desea usted?" he asked. (What do you want?)

"I came to visit my son, Andres Torres!" Guillermo answered.

"The visiting hours are over! There is no more visitation of prisoners today!" he answered sternly, as though he was angry at having been disturbed.

"I just arrived from Galicia after being told that my son had been arrested! Please, sir! Will you please make an exception?" he asked.

The jail keeper looked at him and saw that Guillermo had arrived unshaven and had probably been on the road for several days. After a few moments, he took another look at him, but remained silent until Guillermo reached into his pocket and gave him one peseta! The man took the peseta, put it into his own pocket and told him to follow! They walked down a long corridor that was cold and damp with two rows of about ten cells in each row! It was a very familiar sight for Guillermo as he remembered long ago days when he and Dolores had almost faced the firing squad! Not much had changed he thought! Midway down the aisle the gatekeeper stopped by one of the cells!

"Esta aqui! You have only fifteen minutes!" he said sternly, without any further comments. He unlocked the cell door and allowed Guillermo to enter!

Andres was lying on a small cot that had nothing more than a small comode and an even smaller wash basin inside the tiny room! When Andres saw his father, he leaped off the cot, embraced him and quickly started to explain what had happened! Guillermo couldn't stop thinking about the days when he and Dolores had also shared a similar cell while awaiting the death sentence! Since that time, Spain had abolished capitol punishment! He could see that his son was now sharing the same intense anxieties that he too had shared, in what now seemed like ages ago! Guillermo had to hold back his tears when he saw the sad look on his son's face! He needed to stop talking because of the lump in his throat! This time he knew he was going to need the same strength that he had the day that he and Dolores had waited to be sentenced to death! This, unfortunately, was his son; and, for no other reason, he needed to retain his composure! Also, he needed to have the strength to help him through this period of anxieties!

"I must ask you one question!" Guillermo asked him. "Did you do it?"

"No, father! I have no idea what happened after that young woman left me alone in the plaza! I didn't see her again after she left me to go back to the university!" He paused for several moments; and, for a brief time, Guillermo thought his son was about to burst into tears! His son was much too proud to allow his father to see him crying! "What they said was true! I was washing her clothes when the Guardia Civiles arrived! They had been soaked with blood and if she recovered enough to go back to her room, she would need her clothes! I did undress her; and yes, I did lay her down on my bed! Father, she was badly hurt! Nothing happened! I used the skills I learned while serving in the army to clean her wounds and place ice compresses on her injuries!I didn't cause those injuries; but, unfortunately, she is still unconscious and is unable to tell the authorities what really happened!"

"Is there any way that we can contact a lawyer for you? Perhaps we can speak to someone from the law department of the school and see what they can recommend! You know as well as I that the lawyers in Galicia are very expensive, and we can't afford the costs! For any of them to come here and represent you, we would need to also pay for their living expenses as well as the legal fees and we just don't have that kind of money!" he said.

"I know that! My only hope is that the young woman will soon recover and will be able to explain what actually happened! From what I hear, the trial has been set for two weeks! While the doctors expect her to make a full recovery, they also say that these kind of injuries take time and don't really know how long it will take!"

Guillermo was listening to his son and wished there was something he could do to help! Unfortunately, the poverty they were experiencing together with the high legal costs that would be needed made it almost impossible! He dreaded leaving his son alone in a court full of hungry vulchers who were looking for blood! He knew that feeling only too well! The only comforting thought was that he knew and believed in his son's innocence! Also, he knew that his son had always been a level headed man; and, in the end, he would prevail! If he was convicted his mother would probably have a nervous breakdown which would only make matters worse! After a tearful goodbye, Guillermo left his son and returned to Galicia! All he could do at this point was to pray for a miracle, even though he also knew from experience that miracles do not come easily, especially when dealing with these matters! Andres had put on a strong front! He didn't want his father to see that he was scared to death about what the outcome could be! He had been trained in the law, and knew that in Spain, under the new government, the laws were very specific on criminal matters! If an accused came from a wealthy family, there were many more opportunities for appeals and re-trials; but, if the accused came from a poor family, those avenues were closed very quickly!

Several days before the trial, Andres was just washing up when he heard a commotion near his cell! At first, he paid no attention realizing that these types of commotions happened so frequently that nobody paid any attention to them! This one was different! He heard the unmistakable voice of an old man speaking in broken Spanish as if he had a foreign accent! Before he could see what was happening, the jailer went to his cell and told Andres he had a visitor! Andres was both surprised and startled wondering who it could be who wanted to visit with him so early in the morning! The jailer opened the cell door and in walked an old man, probably into his eighties! He was wearing a white cotton shirt that had not been washed in a long time and a pair of civilian trousers that were wrinkled and worn! Therefore, he stood inside the cell staring at Andres with a large pack of disheveled papers under his arm!

"So!" the old man said with a strange sounding voice! "You are Andres Torres, the man who is accused of criminal charges?" Andres couldn't tell whether this man was making a statement or asking a question!

"Yes, sir!" he replied. "Who are you?"

"My name is Otto Heintz!" the old man said. "You do not know me, ja? My Spanish is not so good but your case is interesting to me! Tell me, do you have an attorney?"

"No, sir!" Andres answered. "I can't afford one!"

"Good!.....good!...." he answered, nodding his head up and down. "I am professor of criminology at the Universidad! I do not know you...but...your case has interest for me!"

"Why is my case of interest to you?" Andres asked.

"I vill tell you!! I have spoken to some of your instructors to see what kind of student you are! You will please excuse.....I do not speak good Spanish! I am a German! I come here during the war and I like Spain very much. So, I stay here! Now, I want to ask you some questions that you must answer for me...ja?"

"Of course, sir! Ask me anything you want to know!"

"Good...good...! I ask you one more question you must answer! Did you do things you are being charged with?" the old man asked.

"No sir! I did not! I don't know what happened to the young lady, but I can assure you that I didn't do it....honest!"

"No need to say honest! Either you did or you didn't! Your instructors have told me that you are a very intelligent young man! You are very quiet in classroom and very shy! You never in any trouble....ja?"

"That is probably true! I came here to study law and not to look for trouble!"

"Ja....Ja....Good...Good! Das ist good! I represent you pro-bono! I no charge you! At my age, money is not important! I, too, am a student of the law and I want to defend that law.....but also.... I need to defend the accused! You see, what the government says is evidence, I find it very strange and surprising! Now...you tell me truth, why you bring the young woman into your room?" Andres watched as the elderly man took out his pencil and legal pad and began taking notes!

"I didn't bring her into my room! She was found by some of her friends and when they saw my room number in one of her pockets, they decided to take her to me! From what I was told, they tried first to take her to the school clinic, but it was closed! That was why they brought her to my room!"

"Yes!....I see....I see....But, tell me, why you wash her clothes?"

"Because they were full of blood stains and she would need them to return to her own room! I had no idea she was badly injured! I also gave her first aid and bandaged up her wounds waiting for her to awaken from the injury!"

"Ja.....Ja....but, you take her clothes off?"

"Of course, I did! With her clothes soaked in blood, I needed to see if she had any other injuries on her body that needed attention! I was a medical corpsman in the Army and I used my medical training to treat her! I did not rape her nor did I do anything other than to examine her body for any wounds!" he insisted.

"You see, that is what troubles me! If you cause injury to young woman, why would you take her back to your room? That is not the profile of a rapist! He would attack her and leave her where she was! It is this part that I find to be most interesting! The government considers this to be conclusive evidence; but, I do not think so! I find it very strange that you bring the girl back to your room! We must prove them wrong, and we must do so quickly! One other thing surprises me! Why are they so anxious to take this case quickly to trial? It is my opinion they would want to convict you before the young woman wakes up! As a student of law, you must know that in Spain there are no appeals! Whatever is decided at the trial must be carried out, no matter what happens! It is my opinion that they want to see you convicted before the young lady wakes up. By that time, the case has been disposed of, and whether you are guilty or innocent does not matter!"

"Why would they be so anxious for a quick trial!" Andres asked, since the previous explanation was not exactly very clear to him.

"Where you come from?" the old man asked.

"I come from Galicia!" Andres answered.

"Ja....ja....now I understand why! You come from the North...ja? If you come from the South, they are not so anxious! Government does not like the people from the North country...so... they make trouble for you....ja?" The old man waved his finger in the air as though he were admonishing a youngster for having done something that was wrong!

"I think I have an idea! If you agree, then, you must do whatever I say without questions...and you must agree to everything I tell the court....ja? If we cannot beat them at their strengths, then...perhaps...we must defeat them at their weaknesses! Do you agree?"

Andres was thinking about what the old man had just said! There was something about his comments that didn't sound convincing; but, then, he really had no other alternative! After all, he had nothing to lose! Of course, if he had a choice, he would have selected an attorney who was far more articulate and was well schooled in criminal law! But now, he had no choice! At least, he had an attorney! He was an old man who didn't speak very good Spanish, but it was better than not having any lawyer at all!

"I have no choice, Professor Heintz!! Of course, I will do exactly as you say!" he replied.

"Good....good....Das ist good! Tomorrow I come back to see you! After I make some notes, then, I come back to see you! We will talk again...ja?"

Andres remained in his cell thinking of what the old professor had told him! Obviously, he had something on his mind that he felt would be of help! He knew from his classes that the trials for criminal offenses were held before a Mariscal who would almost always side with the position of the government! Under the new Spanish laws, the hearings were nothing more than a formality of justice! Unfortunately, the laws were still based on old military interpretations of justice and not on what seemed proper and reasonable for the accused, as it is in most civilized countries. Because the courts were overcrowded and over worked, that aim of the courts were for a speedy trial! Once the sentence was pronounced, there were no appeals or re-trials! If Maripaz did awake from her coma and exonerated him, it would no longer have mattered! There were no juries that might call for a re-trial and reverse the sentence! He would need to spend the time dictated by the sentence in jail, regardless of any extenuating circumstances! It was obvious that the old man, despite his advanced age, had something up his sleeve! He had been teachinjg at the university for a long time! While Andres knew little about him, he had to be a good professor or else the university would have replaced him with a younger man! There were few risks in having this old man represent him! Andres knew that while the evidence was all circumstantial, there was certainly enough to help a prosecutor to convict him! After all, it was all a stacked deck! The prosecutor was a member of the federal government as was the Mariscal! He had already known from his classes that many of these cases were decided in advance, and that the trial was simply a formality for the benefit of the controlled press! It was also intended to show the world that Spain had a semblance of the law and order throughout the land! His only salvation was if Maripaz would awaken from her coma before the trial and would exonerate him! Unfortunately, he had no word as to how she was or whether or not she had shown any signs of improvment. He had made an attempt to obtain medical information, not that he was looking to be exonerated even if it would be helpful! The real reason was that he did like her and wanted her to get better for her own sake, if not for his! It was going to require a miracle or two to help him! One was for her to awaken prior to the trial, and another to get him released from jail and re-instated in the university!

When the old man appeared at the jail the following morning, Andres noticed that he was still wearing the same clothes he wore the previous day! The large pack of losely held papers were under his arm as he sat down and thumbed trhrough the papers reviewing everything that had been said! Andres told him, in detail, about their meeting and about the visit to the Plaza Central! It had been an enjoyable day, amidst the wine and chorizos they had eaten! The meeting had gone well, and there seemed to be a genuine attraction for each other. It had been Maripaz who had walked away angrily from him, all because he had not made a move to see her again! It was not that he didn't want to...indeed, he did! He also knew that money was tight and that he simply could not afford to see her on a regular basis! His own studies of law were intense and he needed to devote as much of his time as possible to the volumes of textbooks that were needed for him to receive his degree! He had hopes that at some future time, he would be able to find work in one of the local law firms which would at least provide him with an income! For now, however, these wishes were beyond question! Also, he even mentioned that she had come from the province of Vizcaya, probably from a wealthy family, even though she had said little about them! They had also not spoken about the Civil War knowing that General Franco had issued specific instructions making it a criminal offense to speak harshly against the new government! During their conversations they had spoken about his military experiences in Korea after being conscripted into the military service! Further, he told him about his medical training but that was all behind him now! He could see that the old man began writing quickly when he spoke about Maripaz coming from Vizcaya! Obviously there had been something of interest that had attracted him!

Andres was feeling depressed and lonely! More lonely
than he had ever felt in his life! His father had already returned to
Galicia; and it had saddened him when he saw Guillermo, a tall,
strappy, hard-faced man, break down and start to cry like a baby,
moments before he said goodbye! Of course he had felt guilty that
he had let his parents down, although his own conscience was clear
that he had done nothing to injure that poor woman!

On the day of the trial, Andres felt uneasy being taken into
the courtroom under an armed guard! At one of the tables, he saw
what he assumed to be the prosecutors looking over their notes and
papers. He already knew that this attention was being given as a
performance for the attending press as a showing of progressive
civil behavior! After all, if the news of the trial was going to be
reported in the press, they wanted to show civility and proper
conduct! It was important that Spain receive a positive acclaim in
the free world, if they had any hopes of being accepted into the
European community! Everyone who lived in Spain knew that
the country was being driven by a military rule, a dictatorship in
disguise! The press had been controlled, and there were curfew
throughout the land for all of the people, and there was no civilian
law that had not been superimposed by military conditions, many
of which had been written by General Franco himself! The world
regarded Spain as a country that was rebuilding after the dismal
effects of the Civil War! They had just recently finalized a lucrative
treaty with the United States for the use of their Air Bases, in the
South of the country! It was a godsend that would provide the
country with an enormous amount of badly needed hard capital for
many years into the future.

Everyone was seated including the Mariscal who was
anxiously awaiting the arrival of the defense attorney! Since he
had already reviewed some the papers prepared by the prosecutors,
he seemed impatient in having to wait in order to begin the trial.
About one half hour later, everyone was startled by a commotion
just outside the courtroom! The door finally opened and in walked
the old man, Professor Heintz, aided by the help of a walking cane!
His white hair was disheveled and uncombed! The suit appeared
wrinkled and without being ironed; and the tiny knot of his tie

was turned carelessly to one side! Under his arm he was carrying a stack of yellow papers, some of which dropped to the floor as he was walking down the aisle toward the defense desk! He paused just long enough to pick up the fallen papers and to apologize to the Mariscal for being late! Andres looked at his defense attorney and was suddenly having second thoughts about having this old man represent him! The old man walked to the front of the room where the defense table awaited him and sat in the enpty chair beside his client! Professor Heintz stopped momentarily to wave at several people that he recognized and who were seated in the court room! All of these delays were making the Mariscal increasingly impatient!

"Will you please take your seat!" the loud, booming voice of the Mariscal could be heard throughout the courtroom!

"Yes....yes....of course! I vill sit down!! Thank you, Don Mariscal!" the old man answered as he carelessly unloaded the stack of papers all over the desk surface. Once the court had been called to order, the Mariscal made a motion with his hand signalling to the prosecutor that it was time for him to begin! A tall, thin, well dressed, middle aged man stood up from his chair, faced the Mariscal and began to outline his case against the accused! The presentation took about thirty minutes while the tall man explained in fine detail what had been theorized and what the investigators had seen when they visited the room of the accused. Andres immediately recognized the familiar faces of the two Guardia Civiles, now sitting in the front row, as being the men that had arested him on the night of the incident! All of the details had been carefully prepared as he made a special emphasis of the fact that the young woman was almost nude laying in his bed as he washed her blood stained clothes in the bathroom! He had been thorough in his presentation; and, even though the allegations were hardly true, Andres needed to admit that the tall man had arrived well prepared and had been careful in stating the facts exactly as they had been presented to him by the arresting authorites! During the presentation, the prosecutor had to pause momentarily as the old man was carelessly thumbing through his papers ignoring everything that was being said! When the initial presentment of the charges was finished, the Mariscal looked over at the old man and asked him whether or not he had listened to the charges against his client!

"Ja....ja...Don Mariscal! I listened to everything.... everything; but I do not believe what he said!" the old man answered.

"What is it that you don't believe?" the Mariscal asked while the audience seated inside the courtroom began to snicker and smile!

"Don Mariscal!" the old man began. "What Mister Prosecutor said was well prepared! He tells an interesting story; but he has not told this court the reason why this young man had done the things he has been accused of doing!"

There was an uneasy silence as the audience waited for Professor Heintz to reveal more information. They all seemed disappointed, even the Mariscal, when the old man took his seat and decided he had nothing more to say at the moment!

"Is that all you have to tell this court? the Mariscal asked. (All the time, the Mariscal was thinking that this case was going to be much easier than he had expected! In a few more minutes the case would be over; everybody could go home, and the young defendant would be taken back to his cell!) The mistake made by the Mariscal was in waiting a few minutes before continuing with the proceedings!

"No!!!" the old man suddenly blurted out as he abruptly got up from his chair, looked over at the opposing counsel and said. "If I were the government, I would take this prosecutor and fire him on the spot for making such a poor accusation!"

The audience was again stunned and once again started to ramble and smile wondering what this old man, who should have probably been retired a long time ago, had on his mind!

"Would you care to tell me why you think the prosecutor should be fired?" the Mariscal asked, annoyed over the laughter of the audience seated in his courtroom!

Andres shot a glance at the prosecutor and saw that he, too, was smiling as was the Mariscal! It was almost as if they were enjoying a private joke, but at his expense!

"Because I think that the prosecutor is totally incompetent, that's why! What kind of prosecutor takes his case to trial immediately instead of waiting for the facts to become clear? Don Mariscal...if I were the prosecutor....."the old man stopped talking as he was interrupted by the Mariscal.

"........but you are not the prosecutor, you are the defense attorney, are you not?"

"Ja.....ja....I am a lawyer for the defense; but, every good lawyer needs to listen to the presentation by the prosecutor! I listen to every word,....and...do you want to listen to what I think?" he asked.

The Mariscal seemed exasperated that this case was taking entirely too long!! "Yes," he finally said. "I'll listen to what you think, but you must hurry it along! I don't have all day!" he ordered.

"Ja.....Don Mariscal! If I were the prosecutor, I would not yet take this case to trial! Consider....sir Mariscal....there are no witnesses! No weapon has yet been discovered that was used in the attack.....and there has been no confession of guilt! The prosecutor tells us a nice story; but he does not tell us how he knows that this young man attempted to murder the young lady, nor does he tells us how he knows that this was the young man who tried to assault her! Why? Everything was because he was trying to help her and was washing her clothes? My housekeeper always washes my clothes....why? Does that mean I am trying to assault or murder her?" He stopped speaking long enough to wait for the giggles and the snickers from the audience, before starting again! "Now, if I was the prosecutor, I would delay this trial until I was absolutely sure of what I say! Why try this man for attempted murder or assault? If the young girl dies, then, he can be tried for murder! If the young girl lives and she denies that it was him, the prosecutor can then drop the charges without looking like a "Mamon" (Sucker or dope!) inside the courtroom! What kind of "Mamon" is he, that is willing to settle on an assault conviction when he has the chance of getting a murder conviction? It makes no sense at all to me!" he said before sitting down.

My God, Andres thought! This old man is going to have me convicted of murder when I had nothing to do with the crime! He was now sorry that he had allowed himself to believe that maybe... this old barrister had a chance of getting him exonerated! Now, it seemed that instead of seeking his freedom he was trying to have him convicted on a more serious charge! He probably would have done better had he decided to defend himself! The truth was that the old barrister had raised an objection that seemed to be obscured by logic and good common sense! On the other hand, the prosecutor was thinking that this had only been a ploy to make him look anxious for a conviction in the eyes of the court. What he had said had been the God's truth, and the old man certainly knew it! There had been no formal accusation for the assault; it would come later! And there had not been any weapon that had been found, but he considered this to be a minor point! Perhaps the old man had been right, after all! What crime would there be in waiting for a few more weeks to bring this defendent to trial? If the girl should die, he would certainly get a better press in the news media; and he would be able to alter the charges to include murder! The old coot had rambled on and on without making much sense; but, without thinking of what he was doing, he had just given the prosecutor a helping hand! He raised his hand to make a motion, but the Mariscal ignored him and asked the old man to continue!

"Don Mariscal....ve are a growing nation of new laws! If we are to be successful and get recognition, we must prove to the world that we are capable of creating new laws that can consider the views of the criminal as well as those of the victim! What kind of society would it be if it considers the condemnation of a promising young man without any real evidence? I have a friend who lives in Switzerland who has been named to the newly formed Commission of Human Rights that extends to all countries! A dictatorship such as Spain cannot afford to apply the laws of a dictatorship without being accused of a violation of civil rights! I have taken this case only so that I could prove my point and attempt to elevate this country to an equal status among other countries of the world!f" Once again the old man paused long enough to notice that he now had the attention of everyone in the courtroom! "We need to make every attempt to condemn the accused as well as to protect the victim, but, we must proceed slowly with the process and make sure that all the rights are protected! Only then will we have the respect of the world around us!"

There was a slight sound of applause when he finished and even the prosecutor was seen nodding his head as if to tell him that he was in agreement! The old man had not been nearly as naive and careless as he appeared. He knew exactly what he was doing and had done his job admirably! Tha Mariscal looked down at the prosecutor and quickly realized that he was now on a crossroad that would probably help him politically in his profession!

"While I do not entirely agree with your views, I must agree that there is some truth in what you say! Since the young woman is still in a coma at the hospital, perhaps it would be wise to delay this trial for thirty days and see what happens to her! Remember that if she should die, your client will be charged with murder!" he said almost as if he was giving a simple threat!

"Ja....ja...I understand Don Mariscal! But if she lives and exonerates my client, then all the charges against him must be dropped!"

The Mariscal made a motion with his hand to the guard ordering the prisoner to be returned to his cell! Andres stood up and was ready to follow the burly man back into jail when the old man stood up again and said to the court. "No...no....no! This is all wrong! You cannot do that! If the client is not being charged with anything at the moment, he must be released from jail and be allowed to return to his studies at the university! If he is returned to jail and the expulsion from the university is upheld, is he not being punished for a crime before he is convicted? This is not the way it is done in most free societies! The accused must be allowed his freedom until he is convicted!"

Once again, the old man was being sly and was making an excellent issue! How could the Mariscal relegate the young man to a jail cell and be expelled from the unversity if he was not yet accused or convicted of any crime? After a brief meeting with the parties involved, the Mariscal finally ruled that the accused should be allowed to remain free and should also be immediately re-instated at the university until the case was decided at a later time!

Andres was beside himself with happiness! He hugged the old man and shook his hand warmly in appreciation of what he had just done!

"Not so fast, young man!" Professor Heintz told him. "Now we must wait and see what happens to the young woman! Let us hope and pray that she awakens from her coma and is able to tell them that you were not the one who assaulted her!"

Andres was hardly listening to what was being said! Only two things were on his mind at that moment! One was to write a letter to his parents telling them what had happened and that he was now able to resume his studies! Second, he wanted to go to the hospital and see for himself how Maripaz was doing! During the time he had been in jail he had asked several times about her condition, but no one had given him any information! Now that he was a free man, he wanted to visit her and see for himself! There were still some elements of guilt thinking that he never should have allowed her to return to the campus by herself! Had he been with her, she would have been safe and nothing would have happened! All that he wanted to do now was to re-establish his relationship with her; and, if she was willing to tolerate his poverty and his studies, she might once again be willing to enter back into his social life! He rushed out of the courtroom and went directly to the hospital with a head full of anxieties!He had already decided that as long as she was in the hospital, he would visit her every day, even if it meant studying in her room! It was important that the first person she saw when she awakened from her coma would be him! Suddenly, he was taken back by a flurry of commotion when he entered the hospital. He saw nurses and doctors scrambling about and running everywhere in an unusual flurry of activity as he got out of their way while going to the elevator! At first he had paid little attention to what was happening! After all, this was a hospital and strange things always seemed to be happening! He stepped out of the elevator when it reached the fourth floor! His heart was in his mouth as he walked briskly down the hallway until he reached her room and saw that the door had been closed with her name on a piece of paper stuck on the outside!

"What are you doing?" somebody yelled as he was about to open the door to her room! "You cannot go in there!!" they said sternly.

"Why not?" he replied. I came to visit the patient who is a dear friend of mine!"

"Because there is 'codigo Azul'" the middle aged nurse dressed all in white answered! He knew only too well that a Code Blue meant that there was an emergency!

"Can you tell me what happened?" he asked.

"The patient has taken a turn for the worse! Her blood pressure continues to drop and she is having trouble breathing! Are you a member of the family?" she asked.

"Yes!" he lied. "I am actually her brother and I must see her!"

"You cannot go in there! Several of our staff is inside trying to help her! I suggest you go to the lounge down the hall and wait! A doctor will come and tell you what is happening! For now, you'll have to wait! I'm sorry, it does not look good!" she said.

"Is she going to die?" he asked.

"We don't know! All that we know is that she is a very sick woman; and, with her blood pressure falling, the outcome does not look good! I wish I could give you better news!" she said as she opened the door and went into the room!

CHAPTER 3

Madrid

The news from the nurse and her sense of urgency had not been what he had expected! Andres was already fighting a sense of guilt that he had at least been partially to blame for what happened! Now that Maripaz had taken a turn for the worse, it only re-enforced his own fears! Everything that had happened in the court room was behind him; and the only thing in his mind was Maripaz, and the danger she was now facing! He wondered if her parents had been notified and hated himself for not having asked her more specific questions about her family! At least he would have been able to write to them and tell them what had happened! The only thing she had told him was that she was from Vizcaya; and he had an uneasy feeling that, like many other Spaniards had done, her parents had probably escaped to the Basque country and from Franco's wrath! If so, it was possible that they would be prohibited from travelling to Madrid in view of the specific instructions that had been issued when the Civil War ended.

Andres was undecided what to do! He could either remain at the hospital or return to the University and seek to be reinstated in his class! It seemed that suddenly all of the assurances he had felt in life had been transformed into a world of confusion not knowing which way he should go! The old man had given him a window of thirty days before the case would again be heard!

Despite his awkward presentation, he had to admit that his performance had been nothing short of miraculous! He made a note to remind himself to write a letter to his parents to tell them what had happened and how he had gotten a reprieve for a short time! His mind was suddenly made up! Since it seemed that Maripaz had taken a turn for the worse, he felt it was his place to remain with her until the crisis had passed! The nurse had told him to wait in the lounge until the doctor came to tell him any news and that was where he should be! After all, it was only fair since he was partially to blame for what happened and no family member was available in this time of need!

The long, dark hallway was practically deserted as he walked a short distance and saw the sign reading 'Lounge'! There were old magazines scattered inside the small room as he sat and waited! It had been a difficult day and he was tired! He would have given anything for a good night's rest in his own bed, but this was more important! There would be time for rest after the crisis was over! The old man, Professor Heintz, had asked him to go to his school office and go over some evidence that he felt would again be asked whenever the trial was held! At least he could rest his head against the wall of the building and close his eyes! No sooner had his eyes closed when a tall man dressed in white came into the room to see him! From a small overhead window, he saw that the sun was shining and that he had been there longer than he thought!

"Are you the young man who is interested in Maripaz Romero?" he asked.

"Yes sir!" he answered. "How is she?"

"What is your relation to the patient?" he wanted to know.

Andres thought for a moment before answering! He couldn't really say he was related, because he wasn't! For a brief moment, he had thought of telling him simply that he was her boyfriend; but, he also knew that it would be a lie! The truth was that he hardly knew her! "I'm her best friend!" he said, almost without thinking. "I'm the only close friend that she has here in Madrid!" At that point he had no idea whether or not he would reveal any information about her condition to him!

The doctor also paused momentarily as if undecided whether or not he should tell this young man about the condition of his patient! Finally, the doctor said, "The young woman is still unconscious but her overall condition has improved! Her blood pressure has been stabilized; and even though we had to do a tracheotomy, she now seems to be breathing on her own and is out of danger! Perhaps you should go home and get some rest, it's been a long night for both of us!"

"When can I see her?" Andres asked. He was thinking that if the doctor was as tired as he was, he might allow him to visit her if only for a few minutes! After all, he hadn't seen her since the night of the incident when he was arrestred and sent to jail!

"She won't know you're here, but I think you can go in and see her! However, please don't stay long!"

"Thank you, sir! You needn't worry, I'd just like to see her and then I'll leave!"

"Are you by any chance the young man that gave her first aid the night of the incident?" the doctor asked.

Andres felt caught in a bind! He didn't know if he should admit that it had been he, or if he should deny the involvment! After thinking it over, he decided to be honest!

"Yes, sir! I was the person who cleaned and wrapped her wounds! I also saw the injury to her head! There was little else I could do except to apply cold compresses and hope she would regain consciousness; but it didn't happen!"

"Well, whether you know it or not, she was lucky to have a friend like you!" the doctor told him. "You probably saved her life by stopping the bleeding! By the way, where did you learn that?"

"I served in the Army medical corp! I was with the Army in Korea!" he said.

"Are you by any chance studying medicine at the University?"

"No sir! I am studying law! I hope to someday become a lawyer!"

"It's a shame! Perhaps you should have gone into medicine! You acted quickly, and you did all the right things! I think she'll be grateful you did what you did for her when she wakes up!"

"Have you any idea when she'll wake up?"

"No! I doubt that anyone can say for sure! She has a minor skull fracture that doesn't look serious! I feel confident that she'll awaken soon! By applying the ice compresses, you kept her from suffering a serious loss of blood! That's what probably saved her life!"

"Thank you, doctor! You've just made me feel a lot better than I felt when I arrived!" Andres said as the doctor shook his hand and walked away!

He entered the room and was shocked and dismayed as he went to her side and saw her eyes still closed! She was pale and withdrawn; but one of the nurses had combed her hair and the only thing he could think of was that she looked so regal, almost like a sleeping princess! He gently held her hand hoping that perhaps she would respond; but, it remained limp and her eyes remained closed! Somewhere, he remembered reading that when a person is in a coma, a visitor should talk to them because sometimes they can hear the person speaking even if they are unable to respond!

"I hate to see you like this!" he murmured quietly. "We had such a wonderful day you and I! It's all because of me that you are in the hospital! I promise that if you wake up and say that you forgive me, I won't ever leave your side again!"

Several moments later, he thought he saw a slight movement of her eye lids! He was hoping that it had been a precursor, and she would open her eyes! He again raised her limp hand to his lips and kissed her gently before letting go of her hand! Andres then kissed his own fingers and placed them gently over her lips as he said goodbye and returned to the University.

It had taken several meetings and a few hassles before he was finally accepted and allowed to continue his studies! The next stop he needed to make was a visit to Professor Heintz! The old man appeared as disheveled and confused as he had seemed inside the court room! The only difference was that Andres now realized that what he had done had been a ploy! In his own way, the old barrister had outsmarted his counterparts who were eager to get a conviction! The elderly man made a motion for him to sit down as he continued to ramble through a stack of yellow papers that had been carelessly spread out all over the desk!

"I am happy that you came!" the old man said, "I have some things to discuss with you! Have you gone to the hospital to visit the young woman?"

"Yes, sir!" Andres answered. "I just came from there! She seems to be the same! The doctor told me that he was optimistic that she would soon awaken from the coma!"

"Young man, tell me! Have you ever heard of a Professor Franz Kruger?" he asked.

"No, sir! Can't say that I have! Why? Is there anything I should know about him?"

"But of course, my son!! Every good lawyer should know about him! He was an old man, just like me, who taught law at the University of Cologne before Hitler embarked on his mission to conquer the world! In those days, the laws were badly tilted away from the defendant! Once a person became accused of a crime, if he happened to be poor, the outcome of the trial would be determined in advance! He would go through the motions, found guilty without any introduction of evidence that might possibly go against the conviction! Unfortunately, the old man died before he was able to put into operation a life long dream of his! It was his view that the rights of the victims of a crime needed to be protected! The system of law became so corrupt that it also became necessary to protect, with equal determination, the rights of the accused!" The old Professor paused for a few moments to study the look on Andres face! "Anytime you have a dictator, (er, excuse me, I meant liberator!) the law becomes whatever you want it to be! We have those same laws here in Spain! It introduces a process that I have been trying to teach here at the University for many years since the Civil War! You see, I came here many years ago from Germany to help a government that apparently didn't want to be helped! Since I had come from Germany, I could not be deported! So, I decided to continue with my crusade hoping to change the criminal statutes without someone punishing me for treason and deport me back to my old country!" Once again he paused, but this time he seemed to be wanting to catch his breath before continuing!

"I realized that I could never change all the laws! In your case, if the trial were to continue, you would have been found guilty and sentenced regardless whether or not the young woman awakened from her sleep! I needed to appeal to the incompetence of the prosecutors, realizing that this was the weakness we needed to face! I vant to give you some advice for free!" he continued. "As a lawyer, if you cannot win, then you must look at what can be obtained by exploiting your opponent's weaknesses! I was able to get a postponement for thirty days and have you freed for that length of time! You have now been re-instated at the university; and, with some luck, the young lady will awaken and will be able to tell exactly what happened! I think that all in all ve had a good day...ja?" he said smiling. Andres realized that what he had told him was more of a statement than a question! His entire outlook had been impressive! With some luck, it would undoubtedly come in handy when he became a lawyer!

"But what happens if she doesn't wake up in the meantime?" Andres asked.

"We will deal with that problem if and when the time comes! For the time being, we need to do whatever we can and hope for some more good luck!" he replied. "By the way, there is yet another question I need to ask! Tell me truthfully, do you like this young lady?"

That was the only question that he wasn't prepared to answer! How could he explain his feelings for someone he had only met briefly? He barely knew her, even though he did know that they shared many things in common! Yes, they had spoken of a relationship! He, too, would have liked to have one, if only he could afford one!! His finances were limited and they would have little money to go out! It wouldn't be fair to her nor to him! His mind needed to remain on his studies! He had suspected that Maripaz seemed a bit high strung in handling her emotions and a tendency to over-react to things! But then many other young women her age did the same thing! So did he like her? Of course he did! After all, she was intelligent and very attractive! She appeared sensitive and

caring! What was there not to like? He had wanted to explain his
own feelings to her when he went to the hospital, but he couldn't
when he saw her asleep in her bed! How could he possibly put
his own feelings into words that made any sense? How could he
convince the old man that he had decided to visit her in the hospital
every day, if only to wait for her to open her eyes? He quickly
realized that he didn't really need to justify his own feelings when
he saw the old man, nodding his head up and down, smiling and
saying quietly, "Ja....ja!"

Andres quickly developed a regular routine! He would
attend his classes in the morning and would meet with Professor
Heintz in his office during the early afternoons! After their
meeting, he would then go to the hospital and would sit by the
bedside hoping she would see him when she opened her eyes!
Each day, the disappointment would get stronger when nothing
improved! Everyone in the hospital had gotten to know and
recognized him! Then they would tell him of any changes as
soon as they saw him arrive! It seemed that the comments were
always the same! Her vital signs were stable and she was breathing
comfortably! Of course, the small white patch in her throat where
the tracheotomy had been performed was annoying to see! Twenty
six days had passed; and on the next day, Professor Heintz told him
that they would need to review the case since it was scheduled to
come to trial again! It seemed obvious by this time that the young
woman was not waking up and the period of postponement that
had been allowed by the court was about to end! Andres dreaded
the reminder, knowing that it was going to again be necessary to
face the same annoying problems he had faced a few weeks ago!

The professor took out an old manila envelope and a pack
of loose papers he had stashed away after their first appearance in
court. Carefully, making sure that nothing had been excluded, he
went over in fine detail where Maripaz had gone, when and what
they had eaten, the reasons why she had decided to walk away
from him and the fateful event of her friends knocking on his
room door and leaving the battered woman at his door! Nothing
of substance had really changed, and Andres knew enough about
law to know that he needed to be meticulously consistent! After

they were finished rehashing everything that happened, he saw
the old man silently staring at him as if he were staring into outer
space! Several moments had passed before his eyes returned to
Andres and he told him, "Ve will fight them on the basis of the
actual or the circumstantial evidence! This is the evidence that may
or may not be what it appears to be! I am not yet convinced that
you would be dumb enough to return her back to your room if you
were the person who attacked her! This is where you do not fit the
profile of a criminal, and this is what we will need to throw back at
them! As a lawyer, you must always remember that where there is
circumstantial evidence, there is also always a doubt.....ja?" This is
the doubt that ve must fight!"

The afternoon seemed so much longer, but only a few
hours had passed when they had finished re-hashing the case! By
that time, Andres was tired and would have preferred returning to
his room and get some sleep! Despite his advancing age, Andres
was noticing something that he admired! Not only was the old
man relentless in his determination, but he also knew the law very
well and was well aware of all of its weaknesses! If only he could
transfer and attend his classes, but he knew that a transfer for him,
in view of the circumstances was out of the question! He would
first need to clear the case against him before contemplating a
transfer! Andres felt so tired that he was trying to decide whether
or not he should go to the hospital! Adding to the misery, it was
an overcast day! Even though he had answered all of the questions
that had been asked of him, he still needed to study for yet another
examination that was to be given the following day! Almost on
impulse, he grabbed his book and left for the hospital! After all,
since he needed to study, he could just as easily study in the room
as he could in his dormitory! In another two days, he would again
need to face the challenges of his young life; but first, he needed to
keep up his good grades and the major test that was being given the
next day!

He got off the 'colectivo', walked into the hospital and took
the elevator to the floor! It was so routine by then that he knew the
steps without any effort! One of the nurses that recognized him
gave him a warm smile when she saw him and gently nodded her

head in greeting! The door to Maripaz's room was closed, the same as it had been the day she had taken a turn for the worse! He felt his heart skip a beat as he slowly opened the door not knowing what to expect! Each day he would stop by a small stand that was selling flowers on the street corner. He would buy a small bouquet and take it into the room! He had been troubled because her room seemed so dark and ugly; and he had felt that even a small bouquet of flowers would at least liven up the dismal color of her room! The door finally opened and he was not ready for what he saw! Her eyes were wide opened and she had turned her head slightly when she heard him entering! They were both staring at one another, not quite knowing what to say! He needed to pause momentarily for fear that his eyes would fill with tears, but, it was Maripaz who first broke the silence when she saw him!

"Esas flores son para mi?" she asked. (Those flowers are for me?)

"Pues, claro que si!" he answered. (Of course they are!)

"Was it you who brought all the other flowers in the room?" she asked. At first, he thought he would not tell her the truth! But almost on impulse, he didn't want to lie to her now that she had finally awakened!

"Yes, it was me!" he told her.

"Pues son bien guapas!" (They are beautiful!) "The nurses told me that a young man was here every day to see me! I knew it had to be you, because I don't know of any other man who would go to so much trouble for me!"

Again, Andres found himself at a loss for words. "Yes, I came every day! I needed to study anyway, so I decided to bring my books and study here! That way I could keep you company!" he told her.

"There you go!! Why is it that you always seem to say the wrong things at the wrong time?"

""I'm sorry for what happened! I never should have let you leave alone! I suppose that in a way, I blamed myself for what happened!"

"That's dumb! Why would you blame yourself? You certainly didn't do it! But there is something that I need to know! Will you tell me the truth?"

"Yes, of course!"

"I was told that when they brought me here, the Guardia Civiles had found me laying on your bed without any clothes! Is that the truth?" she asked seriously.

"That's only partially true! You see, it was your girlfriends who found my room number in your pocket! The school infirmary was closed so they brought you to my room! I saw that you were bleeding badly; and I needed to make sure that you didn't have any other cuts of bruises on your body! I took off your slacks and the blouse you were wearing! It was then that I decided to wash your clothes in the bathroom and wash away the blood! The head of Security and the Guardia Civiles came by and you probably know the rest!" he explained.

"Entonces fue verdad que me viste desnuda!" (Then it is true that you saw me naked!)

"No.....no.....no!" he stammered nervously at what she was insinuating! "Your under clothes were still on!" he said apologetically.

"Creo que eres un sin verguenza!" she said very seriously! (I think you are shameless!)

"How can you say that I was shameless? How was I supposed to stop the bleeding unless I removed your slacks and your blouse?" he stammered.

"Well...then...you obviously had to see my body, didn't you?" she was serious again! She almost burst out laughing, just seeing the nervousness in what he was telling her! She had to do everything possible for him not to see her laughing!

"No....Maripaz!! Te lo juro! I swear to you that I didn't notice your body, honest!!!" he said as he flt the beads of perspiration on his forehead! That was all he needed! First, he was blamed for something he didn't do and now he was being blamed for trying to help her!

"Entonces, porque no!" (Then, why not?) she said, still trying as hard as she could to refrain from laughing! "Didn't you think that my body was worth seeing? Was I that ugly?" she asked. By this time, she could no longer retain her seriousness and she started to laugh! Now he seemed to be so upset and in disarray that she could no longer hold her laughter!

"Pues, si......claro que si...!" he stammered again. "Aw Maripaz, leave me alone! You are making fun of me!" he said finally relieved when he saw her laughing!

"Andres, I know what you did!" she said seriously. "I also am aware of the trouble I have caused you! The people here in the hospital have told me everything! I owe you my life and you can be sure that I will never forget you! I know you told me that you didn't want to be involved with me, and I never wanted anything like this to happen! For whatever, it's worth, I'm happy and grateful that you were there for me! When I get discharged from the hospital, I'll get out of your life and leave you alone just like you wanted me to!"

He went over to him without knowing where he had gotten enough nerve to touch her! Slowly and gently he placed her hand into his! "That's just it!" he told her. "I don't want you out of my life! The reason I said what I did was because I don't have very much money and can't afford the luxury of having a girlfriend! I was embarassed to tell you! Believe me, it had nothing at all to do with you!"

"What makes you think that those things are important to me? Do you think that I need to be pampered and taken to a dinner or a movie? I was just as happy going to La Plaza Mayor and drinking a bottle of inexpensive wine together! Those are the things that I want and really enjoy!"

"And what happens after we both graduate? You will be returning to Vizcaya and I'll be going back to Galicia! Where does that leave us?"

"It will probably leave us both with some wonderful moments that we'll never forget! And who can say what fate has in store for us? I want to see you, Andres! And damn it, I want to see you often!! Also, I decided that I was dumb and foolish to walk out on you at the plaza! I should have remained there and given you the argument of your life!! You know how stubborn we Basques can be; and the Gallegos are not much better! To tell the truth, I think that we need each other, don't you?" she told him.

"Yes, Maripaz! The moment you walked away I realized I had made a mistake! I never wanted you to leave!"

"Then why didn't you come after me and insist that I stay there with you? Instead, you decided to wait until I went to your room, then you undressed me and looked at my naked body! I can't really forgive you for that! I also still think you were being a 'sin verguenza'" she said kiddingly. "But....I was still happy that you were there!"

For the first time in many weeks, Andres was happy! Seeing her alert and speaking had been a Godsend! There was no point in telling her now about his problems with the law! Those things would now be settled with the local authorities! There were still some questions he would need to ask her about what happened! For now, however, he could see that she was feeling drowsy. Maybe, it would be best to let her rest and he would go back to his own room! "I'm going to let you rest, Maripaz! I'm going back to my room; but I promise I'll be back here again as soon as I have my test in the morning!" he said as he got up and was getting ready to leave!

"I have another suggestion!" she said through sleepy eyes. "Suppose you stay here while I close my eyes for a short nap! When I awake, I want to see you! Will you stay?"

"Of course!" he answered. "Of course I will!"

"And one more thing! Instead of calling me Maripaz all the time, why don't you just call me Mari? That's what my parents call me!"

"Okay Mari! Cierra los ojos y duerme! Ya hablaste bastante!" (Close you eyes and sleep! You've spoken enough!)

"Bien........sin verguenza!!!!" she answered. as she closed her eyes with a smile on her face! He sat down beside her bed and opened his textbook!

The following day Andres made his regular visit to the hospital! This time he had decided to take along Professor Heintz! If the record against him was going to be removed, it would be necessary to file a petition in court requesting a complete dismissal of all charges! Under the current law, it was possible that unless there was a 'complete exoneration' issued, there was always a chance that there could be a retrial, especially is some eager prosecutor noticed that the case was still opened and pending! Having a pending legal criminal charge would certainly take away his chance of being admitted to the Organization of Attorney's and could just surface again at a critical time! He felt pleased when he entered her room to see that she was alert and on the road to improvement! Her only concern was in leaving the hospital so that she could resume her studies. By this time she had missed nearly a month and many of the examinations had already been given! Because of her circumstances, the school had allowed her to take her exams after her release from the hospital. Unfortunately, she also knew that she was going to need a great deal of tutoring in order to fullfill her obligations!

After greeting her, the old man began to ask her questions about the assault! Any information she could remember would hopefully be convincing enough to remove all culpability away from his client! Since there had not been any move by the prosecutors now that she was awake and alert, it was fairly obvious that they wanted to keep the case pending for a later time!

"How much of the assault do you remember? the old man asked.

"Not very much! I do remember that there were four men involved in the beating! Two of the men were black and the other two had an olive complexion and spoke Spanish!" she answered.

"Could you identify any of them if you saw them?"

"I doubt it! You see, it was already dark and they took me by surprise! I remember that the assault took place a short distance from the entrance to the main campus of the University! One of the men jumped me from behind and the force of the blow knocked me to the ground! After that, I don't remember very much! I don't even remember being taken to Andres' dormitory room!"

"Do you know if they tried to rape you?"

"I can't say! I don't remember very much about what happened!" At this point, Andres interrupted her.

"When she came into my room, she was still fully clothed! I doubt very much that anyone had attempted to rape her!" he added.

"Y este sin verguenza me quito la ropa!" (This shameless one removed my clothes!) she said, smiling!

"If the prosecutor should come to ask you some questions, I wouldn't like you to tell him that the professor told her.

"Of course not! Professor, I couldn't identify the men and I really don't know what they did to me! I don't think it had anything to do with me as a woman! I believe it had more to do about who I was and where I came from! You see, everyone who knows me knows that I am a Basque! Unfortunately, the Basques are not favorably looked upon by other students!" she told him.

"Ja....ja...I know that! It was probably a social disturbance! I do not believe they took away your pocketbook or your money, did they?"

"No sir! I didn't have a pocketbook nor did I have much money on me! I think I had two or three pesetas and nothing more!"

"Very well!" the old professor said,"I will now leave the two of you alone while I go to the court house and file my papers!" He gathered his papers, shook her hand, and left the hospital.

"Andres, what is going to happen to us? I have a great deal of work to make up; and I won't get much of a chance to see you!" she said. The tone of her voice was telling him that she seemed more concerned with not seeing him than about the work she had missed.

"You will probably need a great deal of tutoring! I could tutor you in my spare time and help you with your studies! At least it would give us the opportunity of being together, even if we had to work!"

She let out a large smile! "I was hoping you would say that! The last time we discussed this subject, remember, you told me that you were too busy to spend any time with me! What made you change your mind?" she asked while edging him on. She already knew that he would get flustered and feel embarassed, but she needed to know whether he was simply helping her out of pity for her, or was it because he wanted to be with her! Damn it, she thought! Why are men so dumb that they never want to reveal their true feelings? Was he helping her because he wanted to be with her or was it because he was still blaming himself for what happened? There was no way of not showing that ugly frown on her forehead again!

"The last time that the subject came up was so long ago that I forgot what I told you!" he lied. "Then I saw you in the hospital and I began to blame myself for what happened!"

"Andres....I don't want your help out of pity! I don't need your pity! I need you to help me, but only because you want to be with me!"

"Mari, what is the matter with you? Have you listened to anything at all that I've said? I thought I told you that I had made a foolish mistake! What more do you want me to say, except that I don't think you've been listening to me!"

"Damn it! Then say it! Why is it so hard for you to say what you feel? Why do you always need to mask your feelings? Don't you know anything at all about women? Don't you realize that there are times they have the need to feel wanted for themselves? You should try it sometime! It may not be as hard as it seems!"

"Of course I want to be with you! I already told you that; but, I also know that you are going to need to work like hell to catch up on your studies and that has to come first!"

"That may be first with you! I know the importance of the work, but, I also need to know that you want to be with me! That is what you refuse to tell me!"

He stared at her and at those deep revealing eyes! There was no need for him to say anything further! She knew then that he wanted to be with her without telling her specifically that she was the only person that he wanted to be with!

Maripaz was making a fast recovery! Within one week, she was released from the hospital and from that time, Andres and she were constantly together! True to his word, he had worked with her and had helped her to catch up with her work, while she helped him with his studies! Little by little, she was getting more interested in the study of law than with her own work. He was always with her,

especially in the school dances! They would always look forward
to the end of the day when they would walk hand in hand to the
park and study whatever work had been assigned to them! There
were times when she would take his hand and could feel him relax
as though it was exactly where it belonged, nestled in her hand!
Even though neither was willing to mention it, they were both
aware that the time was coming when they would be graduated
and would have to make some hard decisions regarding their own
lives and the things they planned to do after graduation! Neither
of them had looked forward to facing this dilemma, realizing that
some things in both their lives would need to change! He had given
some thought about going to practice law in Vizcaya; but he soon
became torn by the thought that his old Professor Heintz had urged
him into continuing his studies in the new law that was intended to
benefit the entire nation! The old professor had told him repeatedly
that if the laws of the country were to change, they would need
a strong, intelligent leader that would pave the way for legal
advances that would take Spain into the foray of nations! They had
to be obviously eager to advance their own laws if they wanted to
equal many of the other free countries of the world that had altered
their statutes about criminology and eventually found their place in
the new world that was forming around them!

One day it was Maripaz who raised the questions wanting
to know what would become of them after graduation? The time
for her graduation was before his, and she realized that she would
soon need to face an important decision that would alter the course
of both lives! "I don't know what to do, Mari! I'd like to stay here
and take some advanced courses, but, I hate to make the decision
that will effect both of us!" he told her.

"Have you considered getting married?" she asked. "We
are both old enough and I think we both know what we want! If
we were married, I would remain here with you and help you with
your work! I had promised my parents that I would return home
after graduation; but, if I told them there was a young man in
whom I was interested, I'm sure they would say that my place was
with you!"

"But how would we live? As long as I am single, I can still live in the dormitories! If we were married, we would need to rent a small apartment for the two of us! This would involve extra costs that I wouldn't be able to afford for a while!"

"My parents are reasonably wealthy! I'm quite sure they would understand! Have you given any thought about going to Vizcaya and practice law in the Basque regions?"

"Why would I want to do that? If I wanted to practice the law, it would be easy for me to return to Galicia! No, Mari, if I am going to practice law, I'll need to remain in Madrid where I can make a difference in the way that the law is being practiced! Professor Heintz has already told me that he thinks I have the capability of being much more than a simple lawyer! He believes that with his help I can make a difference that may change the laws of this nation! Isn't that worth working for? Of course, you would have your studies of the humanities which are equally important; and, perhaps together, the both of us could make a difference!" He immediately saw the old familiar frown on her face, knowing that she was disappointed with his answer. "Would it be so bad if you remained here with me? If we were married,we could be working together and we could still travel to visit our parents!" he added.

"Perhaps we shouldn't think of those things now! We can work them out when the time comes!" she answered.

"But it is still something we need to think about! The time will soon be here! I don't want to lose you, but we do have our careers to think about!"

It was during the conversation that the door of his room opened and his room mate Carlos came in! It had been then first time he had seen her since the night of the dance and was a bit surprised when he imagined that this young, attractive woman was sharing Andres' room! He took one look at his friend and glanced over to where she was sitting!

"You remember Maripaz, don't you Carlos?" he asked.

"Yes, of course! I had no idea that the two of you were so close! Would you want me to leave so you can be alone!" he asked.

"No! We've finished studying and were talking about what will become of us after graduation! We don't know what to do!

We want to be with each other, but now we both have our careers to think about!" Andres said. All of a sudden, Maripaz let out a ferocious scream!!

"Ese...ese es el cabron que me golpeo!" she said, still nervous! (That's the bastard who beat me up!)

"What? Que dices Maripaz?" (What are you saying?)

"It all suddenly came back to me! He was the person that beat me up and put me in the hospital! How can you have such an animal for your room mate?" she asked, excitedly and still very nervous!

Carlos was taken back by the accusation! He had no idea what she was talking about! There had to be some mistake! He had nothing to do with the beating and why was she accusing him of the beating? "Que dice usted, Senorita? No se lo que esta hablando!" (What are you saying? I don't know what you're talking about!)

"Si, ese es.....ese fue quien me golpeo!" (Yes, that's him! He's the one that beat me!)

"I think you are confusing me with someone else! It couldn't have been me!" Carlos told her calmly. He could see that she was excited and nervous! There was no point in acting excited or nervous, especially since he knew that he had nothing to do with what she was accusing him of doing!

"Take me out of here now!!" she ordered."I don't want to be in the same room as this animal!" Andres put his books away and walked out of the room with her! By the time they had reached the hallway, she was crying hysterically and making all sorts of startling accusations! He hurriedly walked her to her room, kissed her goodnight but this time he noticed that she had not returned his kiss! He returned quickly to his room! There was now an urgent need for him to confront his friend and find out whether or not the accusations she had raised were true!

"Carlos, she was pretty convinced that it was you who beat her up! Tell me the truth! Did you have anything to do with that?"

"Are you crazy??" he replied. "I didn't even see her! Besides, on the night she was beaten I went with some friends to the Parque de las Provincias! We were at the Sevilla stand and drank a few Mariposas (Orange juice and brandy!) After a while we walked to the Asturiano stand and drank cider late into the night! I didn't see her at all!"

"She seems quite determined! Is there any way in which you can prove where you were?" Andres asked him.

"Why? Do you think I am not telling you the truth?" He answered angrily.

"No! Of course not! I do believe you, but she seems quite sure of herself! Before I again confront her, I need to make damn sure!"

"Wait!!" Carlos said excitedly. "I think I may have something! he said as he pulled out a pile of small scraps of paper from his pocket. Andres looked at them and saw they were cash register receipts! He looked through all of them carefully until he finally found the one he was looking for!

"Here, look at this! This is a cash register receipt from the Asturiano pavillon! You can see the time, the bill shows that it was recorded at 8:00 P.M. That was long before we returned to the dormitory! Wasn't that about the time she was taken to the hospital? It means that at the time she was beaten up, we were not near her at all!"

"Actually, it was a bit earlier when she went to the hospital! It was around seven when the Guardia Civiles came here and took her away! The incident had to happen long before then! I do believe you, but I'll probably need to convince her that you were no where near that area!"

"How the hell could she blame me? I don't even know her aside from the night of the dance when I greeted her!" he told him. Andres could see that Carlos had been stunned by the accusation, Now he was also worried about what was going to happen!

"She told me in the hospital that whoever attacked her had been a group of four people! Two of the men were apparently black, and the other two had olive complexions! She probably mistook you for one of them since you also have an olive complexion!"

"But she was dead wrong, damn it! I was with one black person and another man who came from Sevilla who also had an olive complexion! There were also a group of three girls who were with us! If you looked at the receipt I showed you, you'll see that it specifically states a group of six people!" Andres took another look at the small piece of paper and saw that what his friend was telling him had been the truth!

"I'll need to speak to her tomorrow and try to convince her! It's quite possible that the only thing that she noticed was the olive complexion! Naturally, everyone she sees with those same dark features will look suspicious! I think that after I explain things to her tomorrow, she will see that she was wrong!"

"I certainly hope so! I don't like the idea of being blamed for something that I didn't do! I would never do such a thing and I thought you knew me well enough to realize that!"

"I do realize it! But I also need to convince her that she is wrong in her identification! Perhaps after I explain things to her, she'll see things our way! I wouldn't worry too much about it! I don't expect to have very much trouble in convincing her!" Andres told him.

Andres could hardly wait for the last class to be over! He had made up his mind that before confronting Maripaz, he would first interview all of the other people that had been with Carlos the night she was beaten! Suddenly, it was quite obvious that he was reviewing the matter, no longer as a friend, but, rather as an attorney! Part of his training as a lawyer had been to search for inconsistencies in any of the accounts from the others! As far as he could tell, he was in the middle of a serious problem! On one hand, Maripaz was quite certain that Carlos had been the person who had beaten up on her! Yet, on the other hand, Carlos had already given him some evidence to support that at the estimated time of assault, he nor his group was anywhere near Maripaz! Someone was either very confused or was not telling the truth! This was now his challenge and he needed to discover the truth before confronting her with the definite details!

He planned to search for all of the other members that had been with his room mate and ask them to account for their whereabouts on the night of the incident! Carlos did not mind giving the names of his other friends to him, because he had nothing to hide! Once he got this information, he felt he would be able to go to her and convince her that the assault had not been committed by any member of Carlos' friends! Once the truth were made known, he felt reasonably sure that he would be able to convince her that she had been wrong in her accusations! Andres was well aware that there were times when she had a tendency to over react and this could well be one of those times. Unfortunately, he also felt that by this time she should certainly have enough confidence in him to realize that he was being helpful but at the same time, very truthful! It seemed to him that this was simply a case of mistaken identity or perhaps possible even the strange phenomenon of thought transparency! It was certainly possible that in her own mind anyone who had an olive complexion would be accused of being the perpetrator! What he needed to do was to convince her that he had looked in to the matter thoroughly and then to disclose what he had found out during the interviews!

When he arrived for their daily walks, he noticed a very different Maripaz! She seemed cold and distant, a far cry from the way she had treated him during their times together! Unlike all of the other times, this time there was no talk about marriage nor did she want to bring up the subject as to where they were going to live! The frown on her face quickly told him as soon as she came downstairs that she was angry! Damned angry!! Andres decided to disregard her anger for the moment as he arrived carrying a legal pad that was full of notes he had taken during his interviews! One look at her and he knew that convincing her was not going to be an easy chore!

"Mari, before we go for our walk, there are some things I think you should know! I need to talk to you!" he said seriously. He realized that he was now being more of a lawyer than he was the person she had wanted to be with following graduation!

"I don't want to listen to anything about what happened last night!" she blurted out. "I know what I know and nothing can change my mind!"

Good! He thought! He had been trying to find the proper words to say in order to approach the subject and now she had just made things easier for him! "Don't you think you should

at least listen to what I found out and what I have to tell you?"
he said seriously. Andres remained calm as he spoke! All of
the psychology he had learned in his classes suddenly began to
surface! The transformation had been instant! He had turned from
a friend to an attorney! He slowly took her hand into his! It was a
simple gesture that she had always done whenever they met! Today,
however, she decided that she forego that sign of affection! If they
were to have any chance of having a decent life together as they
had discussed, she would need to have enough faith to realize that
he was on her side and was not coming to her as an adversary!

"What for?" she asked angrily."I know that it was your
friend who committed the attack!"

"Mari, think about it for a minute! When you were in the
hospital you specifically told me that you unable to identify who
had attacked you because it was dark and the perpetrator had hit
you from behind! These were your words, not mine, remember?
You went on to tell me that everything went blank and that you
couldn't identify who it was! You also said that there were two
black men in the group! From what I've been able to find out, there
was only one black man, and there were also several other young
women in the group!" he said as he looked down at the notes he
had scribbled.

"When I saw your friend, everything came back to me! It
was him and his friends! I don't remember any women being with
them!" she insisted.

"But, these people were at another location, a reasonable
distance away from where the attack took place! I have seen the
cash register receipt to prove where they were and at what time!
Would you like to see the receipt? I can get it for you! On that
receipt you will see clearly the date and the time that the bill was
paid! It is virtually impossible for them to have been where the
attack took place at that time!"

"So, what are you saying? Are you calling me a liar?" she
said defiantly, once again showing that frown on her forehead, a
clear giveaway to show her anger!

"No! Of course I am not calling you a liar! I know all too
well that the assault happened! I am only saying that, on the basis

of what I've been able to find out, I am not convinced that it was Carlos and his friends! That's all I'm saying!" he insisted.

"Entonces estas diciendo que soy una mentirosa! Verdad?" (Then, you are calling me a liar, right?)

"No Mari! I am only saying that I want you to listen to reason! Please, listen to what I'm telling you!"

"And why should I listen?? You weren't the one who was laying in the hospital without knowing what day it was! That was me, or have you forgotten?"

"How could I forget? I was there with you every day, hoping and praying that you would open your eyes and see me sitting there! I realize how much you have suffered and how angry you are, but I can't in good conscience accuse an innocent person for a crime where the evidence shows that it wasn't him!" He was hearing his own voice rising as he spoke! It was something that he had been specifically taught never to do! She was being much too subjective without listening to reason! He had wanted to keep away from telling her bluntly that she couldn't go around accusing people if the evidence didn't support her story!

"Si! Pero a mi no me crees! Yo soy la mentirosa, y el es quien tiene toda la razon! Y porque?? Porque es tu amigo, verdad?" (Yes, but you don't believe me! I am the one not telling the truth! Why? Because he is your friend, right?)

"How can you say that?" he asked, realizing that he was also getting angry at her insinuations! "Haven't I convinced you how I feel about you? Did you forget that we even discussed what we were going to do after graduation? How can you even suggest that I would take his word over yours because he is a friend? He may well be my friend, but, damn it, you are the one I once thought of spending my life with! Doesn't that mean anything?" The longer he spoke, the angrier he was getting and his voice was getting louder and louder! Everything he had studied had shown an emphasis on making certain that facts were correct before making any accusations! She had one hell of a nerve accusing him of placing his friendship with Carlos at a higher level than what he felt for her! It was an insult! He would be willing to forget her blunt comments, knowing that she was upset! But he couldn't forgive the accusations that were unwarranted! Sure, she was angry! She had every right to be! All of his life he had been told how stubborn and self-centered the Basques could be, once they thought they were right about something! Still, it was necessary that he remain calm and try to convince her that she was acting out of anger instead of trying to think objectively!

"Look! I don't want to talk about it anymore! You can believe whatever you want to! I know what I need to do! I know exactly how you think! You are only taking your friend's part instead of mine! Well, you and he can go straight to hell!" she said with furor in her eyes.

At that point she removed her hand from his, went back into her room and slammed the door in his face leaving him surprised and flustered outside in the hallway while other young people were passing by and smiling at the lover's quarrel that was going on! Little did they realize that the argument was much more serious than they could imagine! It consisted of a false accusation that, if not correct, could ruin the future of another person! He stood alone outside her door for several moments, not knowing what he should do or say! Her accusations had made her inflexible; and her last words, if he heard them correctly, had been threatening! When she told him that she knew exactly what she should do, it troubled him not knowing what she had in mind! If she should decide to take the law into her own hands, the results could be devastating! There was little chance that, given her emotional state, he could say anything that would quiet her down long enough for her to listen to reason or could speak to someone else that might be more objective and authoritative that could convince her she was wrong! The only person he thought of who might be able to help him was Professor Heintz! Maybe, if he could convince the old man to pay her a visit and explain his position in a calm manner, maybe she might just decide to listen to him! Several hours had gone by before he was able to see Professor Heintz! Andres waited for him in his office and he finally had an opportunity to calm down and to see things more logically than before. He needed to have advice from someone he could trust; and, the only person he could think of had been the old professor! When the old man arrived and after the pleasantries had been exchanged, Andres discussed everything that had happened to him!

"I don't believe there is very much we can do!" the old man told him. "If she is certain that it was your friend who assaulted her, the law clearly stipulates that he must be detained and charged with the crime! Certainly, you know as well as I that the law is very specific on that!"

"But how can the law be so specific when there is no evidence that he was near the scene of the crime? If anything, the opposite is true! I have interviewed all of his friends who were with him that night, and the story they told was consistent! If anything there are cash register receipts that prove where they were at the time of the assault!" Andres explained.

"Then you must visit your lady friend and convince her of the truth! If the police find out, there will be an arrest and they will believe whatever she tells them! Unfortunately, that is the law, and although it may not be fair at times, it is all we have!"

"But an arrest will more than likely ruin his life! There has to be something else we can do!"

"We can!! We can speak to the young lady and explain to her what you have just told me! Maybe by the time you return, she will be more calm and ready to listen to reason! I'm afraid you are the only person who can convince her!" They had barely finished their discussion when the telephone rang and interrupted their conversation! "What???" he heard the professor say. "That cannot be true! Yes....yes....he is here! Of course I will tell him! He will call you and tell you what he decides to do!" the old man said before hanging up the telephone! Judging by the surprised look on the professor's face, Andres knew that the news had not been good!

"What is it, Professor? I am almost afraid to ask!" Andres said in his usual calm but with caution not knowing what had happened.The professor stared at him for several moments with the look of both worry and concern on his face! It almost seemed that he was looking for a better way to give him some bad news!

"I'm afraid that a problem has come up!" he said. "It appears that your lady friend went to the police and accused your friend of assaulting her!"

"Mierda!!! Mierda!!" was the only thing Andres could say! Why had she done such a foolish thing before all of the facts had been known? Why did she lack the faith in him to look deeply into this case, not as a friend but as a lawyer, before going to the police with evidence that didn't even make much sense?

"It gets even worse, I'm afraid!" the old professor told him. "It seems that the Guardia Civiles have gone to the dormitory and have arrested your room mate! He is being charged with an assault! That was your room mate on the telephone asking for our help and asking for us to represent him in court! I am old and tired, and I have a difficult time fighting these battles on my own! The only way I will represent him is if you agree to assist me! You know, of course, that for you to do this, it is important that you believe in his innocence! Do you?"

"Yes, Professor! I have checked the information for myself, and I am thoroughly convinced that the evidence will show that neither he nor his friends were anywhere near the scene of the assault! I have no idea why she did that without speaking to me again! I realize that she was angry when I spoke with her, but I had hoped to speak to her again after she had a chance to calm down! Maybe, I'll be able to convince her of my findings! At least, I can try!"

"You need to go back and speak to her again! Remember, she has already filed the charges! Of course, just as in your case, the young man will be expelled by the university! I have a feeling that the authorities will be anxious to close out this case with a conviction! His life will obviously be ruined; and, since he comes from the South, no one will really care!"

"Damn it, I care!! I cannot allow that to happen! I'll go and speak to her again! Maybe if I'm lucky she will listen to me this time!" he answered.

"Whatever you do has to be done quickly! Remember, he is already under arrest! There is little time remaining!"

Andres walked out of the professor's office and went directly to the women's dormitory! He knocked on the door several times but there was no answer! Again, he knocked on the door, this time much harder, and there was still no answer. Not knowing what to do or where he could go, he decided on an impulse to walk to the nearby park where he and Maripaz would often go in the afternoon hours after the classes were finished for the day! Beyond what had happened with Carlos, he was still hopeful that there was enough left of their relationship that she might go there if only to relive some of the happier times they had spent together! It had been a beautiful autumn day! The sun was crisp and the air was cool! It was an ideal time for relaxing as he saw many of the other students with books opened and speaking to their friends! It was just the way he and Maripaz would do when they were happy! Maripaz was no where to be found! There was little point in wasting any more time! If he was going to talk to her again and try to convince her that what she had done had been wrong, time was of the essence! He walked away from the park and began walking back toward the dormitory when from a distance he saw her walking in the opposite direction. Andres waited until they were closer; neither of them was trying to avoid the other! It wasn't until they were almost face to face that he stopped walking and stepped in her way prohibiting her from moving forward!

"Porque lo hiciste?" he asked. (Why did you do it?) "Have you any idea of what you've done? You have probably ruined a young man's life for no reason at all! You could at least have told me what you were planning to do!"

"Ya no tengo mas que hablarte!" Hize lo que me dio la gana!" (I have nothing more to say to you! I did what I wanted to do!) she told him.. There was a sarcastic overtone to her voice that was making him angry, but he knew that this was her way! These were times for cool heads to prevail including his own!

"But why, Mari? Don't you realize that they have already arrested Carlos and there is really no hard evidence that he actually was the person who assaulted you! What you did was wrong; and, if you had trusted me, you would have discussed your plans with me before going to the authorities! I have already shown you that it was impossible for him to be at the scene of the assault! He can prove that he was at the park drinking Mariposas! Also, I'm sure that his friends will verify where he was!"

"That may be your story, but it isn't mine! I know for
certain it was he who assaulted me!'"

"Damn it!!! No, Mari, it wasn't! It was someone else but not
him! We can prove that in court!'"

"Do you intend to represent him?" she asked. He saw the
familiar lines of anger on her face as she spoke! Andres suddenly
felt a sick feeling knowing that this was going to be the point in
their life where they would probably be parting company! As much
as he liked her, it was an important time in tune with his ideals
where he was going to need to stand up for what he believed in!
He was firmly comvinced that giving in to her at this time would
proably mean that she would always have the upper hand! Would
she always use this tool to her advantage and prohibit him from
doing that he believed in? How could he pursue his own life if the
only woman he had cared for had no faith in him! God, how he was
hoping that it wouldn't come down to this! Fate had deceived him!
But, if she could be senseless and stubborn, so could he! She may
have been a Basque, but he was a Gallego! Both were known for
refusing to give in on issues that they considered important!

"He has asked Professor Heintz to represent him! The
professor, in turn, has asked me to assist him! Yes, we will both be
representing him! I honestly think you are wrong; and I honestly
wish that you would decide to reconsider! The man is being
accused unjustly, and he needs a defense! Yes, Mari, this time I
will need to go against your wishes!" he told her.

"Then you and I have nothing further to talk about!" she
said with finality, as she walked away without saying goodbye!

He had not spoken to her nor had seen her since the last
meeting in the park when she walked away! It was time for her to
graduate! He had honestly tried to call her on several occasions,
but, each time she was either too busy to answer the telephone, or
else she would ask one of her friends to tell him simply that she
wasn't in her room! It seemed almost odd that the one thing in
common had been their ideals; and, now, it had been these ideals
that wer driving them apart!

News of the graduation had been posted throughout
the university campus and Andres felt that if she decided to

leave Madrid after the graduation, he would probably never see
her again! That was the one thing he didn't want to happen!
Graduation was going to be a joyful occasion, and he had wanted
to be there! Almost on impulse he decided that he would go to the
auditorium and would take a seat in the front row where she would
see him! Once she saw that he had not forgotten her, he felt she
would be receptive to his appearance! After all, the matter that was
now separating them had been minor when compared to the desires
they had expressed about spending their time together! He stopped
by a florist and bought a large bouquet of fresh flowers to give her
on this happy occasion! If nothing else, he had a feeling that she
would be willing to fogive him and to forget their differences. If
it meant that he needed to participate in Carlos' defense, so be it!
He was still a student and would probably be more of an observer
than an actual defense council! It had been such a foolish argument
that it should never have gone this long! Perhaps he had come on
too strong with his ideals! He decided he would kiss her and tell
her how proud he was at what she had accomplished in the hopes
that she would return his kiss and all of the bitterness would be
forgotten! It would be a great time to once again discuss their
plans together, since they had never been finalized when they were
discussed during their courtship! Whatever had happened would
remain in the past where it belonged, and they could now begin
making their plans for their future!

  He sat in the first row of the crowded auditorium holding
the bouquet of flowers and anxiously waiting to see her make
her entrance wearing the cap and gown! There was no way she
could avoid seeing him! He would just smile and nod his head,
a symbol of pride in seeing her graduate on this day! All of the
names were called as he waited anxiously and he watched as all
of the other graduates began to take their pre-assigned places on
the stage. It seemed like forever before he heard the announcer
begin calling out the names beginning with "R"! Almost at the
end of the list, Andres heard the name Maripaz Romero called!
He waited eagerly hoping to get a glimpse of her walking down
the aisle! He felt his heart beating faster with anticipation as the
music played! Her name was again called and again he saw that she

was conspicuously absent! There were a few unsettling rumbles in the audience as the spectators were wondering why this graduate was not taking her place among the others! Andres was worried when he realized that she would not be appearing! He waited until the cermony had ended and walked out of the auditorium still holding the bouquet of flowers. Finally, outside in the hallway he spotted one of her room mates! He went over to the young woman, congratulated her on her graduation, and asked her casually why Maripaz Romero had been absent from this important ceremony!

"Oh, haven't you heard?" the young woman answered surprised that he had not known of her absence!

"Maripaz has been called back home! It seems that her father has become quite ill and she left for home several days ago! Before leaving she made arrangements with the graduation committee to mail her diploma to her home in Vizcaya! I don't think she has any plans of returning!" the young woman told him. "Is there anything I can do?"

"No, thank you very much! I guess she forgot to tell me she wasn't going to be here!" he lied, not wanting to appear embarassed that he had gone to see her with a bouquet of flowers! He glanced at the bright flowers and handed them to the young graduate! "Here!" he said. "You deserve to have these!" he told her as he walked away disappointed that Maripaz had walked out of his life, and he had no way of finding her. Perhaps things had turned out for the best! There were many things on his mind that he would begin working on! These were things he had doubted she would understand! None of that mattered now! All of the differences they had could have been easily resolved! There was little for him to do except to pick up the pieces and continue on with his own life! One thing was certain, and it was something she had probably never known! She had been the only woman he had ever cared about and there would never again be anyone that would take her place!!

CHAPTER 4

Madrid

Andres felt disappointed and sad when he returned to his room! He had promised Professor Heintz he would pay him a visit, but now he was in no mood to speak to anyone! He was also aware that his own graduation would soon be arriving, but he was in no mood to review his work or to study for the major exams that he had to take. Since the time when he had been wrongly accused in Maripaz's assault, the relationship between the professor and him had grown. Unknown to him, the old professor was slowing filling the young lawyers' mind with his own liberal dreams, realizing that his years were advanced; and he would never live to see the changes he thought were necessary. If any changes were going to be made, they would have to be at the hands of a protegee such as Andres who felt the same way he did about the unfairness of some of the laws! Andres had all of the qualifications he had been looking for! The young man was brilliant in his work, resourceful, and determined to make a difference! Above all, he had no selfish motives nor was he driven by the profit motive as so many other young men had been as soon as they graduated from law school. There was also a sense of honesty and seriousness that, in many ways, reminded him of himself when he, too, felt that his own contribution to society would change the world! The young man had come from a poor family of peasants and had only been accepted to study law at the university because of his high grades and his own intellectual achievments. If there was anyone who was capable of carrying out the reforms the old professor had envisioned, it would need to be someone like Andres!

It was late in the afternoon when Andres finally went to see Professor Heintz! One look at the sadness on his face and the old man knew immediately that something had happened! There was no point in asking him any questions! He knew from experience that young men in this state of sadness would prefer to retain his anxieties and all of his problems to himself! He assumed that it had something to do with the young woman who had been assaulted! If so, he would wait until he felt that Andres was willing to talk about it! For the time being, the least he could do was to strengthen his ego and remind him of the good qualities and not to dwell on the feelings of despair for a long time!!

"Have you spoken to the young woman?" the professor asked. It had been asked a lead-in question, but he wanted it to open the conversation between them. Professor Heintz had checked at the university, because if the trial against Carlos went forward, she was going to be needed to testify! The university had told him that she had returned home because one of her parents had become quite ill!

"No, sir!" Andres replied. "I went to see her but she didn't want to discuss the matter with me! I did my best to convince her that she was wrong, but she didn't want to listen to any of my explanations!"

"Perhaps you have underestimated her! Whenever there is such a problem, you need to remember that the victim is always convinced that her own views are true! It is very difficult to convince another person who has been victimized! When you are dealing with a Basque, the problem is always more difficult and you need to be more tactful!" the old man offered.

"It doesn't matter anymore! I went to the graduation like a fool and was told that she would not be attending because she had gone home! I guess now I'll never be able to convince her!" he said.

"One of the advantages of being young is that when a person is young, it is much easier to forgive and forget than when he gets older! Who can say? There may yet come a day when she will be able to forgive and forget! Then, perhaps she'll return! I want you always to remember that you have a perfect right to your own opinions! But, they must be based on what you have learned as being the truth! On the other hand, she, too, has a right to her own opinions, not necessarily because of what you may have told her, but, rather, on what she perceives to be the truth! It seems to me that you really liked that young lady, didn't you?"

"Yes.....professor...you are quite correct! But since she has gone away, it no longer matters! I think that what hurts me the most is that she didn't have enough faith in me to realize that I was telling her the truth! I suppose she didn't trust me enough!"

"Maybe it had nothing to do with trust; but, instead, it had to do with who she thought was right! Actually, she has made the problem with your room mate much easier for us! If she isn't around to submit to cross-examination, the authorities will have no other choice but to give him his freedom! If that happens, you have just won your first legal challenge without needing to go to court! You should be very proud of yourself!" the professor said smiling.

"Winning or losing is not nearly as important as making a difference! We have already seen that many of the laws are wrong and some are even contradictory to society's demands! Those are the things I would like to change!"

"Good, my son!!.....good, ja? Who can say? Perhaps you will be the one to succeed where many others have failed! Only time and hard work will tell!"

Bilbao

It was a rainy day when Maripaz arrived home after travelling in an open decked steamer with all the creaks and noises of a small fishing boat, eager to reach its destination while fighting tall waves and high seas on its way back to a safe harbor. School was now behind her since she had been called home to attend to her ailing father. The notice asking her to come home had been brief! While there had been no signs of urgency, it had not been written as a request but more to convince her that something was seriously wrong and she was needed at home! The graduation and the culmination of years at school were behind her. No one would know that she would have preferred to remain until after graduation and walk down the aisle with her other classmates! Unfortuantely she also owed her parents a debt; and, as far as she was concerned, her family always came first! If only she had the time to say goodbye to the young man she had argued with! Despite their differences she had become attracted to him! He was perhaps the only young man she had met who was always kind, gentle, and sensitive! Also, he had always treated her with care! Now that she was away, she regretted having argued with him so strongly about something she was not even sure of! After all, how many other young men would have had the decency to undress her in his own room without taking advantage of her? Although she had chided him for what he did, she also knew that he was different than most men! Too bad that he was a Gallego!! He would have made an excellent Basque who were known for their sensitivity toward woman! If ever there was a young man she had been interested in, it had been he! But she had lost him through no fault of her own; and now there was little she could do about it except to pick up the pieces of her life and go on!

She was beginning to hate herself for not having given Andres her address! Sitting all alone on the large steamer had given her a long time to think things over! Perhaps she had been impetuous with him, far more than he deserved! In her anger she had accused him of things which after thinking them over, she shouldn't have done! How many other young men would have been as honorable and as sensitive as he had been when she was taken unconscious to his room? Other men would have avoided the responsibility; yet, he had risked being accused, just because he sought to help her! At that time, she had told herself what a great person he was and how much she would want her parents to meet him. Now, in anger, she had done precisely the same thing! She had accused his room mate, knowing only too well that, aside from his olive skin, she had no idea who the attacker had been nor would she be able to recognize him if asked to do so in a court of law! Could it be that Andres had been right all along? Could it be that he had investigated the matter and had wanted to spare her the embarassment of having to identify her assailant in court? There had been no point in worrying now! Quite obviously, she had made a fool of herself and had allowed her emotions to take hold of common sense! After all, she should certainly know that as a lawyer, he needed to work with the truth and with facts that were rational and made sense! Perhaps being a stubborn Basque had taken its toll! There was little chance of ever seeing him again! No doubt he would be successful as a lawyer! He would probably marry some rich woman who would help make him famous and would forget all about the plans they had discussed before she had sent him away! It was fairly obvious that she had just had her first lesson in growing up! It had ended up by costing her a man she would have been proud to have by her side for the rest of her life! Even while going home in the old steamer, she kept looking at the sea and sky and wondering, if somehow, someway he was thinking about her? Did he have any idea how she felt because of her foolishness? Of course not! Why should he? She had gotten exactly what she deserved; and he had gotten what he didn't deserve! All the while she was thinking over and over not only how much she already missed him, but, also, would she ever find another man like him? No! Of course not! Men like him came along once in a lifetime and she had her chance! She made up her mind that she would never allow anyone to take his place! It just wouldn't be fair, because she would always be comparing any other men to Andres! She already knew that they would never equal the person that he was!

As soon as she opened the door to her house, she took one quick look and realized how much things at home had changed! Her mother greeted her warmly; but one look at her father, sitting on a chair with a dark blanket covering his legs, and she could see the change in his appearance and how sick and pale he was! Maripaz looked back at her mother and couldn't control her tears! His face was ashen and pale with deep dark circles under those large dark penetrating eyes that she had always admired! It took several minutes of struggling with her self before she was able to ask her mother the nature of his illness for fear that the facts would be even worse than she expected. She cried and cried while her mother cradled her in her arms, the same as she did when she was a child! There had been only two men in her life that she admired; fate had already taken away one of them! Could it be that the same fate was going to take away the other man in her life?

"The winter has been unusually cold and damp! Your father has been ill with pneumonia! He's been very sick; but, thank God, we were able to give him several 'remedios' that have helped him! The best remedy I could give him was when I gave him the news that you were coming home!" her mother said.

"But, if he was so sick mother, why didn't you ask me to come home sooner? I would have dropped everything and would have come home!" she answered. (All the time she was thinking that had she come home sooner, she probably would have been spared the hurt of losing a person she was fond of!)

"Your father didn't want me to call you! It was important that you complete your studies; receive your diploma! Then you could come home and help him handle the loads of paperwork that awaits you! I wish I could have done more for your father; but, unfortunately, I never learned to read or write! I guess I wasn't very much help to him!" her mother answered almost as if she apologizing.

"It doesn't matter, Mother! I am home now! I'll be able to help you with the ranch!"

"I'm afraid it's much more than that, Mari! You see, things have changed in Vizcaya. Since you went away, there has been a change in our government; and it doesn't seem to be for the better! An organization has been formed, mainly among the young people, called the 'Euskadi Ta Askatasuna' or the E.P.A. as it is known! It was formed because of the moderate actions of the Partido Nacionalista Vasco that was formed under the Government of Franco! A group of young people from Bizkaia and Gipuzkao have been unhappy with the government for a long time! They felt that the P.N.V. was not acting energetically enough to advance the Basque causes! The E.T.A. stands for the Basque Homeland and

Liberty; and it is the only armed group that has been allowed to emerge in the Spanish state!'"

"Why, Mother? I always thought that our government was quite stable! It was one of the few areas of the country that were permitted to retain their own land and had enjoyed autonomy throughout the region!"

"As I have said before, things have changed! The other day one of the ranch hands was in the Western areas and saw that the fence enclosures had been deliberately torn down and some of the sheep were missing! It seems that this is what the newly formed members of the E.T.A. are doing to the ranchers. They want to destroy the large ranches so that the land can then be distributed among the peasants. It's a new wave of crime and your father is much too ill to fight them! Also, some of the ranch hands have left the area and have joined the E.T.A. The problem has now become critical and all of the complaints that have been registered seem to fall on deaf ears!" her mother explained.

"But why? Doesn't the government know the amount of taxes that are being paid into the government by the ranchers? If they destroy the ranches, who is going to pay the taxes that are needed to run the country? Why doesn't the government of Franco do something to protect the ranchers?" Maripaz asked.

"It is because for years the Basques have been demanding complete autonomy! What they have received was only a partial autonomy and the Franco government has no desire to intervene! I have no idea what we are going to do if the current trend continues!"

Maripaz was noticing that while her mother was doing most of the talking, her father was silently listening to every word while seated on his chair. Every once in a while, she would hear him begin to let out a strong, phlegmy cough that would linger for several minutes before subsiding. It was the fierce trembling of his once firm hands during the coughing spells that bothered her! Her father, who had once been the tower of strength, was being weakened by the illness that should have been treated more adequately and much sooner!

"Mother, why haven't you taken Daddy to Madrid to visit a specialist?" she asked.

"Because, under the new rules, he is now prohibited from travelling out of the area! He is forbidden to travel away from here for any reason! To the Falange, he is still very much a traitor! He would risk being arrested and tried for treason if he were caught!"

All of a sudden, thoughts of Andres came to mind! She remembered vividly all of the talks the two of them had during their walk through the park near the university. These were the types of laws that bothered him and that he wanted to change! Damn it, she thought! Why did she need to allow her foolish temper to interfere with their friendship? If she knew how or where to contact him, he might have given her some help in knowing how to get around the law! She was now faced with a growing condition, a sick father; and, yet, she felt helpless not knowing what to do! The more she thought about her limitations, the more she realized that her only alternative was going to be to join the ETA in secrecy, and do whatever she could to help her family! If the concept of the law was to remain out of bounds to her, at least she might be able to convince the leaders of the group to leave her family alone and to concentrate their efforts on the more wealthy ranchers. She knew there would be no point in telling her parents what she planned to do because she had already sensed, by the sound of her mother's voice that both she and her father were steadfast against the new movement. There was no point in telling them what she planned to do since they would never allow her to join the group! If she tried to resist their plans, there was a good chance that her safety would be threatened!

Maripaz had known for a long time that her father had once been a very influential member of the Fascist party! She also knew that he had served admirably as a Mariscal during the Civil War! She remembered hearing something that he had left his post within the new government because of the love he had for her mother. Unfortunately, she had never been able to find out what had happened that had caused him to lose face with the government! When she first heard about it, she hadn't given the matter very much attention, thinking that it had been nothing more than a fairy tale! She did know however that her mother had been active in the underground movement; but she never knew that her father had been prohibited from travelling into other parts of Spain now that the country was at peace! For the next few weeks, Maripaz made many trips into town! Every time there was the slightest reason for going, she had argued with her mother into allowing her to go! It was this time when she would start up conversations with other women during the times they would be buying their groceries. She had used these friendly talks to listen to what the others were saying and try to learn whatever she could about this new movement! In a matter of weeks she learned more things about the Basque movements than she had ever known! If her own plans had any chance of success, it was important that she learn everything she could about her homeland; and why they found the need to struggle with a new behavior that seemed senseless and useless!

Maripaz soon learned that the first activities of the ETA had involved the planting of explosives in the cities of Bilbao, Vitoria and Santander when the movement began in 1959. Stories were also circulated telling how the first military action had been an unsuccessful attempt during 1961 to derail a train carrying Civil War veterans that were travelling to Donostia to celebrate the 25th anniversary of the Civil War. The police had apparently responded by applying road controls, arrests, house searches, and a widespread use of torture on those that were apprehended. As a result, many of the Basques travelled abroad and went into exile! Others who had remained joined the newly formed units of the ETA. A few years later when democracy had again beeen restored, many of the exiles chose to return to Spain! The newly formed democratic government of the nation had granted unconditional autonomy to the various regions of the country. The Basque regions were granted their own parliament and were given control over such issues such as education and taxes. On the other hand the very distinctive Basque language and culture were promoted in the schools. For a minority of the ETA the partial autonomy was not nearly enough! They firmy believed that the Basques should enjoy full independence from Spain; and, to this end, they intensified the violence against the security forces and the politicians! These groups apparently become the main targets of the group!

The former Socialist government of Felipe Gonzalez attempted to combat the ETA's violence by setting up the GAL, an anti terrorist liberation group, that was apparently responsible for the deaths of about 28 suspected ETA members. Secret talks between the ETA and the government were later held in Algeria but failed to bring about an end to the conflict. In July, an estimated 6 million Spaniards took to the streets to condemn the ETA violence, following the brutal kidnappings and the muder of a young Basque politician. This forced the Spanish government to adopt a hard-line approach to all things related to the EPA; and the entire 23 member leadership of the ETA's political wing and their leader Henri Batasuma were all sentenced to a total of 7 years in jail for collaborating with the armed group. It appeared that the armed group had once again gained sufficient strength and had used its power to intimidate many of the prosperous ranchers in the area. Their hopes were of eventually gaining access to their lands and parcelling off their lands to members of the ETA and other peasants who would be compelled to compensate the ETA members with a large portion of their earnings in order to further finance their aggressive activities!

Maripaz had learned everything she could by listening to the townspeople and making note of everything she heard. She quickly realized that as a young woman, recently out of college and lacking any real support, could do little to reverse this trend! If she had any hopes of succeeding, she had little choice other than to join the ETA, attend their meetings, and do whatever she could from the inside to fight the criminals that were threatening not only the other members of the town, but her own family as well. In order to do this, she was going to need to find a way to be admitted to the secret meetings; and with any luck, she might be able to convice the group to leave her family alone and undisturbed! Whatever she did would need to be done secretly, making sure that her parents did not know what she was planning to do! She had become familiar with the evil look of her mother's eyes anytime she mentioned the ETA; and her father was much too sick to show any concern one way or another. She started by finding out where the meetings were being held and soon discovered that many of the meetings were held in the open cafe's in town! The small restaurants that also served a large selection of tapas were outdoor cafes that catered to young people who would come to the coffee shop, sit at a table and talk over the activities that would be taking place. These ideas were then taken over to another major meeting that was held in a secret location every week. Then they would be discussed among the leaders who would decide whether or not they were acceptable.If the thoughts were found to be deserving, they would be discussed among themselves and a decision would be reached. If the ideas were favorable, they would then discuss a method of planning and schedule a specific date when it would be carried out. The entire sequence was much more difficult for a woman in attendance than for a man! Maripaz soon learned that she was going to need to come up with an exceptional idea in order to be invited to present her ideas to a major meeting and become accepted as a member of the group. After speaking to some of the women around town, she learned that one of the small cafes in the outskirts of the city was where some of the members of her age group would meet on Wednesday evenings to discuss their plans. If she hoped to be accepted, she would need to make herself obvious even if it meant flirting with some of the younger members of the group to gain their acceptance! Therefore, she marked down the address of the meeting place and decided she would go there the following week. The only thing missing was the need of having someone else with her! After all, this was Spain; and in Spain good girls did not go to such places by themselves! They would be looked down upon by other members of the city! If only there was someone else she could go with that would agree to sit with her at a table, order a cup of coffee and some tapas! Her own absence from the area while she was at school had made her a stranger in her own home town. The only woman she could think of at the moment was a young woman who worked at the local bakery. On the next trip to the bakery she would ask her to accompany her for coffee! It would be an excellent time for the two women to get better acquainted and might perhaps lead toward going to the coffee shop together! It was a thought, maybe not a very good one; but one worth exploring!

There were also many questions still lingering in her mind about her parents that had never been answered! Most noticeably one had happened the day that she had been re-arranging her fathers' room and had come across two interesting articles that had been tucked away in one of the chest drawers. One of the items was a letter hand signed by none other than General Franco, appointing him as the senior Mariscal of Toledo! As a child, she had been told that he had served as a Mariscal but had never been told that he was personally appointed by Francisco Franco! She could still remember the far away look appearing on her mother's face when she was told about the letter! The only thing she had offered as an explanation was that technically all of the Mariscals were appointed by Franco and that the letter had no other meaning! When she arrived at the university, she had taken several courses in history and learned that only a few people had been personally appointed by Franco. These people who had received appointments were considered as very important officers of the Falange movement! If this was true, then, why did her father consistently avoid speaking about it? Why did he escape to the Basque country before the war was ended? There was no point is seeking additional answers from her parents since she knew that no more information would be given!

The other strange item she had found was even much more curious! Wrapped up in a simple, crumbled up newspaper, she stumbled on a large head mask with only small holes for the eyes and mouth! Because the mask covered the entire head, it almost looked like an executioner's mask she had read about in foreign European countries in centuries gone by! Somehow, she could never imagine her father as an executioner! He was much too sensitive and kind to the demands of others! Besides, there had been no real need for that! After all, as a senior Mariscal for the government, a portion of his job was in pronouncing sentences on people that came before him! Surely, he would have had his own staff of executioners for the people that had been given death sentences for their war crimes! Then, why the mask? The more she thought about it, the more mystery seemed to be attached! Also, why was it so carefully wrapped in newspaper as if preserving both the mask as well as its significance? Once again, she had asked her mother and the answer was vague and not very convincing! Her mother had explained that it had only been a gift from a friend during the Civil War! The abrupt answer and the concerned look on her mother's face when she was explaining the significance soon told Maripaz that her mother was not being truthful! There was quite obvious another significance that was being kept from her! Without mentioning the item, she decided to look into these items on her own! To do this, she would need to be careful that whatever they signified did not reflect on any activities by her parents.

As far as she knew, their story had been consistent! They had told her repeatedly that they had gone to live in the Basque areas with a small amount of money her father had been able to salvage when he was a Mariscal! There was every reason to believe that they had left Toledo in good graces with the Fascist government! Once again, for every question that was answered, another question seemed to appear! If it was true that they had left Toledo with the permisision of the government; why then, had he been relegated to live in the Basque area instead of living in his home in Asturias where both of her parents had been born? Also, why had he been barred from going to Madrid to receive badly needed medical attention needed for his illness? None of the questions had ever been answered to her satisfaction! The more she thought about it, the more confused and angry she became with herself not knowing very much about the background of her parents.Her father was now a very sick man! Most of the strength she had always known him to have had been zapped by his illness; and she could see him getting weaker and weaker as time went on! If something was going to be done, it would be up to her to find the right answers! It might be that she would need to ask more questions in town and to ask the other members of the ETA! She already knew that her parents would resist her joining the unit, but she feared that her fathers physical condition would worsen if he were to find out what she planned to do!

Maripaz's mind was made up! Whenh she arrived at the bakery the following morning, she was greeted by the daughter of the owner who worked inside the small bakery during the day! There had been the occasional exchange of pleasantries each morning when Mari would go to purchase the bread! Today, Mari had other things on her mind and decided she would be more friendly than usual! The young woman was extremely heavy for her age, a sign that she had probably eaten too many of her pastries! Her hair was uncombed and she was wearing a dirty apron over her blue smock! The conversation soon shifted to the fact that this young woman was frustrated because she had no life for herself outside of the bakery when she worked long hours with little recognition! The woman spoke of her desire to be able to go to one of the local cafes just like many other young women her age and look at some of the young men who might also be visiting the cafe! She had mentioned these desires on previous occasions, but Maripaz had simply cast them aside! After all, if she was unhappy she was not alone! Maripaz herself was also unhappy, and she didn't walk around telling everyone in town her own problems! Today, however, Maripaz had other things on her mind! When Olga repeated her wishes for going into town, Maripaz had decided she would sieze the opportunity and offer to go with her! It would be her way of disguising her real motives and might even involve hdr getting acquainted with other young men from the town who were members of the ETA! Maripaz waited patiently for the pastries and the bread she had ordered! Her mother had insisted that the Borona (Brown bread) and the Pan Dulce (Fresh bread sweetened with sugar!) had to be fresh from the oven! Maripaz knew that her father would refuse to eat the bread unless he could still feel the warmth from the hot oven! Good, she thought! They could now speak frankly to one another while they waited for the bread to come out of the oven! Maripaz waited for the subject to come up again, knowing that it would, because the heavy woman would use this time to talk about her unhappiness!

"I become so lonely after working here all day that the only thing I want to do when I go home is to eat!" she admited.

"Creo que necesitas un cambio!" (I think you may need a change!) Maripaz answered.

"Perhaps1 But what can I do? I am here every day fron sun up to sundown! By the time I go home I am so tired that I eat whatever I can and then I go to bed!"

"Why don't you go into town to one of the cafes and talk to some of the other young people?" Maripaz asked, knowing that she was slowly drifting into her plans!

"Because there isn't anyone that has invited me to go with them! I just can't go there by myself! I'll start to eat the tapas! To do that, I may just as well stay at home!"

"That's nonsense!" Maripaz told her. "I never realized that you wanted to go or else I would have offered to go with you!"

"Would you really?" Olga asked. Maripaz was watching her new friend showing a sudden surge of excitement coming over her.

"Pues, claro que si!" (Of course!) Maripaz answered. "If you have nothing better to do, suppose I come after work on Wednesday, and we'll go into town together?" she asked inviting herself and trying to show as much excitement as Olga was showing!

"Ay! Que bien, que bien!! Wednesday is usually the night when many of the young men living in the area go into town and visit the cafes! Who knows, perhaps you and I will spot some young man that is looking for company, eh Maripaz?"

There was a new found gleam in her eyes as she spoke! Maripaz was feeling a bit guilty about goading her on and picking up her spirits, even though she was doubting very much that any young man would really want to be seen in her company! She almost felt sorry for Olga as the guilt was growing with what she was attempting to do! For a few moments, Mari toyed with the idea of telling Olga to wear something attractive, and, for God's sake, comb her hair! She soon decided that to do so would have been insulting and decided against it!

"Okay, Olga! Then, Wednesday night it is! I'll come for you after dinner around 9:00 P.M. and we'll go together! Now, don't let me down! I'll be counting on you!" Mari said, seeing that the Pan Dulce and the Borona had been taken out of the oven and were ready to be taken home! The said their goodbyes with Olga promising her new found friend that nothing would change her mind! Her mind was on the young men she would meet and she hadn't felt so excited in a long time! Meanwhile, Maripaz simply smiled, paid for the bread and left the store with a simple wave of the hand! The next few days went by slower than usual as she was almost regretting what she had done! There were still some reservations about meeting these young men knowing that her mother had cautioned that many of them were terrorists who were only anxious to destroy things that were good! She also wondered if their attempts to gain total autonomy was only really a ploy to justify their own selfish desires? Everyone knew very well that it had been some of these young men who had already killed several influential people that had served the governement of Spain as well as those of the Basque held areas. Nevertheless, it was important that Mari's own true motives remain contained and that she carry through with her plans! It was going to be necessary for her friend Olga not to become so dependent on her that she might destroy what Mari wanted to do!

Her parents showed signs of happiness when Maripaz told them she had made plans to go into town with Olga from the bakery! At least, she had found someone her own age with whom she had made contact and might even serve as a friend! After all, she had been home for several weeks; and all of her time had been spent caring for her father and helping her mother with the daily household chores! At night, after her father had retired, she would take the daily ledgers from the ranch, entered all of the necessary accounting entries, and returned them to where they were being kept under lock and key! This had been a job that had been handled by her father! But with his illness, he had relegated the responsibility to Maripaz now that she was home from school! There was one occasion when her mother had asked her about the young man she had written about when she was at the university! It was a subject that Maripaz preferred not speaking about! Instead, she had told her mother that it had been nothing more than a childish infatuation that had ended as quickly as it began! She felt it important not to reveal any of the details about her being attacked nor how wrong she had been in turning away someone whom she really missed and wished he was there with her! If her mother only knew how much she had cared for him she wuld have regretted writing to her and asking her to come home! Maripaz felt it was best for her not to know how many tears she had shed at night wondering where he was and what he was doing! She often wondered why he had never asked for her address; but those happy days seemed long ago and no longer mattered!

Andres was too good a person not to be recognized and taken by someone else who would give him the kindness and the affection that he deserved! What good would it do for her mother to realize that it had been her fault he had left her because she was so damn temperamental! There was never any doubt he would have been the perfect man for her! Everything had really happened so fast that there had been little time for them to resolve their differences! Maripaz had always smiled at herself whenever she thought about how embarassed she had made him feel when she questioned him about removing her clothes as she lay on his bed! He had never known that she had found the story exciting and often wondered what might have happened had it taken place under differnt circumstances? Could it be that he might still be thinking about her? Probably not! What would she tell him if by chance they happened to meet again? One thing was certain! She had learned a valuable lesson about life and would never make the same mistake again!! What happened to them had changed her disposition! For that, she would always be grateful! He had lost her while defending his friend, and for that, he would always have her admiration!

"Buenas noches, mama! No esperes por mi si vengo tarde!" she told her mother! (Good night, mother! Don't wait up for me in case I'm late!)

"Entretiente, hija!" (Enjoy yourself!) her mother answered. Maripaz put on her best cotton dress, knowing that it would enhance her figure and be more attractive to the young men! She had carefully combed her hair aware that it would be compared when she entered the cafe with her uncombed friend. As she expected, her friend Olga looked not much better than she looked when she was working and serving bread to her customers. It was

not easy to tell whether or not she had combed her hair, not that
it mattered! Maripaz had her own reasons for going and she had
no intentions or having any romantic attractions to anyone! Only
once in her life was she attracted to someone, and he was now out
of her life! The two women walked side by side, Olga doing most
of the talking while Maripaz looked at the other customers who
were sitting and drinking coffee at the other tables. As they passed
several of the coffee shops, an occasional waiter would motion with
his hand summoning them inside! They had carefully scanned
the tables; and, when Maripaz saw that there were no young men
seated, they should shake their head from side to side and move
on to the next cafe! Finally, they reached one of the cafe's and saw
a group of three young men seated at one of the tables engaged in
casual conversation among themselves. They went in and sat at an
empty table near them where they could listen to what they were
saying!

"Mira que bien! Mira a los mozos que estan sentados aqui!"
Olga said. (Look at the young men alreeady seated here!) They
didn't wait for one of the waiters to show them the way. They sat at
the empty table when a middle aged waiter wearing a soiled apron
walked up to them and asked them what they wanted to order!

"Para mi, un capile!" Maripaz said. (Capile, is a cup of
strong black coffee served with an abundance of hot milk and
containing a few drops of annisette or brandy!)

"Con anis o congnac?" the waiter asked.

"Con anis del mono!" Maripaz answered.

"Solo o con bizcochos?" he asked. (By itself or with
pastries?)

"Solo!"

"Y Usted senorita?" he asked, looking at Olga.

"Para mi, igual! Pero con los bizcochos para mi!" (The
same but with pastries for me!)

"Muy bien!" the waiter answered as he rushed away to fill
their order.

As the waiter was taking the order, Maripaz was trying
to listen to what the young men were speaking about. After
eavesdropping for several minutes, she heard them talking about

their plans for robbing a small grocery store. They were intending to enter the store, and steal whatever funds were available. The funds were apparently needed to pay for yet another crime that was in the works for another location!

After the order had been served, Maripaz turned around and faced the young men seated at the next table. "I'm sorry, but I overheard what you were speaking about! Don't you think it is a bit cruel to steal from another Vasco who is struggling to make a living?" One of them looked at her strangely, while yet another turned his head quickly and tried to ignore her!

"Did you hear what I said?" she repeated.

"What business is that of yours?" the man replied angrily. He seemed unhappy that the conversation had been interrupted by a brazen woman who should be at home washing dishes!

"There is no need for you to be so angry!" she said brazenly. "Maybe that is the reason why your dumb movement will never get off the ground! You spend so much time thinking about hurting your own people instead of inflicting the harm on those you really want to hurt!" the tone of her voice had risen and she was just as angry as they had been with her!

"No te metas!" Olga whispered. (Don't get involved!) "These men are vicious and can be very dangerous!"

"Don't be a fool!!" she said loud enough for them to hear. "They are too stupid to be vicious!! Listen to what they're saying! They're talking about ripping off a small grocery store for a few pesetas in order to finance their pranks! Do you really think they are at all interested in what happens to our nation? If they were, they would be thinking about bigger and better things to do that wouldn't be quite as risky!"

The young men at the next table were taken by surprise by the sudden outburst from this strange woman they hadn't seen before! One of them, presumably their leader, since he had been doing most of the talking, looked over at her, smiled and asked. "What would you do that is bigger and better?"

"I certainly wouldn't rob some poor merchant trying to make a living! He is one of us! Why not take your cause to

413

someone who is not one of ours and let our people live in peace!"
she told him.

The group leader quickly realized that this strange woman
was sassy enough and not afraid to confront them! One thing was
certain, the dangers involved didn't seem to bother her! He was
also aware that they were in a public place and in the event of any
disturbance, she could yell her head off and attract some policeman
to come to her rescue! Maybe he should listen to what she had to
say! Who knows, she might have some ideas they could use!

"Why don't we draw our tables together? Maybe you can
join us and give us some new ideas!" he asked calmly. Maripaz
noticed that his facial expressions had not changed while he spoke.
It was hard for her to determine whether he was merely goading
her or if he felt that she might have some new ideas that they could
put to use!

"What do you think, Olga? Do you want to join these losers
or let them continue to make their own plans and hurt our people?"

No sooner had she addressed Olga, she saw the look of fear
appearing on her face wondering what these men would do to them
if she made them angrier than they were! Maripaz got up from her
chair and dragged her table over to theirs and moved the chairs
closer to them!

"So, tell us, what would be in your plans?" the leader of the
group asked her after they were again seated.

"For one thing, why are you punishing our people with your
dumb 'two perronas' robberies? If I were you, my sights would be
set on much greater plans! Think about it, there is a small bank on
the north side of town! Banks have money from all kinds of people,
from here and from other nations! With only one well planned
robbery, you could get enough money to finance your plans! You
would also be stealing the money of the wealthy in Spain as in
some countries such as England and France! If you are going to
take a risk, then, take it!! But take the risk that will pay off good
dividends! You can probably steal more from the bank in one raid,
than if you steal from our own people the few pesetasa they have in
their cash registers! Since you want to protect the Basques so damn

much, protect them and take your frustrations out on the right people!" she told them.

Two of the men were taken by surprise at what she was saying. Only the leader who was listening attentively, occasionally nodding his head up and down, was eyeing her completely to the point that it nearly frightened her. At first, she thought that he was probably undressing her in his mind! If he had any ideas about this, he had better forget them! She had no plans to submit to any of his amorous advances or his fantasies! She had sworn to herself that she would kill anyone who laid a hand on her! As far as she was concerned, there had been only one man in her life that she would have submitted to, and he sure as Hell was nowhere in sight!

On the other hand, the group leader seemed to be impressed by this woman! What she had said made a great deal of good sense! There was really no point in harassing their own people who were struggling to make an honest living! It would seem much better to harass those people that were responsible for their problems and leave their own people alone!

"Would you be willing to come with us to one of our meetings and tell the others what you just told us?" the group leader asked her.

"Is this an invitation? If you intend to listen to me constructively, then, of course I'll go! But if all you plan to do is to make fun of me because I am a woman who should be at home minding her business, then, Hell no! I have no desire to listen to a lot of nonsense spoken by amateurs who aren't capable of knowing the difference between a solid room and an opened door!" she answered.

"No!" he answered. "I think they will listen to what you have to say! If you tell me where you live, I will pick you up on Friday evening. After the meeting I will take you home! Don't worry! I will see to it that nothing happens to you!"

"How can I be sure that you won't rape me or attack me on the way home?" she asked as felt her knees begin to tremble and she felt a need to control them. She didn't want him to see that she was frightened to death by his invitation!

"What we do can sometimes be foolish, but we do it for the right reasons! My wife will also be in the car when we come for you and take you home! I give you my word that nothing will happen to you!" he told her. She could see that the man was serious; and if his wife was going to accompany him, she felt reasonably certain that he could be trusted not to harm her.

"I'll go, but on one condition! You have got to leave the people of this town alone! My father is a rancher who is ill! Someone in your organization has torn away the fence at the far side of the ranch and has stolen some of our sheep! Is your cause against the Basque people or is it against the people that are doing us harm? If you promise to leave the rest of us alone, then, I will tell you my plans. Then, maybe, your newly formed ETA group may even prosper!"

"Do you have any plans for robbing the bank that you called to my attention?" he asked.

"Of course I have! But if you decide to accept my plans, then, it needs to be done my way! Your group has already made too many dumb mistakes! At this moment the entire town is against you because of what you have done to them! When you leave them alone and decide to concentrate your efforts on the right people, our people will consider you their saviors and will even offer you refuge from the police if you need them!"

"Very well!" he said, as he stood up at the table and waited for the others to follow. "We'll see each other again on Friday night and we'll listen to what you have to say! You will become a member of our group and no one will then harm you! We do not commit any harm to our friends!" he said in parting.

"Are you really planning to join their group?" Olga asked.

"Of course!! What do I have to lose? Either I join their group or else they'll steal all of our sheep until we have no ranch! As I see it, it is the better of two evils! Now, I need to make certain that my parents do not find out, and I trust you to keep our secret!" she asked.

"Of course I will! But what about robbing the bank? If they get caught, then, so will you! We've never had a bank robbery

around here! This will elevate the terrorism to a new level! Do you
honestly have a plan?"

"I wouldn't have offered one if I hadn't! I don't give a damn
about the bank! It's my sick father that I'm worried about!"

"I know how you feel! Some of the ETA members have
already robbed the bakery several times and it has hurt our
business badly!" Olga told her as they drank their coffee and
ordered another round of 'capiles' and 'bizcochos' for Lola!

Madrid

Alvaro de Figueroa y Torres was born in Madrid and had
been made a lawyer in 1884, a graduate from the Universidad
Central de Madrid. Afterwards, he travelled to Bologna and
specialized in Political Science where he later received a doctorate
degree. It was in 1890 when he began his political career, always
directed to the Liberal Party of the country and was later named as
the chief lawyer for the city of Madrid. In 1894 he was appointed
mayor and was again appointed to the post in 1898. He later
became the owner of the newspaper El Globo and continued to
promote his liberal policies throughout the country. In 1901 he
was appointed by the government as the Director of Fine Arts
until 1905 when he helped to form the Council of Ministers
which was under the direction of Montero Rios and later was in
charge of the government agencies of Justice. In the year 1909 he
became head of the Congress of Representatives. In the year 1912
the King of Spain requested him to form a government which he
later formed in 1914! Later, he was the Senator of Guadalajara
in 1923, and later, the residing president of the Senate which had
been his role when there was a military takeover formed by Primo
de Rivera. After the Second Republic of Spain in April 1931, he
continued his political career as a Representative of Guadalajara.
Figueroa defended valiantly the throne of Alfonso XIII against all
the Acts and Accusations that were subsequently formed in the
courts during the year 1931. Afterwards, he was established as the
president of the Royal Academy of Fine Arts of San Fernando and
then a member of its history. In time, he wrote many books such
as Notes of One Life 1912-21 which were nothing more than the

political responsibilities of the previous regime.Then, he was given the title by Alfonso XIII as the Conde de Romanones! His presence in the Spanish government was so strong that he was considered an institution rather than an individual! So, he was a monarchist; and those that dared to speak against the throne of the King never had enough nerve to touch the elevation of the Count! In 1937 he aligned himself with the advances of General Franco and became an ancient symbol of the old government, the only member of the Royal House who had served successfully in all three Spanish governments as well as in the Royal House of the King before he went into exile. Then, he served the Socialist Government and the Fascist Movement of Spain. Later, he married the daughter of a wealthy banker by the name of Manuel Alonso Martinez, who became the Condessa de Romanones.

The Condessa's daughter, Lourdes de Romanones, was widowed at an early age! Her teenage son, Jose, had been a mischievous child who had taken advantage of his social status and had become a problem child following the death of his father. He had many scrapes with the law and had barely reached his thirteenth birthday when he and a few of his friends decided to break into one of the nearby stores, tear up the counters, and create a wave of mischief in one of the outlying areas of Madrid. Both his mother and grandmother had scoured the entire city in search of an attorney who would be willing to defend the young man in court. All of their efforts had been in vain as no attorney was willing to approach the young man's defense for fear that word would circulate that they had failed! The laws of the country were absolute and direct! The new decress explicitly stated that any young man who committed a criminal act would need to face the same penalties as those imposed on a hardened criminal committing a similar act! The Condessa and her daughter, Lourdes, had gone from office to office in search of a barrister who might agree to take on the case! On one of their many visits, the attorney had mentioned the name of a relatively new young attorney who worked exclusively with the constitutional statutes. He recommended that they go to him and ask for his help! After giving the two women the young attorney's name and address, they

walked into the small, messy office and met an old man with grey
hair writing something on a piece of paper. The old man stopped
what he was doing momentarily when he saw them! He looked
up and asked them to wait until he was finished! Both women
immediately were annoyed that they had been asked to wait! After
all, didn't this messy old man with grey hair realize that he was
speaking to the Condessa de Romanones and her daughter? He had
some nerve in addressing them with this lack of respect and not
dealing with them as soon as they opened the door to the office!

"What is your name, old man?" the Condessa asked in a
stern tone of voice that showed her anger!

"My name?? My name is Herr Otto Heintz!" the old man
answered quickly and returned to his work.

"Who is in charge of this horrible office?" the Condessa
asked.

"No one is in charge here...ja?" the old man replied,
showing some signs of frustration over the unexpected
interruption. "At this moment...I am in charge! That is...unless you
want to speak to my associate!"

"Sir!" the daughter interrupted, realizing that her mother
had been somewhat cruel in her approach. "We have come here
because someone has recommended you to us! They told us to ask
for Licenciado Andres Torres! Is he available?"

The old man could quickly see that her tone of voice was
much more subdued than her mother. Just then, another door
opened at the rear of the office, and a tall, handsome young man
very polished and well dressed in a business suit walked into the
room.

"There!" the old man said, pointing his finger at him as
if he were anxious to rid himself of these rude people. "This is
Licenciado Torres now; you can talk to him....ja?" he said without
once looking up from his desk.

"Can I be of help to you ladies?" Andres asked politely and
in a calm voice that instantly seemed to soothe their anger.

"Can you be of help??....Can you be of help...?" the
Condessa repeated. "We came here looking for you and...this....
this old man has been very rude to us! Have you any idea who

we are and who I am?" the elderly woman asked in a stern and authoritative voice. She paused before continuing without even allowing him a chance to give her an answer. "I am la Condessa de Romanones, and this is my daughter Paloma! We came here with a problem we need to speak to you about!"

"Thank you for telling me who you are!" he answered calmly but modestly. "I am the person you are looking for! Would you please come into my office where we can talk privately?"

He did his best not to show that he was both irritated and nervous! It was his first experience speaking to someone with a royal title; and, for a brief moment, he felt his legs feeling a bit unsteady as he led them through the open door and into his small office. The Condessa's daughter couldn't help but notice how young and handsome this man was! His manners were excellent; and, although she knew that her mother could often be difficult, he made believe that her approach had been normal and unassuming! He waited calmly until everyone was seated before asking. "Now, how can I serve you?"

Again, Paloma was excited about this young man's manners! It would have been much more normal for him to ask, how may I help you! Instead, he seemed to be paying recognition to their social status by asking, instead, how he might serve them! It didn't take her long to feel attracted to him! Of course, she had no idea how good or bad he was as an attorney, or even whether or not he was even married! Silently, she found herself almost hoping that he wasn't married! Not that it made any difference, but, if he was unmarried, she felt that she would like to know more about him!

The Condessa began to speak, but was soon interrupted by her daughter! "Mother, please, let me speak to Senor Torres! After all, I know more about what happened than you do!" It was a mild reprimand that produced a snicker from the old woman! It was enough for her to see that she was annoyed by the interruption! Not that it really mattered, because, between mother and daughter, these interruptions had happened many times before!

"What may I call you? I know that your name is Paloma, a strange name for a Spanish aristocrat! Perhaps someday you will tell me how you received such an interesting and attractive name!" he asked showing a slight smile as he spoke.

"People usually call me, Dona Paloma! In truth, I actually dislike being referred to as Dona! It makes me feel much older than I am! Because, if you decide to take this case, we may find ourselves speaking frequently to each other, suppose you just call me Paloma!" she said.

"Good!" he answered. "I would like that! Please, call me Andres! As for you Condessa, I have too much respect to call you any other name than the one attached to your title! Nevertheless, I wuld feel honored if you too would call me Andres! That is, if you don't mind!"

The old woman did not answer, but from the corner of her eye she thought she had detected a slight smile! There was something about this young man that was pleasing to her! Perhaps it was his good manners or his respect for her official title! (That's okay, Andres thought! I really don't give a damn whether or not this old bitch likes me! Just as long as she gives us a case that will supply us with enough money to pay the office rent!)

"Sir!..." Paloma began until she was again interrupted!

"Please, call me Andres!" he corrected.

She let out a smile that seemed to be contagious for a moment! She quickly changed her expression to seem more businesslike! After all, she was afraid that she was making her attraction to him a bit too obvious!

"Very well, Andres! I have a thirteen year old youngster who, along with several of his playmates, committed a childish prank! While playing together, it appears that they did something to break the law! The incident was little more than a prank such as many youngster do, but, the truth is that he is in serious trouble and we need you to do whatever you can to help him!"

"Just what was this prank?" he asked as he pulled out a large yellow legal pad and started to take some notes! He was already assuming that this young man had done some mischief, and, it must have been serious for this old woman and her daughter to go around town looking for an attorney!

"Three of the young men walked into a candy store to buy candy! While they were inside, they decided to open the cash register and steal the money in the register! The proprietor then called the Guardia Civil who arrested all three of the young boys! I telephoned the store owner and offered to pay him for the losses; but he insisted that he wanted them arrested for burglary and didn't want to accept the money I offered him!" Paloma explained.

"Where is the young man now?" he asked. "Also, what about the other two boys! Have they also been arrested?"

"No!" You see, only my son Jose was arrested! The owner told the arresting authorities that it had been my son whom he saw taking the money out of the register and that the other boys were only watching! My son was later taken to the precinct and is now being charged with 'Grand Theft'. The other two young men were released to the custody of their parents!"

"So, is your son currently in jail?" Andres asked.

"Oh, heavens no!!" the old lady interrupted. "Have you idea the responsibilities that my title mandates? How could I possibly allow my grandson to be in jail because of a foolish prank?"

This had been his first encounter with aristocrats, and already he didn't like the way in which this conversation was going! He realized that the old lady probably had expected him to be or at least to act, sympathetic; but, he found it hard to act this way whenever someone deliberately broke the law! In his mind, he was already thinking of this young boy as a spoiled brat who had been caught stealing! It was now time to pay the price for this 'childish prank'! It was necessary for him to approach this case with care. He felt himself getting a bit angry remembering how difficult it had been for him to get his education from his parents who needed to struggle for everything they had!

"So, if he isn't in jail, then, where is he?" he asked.

"The poor boy is resting at home! He has become very depressed over what happened and is very upset!" Paloma explained. (Damn it! He sure as hell wasn't too distressed when he robbed the store, he thought!)

"It will be necessary for me to speak to him! When can you bring him here?" he asked. As difficult as it seemed, he did his best to remain calm despite his own feelings!

The fact that Paloma had been smiling at him every chance she got had not escaped him! Now, she was showing him a more serious look leaving him wondering if perhaps he had shown her his own feelings about the spoiled brat! One of the things they teach you in law school is always to conceal your own feelings and to work exclusively with the evidence and the law but nothing more!

"When can you come to our house to interview him?" the old woman asked. "We're willing to pay whatever you ask; but the young man is much too upset for us to expose him to a law office! No, you'll simply need to come to our house and speak to him!" Just listening to what this woman was saying was making him more furious! Now, he knew that he was displaying his true feelings! Paloma made a motion with her hand and ordered her mother not to speak!

"Andres, we should have realized that you would probably want to speak to him! The truth is that he is young and there are times when he can be testy and uncontrollable! You see...he lost his father when he was very young,,,,and....frankly..." she said before Andres interrupted her.

"Yes, I know!!" he said., "I also know that your son is a spoiled brat! The truth is that the money that he stole is considered as Grand Larceny! The law clearly states that anyone convicted of a serious crime, needs to be punished as an adult! At the moment, I have no idea whether or not I'll be able to help him! I do know that it isn't going to be easy and I'm going to need every bit of cooperation you can give me! I'm willing to help! But I can't help him if you are going to tie my hands behind my back and expect me to work miracles!"

"You needn't worry, Andres!" Paloma answered sternly. "You will have our complete cooperation! Please, do whatever you can and I want you to treat him just as you would treat any other client! We should have known better before coming here! You have my absolute authority to do whatever you need to do to correct him even if he gets a bit rowdy or testy! Now, please Andres, tell us that you'll take this case!" Andres saw that she was almost pleading with him not to let her down! There was a certain determination that came over her making him realize that she had obviously had a difficult time with this brat; and she was extending her call for help! It was something that quite obviously her mother had been reluctant to do!

"Very well, Paloma! "I want you to bring your son to my office this time tomorrow! When I speak with him, it will be in private! I want to interview him without anyone being in the room except him and me! I warn you that I may well need to get testy with him if he decides not to cooperate! Do you agree with me?" he asked as he looked directly into the face of la Condessa. The old woman showed surprise by his attitude, but he had the feeling that her daughter knew exactly what he meant and what her son needed!

"Very well, Andres! We'll come back tomorrow and I'll bring Jose to see you!" she said smiling. (Damn, she thought! This man was strict and determined, but he did seem to know exactly what he was doing! She still had no idea of whether or not he was married, but she also felt that he would have made an excellent parent! While on that subject, she was also thinking that he would probably make an excellent husband!)

Andres stood by the doorway watching as they left the office. He couldn't help noticing the difference between the older woman and the daughter; and how difficult it must have been for them to raise a young teenage son without a father. He could see that the old woman, despite her snobbishness, was probably a poor disciplinarian when it came to her grandson! He was also well aware that in most European countries the young men are the preferred gender; and the young girls, more often than not, are treated like second class citizens.

The case was going to be difficult because of the solid rigidity of the law! It had been put into action by General Franco after the end of the Civil War and for good reason! There had been a number of thefts and larcenies, some caused by the intense poverty throughout the country! Some of the thefts, however, had been committed by young people, such as this one, as a prank, hoping they could get away with it or else blame it on someone else! Following the waves of crime, the General Court had issued an edict that anyone committing an adult crime would be tried in court as an adult and receive the same sentences as an adult! At this point, he had no idea into what category this youngster fell into; but he did know that unless he was able to do something, the young man could be facing a jail term of at least ten years! Without having spoken to the young man, he felt a bit sorry for the mother! She was still a young and a very attractive woman who had probably needed to raise her son constantly at odds with what she knew was the right thing to do over the domination of the older woman who would probably resist her punishment no matter what the young brat did! An overpowering feeling came over him as he really wanted to help her! The more he thought about it, the stronger the feeling became.He had a hard time trying to decide whether he wanted to help the young man because he felt sorry for the circumstances that led to his arrest, or was it because he rather liked the boy's mother and wanted the opportunity of seeing her again? She appeared friendly and gracious and wondered if she was really the way she seemed to be? When they first arrived, he had to admit that his legs felt a bit unsteady not quite knowing how to act. The younger woman appeared to have detected his uneasiness and had tried to make him more comfortable! It had been his first interaction with aristocracy; and he wasn't sure whether or not he liked the way it felt!

He walked out of the office and noticed that Herr Otto was still busy at work at his desk! "Vell....vat do you think?" he asked. "Are you going to take the case?"

"I don't know yet! I don't really think I'll be able to help the boy, but, I do feel a bit sorry for his mother and grandmother! I don't think it has been easy raising him since the young woman's husband died when the boy was young!" he said.

"....ja? Vell...you must be careful! Remember, a good lawyer must always think about his client and nobody else! If you are feeling sorry for the mother, you might not be doing the right thing...ja?" Otto told him.

Andres didn't answer! He was well aware of what Otto was trying to tell him! He was treading on thin ice and he knew it! It was more than likely that he would soon start ignoring the first cardinal rule of law! Never to allow anyone else other than the client to influence what you plan to do! Tomorrow was promising to be an interesting day! Of course, he would learn much more about the case after he interviewed the young man! He could only imagine how difficult the interview would probably be, especially if the young man became impatient or unruly! How would he react if he needed to get a bit authoritative with him! Also, he wondered how the other two women in the young boy's life would react if his attentions with young Jose were not quite what they expected?

CHAPTER 5

Anzgoit

The quaint town of Anzgoit is a small farming community located about twelve miles west of Bilbao! Normally, it is a quiet town that is practically deserted as soon as the sun goes down! The young man who had identified himself as Pergo had agreed to pick her up with his car a short distance away from where she lived!Maripaz had asked her friend from the bakery to go to the meeting with her; but she had decdied against it for fear that her parents would discover where she had gone and would be furious when they found out that their daughter had gone to meet with other members of the ETA at one of their general meetings!

Maripaz remained silent while riding in the rear seat of the car! She, too, was having second thoughts not knowing where she was going or what was going to happen! The building where the meeting was being held was an old deserted wooden barn that was showing the usual signs of decay and abandonment with the passing of time! As she looked over the place, she had to admit that the old building seemed ideal for the meeting. After all, it was in a deserted area that was well protected by an abundance of trees and shrubs and out of the way from the inhabitants of the village. It provided the members of the ETA with all of the privacy they could hope for! The inside of the old building was no better than the outside. The illumination was provided by large lit candles that had been set in brass holders on the walls. In the center of the area, there was an old rectangular wooden box, presumably where the leader of the group would present his views while the other members sat on the cold ground because there were no chairs inside. At first it seemed hard to believe that this old haunted place would accomodate a group of would-be terrorists that had already proved themselves successful in terrorizing many of the surrounding communities. They were among the last to arrive as Pergo drove the car behind the barn. She noticed that he gave another member who had greeted them a secret handshake, perhaps a symbol of solidarity among the members. Maripaz waited until she was finally asked to enter and was met with strange stares from some of the other members of the group who were already seated on the floor.She had expected to be met by a large group of people; but, instea, the group consisted of only ten men and two women beside herself who appeared to be either the wives or the girlfriends of the other men.

Pergo walked up to the front of the barn and stood up on the wooden box! At his command, they all recited some poem or anthem that she didn't understand since they were all speaking in the Basque language. After they had finished a few moments later, all of them stood up and began clapping their hands and cheering in a show of unity! She had no idea what all the excitement was about because none of the men were considered to be genius strategists! There was, however, a constant chatter among them! At times, one of the men would raise his voice above the others; and, at times, a few of them would speak at the same time without paying much attention to the main speaker in the middle of the floor. The Basque language is difficult to understand in its own right, and the idea of listening to a group of people saying things in unison or else chanting incantations of some verbal extraction from somewhere made understanding the rite difficult at best! All that she was able to do was to listen carefully, pick up a word here and there, and try to make some sense about what they were saying!

After about twenty minutes, Pergo finally asked for silence and announced that there was a new member in the group who had some ideas that could benefit their cause! He insisted that she be permitted to speak freely and without interruption; after which, she would be willing to answer any questions that they might have! There was some light applause, most among the other women, as Maripaz stood up and walked slowly to the front of the room! She still felt somewhat apprehensive as she looked over some notes she had taken down before being asked to speak. In the short time she had been there, she had already learned a great deal about about the ambitions of the ETA movement. She had learned that the hard core activists actually consisted of about twenty members even though they boasted of having several hundred supporters. It was difficult for the authorities to penetrate the organization because of its non-heirarchial structure! Also, she learned that the members of the organization operated in small self-sufficient cells and had only the most tenuous with the organizations leadership! Someone had also mentioned that while the ETA was operationally headquartered in the Basque provinces of Spain and France, the organization had members and underground supporters in places as diverse as Algeria, Argentina, Belgium, Cuba, Dominican Republic, Germany, Holland, Italy and Mexico. Most of the main activities were usually coordinated from France, although some of the organizational leaders were also suspected of directing the groups activities from Latin America.

Much of the training for its members was received at various times in countries such as Libya, South Yemen, Lebanon and Nicaragua. There were also reports saying that some of the members had sought sanctuary in Cuba. The group apparently had ties with the Irish Republican Army through two groups of the legal political wings! The funding came from Basque supporters, extortion that they cleverly called "Basque Revolutionary Taxes", drug trafficking, kidnapping ransoms and armed robberies. The funds were used mostly to finance such activities as assassinations (mainly among Spanish and French targets) bombings, (lethal and sophisticated) using their favorite explosive Goma 2, as well as other guerilla tactics. The group apparently had recently launched a new campaign of political assassinations, mostly consisting of government officials, security and military forces, politicians and judicial figures. At the time Maripaz had been in attendance, they had been planning the assassination of Admiral Luis Carrero Blanco, who, during that time, was considered to be Franco's likely successor. Several of the members had mentioned the possibility of assassinating King Juan Carlos during a planned visit to Majorca! It was a small group but with very ambitious expectations; and she knew she was going to need to be careful with her presentation! She put down her notes and papers and peered over the group for several moments before she started to speak!

"For your information, my name is Mari! I won't tell you my last name nor anything else about me! As far as I'm concerned, the movement is interesting but is not being well planned. I know that I'm a woman; and, as a woman, I am not supposed to know anything about these things! I've been sitting here and listening to your people recount the stories of about seventeen thefts. Everyone of you was gloating over the fact that you had gained two or three thousand pesetas! There weren't any of you who were smart enough to mention the other side of the story! Nobody mentioned that you had placed yourselves and the group in jeopardy seventeen times for the paltry total of a few pesetas! Frankly, I don't think that the income received was worth the risk! In my opinion, the moves were not only ill planned, but were also senseless! Certainly not worth the risks you were required to take!" She paused long enough to study the looks on the faces of the other group members and wondered if she was getting through to them!

"In the meantime, I have to ask you if it's worth to steal from our own people? To take away their hard earned money in order to finance a project that is supposed to benefit them! Does that make any sense to you, because it sure makes no sense to me? My father is a hard working sheep rancher! You people have destroyed a fence on his ranch and you have also stolen some of his sheep! How much could you have gotten for them, a few hundred pesetas? It only goes to show that your plans are small and whoever designs them is certainly not a progressive planner with any imagination! Have any of you given any thought at all to the small bank at the edge of town? They take in the money from everybody, even from their influential aristocrats of the country that you decry as being your fiercest enemy! If you plan to organize large projects then, you are going to need large sums of money; and you have to think 'big'! Leave our own merchants alone, for God's sake!They are working hard enough to feed their own families! Concentrate your efforts on those you despise and that you feel are the reasons behind all of your complaints!" She could see by the surprised look on their faces that she had been successful in getting their attention! The idle chatter she had heard when she started to speak had now subsided, and there was an absolute silence that was encouraging her to continue.

"I have been inside that bank; and, from what I saw, it can be robbed very easily because it has no 'sereno' (Guard) to overlook who enters and leave the building! If you want me to, I'll make a few visits and draw a diagram of the accesses where most of the money is being held. When the time is right, and I am convinced that it's safe, we'll outline the plan and together we'll commit the first bank robbery of 'Anzgoit'!" There was an eerie silence for several minutes; and then, suddenly, the group broke out in an enthusiastic applause that continued long after she had acknowledged their applause by a simple wave of the hand and had again taken her seat!

"How can we depend on the plans of a woman to accomplish our mission?" one of the vocal group members said.

"Maripaz quickly realized that this person was presenting a challenge to her gender and she found an urgent need to reply with the same tenacity! "Because it was a woman that thought of the plan and not some stupid man! The bank has been there for years; why didn't you think of it if you're so smart?" she said.

There was another round of applause supporting what she was saying! "I'll deliver on my promises for the good of the ETA, but it will need to be done under the following conditions! One, that you leave our local people alone and concentrate your efforts on those that are not Basques! Two, that you stop taking any more foolish risks that will only result in getting more of our members killed!"

Pergo stood up from where he had been sitting! He was pleased with what he had been hearing and the things that this woman had told them certainly made a great deal of sense! "Mari is right!! We cannot afford to go on taking foolish risks! It will be only a matter of time before some of our members will be killed! I say that we allow Mari to tell us of her plans during our next meeting! In the meantime, I move that in the future we will no longer stage our attacks against our own people! How many of you agree with me?" he asked as he saw a sudden show of hands raised from most of the members signifying their agreement!

Maripaz had a smile on her face! She was confident that she had succeeded in her attempt to get them to leave the local people alone! It seemed definite that, in the future, the group would concentrate their efforts against those business that were larger then the small stores that were in the town owned by the local merchants. It also seemed fairly convincing that her father would no longer need to worry about any broken fences nor about his herd of sheep being stolen!

It was late in the evening when Mari was driven home! Her mother had been awake waiting for her! She was not accustomed to see her daughter arriving home late at night, and she had started to get worried. Since she had been at home, Mari was always the first to go to bed; and her strange behavior was becoming more noticeable by the mysterious silence when she asked her where she had been!

"Nowhere, mother!" she said. "I was with the woman from the bakery! At the last minute, we decided to go into town and visit one fo the cafes! Before we realized the time, it was already quite late!" was her only explanation.

At first, her mother had accepted the simple explanation until she noticed as time went by that many of her actions were beginning to change! Maripaz had a regular routine of going into town early in the morning before starting her daily chores. She would wear a clean dress, comb her hair, and go into town by herself and returning around noon! Now, her mother began to notice a change in her personality! She was still cheerful and attentive to her father's needs, but would stay at home during the afternoon hours. Once, her mother had mentioned their daughter's strange behavior to Miguel! His only response had been to shrug his shoulders without offering any further comment. After all,

Miguel felt that his daughter was a young, attractive woman
and deserved to have some pleasant activities away from the
usual chores of her home. Actually, he was pleased that she had
obviously found a friend she could now speak to! As far as he was
concerned, he viewed this as a healthy sign! Soledad, however,
was much more skeptical! Soledad had felt that the changes had
come about much too rapidly, and when asked, she was showing
a marked reluctance to speak about it! During the next few days,
Maripaz would leave the house early in the morning, always by
herself, and walk to the other side of town where the small bank
was located. When she was certain that no one was looking, she
would take out a pad and pencil and would begin writing down her
observations of the people who were working there, the presence
of any security guards, and wrote down what every employee was
doing! She had seen only five employees, and four of them were
women! The bank manager was an old man, probably in his sixties,
and he was certainly no challenge! Since no one had ever tried
to rob the bank before, there was obviously no need for security
guards inside the building. There was another observation that had
caught her interest! Most of the people visiting the bank would go
to conduct their business during the morning hours before lunch!
The bank would then close its doors at noon for the traditional
two hour 'almuerzo' (lunch) and would re-open again at around
two thirty! Maripaz soon decided that the best time for the group
to stage a robbery of the bank would be a few minutes before the
bank closed its doors for lunch!

All of the physical characteristics of the robbery had been
carefully written down in detail on a piece of paper! From what
she could see, it seemed like an ideal situation to stage a robbery!
There was one other thought that came to mind! The memory of
the young man she had met while at college! She remembered
his telling her that the most serious crime a person could commit
was murder! There was no statute of limitations on murder; and
under Spanish law, the penalty for a conviction on the charge of
murder was always execution! Maripaz realized that some of the
young men in the movement were not very intelligent, and it was
important that they learn quickly that no one inside the bank was to

be killed or injured in any way! It was bad enough that eventually the federal police would undoubtedly be summoned from Madrid; and, presumably, the members of the ETA would have the need to scatter and take refuge out of the town before the police arrived!

On the third day, just as she was about to leave the house, she was called by her mother and asked where she was going! "Nowhere, mama! I was only going out for my daily walk into town! I'll be back in a couple of hours!'"" she said.

"You've been going out in the morning for quite a while and you come home several hours later! Don't you think it is a bit unusual? You never did that before!" her mother said.

"For goodness sake, mother!" she answered angrily. "When are you going to learn that I am a grown woman? What is so strange about going out for a couple of hours? I am still here in time to do my daily chores and to take care of daddy!"

"I'm afraid that you may be getting involved with some of those young men who belong to the ETA! They are nothing but troublemakers and I certainly hope that you have more sense than to be involved with them! Remember, most of those men have never worked an honest day in their life and most of them have never even gone to school! Why would you want anything to do with them?" her mother warned.

"What makes you think that I am involved with them? I don't even know what they're doing! The only person with whom I am friendly is Olga from the bakery!" she lied.

"Isn't that a bit strange? How can you be with her in the morning? She is always in the bakery! There has to be someone elese that interests you!" her mother asked suspiciously. She waited a few moments before continuing! She was looking at the changed facial expressions and realized that she was not far from wrong in what she was saying! "By the way," her mother continued. "Whatever happened to the young man you wrote us about when you were at school? You told me once that you would tell me later! Why not tell me now?"

"There isn't anything to tell! It just didn't work out! He wanted to continue on with his career as a lawyer and I was called home! Don't you remember>"

"You never told me! Were you in love with him?" her mother asked.

"What difference does it make? It's all over now and I would prefer not to talk about it!" Soledad was watching carefully as she noticed that her eyes had suddenly become misty as she was speaking. The hurt look upon her face was telling everything! She went over and placed her arm around her daughter's shoulders!

"I think it makes a lot of difference! I can see it in your eyes! Mari. have you ever thought of..perhaps...writing to him and ask him to come to Bizcaya for a visit during the summer months? I think that after everything you said, I would like to meet him!"

"It will never happen, mother!" she said sadly. "We had a silly argument and decided each should go their own way! I doubt he would even remember who I was if I contacted him!"

All of a sudden, she stopped speaking when she saw that Maripaz was unable to hide her tears any longer and began to cry! Many thoughts were on Soledad's mind while her memory went back to her own youth, and the sadness she felt when she was all alone! The only thing she hoped was that her daughter had not made the same mistakes she had made that had ended up causing her a lifetime of unhappiness!

"Mari!! I want you to listen carefully to me! Many years ago, I also made many foolish mistakes that made me unhappy! Perhaps, if you were to tell me honestly what was happening, you could avoid making the same mistakes!" she said. Maripaz suddenly stood up in a rage! She slammed her notebook on top of the table and began yelling at her mother!

"Why?.....Why?" she yelled. "Why should I tell you everything that happens in my life? I am a grown woman and I can do anything I want to do!...No!!...damn it! I don't want to ever talk about it again!" she said half crying while showing her bad temper. Her mother was taken back by the unexpected outburst! She always knew that there were times when her daughter had shown signs of anger and rage, but she never expected that she would have become so embittered by what she said!

"If....you...ever...raise your voice to me again," Soledad said very calmly without once raising her voice! "I want you out of this house! I will never allow you to speak to either your father or me with such disrespect! Do I make myself clear?" By the time she was finished she saw that Maripaz was sobbing uncontrollably! For a brief second she wanted to go to her, put her arm around her like she used to do when she was a child and comfort her! This time, she decided against it! She had no idea what had gotten into Maripaz's mind; but, perhaps, it was time for her to learn a few things about respect!

It was a long time, before Maripaz managed to control her emotions and was able to speak! "There are many things about your own life that you never told me!" she told her mother in a very subdued voice. "Why was it that daddy, a senior Mariscal in Toledo and appointed by General Franco himself, can't even go to Madrid to be treated for his illness? Also, what about that funny mask I saw when I was arranging his clothes? What does that represent and why is it so carefully wrapped? Do you remember when I asked you? You refused to give me an answer!" she blurted out!

"You're right!" her mother said, once again without raising her voice. "I never did tell you, but, I promise, that one day you will know! You have every right to know that our lives were not always as happy as you may have imagined! Unfortunately, that was in the past! Now, we have to worry about the future, your future! I can only hope and pray that you never make the same mistakes we made!" she said somberly, almost as if she was regretting something that still troubled her!

Mari got up from her chair, walked over and hugged her mother tightly. She began to cry all over again! "I need to go now, mother!" she said softly. "I promise to be back shortly! Please.... forgive me....for speaking to you with disrespect! I never wanted to do that; and God knows, you certainly didn't deserve it!Remember mother...you and daddy are all I have! I can't afford to lose either of you!" she said as she hugged her motehr again and kissed her warmly before leaving.

On her way into town Maripaz knew very well why she was angry! Over and over she promised herself that she would have nothing further to do with the ETA! The mere fact that she had gotten them the information about the bank seemed so ugly to her!

She was ashamed at what she had done, even if it were for all the right reasons! Once she gave them the information that they would need, she felt that her committment had been fullfilled! Now it was up to them to leave the local people alone, including her own father who was ill and should not need to worry about his sheep.It was an assurance that her father had needed and she had been successful in getting it for him! But, at what cost???? What they neglected to tell her at the general meeting was that once you are considered a member, there can be no turning back! The only recourse for her not to continue attending the meetings was to come up with some lame excuse and hope it would satisfy the ambitions of the leaders. All that she hoped for was that they would eventually forget about her once they had robbed the bank successfully and would go on their own crusade! All the information she felt they would need would soon be in their hands! It would be up to the leaders to decide when and how they would enter the bank and rob the tellors! As far as she was concerned, her job was finished! She walked to the small cafe where Pergo had agreed to meet her. On the way, she had already decided that her visit today would be short! She would simply tell him of the plans, turn the papers and her notes over to him and would then go home! After the discussion with her mother, she was in no mood to listen to any diatribes about the ETA; and, quite frankly, she didn't give a damn what they did! As far as she was concerned, the group was nothing more than a group of hoodlums! Who cared if they were all caught and killed!

Maripaz saw Pergo already sitting at one of the tables waiting for her. She took her place at the opposite side away from him and handed him a small stack of hand-written notes, outlying everything about the bank! Pergo studied the papers, complimented her on her thoroughness, and told her they would discuss the matter at the very next meeting!

"I'm sorry!" she told him. "My father is very ill and I won't be able to attend!"

"What do you mean?" he answered. Mari noticed that his tone of voice had become angry as he spoke. "These are your plans and you need to be there to answer any questions that the others may have! I'm afraid that you're father is going to have to wait, that's all!" She quickly noticed that his remarks were no longer a request, but a firm command.

"My father is more important to me than all of the plans you people havce for the furtherance of the ETA! Under no conditions will I neglect him, just so I can become a part of your ambitious schemes!" she said angrily.

"You don't understand, Mari! You have now been included as a member of our unit! Once you become a member, there is no turning back! You are one of us!" he told her.

"Like Hell!!" she bellowed. "Now you listen to me! I only agreed to draw up the plans for the bank that your gang is too stupid to work out for themselves! In exchange, you agreed to leave the local merchants and the ranchers alone, or have you already forgotten your promise?" The longer she spoke, the angrier she was getting!

"No, I didn't forget!" Pergo answered. "But if you no longer want to be a part of us, why should we keep our promise to you? Remember, it is your father who is ill...and...I'm certain he wouldn't want to lose any more of his precious sheep!"

"You have no idea who or what I am!" she said, surprising hreself that she was able to mask her anger and speak very calmly but deliberately. She knew damn well that she was so livid that nothing was going to frighten her! "You'd better hope and pray that nothing happens to either my father nor the sheep! So help me God! I have enough money to buy the weapons that I need! I'll kill the whole damn bunch of you if I have to! If you think that I won't, just take another one of our sheep and see what happens! Now take your damn notes and get the hell out of here!" she said as she threw the yellow pieces of paper in front of him on the table, stood up and was getting ready to leave!

"Just a minute!" Pergo told her. She turned around and gave him a dirty look! "I'll be there to pick you up on Wednesday! If you don't show up, I'll be only too happy to explain to your mother how busy you've been getting us the plans for robbing the bank! We'll also tell her how you were the one who planned the broken fence so we could steal a few of the sheep! If you want me to tell your mother how busy you have been, just don't show up!

Also, remember that the story to your mother will only be the first! Afterwards, there will be other visits!" he said. Mari knew how vicious these people could be! She also knew that the threats would be carried out if she didn't show up! Joining the group had been a serious mistake! How could she have been so stupid not to realize the seriousness of what she had done? She had joined the group thinking that it was a way of helping the townspeople as well as her own father, never thinking that they would never allow her to leave the group now that she had become a member.

After a few moments, she finally walked away from him a dejected and torn person! Of course, she should have known that they would carry out their threats. The last thing she wanted or needed was for her parents to know what she had done! The threat of inflicting bodily harm to her father was also a real possibility! He would never be able to fight them off, and they would take advantage of his illness to harm him! How could she ever possibly explain to her parents that what she had done had been for the good of the town? She could never convince them! When she finally arrived home, her mother saw that she was still upset!There was anger and turmoil in what Pergo had told her as she struggled to find a way of getting even!! Never had she imagined that a simple act to help the people of the town would end up in an obligation to become a terrorist over a cause that she wasn't even sure she believed in! Maripaz began to work her chores around the house thinking of things she might do to the group and what they might obligate her to do in the future. For several moments, a thought entered her mind about going to the local garrison of the Guardia Civil and tell them the entire story. Unfortunately, she also realized that before the young men were arrested a great deal of damage cxould be done to her family! If the group were to decide that her future role in the group would be to study potential targets, she decided that she would do so but would remain inconclusive and would outsmart them by directing her views to those areas where they would face the largest risks of being caught!

The ETA group had reviewed the contents of her notes and a special meeting was hurriedly put together that evening to discuss the plans! Assuming that everyone was in agreement, it was decided that the bank robbery would take place the following day! It seemed strange that Pergo, who had taken her list of suggestions, had quickly named himself as being in charge of the assault. Among the male members, there was always a jealousy among them as to who would be in charge. One of their edicts was that a successful assault of a target would elevate the leader to a preferred status in the unit. When one of the members suggested that Pergo should be the driver of the vehicle, he objected to the suggestion vehemently, and told the group that since he was in charge of the robbery, he wanted to lead the assault on the bank. Had things been different, she would have suggested that Pergo, of all people, should not be the leader because he had been known to be more reckless and impatient! Besides, it was also generally known that he was too anxious to fire his weapon at whoever got in his way! In her notes, she had already made it perfectly clear that it would be a terrible foolish mistake if someone decided to injure or kill any of the bank workers!

It was decided among them that only three members would be involved! One would be needed to driver the car while the other two men would enter the bank at the precise time just before the bank workers went to lunch and the bank was closed. They would visit each of the tellers, take their money and run out of the bank! The entire theft would take only a few minutes, assuming that everything went as planned. It was decided that they would not threaten the bank manager who was an old man, unless the amount of money was not as expected. It would only require a few more minutes to threaten the old man if it became necessary, coerce him into opening the bank safe and ran away! Speed was to be of the essence! They would need to leave the bank quickly and drive away before anyone was able to sound an alarm that would ring at the local office of the Guardia Civil!

Another meeting was held early in the morning to review the plans for the heist! Pergo announced to the others that since he was in charge of the mission, only he would be be armed and would be carrying a concealed weapon! Maripaz felt that his last minute decision to carry a gun had been aimed at her because she had specifically recommended that no fire weapons should be

carried by anyone! She already knew that some of the younger
men were much too anxious to fire their guns; and she really didn't
trust them carrying a gun inside a public place such as a bank!
The group put on their bright "red boinhas' (Caps) and drove to
the bank near the noon hour. Pergo got out of the car and glanced
through the glass door and saw that two of the tellers were already
counting their money before going to lunch! He also saw that there
were no customers inside the building at that time! Pergo and
another group member entered the bank and told the tellers that
they were to load all of their money into a canvas bag and hand it
over to them! The robbery had taken under two minutes since the
tellers became startled and eagerly scrambled to place the money
into the bag as directed. The two men grabbed the canvas bags and
ran out of the building and got into the waiting car! Pergo was the
only group member who was dissatisfied with the way the robbery
had gone! He felt that it had been much too easy! Perhaps, had they
forced the old manager to open the bank vault, they would have
gotten more money! He thought that inside the safe there would
be a large cache of money, not to mention the other valuables such
as jewelry and diamonds that customer had left at the bank for
safekeeping!

"Hurry up, Pergo!" One of his companions yelled from the
car! "We need to get out of here quickly!"

"Wait another minute or two!" he yelled back. "I'm not
yet finished!" He went durectly to the old manager who was still
sitting in his small office at his desk! The old man was stunned and
frightened at what was happening in broad daylight! Pergo let out
a smile when he saw the frightened look on the old manager's face
when he stared at the gun he was aiming at him!

"C'mon old man! I want you to open the safe!" he ordered.

"I can't open it!" the frightened old man said, "I must have
the keys to open it!"

"Well, hurry and get the keys! I want you to open it quickly
and hand me everything that is inside!" he said threateningly.

"But...what is inside belongs to the depositors! I cannot
give you the valuables they have entrusted to us for safe keeping!"

the old man said still frightened that the gun would go off and he would be killed.

"Well....it now belongs to us! Hurry up and open it before you make me do something that I don't want to do!" the old man moved his trembling hand slowly down to the top drawer of his desk! His other hand was still raised high in the air, as if he were protecting his face! "Hurry up, old man!! I don't have all day!" Pergo ordered.

All of a sudden, with a desperate burst of speed, the old man drew out a small revolver from the desk drawer and fired off a shot that caught Pergo squarely on the forehead! Pergo made a motion as if to fire his own weapon, but instead, he stumbled two steps back and fell to the floor, his revolver still clutched in his hand! The old man got up from his desk and looked at the assailant lying on the floor with his eyes wide open and a mucous like liquid mixed with blood oozing out of a small hole in the center of his forehead! The two men in their car, waiting for their leader, heard the shot! When they saw the old man running out of the building with two of the tellers behind him, they knew immediately that their leader had been shot! They drove off hurriedly realizing that the Guardia Civil had probably been notified and would soon be there! It was important that they leave the scene of the crime quickly before anyone was able to recognize who they were! They drove the car and parked it behind the old wooden building where it would be out of sight! Several of the other members ran outside to greet them, but they could see by the look on their faces that things had not gone as planned. Quickly they emptied out the canvas bags that were filled with large stacks of pesetas, telling the others what had happened and that their leader, Pergo, had been killed!

"What the hell happened?" one of the members asked, surprised by what had happened. "I thought this was supposed to be an easy robbery!"

"It was!" answered one of the men who was emptying one of the sacks. "We had already emptied the tellers cages, but Pergo decided to stay behind and threatened the manager into opening the safe! The old man just pulled out a gun and shot him!"

There were no signs of sorrow or regret for what happened! Instead, one of the other men in the group simply shrugged his shoulders and said, "Good! That's what he gets from being greedy!" as he continued to count the money inside the canvas bag.

Maripaz was obviously shaken and nervous when she read the newspapers the following morning! There was a lengthy article on the front page telling what had happened; and, how, after many years of being in business, the local bank had been robbed by a group of young men thought to be members of the ETA! Soledead was sitting across from her daughter and studying the expressions on her face as she read the news! Soledad knew immediately that Mari appeared shocked and worried by what she was reading!

"What's wrong, Mari? You seem to be worried about what happened at the bank!" Soledad said.

"Nothing.....it's ..nothing! No! I'm not worried! Why should I be?" she answered with hesitation; just enough to convince her mother that something was wrong!

"Mari, are you sure you had nothing to do with what happened at the bank?" she asked.

The section of the story that had been the most news worthy was that the robbery had apparently been committed by members of the ETA! It was a rising new wave of violence that the townspeople were unfamiliar with and now needed to fear! There was a worried look and a certain unconvincing hesitation that Maripaz had given her mother that worried Soledad! Whatever it was, she knew her daughter and somehow knew that her daughter had been involved! The hesitation of her voice and the worried look on her face had been dead giveaways that she knew much more about the robbery than what she was saying! Soledad's main fear was that Mari had somehow gotten mixed up with the activities of the ETA! As a former member of Los Milicianos during the Spanish Civil War, she was well schooled in what these guerilla activities could do! The ETA was much more dangerous than Los Milicianos had been! They were feared by all of the townspeople who were struggling just to make a decent living from day to day! For the most part, the young members of the ETA were considered to be nothing more than common hoodlums! There was also

some talk that the Federal Government was about to get involved
and take steps to break them up and to arrest the members that
had committed crimes against the community! Soledad had felt
comfortable thinking that her own daughter was far above the other
young girls and there was just no possible way that she would ever
do anything that would disgrace her family. For now, she didn't
want to pre-judge her own daughter as she tried hard to erase those
thoughts from her mind! She thought it might be best to change the
subject rather than to get into another argument with her daughter!
One thing for certain, she thought! She was happy that Miguel
was not aware of what had happened nor of the doubts and fears
she was feeling! It would have been a terrible shock to him if he
ever found out that the daugher whom he loved so much had gotten
herself involved with a ruthless mob whose only intention was to
inflict injury and hardships on people that they didn't deserve!

Soledad waited deliberately for her daughter to get
all dressed up as she always did before leaving the house on
Wednesday evenings! She had repeatedly insisted that this was
the night that she and the young woman from the bakery would
go to the local cafes for coffee! Today, things were different!
From the corner of her eye she was watching her daughter as she
was nervously looking out the window as if she were waiting for
someone. Finally, she heard a car pull up a short distance away
from the house! Maripaz went quickly up to her mother and kissed
her as she always did before leaving the house! She then went over
to her father, gave him a peck on the cheek, and rushed out the
door!

"Don't wait up for me, mother! I may be home late!" she
said as she was leaving.

Soledad reamained looking out of the window and saw
Maru get into a car with several other young people! From what
she could see, there was a man that was driving and another man
and a woman seated in the rear seat. Before the car drove off, she
watched them as they took something out of their pockets and each
of them put on the 'Boinhas' on their heads! What she saw was
unmistakable! The men were wearing the traditional blue caps
while the women were wearing caps that were bright red! There

was no mistake! Soledad realized that she had been betrayed by her own daughter! How could she have allowed herself to join such a radical organization as the ETA? This had certainly not been what she had been taught at home! The sad part was that it was now a subject that would need to be dealt with in serious terms! If, that was what she decided to become, there would no longer be any room for her in her parents home! Tomorrow, she promised herself, the matter would be settled once and for all!

Madrid

The situation in Spain had been slowly improving following the end of the Civil War! Great strides had been made in establishing a new set of rigid Civil Laws which were far more severe than the previous laws had been. General Franco, who had been a military person for most of his adult life, had prepared a format of civil statutes that were patterned after the rules of military justice! As a result, no distinctions had been made between juveniles and adults when it came to being punished for any acts of criminal conduct! He was quick to establish curfews in most of the largely populated areas of the country. Eventually, these became somewhat successful in reducing the amount of crime that had been rampant following the end of the war!

With the economy of the country in disarray and the treasury drained dry by the misconduct of previous officers and the costs of the war, there was little that Franco could do except to hope that eventually things would return to normal. There was massive unemployment everywhere, and, as a way of trying to improve the situation, General Franco passed a law that would allow farmers to pay less in taxes to the state as an incentive to provide more food for the people! With a few exceptions, the General granted amnesty to many prisoners that were still serving long terms from the Civil War! These men were then returned to a normal status of Spanish citizens! One of the lucrative incomes Spain received was in the form of rents from the United States arising from the use of several air bases, mostly in the South and two naval bases. The money that was received came at an extremely critical time, because it helped to replenish the treasury and also to pay for items that were badly needed and had to be purchased from abroad! Thanks mainly to many of the liberal advisors, Franco eventually established normal work days consisting of eight hours, and it was made mandatory that no one would be compelled to work on weekends! All employees had to be granted vacations that were commensurate with the employees length of service. In time, things did improve and the economic situation became more stable! International trade soon began to fluorish, first with France, and then throughout the other countries in Europe and South America! All of the trade standards included deferred payments with reduced interests which allowed Spain the luxury of time to improve the internal situation before having to pay their foreign obligations. The only people who had not seen any of the improvements, had been the farmers that were living along the northern provinces! The entire area had been damaged by a prolonged dry spell caused by the weather! As a result, the lands that had been cultivated mostly by hand had failed to produce enough food for distribution to the other provinces that would have allowed them a reasonable income.The war had taken its toll on these provinces! The casualty losses had been great! There was an acute shortage of manpower! Many of the farmers were much too old and their children were much too young to work the fields! Because of the prolonged dry spell, manpower from some of the other provinces had sought better working conditions in other areas, mainly along the southern coast of the country! Many of those who were able, soon left Spain and migrated to other countries in Europe in search of earning a living that was better than what they could expect in Spain!

Guillermo Torres and his family had fallen on hard times! They had struggled to send their only son to Madrid to attend the University! Silently, they had always hoped that after he received his degree, Andres would return home and establish himself as a lawyer near the town of Guisamo! The truth was that he might have considered this option had it not been for the massive poverty that was being felt by everyone in the area. There would be great difficulties for him if he were to try to make a living out of practicing law! At the insistance of some of his instructors, he had

decided to take additional courses specializing in Consitutional
Law, a relatively new program that while interesting, would hardly
be able to expect to pay for the routine office expenses! The result
was that he decided to remain in Madrid, and with the help of his
German isntructor, together, they had opened a small law office
in an old brick building near the university, where he could be
tutored by his German partner in the specialty that he had chosen!
The parents had not seen their son for almost a year! The only
communication they had with him had been by a regular exchange
of letters he had shared with them. He was well aware of the
poverty they were feeling and regretted their inability to send him
any money to help him start on his way! Andres knew very well
that it was time for him to repay the debt he owed his parents! No
longer did he have the luxury of being selective in the cases he was
willing to take! It was necessary for him to accept everything that
was offered and hope that his work would result in winning which
would allow him to pay the expenses of an office in the large city!

When the Condessa de Romanones arrived with her
daughter for legal assistance involving her grandson, he would
have preferred to say that this area of criminal law was not really
his specialty. It was the thought of an income that encouraged
him to agree to represent the spoiled brat for the elderly woman!
Who could say, the Condessa obviously had many friends around
the country! It was possible that if she was pleased with him,
she might decide to promote his work among her friends and
acquaintences! Besides, there was also the added benefit that she
had taken her daughter with her! A beautiful young woman who
was easy to admire!

It was mid-morning when Paloma arrived at his office with
her son, Jose! His first impression of the young man was that he
was rather large for his age! He had a large head of thick black hair
and a fair complexion! The lawyer extended his courteous greeting
to the mother and then extended his hand to the young man! The
youngster rudely crossed his arms in defiance and refused to shake
Andres' hand! The youngster was chewing a mouthful of gum
and making strange noises with his mouth! Andres felt his face
feeling flushed as he could feel himself getting angry! He waved

his hand at Paloma who quickly excused herself, telling her son that she would return for him in an hour! When she was out of sight, he motioned to the young man toward a small room that he oftened used as a conference room and ordered him to sit down! Andres took out a legal pad, scribbled a few notes and explained that he wanted to know everything that had happened the day of the incident! He watched as the young man was slouched over the desk, still chewing on his gum and making more ugly sounding noises that were a disturbance to them! The young man remained silent and refused to answer!

"I want you to tell me everything that happened that day!" he repeated. "I want you to start from the time you left your house and I want to know the names of the other boys that went with you! Think over the answers carefully before you speak and try to be specific as possible!" Andres asked, however, this time it was more of an order than a request!

"I don't remember!" he finally answered. The manner in which this youngster was acting was obvious that he had not been trained in having any respect for authority! Silently, Andres was thinking of something he had once heard that, a person never gets a second chance to make a first impression! The impression this young brat was making was far from being favorable!

"I asked you to think over your answers before telling me!" he repeated. Suddenly, almost on impulse the young man stood up from his chair; and, in a fit of anger, he grabbed hold of the chair and slammed it to the floor causing one of the legs to break from the frame!

"Ve'te pa'l carajo!" (Go to hell!) he told Andres. "Do you have any idea who I am? I am the grandson of the Condessa de Romanones! I don't have to tell you anything!"

Andres felt himself showing a cardinal sin! Never to allow a client see you angry! It was true that his mother had cautioned him about her son's behavior, but this was something he never had planned on! One thing was certain! He was not about to take any abuse from a spoiled brat, either!

"I know who you are; and, guess what? I don't give a damn! I didn't go to you, instead, you and your mother came to me! Now, before we start, I want you to pick up that chair that you broke and place it into the corner of the room!" Jose saw that the lawyer was talking very calmly, but the look on his face was telling him that it was not a request but an order!

"Pick it up yourself!!" Jose told him. "This is your office, not mine!" he said with sarcasm.

Andres was livid! He had never been a person of violence nor did he consider violence to be necessary when dealing with a youngster! Unfortunately, this was no ordinary youngster! This was nothing but a spoiled brat who was out of control and without any manners, discipline nor respect! Without answering him, he put down the pad he was holding, got up from his chair. Without any warning he took a handful of Jose's thick black hair and slammed his face forward against the wooden table!

"Now! Suppose you pick up that chair and do what I told you! Did you hear me, or would you want me to slam your head again?" The young boy became meek as he slowly bent down to pick up the chair and do what he had been asked to do! "Now, one more outburst from you and I'll throw you and your mother out of my office! As far as I'm concerned, you can all go somewhere else! Do you understand that?"

"You can't do that!" Jose answered in a calm voice. "You are getting paid to get me out of this mess! Now, do your job or else I'll tell my grandmother to find another lawyer!"

"Now, Brat! Suppose you listen to me!! I don't give a damn what you tell your grandmother, that's your business! I will tell you this! If I am going to represent you, you will cooperate completely with everything I say, whether you like it or not! Also, if I ever see another display in this office from you, you won't have to leave! I'll pick you up by the seat of your pants and throw you out of here myself! Do I make myself clear?" Andres stopped for a moment to allow his anger to be known. "There is one more thing! I am not being paid to get you out of this mess! I'm being paid to help you! Quite frankly, I don't really care whether or not you go to jail for ten years! Who can say? Perhaps it will do you good! Now, I suggest that you sit down and think over the questions I asked and then give me straight forward answers! For your information, my name is Licenciado Andres Torres and that is the way you will address me from now on! Is that clear?"

Young Jose was at a loss for words! No man in his young life had ever spoken to him in such a way! Every person he met would treat him as an aristocrat, fearing his grandmother! This man was puzzling! It was obvious that he was not afraid of his mother nor his grandmother! The angry look on the lawyer's face said it all! He decided that perhaps he had better sit down and do as he was told! After they both had quieted down, the interview had gone rather well, after all! He did his best to explain everything that happened that day, and admitted that it had been his idea to rob the money from the cash register! Jose told Andres that when he was caught, he had admitted to the police everything that happened. After the interview had been completed, Andres decided that it was an open and shut case; and there was really little he could do for him except to try to get the required jail sentence reduced!

The interview had lasted about an hour! Both sides looked and acted tired, but, at least, the atmosphere was congenial and friendly! After a few minutes, Jose asked him, "Are you going to tell my mother that I broke your chair?"

"Maybe you and I should get one thing straight! You are my client not your mother! What happens in this office beween you and me is our business and no one else's! If you want to tell her, that's up to you! But no, I have no plans to say anything to her!" he explained.

"Can you help me?" the boy asked. This time, his voice was silent and calm, almost as if he were pleading! The young man's approach was suddenly more subdued! He was asking a perfectly good question that deserved an honest answer!

"I honestly don't know!" Andres told him. "The story that you gave me is not very convincing! If you told that same story to the local police, I don't think they will want to listen to any defense I can raise! The best I may be able to do, is to have you plead guilty and then appeal to the court to reduce the mandatory sentence! Whether or not I'll be successful is anybody's guess!"

Suddenly, Andres saw something that he had not expected! The young boy began to sob uncontrollably! For the first time, he felt sorry for this boy! Yes, he was spoiled and mischievous, but, did he really deserve to go to jail for ten years for a childish prank? It didn't seem fair! The mandatory sentence of ten years was certainly excessive, especially when dealing with a teen age boy! He was also aware that with a mandatory sentence, there would be little he would be able to do to help him! He went up to him, placed his arm around him and allowed him to rest his head against Andres shoulder while he tried to control his sobs!

"That's okay, son!" Andres said soothingly. "It's okay to cry and get it out of your system!" he added much more calmly than before.

Several minutes later the door to the office opened and Paloma walked in to meet her son! Andres explained that he would try to review the arrest order and determine what the young man was being charged with! When he found out, he would then contact her with the results. Paloma smiled and nodded her head as she and her son walked out of the office! He stood at the doorway watching them walk away! From the look on Andres face he could see that his partner was concerned!

"I think you are angry....ja?" he asked.

"Of course I am! This is the kind of case that I hate to defend! The young man commits a childish prank and gets sent to jail for a mandatory ten years! It isn't fair, Otto! These laws need to be changed and there isn't very much I can do about them! I may be able to have the judge reduce the sentence, but the stigma of a conviction will always be with him!"

"Perhaps you are making a big mistake!" the old man answered. "Perhaps you are concentrating too much on the punishment and not nearly enough on the law! If I were to handle the case, I would try to convince the court how the letter of the law is grossly unfair when applied to young people! Even if you should succeed in having his sentence reduced, he will still be charged with an adult crime that will remain with him for the rest of his life! If he is already considered a criminal in the eyes of the law, then, what initiative does he have to correct himself and to turn things around! There is really no incentive for him to do so...ja?"

Andres thought about what Otto had said for a long time before answering! He didn't want the old man to know that at least a part of his anxiety in helping his client was because he felt he would be handsomely rewarded with a badly needed income! Besides, his client also had a very good looking mother and he wouldn't mind at all seeing her again as soon as possible! "Herr Otto, I think you may be right! I may have better luck by challenging the statute than by having the sentence reduced! You have just given me an excellent idea!"

After the brief discussion with Herr Otto, he went back into his office and spent the rest of the day reading his law books! He needed to find a way that would make good sense for helping this young man and any other youngster who might come to him for help! He spent the entire afternoon reviewing his text books searching for answers! His eyes were tired when he glanced at his watch and saw it was time for him to go home! He carefully placed the books back on the shelf in their proper place, put on his suit jacket and was about to leave when the door opened again and Paloma walked in! "Just the person I wanted so see!" she said smiling. "I remember your telling me that you didn't like to interview clients at their home, but you said nothing about clients coming to your office!"

He was momentarily speechless, not knowing what to say! He had no idea what she would want at this time of day when he was about to go home! "Would you like to come into my office?" he asked politely.

"No! Not really! You see, I came here for two reasons! One, to pay you for the chair that my son broke in your office!" she said, handing him an envelope filled with a stack of pesetas!

"That won't be necessary!" he answered. "It's already been taken care of! I am happy that he told you about it! I had left it up to him, whether or not he should tell you what he did!"

"Please, Andres! I want you to accept this! It is only fair!" she insisted.

"No, but I think I may have a better idea! Why not bring your son to this office every day for a month and let him work here and earn enough to pay for the chair? He can do a number of odd jobs, such as cleaning off the desks, emptying the waste baskets and generally run errands for me and feel useful! Would you allow him to do that?"

"Of course," she said excitedly, "I think that is an excellent idea! Besides, it would also give me the opportunity to see you every day!" she said as her face showed signs of being embarassed that she had been so forward!

"Now that we have the first reason resolved, what was the second reason?" he asked, anxious to get away from a subject he had not expected nor did he quite know how to respond!

"The second reason was to ask you to come to dinner and perhaps we can then discuss this legal matter without my mother being there to interfere!" she said flatly. "Now, don't you dare turn me down because I have no intentions of leaving here without you!"

He went back to the lavatory to wash up ! It was also a good opportunity for him to think things over! He had no idea what he would say once he got there nor how he should act! This woman was extremely elegant and charming, but, she was also an aristocrat, and far above his social status! Really, he didn't know how he should act in this new experience! After a few minutes, he decided that the only approach would be the honest one! Once they were at her house, he would simply admit that he had no idea what they could possibly have in common that would make for an interesting conversation over dinner!

"You'll need to excuse me if I seem nervous! You see, I don't have very much experience in dining with aristocrats! I hope that I won't offend or embarass you!" he admitted as she simply smiled and took hold of his arm as they made their way toward the door.

"I doubt very much that you could ever offend me! Just be yourself, and instead of thinking of me as an aristocrat, think of me as being someone you are happy to be with!" she said, making him feel more at ease! They entered the long limosine as she told the driver to take them to a restaurant she had deliberatly selected at the outskirts of Madrid! Andres had heard of the place; but, he also knew that it was very expensive and he could not afford to dine there! She began asking him how the interview with her son had been and the reason why he had broken the chair!

"I promised him that I wouldn't say anything to you! I think it's important that I keep that promise! Let him be the one to tell you if he wants to!"

Paloma had a strange feeling that she was making him nervous, but she reluctantly agreed with his suggestion regarding her son! No body needed to remind her that her son could at times be undisciplined and rude; but, she also saw that in a short period of time, her son had shown a respect and a feeling of trust with him! That, in itself, had been a major accomplishment!

Paloma was holding on to Andres' arm as they entered the lavish restuarant! He was still feeling a bit nervous being with her and noticing this, she did everything she could to make him comfortable in her presence! The waiter, dressed in a black tuxedo came over to them and escorted them to a table that was a bit removed from the others in an area of the building that was almost secluded! The man held her chair while she sat down! He then turned his attention to Andres and asked them what they would like to drink!

"Para mi, un vino tinto!" he said (For me, a glass of red wine!) Paloma made a motion with her hand as the waiter nodded his head. Without the necessity of words, she had signalled to him to bring a bottle of expensive red wine from the wine cellar!

"I am still making you nervous, aren't I?" she asked smiling.

"I'm afraid so! After all, it isn't every day that I get to eat my dinner with the daughter of El Conde de Romanones!" he answered. They spent a considerable amount of time speaking about her son while he explained in detail what he thought he might be able to do and about the things he would not be able to do to help him! When they were finished, she looked at him and gently stroked his arm that was resting on top of the table!

"You must have made quite an impression on Jose, because he insisted that he doesn't want anyone else except you to defend him!" She watched him carefully noticing that he had a very warm smile, especially when he felt embarassed by something she had said.

"I doubt it! We had a few differences at the beginning that needed to be ironed out; that's all! By the way, who was the person that recommended me to you!?" he asked while trying to change the subject! He was not going to tell her what had happened, nor that he had yanked her son's hair when he broke the chair during a temper tantrum!

"It was another attorney by the name of Carlos Perez! Do you know him?" she asked.

"Yes! I know him very well!" he answered. She could see that there were elements of nostalgia as he spoke! Little did she know how well he had known Carlos! So many memories came vividly back into his mind as he remembered how unhappy Maripaz had been when he had defended Carlos against accusations she had made! Also, he remembered how it had been because of Carlos that they had drifted apart even though he had never really forgotten her! "He was my room mate when I was in the university!" he said after a few moments.

"You probably made a good impression on him as you did with me! He told me that you were one of the most honest people he had ever met! That's quite a recommendation coming from someone who was born in Granada!" she said. Andres let out an impish laugh and she could see that he felt a bit embarassed at speaking about himself!

"Andres, tell me the truth! Can you help my son!" she asked bluntly. It came as a thunderbolt from out of no where! It was yet another comment that he preferred not to answer because, honestly, he had no way of knowing whether or not he would be successful in defending her son!

"I honestly don't know!" he told her. "From what I can see, the problem can be approached in two ways! I can enter a guilty plea on his behalf! Afterward, I can then appeal to the presiding judge and ask that the mandatory sentence be reduced because of

his age! There is also the possibility of attacking the justification of
the law saying that it is entirely too excessive for a young child! Of
course, we would also ask that the law be changed in dealing with
juveniles! Whether anyone will be willing to listen or not, remains
to be seen!"

"Which alternative do you suggest?"

"At this point, I really don't know! If I enter a plea of
guilty, Jose will be saddled with a criminal record that will be with
him for the rest of his life! I think that the law is totally unfair in
these situations! On the other hand, if I can successfully attack
the existing law, there is always a chance that it might be changed
when juveniles are involved! If I am successful, and believe me, it
is a big 'if', he would then go on with his life with a clean slate as if
nothing had ever happened!"

"I'd like to know what you would do if you needed to make
such a decision on your own son or a member of your family? I'm
assuming, of course, that you had a son!" She was smiling as she
spoke but Andres quickly realized that this was her way of finding
out whether or not he was married! It was a touchy subject and he
knew that he would need to be careful with his comments!

"I don't know what I would do! It has to be your decision!"
he said.

"Damn it, Andres!! What do I need to do to crack that
mysterious wall around you that refuses to allow anyone to go
inside?" It was difficult for her to understand that he wasn't really
creating a wall around him! He was acting the way any attorney
should act under the circumstances! What was being discussed
was purely business! It was an important decision that needed to
be made! Since she was an aristocrat, he could not afford to lose a
case, being reproached by the Contessa, and probably rediculed to
their friends!

"I didn't realize that I was so transparent!" he answered.
"And since you've asked the question in a round about way, no, I
have no wife, no girlfriend, and no child! Now, have I answered all
of your questions?" he asked smiling.

"All except one!" she answered also smiling. "Why?? You
seem to be the perfect mate for some lucky woman! I need to admit

that Carlos Perez did tell me an interesting little story about you when he recommended you to us! It had something to do with your falling in love with a woman at the university; then, you had an argument with her and she ran out on you! Is that true?"

Andres was startled and confused to know that they had been speaking about him on a personal level! This was highly unprofessional and had it been anyone other than Carlos, he would have probably been angry that so much about his personal life had been revealed to a stranger without his permission!

"Partially!" he replied. "Tell me! Why is the story about my life so important?" he asked! Although he tried to conceal how he felt, he was showing signs of being annoyed that she had inadvertantly sought to learn more about his life than he was willing to reveal!

"Because, to be honest with you, you have even impressed my mother! Believe me when I tell you that she isn't easily impressed!" was her reply.

"She hardly knows me! From what I could see, she certainly didn't seem overly impressed when she first met me!"

"That's where you're wrong! When I told her I was coming to take you to dinner, the only thing she said was that it should turn out to be an interesting evening! You don't know my mother! Ordinarily, she would have been angry to learn that I was going to have dinner with someone she considered to be a bit below my social status!"

"I guess I never really considered social status! You see, I come from a poor family of farmers in Galicia! They needed to struggle hard just to send me to the university! In my opinion, it is hard to find anyone with a higher social status!"

"It doesn't matter much to me either! I became a widow with a baby boy who was only two years old! I had the name, but not very much more! Whatever I have, I owe to my mother!"

"Tell me something! How did you ever get the name of Paloma? That is certainly not a Christian name!" he asked.

"When I was a little girl, my father, the Count, noticed that I was running around everywhere I went! Since I was his favorite daughter, he began calling me 'Palomita'! My Christian name is

457

Eugenia, but I always disliked the sound of that name! So, from Palomita it went to Paloma; and that name remained with me since! Why did you ask? Don't you like it?"

"On the contrary, I think that the name is great! I was just curious, nothing more!"

"Well, you had better get used to it! I'll probably be seeing a great deal of you! There seems to be something about you that has attracted both my son and me! Please, don't think that I am being forward although I have to admit that I do like you! Can I depend on you for dinner tomorrow night?" she asked. The unexpected invitation had taken him by surprise. He had also noticed that she was being a bit more forward than he had expected! There was something about her that was simple yet elegant! Besides, she was also a very good looking lady! There were certainly much worse things in life than to be in her company! If the feeling was mutual, it would only be to his advantage, he reasoned! Instead of answering, he gave her a smile of acceptance!

"I suppose you are the type of person that doesn't like to commit himself, is that it? Well, the least you can do is to ask me out to dance!" she asked as the soft music began to play!

"I'm not a very good dancer! But I am willing to give it a chance if you don't mind!"

She took hold of his hand and allowed him to lead her out to the center of the dance floor! The small orchestra had just begun to play, and it felt a bit clumsy to hold such an attractive woman as she snuggled up close to him! They were so close that he could feel her nearness and smell the sweet, tantalizing fragrance of violets inher hair while it brushed against his face! It felt great to be in the arms of a beautiful woman again as his thoughts went back to the university! Today had been the first time he had danced with anyone since those unforgettable days! He still remembered when Maripaz had asked him out to the dance floor and how wonderful it felt feeling her presence against him! For a few brief moments he wondered what had happened to her and where she was! There were a few feelings of nostalgia as his thoughts drifted back to those long gone days when she had been the only woman in his life that mattered! Could it be that this stranger that he had recently met was now about to take her place? He hoped not! Still the nearness was intoxicating and he didn't want the music to stop playing! There were still mixed feelings within him knowing that he should be thinking about her as a client rather than as a beautiful young woman who had found him equally attractive! He wasn't quite sure whether or not he liked the way he was beginning to feel!

The following day Paloma arrived at his office late in the afternoon with her son. Andres quickly put him to work returning unused books back in their places and straightening out the chairs and papers in the office. The fact that the attorney had deliberately avoided any long conversation with him was that he wanted to wait and see if the young man had told his mother about his behavior in the office! To his surprise, he said nothing! There had been however, a noticeable change in the boy's personality and attitude! The young man appeared courteous and polite, an indication that his behavior had improved since the last time!

"Tell me, Licenciado Andres, are you still angry with me?" he asked.

"No! As long as you treat me like a human being, I'll treat you the same way!" he answered.

"Do you think you'll be able to help me?" For the first time, the youngster was showing signs of being worried at what would happen.

"I'll do everything I can, but I can't promise you anything! You'll need to have faith in me!" he answered.

"I hope you can do something! Yesterday, I heard my grandmother talking to my mother! They said something that if you can't help me, they'll need to find another attorney that is willing to take the case! My grandmother has already started calling some of her friends and asking them for the names of lawyers that might be able to help me! I don't want anyone else, Licenciado!! I want only you to help me!"

The youngster's comments had taken Andres by surprise! During the previous evening, he had been listening to the boy's mother giving him accolades! Now, thanks to the innocence of youth, the young man revealed the conversations that were apparently taking place behind his back! He became angry! Damned angry! Suddenly, he made a final decision! If that was how they felt, perhaps it would be best if they went elsewhere for legal advice! When Paloma came back to take him to dinner, he would be direct and frank with her! There was no point in his handling the case of her son! Perhaps it would be best if they turned the case over to a more experienced lawyer whom they considered to be more competent!!!

CHAPTER 6

Bilbao

Several more reports were published telling of banks
being robbed at gunpoint during the weeks that followed! Soledad
surmised what was happening with her daughter and lived in
constant fear knowing that it was only a matter of time before
the government took an active role in controlling the new wave
of robberies that was now threatening the economy as well as
the safety in the area! From a prank committed by amateurs, the
problem became more real as reports continued to circulate telling
of an increase in the frequency of the thefts! The latest movements
of the ETA were now showing a renewed strength as shown by
the advanced weaponry that was being used as well as the growth
in the enrollment of their membership! The government was well
aware that for an economy to prosper, it would need to have an
active bank system that would serve as a stepping stone to elevate
itself from the economic pressures that the country was suffering.
If the robberies continued, it would only be a matter of time before
the depositors began to lose faith in their banks and would avoid
making deposits in the local banks. In order for any system to
survive, it was necessary to have and maintain a steady flow of
capital! Deposits meant a movement of hard currency throughout
the area! Deposits, of course, meant increased profits; and profits
meant taxes that were necessary to afford the needs that existed,

not only in Bilbao but also in the other provinces throughout the country! The government by itself could simply not afford to maintain economic systems of security in a country that had been plagued by misfortunes created by the previous government. The international income from abroad was limited to the few rents that the government was able to obtain from the treaties with others, such as the United States, for the use of the military air and sea bases!

Every time that Soledad read the newspapers and saw that other women were actively taking part in the robberies, her heart would sink to her feet, realizing that her own daughter was quite likely one of the active members of the movement! She waited for her daughter to come home from one of the usual Wednesday night meetings, knowing it was late for a woman to be walking in the streets at night all alone. It had obviously been nothing more than a lie when she had told her mother about her outings with Olga to the local cafes! There had been times when Maripaz had used this as an excuse to go out; but, when her mother made a trip to the bakery, she saw that the young woman was still very much at work behind the counter and had not seen nor been with her daughter. Tonight she had made up her mind that it was time for another mother and daughter discussion! Of course, she would need to approach the subject with special care, perhaps beginning the conversation by asking about the young man she had fallen in love with at school!

Mari was baffled when she opened the door and saw her mother waiting for her! "Did you have a pleasant evening?" Soledad asked. She was careful not to mention that she had gone to the bakery that same evening after her daughter had left the house and had seen the young woman still working behind the counter!

"It was okay, mother! Olga and I started to talk; and, before we knew it, it was later than we thought!" she said

"Mari." Soledad asked almost with a reluctance to delve into an issue that had been in the past and practically forgotten. "I'd like you to tell me what happened between you and that young man you wrote to us about! From the way you described him, it seemed to your father and me that you had fallen in love with him!

462

How could it be that you ended your relationship and he never once tried to contact you!"

"Oh mother!! Why are you bringing that up again? I already told you that things didn't work out; that's all!"

"Yes, I already know what you told me; but I think it was much more than that!"

"Well, if you must know, I became unhappy when something happened and he decided to take the word of his room mate over mine! That's all! I know I made a mistake; but, it's over! He's probably married by now with a wife and a child! Don't worry! I got over it!"

"Oh, I'm quite sure that you did! You know, there is a story that I think you should listen to! Sit down and let's you and me have a talk!"

"Not tonight, mother!" she said as she let out a loud sigh indicating that she was tired. "Really, I feel very tired and would like to go to bed!" Soledad allowed her eyes to drift down to Mari's pocket and from the corner of her eye she spotted the blue trim of her red "boinha!

"No Mari!!" she said showing concern mixed with anger! "Tired or not we need to have a talk! I don't want to talk to you when your father is here! It would only upset him if he heard what was on my mind!" She motioned to Mari to take a seat next to her! By the look on her face, her daughter knew that this was not going to be a regular mother and daughter talk! This was much more serious and she could see that her mother was angry!

"When I was a little girl, in the Playa de Salinas, my family was very poor! I was raised with a young man my own age whom I really thought I couldn't live without! We even had spoken of one day being married! Then, the day came when he told me that he was joining the Guardia Civil! I was besides myself with anger, not because he was joining the Guardias to improve himself, but because he had the audacity of leaving me all alone! It was a very selfish motive that I had to learn to live with and for which I suffered the rest of my life! In fact, my anger was so severe that when he came to visit me I told my mother to tell him that I didn't want to see him anymore! That was the biggest mistake of my life and it all came about because of my own selfish feelings! You'll never guess what happened to me after that, because things happened that I don't want to talk about! I became a guerilla fighter with the underground and was very active in their movements! One of the worse things that happened was when I became an excellent marksman with my rifle! I was so accurate that I actually enjoyed killing people and taking away lives without any good reason! It was a terrible way to live, that is, until your father came along!"

"So what, Mother? That was all in the past; and now you and daddy are happy together, aren't you?" she asked.

"Ah yes!! But there is more to the story! You see, that young man was your father! While I became an active fighter in the underground, he went on to become the head Mariscal in Toledo appointed to the post by General Franco! Our paths crossed again, but not until I was arrested and sentenced to death! Since your father was duty bound to the government, he wasn't able to pass a death sentence on me because he had always been in love with me! In order to be active, he had to disguise himself with a hooded mask with the cut outs for the eyes! During the day, he would be the Mariscal; and, in the evenings, when we went out on a mission, he would disguise himself as 'El Raposo' so that no one would recognize who he was! Everyone knew that eventually he would be caught; and, when that dreadful day came, he left the area on a boat with the help of his friends and that was when we came to Bilbao! The General was angry, but he didn't come here to arrest him! Instead, he issued a direct order that if he ever should come to Madrid, the Guardia Civiles were given orders to kill him on sight, without a trial! That's the reason why we can't go to Madrid to receive the medical care that he so badly needs. The worse part is that there is nothing more that I can do for him, except to be with him, love him, and be at his side!"

There was a surprised look on her daughter's face! So, that was it! Her own father had been the famous, 'El Raposo'! He had been considered a legendary hero to the members of the Republican Army while, all the time, to the Nationalists, he was considered a traitor!

"Did you know that we read about the famous 'El Raposo' in school?" her daughter said. "I always admired him; but I never dreamed he was my own father! Gosh, I'm so proud of him! Why didn't you tell me before about this?"

"Probably because there was really no need for you to know!" she answered.

Maripaz was still surprised by what she had just been told! "Now I finally know about the mask that I saw wrapped up in his drawer! Thank you for telling me, mother! Don't worry, the secret is safe! I would never tell anyone!"

Slowly, in a move that startled Maripaz, she watched as her mother got up from her chair and walked slowly over to where her daughter was sitting! Without a warning she reached down and yanked the 'boinha' that was barely showing from her pocket!

"Now, do you want to tell me what this is all about? I knew that what you told me was a lie! You were not with the young woman from the bakery tonight! You see, I went to the bakery after you left the house and I saw her still working behind the counter!" she said in a calm voice, but showing a frown on her forehead that Mari always knew it meant that her mother was quite angry! The frown was certainly not of surprise; but even though she was speaking in a calm voice, she knew only too well how explosive her mother could be when something made her angry!

"Yes, mother!! There is no need for any more lies! I am a member of the ETA! Believe it or not, it didn't start out that way! In fact, it began with my trying to do a favor to the town by keeping them away from the ranchers and the merchants! Before I knew what was happening, I became a member of the group and now I can't get out!" she explained. When she was finished, Soledad was no longer able to control her anger! She reared back her hand and slapped her hard across the face with the palm of her hand!

"Have you any idea of what you did? You have disgraced this house as well as your father and me! I can never forgive your deception!"

"Please mother, do you want to listen to my side of the story?" she said through the tears. "Please.....please, let me explain!" she cried.

"How are you going to explain it, with more lies? I want you out of this house by tomorrow! I don't care where you go or what you do! Since you seem to love that group of terrorist so much, maybe they can support you! I never again want to see you in this house! You knew very well how we felt about the ETA! Yet, you obviously wanted to punish us by joining them! I don't think your father nor I deserved that!" Maripaz stood there, stunned and unable to speak! The tears were streaking down her cheeks! Never in a million years would she have expected her mother to throw her out of the house because of what she did!! How could she ever explain, that what she did, had been for the benefit of the entire community! How was she to know that once she joined the group, there was no getting out?

"Very well, mother!" she said after she was able to compose herself! "I'll be out of here in the morning! Since you will probably tell daddy your side of the story, you might also explain that what I did, I did for his sake as well as for yours! For whatever it's worth, I love both of you very much and that will never change! If I should get arrested, I want you to look the other way and pretend that you don't know me! That way, you won't need to feel embarassed! I never wanted to bring disgrace upon you!" she said, as she stormed angrily up the flight of steps and slammed the door of her bed room!

Soledad remained by herself, angry and crying at what she had done! Might it be that this would become yet another mistake in her life that would pain her? What if Maripaz was arrested for her part in the robberies? Could she ever look the other way and pretend that she didn't know her own daughter? And what about Miguel! How would he feel when he knew the truth? The doubts were mounting in her own mind, afraid that she may have over reacted! Now that she had been more in control, it was a strange choice of words that Maripaz had used when she said that what she did, she did for her mother and father! If so, how could she have been so careless and insensitive? The very least she could do was to allow her daughter to explain why she did what she did! She remained all alone downstairs all evening thinking and crying over what had happened! As she sat all alone, her eyes puffy from crying, it puzzled her how much of her past had been inherited by her daughter! Mari had done exactly what she had done many years ago that had given her unhappiness throughout her life! It seemed that her own daughter was now making the same foolish mistakes; and, in silence, she prayed that despite her anger her daughter would have been happier than her mother had been! Perhaps she would feel better by morning and both women would sit down as they had done so many times, and discussed what had happened! As a mother, she would have to apologize to her daughter, if not for her own sake, then for the sake of Miguel whom she already knew would have been devastated by the news of Mari's departure! Would he also turn against her for having asked their only daughter to leave the house? It was early in the morning when she finally dozed off, anxious to sit down with her daughter and make peace with her! Unfortunately, it didn't happen! When she opened her eyes it wa already daybreak! She ran upstair to her daughter's bedroom and opened the door without knocking! One look and she again started to cry when she saw that Mari had already left the house and had taken some of her clothes with her!

Maripaz soon realized that she had made a horrible mistake! It had been one that couldn't be easily rectified! She realized too late that her mother had been justified in what she had done! Her only mistake had been in not allowing her to explain what had happened and the reason why she had joined the ETA, knowing that it was a terrorist group! From now on, she could expect her own life to change! It was going to be necessary for her to take care of herself with a group of other young people who thought they were idealisitic, but instead, were merely looking after their own selfish interests instead of the interests of the people! Many changes were taking place and none of them were positive! When many of the other members realized how easy it had been to rob a bank and how hefty the rewards would be, the membership enrollment of the group began to increase! Where there had been only a few members who would be at the regular meetings, there were now nearly a total of forty new members ranging in age between eighteen and twenty two years of age! Maripaz was the only member of the group with a college education and soon became highly regarded by some of the other members because of her intelligence and for her ability to plan a raid with the utmost of care! Some of the older members were jealous knowing that none of them could match her when it came down to using common sense and careful planning!

It was decided that it would be necessary for Mari to assume some kind of leadership in the group! She soon outlined her own plans, most of them justifiable, that would make her invisable while being certain that she didn't become one of the members who would be going out on the actual raids! At least, if the others were caught, she would remain insulated and could then plead her innocence! She remembered something that Andres had once told her. The worse thing for a person to do was to plead guilty to a crime! Doing so meant that there would be nothing left for the prosecutors to prove in the court room! Explaining her reluctance to the other members, she had told them of the possibility of being caught and taken to jail! She had argued that if she were to be caught and arrested, there would be no one left behind that was capable of planning future raids. It was a weak argument, but, since she was working with a weak group, she knew she could easily get away with her logic! Once this concept had been accepted, it no longer mattered whether or not an y of the others were captured and carted off to jail! The most she could be accused of doing, was in joining the group and nothing more! Anything further that the authorities wanted to pursue was circumstantial and something that she could argue against! In addition, it was important that her name not appear in any of the newspapers, thus sparing her parents from any additional anguish that would come with knowing that their only daughter had been arrested for engaging in criminal activity!

The next meeting had been nothing but a shouting match between a few of the older members and some of the newer ones! The older members had held to the thought that all raids should be planned allowing time between them since they already had all of the money that was needed! The newer members were much more greedy! Their argument was to rob as many banks as possible and as quickly as possible! Some of them even suggested that they return to those banks that had already been robbed and take whatever cash was available and that had been accumulated since the previous heist! There was always an impasse as to which would be the better approach. In all of these discussions Maripaz had chosen to remain silent and allowed the others to decide what they should do! Her participation was only up to the point of any unforseen possibilities and the dangers that might be encountered. They didn't seem to want to accept the possibility that some of the banks had now hired armed guards to protect them against theft! In addition, there was added foot patrols of the Guardia Civiles in all the areas that were vulnerable to attacks! She had easily convinced her self that none of these terrorists were any match at all for the Guardia Civiles who had already been given orders to shoot on sight! She knew that it was only a matter of time before they would be killed because of greed! It would result in another repitition of what had happened to Pergo the day he was killed! If that was what they wanted, then, so be it! At least she would be in the clear!

One of the things that began to trouble her was that some of the members had used their money to buy advanced weaponry for the raids! Some had ordered expensive rifles that were capable of firing in rapid succession thinking they could easily outsmart any of the Guardias! Other members of the group had purchased small hand-held hand grenades that could be easily detonated when entering one of the banks! It certainly wasn't up to her to remind them that the purchase of these weapons would only cause the guards and the Guardia Civiles to purchase similar ordinance that would allow them to fight back! So far, the only group member that had been killed had been Pergo, and already he had been all but forgotten! She was absolutely certain that with the new purchases there would be many more killings as well as an escalation of their attempts to steal from other areas besides the banks! Every day she would review the reports to see if any more sheep had been reported stolen from her parents or if any damage had been reported to any of the fence enclosures around the ranch of her parents. She had sworn to herself that if she ever read such a report she would find out who had committed the incident and would personally kill them herself!

Several weeks later an item appeared in the local newspaper that created some unexpected excitement! On occasion items would be printed telling the readers of large amounts of money that were expected to be transported to and from the local banks! Since many of the banks had been ordered to work with limited amounts of cash, it served as a way for the government to advise their depositors when money was expected to be delivered to the banks so that the depositors who wanted to make withdrawals would know when it was convenient to transact business in a certain bank! Many of the younger members of the ETA group were elated by the news! Some felt that since it seemed so easy to rob money from the banks, it would be just as easy to rob a truck that was transporting cash to the bank! Some of the older group members had voiced some objections in trying to steal money from a government truck! Their voices were silenced by the younger group members who felt that since they were now equipped with semi-automatic weapons and grenades, stealing from the trucks would be as easy as stealing from any of the banks! Something about that news article was troubling as Maripaz listened to the exchange of ideas! It wasn't anything she could easily identify, but there was something about the article that seemed very suspicious! She felt it her duty to advise the group against taking any unnecessary chances that might be needed! All of her arguments had been met with deaf ears as the excitement of yet another lucrative heist began to grow among the members. The words printed in the article were fixed in her mind! She reviewed it many times trying to find out what was troubling her! The mere fact that it had been printed was in and of itself foolish! If the banks were being robbed on a regular basis, why would the government be so foolish as to make a public announcement of when large deliveries of money could be expected at the bank? It just didn't make any sense to her! There had to be another reason for the disclosure and that was what was bothering her! As she re-read the article again, there was something that stood out! On one of the lines, the name of the bank was specifically printed and it said that the delivery would be expected there at about 1 P.M.! Suddenly, everything came back to her in a jiffy! Why would the truck carrying the money chose to make a scheduled delivery at 1 P.M.? Surely they had to know that this was the time when the banks would be closed and the employees were sent home for the traditional two hour siesta! Something was obviously wrong! It might had been an oversight on the part of the planners or it could also be something else! The more she thought about it, the more troubling it became! There had to be an ulterior motive! Could it be that they had ovrestimated the logic of the ETA? Or might it possibly be that the times had been deliberately published, realizing that the ETA would take the advantage of the workers being at home for lunch and would consider the time as excellent in which to plan a robbery? On the other hand, there was also the possibility that when the group went to rob the truck, they would be met with a cadre of Guardia Civiles instead of the stacks of money they were expecting to receive!

Maripaz did her best to interrupt one of the speakers who was eagerly describing the political ambitions of the group! He was speaking to an audience that had already shut out his message, and the only thing that mattered was the large cache of pesetas they were expecting from the haul! She tried once again to get the attention of the group, but once again her message was landing on deaf ears! To hell with them, she said to herself! If they refuse to listen, then, so be it! Let them carry on with their plans and then see what happens! One thing was absolutely certain, there was just no way she would even consider going with them on this raid! Instead, she decided that she would take along her revolver and would observe the heist from a safe distance away! It wasn't that she cared about this group, but, after her mother had asked her to leave the house, she had no other choice other than to turn to them for a place to live!

She was still regretting what she had done! It had been her intention that by directing the group to the banks, they would leave the poor ranchers and farmers alone who were already struggling to make an honest living! Her intentions had, of course, been good; but no one seemed to know that, nor did anybody care! The only person she hoped would have listened had already tossed her out of the house without allowing her the opportunity of an explanation! It wasn't that she blamed her mother; but she felt that there was

an element of unfairness by not allowing her to give her own
explanation to what was happening! The truth was that she simply
hated the movement! It had been started on an idealistic basis that
at first seemed fair; but then, as in most other movements, because
of the infusion of newer ideas and members who had become
trigger happy, the original ideas had long since vanished. Her
temper had become her greatest enemy! It had been her temper
that had turned Andres away from her, and she had been much
too proud to call and apologize for what happened! Now, her own
impatient behavior was contributing to yet another cause that was
important to her! She felt confident that at some point she would
once again become reunited with her parents; but, for now, the
problem needed to take its place on the back burner!

It was early in the morning when the young men who
had volunteered to take part in the assault of the armored truck
began to arrive at the meeting place. The plans had already been
discussed previously and everyone was in agreement that the
major points had all been covered. The only thing left to do was
for them to return to the old wooden barn with large cotton sacks
filled with stacks of pesetas! Maripaz listened to them as they
spoke among themeselves trying to decide who the group leader
would be! After considerable exchanges, it was finally decided
that one of the young men, probably no more that eighteen years of
age, would lead the group in what was scheduled to be the largest
robbery of its kind! Although she was listening carefully, Maripaz
was careful not to interfere! As far as she was concerned she still
felt that they were making a large mistake and would probably
end up in a bloodshed on the clean streets of Bilbao! It was shortly
after the noon hour when the group of four men and their leader
left for town! Maripaz had already decided that she would go into
the public square and observe what was happening! However, she
would be watching from a distance! There was no way that she
wanted to be connected with this theft, especially since she felt
unsure of its success! Today she wanted to be sure that her tell tale
'boinha' remained back at the wooden building, so no one would
recognize her as being a member of the group! There was a feeling
of failure troubling her knowing that the attack had been planned

and orchestrated by amateurs! She went by herself to one of the smaller outdoor cafes at the Plaza de Bilbao. The cafe as well as the plaza was practically deserted since most of the people had already gone to their homes for the customary afternoon siesta! She sat at one of the tables that was facing the bank and ordered a cup of black coffee!

As she was sipping on her coffee she saw the car arrive with the members of the group. Some of the members were getting a bit overanxious while waiting for the armored truck to arrive! Because the bank was conveniently located across from the plaza and situated between several large commercial buildings she had an excellent view without being spotted from across the plaza. Several minutes after one o'clock they heard the rumble of a large truck as it was approaching the area.Maripaz put down her cup and watched as she saw the truck being conveniently parked in front of the bank! It was then that she shook her head from side to side as mistake number one was about to take place! She saw one of the group members who was sitting in the rear of the car getting overly anxious as soon as the truck came into view! When he saw the truck parking in front of the bank, he jumped out of the car, took out a hand grenade and pulled the pin tossing it in front of the truck. The grenade exploded instantly sending an array of dirt and stones high into the air as the truck jammed on its breaks and came to a complete stop. The critical mistake had been that the grenade had been tossed a bit early and had exploded before the truck had reached its destination! Aside of the loud explosion, there had been no damage at all to the truck! What it did was to warn the driver that they were about to encounter trouble and provided them with valuable time to be ready before it reached the bank!

The group of young terrorist realized immediately that they had acted much too hastily and were now faced with the situation of no other alternative than to go on with the assault. The men got out of their car; one of them stood in front of the truck while the others remained poised with their weapons drawn and standing at the rear door! Seconds seemed like hours while the group waited for the door of the truck to open! It was then that mistake number two took place! The back door of the truck opened and a squad consisting of five Guardia Civiles, fully armed, jumped out and started firing their weapons at the group! There was a violent exchange of gunfire; and, by the time the smoke had settled, four of the young men from the ETA were lying out on the street in a pool of fresh blood! Maripaz had seen everything that happened and she almost felt sorry knowing that the massacre had taken place before her own eyes! They had obviously been beaten by the government at their own game! As the Guardia Civiles began searching the victims she saw that the man who had been standing in front of the truck started to run away in her direction. At that time, a young girl of about nine years of age began to run to the other side of the plaza toward her mother who was signalling to her! The man who had been running away quickly changed his direction and began to run after the small girl. Maripaz knew that what he wanted to do was to abduct the youngster and to use her as a shield hoping to escape capture. Seeing what was happening made her begin to move in his direction! As soon as he spotted her, he called out and asked her for help! If she did help him, she knew that he would have told the Guardia Civiles that she too was a member of the group! She could not allow that to happen under any circumstances! He went up behind the child and grabbed her by the arm while the child began to cry frantically and calling for her mother. Maripaz took out a revolver from her pocket, cocked the hammer, and held it tightly in her right hand! With her left hand she anchored her right arm with her left hand firmly beneath her right wrist! The man running away was now close enough that she had him in her sights!

"Alto!" she yelled on impulse. "Deja la nena estar!" (Stop! Leave the child alone!) she hollered. The assailant had hold of the youngster's arm and was tugging at her roughly. "Suelta esa nena!" (Leave the child alone!) Maripaz ordered again! For several moments the man appeared to be confused that this young woman who was supposed to be helping him was aiming her revolver at his head and ordering him to leave the child alone!

"Jode a tu puta madre!" (Screw your mother!) he yelled back, knowing that he was well within range of her revolver.

"I'll tell you once more!" she yelled. "Leave the child alone!"

Again the assailant ignored the warning as he watched her aim her gun ever so slowly, making sure that the child was not in her line of fire! Suddenly, she squeezed the trigger and fired off several shots, each of them finding their mark on the young man's chest! She watched him looking momentarily up at the sky and finally released the young child! Within seconds she saw him take two backward steps and fired off two wild shots into the air before he fell back on the hard concrete plaza! When she reached the body, there were several small holes in his chest, each one emitting a steady flow of fresh blood. She extended her hand to the little girl and slowly led her across to where her mother had been waiting!

Several of the Guardia Civiles who saw what had happened went over to Maripaz and asked if she was okay! Of course, she said! She only did what needed to be done because the young man was endangering the life of a child!

"You saved that little girl's life!" One of the Guardia Civiles told her. "That makes you quite a hero!" he said smiling.

"No! I'm not a hero!" she answered modestly. "My only thought was to save the life of that young child and I was afraid that she was going to be hurt!"

"Can we please have your name, young lady?" the Guardia asked. "When the newspapers print this story, we want to tell them everything that happened and how you saved the child's life!"

"Mi nombre es Maripaz Romero!" she told him proudly. "My father is a sheep rancher and his name is Miguel!"

Maripaz slowly walked away hoping that her mother would read the newspapers the next day and would be willing to forgive her! If nothing else, she had hoped that both her mother and father would have been proud of what she had done! It was almost a ritual that they would look at the news while drinking their morning coffee! The woman who was now holding her little girl in her arms came over and sat at the table. Maripaz quickly ordered a cup of coffee for the woman and a glass of soda for the little girl who had finally stopped crying after the frightening ordeal! "No llores, nena! Nadie te va lastimar!" (Don't cry little one! No one is going to harm you!) she said calmly.

"How can I ever thank you for saving the life of my little girl?" the woman asked as she showed every sign of gratitude she could think of!

"Just take her home and love her!" Maripaz said almost sadly. "That's how you can thank me! I'm just happy that I was able to help out!" she said humbly.

The next morning Maripaz went out and bought copies of the newspapers that had carried the news of what had happened! Now more than ever, she was determined to make peace at home with her parents! What she had done had been a stroke of luck! The government used the incident as a public relations ploy to tell the people how the citizens of Bilbao had become tired of the crime wave, created by the growing numbers of ETA members. Maripaz's picture appeared in all the papers as well as her own account of what she had seen and done! For her, it had been easy! The Spanish government still had a tight control over the news media and would routinely expand any article that would show the Fascist government in its best light!

Mari was thrilled with all the attention! Today she decided that she would visit her parents, show them the news, and ask them for forgiveness! The truth was that she hated the one room pension where she had gone to live! Her appeal for money from the group to pay for the room had gone on deaf ears; and it was only when she threatened to tell the world what the ETA was planning to do that one of the leaders decided to provide her with barely enough money to pay for the one room flat! Today she was hoping that her luck would change and she would again be allowed to remain in her own room and live at home with her parents!

Soledad was also in tears as she read the newspapers and became aware of the heroics of her daughter! Nobody knew how much she had dreaded asking her own daughter to leave the house knowing that perhaps, she should not have been as forceful as she was! She also realized that the dismissal of her daughter from her house was against all of the established mores of Spanish culture; and by doing what she did, had not only been against her daughter but oddly enough, it had also gone against her own heritage! All of these things were playing on her mind when she heard the door open slowly! Soledad wiped her eyes and looked up to see her daughter standing in the doorway. She ran over to her mother, kissed her warmly and hugged her tightly! It felt good just to be in her mother's arms as she went over to her father and kissed him!

"Mari." her mother said, "You have no idea how much I was hoping that you would come home where you belong!"

"I'm sorry if I hurt you! I never wanted to hurt either one of you! I still feel that I owe you an explanation of why I joined the group and why I needed to do what I did to save the sheep from being stolen! I never thought that things would become so messy and that I would be forced into a blank wall with no way of getting out!"

"It doesn't matter any longer, child! I was hurt and angry, but I should have never asked you to leave! Come home, Mari. your father needs you and so do I!" her mother told her. Both women stood in the middle of the floor hugging each other, both promising never to hurt each other again! Then, in a typical Spanish greeting, her mother quickly told her that she seemed to thin and frail and probably hadn't eaten! Maripaz sat at the table while her mother was making her some food! It was a grand time after all, she thought as she opened up and read the newspaper!

"I suppose you already know what happened! I brought you some of the newspapers hoping that you would be proud of me!" she told her mother.

"I already know what you did and I admire you for having done what you did! When I told your father what was in the newspapers, I saw him beaming with a smile! The look of happiness was written all over his face! The only thing he told me was how very proud he was of his daughter! Honestly, Mari. he had me in tears as I saw him happier than I've seen him in a long time!"

"It doesn't matter, mother! What I did or didn't do is now in the past! I just missed being with you here at home, and you have no idea how badly I wanted to return!" she said.

It was the first comfortable evening Maripaz had spent in several weeks since leaving home! All of the comforts she had been accustomed to having were with her! It seemed strange how many things one takes for granted until they are lost, she thought! She promised herself that never again would she make her parents so unhappy that they would ask her to leave! This was her home, and this was where she really belonged! She would be happy even if it meant spending the rest of her life in this house where she had been born and raised! She walked downstairs and sat at the breakfast table with her parents as she always used to do! It was as if nothing had happened! There were together again as a family and this was where she belonged and wanted to stay!

She had just finished her first cup of strong black coffee when she heard a knock on the door! "I'll get it mother!" she said, confident that nothing important could possibly take place so early in the morning! There was a sudden gasp of surprise when she opened the door! There were two Guardia Civiles, dressed in their uniforms standing at the doorway! After announcing themselves, one of them asked her, "Es usted la Senorita Maripaz Romero?"

"Claro que si! Yo soy Maripaz Romero! Porque?" (Of course! I am Maripaz Romero, Why?)

"We have an order to place you under arrest! Please gather your things and come with us!" one of the Guardias told her.

"What????" she yelled. "But why? I have done nothing wrong! Why am I under arrest?" she asked, confused and bewildered that her good fortune was quickly fading away!

"One of the members of the ETA that was shot two days ago was still alive when he was taken to the hospital! He has identified you as being one of their leaders and is willing to testify against you in court!" the guard told her.

"That's nonsense!" she said angrily. "I was not with the group! As I recall I was sitting across from the bank at the Plaza! I was drinking coffee at the time of the assault! I'm quite certain that the waiter who served me will testify as to where I was at that time!"

"Ma'am! That is out of our jurisdiction and up to the Mariscal to decide! In the meantime, please gather your things and

come with us! We have several questions that we'll need to ask!"
he said, as she gathered up a few of her things and left the house
with one of the Guardia Civiles holding on to each arm!

Her mother was shocked as she watched her daughter
being led away as though she were a common criminal! She was
worried and confused not knowing what to think or who she could
go to for help! Her life during the past few days had been turned
upside down! There was a feeling of helplessness that crept over
her and there was nothing she could do! Unfortunately, she didn't
even know the name of a good attorney that she could go to for
help and ask him to represent her daughter! She hated the thought,
knowing that she was going to have to explain to her husband what
had just happened, knowing that he, too,was going to be angry
and confused! Worse of all, he was too ill to represent her in court
when it came time for her to face a military Mariscal!

Madrid

October is not the very best month of the year in Madrid!
There is generally an abundance of rainfall during the month and
the skies are overcast and gray as if to announce the arrival of
another winter! Andres was seated in his office feeling as gloomy
as the weather outside! It had not been a particularly good and
exciting day! He had managed to lose a case in court that he had
thought would be easily won with little effort! But, as it sometimes
happens, the judge simply refused to see things his way! The judge
had been a military man; and judges or Mariscals who came up
through the military ranks seldom see things in terms of being
right or wrong! For them, only the military version of the law is
important! To their way of thinking, the law was always beyond
being challenged!

In an attempt to elevate Spain into an equal status with
other European countries, General Franco had accomplished
great strides! He had been successful in improving the economic
posture of the country by finally creating an economy where
none had existed! He managed to put into play labor laws that
allowed workers not to work beyond forty hours per week! All
employers were compelled to compensate their employees with

at least two to four weeks vacation each year depending on the length of service! While copying some of the employee laws of other countries, he established that after two years of continuous employment with a company, an employer could not simply fire or discharge a person except for just cause. The Department of Labor, another invention of the Spanish government, was then empowered to hold a meeting or a hearing to discuss the reasons for termination! If the cause turned out to be invalid, the employee could not be terminated! It was General Franco's way of offering a guarantee that the employment was permanent! After so many years of both economic and political turmoil, the people were finally anxious to back their government and the new movements that it was offering. The only element of the government that didn't receive the overhaul that was badly needed was in the ara of the common and criminal laws! The existing laws that were still in use were the same laws used by the military; and no efforts were made to remedy, either the arguments or the punishments, many of which were much too severe for the acts performed while some others were much too lenient! As in other countries, when the elements of progress began to expand throughout the country the petty crimes began to increase in number! Franco soon issued a strict edict that controlled the way people were not only to act but also how they should dress! Public demonstrations of any kind were strictly forbidden, and a semi-martial law was established resulting in a curfew at midnight for all youngsters under the age of twenty! Anyone challenging these laws was subject to stiff jail sentences that far outweighed the committed crimes; another result of military jurisprudence! The consequences were feared among the young people while the older citizens were pleased with the implementation of the new edicts! One thing that it did was to curb violence and eliminate petty thefts of innocent citizens and small businesses everywhere!

Andres was not particularly happy with what Jose told him! He had received a set-back in court, and the fact that there was a lack of confidence with the Condessa and her daughter did little to improve the way he felt! After thinking things over, he had decided that there would be no point in continuing on with the case! The strange thing was that he had grown rather fond of young Jose; and, in many ways, he had been looking forward to defending him with his legal problems!

Ordinarily, when Paloma walked into the office he would stand up, shake her hand in greeting and engage in the usual small talk until both of them were prepared to discuss the problems at hand! Today, things had turned out differently! He was in no mood for small talk, and he was certain that she would sense his unhappiness as soon as she saw the look on his face! There was no point in prolonging the inevitable! Today, when Paloma arrived, he would make it a point to get the matter over with promptly so he could get on with other things that were far more important than defending a spoiled brat!

What young Jose had told him had been a blow to his ego as well as the professionalism that he always tried to maintain with his clients! Despite the way he was feeling, he had grown to look forward to her arrival, a hearty dinner and a bottle of good red wine! Paloma was always impeccably dressed, upbeat and happy! Her hair was always neatly combed and she always had the radiance of an aristocrat that was pleasant to the eye! Perhaps, separating himself from her would be a good thing after all! Since she had entered his life, he had little time in the evenings for anything else! He had begun not only to wait for her at night; but he actually liked her company and enjoyed being seen with her. It was always amazing how relaxed she always made him feel, but there had been troubling signs that their meetings were becoming more than simple friendship! They would begin by speaking about young Jose; but shortly, the conversation would change, and they would begin speaking about themselves! There was one thing they had in common; they were both lonely people! There was even a time when they had spoken about their loneliness. She had joked that since they were both lonely, perhaps they should be together! The comment had been said in jest; but he quickly skoffed at the idea by simply telling her that she was too much of an aristocrat and he, too much of a peasant! That comment had also been said jokingly; but he wanted to convey the thought that they were socially different and that any relationship between them would never survive! She had also returned a strange answer! She had said, with a smile on her face that always emitted a halo of light, that perhaps there was a chance! All he would need to do was to be a bit more of an aristocrat, and she would happily learn to come down to his level! It had been this last remark that had spoiled the mood of the evening! Instead of considering themselves as equals as he had done, she was considering herself of a social status that was superior to his! If this was really the way she felt; how, then, could there possibly be a middle ground that would allow them some room for compromise? He quickly changed the conversation after that exchange! He could see by the serious look on her face that she knew she had just made a terrible mistake that was unforgivable!

He was thinking over what had happened when his thoughts were disturbed by the ringing of the telephone in the other office! He did his best not to smile as he was listening to Herr Otto speaking to someone that he obviously didn't like! "Ja....ja...ja! But...but of course I hear you! Vat! you think me deaf? I am not deaf and I can hear you.....besides, you speak too loud!!" he was saying to someone that was annoying the Hell out of him! "Okay.... okay....okay!! Just you vait! I vill go ask if he is in and if he vants to speak on the telephone! Yes....yes....of course, I already told you I hear you very well! Now for once, you lissen to me and I go see if he is in the office and vants to speak mit you!" Andres was still shaking his head and smiling when Herr Otto walked into his office and said, in an angry tone of voice, to speak on the telephone because the old woman was becoming very annoying and he was getting angry!

"Bueno! Habla el Licenciado Torres! Con quien tengo el gusto de hablar?" he asked. (Hello! This is attorney Torres! Who am I speaking to!)

"This is la Condessa de Romanones!" she said appearing to be annoyed." Are you the person who is punishing my grandson by making him clean your office?"

"Yes, I am!" he answered, trying hard not to show that he too was annoyed that she had considered the matter so important that she needed to become involved in something that was really none of her business! "Let me remind you that what I did, I considered it to be the best thing to do for the youngster! I talked about this with his mother and she agreed with me!" The last thing he wanted to do was to appear condescending or apologetic!

"Oh yes, young man!! I know all about that! But never mind! I called because I wanted you to come here to dinner tomorrow! Now, before I give you the details, I want you to know that I will not take 'no' for an answer! Is that clear?" the old woman said.

"No! I'm afraid it isn't clear, Condessa! You see, I have another engagement tomorrow night and I won't be available!" he lied.

The Condessa remained silent for a few moments as if trying to select her words correctly. "Well...I'm afraid that you're simply going to have to break it! I want to speak to you and I want it to be private!" she ordered.

"That's the reason we have offices!" he answered. "Why don't you come here? I'll be happy to talk to you if I can be of help!"

"Listen to me...young man!! If I wanted your help, of course I would come to your office! What I need to tell you is private and there is no reason to go to your office! Now, suppose you break whatever engagement you have and do your good deed by granting an old woman her wish!" It was almost as though she was trying to make a joke of the conversation! "Whatever you do...don't bring that terrible old man with you! My goodness....he can hardly hear me when I am speaking!"

"Okay!" Andres said as he knew he was making a mistake! "Give me the details," he said smiling. "I'll be your guest for dinner!" He had second thoughts about giving in to her request, certain that Paloma had put her up to it! What the Hell, he thought! What did he have to lose? Anything that may have started between Paloma and him was in the very...very...early stages of development, and he had been successful in breaking away from her! He hung up the telephone, all the time shaking his head from side to side and laughing to himself! It certainly had all the expectations for an interesting night! Not favorable...perhaps! But certainly interesting!

Again, he found himself smiling! It suddenly occured to him that he had forgotten to ask the 'old bat' whether or not he should also rent a tuxedo for the occasion?

As he had imagined, the Condessa's house was spacious and elegant! It was located in a rather secluded section in the western part of Madrid that was known as "Millionaires row" ! Surprisingly, when he rang the doorbell on the enormously large wooden door, he had expected that it would be answered by a butler dressed in a formal attire; but, instead, the old woman opened the door herself and greeted him warmly! She led him into a large sunken living room, elegantly equipped with complete 18th century furniture and a deep pile rug that almost made him feel that he was walking on air. She quickly led him off to yet another smaller room that was off to one side, also filled with period furniture but considerably less ornate and more informal!

"Que te sirvo?" she asked graciously. (What can I serve you?)

"Un vino jerez, por favor!" he answered. (A sherry wine, please!)

She went over to a large oversized wall bar, opened up a new bottle of wine and poured two glasses. (Good, Andres said to himself! Only two glasses! This means the meeting is going to be private!) She sat next to him in a large oversized sofa that looked large enough to accomodate several people!

"I guess you're anxious to know why I summoned you here on such short notice!" she asked in the form of an introduction.

"The thought has crossed my mind!" he answered.

"Young man, if you don't mind, I am going to call you by your first name, Andres! You can call me Florencia!" she said.

"Florencia is a charming name!" he lied as she let out a mischievous smile.

"Oh, I'm quite sure that you and many others, including that horrible old man in your office, have called me worse names than that!" she said. They both laughed; but Andres clever enough not to agree or to disagree with anything she said.

"Tell me the truth! How much did you know about my late husband, the Count of Romanones?"

"Perhaps not nearly as much as I should have! I did know that he was well known and very influential! I also know that he had been a senior advisor to the three governments we had in Spain! Aside from that, I'm sorry to say that I knew very little about him!"

"Did you know that he was a staunch liberal during the time when the Monarchy and the Socialist government were in full control? Did you also know that he had the distinction of also being a senior advisor to the Franco govenment before he passed away?" she asked.

Andres had no idea where she was going with this conversation! The truth was that he really didn't care! As far as he was concerned, those days were gone and the Count....whatever his name was....was dead! "No! I'm sorry! I didn't know that! He must have been a remarkable person to fight off the powers that expressed altogether different ideas!" he said. (To himself, he muttered silently, either that...or a damned fool!)

"Oh, he was much more than that!" the Condessa told him. "As a staunch liberal he fought everybody for the human rights of Spaniards. Many of the other politicians would criticize him bitterly, but he was to become a savior in a world of losers! I don't know whether or not I should tell you this; but, in many ways, you remind me a great deal of him! When we first went to visit you, I realized that I had been impudent and stern! I deliberately wanted to be that way because I resented you for reminding me of my late husband! Then, came your manners, your respect, and honesty, always impeccable and sincere! That was exactly the way he was! God, you have no idea how much I searched for reasons to dislike you, but I couldn't! Then, Paloma came and told me that she was very fond of you and that she had been attracted with you as a person! It made me happier than I wanted to be! I began seeing in you the possibility of continuing my husband's work! You are very different from most other attorneys whose only interest is in making more and more money! I have the strangest feeling that money means very little to you, am I correct?" He was amazed and flabbergasted that this old women, whom he didn't really like had decided to be so open and revealing with him! For a long while, he had no idea how he should answer her or even if he should give her an answer! "I see you became silent! That generally means that either I surprised you or else that I was wrong about you! Which is it?" she asked.

"I feel honored by the things you said! Yes, I suppose there is some truth in the things you told me! Condessa, I come from a poor Gallego family that struggled through the bad times and suffered a great deal by the Civil War! You are correct! Money was never really important to us; because, quite simply, we never had any! My interest is primarily in how people are treated! That was the reason I chose to study law! There are many statutes in the books that are much too rigid and too military; these are the ones that need to be changed if only to protect the sanctity of human rights! But, unfortunately, that's another issue! I thought you simply didn't like me and that was why you wanted another attorney to handle Jose's case!"

"What???" she exclaimed. "Why in the dickens would I want another attorney when we already have you?" She seemed genuinely surprised that he had raised a question that she was not prepared for!

"I guess we can blame it on the innocence of youth! Jose had told me that Paloma and you were searching for another attorney! That was why I asked to be removed from the case! After all, if you had no faith in me, why should I waste either your time or your money!"

"What Jose told you, took place before we met you! Tell me the truth! Was that the real reason why you told Paloma that you wanted to drop the case?" she asked.

"Yes, it was! I thought that perhaps another attorney with a different persepctive and with more experience might be of more help!"

"There you go again!! Damn you! Why can't you just be like any other attorney? I can see why Paloma has fallen in love with you!" she told him. He was aware that Paloma and he had become quite close; and he rather enjoyed the feeling that there was finally a woman in his life that seemed to like him for the way he was! Still, hearing about love from the lips of the old woman had come as a surprise! The truth was that even though they had dinner together nearly every night, the serious subject of a steady relationship had never been discussed! There was a look of concern and sadness written on her face when he suggested that perhaps they should not see each other anymore!

"....honestly.....I...had...no...idea!"

"Of course not!" she interrupted. "You wouldn't know love if it hit you over the head! What's the matter with you, young man? Don't you know anything at all about women? The more they argue with you, the more they like you! I know all about her seeing you every night and she told me about your plans and also about Jose! Tell me the truth! Didn't you get tired of such a boring conversation? If you were my suitor, I would have slammed the door in your face for being so stupid!" For the first time, he was smiling while he listened to this woman explain to him about women! It almost seemed that she had been mocking him while at the same time, she was telling him of his weaknesses!

"There was someone I became fond of when I was at school! I got to like her a great deal, that is, until she walked out on me! That was the end and I swore to myself that I would never be hurt again!"

"If you liked her so much, why didn't you go after her? Wasn't she worth it?" she asked almost as though she were scolding him for something he either did or something that he failed to do! He didn't know which it was!

"She went home to Bilbao and she never gave me her address!" he answered almost as though he was apologizing.

"And tell me, young man! What are your thoughts about Paloma? Did you simply shut the door in her face when you told her you wanted out of the case, or were you kind when you broke up the relationship?

"I like Paloma very much! I find her extremely interesting and exciting! I also think she is very beautiful! But Condessa, you know as well as I! I am not nor can I ever be of equal social status!"

"Ah, so that was it! You couldn't stand being the suitor of an aristocrat, is that it?"

"Something like that!" he answered. "I had been hurt once before and I had no desire to go through that ordeal again!" For some unknown reason, he felt comfortable, more than he thought he would, sharing some of his moments with this elderly woman!

"Well, let's go on to something else! You have started to make me angry all over again!" she said with a smile. "What did you do with that spoiled brat of a grandson? He broke your chair but you refused to accept payment! Then, you decide to take him under your wing! Next thing you know, he decides to settle down and he isn't spoiled anymore! Then, he come to me and asks how long does it take for him to become an attorney? It's all because he has decided to practice law exactly the way he sees the 'wonderful' Licenciado do in his office! He told me that he wants to be exactly like you! Do you have any idea how much he has grown to admire you? In a short period of time young man, you have caused chaos to my entire family!" He saw that she was still smiling, and he found her to be easy to speak to!

"Forgive me, Condessa! I never wanted to do that! How can I redeem myself!" he asked mockingly.

"To begin with, you can start by allowing me to take your arm when we go to dinner! I also think that you had better redeem yourself to Paloma and Jose! They are the ones who have been hurt by the news that you were getting off the case!" Suddenly, she got up from her chair, placed her arm inside his as she guided him to the table. "During the meal, I want you to explain to me just how you plan to defend my grandson! Since we are at the table, I think I'd better call Paloma down to join us, do you mind?"

She was certainly a sly old woman but he marvelled at her honesty! She was sincere and direct! There were times when she would be quite flattering; and, at other times, she had the ability of making you feel like a fool without your being aware of what was happening. It had been his first dinner invitation at the home of an aristocrat and things had started off rather well! He took his place next to her while Paloma sat down next to him! Her greeting was guarded but proper while he stood up, took hold of her hand and kissed it gently while staring into her large dark eyes! "I'm very happy to see you again!" he said politely but with honesty. She flashed him a smile as she saw in him a great deal of sincerity that she hadn't noticed before!

"Now, tell me Andres! How would you like us to begin our meal with a bottle of expensive, Rothschild Red wine, Vintage 1906?" the old woman asked! Just then, Paloma interrupted her mother!

"Mother, I think that our guest would much prefer a stiff Duque de Alba, Cognac, followed by a simpe bottle or Marque de Riscal or Sangre de Toro!" she told her mother, glancing over at Andres.

"Good! Now I know I like you! Actually, I prefer Cognac myself! It seems to settle my nerves! I prefer a bottle of simple red Spanish wine over that sour red wine that is supposed to be wonderful because it was bottled a long time ago! Believe it or not! That is precisely what the Conde de Romanones would have done if he were eating with us!" she said.

He had no idea if she was simply trying to impress him with her simplicity or if there was a hidden message! Could it be that she was trying to show him that even aristocrats are not above drinking simple drinks if it pleases their palate? The butler walked in and poured the dark Cognac into their brandy goblets! Andres felt a bit uncomfortable so he decided to keep his eye on Paloma and on what she was doing! This would be a sign for him to follow! All of a sudden, the Condessa raised her goblet into the air and offered a toast! "Para ti, Alvaro! Mi corazon y mi vida! "(To you, Alvaro! My heart and my life!) If Andres was waiting for her to take s tiny sip of the strong cognac, but he was completely surprised! She gulped down the entire contents of her glass in one quick swallow, stopping only long enough to smack together her lips before asking the waiting butler to pour her another which she then swallowed into much smaller sips as did Andres and Paloma!

"This was always something that was private between my husband and me!" she explained. "When he was alive, he also was fond of Duque de Alba! Every night we would have a drink together and toast each other! Our little secret was that the first drink had to be gulped down before ordering a refill! I still do it every time I drink Duque de Alba!" Andres was still surprised at what he had learned from this elderly woman and by her ability to gulp down a reasonable portion of the strong liquid as if it were water! "I guess this is also something else that you and he had in common!" she said, almost as an after thought!

"Now before we get overly sentimental, I'd like you to explain your strategy for defending Jose to Paloma and me!" she asked.

Andres thought about an answer for several moments! It was just like her to spring a complex question at him without any warning! Fortunately, he had done some earlier research and actually he did have a plan put together that he could discuss! "As I see it, we have two options that we can follow! The first option is a bit more conservative! We can enter a plea of guilty for Jose and then plead to the Mariscal to reduce his sentence, offering of course, to make full restitution to the owner of the store! I've already discussed these things with Paoloma!" he told her.

"I take it by the lack of enthusiasm that you don't really care for this option! Frankly, neither do I" the old woman told him. "Now, suppose you explain the second option!"

"You're right! I don't particularly care for that option because it still attaches a criminal record to a youngster that will be with him for the rest of his life! As for the second option, I have found in some of the older law books that there was once a set of laws that were directed toward children. It was designed to protect the rights of youngster who may have committed some childhood pranks where nobody was seriously injured! This group of laws were called, 'La Doctrina de Fastidios Atractivos' (Doctrine of Attractive Nuisances). These laws were intended to protect young people, especially in those case where the owner of the nuisance may have been either negligent or careless! I have also learned that these same laws are in effect in most of the European countries and were also in existance here in Spain until the Civil War when everything was changed! If I am successful in resurrecting these laws again, it could be that Jose will walk away with a clean record and without any punishment!" he explained as he eyed the face of the Condessa who was carefully listening to every word.

"What do you think are your chances of winning?" she asked.

"I don't know! But let me be honest from the start! Many of these laws have not been used in Spain for many years. I haven't any idea how they would be received if I were to introduce them again! I can only say that the other countries of Europe have these laws in operation. What the law says, in fact, is that if an owner of an object that, because of its nature, may be considered to attract a youngster, is left unprotected, the child cannot be held liable for being drawn to that object because he has been attracted to it!"

"Tell me more!" she insisted.

"I have already spoken to the other two boys! Their story was that the cash box was opened and left unguarded when Jose reached in and removed some of the money! The owner had apparently left the cash box unlocked when he left to go to the men's room, knowing that there were youngsters inside the store who were mulling around the area where the box was located. My argument would be that the cash box became an attractive nuisance! Nothing would have happened had the owner been more careful and locked the box before leaving it unattended!"

"Your argument sounds reasonable!" the elder woman said. "What do you think Paloma?"

"Jose has faith in Andres, mother! I think that whatever he suggests would be fine with him!" she answered.

"Andres, there is yet another question that needs to be asked! What happens if we lose?" the elderly woman asked.

"If we lose, we can always return to the first option! That option is always available to us in any appeal!" he replied.

"Speaking to you has made me feel much better! I think that what you have just said is precisely the way my husband would have thought! He was such a fighter and would never give in to a cause if he thought it was unfair! In those ideas, I see him everytime you speak! Paloma, I heartily agree with your choice in having this young man represent Jose! My advice to you as your mother, is that you don't allow this young man to get out of your sight! If I were thirty years younger, who can say, I might decide to compete with you for him! Now, suppose we get on with the meal!

We have already taken up enough time speaking about serious issues, it is time to enjoy the food!" she said.

The meal had been excellently prepared and tasty but not nearly as extravagent as he had imagined! The steaks were certainly large, but he would have preferred a bowl of Caldo Gallego (Galician soup) just like that which his mother used to make! It had been a long time since he had eaten any of his mother's soup! When the dinner was over, Paloma placed her arm in his and led him on a stroll through the different walkways in between the vast display of flowers in every color and type as well as rows and rows of expensive green bushes! Each had been marked with a special tag indicating where the individual bush had been purchased! It was nothing short of a horticultural extravaganza that perhaps someone else would have enjoyed more than he did! In some ways it reminded him of Galicia where there were also many green spaces with trees and flowers that had been a part of his youth. Paloma led him to the direct center of a botannical site complete with a wooden gazebo that had been constructed on an elevated platform that offered a magnificent view of the city of Madrid after the sun went down! "Wow!" he told her. "This is quite a view!" he told her as he looked down upon the city with its massive display of lights.

"I get the feeling that you aren't really very enthusiastic with what you see! Am I correct"? she asked.

"It's not that I am not being enthusiastic, Paloma! I am seeing things that I have never seen before! You already know my background, and it is not exactly filled with as much affluence as you people enjoy! My folks are simple people who had a simple life! I doubt that they even know that there is such beauty in this country!"

"Is that what is bothering you? Andres, are you being so threatened by our social status that you are actually afraid that you might learn to like it?" she asked. trying to goad him into yet another serious discussion that she felt would come up several times again in the future.

"I guess I am a bit intimidated! Wouldn't you be if the cards were reversed? It isn't that I am afraid, it's just that it is something

I never had before nor am I accustomed to having! I am also not quite sure how it might change my life if I were to have it? Am I making myself clear to you, or is it just nonsense?" he asked.

"I don't know! Only you can answer that one! But, I do know this! You thought that my mother disliked you, and you were wrong! She loves you! She thinks you are exactly like my father was in many ways! There are no rules that say that you cannot be both, an aristocrat as well as a scholar!"

"Paloma, what are you trying to say? Are you asking me, would I be happy with this arrangement? I really don't know!"

"I am saying that yes, I do care about you! I have cared about you from the first time I met you! Nothing would please me more than to make you a part of my life! I already know that I need to learn more about you as I suppose you would want to know about me! I also know that Jose would be pleased to have you as a father! He has a lot of respect for you! I can only tell you that these past few days when we didn't have dinner together, I felt lonely and I did miss you terribly! I don't want to feel that way again!" she said.

All of a sudden, this pleasant interlude had become much more complicated than he had thought! In truth, he had also missed their little get-togethers at night! It had been a refreshing departure away from the world of daily problems; and, yes, he had missed her! Unfortunately, he was not quite sure whether or not he could accept what was being offered to him! He still considered himself a simple lawyer from a simple town and playing games of law in a large city! His work was his life and it would always be! Would he ever be able to compromise what he had always been for the benefits that were suddenly being offered to him? He just didn't know!

"Paloma, I do care about you! For whatever it's worth, I did miss you! But, my work is my life and I'm not sure that I can handle both! Many of the cases that I take are those of simple people doing simple things that sometimes go wrong! I'm not quite sure how I would handle being an attorney for people that are aristocrats who routinely expect to receive the most from the very best and at the highest prices! I can't tell whether or not it would make me happy!"

"Why can't you have both? You can have both your work and dedication and you can also have me and my family! Is that so hard for you to accept? Andres, I have enough love for both of us! For whatever it's worth, I can live in your life and be quite happy! All that I need is to have you by my side! I don't even want to make any demands of having you with me all the time! I am willing to take whatever parts of your life you are willing to share! It would make me happy, and it would make my mother ecstatic, knowing she had you for a son-in-law!" she said.

"Are you proposing marriage to me?" he asked.

"Yes!" she answered calmly. "Perhaps not yet, exactly! But yes, somewhere down the line when we both feel comfortable in each other's lives, there is nothing that would make me happier than to become your wife! You would be a very strong part of the famous Romanones family! Your association with the family would, of course, open many doors for you!" she told him.

"I suppose you're right! It would open many doors, but.... would it make me a better or a worse person? That's the question that worries me!"

Paloma noticed that during the time they had been speaking, her hands were still holding his and he had made no effort to remove them! The night was clear and cool and it allowed them to feel the intoxication of the cool autumn winds that intertwined with the fresh delicate aromas of the flowers all around them. The full moon had successfully blotted out the tiny specks of light from the stars. They were both silent and enjoying the magic of the night and enjoying each other in the splendor of the moment. Andres was reminded of her beauty and her elegance! It was certainly a night that was made for other things rather than to discuss their future together! Nobody needed to remind him of the advantages of being married to her! It would have opened an avenue for success that might never come again!Her face was only inches away as he felt her lips getting closer to his! In a sudden display of unity, charm, and womanly intuition that seemed to be urging her on! He went forward just a step, afraid that if he were

to go back, this moment might never come again! Suddenly, he felt
her cool lips on his as they kissed, slowly at first, then increasingly
more amorous as they became locked into a passion that was
overpowering and incontrollable! Slowly, he wrapped his arms
around her, drew her even closer, and kissed her passionately. It
was a moment he would never forget! The thought came back to his
mind of how far he had come since those long ago days at college
when he had felt someone else's lips on his! Those days were now
gone forever! No longer would he be the shy young man from
Galicia who knew nothing about life other than its unhappiness
and poverty. For the first time in his life, he had met someone who
was willing to share with him his dreams, his ambitions and his
determinations for a future that, if handled correctly, would aid
him in achieving all of the goals he had ever invisioned.This was
life at its best! For the first time he felt that the opportunity was
there within his grasp to have everything and anything he wanted
out of life!

They remained at the wooden gazebo for a long time;
each lost in the other's embrace! From the far side of the large
house, a single light was flickering from an upstairs bedroom. It
really didn't matter who was there! This was all a part of his new
life! Andres glanced upward toward the room with the light, but
there was no one watching! He embraced Paloma again and kised
her! The thought appeared as he wondered whether this was a
beginning or...would it become the beginning of the end? He had
come to this house as a professional man with a world of new ideas
that would change his life and, in some small way, perhhe could
also change the lives of Spaniards for years to come! This was his
chance to make a difference and he could not afford to allow it to
pass him by!

Upstairs in the lit bedroom, Andres never noticed the old
woman looking happily from behind a large set of elaborate drapes
eyeing carefully everything that was going on! They didn't see
her smiling at herself and humming an old traditional Spanish
tune, that she hadn't remembered in many years! "Ya va siendo
tiempo!" she said to no one in particular. (It's about time!) At last
she had succeeded in what she had set out to do! No one would

ever realize the countless times she had prayed at the grave of her husband that a man would come into Paloma's life! Hopefully, and if her husband was helping her from above, it would be someone that she would be able to train in her own way and in the ways of her departed husband! At last, she was pleased that this young man was showing signs of promise! With his own ideals he would fit in perfectly into finishing the work her husband had started before his death! Tonight she would be able to sleep peacefully knowing that her prayers had finally been answered. As a starter, she would first train him in the ways of affluence and aristocracy so that her husband's legend would continue! She felt reasonably confident that in a short matter of time. she would make him forget his poverty strickened past while he gravitated toward his new future as a member of the family.Only then, would the ideals that were started by her husband comtinue to grow and the proud name of the Conde de Romanones would continue for many years into the future!

CHAPTER 7

Bilbao

Soledad was crying when she saw the Guardia Civiles
escorting her daughter out of the house! There was a guard on
either side of Maripaz as they courteously helped her into a waiting
car for the trip to headquarters! She was at a loss for words as
to how she would tell her husband what had happened, knowing
that the news that their daughter had been arrested would be
devastating. Anything that happened concerning their daughter
had always been dealt with using extreme care since she knew that
her daughter had always been the apple of his eye! What was now
happening could certainly be kept away from him, nor would the
many other things that would probably surface now that she was
being accused of a crime. The fact that some of his sheep had been
missing had not gone unnoticed; but, Miguel always felt that some
poor family had stolen the and had used them for food! If that was
true, and he believed that it was, then, so be it! They had been lost
for a worthwhile cause! If the sheep had been stolen and sold for a
profit, he would certainly not be as charitable even though he knew
that in his present physical condition, he was much too ill to take
matters into his own hands and deal with what now seemed to be a
growing problem! On his visit to the ranch, he had seen the tears in
the enclosures and the thought that perhaps members of the newly
formed ETA may have been involved since other ranchers in the

area were making similar complaints! In some ways, he had given tacit approval to some of the motivations of the ETA; but the young people who were now in the group were no longer considered to be idealists as the older members had been. The young people who were now the members were nothing more than a bunch of hoodlums who stole and damaged good property just for the sake of stealing or for destruction! In his younger days as a Mariscal he would have known how to deal with the growing problem; but, now, things had changed! If he became too vocal there was a good chance that the thefts and destruction would get worse than it was!

Miguel knew that Soledad's temper had never diminished through the years! What he had learned while visiting the ranch could not be revealed to her for fear that she would be angry enough to take matters into her own hands and create more damage to the area! What he didn't realize was that many of the fears he had for Soledad had obviously been passed along to his daughter! In an effort of trying to do what was good, she had gotten mixed up with this group of criminals for which there was no exit for any members! A serious argument took place when Soledad told him what had happened! His first reaction was one of shock and disappointment that his daughter had gone against his wishes and had joined the violent group! He immediately stood up from his chair, a bit wobbly as he felt his legs beginning to shake, insisted that he wanted to visit her in jail!

"No, Miguel!" Soledad told him. "You are much too weak to visit her!"

"You have a choice," he told her calmly. "Either you take me to see my daughter or I'll go by myself!" Soledad knew very well that when he was determined to do something and announced his plans in a calm voice, he would do exactly what he said he would do! "Nothing is going to keep me away from seeing my daughter!" He reached over in a surprised show of both strength and speed, put on his outer coat, and after stopping for a brief coughing spell, walked out the door with Soledad following a step behind him!

The old jail with its musty odor or urine and decay quickly became reminiscent of the days when he had served as the

Mariscal! He walked up to an elderly man with a large mustache, dressed in a sloppy looking uniform and sporting the stripes of a sergeant on the sleeve of his jacket. The man was looking through a pile of papers on his desk when Miguel walked up to him. The sergeant looked up from his papers and said, "Si Senor!! En que le puedo servir?" (How can I help you?) The man had a robust build, but his approach was serious and professional! Good, Miguel said to himself! This approach would have been exactly what he would have demanded when he was the Mariscal!

"I have come to see my daughter, Maripaz Romero! I understand she has been brought here! I am her father and I'd like to learn the charges against her?" Miguel's tone of voice was calm and direct, but his mission was unmistakable! The sergeant looked at him and realized that this was not the type of man who could be easily dismissed with a quick wave of his hand! This man was articulate and forward, a no nonsense type that had probably been a professional at some point!

"Yes, sir!" the sergeant said. "We have her here! She is here for interrogation and debriefing! As far as I know she is being charged with attempting to overthrow the government, armed robbery, conspiracy to commit a criminal act, and for being a leader of the Basque movement, the ETA!" Normally, the sergeant would not have been as thorough, but this was not an ordinary man. His questions had been well taken; and as a father, he deserved a straight answer!

"Have any of these charges been proven?" Miguel asked.

"Some have and others have not! We did get a 'Boinha' that was taken from her! She admitted that it had been given to her by other members of the ETA! It's supposed to signify identification with the ETA!"

"So, a cotton 'Boinha' given to her as a gift makes her guilty of trying to overthrow the government of the Francisco Franco?" It was now his turn to sound sarcastic!

"I'm afraid I can't answer that, sir! We are holding her for more information! I understand that she will soon be moved to headquarters in Madrid! I'm sure that is where the trial will be held! I'm afraid that is all I can tell you!" the sergeant told him.

"Can you at least tell me if she has been allowed to consult with an attorney? It's my understanding that she is entitled to this! I also believe that you have no right to question her without an attorney being present! May I remind you that the procedures for interrogation are well defined by Codigo XVI, de las penas menales!" The mere fact that this elderly man, who looked ill seemed to know about the Codes covering interrogations, made it obvious that this was no ordinary citizen asking about his daughter! No, this man knew too damn much about the law!

"I don't know about that, sir! I'm sure that her rights under the law are being protected by the accusers! That's all I can tell you!" he explained.

"I'm afraid that isn't enough! You see, I once served as a Mariscal and I know what her rights are supposed to be! This is a woman that was recognized in all of the newspapers several days ago as being a heroine! You are telling me that she was trying to overthrow the government? I hardly find that feasable, don't you?" By the confused look on the sergeant's face, he could see that he had upset the sergeant! He had no idea what he should or should not be telling this knowledgeable parent who was obviously trying to protect his daughter! Still, the crimes she was being charged with were extremely serious; and whatever questions he had should be better handled by his superiors than by him!`

"Sir, I am a sergeant!" he said as he exhaled heavily showing that he really didn't want to continue the conversation for fear that he might say something that he shouldn't say! "I don't give out orders! Instead, I have my orders to carry out! All I know is that she is to be transferred within a few days to Madrid! As for the charges lodged against her, you'll have to speak to my superiors! They are the ones who can give you more answers!"

Miguel became suddenly nervous and found it hard to hide the way he was feeling! The thought of Maripaz being moved to Madrid was making him frantic!God alone knew when he would ever see her again! As a Mariscal, he knew only too well that once a person was found to be guilty, they would then be transferred to some unknown location to serve out their sentence! In many cases, he also knew from experience that many of these people would disappear from the face of the earth and would never be seen or heard from again! He could not allow this to happen to Maripaz, the love of his life! If only he were younger, like in the days gone by, he would know exactly what to do! In those days, the Raposo would have taken care of that situation! Unfortunately, those days were gone as was his strength, and there was really no place for him to turn to for help!

The sergeant led Soledad and Miguel back through the long, dark corridor to the smelly jail cell that he recognized only too well! Not very much had changed since the days when he assumed control of these situations. From a short distance away as he approached the cell, he saw Maripaz laying on the narrow bed as if she were sleeping. The first thing he noticed was that her hair was uncombed and she was now wearing the traditional blue and black uniform of a convict! The uniform was several sizes too large for her slim body! Her face was pale and thin, an indication that she had probably not eaten in several days. As soon as she heard them, she jumped off her narrow cot and began to cry!

"Poppy! Que haces aqui?" she asked speaking through a steady stream of tears.

"I came to see you, my love! I had to come! What happened and what did they do to you?" he asked.

"Nothing daddy! What they did I did to myself! I thought I was doing the right thing for everyone; instead, everything went wrong! Daddy, it's important that you know that I was never a leader in the ETA as they accused me of being! Yes, I was a member, and I told them so, but I was never a leader! I realize that the charges against me are serious and that perhaps, I may never see you again! I may just as well be dead!" she cried.

"Don't cry, Mari! There has to be something we can do! I'll go to one of the local lawyers and ask him for advice! In the meantime, I don't want you to speak to nor to say anything at all to anyone! Listen to me carefully! I don't want you to admit to anything other than the fact that you were simply a customer sitting at the Plaza when the robbery took place! You saw a crime being committed and you acted and did what you considered was the right thing to do! It's important that you stick to this story no matter what they ask you! Is that clear? I'll hire an attorney to come here and then we'll see what can be done! In the meantime, please, I don't want to see you crying! This isn't over yet!" he said reassuringly. To himself, he was silently wishing that he could be as sure of himself as he was trying to be with her! The charges against her were very serious; and he would need to find quickly a lawyer in Bilbao that not only was trustworthy, but also, one who had experience in handling these types of cases!

All of the ill feelings that Miguel and Soledad had exchanged when their daughter was arrested, needed to be ironed out! There was too much to do to waste their time arguing over what should or should not have been! Whatever had happened, happened! As a Mariscal he knew that in these situations it was necessary to buy the best legal advice what was available! He had searched high and low, asking everyone he knew in the city hoping for the name of a good attorney who could be trusted to represent Maripaz! Time was critical before she was transferred to Madrid! He needed to get help quickly! Maybe he should have had some doubts about her activities, but, as a father, he was thoroughly convinced that his daughter was completely innocent of the charges! His only hope was that the publicity she had received when saving the life of a youngster would work in her favor at the trial. Both Soledad and he had visited the offices of more than fifteen attorneys that were supposedly qualified and had been recommended! Unfortunately, none of them had enough expertise in this phase of the law that was going to be required. The new pattern of Civil Law of Spain was in an infancy stage! The rule of laws in existance were those governing bodies under a military tribunal; and there were few attorneys willing to take such a case, despite the promise of handsome fees that would be charged. This area of law was relatively new, and there was still an abundance of existing laws under a military program that many of the available attorneys wanted to evade! Miguel started to hate himself for having allowed his illnesses to take control of his prior behavior, knowing that there had been a time when he would have been far more useful!

"Miguel," Soledad asked. "Que vamos hacer?" (What are we to do?) "We need to do something but no one wants to take this case!"

"I wish I knew!" he answered. "I think she may have a chance if she tells them only what I asked her to do and not to admit anything! If nothing else, it should give us some valuable time in which to find help from other attorneys! Many of the ones we spoke to were hardly capable of defending an animal! I can't afford to put her under their care!" he answered.

In a strange twist of fate, he started to notice that despite his illnesses, the weather had improved and he was starting to feel stronger than he had for a long time! Some of the physical problems had improved and even the coughing spasms that had barely allowed him to breathe seemed to get better as time went on! The only thing that was constantly on his mind was that perhaps he should consider defending his own daughter! He also knew that doing so would have produced the other old saying, 'that he who tried to defend himself usually discovers that he had a fool for a client!' How would he feel if he did defend his daughter and the decision did not go in his favor? It would prey on his mind for the rest of his life, knowing that he had been removed from the matters of law to expect to be effective! No, Mari deserved better! Also on his mind was that, should he chose to defend his daughter, he would need to go to Madrid! What would happen if his past was exposed and the exposure worked against him in court? The courts in Madrid were much more harsh and the punishments more severe than those given out by the courts in Bilbao! The magistrates working the courts of Madrid were professionals! Most of them had also been appointed by Franco, just as he had been before falling out of grace! In any of them were to uncover his past secrets, his past would be used not only to get a conviction on Mari; but, since he had been forbidden from going to the capital city, they could also pursue charges on him as well! The down side was that he knew of no attorneys in Madrid that he could go to for help! After reviewing the qualifications of an attorney in Bilbao that had been recommended to him by a friend, he found out that he had done some work in similar cases where an accused had been charged with attempting to overthrow the government! True, his track record on handling these cases was not very good, but it was the only glimmer of hope he could cling to. After speaking to Licenciado Martinez, he realized that man was much older than he preferred and his approach left a great deal to be desired. His only suggestion was for Mari to plead guilty to all the charges against her and then ask the court to consider clemency on the grounds that her parents were both ill and she was needed at home! Miguel was still reminded of how often he had listened to the same defenses; and, in each case, he had disregarded the clemency defense and had convicted the defendant anyway!

"We can't use that defense!" he said. "There isn't a Mariscal that will accept that testimony! It would be nothing more than a lame excuse that has been too frequently used to be effective!"

"But Mister Romero!" the attorney said, "You must realize that your daughter is indeed guilty of the charges! There is little, if anything, that can be done! Besides, everyone knows that the government is anxiously trying to break up these gangs of hoodlums that are threatening our people!"

"She wasn't threatening our people when she was saving the little girl's life, was she?" he said showing signs of anger. "No, she was saving a child's life!The fact that she may or may not have been a member of the ETA, does not in itself, make her the leader of the group!"

"Yes, but remember, one of the group members that was injured in the shoot out identified her as being a leader! That, in itself, goes to positive identification and is certainly enough to convict her!" he explained.

The more he spoke to this dumb attorney, the angier he became! "Senor Martinez," Miguel finally said, "Tell me the truth! Do you or don't you believe in my daughter's innocence? That's what is important to me!"

"What I belive does not matter! What does matter is what the Mariscal will believe when he listens to the charges! You should know that as well as I since you were once a Mariscal!" the attorney answered.

"As I see it, the only chance we have of saving her is to get the charges dropped before it moves to Madrid! If we wait until then, I doubt that you or anyone else will be able to help her! Now, are you going to follow the defense I asked for or shall I look for another attorney?" Miguel asked. He could see by the look on the lawyer's face that he had been surprised and angered by his comments!

"I've already told you that there is little that we can do! If you want me to take on this case, it haas to be handled exactly as I've explained. We'll just need to take our chances in the sentencing phase and not with the actual trial! The decision is up to you! Unfortunately, your daughter was much more involved with the group than either of us would have preferred. I know that as a parent one always tries to find the best scenario that will produce the most favorable results whether or not they are true!"

"Very well, Mister Martinez! You allow me no other alternative! I will leave her defense in your hands and hope for the best!" He had grudgingly given in to the attorney, not satisified with what he said and wondering if he hadn't made a major mistake in hiring him. Now he felt a defeated man, and was already feeling that he would probably never see his daughter again. Miguel walked away, depressed and dejected, realizing that most probably his daughter would be found guilty of the crimes and would disappear after the trial was held! This had been a familiar pattern with other detainees that had been charged with smiliar crimes.

The laws in practice after the end of the Civil War had been those that were put into effect during the war! Most of the cases were not heard in civilian courts, but were being held in military tribunals! They were guided by the same details and penalties as if the defendents were still members of the military establishment! Miguel knew the practice of these tribunals was grossly unfair even before Maripaz had gotten into trouble. Many of them were much too severe and harsh! In the lower tribunals a total of four military officers would be convened. Most of them were of company grade while one field grade officer would serve as being in charge of the trial. Justice was almost always swift and severe, even in lessor crimes, and there were no avenues of appeal under any circumstances. In the higher tribunals, a panel of eight military officers would be convened and one field grade officer would be in charge. The down side was the fact that most of the officers had little, if any, knowledge of the law and were unable to ask any of the proper questions that would affect the guilt or the innocence of the accused. Because most of these cases were capital cases, many of them would be settled by the death penalty! Once the death penalty was applied there was one appeal that was allowed to these cases after the initial sentencing! Once again, the case would be heard by a panel of officers, who, like most of the others, knew little about legal proceedings. It was against this background that General Francisco Franco boasted to the world about social reforms that he promised would serve as a model for the other European countries!

One other critical observation was in effect! Since most law students and scholars realized that the application of a logical system for legal behavior was non-existent! There was no incentive for incoming law students to practice, as a specialty legal reforms, knowing that the rewards were few because most of the defendents were unable to pay for their defenses. The income derived from defending serious crimes against the state was mainly non-existant! There were few lawyers who were willing to defend a case, especially if the defendent was accused of a serious crime such as the overthrow of the government or the willfull and deliberate destruction of government property! Every day the newspapers would routinely list the crimes that had been committed by people, some because of necessity, and some out of mischief. The federal government had announced an active determination to eliminate the uprising ETA before they became strong enough to commit more serious crimes!

Miguel, because of his experience, knew how the game was played only too well! Since most of the cases were open and shut, any hopes of receiving favorable treatment would depend on a few stacks of pesetas being handed over secretly to the officer in charge. If he had any hopes of succeeding, he would need to play the game! During the times when he had served as a Mariscal, lawyers would often approach him and would offer him 'regalos' or gifts, all of which were nothing less than bribes that were forbidden by the government, but which were accepted quite frequently. He still remembered how he had despised the use of bribes, believing that it defamed the system of government. Now his own daughter had been caught up in a similar situation; and, he, as a father, was hoping it might be possible to bribe the Mariscal that would be assigned to this case? Because the use of any bribes was strictly forbidden, the lawyer would need to apply special caution in approaching this matter! The amount of money was unimportant! He was independently wealthy and could well afford it! The use of bribes might have worked had it not been that any crimes assigned to a Mariscal were much too serious to be susceptible to the use of bribes! The only thing left for him to do was to casually mention this alternative to the lawyer; and let him work out the details as to how to exchange the money successfully, even if there was some doubt that it could be arranged!

"I can probably approach someone sitting on the panel; but, I'm sure you realize, these matters are veru delicate and require a great deal of care and diplomacy!" the lawyer explained.

"I do realize that! It is, however, a possibility that needs to be explored! It cannot be offered once my daughter is taken to Madrid! The Mariscales there are professional who earn their money legally! They could be offended if it is offered in the capital city!" Miguel explained.

"I'll certainly take the matter under consideration and see what can be done!" was the reply. "If it can be arranged, I'll notify you of the details! I'll probably need to use the services of a third party if an arrangement can be made!"

"I'll wait for your answer! Please, don't wait too long! I don't know when she'll be moved to Madrid and it needs to be done here in Bilbao!"

"I'll see what I can do!" the lawyer answered.

Just by listening to his tone of voice, Miguel knew that there was no reason to be optimistic that such an arrangment could be made! He began to hate himself for what he had offered knowing that he was now going against his own principals! Unfortunately, this was his only daughter and there was little

more that he could do! The only alternative that remained was
to hope that Maripaz could offer the investigating authorities
enough information about the group and would permit the Federal
government to make large scale arrests hoping to break up
whatever remained of their group!

Miguel was suffering mixed feelings of distress and anger
when he arrived home! Soledad had been kept busy doing her
house chores, and waited silently for him to say something that
sounded encouraging when he walked in! As soon as she saw the
disgusted look on his face, she knew better than to ask him any
questions! He was aware that this was little he could do except to
wait and hope for good news that the exchange had been arranged!
In an effort to begin a conversation she asked him if he wanted
something to eat! Miguel shook his head and without speaking, he
went upstairs to his room! It had been a trying day! Perhaps the
most trying day of his life! He hated himself for having allowed
his health to fail him at a time when he needed all of his strength!
There was the growing feeling of helplessness coming over him
realizing that there was nothing more he could do and no one else
to turn to for help! His own daughter had inadvertantly become a
criminal of the worse kind, trying to overthrow the government of
Spain! Just the mere sounds of those words were explosive as he
tried hard to figure out how things had come down to this level.
How could he, who had always been a staunch supporter of law
and order and had always obeyed the law, had allowed his daughter
to openly take part in a venture that was treasonous to the state?
It had been easy to blame his wife Soledad! After all, she was
the mother and had always supported her daughter in everything
she did! Could it be that her underground activities during the
Civil War had led to this disaster? Could it be that both mother
and daughter were too much alike? He felt helpless while he tried
desperately to find the cause that had made Maripaz embarass
the family in this remote part of the country which was filled
with proud citizens that had managed to survive the war and now
wanted nothing more than to live in peace with tis neighbors!

The only positive aspect that he had noticed during these
difficult times was that there had been a certain strength he

had felt! There were days when his coughing spells had nearly disappeared and he actually felt better than he had when passing the hours sitting on a chair. There had been times when he had felt like visitng the ranch and had spoken to some of the hired hands about the problems they had faced with the torn wire enclosures that resulted in the diminishing numbers of sheep he would be sending off to the market. The ranch foreman had already quit, opting for another job that paid a better wage than he was able to pay. When this happened, he had increased the pay of the remaining ranch hands; and, for the time being, they now seemed satisfied with what they were being paid! He had ordered their living quarters to be stocked with ample supply of food and beverages! Also, he had made sure that while not extravagent, the living quarters were kept comfortable! Each man had been given his own private section for the time when the work was finished. He also made sure that an ice-man would deliver large blocks of ice daily in order to keep the beverages cool! Still, he knew that the work was hard, the salaries were small, and the competition was strong! The rate of turnover was excessive as each rancher tried to outdo the others by offering better pay and better living conditions. Thse had been some of the chores that Mari had taken over when she arrived from school. She had fullfilled her responsibilities admirably; and, as a rsult, the turnover began to diminish as more and more ranchers from town appeared at their farm seeking employment. Still, now that she was gone, he needed a new ranch manager! He was the group leader that would issue assignments to the others daily. Mari had also been responsible for these assignments; but now that she was not there, those chores had been left to Soledad who was not nearly as efficient as his daughter had been!

Everyday Miguel would read about the assaults on banks and on other government buildings within the city of Bilbao! There were also reports of increased ETA activities in other parts of Spain that seemed more serious than those being reported in the Basque regions of the country. He had contacted the attorney several times but there had been no new information about the 'regalos' that were being offered. There was always the insistence that the problems needed to be worked out at precisely the right moment and only with an official that could be trusted. He had never known how he could possibly trust any official willing to take bribes, but those were the things that the lawyer was being paid to do! The disappointing news came several weeks later when he had gotten up one morning and went off to visit his daughter. The old jailer was still at his desk reading the morning newspaper when Miguel arrived. After all of the visits, he had gotten to know the elderly sergeant reasonably well! They had become friendly enough to engage in small talk before he would lead Miguel to the rear of the building where the jail cells were located. Today, however, there was no small talk as the jailer continued to read his newspaper for a long while after he arrived.

"What's the matter?" Miguel asked. "Aren't you speaking today?"

"Si, senor! Of course, I'm speaking; but, I'm afraid I have some bad news for you!" he answered.

"What bad news? I've already listened to enough bad news today! Give me some good news for a change!" he said, trying to sound humorous while, at the same time, he felt his own stomach tied up in knots without knowing what had happened!

"Your daughter is not in her cell! The federales came and took her away! They have moved her to Madrid!" he said calmly.

"Why??...Why did they do that? I had been told that she wouldn't be moved for several weeks! She is still being prepared by her attorney for trial! Isn't it unusual to remove a prisoner while they are being prepared for trial by their attorney?" he asked. The sergeant saw that Miguel was angry and nervous as he spoke. The handling of his daughter had been most unusual! Under normal conditions, it was customary for the investigators to wait until the defending attorney advised them that the accused was ready for trial before moving them away where they would be deprived of access!

"That's the way it is usually done, sir! Today they just came and took her away, probably to Madrid! I suppose your attorney will now need to go there to finish his work with her!" Miguel realized that he was getting nowhere with the man! He tried his best to remain calm but he could feel his anger rising as he tried not to let it show!

"Do you know where in Madrid she will probably be held?" he asked.

"No, sir! I have no idea! They didn't say anything to me! The only thing they said was for her to get her things together because she was being moved! They didn't say anything else nor did they tell me which jail she was going to !" he answered.

"Do you know whether or not her attorney was told about the move?"

"I don't know! I guess you'll need to contact him and find out! I know that he hasn't been here in several days!" the jailer told him.

"Several days???" Miguel exploded! "Just the other day he told me that things were looking good and that he might have some favorable information for me by the end of the week!" He was careful not to say anything about the 'regalos'! He had been led to believe that everything had been arranged and that a final contact would be made within a matter of days!

"I'm sorry, sir! I wish I could be more helpful! I'm only doing my job! Maybe you should contact your attorney; maybe he can give you more information!" he said as he continued to read his newspaper. Miguel was angry, depressed and bewildered! He had no idea what else he could do except to go home and be the provider of more bad news to Soledad!

Madrid

Andre's life had changed! Paloma and he went everywhere together; and, except for some of the normal functions that came with the 'social status' , he had begun to enjoy her company. Their moments of privacy were few and far between because the Condessa was always finding excuses so she could be with them. She had taken it upon herself to coach him into what he should or should not do in the presence of company! It soon occured to him that she was like two different people, one when she was among her social friends, and another, more down to earth, humorous and caring when she was alone with them! The formal functions he had been expected to attend had not been to his liking! It seemed rather boring to be in the company of many of her friends who only wanted to sit around and chat about their wealth and other mundane matters that had no meaning at all! There were so many other things of interest going on around them; yet, they were oblivious to the other social matters that required their attention if Spain was ever going to become a leader in the European community!

His value as an attorney became greatly enhanced when he was successful in defending young Jose! The old law he had used in the defense of the youngster was still on the books! He had been regarded in legal circles as a brilliant approach, especially among the other attorneys who had never bothered to consider the merits of the law when defending an accused! The Doctrine of Attractive Nuisances had been a Godsend! Before one of the major courts, he had argued that every other country had similar laws and had been used successfully when the occasion presented itself! If Spain ever hoped to prosper, it would need to rely on its children, he argued! After all, it was they who would eventually control the future of the country! If their activities should be curtailed because of a senseless act committed in their childhood, it would stain their overall character for the rest of their lives; and this simply was not fair!

In the case about Jose, he had spoken to the other young people who had been with him. It had been conceeded that young Jose had taken the money, but there was also some degree of negligence on the part of the store owner when he left the cash box unattended knowing that children were playing in the area. A simple act of common sense would have locked the cash box before leaving and would have avoided the problems that happened! Ordinarily, the court would have probably rejected his defense, but since young Jose was a member of an aristocratic family, they had been compelled to listen to his arguments knowing that every newspaper had reported the article about his arrest! It seemed logical to assume that the news media would also be interested in the resolution, something that a military court would

try to avoid! It would not be considered a good way to project a
program of fairness and sensitivity, especially if it meant sending
a youngster to jail for ten years! Adding to the defense was the
fact that restitution had been made and that there had been no
protracted injury to the owner! In other countries, he argued, such
a disposition would have hardly received any publicity, but this was
now modern Spain and publicity; especially if it was good, where
what the government had routinely insisted upon in matters of
social and general interest!

Paloma was pleased and happy with the verdict! For her,
it had been a personal accomplishment that her lover had been
acclaimed and almost elevated to the status of a hero for correcting
something that seemed unfair! The Condessa was among the
first to congratulate him when he arrived back to the large estate.
She quickly wrapped her arms around Andres and told the other
members of her company that this was indeed 'her boy'! She was
proud beyond words as she introduced him to her other friends
with an additional caveat that he would soon become her son-
in-law! This had been something that angered him but he was
much too polite to mention it to anyone! With every introduction
the Condessa would add that, while he was really not a member
of their social class, he was a commoner; but he had all of the
characteristics as if he had been born an aristocrat! Andres felt
threatened with this distinction! It almost seemed that she was
deliberately identifying him as a nobody, and that out of the
goodness of her heart, she had decided to make him a supreme
sacrifice by accepting him as an equal! The distinction was unfair
and he had to fight off the urge to tell her how offended he was!

Andres stood all alone in a corner of the large room,
sipping on a glass of expensive champagne, that he really didn't
like, while the others were mingling among their friends making
small talk and doing everything possible to impress one another! A
group of three newspaper reporters had gathered close to Andres
asking him all sorts of questions and eager to learn of his plans for
introducing other statutes that had been overlooked or forgotten!
These were the issues he had decided to express if the country was
to change from a miltary to a democratic rule! All of his replies

had been carefully guarded before replying! After all, he had no way of knowing where this sudden burst of notoriety would eventually lead! (In fact, he didn't even have an idea of where his life was going to lead!) Every once in a while, another of the Socialites would walk by, extend their hand as a courtesy, and wish him well! In the meantime, both Paloma and her mother were kept busy carousing and mingling with the other guests who had come to show their faces, if not to take part in drinking champagne and eating fresh Besuga Caviar with egg and onions, followed by a drink of expensive imported Vodka in order to remove themselves of the foul smelling fish odors from their breath!

The entire affair had lasted for only a few hours; but Andres was eager to abandon this display of artificiality and return back to his small office and Herr Otto, who would be anxious to listen to all of the details about the legal victory. Strangely enough, he was thinking that a simple glass of red Spanish wine and a few pieces of his mother's home made tortilla with plenty of chorizos would seem more appropriate in celebration of his victory! Andres bowed slowly as he had been taught to do as he said good-bye to most of the guests, telling them he had other important matters waiting for him at the office and he hated to leave such a lovely party! Paloma had noticed the displeasure on his face and silently wondered if perhaps her mother had not gone much too far in planning this celebration? She gave him a peck on the cheek which he promptly returned and said she would call him later in the day when she would have more free time in which to speak!

Andres felt relieved when he opened the door to his office and saw Herr Otto waiting for him! The old man was sitting at his desk reading the articles about his victory in court! He felt a sense of pride with his pupil and wondered if perhaps the time had come for him to leave the office and go out on his own! After all, it seemed likely that Andres' career would now sky rocket with his new fame and new acquaintences! There was no longer any need for him to be there! It was the case where the pupil had now become more proficient than the teacher!

"I have been reading in the newspapers that you are now on the way to the top....ja?" the old man asked.

"Not quite, Herr Otto! There is still much more for me to learn!" Andres answered.

"Vy??" he answered. "Vat has happened at the lunch...?"

"Nothing really! There were a few reporters who wanted to speak to me, that was all!" He wanted to keep away his own unhappiness and how bored he had felt being there in a house full of aristocrats!

"The newspaper says you vill soon marry that...that... woman...ja?" Herr Otto asked.

"Don't believe everything you read!" he said smiling. "Now, come on! Put on your coat and let's go to lunch!" he ordered.

"Vat?? I thought you had your lunch or dinner at the old woman's house! Didn't you eat?"

"To be truthful, I didn't eat very much! They served caviar and expensive champagne, and you know that I don't like either of them! Now, let's you and I go to our favorite place before it closes!" They walked down the street to a small tavern at the end of a small street where the two of them often would go for lunch! After sitting at their table, Andres ordered a bottle of red wine, a Spanish tortilla with onions and chorizos! The old man ordered the same thing! He noticed that Herr Otto seemed to be deep in thought today and was not himself! He was looking down at the table cloth as if he were trying to select his words carefully.

"Andres, I am happy you have come back here! There are some things you and I need to talk about!" Once again he watched as the old man's eyes went back to stare at the tablecloth!

"What is it, Herr Otto? Are you ill? What is it you want to say!" Andres asked thinking that maybe the old man was feeling ill.

"No, my son! I am not ill! I think that now you are on your way; and, maybe, it is time for me to return to the University and let you run the law office the way you want! I think it is time for me to get out of your life and let you do what you think is best! You have opened up the doors of Civil Laws that needed to be opened! This was what we have both been working for! You no longer need me, my son!" he said as Andres watched his eyes filling with tears.

"What are you talking about? Of course I need you! As we get busier with more clients, who else do I have to guide me in the right direction and call me a fool whenever I am wrong? Don't even think about the University; you are needed right here! Herr Otto, for the first time we are now making money with the hopes of making even more! We can't quit now! We have too much work to do!" Andres said as he watched the old man start to smile/

"And vat about that old lady? You know she doesn't like me and I don't like her! I get very nervous when she calls and I answer the telephone!"

"So?......Why should I be the only person that gets nervous? I have an idea! The next time she calls and gives you a hard time, just tell her to go to Hell and then hang up the telephone! Next time she will be more careful!"

"Pheeww!" the old man said, "You make my life very nervous! Ven I get nervous, I want to eat!" he replied.

"So hurry up and eat before your tortilla gets cold!"

No sonner had they reached the office when they heard the telephone ringing and it was Paloma calling for Andres! It was important that he remember the affair on Friday night that needed his attention! He had been hoping that she may have forgotten, but it was obvious that another gathering of the social clan was still on! The next question she asked him was even more surprising!

"Andres, if a woman has all of the requirments for meeting a criteria, why shouldn't she be admitted to a college of her choice?" she asked.

"Paloma, I've told you many times before, please don't ask me questions in riddles! Tell me what is on your mind!" he told her.

"One of my friends called me for advice! I told her that I would need to speak to you! It seems that she filled out an application to attend Medical School at the University of Madrid! Apparently she wants to be a doctor; but they wouldn't accept her application because she is a woman! I hardly think that's fair; do you?"she asked.

"I may not think it's fair! But, if those are the rules, then, those are the rules!" he answered.

"But that isn't fair! Why should only a man be accepted
for becoming a doctor?" There were many things that seemed
unfair! This was one of them! It was true that only a man could be
accepted to attend medical school! The School of Medicine was
opened to women, but only those that wanted to become nurses!
Nobody had given any acceptable reason why, but it was one of
those things that the government agreed because they had never
interfered!

"I don't know why that is, Paloma! Also, before you begin,
let me remind you that those things are out of my field! I happen
to feel that the women in this country are not treated equally as
the men; but those things are for women to fight for and not civil
attorney's!" he said. He could almost sense by the way that she had
presented the problem that since it had been one of her friends,
she had expected him to defend her position! This was an area of
inequality that he doubted he would be able to win!

"Isn't there anything you can do?" she asked as she was
showing signs of impatience.

"No! Those are matters of the University, not a violation
of law! The only people that can fight this bias is the University or
the government. I doubt very much that either of them wants to get
involved!"

"Very well then! If that's the way you feel, perhaps I'll take
up this matter in my own hands!" There was a tone of both anger
and determination. The tone of voice was almost as if she were
accusing him of being complacent or incompetent to handle this
slight problem!

"That's a good idea! You do that!" he answered. At this
point, he was anxious to finish the meal and get back to his office
to do some work he had left behind! Perhaps he might be able to
coax Herr Otto into buying another bottle of wine before they
started working.

Both men were swamped with telephone calls when he
returned to the office! Many of the calls were important! Some
were potential clients who had read about his success in the
newspapers and wanted him to take on whatever legal problems
they had! Many people had considered the juvenile codes a

complete nuisance that was completely unfair! Now that at last
a precedent had been established, many of the calls were from
people who were seeking to have sentences given to their children
commuted or reduced, especially if the youngster had been sent to
long jail sentences for minor crimes! The list of people who sought
his help was large! After reviewing some of the names of the
callers, he could see that many of them were considerably wealthy
and could well afford his services! It felt great, for the first time
since graduating from college, to have the opportunity that every
lawyer craves for! To be able to pick and choose only the clients he
wanted while discarding those that he felt he wouldn't be able to
win! He knew that it was a dream that few lawyers ever reached!
Many of the callers had told him that he had been recommended
by the Contessa! Whatever her reasons had been, he considered it
as just another way of improving his so-called social status that she
had mentioned on many occasions!

     With the growth of his legal practice, Herr Otto had now
become indispensable! Both men loved their work and neither had
much time for anything else! As time went by, he was now able
to screen whatever engagements had been given to him by the
Condessa! His work was continuing to pile, and he was enjoying a
docket full of court cases that remained to be heard! His practice
had grown so much that, in many cases, he was compelled to
recommend plea bargains, something he had despised since he
was in law school! Unfortunately, it had now become a necessary
evil if only to reduce his workload! Even Herr Otto had been
summoned and asked to defend cases in court, something he hadn't
done in years! In one way or another his name was mentioned
in the newspapers every day! Every case he defended suddenly
became newsworthy, especially those cases where he had gone
against the system and had come out the victor! Although he still
retained the small office where he and Herr Otto had started their
practice, he had suddenly begun to wear more expensive clothes!
Arguing against his better judgement, he had also talked himself
into buying a car, convincing himself that it was a necessary tool to
get him to court and to his office more quickly. There was a side of
him that told him that this had only been an excuse! The truth was

that he rather liked his new status and what he had become! Never during the climb to his success had he ever forgotten his parents, who were still struggling to make a life for themselves in Galicia! The amount of pesetas he had sent to them had grown and the amounts were now being sent several times each month allowing them to pay their bills! On one of his visits, he had tried to convince his father to give up the farm land and move to Madrid! Unfortunately, the suggestion had fallen on deaf ears as they chose to remain where they were! It no longer seemed to matter that the land had not been nearly as productive as it had once been! They no longer needed the few vegetables that the ground was grudgingly willing to offer! They now had enough money to buy those food items that were not produced; and some of what was produced made their way to other families who had not been nearly as fortunate!

His courtship with Paloma was ongoing as was an almost daily set of instructions given out by the Condessa while she continued on with the task of giving him an equal status! After several months had passed, there were even rumors being circulated in aristocratic circles that the young Andres Torres was being given careful consideration by the government for a Judicial appointment as a Judge in the Supreme Court of the country! The only apparent set back was that while he had served in the Spanish Army during the Korean war, he had never risen to the rank of officer! Being an officer in the Spanish Army was considered a requisite for being appointed as a Judge! Not that it mattered, he was certain that whatever requisites might be needed for such an appointment, they would be overcome through the manipulations of the Condessa! The strange thing was that he had grown to like and admire the feisty old woman! There had been times when he felt she had interfered entirely too much in his plans as well as his life! It was this interference that often made him wonder how his life would be if he were to marry Paloma? Would she always be planning his life or would she finally give them the space and privacy that every young couple wants and needs? The idea of having someone planning out his life had been new to him and it was doubtful that he would be able to stand this intrusion if it should happen!

The preparations for the wedding were now in the early stages! Paloma had explained to her mother and told her of her own plans for a smaller wedding! After a considerable discussion, it was decided that the Condessa would not hear of it! She insisted that the wedding needed to be held at the cathedral and that the guest list include at least five hundred people! Of course, it was almost mandatory that the wedding ceremony itself would be performed by the Cardinal! The Civil Ceremony would be conducted by one of the senior judges of the Supreme Court! What the Condessa considered as being moderate, Andres felt it to be overwhelming and wondered how his parents, from a simple area, would consider this extraganza the likes of which they had never seen before? Unknown to the Condessa, the idea was worrying him! His father would obviously feel out of place in such a gathering and it was understandable! In Galicia these types of weddings simply did not exist except perhaps in story books!

"Paloma, don't you think it might be wise to wait before making up a guest list? We haven't even set a date for the wedding!" he told her.

"The Contessa has given me instructions that she wants the wedding to be held shortly after Christmas! She wants to be certain that the excitement of Christmas is over and all of the attention can then be directed to our wedding!" she answered.

"I'm well aware of what she wants; but, what is it that you want? Don't you at least have any input for the wedding?" He was annoyed that it seemed like the old woman was directing all of the wedding plans that she should be made by Paloma and him!

"I don't understand why you are always criticizing mother! You know how important it is for her to always do what is proper and correct!"

"Correct for who? Is it for her or is it for us? First of all, I'm going to need to review all of my pending cases before setting a wedding date! Generally, the court likes to dismiss those cases that are carried over from the previous year! I doubt very much that we can get married so close to Christmas! From what I can tell, it seems that the months of February or March may be more convenient for me!"

"I'm going to need to discuss that with the Condessa! She seems to have her heart set on a January wedding!"

"Goddammit, Paloma! Don't you and I have any say to this? All I've listened to is your telling me that your mother says this and your mother says that! When am I going to listen to what you want, or perhaps better still, what it is that I want? I sometimes get the idea that your mother would prefer to have the wedding without having me being present!" he said as she could see that he was annoyed over the conversation!

"It isn't that, Andres! There are some.......rather......standards that people in our circle need to consider! It is expected of us and we would be gravely criticized if we should fail in fullfilling our obligations!" she tried to explain.

"My only obligations are to my clients!" he answered angrily. "They are the ones who need me and my services! All the rest is nothing more than window dressing! It is all an act to impress people that don't give a good damn whether you live or die! The only things they worry about is the type of caviar you will be serving and the name on the bottles of champagne you will be opening for their benefit! Do you really believe that I give a damn about these people? If that singles me out as being a non-conformist in the eyes of your friends, well, guess what? I don't really give a damn! Can you understand that?" She could see that he had become exasperated and completely annoyed by what she said! "I understand that I am a simple man! I come from a simple family who has never known what it is to be wealthy! Their wealth only came from what they did have, a great deal of love for everyone! I can't imagine my parents getting exposed to all the pomp that is being prepared! This is far above their level! In fact, I'm beginning to have my own doubts whether or not I can stand it!"

"Maybe you have forgotten that all of this pomp is going to be increasingly important when you are appointed a Superior Judge! You are going to need to show your gratitude as well as your status to all the right people if you ever expect them to appoint you!

"What???? You mean that I have to become an act so they can decide whether or not I passed my test?? Is that what status is all about? If it is, maybe you can tell the Condessa to forget about my appointment! I would prefer not to become a judge and yet still be my own person, than to be appointed a judge because somebody else has pulled the strings and now the marionette needs to do perform its dance! I think this entire matter is getting out of hand! Maybe we should hold off on the wedding plans until we have time to iron out our many differences!" he said as he stormed out of the house and went home! After all, he was going to be in court tomorrow! As far as he was concerned, the entire conversation had been nothing more than nonsense! It seemed odd the way everything had suddenly changed when they began to discuss the plans for the wedding. He did like Paloma; but he also felt that there were many times when she was much more enamoured with her social status than she was with her own happiness! It was no wonder that her young son, Jose, had been a spoiled brat! He had to wonder the type of man her husband had been? Had he been able to withstand the constant pressures of the Condessa? Was he just a simple 'yes-man' for everything she directed him to do? How would he ever be able to live that way and yet retain his own individuality? Perhaps he was right after all! The wedding should be put off! It occured to him that were many more things Paloma and he disagreed with than what they had in common! What bothered him the most was that he knew he owed his recognition to the Condessa, and it had been because of her that his own status had taken a turn for the better! Andres decided that what he would need to do was to have a long talk with the Condessa and suggest that the wedding be delayed for a few weeks or until he was able to rearrange his schedule! It was a small request; but it was one that she might accept as long as the circumstances were beyond his control, and the delay would not be any longer than a couple of weeks. He made a decision that tomorrow when he went to visit Paloma, he would ask to speak to the Condessa and tell her of his own plans for the wedding! He realized that she would probably be upset, but he felt that it was something that he needed to do, and the sooner the better!!

As his practice grew, so did the the work and time that was needed to handle the growing workload! Unfortunately, everything has its price, and as the demands of his practice grew the amount of available time to spend with Paloma began to decline. The social invitations continued to arrive weekly; but it seemed that he was much too preoccupied with his work to allow him time for the parties and social gatherings that he had always considered boring and meaningless! The few invitations he had accepted had been spent mulling around and making small talk with a few of the guests! In the meantime, he would be constantly looking at his wrist watch and he felt certain that nobody had seen him. The invitation he had received today had also contained a hand written message from Paloma telling him that it was imperative that he attend! There were no other explanations, but judging by the brief note, he was rather definite that it would be a function that he should not miss!

He took one last look at himself in the mirror before leaving! After all, any invitation that required the wearing of a black tuxedo had to be important and he had to make sure he looked his best for the occasion! They had no idea how much he always hated whenever he had to wear a tuxedo! They were always so uncomfortable that he often wondered why aristocrats had selected such uncomfortable clothes to wear in their spare time! One final look at his wrist watch told him that he was already running a bit late! Today's boring gathering was apparently being held in the large meeting room of one of the hotels in town! He had already explained to Paloma that it was necessary for him to complete a few things at the office and agreed to meet her at the hotel later! When he walked in, he was greeted by the usual crowd of people, men and women dressed in evening gowns and tuxedos, each trying to be the first person to grope a glass of cold champagne from the silver tray of a waiter dressed in a white jacket and wearing white gloves while he made his rounds drifting in and out of small groups offering a glass of champagne! Andres had not yet taken a glass of champagne when he realized that the orchestra that had been playing had suddenly stopped and the conductor signalled with the microphone that he had been asked to make a special announcement!

"Ladies and gentlemen, I have been asked by Her Highness, La Condessa de Romanones to make an announcement!" The crowd quickly became quiet, almost as if everyone was happy that there would be a pause so that the vulchers could take the time for another glass of champagne and for a refill from the table of the caviar and vodka! "I have been asked to announce the arrival of the next federal judge for this great country, our own Licenciado Andres Torres!" He said as he extended his hand to where Andres was standing amidst the polite applause of the black dinner jacket brigades! Andres walked up to the stage amidst handshakes and gentle pats on the back as if he were a conquering hero who had just arrived! For a few short moments, he felt proud that someone had taken the time to announce that he had been selected to appear as a judge in the highest court in the country! It was a secret ambition of his that had been nothing more than a dream; but now that it had happened, it no longer seemed nearly as important as he had envisioned it would be!

"I want to thank all of you, but, as far as I'm concerned, there has been no official announcment!" he said to the crowd of well wishers.

All of a sudden, there was a burst of activity where the Condessa had been standing! She had arrived all dressed up in a powder blue evening gown! She moved quickly as she made her way through the crowd and took the microphone away from the hands of the orchestra conductor! "The appointment has not yet been officially made; but, I can assure all of you that before the end of the week, my dear Andres will become a new judge!" she announced proudly almost as if she had received some secret information that the appointment was a done deal and it would soon be made official! There was another round of polite applause, this time a bit lighter than the last while the Condessa was assuring the crowd that she had everything under control!

"Now that you have met him, I want all of you to return to what you were doing! Enjoy the food and beverages and help me to introduce him to our very special people at this time!" Andres felt too embarassed to remain on the stage with the Condessa! Instead, he walked away from the microphone while another wave of well wishers came up to him, shook his hand and wished him well! Slowly, he made his way to where Paloma was watching; he took her by the arm, and began to dance with her as the music started to play!

"Why didn't you tell me this was going to happen!" he whispered as he moved closer to her so that he could whisper in her ear without being noticed.

"Isn't it wonderful, darling? Just think! You are about to be named a judge on the highest court of the land! Oh, it isn't yet definite, but my mother has arranged everything for your appointment! As soon as ti becomes official, we'll have another, much larger party that I'm sure you will enjoy!" she whispered quietly in his ear!

"Paloma, you won't like what I am about to tell you! I don't think I am quite ready to be a judge!" he said. There was something about his tone of voice that always surfaced whenever he was angry or upset! Although he always spoke calmly, he was always very decisive. She had learned to identify his voice and to know exactly what he was feeling! It had been a tactic he had learned in law school and he had used it successfully throughout his career, especially when he was arguing a case in court!

"That's nonsense, darling! I think you're ready and I know that mother feels the same way!"

Andres gave her a stern look but didn't answer! This entire charade had been nothing more than a preconceived gathering of vulchers; giving them a chance for a look at the commoner! Everyone knew that once he became a judge in the highest court of Spain, the time available for these affairs would be limited, lest he be accused of allowing himself to be used while making any decisions that might affect any of the group members!

It was a cold, rainy day when he received a telephone call from the office of the President Judge, asking him to appear in his chambers at nine o'clock the following morning! There were some disturbing thoughts thinking that this could be the day that had been selected by the Condessa for the formal swearing in ceremonies! Once again, they had allowed him little time to prepare an acceptance speech in the presence of what he knew would be a court room full of people! All of the other ten Superior Court judges would more than likely be in attendance, not to mention the large variety of newspaper reporters anxious to send their story off to their offices in time for the morning circulation! As he always did whenever he went into a court room, he was wearing the dark suit of a professional, freshly ironed white shirt and matching tie! It was a bit late when he finally arrived inside the Court House steps opening his umbrella and hoping it would shield him from a drenching downpour that was falling! A large gathering of reporters quickly encircled him stopping him from moving forward! Each of them was trying to get his attention, asking him the same questions over and over. Were the rumors true that he was about to become a judge? Had he given any thought to the notion that he would be the youngest judge to sit on the bench? There were also the more disturbing questions that he refused to answer! One of them being was it true that the Condessa de Romanones herself had been the person that had arranged for his quick elevation to the present post? Was it also true that he was about to marry the Condessa's daughter in the near future?

He was overwhelmed and bewildered by all the attention and he felt a little angry and annoyed realzing that his dark suit was getting wet and he was unable to go in out of the rain! There was no dodging this crowd of reporters who were only doing their job and looking for news! After all, anytime that anything happened to the aristocrats, it was always a major news story! Andres waved his hand and asked for silence as he went one step upward and faced the sea of reporters face to face! He didn't quite know how he should answer many of the questions, nor did he really know the reason why he had been summoned to the chambers of the President Judge at thyis time fo the morning! True, he did have his suspicions, but he also knew that it was a long way between suspicion and fact! Suppose there had been another reason for being called to the court house? He would have looked like a complete fool if he answered their questions incorrectly!

"Ladies and gentlemen!" he began acknowledging them graciously. He had been well trained in these matters and had also been taught how to confront an inquiring group of reporters. "I'll make a brief statement, after which I am expected to go 'in chambers'! It is true that I have been summoned by the Juez Supremo, but, I have been told absolutely nothing what this is about! I have no way of knowing why I was asked to come here! If you will now allow me to go inside, I promise to give you another statement when I leave!" he said.

Little by little the crowd began to step aside and a few reporters began making an opening, allowing him to enter the building! He ran up the slippery marble steps, closing the umbrella as he entered and leaving the large water fountain with all of the marble lions and tigers behind as he approached the large wooden door at the top of the spiral staircase! Once he was inside, he ran up another winding staircase to the top floor, returning the nod to some of the people that were nodding at him as he raced down the long hallway to the large room at the end! There was a large painted sign on the door that read simply, Juez Supremo! He paused for a moment not knowing whether or not he should barge in or knock first before entering and wait until he was called inside! He needed to make a quick decision! He quickly decided to knock on the door and wait to be asked to enter! The large, shiney brass fixture made an ugly sound, he thought, as he knocked gently and waited for an answer! "Come in!" A voice said from inside! Andres knocked again and waited hoping that someone would have the courtesy of coming to the door! After all, he knew it was normal protocol not to barge in on the Chief Judge! Those things were not supposed to happen! Andres opened the door slowly as a group of well-wishers immediately surrounded him shaking his hand and patting him on the shoulder! Paloma walked over to him, took him by the arm and led him to a large man, dressed in a black robe who was speaking with the Condessa!

"Your honor!" Paloma said as she interrupted the conversation between the Chief Justice and her mother! "May I present to you, Licenciado Andres Torres!" she said as the large man shook hands with the newest member of the court and draped his army around his shoulder!

"I'm honored to meet you!" Andres said graciously. It surprised even him that the words had come out automatically as if they had been implanted purposely so that they would come out at just the right moment!

Almost as if the program had been well rehearsed the Chief Judge told the others in the group. "Okay, now that we're all here, I think it is time to begin!" It had probably been intended as a courteous request, but everyone knew that when the request was made by the Chief Judge, it was no longer a request but an order! The other five judges, each dressed in a black robe, put down the glasses of champagne and walked out ceremoniously to the middle of the large room! It seemed interesting that the Condessa had remained at the side of the Chief Judge and had not moved away from him when he went out to the center of the room! The large man, made a motion with his hand for Andres to stand in front of him! He waited several moments while everyone took their place and Paloma handed the Chief Judge a large Bible from the top of one of the desks.

"Fellow Judges!" the head man said with a great deal of professionalism. "It gives me great pleasure to welcome into our court a new member who has distinguished himself by his work in the field of Civil Law! He has come to us highly recommended by Her Highness, La Condessa de Romanones! If you will bear with me a few moments, we can conclude our business and all of you can return to your refreshments!" he said as they all began to smile.

Andres glanced over at the Condessa, dressed in her evening formal attire and wearing a corsage of expensive orchids. He watched her signal to Paloma to go stand next to Andres, so that the court photographer would have a much better view of the entire group when he took the photographs which would later be distributed to the press! The Chief Judge cleared his throat several times as if he was about to make an important announcement or make a major speech; instead, while holding the Bible, he asked Andres to place his right hand on the large black book! Andres

still was showing a surprised look, knowing that these honors
did not come easy! It was obvious that the Condessa had been in
charge of the arrangements and the only thing that was expected of
him was to be certain that he didn't embarass her in front of these
gentlemen!

"Espera un momento, Senor Juez!" she said as she
motioned with her hands that something was not to her liking!
"Before you begin, I would like to have a photograph taken with
the new Judge and myself! I would then like to have another
photograph given out to the reporters, showing the new Judge
standing beside me, and also with you and Paloma in the picture!
After all, since he is going to become a part of the family, we may
as well take this opportunity of introducing him to the public!"
Once again, she was giving out the orders while everyone took
their positions and did as they were told. It seemed important to
the elderly woman that everyone was in place so that the Condessa
would have her photograph taken before the actual swearing in
ceremony!

So, that was it, Andres thought! It was but another charade
carefully orchestrated by the Condessa! He was feeling his face
getting flushed with anger! The more he thought about what was
happening and how he was being controlled, the more he felt that
anger was taking over control of his senses! It had been another
of many set-ups by the Condessa and yet demonstrative enough
so everyone knew that she was in control of this moment and of
his future! What angered him even more was when he saw that
Paloma was obediently doing everything the old woman asked her
to do! It was almost as if she had become the Grand Maitre'D of
one of her many household extravaganzas! The honor had been
great and would have been even greater and more meaningful
had it been awarded to him by virtue of his own merits! This was
not an honor! It was nothing more than a well rehearsed charade,
a payment that someone in higher circles needed to repay the
Condessa! This had nothing at all to do with him! He was nothing
more than a pawn as were all the others!

Andres waited until all of the photographs had been taken
before signalling to the Chief Judge that there was something he

wanted to say! "Your Honor," he began slowly. "I am honored by this appointment and I am grateful to you and to everyone here for allowing me these few moments before the ceremony!" The Judge was smiling as he looked at him then glanced over at the Condessa and nodded his head, obviously pleased with the way everything was turning out!

"Unfortunately," Andres blurted out in a move that surprised everyone. "I cannot go on with this charade! In my heart I know that I am not yet prepared to assume this great responsibility! For me to accept this challenge would be a great disservice to this court, and this is something it does not need nor deserve! Perhaps there will come a day during my lifetime when I will be worthy of this honor; but,unfortunately, this is not the day! I would there respectfully suggest that my name be removed from consideration and that this meeting be ended! Thank you, your Honor!" he said as he remained silent allowing everyone to know that this had been the end of his little speech! The other Judges began whispering among themselves, looking stunned and surprised, not quite knowing what to say! Paloma stood facing him, her hand firmly placed over her mouth, stunned by what he had done!

"Andres," she finally said loud enough for everyone to hear. "What are you doing? Have you any idea how hard my mother has worked in convincing the court to make this appointment? How could you do this to her?" she said as she started to cry.

"Ay que verguenza!! Dios Mio!!! Dios Mio!!" the old woman shouted also stunned beyond words. "Que verguenza!! Paloma, quiero que te despidas de este cabron! Jamas lo quiero very en mi casa!!" she said angrily. "How embarassing! Paloma, I want you to get rid of this bastard! I never again want to see him in my house!) "After everything I did for you, this is the way you repay me for my kindness? By embarassing me in front of my friends? Have you any idea at all the many times that you have embarassed me and yet I still wanted to believe that I could mold you into becoming one of us? What have you done to me?" she said. Andres saw that the old woman was crying hysterically and yelling at the same time while the Chief Judge was already starting to slowly remove his black robe!

There was no point in remaining, Andres said to himself! Things were obviously not quieting down and there was still much work that needed his attention at the office. It would have been easy, if not tempting, to get into a shouting match with the Condessa; but he knew that she could be relentless and it would continue as long as he remained there.The best thing for everyone, was for him to leave the court house and return to his office! "Are you coming, Paloma? Or are you staying here?" he asked. Paloma was still crying and didn't answer! When she didn't make any move toward him, he turned around and started walking toward the door! Just as he approached the door, he heard a screeching yell that startled him! Andres turned around just in time as the Condessa was holding her hand over her heart! He could see that her face had become contorted and she was obviously in severe pain! He rushed back to her just moments before he watched her body slowly slump to the floor, her hand still clutched over her heart! All of the others in the group ran to her side! The Chief Judge bent down over the Condessa's body and started to speak to her trying in vain to get her to respond, but there was no answer! He tried again while Paloma was gently stroking her mother's face, pleading with her mother to open her eyes! Andres walked over to the old woman and gently placed his hand at the side of his neck! His hand remained there for several moments as he watched her face become ashen and unresponsive! After several moments he nodded his head from side to side while the others looked in horror and shocked at what was happening before their eyes!

"Gentlemen!" Andres said calmly without raising his voice, "I'm sorry to say that La Condessa de Romanes is dead!" he told them sending a steady stream of shock waves to everyone inside the court house! There was really no point in leaving now! It would have only been a discourtesy to the Condessa; and, whatever their differences, she deserved his respect if nothing else! Besides, he already knew that he was going to be summoned to make funeral arrangements! Paloma was much too shocked to speak and he knew that she was going to need all the help she could get now that her Mother was no longer with her!!

CHAPTER 8

Bilbao

Miguel, an early riser, was up long before Soledad began making their breakfast! It was a regular ritual that he looked forward to each morning but these had not been normal times! Never before had there been so many arguments in the household between them and it had taken its toll on the happiness they once shared! There was a cool atmosphere between them where none had ever been! In the typical Spanish tradition, Miguel had argued that whatever went wrong inside the house was always the woman's fault! It had to be the product of something his wife had done or what she had failed to do as a wife and a mother! In some ways he felt that had Soledad given Maripaz more supervision, perhaps nothing would have happened! It didn't matter when articles in the newspaper repeatedly made mention that the present day youth were facing difficult times! Many of these young people still lived with their families who were poor and had little money to spend on items that were not essential! What neither he nor Soledad had stopped to consider was that what Mari had done, had been with good intentions! Farming and the grazing of sheep were the back bone of the community; and in order to find out what the ETA was doing to the ranchers, the only practical way was to join the group but being careful not to become too much involved, especially if they were contemplating any illegalities! Mari's own interest had started when she saw that the wire fence enclosure at the far side of the ranch had been deliberately torn down and several of the prize sheep were reported to be missing! Other sheep ranchers living in the area had also been reporting these losses; but they had been much too frightened by the threats of the ETA to voice their anger at what was happening! Her intentions had been admirable! She had sought to protect the local ranchers knowing only too well that the ways of the ETA would not diminish, especially as long as they continued to show a growth in the enrollment of the group. It was Mari's feeling that if they should continue to attack at the strength of the community, then, what strength could the ranching community hope to preserve? She had reasoned that if attention was diverted away from the local ranchers and concentrated on a more rewarding target, the community as well as the hard work of her father could be spared!

At first, Mari had felt that some of the demands had been reasonable! She agreed that it was up to the government to provide the measures that would enhance employment, especially in some of the badly deteriorating remote areas of Spain! To date, all of the emphasis of the government had been directed toward the larger cities such as Madrid, Barcelona, Granada and Valencia, but little emphasis was given to the Basque areas! Part of the failure had been the result of a slow down in the economic growth of the country! A much larger part of the blame was attributable to the inherent lack of interest on the part of the government to improve the living conditions in Vizcaya. After all, it was generally known that Vizcaya, as an entity, had never been among General Franco's favorite people! The fact that they had sought to secede from Spain and establish their own country had been met with a fierce denunciation on the part of the country to avoid all social and economic contacts with the Basques from the other regions of the country! One of the things that troubled Miguel was that Maripaz had been singled out as an ETA leader! She had been accused of being a symbol to others and it was expressely announced that any such conduct against the existing government would not be tolerated! As a Mariscal of the past, Miguel was well acquainted with the law! He was also aware that the evidence against his daughter was flimsy at best! All that they had against her in soft evidence was the word of a captured member of the ETA who had identified Maripaz as one of their leaders. As far as Miguel knew, there had been no reports of any hard evidence lodged against his daughter! To use hearsay information as being truthful was unthinkable! Had there been any hard evidence against her, the trial would have been held quickly! The mere fact that many weeks had gone by and still no trial date had been scheduled soon convinced him that his own personal evaluation of the case was probably correct!

Soledad had not been aware of how many nights he had remained awake thinking of possible ways of helping his daughter! The lawyer he had hired in Bilbao had been worthless; and the other attorneys in the city were either too busy with more rewarding cases than to spend their time and efforts in a criminal case where they knew that any valid defense would probably remain unacceptable in court! The government was always eager to arrest anyone remotely associated with the group hoping that by doing so they could make an example of them and then posting their activities in all of the country's newspapers. This was yet something else that had bothered Miguel! After the apprehension of his daughter, there had been hardly any mention at all of Maripaz's activities! It seemed obvious that no new evidence had been uncovered nor that she had given them any incriminating evidence that might be subsequently used against her. Without saying anything to Soledad, he had made a firm decision! He had decided to go to Madrid and visit his daughter! The risks that he would be facing meant nothing! Even if he were arrested on some frivolous charges in Madrid, he felt that seeing his daughter certainly outnumbered any risks he might have to take. It had already been several months since he had seen her and the truth was that he missed her very much! Knowing how cruel some of the jailers could be, he wondered how she was being treated, both physically and mentally by some of these people who could act like animals while guarding young women! The fact that Maripaz was a very attractive young lady certainly would not make things any easier for her!

It had been a few days when Soledad had gone into town to buy groceries! He had not said anything to her but had used this time to search among his friends for someone who could make up a fake identification card using a fictitious name! There were several printers in town who would specialize in making false documents. Most of their work came for the members of the ETA who wanted to conceal their real identities. In order for the printers in Bilbao to earn a living at their trade, it was almost imperative that they resort to those illegal practices which would provide them with a limited means of support! The printer he had selected had come highly recommended by one of his friends and was purported to be among the best of the trade! Miguel had been told that the production cost of these false credentials would be enormous, but he also knew that if you wanted the best, you would need to pay their prices! In preparing for the fake documents, he had allowed his hair to grow a little longer than before and had decided to grow a large mustache in order to hide his facial characteristics. He had also taken on the assumed name of Miguel Vallejo. Why he had selected such a name, he had never known! One thing was certain; he didn't know anyone with that name! When Soledad had asked why he was now growing a mustache, he merely told her that he wanted to alter his appearance and try to do something different! He never really knew whether or not she had believed him! Unfortunately, there were many other things in the house that were cause for arguments! The last thing she needed was to have something else to argue about! It wasn't at all like her not to make some remarks nor to offer any comments! Miguel was careful not to be well dressed so he didn't attract any unwanted attention! In fact, today he had decided to wear an opened collar shirt! There was a sudden surge of excitement that came over him as he remembered the days when he was strong and capable of activities that had long since passed him by! The mere thought that, in some ways, he was actually returning to those days, gave him excitement and an extra bit of energy that he knew he was going to need in order to carry out his plans!

"Where are you going all dressed up?" Soledad asked when she saw him.

"I'll be going away for a few days! Please take care of things until I get back!" he told her. There was not very much more that he needed to say! She knew all too well where he was going! There was really no point in trying to stop him! Experience had taught her that once his mind had been made up, he was much too stubborn to change it!

"You're going to Madrid, aren't you?"

"Yes!" he answered. "I'm going to see my daughter!"

"Do you realize what can happen if you should get arrested for something minor? I thought that we had both decided that neither of us would return to Madrid because it was much too risky! Remember, you couldn't even go there for medical treatments because of the risks! Now, you are facing those same risks! Don't you think that maybe I should go with you? After all, I'm anxious to see her also!" He knew that as a mother, she was anxious to see her daughter! For a moment he realized it had been thoughtless and selfish of him not to arrnage for a fake identification that she could use!

"Soledad, I've arranged for a fake identification card using the name of Miguel Vallejo! I don't think it would be wise for us to travel together! Why don't you go to the printer and ask him to make a fake identification for you! We'll leave separately and meet at the Plaza de Espana! We'll rent a pension there and no one will ask us any questions! I'll leave first by train and then you follow in a couple of days! I know I should have known better! I also am sorry that I blamed you needlessly for what happened to Mari! I never should have done that! I know damn well that whatever happened was not your fault!" he confessed as he saw her eyes fill with tears!

"Miguel, have you any idea how much I want to see our daughter? I realize that you blamed me," she said through a steady flow of tears. "Perhaps some of it may have been my fault! God knows how many nights I laid wide awake wondering and wishing that things could be different between us, the way they used to be! You also need to remember that whatever she did, she did for us and not for her! If we continue blaming each other, then what's left for her? I would like to see us join forces just like we used to do and see what we can do to help! I wish that I shared your understanding of these things and could offer more help! Unfortunately, I can't, and it eats me inside knowing there is little I can do for her! I can't offer her any legal advise! That is where she needs you! I just cannot believe that there is nothing that we can do!"

The look of remorse was written on his face! "In my younger days, I would have known exactly what to do, but those days are gone! I am too old to do her any good!" he said almost as if he were apologizing for something that was beyond his control.

"I refuse to believe that!" she said with determination. "You may not be able to help her with your strength as you once did for me, but you can certainly help her with your mind! Maybe in Madrid you will find an attorney who is well trained in these matters and may be able to help! We need to try to do something besides fighting among ourselves over who is to blame for what happened!" It had been the first time in a long while that the two of them had sat down and had spoken intelligently without fighting! Soledad remained silent waiting for a reply as she gave him a warm smile! It was then that he walked over to her, placed his arms around her and held her close to him for several moments.

"I just saw you smile!" he said. "I thought you had forgotten how to show your teeth!"

"Do you remember the day when I told you that I would never stop loving you? I told you then that I would always be there to protect you! Strange, how long ago those days now seem", she said. He took hold of her arm gently and stared for several minutes at the large scar on the inside of her arm.

"That was a pretty dumb thing you did!" he said kiddingly, still looking at the scar.

"It might have seemed dumb to you but not to me! It meant that our blood was flowing as one person! The strange thing is, we've always been united, that is, until this happened! Afterwards, everything seemed to change!"she said.

"No, Soledad! Nothing has changed! You're right! We do need that same blood to flow through our veins once again!" he answered, still holding her close to him.

"Please, my love!!! Please be careful! I'll be worried until I see or hear from you! Will you call me as soon as you see her?"

"Of course I will, providing I can get a line to Bilbao!" he answered as he kissed her goodbye and went off to the train station, carrying a small suitcase for his trip to Madrid.

Sitting in the crowded waiting room at the station gave him time to take stock over his life and how much things had changed! There had been a time when he had been full of energy as well as physical ability and had used these gifts to their limit! Now, he no longer had that same energy for even the stamina to perform simple tasks. His greatest worry while waiting for the train to Madrid was that he would not be able to escape detection of some eager Guardia Civil who might recognize him despite his changed looks! He had purchased a pair of dark sunglasses that were in vogue; but he knew that there was still the possibility that the mustache he had grown for the trip would disguise his face enough if someone from out of his past should recognize him. There was no point in worrying about these possibilities now, it was too late to be worried! He was on his way to Madrid by himself! It was a trip that he absolutely needed to make if only to show love and support for his only daughter!

Madrid

Just as he had expected, Andres knew only too well that the funeral of the Condessa was going to be the funeral of all funerals as the ever intrusive Condessa was finally being laid to rest in an open casket that was to last for several days! Everyone who was anyone in society had been in attendance; and he found it hard to distinguish who had and paid their respects showing their sensitivity and those that had only come to make an appearance and imbibe of the caviar and champagne that was always served at these functions. These were the so-called social friends who were seated in the rear rows of chairs at the funeral parlor and speaking loudly, completely oblivious to what was happening. Paloma had done everything she felt the Condessa would have wanted and had held her end much better than he had expected! It was obvious by the way she knew exactly what to do that she had been schooled by the old gal long before it became necessary for her to show what she had learned! She knew how to greet the people, how to show her sorrow and at the same time flash them a smile! It was almost as if she were playing a game of acting both happy and sad at the same time! Perhaps this was the way these things were done in social circles, he thought!

There had been more than a few angry stares directed at him when it was known that it had been suggested that he should offer the eulogy for the Condessa but had turned down the offer! There were certainly enough people in attendance who had known the old woman better and longer than he. He felt that these friends were better prepared to offer one of the often-used eulogies that had been repeated on other similar occasions. It wasn't that he wanted to be deliberately disrespectful nor that he didn't like the Condessa! She would never know that as time went by he had found her to be extremely interesting, but her determination of taking over another person's life had never wavered! She could be and certainly was very controlling! He sat in the large room all alone while Paloma was standing at the foot of the open casket dressed entirely in a black lace dress, complete with a black view over her face, black shoes and a wide brim black hat and gloves! He watched her as she greeted each and every visitor with courtesy and respect! Occasionally, she would give someone a slight peck on the cheek or shake someone's hand! The list of people that attended and their lists of liturgies was endless and each had to be limited to only five minutes. Never in his life had he ever seen such lavishness at a viewing as visitor after visitor left their seats and walked slowly and solemny to a small podium that had been set up just far enough in front of the casket so that the lengthy recitations would not disturb the rest of the honored guest, who no longer cared, one way or another, what was being said!

Many of the things that were said were true; but he found it interesting at how many pleasant and nice things are said about a person when they die! He heard not a word about her arrogance nor about her dictatorial manifestations about a woman who had spent her entire life ruling and dominating the lives of others! It seemed rather strange that only one of the many eulogies that had been offered had made any reference at all about her being with God! It was strange that for someone who had apparently been so good and so righteous, no body had bothered to recommend her to God! How could this be??? Maybe it was because everyone knew that if it was God who had called her, she would more than likely be arguing with Him on high and doing her best to take over the reins of heaven! Dread the thought, he said to himself! It might be that God might get tired of her and send her back to earth to join the speakers that told everyone how righteous she had always been!

The truth was that she had actually been very good to Andres! She had been among the few people who had, from the beginning, shown and faith in him! It was because of her that he was now a wealthy lawyer; and even Herr Otto, who really never liked her, was now making more money than he had ever made in his entire life! Their legal practice had grown so much that they had even started to hire fresh new lawyers, recently out of law school, who seemed to be interested in the practice of civil law! In order to accomplish this, he had left it up to Herr Otto to train the new applicants in their conference rooms before arguing actual cases! The practice as well as the knowledge of the law was one thing, but the way a defense was presented in a court room was something that couldn't be taught in law school! Either a person had what it took or he didn't!! Those that seemed promising were quickly hired; and those that didn't meet their standards were soon dismissed and told to practice law somewhere else!

Paloma had made it certain that Andres wore a dark suit and black tie for the viewing as well as the funeral! There had been a slight argument when he drew the line, suggesting that he should also wear a black arm band as a show of mourning and respect! Her insistence of the armband had started an argument that he was able to win! Unfortunately, there had already been several other arguments concerning what he considered to be trivial matters that didn't really make much sense! After all, what difference did it make if the cars that were to transport some of the people were large or small? She had insisted that the large cars would be for those of a higher social status. As far as he was concerned, all that was important was that they had cared enough to accompany them

at the funeral! He felt corrected when she tried to explain that his
opinion was not enough! There simply had to be a list of people
who were expected to ride in the plush, long black automobiles!
Others who were of a lower social status were to be driven in other
black cars, much smaller in size, and sharing the ride with other
visitors! The other argument that began was when Paloma decided
on the number of professional mourners that should be hired!
When he lived in Galicia he had heard of such things at funerals,
but he had always believed that the stories he heard were untrue!
Not so!! Paloma insisted in hiring not less than twelve mourners,
divided into groups of three, each one chanting and lamenting for
two straight hours before being relieved by the next group of three
mourners!

As he sat by himself in the front row, occasionally greeting
someone that he knew or who he had seen before, he was getting
a headache just by listening to the monotonous eerie chants of
these professional mourners all dressed in black! It was difficult
for him to understand how these people could do this for a living
day after day! After a while, he decided to go outside for a breath
of fresh air! The repugnant odors of the many different flowers
were starting to make him feel nauseous and he needed to get
away! Outside, he went over to the corner newstand and bought a
newspaper to occupy some of his time! Thank God that Paloma
had not seen the smile on his face when he saw all of the articles
reliving the Condessa's life as well as her contributions to Spanish
aristocracy! In articles below the accolades for the Condessa.
there was a small picture of him and Paloma identifying him as
the future husband of the Condessa's daughter.What surprised
him the most was that the article had even shown the date of the
wedding and where it was going to be held! It seemed even more
strange that the newspaper had known more about his wedding
than he himself had been told! There was, as yet, no way of telling
what effects the untimely death of the old lady would have on
his wedding! Not that he was against any delays! At this point he
wasn't yet certain whether or not he was prepared for, wanted or
needed the type of lifestyle that awaited him!

Inside the funeral parlor all of the visitors and the mourners had been summoned to their places when the Cardinal arrived to recite the rosary as well as the prayers for the dead! The room quickly became eerily quiet as His Emminence recited, in careful detail, all of the mysteries of the rosary as well as some mysteries that Andres never knew existed! When he concluded his services and was addressing the crowd, Andres was trying to determine if the Condessa had been recommended for heaven, or if she was running for political office! If she was being recommended for heaven, Andres had little doubt that she had already been given her harp and her wings, and now all that was left was for the Vatican in Rome to recommend her for Sainthood! If, on the other hand, she was running for a political office, there was good reason for General Franco to worry about having a successor!!

The long line of mourners in the funeral procession was even more elaborate than the viewing! Andres was among the last persons to ride in a large car and he had stopped counting after seventy five cars! He was surprised to know that there were so many black limousines in the city of Madrid! Every person that was titled had his own private car and only the non-titled were destined to ride in the smaller cars that had been rented for the occasion! Paloma and her young son, Jose, were in the lead car, and it appeared to Andres that the lead car would probably arrive at the cemetery before the last of the line of cars had begun their trip!

The Condessa was laid to rest in a large pavillion that had been reserved exclusively for the Romanones family! All of the other family members that had gone to their final resting place before the Condessa had been interned in that old, musky mausoleum that had several other caskets resting into a niche on the wall, each one bearing the prominant name of the member of the Romanones family! All the time he was there, he was wondering if, when, he died, he too would need to be resting in such an awful place among strangers that he didn't really know? He rather hoped that he wouldn't; knowing that he wouldn't have been happy with the company! As far as he was concerned he would prefer to be laid to rest in a private plot where he knew nobody and where he might still be able to pick and chose those people that he wanted to befriend! This was something that he needed to remind Paloma about, to be sure that he was interred with people that wouldn't aggravate him as much in eternal rest as they had done when he was alive!

The long procession of cars stopped just outside the large, granite mausoleum! Paloma was the first to leave the car followed by a steady parade of mourners walking slowly who had come to the funeral! Andres got out of the car, and went to the side of Paloma! He took his place at the far side of the large granite structure while the Cardinal, dressed in his bright red garments, recited the final prayers, sprayed the casket with holy water; and the old lady was finally put to rest in an empty niche in the wall that had apparently been reserved for her! Only then did another thought come to mind! Why was it that anytime that a Socialite had died, the Mass and the prayers over the deceased were always performed by a high official of the church? Did this mean that the person who had died was personally escorted into heaven because a high official of the church had said the Mass? Why was it that whenever a poor peasant died, no Cardinal was ever in attendance? That only happened when the decedent was someone of a higher Social status, or it was someone who was well known! He needed to remind Paloma that when he died, only a Cardinal dressed in red garments was permitted to say the Mass over his dead body! He wanted to be sure that if there was anything to this mystery, once the Cardinal said the Mass, it would provide him with a free pass into heaven! After the prayers and a sprinkling of holy water, the bronze casket of the woman was carried across two large metal supports where it would finally rest in peace!

There were a few somber faces, but he would see in the faces of some of the others, that they were anxious to go somewhere and celebrate either the death or the new life of the deceased! Following the funeral, everyone was invited back to the house and the only person that was still dressed in the traditional black dress was Paloma! All of the other vulchers could hardly wait for the corks to pop and the besuga caviar, the imported Russian Vodka and a large array of Queso Manchego were being served for everyone! Back at the house, Andres saw that there were no tears, no sorrow and no remorse! The charade had ended and it was now the time to celebrate! The vulchers dug into the caviar and champagne as if they had just been released from a cell of abstinance and were starving for food! Paloma and the servants were kept busy serving the trays of food and making small talk with the visitors that had chosen to return to the house! Andres grabbed a glass of champagne and decided to go outside into the gardens thinking about the ceremony he had just witnessed! He wondered if, indeed, anyone other than he really gave a damn that the old matron of the house had just been buried? It was several hours later when the last guest finally left the house. All of the caviar had been consumed and since there was no more left, there was no point in remaining! He walked out the door, giving Paloma a peck on the cheek and shaking Andres' hand! Once again the guest had expressed his sorrow, offered his help if it should be needed, and went on his way!

"Don't you think it was a wonderful tribute to mother?" she asked when the last guest had departed.

"It was a tribute!" Andres answered. "Whether or not it was wonderful depends on what your mother would have wanted!"

"Andres, I need to tell you something that I hope won't hurt your feelings!" she told him. "You know that in Spain there is a period of mourning of one year for members of the decendents family! This means that we'll have to wait a year before we marry! Do you mind?"

"No! Of course not! If you think we should wait a year before being married, then, so be it! After all, she was your mother and you know what is best!" he told her.

"I would also like for you to do one more thing for me in honor of my mother!" she asked. "I would like you to wear the black arm band on your right arm during this time of mourning! It would mean a great deal to mother and it would also mean a great deal to me!"

"Paloma, what you wear on your arm has nothing to do with how you feel! Remember, I am an attorney and I need to be in and out of the court house! I can't walk around with an arm band just to show the world how I feel!" he explained. She had taken him by surprise, especially, since they had already discussed this option before the funeral! He thought that the matter had been settled but here it was, surfacing again!

"And, just how do you feel? Why are you so ashamed to show people that you are in mourning for your future mother-in-law? Is it too much to ask?" she said, annoyed that he had again refused her.

"Frankly, yes! I think it is! First of all, I don't belive in showing your sorrow on the sleeve of an arm that means absolutely nothing! Secondly, I doubt very much that any of your friends will give a damn after today!"

"If you won't do it for her, you might at least do it for me!" she said angrily.

"I can't promise you that! I'll wear one, however, when we are out on Social functions; but I won't wear one when I'm working!" he insisted.

"I don't know why you refuse to humor me! Have you forgotten that you are the reason why my mother is no longer with us?" she said testily. Andres was livid! So that was her little game, he said to himself! In her own way she was blaming him for the Condessa's death, and he didn't think she was being fair with him!

Everything had changed at the Romanones household after the Condessa died! Everytime Andres and Paloma had an argument, she had taken it as a personal affront against her mother; and the results were that each was going their own way and spending less time together! Andres was kept busy with his law practice while Paloma did her best to assume the duties and responsibilities left behind by her mother. Arguments began nearly everytime they were together, or whenever he told her that he would be unable to be at a function because of pressing legal work that he needed to do! Paloma would then attack him at these times by blaming him for the sudden death of her mother! She had been unable to understand that in refusing the judgeship of the court was because he didn't feel ready to take on such a challenge! The truth was that he was well aware of the many doors that had been opened for him because of the Condessa! Even though she could be conniving, manipulative, and controlling, the truth was that he

had grown to admire the old woman! Not even the advanced age
had been able to quiet her zest for life! Wherever she was, there
was little doubt as to who was in complete control, and he rather
liked that in a woman! Many times he had wished in silence that
Paloma could be more like her mother! Unfortunately, she had
allowed herself to be dominated by her mother; and, at the time
of her death, Paloma was feeling her loss knowing that she no
longer would have anyone to control her every movement! Now
had come her struggle to accept the responsibilities and duties
of the aristocracy; and, frankly, the harder she tried the more
unconvincing she became!

Andres doubted that either she or her mother had ever
understood when he explained how he had come from a simple
and uneducated family Their only wealth had been the love and
care they had given to all of the members of his family! At first, he
had been disappointed when Paloma told him about the period of
mourning and that the wedding would have to be postponed! Now
that she had so often blamed him for the death of the Condessa,
he was rather pleased that the wedding would have to wait! He
was being challenged by his ability to become an aristocrat and he
didn't know shether or not he would ever be up to that challenge!
For one thing, his own view of their coveted circle of friends was
much different than Paloma's! Throughout the time he had known
their friends, he had always considered them to be nothing but
'users'! They were nothing more than people who would constantly
use whatever status they held to take advantage of others less
fortunate, just because most of them were wealthy and could afford
to take advantage of their social status! Perhaps things would
change by the time the mourning period was over! At least it would
give him something to hope for!

In another section of the city, known as the famous Plaza
de Espana, Miguel was seated in the small one-room pension he
had rented! At least the 'pan dulce' they served with coffee each
morning had been freshly baked! The small room, designed for
transients, was unattractively furnished with a few pieces of odd
furniture that seemed to have come from another century! At the
end of the hallway there was a small bathroom, equipped with an

old fashion bathtub and a hand held shower! The bathroom was intended to accomodate the guests living in the remaining eight rooms on the floor. After the first night, Miguel became quickly aware that he would need to get into the bathroom early in the morning in order to take his shower before the other guests began their march to the small room! Whoever arrived first was rewarded not only with the use of the bathroom, but also a limited amount of hot water to be used for bathing! It was a much different from what he was accustomed to in his home in Bilbao, where all of his needs were at his fingertips.

He had already walked the streets by himself visiting the offices of many attorneys that had advertised their expert services in the local newspapers! All of his visits had fallen on deaf ears, as each attorney after listening to his story would systematically turn him down! The excuses were always the same! Either they were much too busy to handle the case, or else they lacked the experience of taking on the federal government on the matters of terorism! Not one of them had shown any interest at all in defending Maripaz! Everyone knew that the issue about the ETA had been a sore spot with the government and nobody wanted to take on any added pressures in defending a young woman whom the government felt was guilty of a crime! To most of them, it was not a matter of money! Instead, it was a matter of taking a case that they felt could not be won at any cost! It had come under the specialization of someone well versed in Federal law! While all criminal activity was normally handled under the Federal Law statutes, most cases involving people who had been charged with the attempted overthrow of the government were nearly always heard in a Military court; and most attorneys knew from experience that military tribunals seldom ruled in favor of the accused!

After the first day, Miguel had been successful in visiting his daughter every day! Of course, there needed to be a small pay-off or a "mordida" as it was called, to the jailer! The money had practically brought him a sense of friendship with the jailer making things easier for both of them. Every day, he would be met by the jailer who would then escort him to the cell where Maripaz was being held. The murky building was old and poorly maintained! There was almost no illumination and there were foul smells and unpleasant aromas of disenfectants that made him nauseous whenever he entered. Miguel was shocked and upset when he first saw Maripaz dressed in a yellow one-piece jail suit with large black lettering on the back of the uniform that read, "DDD" (Dormitorio de Damas). The tiny cell, a mere four by six feet, barely allowed her enough room to move around! Each cell was equipped with a tiny wash basin and toilet that was leaking water each time it was flushed! Although he was well aware of the lack of comforts of his daughter, it was hard to imagine any convict, or any other human being, being treated so poorly while in captivity. Maripaz seemed depressed and he could see that she had lost all of her aggressiveness! She was no longer the happy, smiling young woman she had always been! As he came closer to her, he could smell the foul odor of perspiration, probably because of working long hours in the hot confines of the jail laundry! Her hair, that she would always comb each morning was now disheveled and uncombed and her complexion was pale! The only emotion she would show was a steady stream of tears that began when she saw him for the first time! After that day, she showed no ambition nor any desire to fight for her freedom! All of her drives had been taken away from her! It seemed that she had already accepted her role of being a criminal, and seemed determined that her destiny was to spend the remainder of her life in jail!

The first time he went to visit her, he saw that there were ugly scars on both wrists! As a Mariscal he had seen these things before and realized that she had probably made an attempt to take her own life! Although the attempt of suicide was a worry, he decided that it was much too delicate a matter to mention while in her presence! His aim was to offer her encouragement and now he too felt discouraged because no one seemed to be willing to help her! Today, he had already decided that he would need to tell her the truth! It was something he hated to do and he wondered how it would effect her! He would tell her bluntly that all of his efforts of hiring an attorney had been futile! There was really no place else to turn; and, yet, seeing her like this, he just couldn't walk away and leave her alone! He would need to remain there with her, but he had no idea for how long! Many of the things he saw had been kept from Soledad! He had decided to tell her the truth, but only after he was home knowing how badly the news of how she looked would affect her mother!

The daily newspaper that was slipped under the door to his room was but one of the few perks that came with his rent! Miguel opened the newspaper as he did each morning and began to look through the articles for any news that would be of interest. After breakfast, he knew that there would still be time to kill before going to the jail to visit his daughter! The entire first page of the newspaper was devoted to the death of some old woman that he didn't even know nor had he ever heard about! The news had been explicit to mention the lavish funeral and the number of influential dignitaries that had come to pay their respects! His only interest as he nodded his head from side to side was how there could be so much oppulence in the world suffereing so much misery and starvation! His eyes drifted down one of the columns to a small picture and an article that seemed of some interest! It was the photograph of a handsome young man who was considered by many to be a legal genius! The woman at his side was apparently his intended bride! The article said something about their intention to marry after an initial period of mourning! Who gave a damn about these people, he asked himself? During his past he had seen and had dealt with many of them; and, for the most part, he considered them to be nothing more than human parasites who preyed on whoever they could use of whoever served the most expensive champagne! The young man's name was Andres Torres and he specialized in Consititutional law! The article also explained how he had turned down a federal judgeship just because he didn't feel he was properly trained to cope with the responsibilities that the job entailed. At least the young man seemed to be be admirable! From what he had heard, not everyone had the opportunity of turning down a judicial appointment, especially if he was to be the son-in-law of the famous Condessa de Romanones! There was some mention that the young man had come from a small town in Galicia and had been educated at the

Universidad Autonoma de Madrid! If he was so damn poor, how
in the hell did he ever get mixed up with that group of parasites,
he asked himself? It seemed that he was practicing law with an old
professor who had arrived from Germany during the Civil War!
Suddenly from out of nowhere an idea came to mind! Why not
look this young man up and ask him for advice? If he had the balls
to turn down such an important assignment, he was obviously an
idealist and might be able to steer him in the right direction! The
worse thing that could happen was for him to join the chorus of
other attorneys who refused to handle the case! What the hell, it
was certainly worth a try! He had nothing at all to lose! He cut out
the article and started to thunb through the local register looking
for an attorney by the name of Andres Torres! Today, he didn't
know it yet, but he was going to be visited by yet another new
client!

Oficina de Lic. Torres y Heintz

Miguel knocked on the door three times before he heard
a voice with a thick accent asking him to enter. After introducing
himself to Herr Otto, he asked if he could please talk to
Licenciado Torres! The old man asked him politely if he had an
appointment! When Miguel told him that he had no appointment,
the old man offered some excuse telling him that the Licenciado
was busy with other appointments and would not be able to see
him today! All of the optimism he had before coming to the
office began to fade as he felt himself getting defeated again. His
hopes had soared when he read the article especially knowing
the reputation of the Gallegos in helping their fellow citizens. It
appeared that his final hopes had just been dampened with the
denial! Gently, Miguel slowly lowered his head between his hands,
ashamed that this old man would see him, a grown man, crying!

"Pheeew!" Herr Otto said nervously. "Vat is dis? Tell me,
vy you cry? Is something wrong...ja?"

"It's only that I have a serious problem and no other
attorney wants to handle it! My last hope was that Licenciado
Torres would see me! I guess it was too much to ask on such short

notice! Thank you......." he said as he turned around and was about to leave.

"Vait!!....Vait!.....Vy do you get discouraged so quickly? Vy not take a seat in the office and ven he can.....he vil see you....ja? I promise you! Now....you must stop crying......men are not supposed to cry!! Ve must be strong...and....you too must be strong! Now... stop crying and I vill see to it that Licenciado Torres vill meet with you! Maybe...it vill take time...but....I promise you...and, I always keep my promises...ja?" he said as he tried to give the new client some words of encouragement! Miguel felt a bit better already! This nice old man.....whoever he was....was a sly old fellow! He knew exactly how to make people feel comfortable and comfort was something he hadn't felt since arriving in the capital city!

It seemed like hours before he finally saw a tall young man, handomely dressed in expensive clothes come out of the back office. "Herr Otto!" he said, "I expect to be gone the rest of the day...."

"No...No....No!! You cannot go yet...ja? This man has been waiting here for hours to see you! I promised you would talk to him as soon as you were finished! Andres...please, you must see him! I think maybe he has a serious problem....ja?"

Andres looked at his partner and let out a smile! It was just like him! No matter how busy he could be, nobody who walked into their office with what seemed to be a serious problem would leave the office without being seen. This had been something they both had been serious about and there was no point in arguing with him! The small gathering that Paloma had arranged for many of her friends in memory of her mother's death on the one month anniversary would need to wait! This frail looking man, whoever he was, obviously needed his attention! Besides, Herr Otto would have a fit if he was turned away without first being seen!

"Okay, Herr Otto! You win again!" he said smiling. "Please come in, sir!" he said as Miguel followed him into the office at the rear of the building and closed the door behind him! Andres motioned to him to sit down across from the large desk as he took out a yellow legal pad and pencil and started to take notes! "Now sir, what seems to be the problem?" he asked.

"My name is Miguel Romero! We live in Bilbao, and I was once the Mariscal for the government during the Civil War! The problem is....that....my only daughter....is...in serious trouble!" he said as he felt his own voice start to quiver as he spoke. Andres did not look up but continued writing on the pad!

"What is your daughter's name?" he asked.

"Maripaz Romero!" Miguel answered. If Andres was suddenly shocked, he made no attempt to show it! The only visible sign of a surprise came when he stopped writing for several moments before raising his eyes and looking at his client. "She has been charged with terroristic activities and to overthrow the Spanish government!" Miguel added.

"Those are very serious charges! Is she under arrest?" he asked.

"Yes, sir! She was arrested in Bilbao and later transferred to Madrid!"

"Have you seen her and have you spoken to her since she arrived?"

"Yes! That was why I came here! I saw her yesterday! Today, I have been sitting in your office all day waiting for you! I'm sorry if I disturbed your plans!" Miguel told him.

"My plans are unimportant! What is important is that I need to know everything that happened in your own words! When we are finished, you and I will go to the jail and visit your daughter! Is that okay with you?"he asked.

"Yes, of course! But the visiting hours are over and I doubt very much that they will allow me to go in for a visit!" Miguel answered.

"You will go with me! I can assure you that you will be permitted to enter! I need to know everything that happened! First, I want to hear it from you! Then, I will need to hear it from your daughtert!"

"I have tried to find an attorney in Bilbao that would represent my daughter but no one would consider taking her case! I also tried to find one here in Madrid and again nobody wanted to represent her. You were my last ray of hope, and I found your name by reading the article in the newspaper!"

"Well, for whatever it's worth, I have no idea what the problem is! However, from this moment on, I assure you that you now have an attorney who will represent your daughter!"

"I am willing to pay you whatever you ask!" Miguel said.

"That won't be necessary! Money is not an option! Please sir, I would prefer that you didn't ask me any questions! I have my own reasons, but I assure you that she will not be alone!" he said.

On the way to visit Maripaz, Andres was filled with anxieties! It seemed strange the way fate deals with certain things! Even as they walked he could feel his legs getting a bit wobbly, and there were cold beads of sweat as they walked! The truth was that he had never forgotten her; and while he certainly knew how stubborn she could sometimes be, he wondered how an intelligent woman such as she could have allowed herself to be in so much trouble that she might easily spend the rest of her life in jail! The most troublesome part was in realizing that after Miguel had esplained what had happened and the reasons why and how she had been arrested on nothing more than hearsay evidence, he had no idea what he was going to be able to do for her! As a lawyer he knew that the penalties for these types of crimes were harsh and severe! It was the government's way of discouraging other young people from taking part in actions against the government!

When Andres asked to see Miguel's identification card, he noticed immediatelky that the name on the card was different from the one he had been given! When Miguel tried to explain, Andres interrupted quickly. not wanting to be told the reason why there were two different names! Obviously, the card he was shown had been a fake, and if he was aware that his client had a false identification card, as an officer of the court, he had an obligation to turn the matter over to the proper authorities! If, on the other hand, the truth was not known, he couldn't be charged with harboring a criminal or as a co-conspirator! His attention was directed to Maripaz, and he also knew that the resolution to her case was going to take a long time. Judging by the looks of this man, he was frightened and troubled thinking about his daughter, and had every right to be! He could also see that the man was ill and in need of medical assistance!

The two men entered the jail! Andres quickly told the jailer that he had been appointed as the attorney for Maripaz Romero and that he wanted to visit with his client! His comments were not a request; instead, it was a demand knowing that the jailer would have no alternative but to allow them to follow him into her cell!For a few moments, Miguel had forgotten how putrid and annoying the jail cells could be! It had been a long time since he had visited a jail! Andres followed him, remaining a step behind! When they reached the cell, it was Andres who turned and faced the jailer asking him to leave him alone with his client. As soon as the door was opened, Miguel was the first to enter the cell and hug his daughter! Andres remained behind him and had not yet been seen by Maripaz!

"Esta bien!" Andres said to the jailer. "Leave us alone!"

When Andres turned his head and faced Maripaz, he could hardly believe the way she looked! She was dressed in the familiar jail suit, soiled and unclean from her work! Her face looked shallow and pale, her hair uncombed, and there even seemed to be a passive look about her as if she no longer cared whether she lived or died! He stared at her , standing directly in front of her just a few short steps away! She took one look at him, her face covered by her hands as she began to cry! At that very moment he wanted to take her into his arms and reassure her that everything was going to be okay! But unfortunately, he couldn't do that! She was now his client, and he, her attorney! He needed her to be at her very best if he had any hopes of defending her successfully, even if it meant making her angry from time to time!

"Oh, my God!!! Oh, my God!!!" was all she would say. "How did you fine me?" she asked through her tears.

"Que haces aqui?" (What are you doing here?) he asked. Miguel was shocked as he saw that this was not a first reunion! These two people had obviously known each other from before; and judging by the looks on both their faces, they were both surprised and upset! Maripaz took another look at him and was unable to keep from crying, ashamed that he was seeing her this way! Slowly, she took a step forward in his direction afraid to touch him for fear that it was all a dream and that he would suddenly vanish if she became awakened! Instead, he moved forward toward her and embraced her with his arms and drew her even closer to him! There was no need for either to speak! Their response in being in each other's arms said it all!

"I'm going to dirty your suit!" she said as she tried to joke with him. "I don't want to do that!" she said, almost as if she was being apologetic that he had been enticed to put his arms around her and draw her near to him!

"If the suit gets dirty, I'll have it cleaned!" he told her. "I need to know how you got yourself into this mess?"

"It's a long story, and probably one that you won't believe!" she answered.

"Look, Mari, I'll be back tomorrow morning! We have a great deal of work to do! The first thing I want you to do is to put on some clean clothes, wash your face and comb your hair! I don't mind telling you that you look like hell and I don't want to see you this way!" he said.

"Damn it! You haven't changed at all, have you?" she charged back. "Why don't you try working in the hot laundry room and then being accompanied back into this hell-hole! For sure, you wouldn't be wearing those expensive hand tailored suits!! I assure you that you wouldn't look any better then me!" All the time she was speaking, he noticed that she hadn't let go and was still holding on to him! Meanwhile, he stared at her father who was still stunned and amazed by what he was seeing! Andres shot him a smile and winked at him! Her reaction was exactly what he had hoped for! He had arrived and had seen a depressed and defeated client! If he had any chances of winning, he was going to need her to be her old adament and defiant self!!

"How did you find me?" she asked him in a softer tone of voice.

"I didn't! Your father found me and I'm glad that he did! Why didn't you get in touch with me when this happened?" he asked, still holding her against him.

"I didn't know where to reach you! Besides, after what I did and the way that I left without even saying goodbye, I had my doubts that you would ever want to see me again! I also read in the newspapers that you are no longer the Andres I used to know! Now, they are calling you the 'boy genius', and about to marry the daughter of the Condessa de Romanones! The last thing you need would be to have me as your client! I would probably ruin your reputation!"

"Let's get one thing straight!" he wanted to sound serious if only to convince himself that she was now just another client, but he knew better! "I am not yet married and let me be the one to worry about my reputation!"

"Andres," she answered almost in a whisper. "I would never want to embarass you! You certainly don't deserve that, especially from me!"

"Let's put that all behind us for the time being! At the moment, there is a lot of work that still needs to be done! Besides, you still have a lot of explaining to do!! I want you to get a good nights rest and tidy yourself up! When I come back tomorrow I expect to see you at your best! I want you to be angry and opinionated the way you used to be!" he said.

Miguel noticed that the two were still in an embrace! It seemed that neither wanted to be the one to break away! There could be no mistake in what he was seeing! It was obvious that his daughter and this young man had met another time, another place! It was also obvious that they had been much more than just friends! Finding this young man on an impulse had been a sheer stroke of good luck! For the first time, he felt confident that he could return to Bilbao with a renewed hope that his daughter, for the first time since her arrest, was finally in excellent hands!

Andres arrived at the jail early the following morning! For the first time he felt pleased that he was going to visit his client! Anytime he had an early morning meeting with a client, he was always reluctant to go, knowing that he was going to meet someone that was obviously not happy and loaded with questions that needed to be answered. No sooner had he arrived at the jail cell, he could see that there had been a change in her appearance! She was now wearing clean clothes! Her hair was combed and neatly pulled back into a bun! For a moment, his mind returned to the happy days at the university knowing that this was the way she had always worn her hair because he liked to see her this way! He fought off the urge to be more friendly, but this was now business and it had to be treated as such! There was no embrace nor any sign of affection as he tried hard to convince himself that despite what he felt, she was still just another client!

"Mari. I've taken your father to the train station! In view of the circumstances, I thought it would be best if he returned to Bilbao! He seems to be in poor health! Now that I am here, there is very little for him to do!" he said.

"His health has been poor for some time! You may not believe me; but, he is the reason why I had been urgently called back home when I was at the university! I'm very worried about him and my being arrested only made matters worse!" she explained. After a brief pause, she added. "He needs desperately to be seen by some of the specialists here in Madrid; but, he already took an awful chance by coming here! Has he explained to you the restrictions the government imposed on him when he escaped being arrested and settled in Bilbao?"

"No! But to be honest, I rather suspected something like that! I decided that he would be much safer back in Bilbao now that he knew I would be handling his daughter's defense!" He made a motion to the jailer that he wanted a private room where he would be able to speak freely and openly with his new client! The jailer opened the cell door and led both of them to another small room on the second floor of the old building. The room was sparsely furnished with only a small desk and two wooden chairs! He shot a glance upward and noticed that at least he had better illumination than downstairs as they took their seats!

"Mari, you understand, of course, that I may need to ask you questions that are of a personal nature! I'm sure you realize that this case is quite complicated and I need to know everything that happened! Please, I don't want you to be offended by anything that I ask!" he explained. "Tell me, how did you meet these people from the ETA? Tell me, honestly, did you have a relationship with any of them?" he asked.

"What???" she said in a tone of voice that was almost a scream! "What do you think I am? How could you ask me such a dumb and foolish question? Andres, regardless of what happened between us, there has never been another man for me after you! I just never met another man who was able to match your standards! No! There was no relationship!" For several moments, he had to convince himself whether the question had been legitimate or had he asked it for selfish reasons! There was a side of him that wanted to take her into his arms and reassure her that everything was going to be okay! Unfortunately, he couldn't do that! Once again he found the need of reminding himself that she was simply just another client!

"I'm sorry but I needed to ask, but I certainly didn't mean to offend you!:" he said as an apology.

"It all began when a friend of mine who worked in a bakery and myself went to one of the local cafes! It was then that we heard a group of young men sitting at the next table talking among themselves! From the things they were saying, we knew immediately that they were members of the ETA! This was at a time when the group was stealing sheep from the local ranchers and tearing down the barbed wire enclosures. Some of the sheep would simply wander away while others were stolen and sold for money to other ranchers. After speaking to them, I realized that the money was being used to finance terrorism." She paused for several moments, as he carefully wrote everything down on a yellow pad! "I admit that I was the person that suggested to them that instead of stealing from the local ranchers and ruining their survival, perhaps they should think of diverting their attacks against one of the smaller banks! I believe that one theft of a bank would serve to stop the thefts that were being committed! But, it didn't stop there! The robbery at a small bank had been easy, so easy in fact, that they continued to rob other banks in the city!"

"Did you go with them on any of the robberies?"

"Certainly not! You know as well as I that the women are never invited to these activities! I was however awarded one of the 'boinhas', in recognition of my contribution! Aside from attending some of their meetings, I had no other involvment with them!"

"If you had no other involvment, why then, didn't you stop attending their meetings?" he asked.

"I tried!! I really tried!! I was told that once a person belonged to the movement, there could be no turning back! They threatened me and my family with physical harm! I became caught up in a wave of criminal behavior from which there was no exit!"

Andres nodded his head gently and continued to write everything down! He applied a small asterisk to this statement! If he was successful in getting a pre-trial hearing, he would need this as a defense! It was obvious that she had been intimidated by the group and needed to continue as a group member if only to spare herself and her family from the threats!

"I want to know everything that happened on the day you were arrested! Your father explained that the newspapers had written articles that you had saved the life of a youngster and killing one of the members of the ETA! Do you remember everything that happened that day?"

"How can I not remember? It was the first time in my life that I ever killed a person! That bastard was going to harm a little girl! I had my gun inside my purse and I told him several times to let the little girl alone! He was holding her by the arm, so I asked him again! That was when he began to laugh at me and completely ignored my warnings! I became angry and aimed the gun! I then squeezed the trigger! The ETA member died quickly!" she said.

"Mari, has anyone abused you or offended you while you were in jail?" he asked, hoping that she had not been abused as some women were by the guards, especially when they were taken to the jails in Madrid. Once a person was taken to one of the jails in Madrid, it was assumed that she would be spending many years in jail!

"No!" she answered. "I can't say that I have! I was interrogated every day for a while! My father had advised me not to give any more information that could be incriminating! They did, however, make references saying that I was a traitor and would probably remain in jail for the rest of my life! But no one has abused me! Why did you ask?"

"Nothing! It's just something that we always ask, in case there are abuses that we need to be aware of!" he lied.

"Andres! I need to know the truth! Can you help me? I don't think I can stand being locked in a jail much longer!" Andres had seen the slash marks on her wrists! This was the reason he had asked if she had been abused! It would be just like her to take away her own life! Now that he found her, he wasn't about to let her go! He decided against mentioning the scars or asking her how she had gotten them! If she chose to explain them, he was willing to listen, but he preferred not to mention them unless he noticed something that didn't seem right! For the moment, everything was fine!

"You know that I have always been honest with you! I was even honest the day you got angry at me and walked away, do you remember? The truth is that I don't know how successful I'll be in helping you! The charges that have been lodged against you are very serious! It makes no different whether or not they are true! All I can promise you is that I certainly didn't take this case for money! Your father walked into my office! As soon as I learned that you were his daughter, I wouldn't say no to him! In order to help you, there is going to be needed a great deal of legal maneuvering that needs to be done! I'm going to insist on a pre-trial hearing; but, in order to do this, I need to make certain that the pre-trial arguments are heard by a judge that I consider to be reasonable and unbiased! You may see a series of postponements until I am awarded a judge that is to my liking! No matter what happens, I need you to promise me that you won't do anything foolish! You're going to need to trust me and to work with me! Can you promise me?" he asked.

"I suppose I know why you ask me those questions! You have seen the scars on my wrists, haven't you? she asked as she turned up her hands and showed him her wrists again!

"Yes! Now that you have shown me, I need you to promise me that you'll never again try to take your life no matter what happens!" he told her.

"Why, Andres?" she asked. "What difference does it make? My life is over! Just look at where we are! We were once lovers and now I am nothing more than a client! You have become a famous attorney and about to marry a socialite that is capable of giving you everything you need! I have nothing at all to give you! I can't even give you....myself!" she said as she began to cry.

He looked at her not knowing what to say! In his mind he was wondering if she knew that he was feeling sorry for her? If so, it was certainly something she didn't need to know! What she was telling him had at least been partially true! Paloma was certainly capable of giving him everything he wanted or would ever need! Money was certainly no longer a problem! By this time he even had enough money to spare making certain that his parents would never again need to struggle just to survive! The things she said mattered a great deal to him and were fixed in his mind!

"Mari, you are so wrong!" he told her. "Your life is never over as long as there is a breath of life left within you! You are also correct that I am about to marry a socialite who can give me everything I need! Unfortunately, the things she cannot give me are the times you and I had together in college! As I look back, I think they were the happiest days of my life! The one thing I never realized was how much I was going to miss you until you left school without saying goodbye! It seems strange that we never once mentioned where either of us could be reached! As

I look back, I guess it was probably because we both felt that we would never be separated! Besides, I guess you were too angry to even give a damn about me! Nobody knows what the future holds for us! Who would have thought I would have you for a client after all this time? One thing we both know and can't deny! If one of us is not there, then, the future becomes very bleak! And you are quite right, the socialite can give me everything..... except.....perhaps.....what I need most!" he said, without finishing the sentence. Then, quickly, he decided to move along and explain parts of the case. "There is a possibility....and, mind you....only a possibility, that I might be able to convince a judge to release you into my custody while the trial date is pending! How would you feel about being released into my custody if that were to happen?"

"Andres, I could never afford to pay you room and board! My parents have suffered enough! Of course, they would want to help me, but you know as well as I that things here in Madrid are more expensive than they are in Bilbao!" she told him.

"Over our office there is a small apartment that consists of two rooms! If we are successful in getting you released, you could live in those rooms! During the day, you could help Herr Otto in the office with his paperwork! I'm sure you and he would hit it off wonderfully! Then, you could accompany herr Otto and me for meals! In other words, you would be earning your keep since you won't be able to leave Madrid while the trial is pending! It would be your decision to make!" he told her.

"And how do you expect to explain me to your future wife if she comes to visit and finds me working in the office?" she asked with a sneer.

"I'll simply explain that you are a client and that your're earning your room and board!"

"Will she accept that explanation?? I sure as hell wouldn't!" she told him with a smile.

"It's about time I finally saw you smile! I thought that maybe you had forgotten how to smile!" he said with just enough sarcasm for her to know how he still felt! He had told her this many times before when there was no money, and yet both of them were happy with each other! "I'll be back tomorrow! I want to know everything about the day that the ETA members were ambushed by the Guardia Civiles! In the meantime, I'll be filing a motion in court for a hearing and see what judge has been assigned to hear the case! Also, remember! You promised me that you wouldn't do anything foolish!" he said in parting as he got up from his chair and was getting ready to leave! In parting, he asked, "Is there anything you need or want me to bring?"

"No!" she said softly, almost in a whisper. "What I need you can no longer give me!" she told him as he raised his hand to say goodbye and signalled the jailer to open the cell door!

Bilbao

Miguel arrived tired and hungry after the long two day train ride! Soledad had been worried, especially since he had promised to call her but there had been no call from Madrid. At least there was some satisfaction when she saw that he seemed pleased and upbeat with his visit to Maripaz! He started to explain his disappointment in not being able to find an attorney who was willing to take her case. It had been a stroke of luck that he had bought a newspaper and came across the name of a lawyer who specialized in crimes against the Spanish government. The young man had taken on the case as soon as he explained what had happened!

"Did he tell you that he would be able to help her?" Soledad asked him.

"No! He didn't say specifically what he could or could not do! I did go to visit her with him and he agreed to take the case! He made me feel a bit strange because they were looking at each other as if they had known each other from before!" he explained.

"What makes you think that?"

"I don't know what it was! It was just a strange feeling that came over me, nothing more! It was strange that I left there feeling completely comfortable that the young man was going to do everything within his power to help her!"

"Yes, and how much is it going to cost? I wouldn't mind paying for the expenses if I felt comfortable that he was going to be of help! Have you forgotten what happened with the other attorney you hired to defend her? He charged us a great deal of money; and, in the end, they ended up by transferring her to Madrid!"

"That was the strangest part of all! As soon as I told him her name, he looked at me and immediately told me that he would be her lawyer without asking any more questions! He also explained that he would take the case, pro-bono and that there would be no cost!"

"Hah! And you fell for that? Whenever they say that there isn't going to be any cost, that is when the costs become excessive! I only hope that he doesn't abandon her the way the lawyer did in Bilbao! How did Maripaz feel about him!"

"She seemed to be very happy with him! At the beginning she seemed a bit apprehensive, but later as he started to talk to her, she seemed to be very comfortable with him!"

"We'll see, Miguel! We'll see! I only hope that she isn't disappointed and tries to take her life again! That's the greatest worry that I have! She tried it once before and I am afraid she'll try it again!" Soledad said.

"I don't think so!" Miguel answered. "I have a strange feeling about this man! The newspaper said he is considered to be a 'legal genius'! He is young, very handsome, and dresses very well!"

"Huh!! Those are the worse kind! They look good....talk good....and handsome! God only knows how much it is going to wind up costing us! I wouldn't care if I felt comfortable that he would be able to help her! But what do we do if he can't? She'll probably go to pieces thinking again that her life is over!"

"You may be right! All I can tell you is that I left Madrid feeling satisfied that the young lawyer would do his best to help our daughter!" he insisted.

"And what is this 'Mister Big Shot's' name?" Soledad asked. She was still feeling pessimistic that this young unknown lawyer would have enough knowledge and experience to help her little girl!

"His name is Licenciado Andres Romero! From what I read, he is going to marry the daughter of the Condessa de Romanones, after the mourning period is over!"

"Huh!! He was probably the person who killed that horrible old woman! He has to come from money! What family does he belong to?"

"I don't know for sure! I thought I read or heard him say that he wasn't a member of any influential family and that his parents were farmers in Galicia!"

"That's all we need!" she answered with sarcasm. " ..... to have a stubborn Gallego for a lawyer! Wasn't there anyone else available that you could have gone to?"

"He certainly can't be any more stubborn as a Gallego than we are as Asturianos!" he told her smiling!

CHAPTER 9

It is rare when a monarch is not born in the country he will one day rule! When Juan Carlos Alfonso Victor Maria de Borbon y Borbon was born in Rome, Italy in January 1938, any chance of him becoming a successor to the Spanish throne looked remote. His grandfather, Alfonso XIII, had been forced into exile in 1931 following two decades of turbulance for the Spanish monarchy! The former king, Juan Carlos I, had died in 1941. Five years later, all of the other remaining members of the king's family had moved to the Portuguese capital of Lisbon. In accordance with the wishes of his father, part of his education was to be in Spain. The nine year old future monarch, still dressed in short trousers, arrived in Madrid for the first time in 1947. After finishing his secondary school education in 1954, the young prince entered Spain's premier military academies, and graduated as a naval, army and air force officer complete with pilot's wings! He then later completed his education at the prestigious Complutense Universidad de Madrid where he chose to major in Political and International Law, Economics and Public Spending!

In 1962, the dashing Spanish royal prince married Princess Sofia of Greece in the capital city of Athens. Three children would soon follow, Elena, the eldest daughter, was born in 1963, and would later be followed by two other siblings, another girl, and a son! In a move to assure the country's stability after his death, General Francisco Franco, then the head of state, designated an apparently pliant Juan Carlos as his successor during the late 60's! The young prince was carefully groomed for his new role and began his public life in earnest, making official trips on behalf of his country both at home and abroad! General Franco had ignored the successory rights of Juanj de Borbon, the father of Juan Carlos, and sought to educate him as his successor for the maintenance of the regime. During the dictatorship, Franco created the title of Prince of Spain for Juan Carlos. He started to use his second name of Carlos in order to assert his pretensions to the heritage of the Carlist branch of his family. Franco, for a long period of time, had toyed with the idea of conceding the throne to Juan Carlos cousin, Alfonso de Borbon Dampierre, because he felt that Juan Carlos was much too liberal a scholar to be the successor of a fascist government!

Andres was no stranger to Prince Juan Carlos! He had met the prince on several occasions in the Romanones mansion just outside of Madrid! Their first meeting had been at a formal gathering in which the prince had appeared in his complete military uniform. Andres had stood alone looking at all the socialites that were present and who had a daughter within the age of the prince, have their daughters parade before him hoping to catch the roving eye of the future king! He had been sitting alone in the large patio in the estate sipping on a glass of Dom Perignon champagne when someone walked up to him and said, "You look almost as bored as I am!" Andres turned his head only to see the prince standing alone in the patio with him!

"Paloma tells me you are Licenciado Andres Romero!" the prince asked. "I understand that the two of you will soon be married, is that true?"

"Yes, on both counts, your Highness!" Andres replied.

"I am happy to meet you! I was told that you had turned down the judgeship in the Supreme Court! May I ask why?" he asked.

"I'm afraid it would be a long story! Much too long to go into detail! I'm afraid I would be seriously reprimanded if I were to discuss my ideas with you at this time!"

The prince was noticing that Andres was smiling as he spoke! "Confidentially, I think we are both bored! Perhaps a lively discussion is just what we need to lift our spirits!"

"How can you be bored, your Highness? Every woman who has been blessed with a daughter has come here and put them on exhibition hoping that you would make a selection to become your princess!" he said. Suddenly, the prince let out a hearty laugh!

"That is what is boring me! It almost seems as if I am on exhibition! Trust me when I say that someone is watching our every move, hoping that one of us will stumble and fall so that the news media can print how we had entirely too much to drink!"

"For my part, I'll surprise them!" he looked down at the half empty champagne glass in his hand. "I don't even like the taste of this stuff!" Andres said.

"What do you prefer?"

"For me? I would prefer a brandy glass with some Duque de Alba cognac!" he replied.

"If you can keep a secret, I'll be honest with you! So would I!" he took another sip of his champagne! "I came out here on purpose! Paloma tells me that your specialty is Civil Law! I, too, am very interested in this specialty! You see, someday, if and when I become king, I hope to establish enough democratic reforms to change the reputation of Spain before the world!"

"That can be a very ambitious task, your highness! Still, I commend you for your position! However, as long as we have every criminal act or every misdemeanor trial under military law, how can democratic forms ever be established? One is inconsistent with the other!"

"Perhaps we could have Paloma invite both of us one day when no one else is here and we can sit down and have an honest discussion! I would love to listen to your views! You know as well as I that I have been trained by the General in his own way! There has been some talk that he might assign my cousin Alfonso to the throne! It is his decision to make! The General says that I am much too liberal for Spain! Unfortunately, I happen to see Spain in a much different way! If we ever expect to gain any respectability in

Europe, we need to change our views! What do you say? Do you think there is a chance that you and I can get together?" he asked.

"If your Highness so orders, I will be happy to obey!"Andres told him. Once again the prnce began to smile!

"I don't believe in issuing orders! By the way, your name is much too long for me to keep addressing you as Licenciado don Andres Romero! Would you mind if I call you Andres? In return, whenever we are meeting in private and drinking our cognac, suppose you leave out the prince part and just call me Juanito!"

"Very well, your highness! Perhaps I can set something up with Paloma!"

"No! Don't you do it! I'll do it! If you tell her, she will want to set up another gala affair and invite half of Spain to attend! I want it kept quiet and personal! I'd like to get your views especially because of your interesting background!" Andres was feeling a bit perturbed! He didn't want to appear disrespectful, but it was the change in his tone of voice that disturbed him!

"Is my background so strange that it needs to be examined under a microscope?" he asked.

"On the contrary! Yes, perhaps you should be examined because I have always believed that people from all walks of life should be able to advance themselves! From what I heard, you are a perfect example! If one day I should become king, I would want the people to know that I am a king for all the people in Spain, and not just the few that were here tonight showing off their daughters! Is that so strange?" the prince asked.

Just as he was about to answer, Paloma came outside and interrupted their conversation! "Andres, you must come inside! There are people who want to meet you! And you, your highness, people have been asking about you!" she told them as they both looked at each other and shrugged their shoulders! Paloma was taken by complete surprise not knowing what they meant!

The prince shot a glance over to Andres and gave him a mischievous wink! "We will do as you say; but first you'll have to promise to have me over during the weekend! Please, Paloma, this time, no gala affair! I want you to invite Andres and me! Just the two of us and a bottle of Duque de Alba! Do you think you can arrange this for us?" he asked her smiling.

"Certainly, your Highness!!" she said surprised that the prince had made such a request! It must be that he and Andres had something to speak about and he didn't want a large audience. "I would be happy to do as you ask! I will speak with Andres and see how it will tie in with his schedule!"

"Oh nonsense!!" he answered. "We've already gone past the discussion stage; haven't we, Andres? Perhaps I have a better idea! Why don't you let Andres and me alone while you go and visit some of your friends? I think I would like that even better! How about you, Andres?"

"Your Highness, believe me when I say that nothing would please me more!" It was said with sarcasm that caused the prince to smile! Meanwhile, Paloma took each man by the hand and gently guided them to the dance floor! The music had started to play and there were a few young ladies on the floor waiting for the prince to ask them to dance! One of the young woman quickly bowed before him and took hold of the prince's hand as they started to dance! The prince, as he was being led to the middle of the dance floor, looked over his shoulder and saw that Andres had remained behind.

"Que suerte es la tuya!" (How lucky you are!) he said smiling! His tone of voice was very low, making certain that only Andres had been listening to him! Andres nodded his head, made a face and returned the smile!

It was a bright, sunny day when the two men met at the Romanones Estate on Sunday morning! Unknown to the prince, Andres had already had a strong argument with Paloma over the way he was dressed! She had insisted that he wear a tuxedo and black tie since the meeting was a private one consisting only of the two men. Paloma had insisted that the prince was a very important man and whenever one had the occasion to meet with him, one should always be formally dressed! It was only after he insisted adamently that he refused to wear a tuxedo! The prince and he had discussed the matter between themselves and both agreed that the meeting would be informal; and each man would be free to express his own ideas in confidence and without any outside interference by anyone, socialite or peasant alike! After the argument, Paloma was surprised when she saw the prince drive up to her estate in his own sports car and was quickly ushered inside by one of the servants. To her surprise, he was dressed in an open collar sport shirt and an old pair pants that hadn't felt a hot iron for quite some time. It surprised her that he looked anything but regal in his dress! The other surprise that left Paloma speechless and unable to speak was when the prince went up casually to Andres, shook his hand, embraced him and called him by name. "Hola Andres!! Que tal, como estas??" he said.

"Pues, muy bien, Juanito!! Aqui te estaba esperando!!" (I was waiting for you!)

Paloma nearly went through the floor when she heard Andres calling the prince by his name Juanito! It was well known among aristocratic circles that nobody called the prince by name! The two men walked off into the library! Andres walked over to a large wall cabinet and took out a new, unopened bottle of Duque de Alba Cognac! He then took two goblets and poured healthy portions of the dark liquid before handing one of the goblets to the prince.They touched glasses as if they were proposing a toast to someone, then sipped it after Andres closed and locked the door of the large room.

The prince began the conversation by asking Andres how he felt the direction of the country was going? Andres immediately saw this as a loaded question that required maximum care before answering! After all, he relaized that he was speaking to a man that had been personally groomed for the return of the Monarchy; and, even though he felt the need to be truthful, he was careful not ot be overly critical of the evolution that the country was currently taking!

"I believe there has been a great deal of improvement; but most of the improvements have been in the larger cities and little attention has yet been given to the northern provinces!" he said. "From what I have determined, the poor are still poor! I've been hearing that there has been little improvment among the farmers who are trying to produce enough vegetables for market!"

"Be more explicit!" Juanito asked.

"For one thing, we are importing entirely too many fruits and vegetables from other countries, instead of encouraging our own people to become more productive! For example, are you aware that over eighty percent of the tomatoes are now being imported from France! Of course, there is also the imports of beans, lettuce, cabbage and kale. From what I've been able to learn, the reason that the imports are so heavy is because they are cheaper to buy than to produce locally! All of this is great for the French; but, with the vast amount of imports, there is little incentive left for our own farmers! It seems that no one has stopped to think how much of our currency is being siphoned out of Spain to pay for these items! I believe that if we were to produce more vegetables, and, of course, assuming that the farmers are paid an honest wage, the money would be turned over inside of our own economy and the farming communities in the north would also fluorish! As things now stand, the farmers feel no better than the way they did before the days that led into the Civil War! It frightens me that there could very possibly be another revolution in the future just as we've seen in the early thirties when everyone was starving!"

"You present an interesting argument, Andres!" the prince told him. "If I am appointed King, I plan to introduce a constitutional Monarchy that will also include an economic plan that will benefit everybody!"

"Yes, but how long do you think it will take? How much damage will there be before that happens? The term of a Constitutional Monarchy sounds very impressive; but, let's be honest, how many Spanish people will really know what that means? Also, how many will really care? What the people want is to see the results, not the interpretations! If that is the type of government that will be selected, then reforms in the laws that govern our society must also be introduced! How can we have a Constitutional Monarchy and still be using old Military Laws to govern Civil Behavior? Military laws are intended only for military use! What we need to do is to establish a system of civil laws that will be expressely used for civilians!" Andres explained.

"I'm afraid that your recommendations would take even longer! We need to maintain law and order and the best way to do that is by applying the same hard laws we currently have on the books!" the prince replied.

"No, Juanito! Your explanation simply can not be! The laws that we now have are wrong for any society, other than for the military! For example, the General has repeated over and over that there must be amnesty for everyone who served on the opposite side of the Civil War! The fact remains that what is in effect is a 'selective amnesty' and nothing more! No society can offer an amnesty and then, without any justification, make it selective! This opens the door to a great deal of speculation! As long as there is either a conditional or a selective amnesty, then, who is to receive the benefits? Actually, I have one such person in mind! He served the fascist movement admirably for many years! Because he escaped to a city under Basque control, he was forbidden to enter Madrid for any reason! Now, he finds himself in need of medical care but he can't enter the city! Where is the amnesty? Why should he not be able to get those medical treatments that are necessary for his survival?"

"Is this one of the cases you are currently representing?" the prince asked.

"Not yet, but it may soon become one! If it does, I'll need to present the argument to the Superior Court for the defendent in absentia! I can't even allow him to testify on his own behalf for fear that he may be arrested! Is that amnesty? I think that if we are going to provide amnesty, every citizen in the country needs to be covered by the same laws. Those are the things the people will long remember and will ultimately contribute to the growth of this great country! If not, I'm afraid that Spain may well be doomed to failure; and another revolution such as the one we had may not be out of the question!"

"But Andres, you are speaking of a specific case! Of course, you know as well as I that there will always be exceptions! This is so in every society!"

"Yes, but remember! Every specific case becomes an exception! If there are too many exceptions, then, the specific cases take on an entirely new importance! To some extent, isn't that what is happening in the Basque areas of the country?"

"That's an entirely different story! The Basques have been at war with the Spanish government for many generations! That will never change and you know it!"

"That may be true, your Highness, but you have to admit that the government of Franco has been more than tolerant with them! In my opinion, we simply cannot afford to have a divided Spain! Either we all survive as one or we'll all perish as one! In my opinion, I have always felt that the Franco government has been far too tolerant with them! That is what is giving Spain a 'black eye' in the eyes of the world!"

"On that I do agree with you! I can't understand why the Franco government has not shown more resistance to their movement!" the prince told him.

"Do you want to listen to my theory, or do you simply want me to agree with you!" Andres asked.

"On the contrary! I want to listen to your theories! They are important to me!"

"Quite frankly, I don't really believe that the government quite knows how to deal with the Basques! I have a case right now, that is pending, where a young woman is facing a long prison term just because she attended a few of the meetings of the ETA! All of the evidence that has been compiled against her is based entirely upon hearsay, but I can't get the court to at the very least, give her a pre-trial hearing! It seems to me that all they want to do is to put it off for as long as possible! As a result, I may need to go into the Superior Court just to get a pre-trial hearing! In the meantime, the young woman is in jail and has no idea when she will be going to trial! What that tells me is that they simply don't know how to handle those problems! They prefer to let the young woman waste away in jail than to allow her to have her day in court! As an attorney, does that make any sense to you?" Andres asked.

"So, what do you intend to do?" the prince asked.

"I have no other choice but to appeal to the Superior Court and ask for a pre-trial hearing! If I am refused, I'll then ask that the defendent be released for a lack of evidence!"

"That is not a good way for our legal system to be working! I have to admit that if I were in trouble, I think I would want to have you defend me!" the prince tolf him.. "By the way, would you be interested in serving on the board of Judicial review? It's a very prestigious board, you know! You could be exactly what they need to stir things up!"

"No, your highness! That just is not for me! I prefer to conduct my work as I have been!

I am very much for the people of Spain! I don't think I could ever take all the bureacracy in that room full of 'stuff shirts'!" Andres said. He watched the prince flash him a smile before asking, "May I pour you another glass of cognac?"

"Of course! Why do you think I came here?" he said jokingly. "Tell me something, Andres! Let us assume that I were to be named as King of Spain! I know that, in itself, is a remote possibility; but, if I were, would you be willing to accept a post in my cabinet in the office of Legal Reform?"

Damn, this was a loaded question, he said to himself! How could he ever deny the wishes of his King if he was asked to participate in one of his cabinets? He just couldn't! Those things were simply not done! He could never turn down the request of a King, no matter how friendly he had been with him!

"Your Highness, it would depend on what responsibilities would be assigned to me and the manner in which I was appointed! If I were appointed because you believed that I was the best man for the job, of course, I would accept in a minute! I would also need to have some input about changing some of the military laws that are currently being used! The appointment would need to be based upon my work! If I knew I was being appointed only because someone had recommended me, I would be nothing more than a figure head, I'm afraid I would have to refuse, your highness!"

"Maybe you better be thinking about it! If I happen to be named King, I'm going to expect you to change all of the military laws over into a civilian arena! I don't expect to take no for an answer!" the prince told him. "Besides, I'm going to need a Duque de Alba drinking partner, and what I don't need is to have someone that is going to 'yes' me to death! Those are the things that drive me crazy!"

"Juanito, on a personal level, I would be proud to be your friend! On a more serious level, as an official member of your group, I would only accept an appointment if I felt I could help you get your own ideas across to those who will be running the country! I get the feeling that your ideas are very much the same as mine!" he answered.

"How would you like to go sailing with me next weekend? I have a sailboat in La Coruna, and I'd like us to spend the day together! I am still anxious to learn how you managed to win the case against Paloma's young son!" Andres looked at him rather strangely. He was surprised that the prince had known about the case concerning young Jose!

"I'm afraid that would be considered priveleged information! Only Paloma or her son can tell you what happened!"

"Nonsense, I already know all about it! As an attorney, I am anxious to learn more of your strategy! Now, will you come with me or not?"

"Of course I will, Juanito! As long as we take along a bottle of cognac and not champagne! Will anyone else be going?"

"No! Just you and me! Besides, isn't that where your people are from?"

"Yes!"

"Good! Before we sail, suppose we stop off and meet your folks! Besides I haven't eaten a dish of Caldo Gallego in years! Do you think they would mind?"

"Mind?? They would be thrilled! They've been an avid supporter of you and your family for many years! I have to warn you, however! They are simple people who live simple lives! The only thing they have to give is love, and of course, a large plate of Caldo!" he said.

"Then, who can ask for more?" the prince said before changing the subject when Paloma interrupted their conversation and asked them if they wanted to eat! She had already spread out the usual caviar and vodka! The prince, who seemed to be feeling the effects of the Duque de Alba, looked at Andres and smiled.

"Oye Andres! Prefiero una tortilla con gambas al ajillo!
Que te parece?" (I would prefer a tortilla and some garlic shrimp!
How about you?)

"Igual, su alta! Que te parece so hoy seremos simplemente
obreros! Vamos a dejar la alta sociedad para otro dia!" (I feel the
same way! Today, we'll be simple ordinary men and leave the high
society for another day!) he told him.

Corte Mayor, Madrid

As usual, Andres had spent a great deal of time and had
appeared in court well prepared! He had faced a great deal of
opposition trying to have the case heard in one of the senior
courts! It wasn't until he threatened to file an appeal to the Federal
Government that he finally received the notice advising him of
the willingness of the court to hear the pre-trial case concerning
Maripaz Romero! He reviewed the case with Herr Otto and with
Maripaz, who was showing less interest than he had expected
in what was happening! Andres had spent the day briefing his
client on what to expect, but she was showing a lack of real
interest in what he considered to be a major move in her favor!
Although she had said nothing, Andres felt that she had already
resigned herself to spend many years in jail, He had gone to visit
her every day! It had been a form of departure from what he had
undergone at home, especially on those days when he had told
Paloma that he needed to be absent from an important gathering
at the Romanones' Estate! It wasn't that he didn't want to attend
nor did he want to seem disrespectful to the gathering of socialites
that were expected to attend! The truth was that he had nothing
in common with those people and considered them boring and
uninteresting! At least whenever he was with Prince Juan Carlos,
the conversations were always animated while they spoke freely as
two intellects and discuss the country and all of its problems from
two separate points of view. The people attending the gatherings
knew little and cared less about the problems that the country was
facing! As long as there was a sufficient supply of caviar and Dom
Perignon champagne, nothing else about the country seemed to be
of any interest!

When he went into her cell, he saw that she was well dressed! Her hair had been neatly combed and she had even applied a light shade of rouge and liptick, just enough to make her look more presentable in court!

"You look wonderful today, Mari!" he told her. "You almost remind me of those days when we would go for our long walks in the park! Do you remember?"

"I've never forgotten!" she answered sadly. "Andres, I know that you want to help me and I appreciate everything you are doing! But I can't get over this feeling that my life is over and whatever happens will no longer matter! I'm grateful for all you've done, and I will never forget you! I just have this feeling that the court won't change its mind!"

"I'm sure as hell happy that I am not a pessimist like you!" he told her. "I am always optimistic with any of my clients! Suppose for a moment that the court decides to release you in my custody while the trial is pending! Have you given any thought to living in the apartment above my office? It may not be very glamorous, but you would have me for company!"

"I will do whatever you want me to do! If that is where you want me to live, then, that's where I'll live! I won't have any other choice!" she said coldly. She noticed a look of diappointment on his face with her reply. It was no secret that he had expected her to be more animated and excited about the fact that they could be together once again! "I guess I've disappointed you again, haven't I?" she said sorry that she had made him unhappy.

"It doesn't matter!" he answered just as coldly. "I've been disappointed before, once more won't make any difference! I just thought you would be happy to live upstairs and know that I was only a short distance away, that's all! I guess I was wrong!"

"How am I supposed to be elated? I realize that you are about to be married to a socialite whom I can never equal! I've already accepted losing you because of my own negligence and stupidity! I would never stand in your way, but it doesn't change the pain that I feel! My feelings for you have never changed and probably never will! Not that it's going to do me any good! I've lost you and I accept my loss! My life at the moment has no meaning!

If you are successful and get me out of jail, I'll wait until after the trial; and, if I'm lucky, I'll return to my home in Bilbao! In the meantime, you'll be free to marry your countess and forget all about me!"

Little did she know that he wanted to tell her how wrong she was! What she didn't know was that with everything that happened in his lifetime, the truth was that he had never forgotten her and was determined never to allow her to leave for Bilbao without him! Unfortunately, he was an attorney! As an attorney, he needed to concentrate on the case he was defending and had little time for sentimentalities! After the trial, and, assuming that he was successful, there would be enough time to pick up the scattered pieces of his life. For the time being, he needed to do his job as well as he could and do whatever was possible for his client!

After a third deliberate cancellation, he was finally granted a judge that was willing to hear the case and who had the reputation of appealing to a defense attorney! Any hearings on a pre-trial motion were always susceptible to changes; and it wasn't unusual for a defense counsel to delay a trial date for a judge that might be more favorably inclined toward the best interests of everyone! Of course, under military law, once a trial date had been set, there could be no cancellations except for extreme circumstances or for a major force! Those dates were set in stone and would not be changed under any condition!

Judge Velazquez was an old manwho was set very much in his ways! Rumor had circulated that he intended to retire from the bench in another year! He had a reputation for fairness and logic and had often taken the defendent's part whenever he felt there had been impropriorites, or if he felt there was a lack of evidence resulting in a conviction! Andres had tried earnestly to get the records about Maripaz's arrest, hoping to learn the type of case they were charging her with, but all of his best efforts had gone in vain! The fact that none of the prosecutors had been willing to submit any concrete evidence coupled with the fact that no date had yet been asked for a trial, led him to believe that the evidence against her had been fragmentary, vague, and exceptionally weak! He had argued cases before Judge Velazquez on many occasions, and from experience, he always felt that he was one of a few judges that he admired for the way he conducted a case in his court room! If anyone was going to argue a case in his court, whether for the state or for a client, he had better do his homework and come to court well prepared! If not, he would be chastized by the judge who would then dismiss the charges! This was exactly the type of judge that Andres had been hoping for and was ready to argue the case against Maripaz!

The small courtroom of Judge Velazquez was sparsely furnished with old fashioned wooden furniture, probably left over from the Civil War! Only a few spectators had gone to hear the proceedings; after all, this was only a pre-trial hearing involving a woman from Bilbao! As far as the news media was concerned, Bilbao was at the other end of the country. The fact that a woman was on trial meant very little unless she had done something spectacular that merited closer attention! These pre-trial hearings were common place and were hardly ever mentioned in the newspapers.

After the initial reading of the charges, the Judge had motioned to the prosecutors to present whatever evidence they planned to use against the defendent! Andres was busy listening to the charges and at the same time, keeping an eye on the Judge for any tell tale signs of preferential treatment to either the prosecution or the defense. The initial charges were that the defendent was being charged with crimes against the government! She was being accused of being a leader in the terrorist organization whose aims were to overthrow the government of Francisco Franco! It almost seemed humorous to Andres when he heard the eloquent charges of a tall, distinguished prosecutor who chose to be specific in referring to Francisco Franco by name, rather than to simply accuse her of trying to overthrow the government! He jotted down a few notes on a legal pad and was careful not to interrupt any of the testimony! It was more important that the prosecutor complete his opening remarks uninterrupted, by doing so, the case would need to be exposed in its entirety, rather than to have it explained in fragments only to have the brunt of the charges made in an open court during the actual trial! When the prosecutor had been finished, the Judge had asked if he wanted to add any other comments to his case! The prosecutor looked over his notes and simply said, "No, your Honor!" The Judge gently nodded his head before making a motion to the defense to take the stand! Andres waited a few moments as he reviewed his notes before walking up to the small podium before the court! As he walked up to the stand, he took one look at Maripaz and saw that she was anxiously waiting to listen to what he was going to say!

"Your honor," Andres began, "I have listened to the opening statements given by the prosecution! In order to preserve both the integrity and the time of this court, I wish to file a motion for the immediate release of my client into my care!" he said. There was a buzz and whispers from the people that were listening! All were surprised that without offering any rebuttal to the charges, this attorney had instead gone for the jugular and asked that the defendend be released, an act that was virtually unheard of and unknown in legal circles! Andres watched and waited for the response while the Judge and the Prosecutor looked at each other, each showing signs of surprise and bewilderment over the strange request!

"Those are very bold motions that are a bit premature, don't you agree, young man?" the Judge admonished, "It seems to me that your client would be better served if counsel, at least, tried to repudiate the charges, don't you agree?"

"No sir!! I do not!!" Andres bellowed making certain that everyone in the court was listening to him. This was his moment to apply pressure to his case and he didn't want anything or anybody to spoil this moment for him! "From what I know and heard about this case, your honor, there is no case! For your information, we have filed request after request for signs of any evidence to be used but have received no reply! In addition, there has been no evidence presented here or in any other court for that matter against the accused! In the absence of specific testimony, I must assume that there is no hard evidence available that would convict my client! Unless more specific information can be produced by the prosecution at this time,I must submit to the court that the defendent must be released for lack of evidence, your honor!"

The prosecutor was taken by complete surprise! Surely this was a ploy to catch the court off balance! Everyone knew that the hard evidence was only presented at trial and never during the pre-trial hearing! He leaped up from his seat and started to wave his arm! "Your honor, this is preposterous!" he shouted."For the court's information, this woman has been accused of being, not only a member, but a leader of the feared organization the ETA! Everyone knows that the aim of the ETA is to overthrow of the government!" the prosecution protested emphatically before once again taking his seat!

Good, Andres said to himself! This had been precisely what he wanted to hear! Obviously, the prosecution had taken the bait!

"Your honor, my client has already freely admitted that she did, in fact, attend to some of the meetings of the ETA! May I remind the court that there have been many young people who have attended the meetings, but none has been brought to trial! I find the charges by the prosecutor to be preposterous! Your honor, may it please the court, every Spaniard knows that in Spain no women is permitted the dignity of being a leader in a male dominated society! Therre is no society in Spain that regards any woman as an equal in a male organization! How could she be? May I also add that my opponent failed to mention to the court, how moments before an exchange of gunfire between the ETA and teh Guardia Civiles in Bilbao, my client was sitting alone in the plaza watching what was happening! I wish to emphasize that she was not, I repeat, was not a party to the criminal activity that the ETA was involved in! At that time she shot and killed a member of the ETA and was subsequently reported in all the newspapers as a heroine for having saved the life of a young girl that was about to be taken hostage by one of the group members! I submit, your honor, that all of the pertinent data about this case was deliberately withheld from this court! Only those facts that are persuasive to the government have been revealed and this is completely unfair to the defense!" he said.

All of the facts concerning the case were now clearly exposed; and judging by the surprised look on the judge's face,

Andres watched the elderly man on the bench looking at Maripaz with sympathetic eyes! Andres quickly went over to the defense table and took out all of the newspaper articles and photographs taken shortly after the robbery. Each of the articles was praising Maripaz for what she had done and the way she had defied the assailant when he tried to take the young girl as a hostage!

"Were you aware of these articles?" the judge asked the prosecutor.

"Yes, your honor!" he answered softly.

"Then why were they omitted from your presentation and brought to my attention? Frankly, I still fail to know why this young woman has been arrested and is being held over for trial? Unless you can provide this court with additional testimony showing that what she did was detrimental to the best interests of Spain, I see no reason why she should not be released into the custody of her attorney! I doubt very much that a young woman who is so responsible would decide to leave the area in order to avoid a trial!" the judge said.

Before the prosecutor, still stunned by the turn of events, had been able to register an objection, the judge had already slammed the gavel on the top of his desk and was asking the court bailiff to present the following case! Andres walked over to Maripaz, embraced her and led her out of the courtroom with his arm around her waist!

"What happens now!" she asked. After all, everything had happened so quickly that she was totally confused by the various exchanges that had taken place!

"You pack your things and notify your parents that you are free! I'm sure they'll be anxious to hear from you! In the meantime, you will be living upstairs from our office! You can work in the office as a receptionist! My partner, Herr Otto, hates to be answering the telephone! Maybe you could do that for us! It would be your way of paying for legal services!" Andres told her smiling.

"Andres, I would love to do that! But do you think that Herr Otto and Paloma would be willing to give me the privelege of working for you?"

"I think I can vouch for Herr Otto! As far as Paloma is concerned, I'm quite sure she has many more important things to do! I doubt very much that she would care one way of another!"

"Even if she realizes......that......I am still in love with you?" she asked.

This had been precisely what he wanted to hear! Unfortunately, this was not a social gathering! This was business! There would be time for other things at a later time! For now, it was important that he act the role of attorney! There was still a great deal of work to be done! There was just no way he could afford to become involved in affairs other than the law!! At least he knew that she still loved him! He had always felt the same way! Now the only person standing between them was Paloma! He would need to come up with a way of telling her the truth!

"Mari," he said seriously, "I'm speaking to you as your attorney and not as your lover!" he began. "What I do and the way in which I conduct my legal business are the affairs only of myself and Herr Otto! As long as he is pleased with your work, that is all I care about! What Paloma thinks or feels has absolutely nothing to do with the way I conduct myself in the courtroom!"

Galicia

Guillermo had always hated the thought of being dressed up when he was at home! Today that he needed to travel to Madrid, there was no way that Dolores was going to allow him to go to the capital city without wearing a freshly ironed suit and a shirt and tie. They had received the letter from their son mailed several weeks ago telling them that his future bride, Paloma de Romanones, was anxious to meet her future in-laws prior to the wedding! Andres and Paloma had several serious discussions about having his parents visiting them, but Paloma had insisted on the visit of his parents. He had argued repeatedly that his parents were simple people and that they would feel inadequate and out of place meeting anyone who was of a higher social status! They were simple people and preferred to remain the way they were! Paloma had repeatedly countered that if they were to be related as a family, she certainly had the right to know them before they were married!

After all of the discussions had been exhausted, Andres finally gave in and agreed to ask his parents to visit them in Madrid; but only if she promised that the visit would be a private affair between her family and his! He did not want her to spring one of her favorite surprises and arrange at the last minute a large gathering of her close friends who would use the occasion to examine and laugh in secret at these peasants from the northern provinces! The truth was that Andres had grown to despise her friends and had always believed that his parents, with all of their simplicity, had more class and more sensitivity than most of her friends who were always willing to accept an invitation to these gatherings providing there would be ample supplies of cognac and champagne, not to mention a healthy serving of expensive caviar to feed their faces! If only Paloma realized how much Andres despised those people and how much he hated being in their company! He had even gotten to despise their false declarations at the end of each gathering when they would tell the hostess how much they had enjoyed the party! All the while, in silence, they were probably wondering when the next gathering would be held!

Andres knew that his father could often be outspoken! He would never tolerate any critical comments from anybody in the crowd, no matter who they were! If anything, Guillermo had always had a reputation for saying exactly what was on his mind without restricting his comments in anyone's presence! The strange thing was that this had always been one of the qualities that he always had admired in his father! Now, he was genuinely worried! The people that Paloma would gravitate to were brusque and outspoken and were sure to say something to upset his parents when they went to the house to meet the other members of the Romanones' family!

It was a long, uncomfortable train ride, and Dolores and Guillermo were tired and restless, when they arrived from the northern province of Galicia! Andres was at the station waiting for them and had been looking forward with guarded anticipation to their visit since he hadn't seen them in a long time! He had been feeling guilt over not visiting them despite his promises, but something always ssemed to come up that would prevent him from going!

Dolores was wearing a simply cotton dress, but it was the angry look on his father's face that troubled him the most! Guillermo had arrived wearing a dark jacket that was several sizes too small and a tie that was soiled and had seen much better times! After embracing them, he immediately went to straighten out Guillermo's tie moving the tiny knot a bit closer to the center of the yellowish collar of the shirt. At first he had expected his father to push him away, as he often did when he was at home but today was a special occasion and he was much too happy seeing his son after a long absence! Then, Andres took the small suitcase and put it into his car, driving the streets of Madrid until he arrived at the luxurious Ritz Hotel near the large marble Fuente (fountain), a short distance away from the world famous Prado Museum of Art! Andres had made both the selection of the hotel as well as the reservations! He began to smile when he saw the surprised look on his parent's faces as they eyed the large, majestic hotel lobby. Once they were settled in their room, he took them for a short walk to his office where he introduced him to Herr Otto who was busy thumbing through papers on his desk! The two men shook hands warmly; and seeing the inquisitive look of both men, it seemed like a cordial friendship was in the making! Andres pulled over two wooden chairs for his parents at about the same time as Maripaz appeared carrying a tray containing several cups of hot coffee!

"Senor Torres," she asked politely. "Desea el cafe con leche y azucar a desea algo un poco mas fuerte?" she asked with a smile on her face! (Would you like your coffee with milk and sugar or would you prefer something a bit stronger?) Guillermo flashed the attractive young woman a warm smile, pleased by her warmth and her apparent good manners!

"Pues, prefiero algo un poco mas fuerte,Senorita! Que me ofreze?" he answered. I would prefer something a bit stronger! What do you suggest?) Mari reached into a wall cabinet in the small room they often used as a kitchen and removed a half emptied bottle of Duque de Alba, cognac! She slowly removed the cap and started to pour the brown liquid into the cup of coffee!

"Digame cuando sea bastante!" she said. (Tell me when it is enough!) Guillermo flashed her another smile and motioned her to stop when he saw that the cup was filled!

"Cual es tu nombre?" he asked her. (What is your name?)

"Maripaz!" she answered. It was always considered a common courtesy to ask someone their name when they were pleased with a service!

"Oye, Andres! Porque no me dijiste que tenias una guaja tan guapa trabajando aqui en tu oficina?" Guillermo praised her beauty loud enough for his son to hear him! (Why didn't you tell me that you had such a good looking girl working in your office?)

Andres was surprised, and for a few moments was without words! He didn't really want to tell him that she was his client and that she had been released to his custody by the court! He knew that doing so would have been an embarassment to Mari! Now that she and his father seemed to have hit it off well, he didn't want to cause her any embarassment, especially in the presence of his parents!

"La muchacha vive arriba y nos ayuda en el despacho!" (The young woman lives upstairs and helps us out in the office!) he answered, speaking as seriously as he could! At that very moment, he was not at all aware of the implications of his words! It had seemed to be an appropriate thing for him to say in the absence of the truth!

"Ah, si! Ya entiendo!" the father answered. He was smiling mischievously at his son and all the while winking at him! Andres quickly realized what he had said and was a bit embarassed! Unfortunately, it was too late! The damage had been made! He looked over at his mother as if he were asking for her help, but she only smiled and gently nodded her head as if agreeing with Guillermo! Mari, on the other hand, was seeing exactly what was happening and was loving every minute of the charade!

"Te preparo un cafe para ti, Andres?" she asked. (Shall I prepare a coffee for you?)

Andres, still embarassed by what he had say, nodded his head as his father broke out into a hearty laugh! In his mind, the embarassment appearing on his son's face had been enough to confirm all of his suspicions about this young woman! In his own mind, he was telling himself that if she was a worker, why would she be living upstairs and why would she be addressing him by his first name? No, there had to be something else that was going on between his son and this young woman! At least, he felt that if, in fact, he had chosen her to be his mistress, he had chosen well! She was not only attractive, but she seemed to be sensitive and 'carinosa'! Yes, he thought! His son had certainly chosen well! The only problem that worried him was what was going to happen if and when his fiancee found out about her? But then, he had confidence in his son, knowing that he was much too smart to allow himself to be caught in a love triangle! Besides, so what if he were to get caught? He could have certainly done much worse than this young lady who was so gracious and attentive and who made an immediate favorable impression on both his parents!

Maripaz was constantly at their service and making certain that their cups of coffee were kept full as Andres and his parents began speaking about everything they could think about and of the way things had been going on in Galicia. After several hours of chatter, the men decided they were hungry and agreed to go out for something to eat! Of course, it was well known that in Spanish society, women seldom interrupted their husbands whenever they spoke.Andres had said something about going to one of the expensive restaurants in the downtown area of Madrid, but Guillermo expressed his desire for one that was simply, informal, and that served an abundant offering of sardines on the grill and a hot dish of Caldo Gallego (Galician soup!) Andres thought about it while he tried to remember a restuarant that catered to Gallegos but none came to mind! After all, it had been many months since he had gone to a restaurant that was informal yet appealed to the tastes of Gallegos! Only when she saw him thinking about where to go did Maripaz interrupt him and suggested that they go to the now famous Parque de Espana that was located near the university! It seemed strange when she recommended the park because this had been the park that Mari and he would always go to when they attended the University! The recommendation had been done on purpose knowing it would bring back many memories to both of

them! It was odd that he hadn't visited the park since those happy
days at school; but he could still remember how many hours he and
Mari would be seated on the park benches studying their work and
admiring the beauty of the park!

The history of the park was interesting! It had started many
years ago because there were many people unemployed! Someone
within the government initiated the idea of converting the park
into a national park of all the various provinces of the country!
The largest portion had been sub-divided into eight separate
sections, each one representing one of the major provinces of
Spain. One of those areas was the province of Galicia. The area
consisted of a large oversized tent that served many of the most
well known dishes of that particular province. It became an instant
success as families would travel to the park and spend many hours
admiring the beauty of the flowers and the brush while, at the
same time, sampling the many delicacies of the different areas.
Even though Andres was certainly well acquainted with the park,
he had forgotten about it until Mari made the suggestion that
they go there.He had looked at her but had not commented on her
suggestion! It was almost as if he began to suddenly remember the
days of their past when their lives had been so different but simple
and uncomplicated! The world seemed so much more beautiful
then, and both of them were so much happier! How sad it was that
nothing ever stayed the same and that everything would eventually
change, some of the changes would be for the good while others,
would not be nearly as pleasant! He had been able to go from being
a student to a successful attorney, a rise that came practically
overnight! Now here he was about to marry into one of the most
afffluent families of Spain! On the other hand, he thought of Mari,
who had shown so much promise! Now she was about to face a
trial for criminal behavior that, for the moment at least, appeared to
be unjustified!

"No!" Andres said."I don"t think it would be wise to go
there!"

"Porque, neno?" Guillermo shot back! "It seems like an
excellent idea! If we went to the park, I could remove my jacket
and tie and be more comfortable! Besides, I also think your mother

would enjoy eating a few sardines and a dish of caldo! Que te parece Dolores?" (What do you think, Dolores?)

Dolores looked at her son and then she looked at Guillermo and could sense that Andres seemed uncomfortable with the suggestion! The more Andres hesitated about going to the park, the more Guillermo insisted on going there for dinner! Maripaz felt happy for having made the suggestion, and could see that Andres was deep in thought! There had been no malice but the recommendation was made with a specific purpose in mind! She was hoping that some of the pleasant memories they had shared when they were young would come back to him! After all, they had spent many hours in that park and had always considered that park to be their own!

Her thoughts were suddenly interrupted when Guillermo called out to her to settle the dispute! "Maripaz, que dices tu? Me parece tu idea excelente!" (Maripaz, what do you say? I think you had an excellent idea!)

"No, se, Senor Torres! Creo que la decision tiene que ser de ustedes y no de mi!" (I don't know Mr. Torres! I think the decison should be yours and not mine!) she answered while looking at Andres who was still undecided as to whether or not to go there!

"Como no, nena!! Ven con nosotros que yo les estoy conbidando! Quiero que vengas con nosotros! Anda, ponte el saco que have frio!" Guillermo ordered much to the surprise of Andres! (Why not, girl! Come with us, I am treating all of us and I want you to be with us! Come on, put on your coat, it is cold!)

Maripaz was also surprised with the invitation! She expected Andres to offer an excuse, any excuse, saying that she could not go with them! Although he looked undecided as to what to do, he said nothing! As for her, she didn't want to seem ungrateful to this gracious man even if the frown appearing on Andres' face was telling her a different story. Obviously, he didn't want her to go with them! Not that it mattered! She knew that she had done the damage! There were too many pleasant memories for them in that park to be easily forgotten. Dolores was torn between the look of confusion on her son's face and the indecision on the face of this poor young girl! Why shouldn't she go with them, she thought? She seemed frriendly and kind; besides, she could keep Dolores company while Andres and his father were quickly trying to catch up on their discussions, especially now that the cognac was taking its effect!

"Si tu no vienes, pues yo tampoco voy!" Dolores said. (If you won't go then, I won't go either!)

"Anda, anda, conho!! Ya esta listo! Ponte el saco de una vez y viene con nosotros!" Guillermo said loudly. This time it was no longer a request but a firm order to this young woman! (It's settled, damn it! Put your coat on and come with us!) Reluctantly, she looked at Andres who was nodding his head in agreement! She knew that he wouldn't dare go against his father's wishes! Maripaz quickly went upstairs to her room, combed her hair, powdered her face, and came quickly downstairs wearing her jacket! Jokingly, Guillermo grabbed her playfully by the arm and said to her. "Yo voy contigo! Eres mas guapa que mi hijo!" he said laughingly. (I'm going with you! You are better looking than my son!)

Despite all the indecisions and confusion of whether or not she should go with them, Maripaz had enjoyed herself in their company! The evening was going by much faster than they had expected nor wanted. They walked slowly, laughing and speaking loudly through the park! Every once in a while, Mari would catch a glimpse of Andres' eyes on her whenever they walked past a spot or something familiar that served as a reminder of days gone by! They took their place at one of the outdoor kitchens called, El Rincon de Galicia! Guillermo no longer felt homesick, especially when he saw a large burly man wearing a dirty white apron standing by a coal stove cleaning fresh sardines and cooking them in olive oil and garlic and placing them in front of them as soon as they were cooked. Guillermo had already eaten two large bowls of caldo that was served with a fresh bottle of wine. It wasn't long before they all started to sing many of the old Gallego songs that Andres soon remembered as being sung by his mother when he was a child. For the first time in a long time, they were genuinely happy as the wine began to work its magic. The greatest difference was in the way that Andres was suddenly treating her! There was a kinder and more gentle behavior that had not been present at the office! It almost reminded her of the kindness he had always shown to her when they were young! Guillermo stood up and began dancing La Jota! He took Maripaz by the arm and the two of them were dancing until Guillermo became tired and insisted that she finish the dance with Andres! When she saw Andres shake his head, she walked over to him and grabbed his hand, forcing him to dance with her!

"I guess some things tend to repeat themselves!" he said to her when they were dancing. "I seem to remember a time long ago when you also took me by the hand and led me to the middle of the dance floor! Do you remember?" he asked her as they hopped to the beat of the music.

"Andres," she said softly. She was speaking barely above a whisper not wanting Guillermo to hear what she was saying. "I've never forgotten anything we ever did together! Have you ever stopped to think how happy we were back in those days?"

"Of course!" he answered laughing. "I was a hell of a lot happier in those days than I am now!" he admitted much to her surprise. For man who was so careful with his own emotions, he was making a statement that was making her both happy and sad at the same time. After all, why would a man who had everything including fame, money and about to join one of the wealthiest families of Spain be unhappy? He should have been overjoyed by his good fortune! No one knew better than she that he deserved nothing less than to happy!

"I would never want you to be unhappy!" she said seriously. "You deserve your happiness! You'll see, everything will change once you're married!"

Suddenly he stopped dancing and stood silently looking at her in the middle of the small dance floor! "Oh my God!" he said. "Damn it! You've just reminded me that I was supposed to go to Paloma's house after I went for my parents! I guess just seeing them and being with them, reminiscing about old times, made me forget that I had promsied to be there! Tomorrow is the night for dinner at the Romanones Estate where she'll meet my parents for the first time! She certainly won't be happy that I forgot to go there tonight!"

"What will she do and why should she be angry? After all, you hadn't seen your parents in a long time! You had every right to be with them!" she said almost as if she was encouraging him into thinking that he belonged where he would be happy!

"I'm afraid you don't know Paloma!" he said. "She can get quite angry when things don't go her way! Tomorrow, she will probably come to the office like a house on fire and give me hell for not being there tonight!" He told her as a mere comment, but he wasn't showing any particular concern that he had forgotten to go to her house this evening!

"Does she make you happy?" Maripaz asked, not knowing where or how she had gotten up the courage to ask him that important question. Now that she asked, she was almost hoping that he would say no, Paloma did not make him very happy!

"Sometimes!" he answered. He became silent a few moments before continuing. Then he added, "She sure as Hell isn't going to make me very happy tomorrow night!"

"Do you want to go back to the office and telephone her! You can always apologize for overlooking what you promised!" she said.

"No!" he said simply without any hesitation or emotion. "This is the first time in a long while that I am really enjoying myself! There is no point in returning now!" he replied. She could see that he was indeed happier than she had seen him in a long time! Obviously, the wine and the cognac were still working their magic!

"Are you really enjoying yourself with your parents?"

"It isn't only them, it is also with you! I had almost forgotten how relaxed and happy you always made me feel! It's so unfortunate that everything had to come to an end!"

"Maybe we had best return!" she said reluctantly. "I think that the cognac and the wine are making you say things that you'll regret tomorrow! I think it's best that we go home!"

"Yes, there is always the chance that tomorrow I may be sorry for the things I said today! But at least for today, I am happy and happy days don't come around very often these days! We need to take advantage of them whenever we get them! Tomorrow, I'll listen calmly while Paloma gives me hell! But you know something Mari?? All of the terrible things in the world can never take away the happiness that I feel tonight! That alone makes me a hell of a winner!" he said as she looked deeply into his eyes! There were so many things on her mind that she wanted to say!! Damn it! He had no right being with that other women! He belonged with her! He had always belonged with her! Yes, she had made him unhappy and had even lost him! She had made a mistake, and if God can forgivem then why can't he! She was undecided whether or not she should simply go and take her place next to his father! Just as she was about to turn around, she heard him say! "C'mon, Mari! They are playing a slow number! Remember the way you taught me to dance to the slow music? Well, guess what?? I am now ready for another lesson!"he said as he took her into his arms and began dancing cheek to cheek while the music played on and his parents were looking at them! They were seeing their son happy and exhuberant and enjoying every minute of the evening with this young lady! Could it be that he was making a big mistake in marrying someone else? Would his wife ever succeed in making him as happy as he seemed at this moment? Even if he didn't love her completely, perhaps he could learn to love her as time went by! Guillermo was ecstatic seeing his son with this young woman, but Dolores was more concerned with what she was noticing! Could it be the wine and the cognac or was it his heart that was telling a much different story??

Andres arrived early at the office! His head was splitting with the effects of the wine and the cognac from the previous night. Today was the day that he had decided to submit his argument to the court and ask that all the charges against Maripaz be dropped. He was well aware that he would have no choice but to listen to the constant badgering of the prosecutors and to the presentation of any additional evidence against his client! The judge had agreed to listen to his plea and would hear the case with only the two lawyers present. The defendent would be excused from attending since the matter was between the lawyers and there was really no need for her to be in attendance! Andres had done his homework and knew that, at this time, the odds were in his favor for a full dismissal of the charges; unless, of course, the prosecution was able to provide the court with evidence in support of the charges against his client! He knew how the matter should turn out; but, unfortunately, he also knew how sometimes there can be surprises that change the turnout of the case! In secret, he was almost wishing that the case would be postponed for another day! This would allow Maripaz to continue working in his office where he would see and be with her every day! The inevitable was what he feared the most! If she were exonerated, she would be free to leave Madrid and return to her home in Bilbao and take on her life with her parents. He knew it was wrong for him to have these selfish motives! After all, it was necessary that he consider the welfare of his client and put aside his own feelings and emotions. Last night was now history! Perhaps it had been the liquor that had contributed to the euphoria of the evening! Now that the effects of the alcohol had worn off, it was time for the world of reality to return! As soon as he arrived at the office, the telephone began to ring and he knew immediately that it was probably Paloma questioning him about the previous evening! He already knew from previous experiences that no excuse was acceptable in these situations, so there was no use in offering any! One thing was certain, he was in no mood to argue with her as he often did whenever she took him to task for something he hadn't done!

"I'm sorry, Paloma!" he said pleadingly, after listening to her ranting and raving about having forgotten his promise! "Listen," he finally told her. "I can't argue with you at the moment! I am preparing a case for court and I can't afford to be distracted!" In silence he was wondering what she would have said, had she known that he was not only with his parents but had also spent a wonderful evening with his client? "I already told you that I was with my parents whom I haven't seen in a long time! We had a few drinks with my parents and before I knew it, the evening simply slipped away!" (Well, he thought! At least part of the story was true! The evening had been one of the happiest in his life, and God how he hated to see it end so quickly!)

"Yes, yes, yes! Of course!" he said. "My parents and I will be there for dinner tonight! No, I promise not to be late! You too must remember your promise to keep it simple as we agreed!" he told her, hoping she would take the hint and get off the telephone.

Her call had come as expected even if her rebuke and anger had been tempered by the fact that he had agreed, at her insistance, to have dinner at the house and to introduce his parents to their future daugher-in-law! He looked at his watch and noticed that it was getting late for his ten o'clock appearance at the court room! All of the paper he would be needing for court had been arrnaged into a neat pile as he told Herr Otto that he would be returning to the office after the case was heard. He glanced over at the staircase before leaving, noticing that Maripaz had not yet come down to the office! There was a part of him that was expecting the worse scenario and would be missing seeing her smiling face each morning! All the time he was gathering his papers he had been almost hoping that she would be there to see him off and to wish him luck!

His head was still feeling the effects of the alcohol when he entered the courtroom! Only the bailiff and the prosecutor arrived before him and both were busy looking through their papers before the judge entered! He nodded his head courteously at the bailiff before going over, greeting the prosecutor and shaking his hand! Soon afterward, the door opened and the judge arrived, just in time, something he knew was a rarity especially among the senior judges of the court. He opened up his own portfolio in their presence, glanced over the contents probably familiarizing himself once again, and gently banged his gavel bringing the court to order! The slight sound of wood against wood was enough to make Andres close his eyes because it was adding to his discomfort! The judge was quick and to the point! He asked the prosecutor to show cause why the defendant Maripaz Romero should not be released from any custodial restrictions in the absence of more specific evidence substantiating the charges against her! The prosecutor stood up, cleared his throat as he began to look through some of the papers on his desk!

"Your honor," he began after looking through his papers. "I ask the court's indulgence, since this case is still in the initial investigative stages! We ask that the charges that have been lodged against the defendant be retained and that this hearing be delayed for an additional ninety days!" Andres wanted to interrupt, but after seeing the angry look on the face of the judge, he decided to let the presiding judge present his comments!

"How long does it take to investigate a case?" the judge asked, showing his annoyance! "I gave a specific order for you to submit whatever evidence you had come up with at this time! I am of the opinion that your failure to show any evidence seems to me that none is available! If none is available, then, why was the defendant charged? Am I correct or have I missed something?"

"Your honor, may it please the court, this court is very complex! It has to do with a defendant that resides in the Basque region and we have been expressly tolds to exercise extreme care before taking a defendant to trial! We have not yet terminated our investigation!" he said. (Good, Andres said to himself! He had just committed serious damage to his case, but it was not yet time for him to interrupt!)

"I think you have had more than enough time in which to present your evidence! Unless you are able to do so, I see no reason why this woman should remain in detention!" the judge told him.

"Your honor, the prosecution is in agreement with the terms that have been issued by this court!" the lawyer told him. He was more eager to let the matter remain as it was at the present time with the defendant released into the custody of the defense counsel!

"Your honor!! I object!!" Andres bellowed so loud that the outburst had taken both the prosecutor as well as the judge off guard! "Since when are we compelled to keep a possible defendant in custody without any specific charges? I move that she be immediately released from any and all custodial arrangements and that the charges against my client be dropped because of insufficient evidence!"

"But your honor!" the prosecutor remarked. "What was done has been done in accordance with existing statutes! This is a crime against the government and we maintain every right to detain the defendant in confinement until a decision is rendered in one direction or another!"

"On the contrary, your honor! Ordinarily, I would agree that what my opponent has said is true, but it is the truth only because my client is being tried under the statutes that were established during the Civil War! Those were military laws that were only applicable to crimes against the government while the transition from a military to a civilian code was taking place! By my opponent's own admission, he has already stated that the government has ordered a reduced enforcement to the Basque regions! This, I understand, had been issued in order to reduce the unrest and the unhappiness that exists in that area! In my opinion, this is nothing less than selective prosecution which I remind the court is illegal! If we are to return to a more democratic form of government, we must treat our people equally, but we must treat them as civilians and not as military citizens! I find it appalling that because a person attends a meeting of unhappy citizens that this is considered a threat to this nation! If that was the case, every young person in the country that is unemployed would be subject to arrest! We would need to built jails throughout the country only to accomodate all of the arrests!" Andres paused just long enough to study the surprised look on the judge's face!

"In any democratic society, the people must remain free until they are proven guilty beyond any reasonable doubt! May I remind this court that the only evidence we have heard against this defendent is the hearsay of a person whose credibility leaves much to be desired! I move that my client be dismissed from any and all restrictions, either present or future, until such time that proper evidence can be provided that would be more incriminating than what we now have!" Andres said. The prosecutor again stood up and was getting ready to raise an objection when the judge quickly asked him to take his seat!

"I am compelled to agree with the defense! We cannot and should not, as a society, incarcerate people simply on the whims of hearsay when there is no hard evidence to substantiate the charges! In a military tribunal these things are allowed, because a soldier must take an oath not only to safeguard but also to uphold the government as well as the contitution! In a civilian court, the law is changed! It is up to the court to decide the guilt or the innocence of its people! Society has taken no oath either to the government or its constitution! It is, therefore, not unlawful for any person to attend meetings or to voice their objections as if they were in the military! I am therefore directing that the defendent be released immediately from any custodial restrictions and am ordering that all the charges against her be dropped! Is that clear, Mister Prosecutor!" he said angrily.

"But....but.....your honor! I must insist that....." the prosecutor tried to say before he was cut off by the judge.

"The decision has been ordered! This court stands adjourned!" the judge said as he stood up from behind the desk and walked back into his chambers!

Andres had quickly recuperated from his headache when he heard the disposition by the judge! He went over in his mind how he would break the news to Maripaz; and he wondered what she would decide to do now that she had been released from his custody and was free to return home? In silence he was hoping that she might consider remaining in Madrid! Unfortunately, his pending marriage to Paloma was also on his mind! Once the marriage had been completed, it would probably eliminate all of his chances to see her! His only salvation to prolong seeing her would be if he could defend her father against the old case against him. It would take some time to get a judgment allowing Mari's father to go to Madrid for medical care! There was always the chance that if he was persistant enough, she might agree to remain working in the office while he worked the legal details of her father's case! Nobody needed to remind him that having Mari in his office where he would see her every day was a dangerous step! He also knew that now that he had met her again, he hated the thought of her leaving and returning to Bilbao!

Romanones Estate

It was shortly after dark when both Guillermo and Dolores arrived at the Andres law office! There had been a series of discussions between his parents as to what Guillermo would wear for dinner at the estate! He had taken with him only one suit that was several sizes too small and the white shirt with the old fashioned tie was not suitable for such an occasion. After all, this was going to be a dinner offered in his honor and it was intended to be an informal get-together of the two families, hoping they could finally meet and be acquainted with each other. Also, Paloma had insisted that since Andres and Paloma were to married, it was proper that they should have a gathering between the families.

From the start, Guillermo had shown his unhappiness with the arrangements! His agreement to attend had only been at his son's insistence at what was described as an extension to his family! As soon as Andres parents arrived, Maripaz quickly took out clean coffee cups, brewed a pot of fresh black coffee, and poured a generous portion of cognac into the cups. She had met the parents at the door and had given them each a peck on the cheek, smiling and welcoming them until they waited for Andres to come out of his office and join them. Andres took one look at his father already dressed for the occasion and wished he had thought of taking him to a men's store and bought him a new suit! The thought had crossed his mind, but, he also knew that his father was sensitive to those things and would have been insulted had he made such a suggestion! He loved his parents too much to cause them any grief or insult just because Paloma might not like the way they were dressed.

Andres had not yet told Maripaz the news of what happened in the court room! When he returned, she had asked him how things had gone, but he simply told her that the judge had decided to once again delay his decision for another day! He already knew that she would be elated with the results; but this had been her day and she deserved something special in celebrating the resolution of her case! It was important for him to see that she was elated, and, that in some small way, might even express how much she needed him! Perhaps he needed to hear that assurance or perhaps he needed to hear it for himself! He would never know for certain! His thought was that in postponing the good news until tomorrow, he and Mari and his parents could celebrate her good news by having dinner at the Parque de Espana! He had enjoyed his previous visit to the park and he knew they had also enjoyed going there! Besides, he could also see that his father had been taken in by the young woman and there was no way he would agree to go there unless she went with them! In that case, the invitation would need to come from his father instead of from him! It would give him some consolation knowing that his father had invited her! Of course he would need to live with that arrangement even if he also knew that he was treading on dangerous ground!

Andres had insisted on going to the Romanones house for an informal dinner. They had both agreed that it would be simple and private! Andres already knew that his parents would feel very uncomfortable in a houseful of people, especially if they were dressed in black tuxedos! Also, the snacks that were served never changed! There would be portions of caviar and loads of champagne for the guests! His father, although in Galicia had eaten a great deal of fresh fish, caviar was something he had never tasted nor did he have any desire to eat fish eggs! As they got into the car and were driving off to the estate, he could see that his father was feeling nervous and getting a little restless while his mother was doing her best to settle Guillermo down before meeting his future daughter-in-law!

They drove past the famous Plaza de Espana and Guillermo remarked how much it had changed from when he remembered being there with the Guardia Civiles! There was an abundance of outdoor cafes, each with a large shade umbrella shielding the patrons from the warm Iberian sun! Many thoughts and memories came back to Guillermo as he remembered the large crowds of people that gathered there in the pre Civil War days, hoping that some sensitive politician would come out to talk to them and answer their pleas for assistance to erase the hunger they were feeling! Yes, times had changed indeed, he thought! There were no longer any crowds, only a few stragglers who had gathered to eat their Spanish tortillas and drink the wine! The local musicians called "la tuna" was hopping from table to table singing some of the old melodies gathering a few pesetas from the avid listeners! This was the Spain he had fought for and which would have existed then had it not been for the ruthlessness of the politicians who were trying to establish a form of government that cared little about the needs of the people.

Both he and Dolores were amazed by the number of cars on the streets! Those days of travelling by horseback had obviously ended, giving away to a new method of transportation that was virtually unknown just a few years ago! Even the car that his son was now driving seemed to be an invention from another planet as he maneuvered the car in and out of traffic through the busy downtown streets of the city. They travelled into the main avenue that led them out of the city until they passed by the University of Madrid where Andres had studied and had received his degree in the law! It was a new Spain, Guillermo said to himself! He still was not quite convinced whether the new Spain had been created as an improvment or whether at some point, it would all crumble again and revert back to the old miseries and the human problems of the past!

The Romanones' Estate sat in a large tract of land at the end of a long cul-de-sac that wound its way through the plush greenery until it ended with the wrought iron gates that opened automatically whenever a visitor was coming. Beyond the gates, were the well manicured floral gardens that were on both sides of a concrete path until the reached the large white stone estate, complete with long upright pillars that marked the way to the oversized door made of expensive imported wood! The butler quickly appeared, fully dressed in formal attire to take the vehicle to be parked behind the white mansion. Andres greeted him and shook his hand and then stared with his blank expression at the other two passengers that were in the car. Andres ignored the stare! Instead he led his parent beyond the door and into the large white sitting room! As soon as the door opened, he could hear the sound of loud voices coming from inside! People were talking and laughing! He was furious, but, with his parents walking behind him, he knew that it was necessary for him to disguise his feelings! There was no point in making them any more nervous and jittery than they were already feeling! Inside the enormous foyer that led to the receiving room, he saw the same crowd of people he had seen many times before! The men were all dressed in their evening formals and the women were showing off their new evening gowns as they tried their best to outdo each other!

Paloma went up to him, gave him a peck on the cheek and took him by the hand! She took one look at his parents and Andres could see that she was eyeing them from head to toe, asking herself were these people actually his parents or were they just two farmers he had picked up along the way? There was no cordiality nor any courteous handshake nor any pecks on the cheek! In reading her mind, Andres could see that she was regarding them as two foreigners or poorly dressed peasants who very simply did not belong there! The absence of her manners was obvious as she ignored them completely and turned her attention to Andres! It was almost as if they were not there at all! In a show for attention, she took Andres by the hand and led him inside, leaving his parents alone to walk behind them. Guillermo was already regretting having come! He would have preferred to go to the Parque de Espana and enjoy another pleasant evening with his son and his young mistress, whoever she was! When they reached the far side of the meeting room, one of the waiters dressed in his white jacket was holding a tray of half-filled glasses with champagne and milling around the crowd. Andres stopped the young man, took a glass of champagne and handed it to his mother! Then, as the young waiter was about to leave, he asked him to wait! He took another glass of the yellow liquid and handed it to his father! Afterwards, he took a glass for himself! None of the other guests had spoken to them nor did any of them make an attempt to greet them. The guests were much too busy filling their stomachs with caviar, onions and egg yellows, chasing the food down with imported vodka that had been purchased just for this occasion. For the first time, Andres and his parents fell awkward and unwanted! The dinner had been intended for his parents; yet, there wasn't a person in the group that stopped eating for just a moment to greet them. It was almost as if they weren't there at all! Guillermo felt uncomfortable and whispered to his son that he wanted to leave this place!

"Todavia no padre!" Andres told him. "Vamos esperar un poco mas!" (We'll wait a while longer!) He watched Paloma at the other side of the room speaking animatedly with a group of new arrivals, kissing the men and gushing falsely over the dresses that

the women were wearing. He waited until she was finished greeting
them before leaving his parents momentarily to walk over to her.
Andres could see that his own glass was empty! He again stopped
the young waiter and took another glass from the tray and handed
it to his father! Guillermo took the glass, sipped the champagne
and then whispered to his son, "No me gusta esta bebida tan agria!
No tienen vino?" (I don't like this sour drink! Don't they have any
wine?)

"No, father!! Here they only drink champagne! The wine is
only for the workers!" Just as he was aproaching Paloma, he heard
a group fo three of the guests filling their plates with more food!

One of the men said to the others, "......I guess that young
man doesn't own a tuxedo!" while he stared at Andres.

"Yes, but look at the old man!" said one of the other two
men. "He looks as if he just came in from the farm after milking
the cows! I wonder if Paloma really knows what she's doing,
marrying him! Andres had heard them! They were speaking
loudly, probably feeling the effects of the champagne. Instead
of going over to Paloma, instead, he went directly over to the
men who were still filling their plates. He paused momentarily!
He knew that it was necessary for him calm his anger! After a
few moments, when he felt more composed, he put down his
champagne glass on the table next to the plate that was filled with
food. For several moments, he remained there staring at them!
They realized that he had overheard their comments and were now
squirming out of his way, not wanting to face him!

"Hey, you! Don't you walk away, I have something to say!"
Andres said angrily. "For your information, I do have a tuxedo!
Unfortunately, I happen to be one of those people that works for
a living!" He then grabbed the man that had spoken unkindly
about his father! "This man whom you think comes from a farm
happens to be my father! He has more sincerety in his little finger
than you have in your entire body! How dare you insult him!
You say one more word against him, and I'll shove that pig pen
you're holding down your throat! This man has kindness, love and
sensitivity; something you wouldn't know anything about! Those
happen to be the values that he has taught me! Of course, none of

you bastards would know anything about that; because your only interest is waiting to see who is going to invite you to their house to fill your fat bellies with food and drink! Most of you have never worked a day in your lives! You were born parasites and you'll die being parasites! I suggest that you look into the mirror before speaking about other people! Take a look at what you see! A bunch of worthless pretenders who are nothing but leeches hanging on to whoever wants to feed you! You know what? Just the sight of you makes me sick! As far as we're concerned, you can all go straight to hell!" The man whose arm he was holding squirmed momentarily trying to get out of his reach! Just then, Andres picked up the dish from the table that was filled with caviar! In one quick movement, he took the dish and smashed it against the person's face! Food was falling everywhere! His face was full of yellow eggs and onions, and the caviar was all over his fresh starched white shirt! Andres waited for a moment, hoping he would try to defend himself, but he didn't! Instead, he began to sputter, trying to brush away the food that was on his tuxedo!

"C'mon padre! Vamos de aqui! Esta gente son nada mas que mierda!" Andres said. (Come on father! These people are nothing more than shit!)

Seeing the commotion he had caused, Paloma was embarassed and came running over to him! "How could you insult my guests, Andres? I demand that you apologize to them immediately! I won't stand for any disrespect from you in this house!" she told him.

There was fire in his eyes as he looked at her! He knew exactly what he wanted to say to her, but he also knew that he was too much of a gentlemen! He had made his point and that was all that mattered! Instead, he looked at her! "Apologize to those parasites? You have to be kidding! As far as I'm concerned, they are the scum of the earth; perhaps that's why you all seem to get along so well together! You can have them, Paloma! My parents and I are getting out of here!" he said as he walked toward the front door.

"Andres, if you leave this house, you never need to return! Do I make myself clear?" she said as she scolded him almost as if he was a child that needed to be scolded.

"I understand perfectly! Please, don't worry! I won't be annoying your friends any longer!" Andres replied.

"Remember our wedding!" she said. "These friends will all be attending our wedding! We can't make them angry! We need to treat them as guests!"

"I remember the wedding! At this point I don't think it would be wise for us to marry! As for your friends, remember, they are your friends, not mine! It is up to you to treat them as guests! Let's go mom and dad, this place is making me sick!" he said as he took his mother's hand and the three of them walked out the door and asked for their car!

"You'll be sorry!" she yelled back. "You'll come running back to me, but you will never come into this house again!" she shouted angrily and loud enough for all of the guests to hear!

"I doubt it, Paloma! As for allowing me inside your house, I wouldn't advise you to be waiting at the door for me to return!" he said as he slammed the door behind them.

When they were outside waiting for their car, Guillermo looked sadly at his son! He was sorry that he had come to Madrid! He should have known better than to come here! Andres was no longer at the same social level of his parents! He had climbed to a much higher plateau and it had all been due to his hard work and his success as a lawyer! True, he had been about to marry into a very influential family; and now, because of their visit, the pending marriage had been ruined!

"Lo siento, Andres! Seria mejor si no vinieramos aqui!" (I'm sorry, Andres! Maybe it would have been better if we had not come here!) his father said.It had begun with a night full of promises and with happiness and now everything had taken a turn for the worse! He couldn't help but to wonder how this turn of events would affect his son!

"No, father! I am happy you came! I was finally able to see that perhaps getting married might have been a terrible mistake! Having both of you here with me made me realize many things in my life that I had overlooked before! I'm sorry that you weren't able to have dinner as planned! How would both of you like to go to the Parque de Espana and eat some sardines and caldo for dinner?" he asked.

"I think it would be an excellent idea! But first, how about if we go back and get that young woman who works in your office? At least when I saw you with her, I saw you smiling and happier than I've ever seen you! That's the way I want to see you all the time, my son!" Guillermo told him while Andres smiled and nodded his head but without answering!

CHAPTER 10

Madrid

Several weeks had passed since the argument with Paloma. In a move that surprised Andres, she had refrained from calling him as she did several times each day, nor had there been any contact between them. No one needed to remind him that he had committed an unpardonable sin by embarassing her friends. Perhaps he should have been able to control his temper; but he couldn't stand idly by and allow those men to ridicule his own father! When he left the house, he had made up his mind that he wouldn't apologize to any of them. If anything, he felt that both he and his father had been owed an apology by her guests and she should have said something pleasant to his father! After all, she was the one who had invited them after promising Andres that the dinner would be a quiet affair between the two families and no one else.

When she was convinced that Andres was not about to call or to apologize to her, Paloma finally decided to call his office. Once again she was taken back when her call was answered by a young woman, very polite and seemingly quite polished in her speaking. She found it a bit strange that Andres had not said anything to her about having hired a woman in the office nor had he said anything else about her! In the past, she had always been directed to the the cranky old German immigrant who always

sounded obnoxious and rude, something that both she and her
mother had always detested from the moment they had first met
him. The words her mother had told her were firmly implanted on
her mind! She had once said that whenever she made a business
call it was necessary to always be on the offensive if she expected
to get immediate results! Today, she had decided on what to do
after the call. She went to the office wanting to see this young
woman for herself. Only then would she be able to determine
whether something else besides her secretarial skills were
distracting Andres!

All of the anger they had felt at the hands of Paloma's
friends was quickly forgotten when Andres finally explained to
Maripaz the results of her case! Until now, he had been careful
not to say anything for fear that she would decide to return to
Bilbao. Something within him was telling him not to let her leave
again. Fate had worked its miracle and had brought them together
again and he wanted her to remain in Madrid where she would be
with him! When Guillermo suggested it would be a good idea for
all of them to return to the Parque de Espana and celebrate their
good fortune, no one resisted! His father had been careful not to
make any comments about this young woman. The last thing he
wanted to do was to interfere into his son's personal life! The only
observation he had seen and had discussed with Dolores was how
happy their son always seemed when he was in the company of the
young woman. Whenever she was with them, he had no problems;
and even the unhappy moments he had suffered at the hands of
Paloma's friends had been forgotten! Adding to this was the fact
that his parents had also liked Maripaz! She was not only charming
and attractive, but also very respectful and mannerly. They had
seen the look on their faces whenever Andres eyes met hers!
There was the certain unspoken language that lovers alone can
understand. This woman was not a mistress as he had first thought;
she was obviously someone he had known and had obviously fallen
in love with!

Guillermo felt happy when he saw his son dance the night
away, drinking a healthy share of red wine and eating freshly
baked sardines! He seemed so different than when he had been

at the Romanones Estate! Simply put, he didn't feel that his
son belonged there with the so-called aristocrats whose only
conversation was to criticize everyone who was not a member of
good standing in their circle of friends. Guillermo had thought
of talking to his son if only to tell him that for a man about to be
married, he didn't appear to be very happy. It had only been at the
insistance of Dolores that he had decided not to say anything for
fear that Andres might get angry!\. After all, it was his decision to
make! If that was the life he had chosen, then, so be it! Who was
he to criticize? After the wedding, he and Dolores would return
back to Galicia and their contact with anyone of the Romanones'
family would be non-existant! The relief came after the argument
at the Romanones house! He saw a remarkable change in his son. It
was as though a heavy load had just been lifted from his shoulders!

It was almost noon when the long chauffer-driven
automobile arrived at the office! Looking through the window they
watched anxiously when Paloma left the car and the handsomely
paid chauffer held the car door open for her. Herr Otto had also
seen her arrive and was feeling nervous! Maripaz had been
arranging some files working with Herr Otto, with whom she had
established a mutual liking, especially when she decided to call
him 'Abuelito' (Grandfather) The name was given to him with
affection and it was appreciated especially since Herr Otto had no
other living relatives either in Spain nor in Germany. It made her
laugh whenever she would make a fuss over him watching his face
turn red with embarassment, only to be followed up with a kiss
she would give him on the cheek! Despite his protests, he enjoyed
the attention and they had become very close working together in
the office. Maripaz had learned a great deal working with them
and her presence had been a godsend in many ways! It was as if
a new ray of sunlight had come to the office with her presence!
Andres had, for the first time, started to look forward of going to
the office if only to listen to the idle chatter of Maripaz and Herr
Otto discussing meaningless subjects over a cup of coffee before
locking himself in the backroom office and returning to his work.
Being in their midst had been an excellent precursor for starting
the day's activities!! Paloma walked into the office and saw the

old man gazing nervously at her! She quickly asked where Andres was because she wanted to speak to him. Something about his nervousness caused her to smile knowing how intimidated he always seemed when in her presence. What she didn't know was how much the old man disliked her and her entire family! He accepted the fact that all of them were beyond his social reach and common sense had warned him to have as little as possible to do with them. Today, he had been unable to dodge her approach.

"I'm sorry!" Herr Otto explained. "Licenciado Torres is working in his office. He has left word not to be disturbed unless it is someone who has an appointment to see him."

"What do you mean, unless I have an appointment?" she asked with her usual sarcasm that the old man always disliked! I want you to go back and tell him that I want to see him immediately! Do I make myself clear?" she said showing her anger with his comments.

"Ja....ja...I hear you, I hear you! But I was instructed not to interrupt him for anyone! Now, do I make myself clear?" he answered, almost mimicking her. He had no idea where he had finally gotten enough nerve to say what he said.

"How dare you??" she answered angrily as she walked right by him and stormed angrily into Andres' office! The young attorney was seated at his desk and Maripaz was sitting next to him discussing some new instructions he was telling her regarding one of his pending cases. Paloma took one look at Mari and realized that she had good reason for being jealous. Nothing had been said, but intuition told her immediately that something strange was going on that he had not told her!

"Would you mind telling me why I am being treated like a stranger?" she asked. There was still anger in her voice, but much of the fury had left her after seeing the young woman seated next to him. "I asked that worthless old man to get you and he deliberately refused to do so! Does he have any idea who I am? Does he know that we are going to be married and I only wanted to speak to my future husband?"

Maripaz took one look at her! It was enough for her to be convinced that this woman should not be married to her Andres!!

Her Andres, she mused! It was the first time she had thought of him as being her own Andres. There were many thoughts on her mind that she would have wanted to tell her; but the angry look on Andres' face was showing her that he was about to tell her some unkind words of his own and without her help! She smiled courteously, got up from her chair and walked out of the room closing the door behind her.

Andres made no attempt to stand up to greet her. In the few weeks they had been working together neither Andres nor Maripaz had spoken about themselves nor of what was going to happen to them! One thing Mari knew for certain. She was happy with him and knew that he was happy with her! The only thing standing in their way was the intended betrothal with this woman. It was something that, as much as she would have liked, she decided it wouldn't be fair for her to interfere! If and when they were married, all of the closeness they had shared would be ended! It had been something Mari had thought about quite often; but she also knew that any changes would have to be made by him and without any interference from her! This unanounced meeting would probably turn into a showdown and she had no idea how things would finally turn out! She was silently hoping and praying that Andres would decide to terminate his relationship with this woman realizing that he could never be happy if he were married to her. Despite his calm exterior, she knew that Andres did not like to be controlled by anyone. She had learned this the hard way after they separated when they were both in school.

"No one is treating you like a stranger," Andres said calmly without raising his voice. "You are always welcome; it's just that today is simply not a good day for a visit!"

"Don't you think that we still have many things to discuss about our marriage? Time is getting short, you know?" she asked sarcastically.

"I think we've already said everything there is to be said. I thought I told you that there wasn't going to be a wedding." he said. He paused for several moments to study the look on her face for any signs of emotion, but there were none. "I realized the night of the argument that we really had little, if anything, in common.

I didn't like the way that my parents were treated by your guests, nor the way they were also ignored by you. I thought it was rude, tasteless, and without manners! I don't even think your mother would have been as cruel as you were! What more is there to say?"

"Have you any idea the expenses we have already paid out in advance for the wedding? The invitations have already been mailed and all of the arrangements have been made for the ceremony and the reception. You saw the guest list! What about all of the important people that were invited? How do you suppose it will make me look if everything is cancelled because of a silly argument? This could have a disastrous effect on your career, you know?" The way she had spoken had been a veiled threat that she felt would have gotten his attention.

"I would hope that my career is being influenced by my success as an attorney. Not because of your contacts." he told her. "As for the expenses, I'd like to remind you that never once did you talk to me nor asked me what I wanted or whom I would have wanted to invite! The arrangements were all yours, not mine."

"Ah! So that's it! You just want to get even with me, is that it? Well, I won't stand for it! Just remember, I made you what you are and I can ruin you the same way! Have you thought of that? It's probably because you want to take up with the young girl in your office, but think of it? Will she be able to make you happy? Will she be able to recommend wealthy clients to you? And, also, what happens when she gets tired of you? Will you come running back to me? I want you to think over what I am telling you. Once I leave here, you and I are finished! There will be no wedding; but, rest assured, I'll get even for the embarassment you have caused me! You had no right bringing that......that....rugged looking farmer into my house! Have you no shame? Why he didn't even have the proper attire to wear! He was nothing more than a peasant who had no right being in our home!"

Until that point, Andres had spoken calmly. True, he had been firm in his comments not wanting to make her any angrier than she was. Now, ridiculing his parents, she had gone a bit too far! She could say whatever she wanted about him, but he would never allow anyone to attack his parents!

Only then did Andres stand up. "Just who in the hell do you think you are? What makes you think that having a title makes you such a superior person? The person you referred to as a peasant and a farmer happens to be my father! You seem to forget that I am what they have always been! Like it or not, I was raised by them and they were the people who struggled to provide me with an education. They are good and decent people, much more decent than those hypocrites you associate with who haven't ever worked a day in their lives. They are too busy drinking your expensive champagne and feasting on your caviar. Have you ever stopped to imagine what would happen if you were to suddenly stop supplying the champagne or the food? They would drop you like a hot potato and search for some other generous bitch willing to feed their greedy bodies! No, Paloma, I am happy being what I am. You belong with them, not with me. You deserve each other! There can be no wedding. It would be nothing more than a mockery. Besides, there is someone else outside of your circle of friends who would gladly move heaven and earth just to make me happy. Could you ever be as generous? I doubt it! Go back to your friends and hope that ill fortune never comes your way! I doubt you could ever survive if it ever did." he said.

She could see by the look on his face that he was probably angrier than she had ever seen! This was a far cry from the soft spoken, calm gentlemen she had known. Well, what could she expect? He was simply a peasant and just like his parents or that little whore in his office. She should have known better than to come here. "Our relationship is over!" she said with a firm finality. "But you haven't heard the last of me! I'll make you pay dearly for the embarassment you have caused me. The Contessa de Romanones will not be humiliated in this manner!" It was a threat that he knew she would try to deliver. At least he felt happy and satisfied that their relationship had finally come to an end. She stormed out of the office taking one last look at Maripaz and telling her in parting, "Go ahead, whore! Since you want him so badly, you can have him! Let's see how happy you make him when he gets tired of you!" she said as she quickly got into the large black car and drove away. For several moments, Maripaz had thought about answering her; but since she had been listening to everything that went on, she decided to let things quiet down before going to see Andres.

"I'm sorry you both had to listen to the outburst," he told Herr Otto and Maripaz.

Mari was looking at him, not quite knowing what to say. Then, after thinking her words over carefuly, "Did you really mean the things you told her?"

"Every last word!" he answered smiling. "Why? Why are you asking?"

"I'm talking about the part where you told her that I would move heaven and earth to make you happy. Did you really mean that?"

"Of course, I did! Damn it! Don't you think that I know you well enough by this time to realize that?" There was still the sound of anger in his voice as he spoke.

She gave him a smile. Then she went over to him slowly and said in a calm voice. "I'm going to give you something I've been wanting to give you for a long time!" she said. She reached over and kissed him gently on the lips. In a response that she hadn't expected he returned the kiss. Suddenly, almost on impulse they each took a step backward and stood looking at each other. Then, in the presence of Herr Otto, she placed both arms around him and kissed him again. This time the kiss was much longer and with more feeling as he hugged her tightly; something he hadn't done since their days at the university.

"This is something I should have done a long time ago!" he finally said.

When they had finished, they both glanced over at Herr Otto who was showing his embarassment with the show of emotion. "You are blushing! Are you surprised, Abuelito?" she asked smiling.

"Shush......am I surprised? Am I surprised??.....No! I am not surprised! You see, I have known for a long time this was going to happen! Perhaps....even...before you knew it...ja? I teenk maybe it is about time...ja?" he joked back.

"C'mon, both of you!" Andres ordered. "I think I've had enough excitement for one day! I think we should all go to lunch, enjoy a bottle of good wine and some tapas! How about it?" he asked.

"What do you think your parents will say when you tell them that the wedding has been cancelled?" she asked him.

Andres was laughing as he answered, "At this point I am more worried about what they'll say if you and I don't get married!" he shot back! "I think you already know how my parents feel about you. I have a feeling they will be quite happy with the news."

"Is this your way of asking me to marry you?" she said kiddingly.

"Of course it is! My God, Mari! Don't you realize that I have never gotten over you? How in the Hell could I possibly marry anyone else but you?" he said, placing his arm around her waist while Herr Otto was nodding his head as he locked the door to his office.

"Perhaps we should take the rest of the day off.....ja?" Herr Otto said.

"Ja....!!!" Andres and Maripaz said at the same exact time, laughing as they went toward their favorite tavern.

"No...No....No!!!" Andres said emphatically. "Today, let's not go there! Instead, let's go to the Parque de Espana! Herr Otto, have you ever eaten grilled sardines in olive oil?" he asked. The old man nodded his head, telling him that he hadn't. "Good!!" Andres answered. "Today, you are in for a special treat!"

"Whew..." the old man muttered. "I am much too old for special treats...ja?"

"Que va, abuelito! Jamas seras demasiado viejo para nosotros!" (Never! You will never be too old for us.) she said, kissing him gently on the cheek.

Guisamo, Galicia

News of the forthcoming wedding came as no surprise to Guillermo or Dolores. Only Dolores had some reservations wondering whether or not her son was doing the right thing. It

wasn't that she disliked Maripaz; they had both liked her very
much! Her only concern was in wondering if the wedding had not
been planned hastily because of Andres' breakup with Paloma!
The truth was that Andres had never told them that he and
Maripaz had been lovers when they were both at the university
as youngsters! She had been introduced to them as an employee
and the truth was that they knew very little about this young
woman. The only thing they had learned was that she had been a
client and had been in some trouble in her hometown of Bilbao.
No one had asked; and of course, she had no reason to offer how,
following a brief confinement period she had been accused of
a felony and had been taken to Madrid to be tried in the Corte
Superior! Even through her silence, Dolores knew enough about
the system to realize that in order for her to be taken to Madrid,
the charges lodged against her had to be quite serious! One of the
things that troubled Dolores was that there had been no mention at
all about her parents, who they were or what they had done for a
living. She also knew nothing about their background which was
always important to a Spanish parent! Guillermo felt differently
than his wife. There had been a few occasions when he had raised
a question with his wife; but, for the most part, he had liked the
young woman from the beginning and nothing else mattered!
Much of what he had seen had been unimportant. The only thing
that really mattered was the happiness he had seen in his son's
eyes when they were dancing and she had gone with them to the
Parque de Espana. As far as he was concerned, any woman who
could bring so much happiness to his son was certainly acceptable
to him! It didn't even matter if she had been his mistress. After
the encounter with the aristocrat his son was about to marry, the
young woman had been like a ray of sunshine. If it were up to
him to choose a wife for his son; and he had to choose between an
aristocrat and the mistress, he would have easily selected the young
woman. Of course, he also knew that there would come a day when
the parents would have to meet if only to eye each other from head
to toe and decide among themselves whether or not the opposite
spouse was deemed acceptable parents for the offsprings that were
sure to follow. Spanish customs could not be changed or altered,

and that was the way it had to be! In the letter Dolores had written her son she had expressed her own reservations about the quick marriage; but, she also told him that his father was elated with his choice for a wife! As long as the young woman was capable of making him happy, that was the only thing that mattered. As far as they were concerned, her introduction into their lives had been pleasant and they were both thrilled that there was to be a wedding after all, even if it wasn't the one they had expected.

Andres seemed happier than he had ever been since his days at the university when the money had been scarce and time was precious! Now, grateful for his own success, he had money and the lack of time was no longer the hindrance it had once been. Of course, he had noticed, however, the decline of new legal cases following his argument with Paloma. As some of the older cases were resolved, the number of new cases, especially those coming from Paloma's friends, had come almost to a stand still! These had been important because many of them involved large sums of money. The cases he was now receiving were quite small by comparison, many of them uninteresting but at least it provided the income that was needed for the rent! Andres had the good fortune of establishing himself by taking on cases that were difficult and complicated, most of them dealing with civil rights, or other inadequacies within the law that needed attention if the country was ever to develop into a democracy within the European community. As an attorney, he was now compelled to take on an abundance of criminal cases and other minor infractions, most of which were necessary in order to maintain his practice.

Word had spread consistently among the citizenry about articles written about him in the newspapers telling of his success in defending cases of people that had been charged with crimes against the government. As a result of this publicity, there had been a steady stream of people, many of them young people, arriving legally or illegally from the Basque regions, who constantly sought his help! Many of them had been citizens, badly in need of his services, and most of them unable to pay for legal services. The result was that he had bene loaded down with work, but little income that would justify the many hours he had spent with his practice! Much of the misfortune had been attributable to Paloma's threats. In many ways she had succeeded in bringing him down to an unwanted level of mediocrity that was no better than what was practiced by some other attorneys in Madrid.His life had changed and had taken on a new meaning. The only positive aspect had been when Mari had promised him not to leave Madrid! At least this gave him the opportunity to spend more time with her.

There had been only one disagreement. It had been on the day she had asked him when they would be married? He had realized for some time that eventually she would ask that question, but, when it happened, he was totally unprepared for what to answer! If he had any hopes of keeping her this time, he was going to need to come up with some valid reasons for the constant delays. So, he waited deliberately until one evening when the two of them had gone to a local restaurant for dinner. Andres had been feeling a bit depressed and worried that the infamous day of the wedding was going to become the topic for discussion as it often was on other occasions. It was unusual for him to order a bottle of wine without also ordering a healthy supply of tapas to go along with it! Today, the tapas had not been ordered, only the bottle of wine! Mari noticed immediately that there was something bothering him. At first, she thought it was the wedding; but, after seeing how nervous he appeared as he sipped on the wine, she realized that the subject was serious.

"Que pasa, mi amor? Porque te veo tan nervioso?" (What is it, my love? Why are you so nervous?) she asked calmly. She could see that he needed to be calmed down and it was her duty to communicate freely with him on whatever was upsetting him. The thought of her own mistakes many years ago were still vividly implanted on her mind, and it had resulted in her own unhappiness. She was determined not to make the same mistakes again!

"Mari," he said softly. She watched anxiously while he decided to play with his fingers as he spoke. "I know you are anxious for us to marry! What I need to tell you is not easy for me! I wanted to come here alone with you hoping that after I explain my reasons for putting off the wedding, you will understand and won't be angry."

The indication of a 'delay' suddenly ripped into her like a dagger! She still remembered how once before he had told her of a delay! They were at school and had spoken about getting married. When he was confronted with the subject, he became suddenly uncomfortable as if he wanted no part of it. Could it be that he was now having the same anxieties he had then? Ordinarily, she might have walked away from him just as she had done before! This, however, was a new Maripaz and things were so much different than they had once been.She had matured and was now able to handle any rejections or adversities in life. She had the bitter lesson of having to learn tolerance the hard way! This time the situation was much different! They were both older and wiser, more settled in their ways; and there were no problems about the need of making a living. True, she knew already about the reduced income, but she also knew that he was still making enough money to support the two of them. She was far from being another Paloma who he had once planned to marry. With her, there would be no demands! The only thing she needed was his love and knowing that he would always be with her. Instead of expecting her to be angry, she remained calm and settled without showing her obvious nervousness.

"Why do you want to put it off?" she asked. "We've already told our parents that we expected to marry. What excuse would you want me to use?" Her presentation was much different than he expected. He knew that it was he who wanted the delay even though both their parents had been told of their intentions! What did he possibly want to tell them now, she wondered? Since he was the one that wanted the delay, she felt it should be up to him to write a letter to both parents and explain it to them.

Suddenly, he took her hand and held it tightly as he tried to find the proper words to say! "Mari. when I offered to defend you, I have to admit that that I had an ulterior motive for doing so! It wasn't that I didn't want to handle your case, that was never an issue. The problem was that there was no one I had enough faith in to defend you other than myself! When your father came and asked me for help, I saw that the poor man was ill and needed medical care that he obviously wasn't getting back in Bilbao! The concept of amnesty is a legal term that means forgiveness. If that forgiveness is either sporadic or selective, then it can no longer be an amnesty! When a soldier enters the military he takes an oath to protect and defend the country against anyone who would destroy the consitution or the country itself. Under the current law, if you had been a soldier, they could have incarcerated you for a long time, even without the necessity of a trial. The argument would have been that since you had attended a meeting and had discussed the overthrow of the government, you would be required to defend the country against any such attacks. Fortunately, civilians do not have the same obligations since they take no such oath! In a democracy people are permitted to travel freely wherever they wish without any restrictions. I had already decided that if I were successful in getting you released, it might also pave the way for defending your father. In my judgement he is no longer a soldier! Why then should he be restricted from doing something that he wasn't obligated to do?" Andres paused momentarily and took another sip of wine before continuing.

"Assuming you would want me to defend your father...." he said smiling. He already knew damned well that she would never allow anyone but him to defend her father. "This is something I would raise as an issue! However, if we were married, the prosecution would probably argue that I had a dual purpose or perhaps even a conflict of interest! They would justifiably argue that since he was my father-in-law, I would have an ulterior motive for having the restrictions eased. Before you begin....I know exactly what you are going to say. You are going to tell me that it is a lame excuse! And, maybe you're right! It may well be a lame excuse, but....it is an excuse never-the-less! This is why I would prefer that we get married after the case against your father has been settled. Until then, I'd like you to remain here in Madrid with me. I may even try to have your parents come here for a while. He can always use a disguise just as he did that day he came to see me at the office. Getting them to leave Bilbao and come here will be your job. You may need to convince him that we need his presence here."

"But isn't that dangerous? If he is recognized, he would probably be arrested!" she told him.

"Of course, there are risks! Yes, that would probably happen. You need to remember however, that he arrived here by himself and in a disguise only to see you. He was then able to return to Bilbao without any trouble. There is no reason why he shouldn't be able to do that again. Mari, let's face it! He is a sick man! Without the proper care, he is going to die! I listened to the way he was coughing and the difficulty he had in reaching for air! Those are dangerous signs; and, remember, he isn't getting any younger! I think it is well worth the risk." he explained. He waited patiently for her answer while she was trying to digest everything he had said.

"Do you trust me enough to defend him or don't you?" he asked as he interrupted her thoughts.

"Are you crazy?" she shot back. "I wouldn't think of having any other attorney but you defending my father; you know that! My greatest problem would be in getting him and my mother to come here."

"I have an idea! We really should have a little get-together with both parents in the Spanish tradition! This way the consuegros (in-laws) would have a chance to meet each other and help in making the preparations for the wedding! I know I can convince my parents to come here from Galicia. It would give your father and mine a chance to become acquainted and discuss old times! Isn't that what older people usually talk about?"

"Have I ever told you that you're a genius?" she said brightly. She should have known better! It would be just like him to be thinking about other people and not himself in delaying the wedding date! "I think that is a great idea! The only problem is where will we put them up?"

"I thought we could rent a suite of rooms for them! You could stay with your parents; and I, of course, will stay with mine!" he said as she started to give him a mischievous smile.

"What's so funny?" he asked seriously.

"I have a much better idea! Do you want to hear what it is?" she asked as she gave him another smile. This time it was a sly movement that was both devious and devilish. It was the type of expression he had always enjoyed seeing on her face!

"Never mind!" he said with a devilish scowl! He knew exactly what she meant! He was also aware that this was an extremely important matter that would probably effect all of their lives.

"Just remember, you did undress me once, or have you forgotten?" she said kiddingly, knowing that this would cause him embarassment!

"No! I didn't forget! I suppose you'll never let me live that down, will you?" he said smiling.

"Never!!" she said defiantly with her hands placed firmly on top of the table. "You can count on it! Are you quite sure that is the real reason why you want to delay the wedding? Are you certain that you don't have another ulterior motive just as you did when we were in school?"

"How could I possibly have an ulterior motive? I already told you that I would be willing to marry you just as soon as your father's case is settled!"

"Okay!" she answered still smiling. "I happen to agree with your reasoning. As long as you remember that I have no intentions of letting you out of my reach again!"

"Nor will I ever want to be outside your reach! I lived through that separation for many years; and, believe me, I know how I felt!" Just then, the waiter appeared carrying a large tray of food!

"I hope both of you are hungry!" he told them as he began to spread out the dishes on the table.

They had been successful in reserving a suite of rooms in the deluxe Palace Hotel located in the heart of the business district in downtown Madrid. The large hotel entrance was located on the corner of a small street, just one block away from the famous Del Prado Museum of Art. He had deliberately chosen the Palace Hotel mainly because it was conveniently located in the center of the large city. Andres had told himself that it would be an excellent location from which they could take a daily walk up the street a short distance away. Just another short walk would take them into what he thought was one of the finest eateries in all of Spain called the Sixto Gran Meson. The large concrete fortress had once been a convent for an order of nuns who had moved to a more practical location in another section of the city. Many of the large frescoes and paintings hanging on the walls had been well preserved and had retained the quaint ambiance of the building. Andres and Maripaz had reserved a small room on the third floor of the old convent, allowing them privacy and seclusion away from the wine drinkers that would routinely stop by after work to sip the wine and sample a large array of tapas that had been prepared from all of the provinces of the country. Guillermo and Dolores had accepted the invitation of their son without hesitation, especially when they knew that Maripaz was going to become their future daughter-in-law! She seemed so different from what Guillermo had experienced at the Romanones estate. It was immediately obvious that it was Paloma who did all of the planning at her house thinking about only the comfort and enjoyment of the evening among her discourteous friends. This simple arrangement seemed like such a far cry from the elaborate extravaganza that had been prepared for her friends and guests that had already been invited to the wedding!

Ordinarily, Andres had planned to go alone to meet his parents; but, this time, it was Maripaz who had insisted in going with him! She had already met his parents and she also knew that his father was very fond of her and she of him! Andres did not object when she told him that it was her duty to meet them especially since she was going to become a part of their family. They spotted Guillermo and Dolores who were among the first travellers to exit the train. The first thing he noticed was that his father was wearing the same wrinkled suit he had been wearing on his previous visit. Today, for some reason, he had decided not to wear a tie, insisting that the piece of cloth wrapped around his neck reminded him of the noose hanging around his neck before a person is put to death by hanging! As soon as he spotted Mari, he ran over to her, hugged and kissed her warmly as she wrapped her arms around him and held him tightly. Andres kissed his mother before taking the small suitcase they had brought with them!

"Oye, nena!" Guillermo said as soon as he saw Mari. "No sabes lo feliz que estamos que vas ser nuestra nuera!" (You'll never know how happy we are that you are going to become our dauther-in-law!) he said warmly.

"Y yo tambien!" she answered. "Que van ser mis suegros!" (And me too, knowing you are going to be my in-laws!)

After the brief formalities, they all drove off and went directly to the law office where Guillermo greeted Herr Otto with the same fond warmth and friendship he had shown the elder man before. Both men exchanged greetings as if they had been long lost friends!

"Guillermo, please, please you must hear me!" Herr Otto said. "Did you know that your crazy son wants me to be his best man at the wedding? Whew....I have no idea what I am expected to do! I think maybe...your son is crazy....ja?"

"Crazy???" Guillermo answered loudly as he began to laugh. "We think that is one of the wisest decisions he has ever made, except, of course, when he decided to marry Maripaz! But tell me, Herr Otto, who else could be a better best man than you?" Despite his comments, he had seen the proud look on Herr Otto's face when he spoke. It was perfectly obvious that the elderly man had been pleased that he had been asked to participate at the wedding!

"But....but....I do not know what I am to do!" Herr Otto answered.

"Aw!! That is the easy part!" Guillermo explained. "First, you go to the Parque de Espana! Of course, I will also need to be with you! Then, all of us eat grilled sardines with several bottles of wine! After that....you will have no problem and will know exactly what to do!" he said as they all broke out into laughter.

The old man walked over to the door, drew down the shade and locked the door! Why not, he thought? The anticipated arrival of any new clients had already dwindled down and none of the older ones were expected! They all went upstairs to Maripaz's small apartment. She quickly opened a new bottle of Duque de Alba cognac and poured a healthy portion of the liquid for the men. After which, she opened a bottle of wine for Dolores and herself!

This time it was the older man who first raised his glass and toasted the young people with a life of happiness!

When they had finished, Herr Otto took hold of Andres by the arm and worked him away from the others. Almost in a whisper, he said, "While you were gone, I received a telephone call for you but I don't know who it was! He told me to tell you he would call you later! His name was....Prince....Prince....something or other!" he said unable to remember the caller's name.

"Was it by any chance, Prince Juan Carlos?" Andres asked him. If so, he was surprised that the Prince would bother calling him! After all, he hadn't heard from him in a long time, and, certainly had to know that his proposed marriage to Paloma had been called off.

"Ja.....ja....dat is it! Das is vat he said!! He said something like Prince...Prince....Juanito or something like that! I just do not remember!"

Andres was shocked that he had called! There was no way of knowing what the Prince could possibly want with him? It had been some time since he had last seen of heard from him; and he had to know that the wedding had been called off. He also needed to know that he no longer considered himself to be the legal genius everyone had once thought he was! His practice of law was in a state of rapid decline and now he rarely saw his name mentioned in the newspapers with the same frequency as it had been when he was about to marry Paloma! Well, he thought! Whatever he wanted, he would call again if it was important! More than the others, it was Maripaz who was the most concerned about the call. There was a devious feeling going on inside her that was telling her that Paloma had probably contacted the prince, asking him to arrange a meeting with Andres in the hopes of re-establishing their relationship! Whatever it was that he wanted, there was little she could do about it. In many ways she felt certain that Andres had always loved her and only her! Still, there were those annoying twinges of jealousy and suspense wondering why she would ask the Prince to resolve something that was so personal.

There was no time to spend worrying about the prince! Her own family would soon be arriving on the evening train from

Bilbao; and she and Andres would return to the train station to meet them! There were so many things to do and so many anxieties inside of her that she no longer had the luxury of worrying about time. The truth was that it had been ages since she had seen her mother! She and her mother had always been close and it seemed that everything had changed when she was in trouble. She was both nervous and anxious to see her parents wondering whether or not they would approve of the young man she had chosen to be her husband. Spanish people had a reputation for being kind and generous; but, they could easily be strange and removed, especially when they were in the company of someone not to their liking! Her parents were certainly no different than any other Spaniard! Of course, her father had met her young man and both had taken an immediate liking to each other. It was her mother who worried her the most! She had no idea what she would do if for some unexplained reason her mother decided that Andres didn't seem suitable to be her husband! If that were the case, she would have no other alternative than to rely on the influence of her father. Unfortunately, he was still quite ill and he needed to avoid any unusual excitement that might provoke his coughing spasms and chest pain to get even stronger. It was going to be difficult to explain to her mother that she had loved Andres from the time when they were both at the university. They had also endured many dark times that had been kept away from her mother, especially such as the time when she was attacked when at school! She thought it best then as well as now that there was no point in telling her mother what happened! What good would it do them now to know that she had been in a coma for several days and it had been Andres who came to visit her every day?

After several strong refills from the bottle of cognac, Andres and Mari left for the station to meet her parents. It seemed strange that after not having seen her mother fror a long time, she still felt strange and nervous about seeing her.Andres had watched her toying with her fingers and had tried to settle her down, but it had been no use! This was a special occasion and she had every right to be nervous. She could feel her knees start to tremble with the excitement and becoming weaker with anticipation of their arrival.

Crowds of people had assembled everywhere, some of them going on and others getting off the arriving train. Most of the people wer either friends or relatives who had come to meet the passengers. It seemed like hours as she carefully looked at each departing face afraid she might lose them in the crowd. Andres could sense how she felt as he held on to her hand in an attempt to quiet her anxiety. After several long moments, they finally saw an elderly couple walking slowly toward them, the man being held by the arm of a woman. It was difficult not to recognize her father, especially when he began to cough. Tears began to roll down her cheeks as she noticed immediately how much her mother had aged since she had last seen her. Andres walked slowly toward them, then a bit faster while being tugged by Mari who was almost running to hug her mother. Miguel let out a smile when he saw Andres walking toward them. In one swift movement, he turned away from Soledad's supporting arm and quickly embraced his future son-in-law, gratefully thanking him for having gained his daughter's release! Mari. on the other hand, was still hugging her mother as both women were sobbing uncontrollably as many of the other people at the station were looking at them and smiling!

It was a long while before both women were finally able to control their emotions! "Mami," Maripaz said. "Quiero que conozcas mi futuro esposo, Andres!" she said with pride. (I want you to meet my future husband!) Andres extended his hand courteously to the woman. It seemed awkward as he tried to think about what to say or how to address this lady. In one swift movement she settled the problem for him! Soledad took his outstretched arm and embraced him! Before he had time to react, she was kissing him on both cheeks.

"My husband has told me everything you did for our daughter! How can we ever repay you?" she said calmly, but unable to conceal the tremor in her voice as she was speaking.

'Senora," he said as elegantly as possible. "Ya me han pagado! Quisiera tener su permiso para ser el esposo de su hija?" They would never know that this was the part of the greeting that had made him nervous. According to Spanish tradition, he knew that at some point he was going to need to ask their permission to marry Maripaz! Now that he had just asked for her hand, he was finally able to relax! It seemed like such a strange and peculiar place to observe this necessary ritual, but it had to be done, the sooner the better!

"Nuestro permiso con la bendicion de Dios es suya! Ojala que tengan una vida feliz y placentera todos los dias de vuestra vida!" she answered. (Our permission and God's blessing are with you! We wish you a long and happy life for as long as you both shall live!)

It was the automatic response that is always given to the children by their parents, but, the way she said it had taken on an entirely new meaning. There was a certain emotional sincerity and frankness that he admired immediately. Without answering, he reached over, hugged her tightly and kissed her again. Maripaz also felt relieved now that the expected ritual had been said! She knew of course, that this time would come, but there was still the feeling of nervousness not knowing how her parents would react! It felt good finally to be able to relax.

Andres took the suitcase as they walked slowly from the train platform to their car. Even though he remained silent, Andres could see a change for the worse in her father's appearance. In the few weeks that had gone by since he last saw him, Miguel looked much thinner and more sickly than he remembered! He started to think that perhaps delaying the wedding had been for the best after all. As soon as possible he planned to sit down with his future father-in-law and discuss his plans about his case. One thing was certain; this man was in desperate need of medical help! The sooner he could start receiving it, the better off he would be. Of course, as an attorney, he was already anticipating an uphill battle, but it would be one of those necessary evils! He also knew that if he was successful, the government would be left with no other options but to change many of the military laws currently in place and exchange them with new statutes that were more in line with the other democracies of Europe. Assuming that General Franco was being honest with his people; and what he had said about changing Spain into a leading democracy, it had to begin by changing many of its current laws. It seemed a bit strange at the way that fate sometimes works its magic. During this time, he had been happier than he could ever remember! There had been times when he had enjoyed an abundance of money and many new important clients, yet he remained unhappy and the money did little to change the way he felt.Now that the money was scarce, he had finally found the one love of his life; and he could hardly wait for all of his wishes to be answered and take his college sweetheart as his wife! Who could possibly ask for more, he asked himself?

Andres stood by Miguel's side and helped him out of the car when they reached the office.The fact that the man looked tired and frail did not go unnoticed! He took hold of his arm gently and helped him up the stairs to Maripaz's apartment where he knew that Guillermo and Dolores had been waiting anxiously for them. Andres had initially thought of knocking on the door but soon decided against it! He unlocked the door and allowed Mari to enter first. She was followed by her mother Soledad and then by Miguel and Andres. When the two men had entered, Miguel was the first to spot Guillermo sitting on a chair and sipping on a glass of wine! Miguel was suddenly frozen where he stood, unable to speak and almost in a state of shock! When he saw him, Guillermo also stood up and nearly dropped the glass from his hands! Suddenly, Miguel suffered a severe coughing spasm, feeling as if his heart was about to burst, beating harder and harder! Without realizing what was happening he felt his knees grow weak, and for a time he felt as if he were going to pass out! Both men remained standing within inches of each other and staring motionlessly at each other without speaking, to the surprise of the others! Only after a long time did Guillermo begin to nod his head, unable to believe what he was seeing as he stood eye to eye with Maripaz's parents. Could this have been an unreal dream and would soon awaken to find it was not true? Finally, when reality began to replace the shock the two men took a small step toward each other.The men embraced and both men began to cry as they held each other closely for fear that the other might disappear while the others were looking astonished by what they were seeing. The tears were flowing down their cheeks unable to believe that after all these years, fate had once again brought them together. Guillermo held on tightly to Miguel as he helped him to a chair next to him, arranging a pillow behind his head making sure that he was comfortable. There were so many stories each of them was anxious to tell their children that it was difficult to find a place at where to begin! One of the men was strong, burly and healthy, while the other had become weak, thin and frail! Dolores also nodded her head and started to cry when she saw Miguel and Soledad standing beside them. Miguel had spared their lives and they, of course, had never forgotten. Maripaz, Andres and Soledad probably knew nothing about the outpouring of happiness, sorrow, that had come to them so unexpectedly. It had been something they had never expected nor had ever seen before!

"I should have known that Maripaz had to be your daughter!" Guillermo said to Miguel after the tears had stopped and both men were holding hands as if they were young children. "Who else would ever have the determination and the strength to do what she did? Yet, never once did she ever lose her sensitivity nor the love for her parents!" he said.

"And you?" A suddenly rejuvenated Miguel asked. "How did you ever raise such a wonderful man like Andres? He is as determined and as stubborn as you have always been!" Miguel said smiling. "Do you think that perhaps God has planned our fate, mi hermano?"

Maripaz and Andres were still shocked and speechless with the outpouring of love they had just seen. Actually, they both felt that the two men had obviously shared a secret, but, how could it have been so great and profound that it bewildered all of them? Many old stories began to be sifted through Mari's mind! All of a sudden, she turned to Andres and said, "Do you remember me telling you about a person that had saved my parents life and helped the underground during the Civil War? Do you remember how you thought it was nothing more than a foolish war story when I spoke of a man who wore a mask over his face and had become a fearless fighter known as 'El Raposo'? Remember, how you laughed and scoffed at me?" she said.

"Of course I remember!" he answered. "I don't understand what this has to do with our parents?"

"My father was 'El Raposo'! He was also the chief Mariscal for Toledo!" she said proudly. "He and your father had been inseparable long before the Civil War when they were both members of the Guardia Civil! What you probably never knew was that your father and mother had been scheduled for execution by a firing squad! It was my father who spared their lives and went on to become an active member of 'Los Milicianos', helping the cause against Franco! Because of this, he was branded a traitor and needed to escape to Bilbao with my mother.Also, it was because of this why he is not permitted to leave Bilbao and travel to Madrid!" she explained.

"I can't believe it! And you, Dad, you mean to tell me that you were his best friend?"Andres asked, still shocked by the things that were being revealed after so many years.

"We were more than friends! We were like brothers! There wasn't anything either of us would not do for the other! That was how close we were and how our lives were miraculously spared!" Guillermo told them.

"And I want Guillermo to explain to you how we managed to use our hard earned pesetas, turning them into perronas just so we could feed the hungry people!" Miguel added laughing.

"Wait just a damned minute!" Guillermo added as a new thought came to mind. He stood up and took something out of his pocket! Whatever it was, he had turned toward Miguel, took hold of his hand and opened it to everyone's surprise! "Do you remember this half-perrona?" he asked his friend. Miguel looked at the half coin for a long timebefore taking it into his own hand. The images had now faded after so many years had gone by. Still he looked at it lovingly as if it were a piece of gold! Slowly, he reached into his own pocket and took out the other half of the same coin! It had been a relic from the past that both men had always cherished and had always carried it on them wherever they went. "Como no me voy acordar? Siempre estuvo conmigo donde quiera que fui!" (How could I ever forget? It has always been with me wherever I went!)

All of a sudden, the words came easily as both men were speaking rapidly, recalling old times and stories that had long been forgotten. It was almost as though they had never been separated! Each wanted to know what the otehr had been doing and why they had lost contact with each other after the war! The women were much too busy speaking about the coming wedding; and, suddenly, the only two people that felt like strangers in their own home was Andres and Maripaz! They knew better than to try and interrupt their happiness! All of a sudden, Mari noticed that her father suddenly looked and felt better and stronger; obviously, he had just received the right tonic by seeing his old friend again after so many years.

Andres placed his arm around Maripaz and told her quietly. "I think we're going to need more wine!" he said smiling.

"Have you any idea at all how happy I am with this surprise? And look at my father, will you? Suddenly he looks much stronger and he is even smiling! I think that seeing your dad was the best medicine anyone could have given him!" she said.

Herr Otto said his goodbyes and left the house with Andres who was driving him home. He knew his place, and also knew that this happy occasion was no place for outsiders. It was a time for family and this was one family that certainly deserved to be together!

Oficina de Licenciados Don Andres Torres y Heintz

It was late the following morning when Andres drove the parents to the rooms being reserved for them at the Palace Hotel! Both Guillermo and Miguel had spent the night speaking to each other and reliving their old times, but none of that mattered! Whatever may have been the problems they had endured were well worth the reward in seeing both parents happier that they remembered seeing them. Even the curious stares of the other hotel guests did nothing to distract their never ending stories about the past as they went over everything they had done, where they had been, and all of the things that were right and wrong with the current government. In passing, they even discussed what it would take for all of them to remain together now that fate had treated them kindly and had reunited them once again! What Mari found to be surprising was that her father had suddenly developed a sudden surge of unexplained energy and he even looked physically better that he did when they first arrived at the station!

Maripaz had gone with Andres to the Palace hotel so that she would be free to make the final arrangments for dinner! Everyone was looking forward to the happy occasion knowing that it would be a wonderful time for both families to become re-acquainted with each other. Guillermo had made it a point to remain by Miguel's side at all times! He had taken his arm as they rehashed their old stories about their past! Soledad was also astonished to see the sudden surge of energy in her husband as he remained oblivious to everything else that was going on around him. When Maripaz made the suggestion that they all go to a nearby restaurant, both Guillermo and Miguel had already decided to remain at the hotel and told the women to go without them. It was Guillermo who told him that the long dry summer was about to end and give way to the frosts of winter! It had been the northern provinces that had suffered the most severe droughts and the yield of the vegetables for the winter was at an all time low! Even while Guillermo was speaking, Miguel's mind was trying to think of a plan that could be beneficial to both families while at the same time relieving Guillermo and Dolores from the inability to grow more vegetables. One thing was certain! Both men were far at their best when they were in each other's company. It seemed strange to Andres to listen to his father refer to Miguel as 'Flaco'! It was a name that Miguel had removed from himself many years ago and just the sound of that name brought about a wave of pleasant thoughts and memories that had been long forgotten. The truth was that he rather enjoyed listening to himself being referred to by that name again! Everytime the name was mentioned it returned them back to earlier days when everyone knew him by that name! In later years, when he became known as 'El Raposo', that too had been a feared reminder of the past!

Although Andres had spent much of his time with their parents, the piles of work on his desk was getting higher! He had tried to ignore his legal work, but he knew there would come a time when the time for ignoring his work would need to come to an end! Although none of the new cases he received were financially rewarding, both he and Maripaz knew that they were adequate to support them and to pay for the rent of the office, and that was all that mattered. He had barely finished reviewing one of his legal briefs when he was suddenly disturbed by the ringing of the telephone!

"Andres, que tal? Como estas?" the voice on the other said said to him. At that moment he did not recognize the voice even though he had to admit that it did sound familiar!

"Bien, gracias!" he answered politely. "Con quien tengo el gusto de hablar?" (Who am I speaking to!) He stopped speaking when he heard the person on the other end let out a loud laugh! For a moment, he still thought he had recognized the voice but he was now wondering who would be calling him at this hour!

"Ya te olvidaste de Juanito?" (Have you forgotten Juanito?) the other person said to him! Of course he recognized the voice! How could he not recognize the voice of the Prince of Spain? It had been a long time since they had spoken to or had seen each other! So many things had happened since the two men had gone sailing in the cool, clear waters of the Mediterranean. Memories of those happy times came vividly back to mind. It had been a long time indeed! It didn't come as a surprise that Andres had not heard from the Prince after the flare up with Paloma. Andres had simply assumed that Paloma had performed her evil work and he had accepted what she had done.

"Of course, your Highness! How could I ever forget you?" It had sounded more as a courtesy reply; but, the truth was that he had indeed missed the many discussions he had with the Prince! Besides, the two men had been very fond of one another! "It's always a pleasure to hear your voice! It's been a long time!"

"Yes, it has!" the Prince answered. "Andres, I'm going to be brief and to the point! I need to meet privately with you at your convenience, of course. Tell me, where can we have one of our informal talks, just between the two of us? It is important that we get together! There are a few things that I need to discuss with you and get your opinion. Can you make yourself available?"

"I'll be available whenever you like, your Highness!" he asnwered. "Believe it or not I have a great deal of time on my hands these days! I suppose you know that the wedding with Paloma has been called off? Some of my best clients were her friends. When we went our separate ways, some of my office work went with her, I'm sorry to say!" He was certain that the Prince already knew what had happened. Everyone that was inside her social circle would have known that they had broken up. It was strange that the Prince had decided to call him; but, then, he had always been much different than all the others. Maybe he should have known better! The Prince was not the type of person that could be easily swayed by aristocratic titles! Whatever had been his reason for calling, Andres had genuinely enjoyed the Prince's company and he was happy to listen to his jovial voice.

"Oh, of course, I know all about that! That is one of the reasons that I decided to call. I'm anxious to speak to you now that I know you have more time on your hands. I'm certain that you don't miss being bored like we both were the day when I first met you!" he said laughing.

"Suppose I call you. Perhaps we can meet at the Palace Hotel! My parents and my fiancee's parents are both staying there. Maybe you can come disguised with a pair of sunglasses and a hat. This way you can escape being recognized, your Highness!" Andres told him.

"You know, that's a good idea! That is, provided you remember to bring a bottle of Duque de Alba with you!" The Prince was still laughing while he spoke.It made Andres feel elated that he was still being remembered by this kind and wonderful man and that nothing had obviously changed between them.

"As Spaniards, your Highness, you know very well that we have a difficult time speaking unless we have a bottle of that dark liquid with us!" He could hear the Prince laughing harder at the other end of the line.

"Listen, will you forget that your Highness, stuff? This is only you and me, remember? No public forum for us to speak to one another!"

"Very well, Juanito! Suppose I call you later on?" he said as they ended their brief conversation. Andres remained looking at the telephone wondering what the Prince wanted to discuss with him. It was highly unusual for a future King to call one of his subjects on a personal basis! Ordinarily, he knew that the Prince would have probably gone through an intermediary and have him arrange an appointment. It did seem strange that the Prince had made the call personally and had even offered to meet at a place of his choice. Could it be that it had something to do with Paloma? Maybe she had decided to use the Prince to patch up their broken relationship! No, he said to himself, after thinking it over. She would never do anything like that. She was much too proud for that to happen! Not that it really mattered! He had already made his committment to the only woman he had ever loved and was pleased and happy with his choice.

It was a few days later when a large sports car drove quickly up to the entrance of the Palace Hotel. A tall, elegantly dressed young man, donned in regular sports clothes and sporting an expensive baseball cap and dark sunglasses walked away from the car and made his way through the crowded hotel lobby. He knocked on a door of one of the rooms and looked around him making certain that no one had spotted him! Andres opened the door and closed it quickly when he heard the sound of footsteps coming down the hall. The tall young man walked right past Miguel and Guillermo who were caught up in the midst of a serious conversation, drinking wine and oblivious to the new person that had just arrived. The tall stranger, glanced at them, flashed them a brief smile and said a quick 'hello' while Andres quickly whisked him away into one of the empty adjoining rooms. If the two men were aware that there was a stranger in their midst, they never acknowledged it at all!

Once inside the room, Andres opened up a fresh bottle of cognac and poured two large drinks! "You look great dressed in those clothes, Juanito!" he said jokingly after the Prince had removed his cap and sunglasses. "Did anyone recognize you downstairs?"

"I don't think so! I came up quickly and nobody bothered to notice!" both men embraced briefly before Andres pulled up a comfortable chair for his guest!

"Andres, I needed to see you because I have some important information! You'll need to promise me that what I will tell you will be kept a secret until the news is officially released to the news media! Will you give me your word?" the Prince asked.

"Your Highness, how can you possibly ask that? Of course, anything you tell me will be treated confidentially! I would consider it as being priveleged information, as if if it came from one of my clients!" Andres answered.

"Good!" the Prince answered. "As I'm sure you already know, the Generalissimo is in very poor health! I have been called to his estate and he told me that a decision had been made as to whom will remain as King after his death! Apparently, he has made his decision and wants me to rule as King of Spain and will make those conditions known in his final instructions!" the Prince told him. He paused for several moments as if to study what Andres' reaction would be. He was pleased when he saw that there was no reaction at all! This was what he had been hoping for!

"I am honored, your Majesty! Not only am I honored, but, as a fellow Spaniard, I am also pleased that the Generalissimo has made a very wise choice! I am prepared to serve you in any way I can."

"Good, I was hoping you would say that! You see, I really came here in search of your help!" Andres looked at him inquisitively and took a brief swig from his brandy glass as they both became silent. Of course, he was anxious to know what it was that the future King of Spain could possibly want from him before being crowned King. At least, he was happy that whatever he wanted of him, apparently had nothing at all to do with Paloma.

"Andres, please, sit down! There are things I want to discuss with you." the Prince said while Andres poured himself a refill of cognac and sat down next to him. "One of the first things I plan to do when I am made King of Spain is to correct many of the flawed laws we have in this country! I totally agree with you as you once told me that our laws are old and archaic. Many of them were designed for the military and are grossly outdated. If we intend to move forward to a democracy, the entire legal system first needs to be refined and restructured. I want the military laws that currently rule our country to be retained, but only for the military! What I would like to do is to form a new legal department called ***Consejo Estatal de la Justicia*** for the entire country. I have selected you to head the new board I will be forming. Can I count on you to do this?" The Prince remained silent watching the expression on Andres' face carefully as he pondered the question for several moments before answering.

"Your Highness, I am honored by the confidence that you have in me, but I also believe that if I were to accept such an appointment could also be considered to be a conflict of interest for me. Remember, most of my practice has been devoted to those cases that involve crimes against the government! Any laws that would be recommended for a change would meet with strong opposition from those who are in favor of military rules of engagement. In fact, they would consider themselves to be unfavorable represented in any subsequent tribunal concerning these statutes!" Andres explained.

"That's precisely where you would come in! It would be up to you to form a committee made up from all of the different factions.This way, everyone would be evenly represented. I needn't tell you that you would have my complete backing in anything you should decide to do. The only downside is that I would expect you to give up your own private practice temporarily while the transition is taking place; of course, you would be handsomely paid for your work!"

Andres looked at him, and let out a deep breath while he thought about the proposal! It was a wonderful opportunity that would be hindered only by the dissents and reprisals from those that were against such changes. "Your Highness, with deep gratitude for your faith and confidence in me, I doubt very much that I would be able to serve you favorably in this matter! I think it would be best for both of us if I simply turned down your offer!" There was a serious frown on Juanito's face knowing that this person in whom he had confided and considered a close friend was about to turn down his request. The smile on his face had disappeared and he was no longer smiling! For a long time, Andres was left trying to decide if the Prince was angry with him or just disappointed by his refusal!

"Andres," he finally said, "Let's dispense with formalities! I'm asking you to do this as one friend to another! After the many ideas we have exchanged, do you honestly believe that I would trust any of the aristocrats from the Romanones estate with such an important project? They would decide their decisions to whoever gave them the largest can of caviar, or a bottle of imported Vodka! I don't know of anyone better suited than you to carry out this important responsibility! Of course, you also probably know that, as your King, I could order you to accept this challenge!" he told him, even though Andres knew that he was kidding. The King would never order a person to head such a project, not this King, anyway! Andres knew only too well that this King was much too regal to order someone to do a job that was against the person's will.

With everything that was said, Andres also knew, that modesty apart, he was probably one of the best attorneys in the land to handle this project. He thought about it over and over in his mind, pondering over the positives and the negatives of the assignment, until suddenly, from out of nowhere another idea came to mind!

"Your Highness," Andres began. "I think I might be able to accept your offer; but, as a friend, I would need to ask you for a favor in return!"

The Prince looked at him inquisitively. The surprised look on his face told Andres that he hadn't been expecting this reply.

"I have a client, in fact he is the father of my fiancee, who served as a Mariscal during the Civil War! I understand he served as the Mariscal of Toledo! Because of his activities in working with the Milicianos, he was forced to escape to Bilbao in order to escape punishment. He was then told not to leave the city of Bilbao during his lifetime! I know that our present government has issued amnesty for everyone that fought in the war. It is my intention to petition the court in defense of this man. I feel very strongly that he has become a victim of a 'selective amnesty'! He is now quite old and very ill! He needs to travel to Madrid for medical treatment; but, unfortunately, he is not permitted to travel!" Before he had finished the Prince quickly interrupted him!

"What is the name of this person?" he asked.

"He was a Chief Mariscal Miguel Romero! He is also one of the two men you saw in the next room when you arrived!" Andres told him.

Andres watched carefully as the Prince wrote down the name of the person on a piece of paper as they were speaking! "There is more to it! You see, he was also known as 'El Raposo'!"

"What???" the Prince said. "I heard about a person known as "El Raposo"! I always thought he was a legend and not a real person! Are you sure?"

"Oh yes, I'm quite sure! He gave a lot of trouble to many people! No, he was very real indeed!"

The Prince started to laugh!! "If what you're saying is true, he was quite a hero! Tell me, do you think it would be wise if I went into the next room and shook his hand? He had one Hell of a pair of 'cojones'! They certainly don't have men like that today!"

"Of course you can do as you like! Just remember, he came here illegally, so, I wonder if shaking his hand would be the thing to do! The truth is that he became one of those victims for which there was no amnesty!"

"So?" the Prince told him. "I don't understand what the problem is. All that he needs is for me to grant him a safe conduct pass to travel wherever he chooses! That's easy enough! I can have it typed out and signed and have someone deliver it to you tomorrow! If the man needs medical care, by all means, see that he gets it!" the Prince told him as if it had been no trouble at all!

"Your Highness, if you would do that, I..........." the Pricne suddenly interrupted him again!

"What is this 'Your Highness' business? I thought we had all of that straightened out and that I was Juanito? Well, guess what? I'm still Juanito! That hasn't changed at all!"

"Juanito, if you give me that pass for Miguel, I will be more than willing to accept the position you have offered me!" Andres said.

"Good! Then it is all settled! The pass you need for 'El Raposo' will be in your hands tomorrow! Once the authorization is in your hands, there will be no need for you to represent him in court!"

"Not so, Juanito! If you provide him with a safe passage, it will allow him to travel to Madrid for his medical care; but, the blemish on his otherwise excellent military record will still remain! He would have a passage permit, but still would have no amnesty!" Andres said.

"He would if I were his attorney!" the Prince joked. "Also, if you wait until the transition takes place, the amnesty on his military record would be automatic and cleared! Don't you just hate these damned attorneys who always need someone to tell them what needs to be done?" he said laughing.

"The only thing I can say is that I'm happy to be your friend and not your adversary!" he replied. "When do you want me to start?"

"You can begin immediately! I would prefer that it be started quietly at the beginning until the appointment becomes official! And by the way, I already know that you are no longer considered an honored guest at the Romanones' Estate! Aren't you happy?"

"Very happy, your Highness! I am also grateful for your confidence in me!" Both men raised their glasses and toasted the new program that was now in its infancy! The Prince then placed his cap back on his head and slipped on the pair of dark sunglasses. When he walked into the other room, he saw that both men were still talking continuously! The only thing he could do was to wonder about the stories these two old soldiers were telling! For a moment, he almost felt tempted to let himself be known, but, at the last moment, he decided against it! Instead, he walked over to the thin and frail looking man that was seated on one of the chairs! In a swift motion that interrupted momentarily the conversation, he bent over the frail looking man and shook his hand warmly! He held on to Miguel's hand for several moments before saying to him. "Welcome to Madrid!" he said in a very unimpressive tone of voice that startled Miguel!

"Gracias senor!" the frail looking man replied. "Con quien tengo el gusto?" (Who are you?) he asked.

"Un amigo, don Mariscal!" the Prince answered smiling. "Solo un amigo!" (Just a friend!) With those words, he nodded his head as the tall, burly man and walked out the door! Miguel remained silently looking at this stranger that had just shaked his hand! Never would he have imagined that he had just shaken the hand of the King of Spain!

Andres was smiling when he saw what had happened! He stood there thinking alone for several moments reviewing the conversation! It was not only a challenge but also quite an honor to be selected to head the new department. His mind was quickly turning as he thought of where he would begin and who he would need to hire to help him with the new department. The more he thought about it, the clearer it became that most of the newer cases that he was handling were coming to him from the Basque country. Perhaps it would be a good idea to open up a branch office in Bilbao and leave the Madrid office to be handled by Herr Otto. It would be up to Herr Otto to screen new applicants from the law school of the university and provide them with the necessary experience they would need as they did most of the research! Many of the cronies that were friends of Paloma were also attorneys, but most had specialized in civil and corporation law and were not suited to handle the simple criminal cases. There would come a day would he was going to need to confront them and he already knew that the legal exchanges would be anything but amicable. Of course, he would be well paid for his services; but, eventually, he also knew that he would receive the recognition that would come with his new appointment. It was one thing to serve as a member of the court, but quite another to have been appointed by none other than the future King of Spain!

There was also another thought that came to him! Since he would be involved in changing the laws from a military to a civilian jurisdiction, he would also need to hire someone on his staff that was well versed in military law! The more he thought about it, the more he realized that he also had an expert in the field of military law and its applications at his disposal. Who better than his future father-in-law to hire as a consultant? Having served as a Mariscal, no one knew the military laws better than he! All of a sudden, he felt pleased with his new assignment! He already expected that it would be a success because he had an excellent staff behind him and would make it succeed!

That evening when all of them had gone out for dinner, Miguel decided to wait until they were all seated and paying attention before springing another surprise on them. All of them were surprised when he asked Andres to draw up a partnership agreement naming both Guillermo and himself equal partners of the sheep ranch in Bilbao! It was something that had been on Miguel's mind since meeting Guillermo and after thinking it over carefully, it was something he wanted to do! At first, there had been some resistance from Guillermo when he first proposed the idea, but after a lengthy conversation he was finally able to convince his friend to to move out of Galicia to the ranch in Bilbao where Guillermo would work as ranch manager! The reluctance from Guillermo was because he knew that he knew nothing about sheep ranching! Still, it was Miguel's idea that with both of them working together, they could make the ranch grow again as it had in those early days before he became ill. Certainly, they had enough experience working together in adverse conditions during the difficult times in Spain. There was no reason why this newly formed partnership could not become successful! With Miguel's knowledge of farming and Guillermo's brute strength, it seemed like a perfect solution to a growing problem. After all, he knew his own limitations and could no longer tend to the ranch! It was a job for a man! How could he possibly expect Maripaz or Soledad to work the ranch every day? Besides, when Maripaz married Andres, she would probably be much too busy taking care of their children to worry about the sheep ranch! On the other hand, Guillermo insisted on one condition that needed to be met! He wanted it specified in the agreement that he would be able to take care of Miguel and would be allowed to accompany him on the days when he would need to travel to Madrid for his medical treatments! Now that the Prince of Spain had given him a safe passage, there was no longer any fear of doing something that was illegal!

Andres had already filed a petition in court asking that his father-in-law be granted full amnesty in accordance with the provisions set forth by General Franco after the end of the war. He had studied and reviewed all of the existing statutes and had every reason to believe that now that he had safe passage, his amnesty would be complete! Andres had already decided that, if he were successful, he would use this case as a precedent for other pending cases where the rules of amnesty had not been applied to other citizens of the war for whatever reasons! It was several days later when they finally noticed an article in the newspaper that Licenciado Andres Torres had received a recommendation to become a *Juez Superior* in Spain's highest court! Strangely, it had been the same appointment he had once turned down, but now he felt sufficiently capable of accepting the new challenge! Besides, his new role of being a husband and a father was going to increase his responsibilities and would require additional expenses! The role was largely ceremonial; but, the fact that the recommendation had been from the Prince of Spain meant that the new assignment would be granted quickly.

Most of the plans for the wedding had been completed and both Andres and Maripaz were happier than they had ever been! In their discussion with the other family members they had decided on a simple wedding attended only by their families; and, of course, Herr Otto who had agreed to be their best man! It had been a title that he feared but had accepted despite his own insecurities, afraid that he would fail them at the last moment! "Don't worry, Herr Otto!" both had told him. "You are going to be great, we both know it!", hoping to give the elderly statesman some badly needed encouragment!

"Before the ceremony, we'll give you a large glass of Duque de Alba! That should settle you down and calm your nerves!" Andres said.

"Whew..." the old man replied. "I am not so sure! Maybe we should try a bottle of good German Schnopps....ja? Perhaps that would be better!"

"If that's what it takes, Maripaz and I will bring a case for you!" Andres said laughing.

Andres and his future wife walked out of their office hand in hand as if they were two teenage youngsters experiencing love for the first time. Once that were outside, it was Andres who paused momentarily and gazed at the sky! He saw that the sun was unusually bright that day and there wasn't a cloud in sight! Gently, he blinked his eyes and stood looking at Maripaz!

"What were you looking at?" she asked.

"I was staring at the bright sun! Do you realize that all of **The Shadows of the Sun** have suddenly disappeared? The vivid green colors of the hills and the valleys of this great country seem more vivid than I can remember! It's almost as if the sun can hardly wait to show off its brilliance throughout the entire Iberian peninsula!" he told her.

CHAPTER 11

The wedding was small and basically uneventful! Just as in the other European countries, the wedding nuptials in Spain had been attended by a small number of friends that had been invited to both the civil and the religious ceremonies! The civil portion of the marriage was performed in the office of the General Judge of the Province. It is imperative that this segment of the ceremony be performed before the religious ceremony takes place! This process called, El Casamiento del Ayuntamiento" is a sacred vow offered by the participants to fullfill all of the requirements of the State! Since divorces were not legal, both parties had vowed to fullfill their obligations to the marriage and to remain married to each other unless compelled to separate because of death or desertion of one of the spouses! It was a serious obligation that they had taken with the understanding that the parties are to remain married until death! Once this segment of the ceremony had been performed and witnessed by the presiding Judge, they are then allowed to offer obediance to church laws and repeat their vows in the presence of a priest!

It wasn't that either Andres or Maripaz had needed to make those vows! They had been lovers since their college days and neither had any doubts that they would be happy for the rest of their lives! Unfortunately, now that he had received an appointment from the Prince, his time was limited and they had little time for a homeymoon! They had discussed the possibility of perhaps going to the Southern part of Spain and enjoy a few days of sunshine; but, when Andres told her that he would be unable to go, it didn't really matter! All that was important was that they were now married, that all of the dark clouds over them had been dispersed and could begin living out their lives in each others company! As a substitute for their honeymoon, they decided instead to take a few days and visit Bilbao! Maripaz offered to be his guide and show him all of the beauty of the city!

Andres and Otto had discussed the possibility of establishing a branch office in the city of Bilbao! It was a matter of both economics and convenience! Since a large portion of the cases they were now receiving were criminal, many of them had been referred to them from the Basque region of the country! They decided that it would be more convenient and less costly to maintain a branch office, rather than to have themselves travelling into the Basque areas, or have their clients travel to Madrid when a case was being heard in court! Before his marriage, Andres had offered the suggestion to the President Judge that a court be established in Bilbao in order to hear the case originating in that area. When he had presented his case, the President Judge had agreed that building a court house in the area would, in the long run, prove more efficient and less costly. Andres offered to move to Bilbao where he would be able to handle his law practice as well as work on the project that Prince Juan Carlos had given him. The work that the Prince had given him could be performed just as easily in Bilbao as in Madrid! He also knew that Maripaz would be much happier living where she was born than if they were to make their home in the congested city of Madrid! As a matter of convenience, he also knew that his mother and father were preparing to sell their property in Galicia and move to Bilbao where they would be together with his in-laws!

When Herr Otto and he had discussed the idea at the beginning, they decided that it might be best for Herr Otto to reamin in Madrid and be in charge of that office! The case load had increased again; and they both knew that in order to remain successful, they would need to hire several more attorneys to help Herr Otto with his work load! At first, the old man had offered some reluctance on taking on additional responsibilities; but, after a while, Andres had convinced him that Otto was the only person he would trust to operate that office efficiently! His comments had brought a smile to the old man knowing that his partner was showing his faith and trust! As far as the families were concerned, Herr Otto was simply another family member, especially when Maripaz would call him her Abuelito!

They had taken some trips to Bilbao but the trips were tiring! Herr Otto was getting along in years and could not be expected to travel as often as necessary, and he was the only other person to help Andres share the travelling! There had also been the presence of grey in his temples, a stark reminder that Andres was no longer the young man he had once been! The sad part was that he knew that hiring attorneys was not going to be easy! Most of the young people who had graduated from the School of Law were preferring to work in the fields of Domestic or Corporate law, where the work was more leisurely spaced and the income was greater. In working with Consitutional or Criminal law, the income was greatly reduced and at times they would be compelled to take on pro-bono cases whenever a client lacked adequate financing to pay for their legal services! Not that he really blamed them! Perhaps, if things had been different in his own life, he too may have considered the same option! Whichever attorney he chose to hire would need to be someone who loved those elements of the law that were intriguing and interesting but not necessarily rewarding! Also, he would have to match the interest that Herr Otto always had as they would need to devote a great deal of their time to their work!

On October 30, 1975, Generalissimo Franco was near death! It was time to concede his power, realizing that he was now too ill to govern the country! The momentous decision was made and he finally restored the Monarchy to Spain. The recipient of the award was Prince Juan Carlos, whom he had been grooming to become the fascist successor. Juan Carlos, in a move that was contrary to the wishes of the conservative elements of the country, quickly put into place democratic reforms, especially among the ranks of the military who had been expecting him to maintain a fascist state! He promptly appointed Adolfo Suarez, a former leader of the Movimiento Nacional, as President of the Spanish Government! By 1978, a new consitution had been promulgated that acknowledged Juan Carlos to be the rightful heir of the dynasty as well as the King. There was an attempted coup on February 23 1981, in which many of the existing courts were seized with gunfire in the parliamentary chambers. For a time, it seemed that this coup would derail the process until the unprecedented television of the King calling for the unambiguous support of the legitimate democratic government! Andres aided the King by joining with him to call the senior military figures throughout the country, many of whom had been told by the coup leaders that he was supporting them, and to tell them in no uncertain terms that they must defend the democratic government!

Shortly after he became King, there was one Communist leader (Santiago Carillo) who nicknamed, 'Juan Carlos the brief', while making a bold prediction that he and the monarchy would both be swept away with all of the remaining elements of a fascist state. It wasn't until 1981 that the same leader, following the collapse of the coup, in a clearly emotional state told the television viewers, "God save the King!" If the public support for the monarchy among the democrats and the left wingers before 1981 was conditional, after the King's handling of the coup, the support became unconditional as well as absolute with a former senior leader of the Second Republic telling the television viewers, "We are all Monarchists now!" In spite of those declarations, it soon became a common phrase that many of the Spaniards who were not really Monarchists became instead, "Juancarlistas"!

It was another difficult time for Spain while the transition was taking place. All the eyes, not only of Spain, but also of the world, were on the young King, anxious to see how he would handle difficult situations. When the attempted coup was started, he immediately called upon many of his supporters for advice! Among the first to be called was Andres Torres! One of his first moves as King was to personally review all of the statutes that had been altered from a military to a civilian change! With the help of Andres, they announced that the penalties for breaking any of the ciminal laws would revert back to the punishments given during civilian rule! Many of the emphasis was directed to those that had been charges in public demonstrations, destruction of property, whether to another citizen or pertaining to the government! In addition, thefts and grand larceny statutes were strictly enforced and curfews were announced throughout the land!

It seemed strange to Andres seeing many other people referring to the King as 'your Majesty', while he, a lifelong commoner,was among the very few that were permitted to address the King by name. Whenever a problem came up that required attention, it was Andres whom he would go to for a final decision or a resolution to the problem. The small group of supporters and confidants spent many sleepless nights trying to enforce new laws that were supposed to be for the benefit of the country! The group had been sworn to secrecy, and the only thing Maripaz knew was that her husband was spending more time with the King than with her!She began to feel lonely and out of touch with what was happening! These were difficult times for the new King and the eyes of everyone were upon him to see how he would handle the crises thrust at him early in his reign! He ordered the arrest of people who disobeyed the orders, but he also demanded that all prisoners be treated with kindness and care! He felt it was more important to remove these law-breakers from the streets than to impose strong penalties that would mar their record for the rest of their lives. In a short period of time, the citizenry began to side with the new jurisdiction and the merchants encouraged the King to continue because it gave them safety to their shops and stores and were able to remain open while the unrests were going on!

Within days, the unrest began to quiet and order was finally restored throughout the country! Most of the trouble-makers had come from Vizcaya and some from the Southern provinces; but, when they failed to gain the support of the people, those also began to subside and the country was once again at peace! The accolades for the King were numerous; and, for the first time, the Spanish people were supporting the new policies. Even the attempts by a few left-wing organizations, seeing that their attempts were failing, began to throw their support behind the new monarch and began to pledge support to the young King! He had come through victoriously in his first major crises! When the people who had been arrested learned that they had been given amnesty, they too quickly decided to support the new monarch! Thus, the newly established constitution had met its first challenge and had survived the test! Thanks to King Juan Carlos and his small group of confidants, peace and the beginning of prosperity returned to the country. It became the beginning of the Constitutional Monarchy which still exists and is very much in place!

It had been a difficult time; and, for the first time, Andres felt tired both physically and mentally exhausted! Every time he looked into a mirror he would see more and more grey hair in his temples! He knew that time was passing him by and it was time for him to return to a more subtle lifestyle with his wife and young daughter! After several discussions with Herr Otto, they agreed to search for a new attorney to help them handle the work load in the Madrid office. His mind had been made up to move his family to Bilbao where he had accepted an assignment as Chief Justice for the province! The few applicants that had applied for the job in Madrid were soon disappointed when they learned what would be expected of them. Some of the applicants were only interested in obtaining large incomes and few responsibilities! One thing was certain, none of the applicants were willing to perform the strict qualifications Herr Otto and he demanded!

Andres was sitting alone in his office! It had been a tiring day; and even though the sun was setting in the western sky, it was a sign that autumn would soon be arriving! Still there were no solutions to the problem of hiring a new attorney. As he sat in silence, there was a multitude of thoughts running through his mind when he heard a strange noise and saw the front door of the office opening slowly. It seemed strange to see a tall, well dressed young man walk in! His first observation was that the young man was extremely handsome and his hair was neatly combed! He was dressed in an expensive dark suit that was probably tailor made just for him! His white shirt was stiffly starched and he was wearing a set of expensive gold cuff-links that were exposed at the end of the jacket sleeves!

"Yes!" Andres asked. "What can I do for you?"

"Sir," the young man replied. "I came to apply for the job!"

"I assume you are an attorney! Where did you graduate from and when did you graduate?" Andres asked. He already was convinced that this young man was too well dressed to fit the job they were offering! There was just no way in Hell that he would be able to afford the type of clothes he was wearing by working in Criminal and Civil law!

"Yes, sir!" the young man answered politely. "I am an attorney and I graduated with honors from the Universidad of Madrid! I have also specialized in the fields of Criminal and Civil law!"

Well, at least he had specialized in the fields he had been looking for, Andres thought! "What makes you think you would like working here? You know that most of our clients have been accused of criminal behavior problems! I don't think you would be able to afford to wear tailor made clothes with the income available from many of the cases! There is an unusual amount of work that is done pro-bono! Personally, I think you may be better suited for corporation or some other type of law that is more rewarding!" he said.

"No, sir! I am aware that the pay may be small at first, but this is the type of law that interests me! If I'm going to be the type of attorney to handle the types of cases you and your partner handle, then I think this is where I need to start!" the young applicant said. There was a sense of determination that was almost annoying, but interesting, none-the-less! (Well, at least this young man is saying all the right things, Andres thought!)

"You'll have to forgive me, but I still don't think you would be suited to work in this office! There is nothing specific, except that you are too well dressed and probably well trained in your field! What we are looking for is a young man that we can train in the types of law we normally handle! To do that, I'm afraid that the pay scale would be too disappointing; and you would end up leaving us as soon as you received some experience! No, young man, I don't think we can use you!"

653

"I'm sorry, sir! Please, forgive me for being insistant! Yours is the only organization that I want to work for!"

"Have you tried getting a job somewhere else?" Andres asked. He was feeling a bit annoyed that this interview was taking much more of his time than he would have wanted! After all, he already told this young man that he was not the type of attorney he and Herr Otto were looking for!

"No, sir! I haven't gone anywhere else looking for work! This is the only place I came; and, if you don't mind my saying so, I disagree with your motive in refusing me employment! Money is not a problem! That is not my motivation! Yes, I do realize that I will need additional training! I also know that you are the only person who can give it to me! That's why I'm insisting that you reconsider your denial!"

"What makes you think that I should be the one to give you training and experience? There are loads of attorneys in the city who are equally as capable and who can also pay you a much higher salary!"

"That's probably true! But I prefer having you as my mentor and I only hope that you won't turn me down again!"

"I don't think you heard me!" Andres said, beginning to get annoyed with this young man's insistance! "I just can't see where the practice of our law is going to be beneficial for you! The salary will be small and the working hours will be long! I can't see how you can fit in with our schedule! I suggest that you find another law firm that can be more suitable to the things you are accustomed to!"

"And I don't think you heard one word of what I said!" he said almost sounding defiant. "I already told you that the money is not a factor! I am well trained in your type of law, and yours is the only company I'm interested in joining! How else can I convince you of what I want to do and where I want to work?" the young man asked.

Andres was unprepared for this discussion! He was thoroughly convinced that this young man, whoever he was, was not suitable to practice law with them! Still, the man was stubborn almost to the point of being insolent and stubborn and had made a convincing case for himself! It was hard to turn him down again! After all, it was true that they needed another attorney tro help Herr Otto in the office! Besides, he rather liked the fact that this young lawyer was insistant and wouldn't walk away from a denial! This was a quality that might serve him well when arguing a case in court!

"Very well, young man! You've made a compelling case for yourself! I still think I may be making a mistake by hiring you; but I'm willing to take a chance as long as you know what the guidelines are! Tell me, when can you begin?"

"I can begin tomorrow!" the young man answered. Andres remained staring at him for a long time! There was something about this young man that seemed oddly familiar! Perhaps it was his warm smile he showed all the time they had been speaking! There was a certain stubborness that came through that he liked!

"Very well!" Andres finally told him, with a deep breath as the young man turned his back and was about to leave! "One other thing!" Andres said. "What is your name?"

The young man turned around and looked at him, the smile still on his face. "My name is.....Jose...de....Romanones! I believe we have already met, sir!" he said, breaking into a broad smile.

Andres was in shock!! Of course, now he knew where and when he had seen this young man before! It had been many years since he had crammed his head forward in anger when he broke a chair in the office! At that time, he was nothing more than a spoiled brat that belonged to aristocratic circles. He did remember, his mother telling him that he had wanted to be an attorney just like Licenciado Andres! He looked at the young man and nodded his head! There was a broad smile on his face as he nodded his head approvingly! "I think you may be right, Jose! You may be just the man that we need to work in this office! I'll be waiting for you tomorrow morning! I'm also sure that Herr Otto will also be happy to see you! Please forgive me for not recognizing you! Unfortunately, my mind is not quite as sharp as it used to be! Tell me, does your mother know you were coming to see me about a job?"

"You know my mother! As soon as I graduated from law school, she was ready to set me up in a large office in the center of Madrid! She was a bit disappointed when I told her of my plans! After all, my grandfather spent his entire life trying to enforce liberal policies! I had to learn the hard way from one of the best teachers in the business! Besides, don't forget that I worked in this office as a youngster! I know quite well what goes on here! No, Andres! I want to be a lawyer like my grandfather and like you! That's why I fell strongly that this is where I belong!" he said.

"Hasta manana, Jose!" Andres told him, still stunned at seeing him after such a long time! It seems strange how fate sometimes works in our lives, he said to himself! Who would have thought that this young man would want to devote his life into helping others in need? Never in a million years did he think this would happen! He was thrilled and satisfied that he had finally found just the man they needed for the office; and he couldn't be happier with his choice!

Jose was still looking at him when he gave him a mock salute with his hand as he opened the door! "Hasta manana, my jefe!" he said, as he walked down the hallway and out of sight as Andres remained still looking at him and nodding his head, unable to believe what had happened!

EPILOGUE

The unsettled political situation in Spain had ended and the country was now making a serious attempt to create a democratic state in the democratized areas of Europe. Andres was keeping busy still altering the old laws, writing new ones, and replacing some of the old statutes with new ones that were more in line with the current needs! The number of arrests had dropped considerably as more and more people were happy with the way the country was going; and few people were seeking to ruin the gains that the country had made in a short period of time!

Andres was seated at his desk, deep in thought wondering where all the years had gone, when a note was received from the King! With Maripaz now expecting their third child, he was in no mood to take the long train ride to Madrid! The King had been well aware that Andres had always been one of his most ardent supporters and their friendship was as strong as it had always been. He had been a staunch supporter of the King during the attempted coup, and in forming a new Constitution for the country! Despite everything that happened in the attempt to dethrone the Monarchy, Juan Carlos had survived the passing of time! For his part, Andres was happy being one of the senior judges in the Supreme Court of Spain!

Andres was surprised that the King would once again contact him! It obviously had to be something important! The only calming item was that the note had been addressed to both names, Judge Andres Torres y Maripaz Torres! When he nervously opened up the envelope that he saw had been sealed with the seal of the Monarchy he saw that it was an invitation to visit Madrid on a pre-established day! Protocol would direct that when the King gives a specific invitation to both he and his wife, it was something that couldn't be refused or turned down! It didn't matter that his wife Maripaz was eight months pregnant with their third child! Neither of the two seemed eager to make the long trip to Madrid! They prepared their suitcases and left the next day in compliance with the King's instructions! Once they arrived at the capitol city, tired and haggard, they were met at the station by one of the King's consorts who quickly hustled them away to the Palace in the outskirts of the city. Times had really changed, he noted! The man who had once been a dear friend and ally was now the leader of the country!

He entered by way of the large courtyard and into the newly furnished receiving station. The long center rug was a thick red pelt! Andres walked dutifully with his wife behind the consort as he was led down the long corridor to a large podium and stage. That was when he saw the King seated, dressed in full military dress, with his blue and gold epulets on his shoulders. There was also a large golden sash that ran from one shoulder to the opposite side of his waist where it came together with a wide gold belt at the King's mid-section!

"Your Majesty!" the Palace crier announced with dignity and formality when the guests were facing the monarch! "Licenciado y la Senora Maripaz Torres, estan a su servicio!" he announced with all of the righteous pomp normally required from a court crier.Both Maripaz and Andres walked slowly after receiving the nod from the crier until they reached the edge of the platform and both of them bowed courteously before the King! The King stared at them, and, unseen by anyone else, gave Andres a faint mischievous smile which Andres quickly returned!

"Do either of you have any idea why I have summomed you here to Madrid?" the King asked, still smiling.

"No, your Majesty! We were both surprised by your kind invitation! We are both, eager and willing to answer your Majesty's request and to abide by Your Majesty's wishes!" At first, Andres thought that he may have been a bit too majestic with his response, and he was wondering if, silently, his friend Juanito was having a good laugh!

"I would like both of you to move a bit closer!" the King directed. Andres and Maripaz obeyed and took a step closer to where the King was seated! He was only a step away and it seemed strange to see him in this type of surrounding!

The King stood up from his chair and addressed them both! "Licenciado Guillermo Diaz de Torres, I hereby proclaim that from this date forward, you shall be known as and be recognized as *"Conde de Vizcaya y de las provincias de Guipuzcoa y Alava"* Congratulations, Senor Conde!" the King said.

Andres raised his eyes slowly and looked at the King unable to believe what was happening! Never in his wildest dreams had he ever suspected that one day he would be granted a royal title! Maripaz was looking at her husband proud and beaming, smiling from ear to ear! Never had she been as proud of her husband as she was at this moment! He reached over to her when he saw tears streaking down her cheeks! Softly and gently, he wiped them away with his finger and smiled at her!

"A su orden igual que siempre, Su Majesta!" (At your order, as always, your Majesty!) Andres replied softly in a voice that was quivering and calm while his eyes glanced at the King's face!

The King smiled at him and nodded his head, motioning with his hand for Andres to come closer! The King extended his hand and Andres held it dearly for several moments! When the King saw that no one was close enough to him to see what he was about to do, he whispered in Andres'ear! "Afterwards, you and I will have a private celebration with our friend El Duque! Is that acceptable to you?" he asked, still flashing him the mischievous smile that Andres still remembered from the day he had been sitting alone in the gazebo of the Romanones' estate; and Juanito came up to him and asked if he was as bored as he had been! Strange, he thought, how all of these things that had once been taken for granted had come back to him at this moment!

"An excellent choice for company, your Majesty! I think that, all things considered, the Duque could make an excellent companion!" he answered. He was also smiling when the King gave him a sly wink the moment he felt reasonably comfortable that no one had seen him!!!!

ABOUT THE AUTHOR

After working as a Senior Executive for a leading Bio-Technology company for over 30 years, his work has taken him to almost every country in the world when situations required his attention in times of stress, turmoil and catastrophies! Now that he is retired, he has taken to writing novels! Many of his stories are based upon situations that actually happened during the course of his travels!

Jack Sariego was born of Spanish parents who migrated to the United States many years before the Spanish Civil War! Most of the incidents in this book are based upon stories he was repeatedly told by his parents when he was a youngster in his teens! The historical elements of this novel are factual and have been well documented in the historical archives of Spain! This is his first novel of historical fiction! Many of the characters are real and most have contributed to the evolution of Spain after the devastating war that left Spain in shambles! Although the names have been changed for obvious reasons, they were never-the-less very real and lived their lives to the fullest! They loved, they hated; they won and lost, helped and were hindered in their strife to improve the country they had always loved and cherished!

The author is currently working on another novel titled. "Tarnished Sunset" that is being prepared for publication and is based upon problems he ran across while traveling to the Amazon jungle in Brazil and becoming exposed to the manufacturing of illegal drugs!! His interests are vast and varied! He is interested in the sciences, the law, classical music and politics! He is anxious to write more novels about incidents and problems that actually occured during his travels, especially when he was called to travel into the troubled areas of Lebanon, Iran, Israel during times of extreme stress and turmoil!

Jack is a decorated Air Force officer who fought during the Korean War! He has been credited more than 45 bombing missions over North Korea! Among his many decorations are the Bronze Star for Valor, two Air Medals, two Commendation Medals, and the Korean War Presidential Unit citation! During his military tenure, he was also an Air Intelligence Officer!

The author is a graduate of Temple University in Philadelphia and lives with his family in Philadelphia where he was born and raised!

LaVergne, TN USA
13 February 2011
216398LV00003B/112/A